doona

50
11 3

doona

Anne McCaffrey & Jody Lynn Nye

ACE BOOKS, NEW YORK

An Ace Book
Published by The Berkley Publishing Group
A division of Penguin Group (USA) Inc.
375 Hudson Street
New York, New York 10014

PRINTING HISTORY
Ace trade paperback edition / February 2004

Library of Congress Cataloging-in-Publication Data

McCaffrey, Anne.
  [Crisis on Doona]
  Doona / Anne McCaffrey and Jody Lynn Nye.— Ace trade pbk. ed.
    p. cm.
  ISBN 0-441-01131-4
    1. Space colonies—Fiction. 2. Science fiction, American. I. Nye, Jody Lynn, 1957– II. McCaffrey, Anne. Treaty at Doona. III. Title.
PS3563.A255C64 2004
813'.54—dc22   2003062965

PRINTED IN THE UNITED STATES OF AMERICA

10 9 8 7 6 5 4 3 2 1

contents

Crisis on Doona

chapter one

"Mayday, Mayday," a voice repeated over and over again in Middle Hrruban through thick static on the audio pickup. "Anyone who is within the sound of my voice, Mayday! We require assistance. Our ship is down and damaged. Mayday!"

Todd Reeve and his friend Hrriss, at the controls of the Alien Relations Department scout ship *Albatross,* stared at one another in surprise. It was impossible to tell if the speaker was male or female, a Human like Todd, or a catlike Hrruban like Hrriss. The message repeated, sounding more panic-stricken.

"Where's that coming from?" Todd demanded, scanning the readouts on his control panel. They had just emerged from the second warp jump on their journey back to their homeworld of Doona from a diplomatic mission on the nascent colony world of Hrretha, and had not yet taken bearings on their position to initiate the third.

Hrriss's retractable claws extended as he reached for the controls. There was a low humming as the ship's benchmark program triangulated the distress signal and readings began to register. The readouts indicated they were positioned beyond the envelope of a star system whose blue-white primary glittered coldly on their screen. "Not too very frrr away. It comes from the vicinity of this sssystem's fourth planet," he said in a low, cautious voice that resembled a cat's purr.

"We've got to respond," Todd insisted at once.

Hrriss shook his head, his pupils widening over green irises. "Todd, we cannot. We bear the markings of a Trran ship, your Alrrreldep, and this system is interdicted by the Hrruban exploration arm. It would be a violation of the Zreaty of Doona to enter this sssystem."

"But it's a Mayday! You have to answer Maydays," Todd insisted, staring at his friend in disbelief. "The oldest naval laws on Earth required it. Space laws can't be so rigid as to deny assistance in an emergency. Someone's in trouble! They need our help. Why is this one interdicted?" Todd demanded. "What's so dangerous about it?"

"Explorers from my people have claimed this system, called Hrrilnorr, for mineral exploitation, but also perhaps for colonization," the Hrruban explained.

In the Archives established on the Treaty Island back on Doona/Rrala, extensive records were kept of the status of various systems in each species' chosen sector of exploration. Though Doona was cohabited by Humans and Hrrubans, each race had committed to a Treaty specifying separate territorial rights to all other claimed systems.

"There are trace radioactive elements on the inner, solid worlds," Hrriss went on. "The Byzanian Glow Stones of the fourth planet have a curious, milky glow, most beautiful to look upon. They had a strange, mesmerizing effect upon my people, but even more odd upon the analysis equipment they carried. The glow affects short-term memory of both people and things. Until the effects have been proved hrrrmless, no one may enter here."

Hrriss regarded Todd, his closest friend of either species anywhere in the galaxy. They both knew how Treaty Law read. Violation of a system claimed by the other species was an overt act of hostility, which could end in war. The penalties for infractions started with grounding of the ship, and could end with them in prison on a hardship mining colony, or worse yet, remanded to Earth and Hrruba, separated forever.

Todd set his jaw. "If we start ignoring fellow beings' cries for help, we're no better than Rralan snakes. Someone's in trouble. We heard it. The voice said 'our' ship. 'We' require assistance. So there's more than one of them! We have to help."

Hrriss shook his head slowly, clearly uneasy. Todd took charge.

"Look, it's my responsibility. The ethics of my culture require me to act." He prodded his chest. "I'd never forgive myself for ignoring that call and letting people die. Besides, we're in this sector of space and we could be in bigger trouble for ignoring a Mayday—if someone else comes by."

Hrriss regarded his friend somberly. "This is not a very well travelled area and the system is interdicted." Hrriss then saw how Todd's jaw was set and the implacable expression on his face and knew that his friend would not yield. So the Hrruban gave a slow nod of acceptance. "We have both heard the Mayday. I will say that I insisted on answering though you argued that the system was interdicted!" The Hrruban dropped his jaw in his distinctive grin. "It is better thus. The initial blame is mine, for this is a Hrruban system. I convinced you we must respond."

Todd's expression cleared immediately and he gripped his friend's shoulder in relief and approval. "I'd rather acknowledge my own errors, Hrriss, but your idea makes too much sense in this instance. So, just this once, I'll let you carry the can for one of my bright ideas. Anyway, the ship's recorders are . . . Wait a minim . . ." He tapped the small illuminated dial on the panel between them. "Log's not recording, Hrriss. No movement whatever on the VU meter. Those flaming Hrrethans . . . I told them the *Albatross* had been serviced before we went out on this jaunt . . ." As he grumbled, he lifted himself out of his chair. "I'll go see."

"That recording is important, Zodd." Hrriss called after him.

"Don't I just know it?" Todd hurried down the narrow companionway to the engineering compartment, growling Hrruban curses under his breath.

Duplicate meters to those on the pilot's consoles were attached to the front of each panel in the rear section. Todd dashed past the standing cases that operated space drives, life support, landing gear, food service to a blue and pipeclay cabinet. The feed switcher in the center of the panel was on the correct output. The dials were jumping, following the audio of the Mayday call still blaring over the speakers. Obviously the power was running. Only one set of dials wasn't working, the one attached to the holographic log recorder at the foot of the panel.

"Wouldn't you just know? Those Hrrethans aren't worth the leather they belt with!" Todd groaned. Every system had been in perfect working condition before the Hrrethans insisted on the mechanical-overhaul courtesy.

Frustrated, Todd kicked the front panel of the device and turned to look for the toolbox. With a wowing sound like a bear waking up from hibernation, the recorder started to move again, its disk turning and needles moving. Surprised, Todd glared at it and stalked disgustedly back to the pilot's chair.

"The good ol' reliable correcting kick. Try it again, Hrriss."

"A-OK now."

"Them and their 'courtesy,' " Todd muttered, watching the VU activity as the Mayday was now obviously being recorded. That "courtesy" had been yet another delay when he was fretting to get back aboard the *Albatross* and out of the tight uniform he had to wear on such occasions. Sometimes the courtesy appearances that he and Hrriss had to undertake as representatives of their respective cultures were unredeemed boredom as well as too much spit, polish, and restricting clothing: This latest jaunt to open a new transportation facility at Hrretha being an excellent example. "Wonder how long that Mayday's been bleating?" From his training in space flight, he knew the fate of spacers whose life support ran out. Recorders on passenger liners kept on until power was exhausted. Others ended when no more activity was recorded by the life support systems. "I'd hate to think we'd jeopardized everything for a cargo of corpses."

"We will assume rescue is required," Hrriss said. He transmitted a reply. "Stranded ship, this is the *Albatross*. We rrreceive your message and are coming to help. I will make the course correction," Hrriss added, working without looking up.

As they passed through the heliopause, a wild wailing made the cabin speakers vibrate unpleasantly. Hrriss's ears flattened against his head, and his eyes narrowed.

"Perimeter buoy," he said, wincing. "I knew we ought to be close to one. Can never dodge them. Good engineering. Records even the most fleeting pass," he said, reading the control panel, "and our entry. It will also broadcast a rrrecord of the intrusion to the Zreaty Island beacon," he reminded Todd, his tone gloomy.

"So? It's not as if we didn't expect one," Todd said, his eyes on the screen. "We're committed now." His remark was more statement than a request for agreement.

The blue-white sun was a dwarf, much the size of Sol in the Earth home system. The *Albatross* had come out of its jump directly above it, so that the computer-plotted ellipses of its seven planets spread out below the ship like ripples in a pond. The Mayday originated from the fourth planet from the sun, a small, solid sphere with a ring of eight small and irregular satellites. The triangulation crosshatches appeared on the viewscreen and closed down on a point near the planetary equator, and just passing into the night meridian. Anxiously they watched the blip disappear around the planet's curve. Todd adjusted the *Albatross*'s course to meet its orbit at the earliest possible moment.

Though it took a long time for the scout to cross the distance to the fourth planet, neither Todd nor Hrriss moved. Todd leaned forward, elbows on knees, watching the planet and its moons grow on the viewscreen. Unconsciously he rubbed at his neck where the tight formal tunic had rubbed the skin. Even though he was now in the comfortable one-piece shipsuit, he still felt the constriction. Another reason he loathed these formal occasions. Why they never made the collars or sleeves with sufficient material to encompass one's neck or biceps Todd could not figure out.

Hrriss sat, apparently at his ease in his impact couch, but his tail tip switched back and forth, revealing tension.

"That buoy was alive and kicking, so no smart marauder has tried to blank it and get in for a quick decco. Of course, if any of those stones turn up on the market, the vendor's in real deep kimchee," Todd said, shooting Hrriss a mischievous grin. "Or maybe they'll try to tell us that their equipment's malfunctioning and they didn't 'hear' the buoy." His grimace was mocking as he shoved a finger in his ear, pretending to clear it of a deafening obstacle.

"I am still uneasy myself about entering here," Hrriss admitted. "Zomezing makes my hackles rise." He shook his maned head and then extended both long arms in a gesture of futility. "But we have no choice if lives are at stake."

"This shouldn't take that long," Todd said reassuringly, making sure the *Albatross* was on course. "Not more than a few hours. In any case, a rescue is surely a defensible reason for breaking prohibition." He sighed, once again easing the soft collar off the back of his rubbed neck. "I'll be glad when we can slough this sort of duty off on someone else. J hated leaving home while all the Treaty Renewal debates are going on. I was needed there," and he jabbed a finger in the spatial direction of Rrala, "not there!" A second jab, contemptuous this time, was for the system they had just left. Todd's eyes locked on the viewscreen showing the fourth planet, and he began to tap his fingers impatiently on the console.

"Will only your two hands hold back the flood tides of disaster?" Hrriss asked him teasingly, to relieve the tension.

Todd turned red and laughed sheepishly. "Hope there's no flooding at all. But you gotta admit, Hrriss, I speak the best formal High Hrruban of anyone on the Treaty Island."

"That I do admit," and Hrriss's eyes glowed warmly. "Did I not help teach you myself?"

What Hrriss did not add was that, in many eyes, Todd was the first real Doonan. The experts said you couldn't true-teach another language to an adult, but a very young child could assimilate one as if it was his mother tongue. Todd, with his booming voice, far-ranging ways, and quick mind, was the first Terran totally at home on Rrala, the Hrruban and official name for Doona. Life on Earth was too confining, too rigid for the six-year-old he was when he arrived on Doona. He was thirty-one now. His swift adoption of Hrruban ways and language, and his innate courtesy, made him, when he came of age, a natural choice for Alreldep's diplomatic service. Over the years, Todd had been careful to be most punctilious about courtesies and laws, schooling himself to ignore slights and insults that often roused his hot temper and begged for retaliation.

"I feel as you do about the Zreaty negotiations," Hrriss said firmly. "The arrangement must continue. I cannot conceive of going back to Hrruba. My life is on Rrala. My career, my family, my hrrss . . . and my best friend." His grin exposed awesome teeth.

Todd grinned back. "Mine, too. Well, you'd think that twenty-five years of peaceful coexistence between Human and Hrruban on Rrala would convince them," Todd offered. "The trouble is, we're the ones living with it. I'm worried about the politicians, too far removed from the situation, who have power over it. They're liable to dissolve the Treaty without considering the effect on the people already involved."

"Zat is undoubtedly trrue," Hrriss acknowledged. "We have been on enough diplomatic missions to see where the distant governments have made purely political decisions that are irrrrelevant to the true needs of the colony. Theirr continued meddling without sufficient investigation borrrderrrs the rrridiculous."

"In the words of an unknown but often quoted Terran philosophist 'ain't that the truth!' "

As the first successful attempt at colonization of a nonmining, pastoral world, Doona was the natural focus of much curiosity and speculation on Earth. The Space Department and the Colonial Department of the Amalgamated Worlds were beside themselves with pride and worry lest the experiment prove to be a failure, after all, leaving them without sufficient funding or approval to send more missions and colonists into space.

Spacedep, as represented by then-Commander Al Landreau, had suffered humiliation in the Amalgamated Worlds government when the first Terran colonists found a Hrruban village on Doona across the river from their own landing site. No habitation had shown up in any of Landreau's scans, but the village was discovered very much an inhabited site. Because it was Ken Reeve—and his six-year-old son, Todd—who had managed to prove that aliens were, in fact, resident on Doona, Landreau resented the Reeve family more than any of the other eleven original colonists. Not only did the mysterious appearance of an alien species on Doona seriously compromise the Phase I operation under Spacedep, and Commander Al Landreau; but also the repercussions reverberated through the Colonial Department (Codep) for permitting Phase II to be initiated and colonists placed on the planet. The most stringent rule of the Terran Colonization Plan was to avoid planets which harbored another sentient species.

Landreau was not actually at fault. The Hrrubans had not been "in residence" at the time of his extensive survey. By matter transmitter, the Hrrubans had moved their entire village back to their home planet of Hrruba, since the winter months on Doona/Rrala were long and harsh. But Landreau neither forgot nor forgave the humiliation of being wrong.

However, the visionary leaders of both species had decided to make the best of this coincidental colonization: to prove that two alien species could interact without exploitation or contamination. Doona/Rrala became the vital test for Human and Hrruban.

The original colonists of both species were allowed to stay, and more of each species joined the project, under the loosest of control by their respective governments. Both races were determined to make this project work and prosper. And they were scrupulous in keeping to the rules laid down by the momentous Decision at Doona, where a six-year-old boy translated the relevant clauses.

The original twenty-five years of that Decision were nearly over and renegotiation soon to be discussed. Both Todd and Hrriss knew of the recent incidents which they were certain had been arranged with the express aim of creating dissension between Hrruban and Human, rupturing the Treaty, and, more important, preventing a renewal of the unique settlement on Doona/Rrala.

Over 100,000 settlers, Doonan and Rralan, now lived on the beautiful planet, year in and out, benefiting from their complementary skills and strengths, and surviving the intense and bitter winters by mutual support. If the Treaty was not renewed, the settlers would be forced to return to homeworlds with which they were no longer in charity. More heart-rending, staunch friends would be forever separated: like Todd and Hrriss.

All the while that Hrrubans and Hayumans lived in harmony on their planet, space exploration had exploded in all directions—always aware that each species was forbidden to explore sectors clearly marked with space buoys of the other.

Although Landreau never forgave either species, he had gone on to discover so many other systems and planets useful to his own kind that he quickly achieved the rank of Admiral. In a way he owed that to the Decision at Doona, which had brought him to the notice of his superiors. His own efforts had kept him in a highly visible situation. Judicious manipulations on his part, the tacit assistance of powerful companies interested in acquiring rich planets, moons, and asteroids, and diplomatic overtures to high-ranking government officials had resulted in his promotion to the head of Spacedep, twenty-two years after the Doona affair.

Landreau had looked for, and found, others who shared his dislike of the

Doona Decision. Some purists had always argued that a treaty promulgated through the linguistic precocity of a kid had to be defective. Certainly that most honest and unambiguous of treaties proved troublesome to some ambitious and aggressive Humans.

Landreau carefully cultivated such officials, always seeking a way to burst the Doonan idyll—and avenge himself on the Reeves. Subtly, of course, for he would not risk his current high status: especially one which allowed him the facilities of Spacedep's far-flung resources and highly skilled and trained personnel. If some of the immense budget available to Spacedep's Commander in Chief was siphoned off to explore a way to achieve personal vengeance, it was admirably hidden in the morass of official reports, payments, and analyses.

There was, however, another covert reason for subverting the Doona Experiment: Hrrubans and Humans, dissimilar in form, needed similar worlds to colonize, and for the same pressures. If Doona failed, all terms of the Treaty were null and void. The forbidden sections of space would be open once again to Admiral Landreau's mighty vessels and well-armed fleets, and if the rich world was already inhabited by a Hrruban colony, tough on them! A few well-placed germbombs and the Cohabitation Principle was invalid. Unless, of course, other factions of Earth's government could be persuaded how archaic the principle was and rescind it. How much easier would life be on Earth if one could ship out the unwashed masses to fend for themselves on new worlds with viceroys to skim the riches off the top.

The Doonan settlers were certainly aware of Admiral Landreau's hatred, and his machinations, and there were many adherents on both home worlds that did their best to neutralize some of the worst of Landreau's subtle campaign in various government offices. Though Ken and Todd had never vocalized it, they knew that they were Landreau's particular target. Landreau regarded Todd as an incorrigibly wild brat who went native with distressing speed after landing on Doona. Todd's assimilation of the formalities of High Hrruban diplomacy at the age of six, Landreau dismissed as a fluke.

Hrriss, now nearly thirty-five, always had a cooler way of interpreting a situation than his tall friend. Hrrubans were unassailable by any power from Earth. By Treaty agreement, the arm of the galaxy which the Hrrubans chose to explore was off limits to Terrans. Hrruba's home system was protected by the same Treaty. Any incursion into either sphere would be an act of war. Even Landreau in his obsessive hatred for the Reeves would hardly start a war between the species to get at a single family. Though Hrruba was run by a bureaucracy of great antiquity fully as cumbersome as that of Earth, it was directed gently by one mind whose interests allowed expansion and alliance to proceed. Hrriss and his family were unlikely to be removed from their home for any reason less serious than war. It brought Hrriss's need to defend to two foci: Zodd and the Rrev family.

"I know Landreau's working every angle to spoil our chances if he can," Todd said. "But the Doona Experiment is doing incredibly well, and everyone on Earth knows it. There would have to be an awful stink raised to bring the Experiment to an end at this point."

"A diplomatic insult, perhaps?" Hrriss suggested delicately. "A wedge need not be a large one to drive two elements apart. On Rrala, Terra, or Hrruba, it makes little difference."

"Well, if Landreau thought he could start one on this latest diplomatic mission of ours, he failed." Todd grinned. "Rogitel of Spacedep sounded like he wanted to start an argument with me at the banquet on Hrretha, but I pretended to be bogged down in protocol—fardles, I know all the moves better than he does," Todd said with a snort, his eyes on the screen. Their quarry had reappeared on their side of the planet, and its orbit remained unchanged. "So I got him talking about exploration in the Eighth Sector—safe enough topic."

"I told you it would be useful to know those details," and Hrriss dropped his lower jaw in the Hrruban grin. "He tried me later. I refused to be insulted when he called me a would-be Hayuman. If he wishes to create an incident, he will have to try harder." Hrriss's wide pink tongue now licked his upper lip, a further sign of amusement. "Varnorian of Codep asked me if it was true that you were applying to join a Hrruban colony to escape penalties from Earth. As if that would not be a Zreaty violation."

"Glad you batted that rumor out of court. I heard a smitch of it, too, and disavowed it with all the innocence at my command." Then Todd snorted. "Anyone who knows me knows better than to try something that simple on me."

The *Albatross* had closed to within thousands of kilometers of its goal. It was easy to swing into orbit from planetary north. The scout had been designed to pass through atmosphere as easily as it did through the frozen void of space. It swept low, across the top of the envelope of atmosphere, above the mass of clouds enveloping the small planet, angling toward the signal.

"If you keep a sharp watch portside, Hrriss," Todd said, his own eyes on the starboard, "maybe we can catch it first time round and not waste too much time in-system."

It was Hrriss who first set eyes on the source of the distress signal.

"Zzhere!" he hissed, pointing with one of his extended claws. Todd marked the trajectory of the floating craft, perched just on the edge of orbit. It was too far away for the cameras to discern much detail about the ship itself, but one thing was clear: any passengers would soon become cinders. The orbit had decayed so much that in only a short time, their ship would be inexorably caught by the planet's gravitation and fall, burning, into the atmosphere.

"Hey, what if we dip below them and drop a tractor cable?" Todd suggested. "You know, that's awfully small for a ship, even a scout."

"And bigger than the average escape pod," Hrriss said, his tone thoughtful.

The size didn't seem unnatural. Hrruban and Hayuman exploration teams flew variously sized scout vessels. The difference was that the Human teams were larger, or doubled up in specialties. Hrrubans sent out the minimum crew needed to make a primary judgment on a planet. When they found one that warranted a full-team investigation, they dropped a one-way transportation grid to the surface and then 'ported in the appropriate personnel. "It must be Hayumans, then, or they would not still be here calling for help. Standard procedure for Hrrubans is to drop a temporary grid and 'port home safely."

The *Albatross* used the gravity well of the Hrrilnorr IV to brake its speed. The next time it passed within visual range, Todd was able to plot a course to follow their quarry.

"I have initial telemetry readings. No atmosphere leak from the surface of the craft," Hrriss said with relief, reading from his scopes for traces of gas.

Though the craft had been able to retain its structural integrity, it was in grave difficulties. Rather than describing a smooth orbit, the speeding vessel jerked and stuttered its way around the fourth planet, as if pulled this way and that by divergent gravity fields. It passed over the day side again. Hrriss and Todd were blinded by the glare of planetary sunrise.

"Attention, the ship," Hrriss spoke urgently into the comunit, using Terran, broadcasting on all frequencies. "We are the scoutcraft *Albatross*. We are here in answer to your Mayday. Can you read us?" He repeated the hail several times, and then in Hrruban. There was no answer.

He pushed up the gain on the receiver. Nothing came from the speaker but atmospheric noise and the repeated Mayday message.

"They could have lost all communications but the beacon," he said, plainly worried. "If their life support is already gone . . ." Hrriss trailed off and pointedly did not look at Todd.

Todd blanched at that possibility and bent over his controls, trying to keep his face expressionless. "We can spring the tractor line on the craft and haul it in. Passengers could use life suits to access the *Albatross*'s lock." Hrriss nodded approval of the strategy. "Hope it's not too late."

As if taking the pilot's words as a challenge, the small dot on the horizon appeared to fall out of orbit, heading like a meteor for the brilliant white layer of clouds below.

"Oh, no, you don't," said Todd, seizing the manual controls.

Todd drove the scout hard after it, hoping the damaged vessel would not pick up too much speed from the gravitational pull until the *Albatross* could swoop in on it. He toggled the magnetic tractor net into alert status. They were dragging through the top of the atmosphere now as the *Albatross* pursued its quarry, still kilometers ahead. His hands were a blur on the keyboard. Hrriss kept calling out to the ship in both languages, hoping for a reply from the craft ahead. With the sun reflecting off its surface, it was impossible to see more than a vague shape. Hrriss kept requesting on all frequencies for details of the damage the lone ship had suffered.

In the midst of the dense clouds thousands of meters below, Todd at last urged the *Albatross* ahead of the speeding hulk. There was a powerful jerk that bucked them around in their seats when the net of magnetic lines engaged the metal hull of the other.

"Gotcha," Hrriss said, his teeth snapping in triumph.

"Great. Now let's just tell those guys to drag ass over here."

Once Todd headed the *Albatross* back into space, the two men turned the external camera onto their prize, and irised down the lens to counteract the glare. There was a silence and an air of angry disbelief as they stared at the object the tractors had brought in. It was cylindrical in shape, the length of their own scout, and not unlike the escape shuttle they had mistaken it for. What their efforts had acquired was a full-sized orbital beacon, an unmanned buoy similar to the ones hanging above and below the proscribed system, still screaming out its Mayday message on the *Albatross*'s receiver as they stood staring at it. The needles on the VU meters leaped back and forth in their glass settings.

"So we've been suckered into an interdicted system by a recorded Mayday," Todd said, unbelievingly. "I'll report this illicit use all the way to . . ." He paused, since the top of Spacedep was Al Landreau and he knew what short shrift that report would get. "We have fallen into deep kimchee, my friend. I should have listened to you."

"No, friend Zodd, you listened to a distress call and acted conscientiously," Hrriss said with a heavy sigh. Neither needed to discuss the ramifications of this.

"Let's get this sucker hauled in and see if we can salvage that Mayday beacon. That'll add credibility to this incident."

"Good thinking, Zodd," and Hrriss programmed the winch for a slow wind while Todd monitored the progress from the external camera.

"Hold it!" Todd held up one hand. "There's something attached to it. Oh-ho! Double trouble. Did we record the capture? Good. Unless I'm vastly mistaken there's a device riding along a very suspicious-looking thickening of the longitudinal spar. That thing is rigged to blow on contact!"

"Rrrreelease," Hrriss said, almost spitting in disgust at the stratagem. "Can you get a close recording of that section?"

"I have so done." Todd was immensely satisfied by that much of this episode, but as Hrriss plotted their course out of the area, his elation drained from him. "Someone's been getting awful clever, Hrriss. Our course was known from the time we left Doona, so there was plenty of time to set this up where we'd stumble into the trap on our way back from Hrretha."

"All too trrrue." Hrriss nodded, his expression as bleak as his friend's. Even the markings on his intelligent felinoid face seemed to have faded in his concern.

"I could wish boils on the hide of whoever perpetrated this. We could have been killed!"

"Waz that the object? To kill us? Or to lure us into interdicted space?"

The eyes of the two friends met—the yellow-green and the clear blue.

"I know someone who wouldn't shed a tear at my demise," Todd said grimly.

"I have similar well-wishers," Hrriss replied, tapping the console with the tips of his claws in a rhythmic fashion.

"Our deaths wouldn't mean as much as our broaching interdicted space," Todd began, rubbing his chin. Stubble was developing, and there were moments, like this, when he wondered what he'd look like with a full beard, or at least sufficient face hair to make him more Hrruban.

"But not only is there prrroof of our samarrritanism, but also I, Hrriss, made all the vocal contacts."

Todd dismissed that notion. "Everyone knows we're together, so I've certainly been wherever you were, legal or not. What I don't understand is exactly why the tactic was planned in this fashion. Was killing the real end? Or discrediting us?"

The two exchanged few words on the rest of the journey back to Doona. Both of them were deep in thought as how best to mitigate their situation. Violating one of the main stipulations of the very agreement they were hoping to see renewed this year was not good, however inadvertent.

"Have you convinced yourself that the recording is enough, Hrriss?" Todd asked after they had identified themselves to the Doona/Rrala buoy.

"Our people will believe us."

"Let's devoutly hope that's enough. Too bad that false beacon didn't blow up. We could at least have brought a section of it home as additional proof."

"We *do* warn everyone that there are bogus Maydays out there!"

"That is obligatory. Bogus or not, we were in the right to investigate," Hrriss said one more time. "A cry for help from other space travelers is not ignored with impunity."

As soon as they landed the Albatross back on Doona, they contacted the tower. Linc Newry was on duty.

"Can you rustle your stumps, Linc?" Todd asked. "We got an official report to deliver."

"Official? Huh? Nothing to do with the Hunt, is it?"

"Not really, but it'd be great if we could get through landing procedures and decontam and get the Hunt properly organized," Todd said with an encouraging grin.

"I'm coming," Linc said, and obviously switched to a handset for he continued talking. "As you're just back from that Hrrethan shindig, I think it'll be okay if I just seal the lock on the *Albie* and we can do the decontam and stuff when the Hunt's over."

So Todd and Hrriss gratefully disembarked, watched the seal be affixed to prevent entry, and, thanking Linc for his courtesy, hurried off to find Ken Reeve and detail the Mayday incident.

"Genuine or not, you have to answer a Mayday signal," Ken agreed, though the affair obviously troubled him. He smoothed his hair back with a resigned hand. His thick, dark hair had receded above his temples, and lines were beginning to etch the fair, sun-weathered skin near his eyes. He and Todd were of a height now, but often, when he was confused and worried, as he was now, Todd felt himself still the small boy and Ken the adult. Maybe he relied too much on his father's wisdom where experience and the study of law didn't provide the answers. Hrriss sat beside him, his yellow-green eyes unwinking as he stared at the floor between his feet. Ken could tell the Hrruban was worried, but he was not as prone to outbursts as his son.

Todd's eyes were fixed hopefully on his father's face. Ken shook his head and sighed. "Wise of you, Hrriss, to handle all the oral transmissions. Let's hope that the pictures of that device and the possibly explosive ribbing show up." He gave his head another little shake. "Such contingencies will have to be written into the new Treaty, allowing for legitimate rescue efforts and specifying penalties for abuses. I shall suggest the modification myself to Sumitral at Alreldep. But I cannot be easy that the incident was there, waiting to trap the unwary." He paused again, holding up his hand when Todd opened his mouth. "Were there any other representatives at the Hrrethan ceremonies likely to have taken the same warp jumps you did?"

Todd looked abashed. "Dad, I just wanted to leave. My neck was rubbed raw and it was bad enough those Hrrethans insisted on giving the *Albatross* a clearance . . ."

"They insisted?" Ken asked, his expression alert.

"Yes, and we told them that Spacedep had already cleared the *Albatross* . . . Oh, I see what you mean. The recorder could have been tampered with there. You think we were to be the victims?"

"We were not the only ship likely to pass that system," Hrriss said in a slow thoughtful tone. "I will inquirrre. It is worrth that much. And discreetly." He dropped his jaw at Ken. "When one *is* hunted, one generally senses pursuit."

"Then I can leave you to mention this to Hrrestan?" Ken asked. Hrriss nodded. "I shall inform Hu Shih. That will satisfy the necessary protocol. Investigations can be initiated . . ."

"Just don't let that sort of time-wasting stuff interfere with the Snake Hunt, will you, Dad?" Todd was clearly apprehensive. "It's only two weeks away and we've a lot to do."

Ken smiled. "The Snake Hunt is too important to the Doona/Rrala economy to have its leaders absent. I'll handle all the necessary reportings. And inform Sumitral. He warned me to expect trouble from unlikely areas. Cunning of our detractors, isn't it, to start a controversy over a Samaritan issue! And it has the flavor of something the segregationalists would try."

"The group that think Hrruba is only being friendly to get their claws into the best star systems?" Todd asked with patent distaste.

"Or perrrhaps," and Hrriss let his fangs show, "it is those who sense we are arming ourselves for the conquest of your home planet."

"No one takes that foolishness seriously," Ken said quickly. "You don't even know where Terra is."

"Nor you Hrruba," and Hrriss winked.

Ken and Todd both laughed with their friend, whose full-throated chuckle would have sounded to many like an ominous growl. Laughter eased the tension lines from Ken Reeve's face.

"Go on, the pair of you. We'll deal with the matter after the Snake Hunt. Which is going to be brilliant this year, isn't it?" He pinned the two friends with a mock-stern glare.

"Absolutely!" The friends chorused that assurance and left Ken's office.

In only a fortnight's time, Doona would be inundated by foreign dignitaries and guests eager to witness, and participate in, the famed Doonan Snake Hunt. Hundreds of people would converge on the First Villages for the semiannual migration of the giant reptiles, and Todd and Hrriss were in charge of coordinating the Hunt. Which was not so much of a hunt as a controlled traffic along the snakes' traditional path.

While there had been intense arguments both for and against annihilation of this dangerous species, the conservationists—many of them colonists—had won. The immense snakes were unique to the planet, but their depredations, which affected only one area of the main continent, could be controlled. The reptiles ranged in size from two-and three-year-old tiddlers of three to five meters in length to immense females, nicknamed Great Big Mommas, growing to twelve to fifteen meters. They had incredible speed and strength and, although they ate infrequently, they had been known to ingest an adult horse or cow in one mouthful. Their vision was so poor that they could not see a man standing motionless a few feet from their blunt snouts, but they would strike at any movement: particularly one that gave off an enticing odor.

Their traditional route from the sea to the plains just happened to lie by the river farms of the settlers where quantities of livestock grazed, too numerous to be shut up during the migration. So the settlers had devised a method of herding the snakes, making certain by a variety of means that few escaped to wreak havoc among the herds and flocks.

At first the settlers resorted to crude methods of keeping the snakes in line, destroying far too many for the conservationists' peace of mind. Then hunters from other planets learned about the drives, as they were originally called, and begged to join in for the thrill and excitement of adding such a deadly specimen to their trophies. These men also had some excellent suggestions to give the Doona/Rralans, gained from similar drives of dangerous species to which Ken Reeve, Ben Adjei, the colonists's veterinarian, and Hrrestan listened with interest.

"Make it into a real Hunt," they were advised. "Attract the thrillseekers and you'll not only make some money out of it, but you'll have enough help to keep the snakes on the right track."

So the Hunt became an organized sporting feature; one which put considerable credit into the colony's treasury and one which became safe enough to advertise as a spectator sport for those who wanted titillation without danger.

At first, Ken and Hrrestan, with Ben's advice, organized the Hunt, but gradually, as Todd and Hrriss showed genuine aptitudes as Hunters and leaders, the management had been turned over to them. Much had to be arranged to insure that injuries were reduced to a minimum; that visitors were always teamed up with experienced Hunters or in safely prepared blinds; that the horses hired out were steady, well-blooded animals, accustomed to snake-stench and less likely to plunge out of control and drop their riders into the maw of waiting Big Mommas. There were hundreds of minor details to be overseen by Todd and Hrriss before Hunt Day.

When Todd and Hrriss got to their office, they found that much had already been put in hand by their assistants, based on assignments and duties from the last Hunt. Scouts had been given their posts in the salt marshes from which the migration began. Every homestead within ten klicks of the long-established route had had fences, walls, and buildings reinforced. "Sighters" who would fly above the swarm and monitor its progress had been chosen and their aerial vehicles serviced. "Lures" had volunteered. Mounted on two-wheeled motorized rough country bikes, they were specially trained to lead maverick snakes back to the main swarm and to kill snakes that could not be turned. Lures usually performed what had become a rite of passage for young Doona/Rralans: capturing or killing two snakes on a Hunt, or succeeding in stealing a dozen eggs from the marsh nests. In fact, this rite had become an honor sought after by hunters of every system. Many now came just to win accolades as proof of courage and to have their names added to this new legend.

Those who did not wish to expose themselves to physical danger were accommodated in snake blinds, built along, but back from, the river trail. From these, spectators could enjoy this unique sight and excitement. The blinds were sturdily constructed of sealed rla wood, strong enough, though in truth any Great Big Momma Snake could have knocked one into splinters with its powerful snout. However, experiments with various odors had proved that a heavy citrus smell liberally poured on the outside of the blind covered the scent of the juicy morsels within and was a powerful deterrent to the snakes.

Twelve Teams of from twenty to forty horsemen and women rode in escort of the snake swarm. Clever riders on the quick, well-trained horses could head off renegades or stragglers, for some of the tiddlers were always breaking off the main group, looking for something to eat. These were considered fair game for Hunters wishing to kill, or capture, in proof of their prowess.

Approved weaponry—for the Treaty did not permit heavy weapons in the colony—were projectile rifles, metal-headed spears, compound bows and arrows, and any sort of club (though bludgeoning a snake to death, even a tiddler, was extremely dangerous.) Crossbows were the most popular for a quarrel could penetrate right through a snake's eye to its brain. The only problem was to then keep out of the way of the thrashing body in its death throes.

The worst headache for Todd and Hrrestan was still the composition of the Teams, for they had to intersperse novice and experienced Hunters without jeopardizing team effectiveness. There were also some "solo" or small Teams of off-world hunters but they had to produce qualifications to hunt on their own: proof that they were experienced riders and projectile weapon marksmen; preferably letters from other authorized Hunts or Safari Groups.

As Todd scanned the list of those on his Team One, he noted with satisfaction that Kelly Solinari was on it. So, she'd be back from Earth! She'd be a good team second, even if she had been away from Doona for four years learning how to be a good diplomat at Alreldep. Another name, scrawled so badly that he couldn't quite decipher it, was new to him but documentation showed that this J. Ladruo had participated in several well-known Safaris. Well, Team One had to take its share of novices.

He put that minor detail from his mind and went on to designate the places where they'd have to place charges that could be detonated to startle the snakes back into line. Usually the Beaters managed that, with drums, cymbals, flails and small arms fire, but he pored over the accounts of the last Hunt, to see where breakthroughs had occurred and how he could prevent them. He almost suspected the snakes of rudimentary intelligence the way some evaded Teams and Beaters. He'd begun looking at meteorology reports, too, for a wind from the wrong direction would make a shambles of the most careful plans. Drafting contingency plans for windy conditions was his next task.

"The first Hunters have arrived," Hrriss told him, coming in with their documents.

Todd looked up, startled. "So soon?"

"Zooon?" Hrriss dropped his jaw in a grin. "You've been working too hard, my Zodd. Only two more days before the deluge!"

Todd groaned as he took the papers from Hrriss and checked the names off against the Hunt application list. Then he brightened. "Two more days and Kelly'll be home."

Hrriss's grin deepened. "You'll be happy to see her?"

"Sure, she's the best second I ever had." He didn't notice the odd look his friend gave him.

Of the many people making their way to Doona for the Hunt, Kelly Solinari was probably the most excited. She couldn't wait to breathe fresh air again on Doona. On Earth, you felt that taking a deep breath was a crime against your fellow humans and besides, it didn't smell good so why contaminate your lungs with government issue. She knew that Earth's air had improved with stringent reductions of pollutants and the careful control of waste products but her lungs didn't agree. She was also looking forward to eating "real" food again: the absolute calorie rationing on Earth was nothing short of a sophisticated form of starvation. For a born Doonan such as she, these four years were a prison and she was about to be set free.

There had been a lot of change on Earth since her father and mother had left the stagnant, crowded planet: and they'd been considered radical for wanting to emigrate. Now there was an active desire, especially among the young, to break away from their crowded, depleted home planet and go out to settle among the stars. New opportunities had created an aura of hope, lightening the general gloom of the population. The success of the Doonan experimental colony begged the question of when more planets would be made available. Without the Hrruban element, of course.

In the back of every mind lingered the warning of Siwanna, the awful memory of the destruction of another race. In Kelly's diplomacy courses, the Siwanna Tragedy was brought up again and again to warn the eager young diplomats-to-be that such an error could be repeated. It had been an unforgettable and tragic shock that the Siwannese had suicided as a race when the colonists from Earth encountered them. They had been a gentle people, with too fragile a culture to survive contact with another intelligent species. Siwanna was empty now. Codep had erected a memorial to the race there, and had forbidden anyone to settle on the world whose inhabitants had been accidentally destroyed. And that was the beginning of the Noncohabitation Doctrine. No Human colony could be initiated on any planet already inhabited by sentient beings.

The Hrrubans' strong culture and identity made them, in the administration's eyes, a statistical rarity. The Doona colony was an exception, where colonization teams from two cultures had met accidentally. The first-contact groups were to regard all new races as fragile and potentially self-destructive. Depending on which teacher you were talking to, this meant Hrruba was Earth's partner in the great task of opening up the galaxy for exploration and colonization. Or, conversely, Hrruba was an obstruction to Earth's efforts. Kelly, who had been born on Doona, and had more Hrruban than Earth-born friends, was always ready to defend her Hrruban mates, and no one could match a Doonan in an argument.

Younger Terrans and her classmates generally shared her views. They wanted to see Humans allowed to live and prosper on new worlds. In the back of their minds was the idea of meeting and making friends with new alien races, though that thought was rarely voiced, not with so many older folk with ingrained habits ready to report them to noise monitors for loud talking. Who could have a decent argument in whispers?

It was so good to be home, even if Doona was crowded this season! Well, crowded for Doona, but only marginally inhabited compared to Terra. Kelly stared out of the hatch at the swarming mob on the landing field waiting for friends and family. It looked as if every single Human on Doona, all 45,000 of them, must be waiting to greet someone. There was even a cluster of Hrrubans, who enjoyed the spectacle of homecoming for its own sake.

She searched the crowd eagerly, hoping to see her own loved ones after her long absence. She'd be unlikely to see them, lost as they were in the mob of welcoming committees waiting to greet die important visitors who had traveled with her from Earth for the Snake Hunt. It had meant more ships coming in, a cheaper fare for her in consequence. And, to judge by the shuttles bearing the markings of other systems, Doona was already awash with those eager to be part of this primitive event.

One of her fellow passengers, Jilamey Landreau, had bored everyone at their table with his simulated-hunting triumphs. He considered that it was essential to his consequence to be at the Doonan Snake Hunt and kill "one of the big ones." Preferably from horseback, to prove his prowess against a living target. Even as they were making their way down the gangplank, he was still blathering on about it to anyone who would listen.

Kelly, who had hunted snakes on horseback herself, had been the patient listener many a time. She'd recognized his name and decided that it was smarter for her to play it cool in his presence. Her diplomatic training had taught her how to hold her tongue. She was also too kind to make fun of someone who had so far defeated only computer-simulated prey.

She turned her back on him gratefully when her mother and father, Anne and Vic Solinari, approached her from the other side of the field, crying out their welcome, gesticulating for her to notice their position.

"Sweetheart!" Anne said, gathering her into her arms. "Oh, Kelly, welcome home!"

"Oh, Mom," Kelly said, hugging her mother and suddenly feeling like a little girl again. "I missed you. Hi, Daddy."

"You look so grown-up," Vic said, embracing his daughter in turn. "I wasn't sure we'd recognize you. You look just fine. How was the trip?"

"Long," Kelly said, wrinkling her nose. "Cramped. Very smelly. All they had was canned Earth air."

Vic laughed. "It's the second thing that's kept me from taking a trip back to Earth: the first is living in the crowded conditions. I sure don't miss those little granite boxes! Well, come on! Your brothers and sisters are waiting to hear all about what you've been up to. All voice and video this time, not taped transmissions."

"Am I okay for Team One, this year, Dad?" Kelly asked urgently.

Her parents laughed. "Formal notice came last week," her father said, ruffling her hair. "And Michael's kept that Appie mare of yours exercised and has kept your snake-skin in her stall so she won't disgrace you, us, or Todd."

Kelly breathed out a huge sigh of relief. "I was afraid we wouldn't land in time."

"Afraid Todd wouldn't remember to put you on his team?" her mother said with a raised eyebrow.

"Oh, mother!" Kelly was glad of the excuse to go search for the luggage the handlers had just dumped on the tarmacadam.

Kelly finally found and threw the bags into the back of the family's power sled. It was exhilarating to be back on Doona. It couldn't just be the weaker gravity or the invigorating pure air that made her feel so light. She was happy.

As they flew toward their ranch, her mother and father pumped her for data about her life over the last four years. She didn't stop talking for one moment all the way home. The weather was gorgeous, and Vic kept the top of the sled down so they could enjoy the sun.

Then he was turning the sled into the gate of the family ranch, some klicks distant from the original First Community buildings. The new town had been built some distance from the original colony site, out of the path of snake migration. Their ranch abutted the Reeve farm on one side and the Hu property on the other. Behind them was the red sandstone back of Saddle Ridge, no-being's-land except for the wild animals native to Doona. Beyond that and the river was the Hrruban First Village. Every landmark came rushing back to her like the tide coming back up the Bore River from the distant sea.

She knew her mother and father were struggling against laughter as she kept inhaling and exhaling until she was hyperventilating. But she couldn't seem to get her lungs cleared of all that stinking canned air. And she couldn't keep from swiveling her head about her, wishing it were on a 360-degree socket. The sheer space, just loose and lying around, was a sight for her eyes.

Student housing allotment on Earth was very cramped, even for a junior diplomat trainee in Alreldep. No special treatment was given one who had graduated with honors or taken the advanced degree in only a year. She had had to endure the same tiny quarters as any other beginner in what she liked to call Diplodep. She had missed having room to stretch out, and the view of faraway horizons. She had longed for that almost as much as she had missed her family. And Todd. And today was the Hunt.

They were nearly at the ranch house now, and Kelly felt her heart pounding for pure happiness. Two of the farm dogs paced the sled, barking their heads off. Kelly leaned out, calling their names and trying to pet their heads as they ran.

Vic coasted the sled to a stop in between the house and the barn. When he turned the ignition off, he gave Kelly one more quick hug.

"Welcome home, sweetie. Hey!" he yelled at the house. "Lookit what I brung home!"

Joyfully, Kelly leaped out of the sled and into the arms of her brothers and sisters. The two smallest, Diana and Sean, tried to jump into her arms. The dogs raced around them, barking and jumping and trying to lick her face.

"Hello, coppertop," she hailed her brother Michael, who waved from the door of the barn and hurried up to meet her. Michael was a year her senior, but they had always pretended to be twins. Their faces were very much alike, with broad foreheads, wide golden hazel eyes, and strong pointed chins. His hair was as fiery a red as hers and just as thick. Their mother always said they reminded her of two matches in a box. Their father, more kindly, merely called them autumn-colored, to suit their autumn birthdays.

"Hi, hothead," Michael said with a broad grin on his face, swinging her around in a circle. He was a very junior veterinary resident, working under Ben Adjei at the Doona/Rrala Animal Hospital. Michael was still clad in his white tunic, but was stripping it off as he steered her toward the house. "Hurry up and change into your gear. They're going to start Gathering the Hunt at twelve hundred hours. Go scrub the ship stink off your skin, or the horses'll run from you, not the snakes. Unless you're too tired to participate?" he asked teasingly.

"Not a chance!" Kelly said, wriggling free and heading toward the house. "It's what I hurried home for! Oh, how I've missed Calypso."

"That's what Todd said you'd say." Michael nodded, helping her carry her bags. "Still horse crazy after those years of horseless Earth?"

"Thank goodness, he and Hrriss got back from that Hrrethan assignment," Kelly said, ignoring her brother's jibe. "Wouldn't be a proper Hunt without them leading it."

As soon as she had showered in unlimited hot water and dressed in comfortable well-worn clothes, Kelly raced out to saddle her bay mare, Calypso. The mare gladly accepted the present of a couple of carrots and nuzzled her mistress's hand. Kelly just hoped that she hadn't forgotten too much in her years away. But Calypso would take care of her: she usually did. And there was just time left to get down to the Assembly Hall.

Vaulting into the saddle, Kelly kneed Calypso forward, toward the fields leading to the village common. After living on earth for a time, it was hard to readjust to so few people per square kilometer. By law, there could be only as many Humans as Hrrubans. After the Decision came into effect, more Humans had had to be imported to equal Hrrubans, and four more villages' worth of

Terran colonists—out of the millions applying—had come to Doona/Rrala. Even so, the combined population made little impression on a planet whose diameter was three thousand kilometers greater than that of Earth.

Kelly was proud that her mother and father were two of the original colonists. Over the quarter century since that historic Treaty, Admiral Sumitral of Alreldep had continued to negotiate with Hrrestan, Hriss's father and chief of the Hrruban village elders, to make room for more Humans who wanted to leave overcrowded Earth and more Hrrubans with a similar desire. The talks had been successful, and the population of Doona had increased a thousandfold. Men and women who had lived in cramped, crackerbox-sized apartments on Earth had built homes and ranches in the fertile river valleys and settled down with room to stretch out.

No limit had actually been set on how much land each settler could claim, so long as waste, pollution, and senseless destruction of resources were avoided. As well as the native urfa, Vic Solinari, who had come to Doona as the storemaster, had elected to raise sheep and goats, his share of the precious breeding stocks sent from Earth. To keep the grasslands healthy, he rotated their pasturage every season to another part of their land. Typically Doonan, he also had a stable of horses, Kelly's favorite animal as well as cats and dogs.

It had been four years since Kelly had seen a living animal except Humans and Hrringa, the lonely Hrruban minding the transmitter grid in Alreldep block. Elated and exhilarated, she screeched greetings to a flock of goats milling around in a pen, and sighed with happiness as a cluster of young colts galloped in play across a fenced meadow not far from the house. It was wonderful to be home. Kelly legged Calypso into a canter down the hill toward town, revelling in the rhythmic gait and the joy of being back in the saddle again.

chapter two

Dr. Ben Adjei had estimated the day this year—and he hadn't been wrong in twenty years—when the great reptiles would migrate from the salt marshes to the low-lying desert fifty kilometers inland to lay their eggs. Only off-worlders bet against him, the local population shrewdly inciting them to do so.

A Sighter had landed her small copter behind the Reeve ranch house early in the morning to alert Todd that the egg-heavy female snakes were arriving in the desert and beginning to burrow into the dunes. Immediately, Todd called a meeting of leaders of the Hunt at the colony Assembly Hall. They had gathered from all over Doona and had been staying in or around First Village for the last few days, in case Ben Adjei's estimate was off a bit.

For the past fifteen years, Todd and Hrriss had been in the first line of hunters. Their rapport was instinctive: they seemed to read each other's mind. They never took unnecessary chances or risked lives, theirs or others. Their impressive tally of kills and captures of the dangerous reptiloids had reached legendary totals. As they grew to an age when their parents would permit it, they came to lead the Hunt and had done so now for ten years.

"You could see them in the underbrush, swarming toward the sands," Lois Unterberger informed the leaders who had congregated at the Reeve residence, the usual Hunt headquarters. Excitement made her brown eyes wide, showing white all around the irises. Her dark hair was intricately braided and pinned tightly to her scalp. "Hundreds of them, like a river, pouring onto the dunes and disappearing into burrows. I followed the leading edge all the way from the salt marshes. Hrrel is still in his copter over the dunes, watching until I get back."

"This is it," Todd said excitedly. "Lois, you fly back and keep an eye on the snakes. We've got to know the minute they start to leave. Dar," he instructed another Sighter, "go and check the snake blinds along the way to make sure everyone knows the snakes are coming and to stay inside. Take two of the Lures with you, and drop them at the vulnerable points we discussed."

"Gotcha! I'm away," Dar Kendrath said, dashing for his small craft.

"And keep in touch!" Todd called after him. "We need to know the moment the snakes start to move out!"

Dar threw him a salute from the seat of his copter as the vehicle took off.

"We're ready," announced Lou Stapley, who was in charge of the Beaters, who helped to keep the snakes in train by thrashing the undergrowth with flails or beating drums and cymbals.

Wranglers, very experienced riders, were in charge of each horse platoon. Their main concern was spotting the nervous rider who could panic his mount. Or a horse who suddenly decided he had had quite enough snake hunting in his lifetime.

Hrrula, one of the Reeves' oldest friends, was both the leader of Team Two and a Wrangler. "Everrryone is prrrepared," he assured them.

"Great," Todd said, checking them off on his list. All the preparations were falling together nicely.

"We've got the pass blocked toward the Launch Center," Jesse Dautrish said, scratching his jaw. "Let's hope it looks impassable to snake eyes. But it won't take long to clear it after the Hunt's over. The bridges have thorn barricades as well as mines, just in case the snakes try to cross the easy way." Though the snakes could swim, the banks of the rivers upstream were too sheer and deep for them to get a belly-hold. "I need another shower," he added, scratching his waist. "Damn dust settles in every pore."

Jesse's assistant, Hrrol, brushed at her short, tan fur, sending up clouds of dust. "All the charges are laid near rrrsidences and rranchess," she said. "Here's your copy back, Hrriss."

"Well done," Hrriss told the attractive Hrrol, and passed the list to Todd.

"Okay, okay," Todd said, calling the Hunters to order. "Let's go. Spread the word, we gather the Hunt at noon, and we'll ride out as soon as we get the word from the Sighters. Robin, see you at the feast later."

"Right, Todd!" called Todd's youngest brother, running for his horse. "Good hunting!"

Todd and Hrriss saddled their mounts and rode to the Assembly Hall to wait for the rest of Team One. Horses were still the primary form of individual transportation on the colony world. Doonan-bred horses were one of the colony's most important assets and trade goods, especially on Hrruban-settled worlds. Hrrubans were fascinated by the gentle quadrupeds, and were natural riders. The breeding of horses, rescuing the beloved animal from near extinction by careful genetic husbandry, was done on nearly every ranch on the planet, both Human and Hrruban. The Doonan style of saddle and bridle included gems and other valuable pieces easily obtained from the planet's generous storehouse of precious minerals.

The style, which echoed the formal wear of the Hrrubans themselves, seemed unbelievably ostentatious to denizens of Earth, to whom a single one of these gems represented additional comforts not yet purchased. When gems could be picked up in riverbeds and rift bottoms and polished with little effort by the finder, it was difficult for young Doonans to take the awe and greed over such trinkets seriously. Todd was proud of the way his gray gelding, Gypsy, looked in the new tack he'd made, aglitter with gilding and pretty stones, many of which had no commercial value, but some of which were worth enough alone to buy a change of status on Earth.

The colony folk had also rediscovered handcrafts. Doonan/Rralan crafts were so well thought of that goods of that origin commanded a good price offworld: pottery; needlecraft; weaving; stone, metal, and wood sculpture; jewelry; and leatherwork. An object made of the porous rla wood could be dyed in rainbow colors before it was painted with rlba sap to seal and harden it to the consistency of stone without the weight. Todd's saddle frame was made of rla, giving him a sturdy seat that required no effort for his mount to carry. He needed to travel light, because the Hunt was hours of hard riding.

Gypsy danced beneath him as other Hunters and their horses gathered around them on the common. The gray gelding had caught some of the excitement Todd was feeling. The hard work of the last two weeks was about to pay off. He and Hrriss exchanged grins of relief.

"Do you know, for a while I was afraid no one else was coming when the shuttles were late arriving?"

"Not coming!" the Hrruban echoed, mocking disbelief lighting his eyes. "Many spend the time between Hunts looking forward to the next one."

A slender horsewoman on an Appaloosa mare rode down the hill toward the square, standing in her stirrups and waving. Todd recognized the flame-bright hair on sight and vigorously waved back.

"Hey, Hrriss, Kelly made it back!"

"Good!" Hrriss said, raising his own long arm to return her salute. "One more good backup rrriderr to keep order among the aliens."

"Hey, gal, welcome home," Todd shouted when she was near enough to hear him over the pounding of Calypso's galloping hooves. "Mike said you were trying to make it in time for Hunt. And you haven't changed at all!"

She plumped back in the saddle, to signal the mare to halt, and eased her between Gypsy and Rrhee, Hrriss's mare. Now, grinning, she snapped her fingers, her expression mock-wistful. "Gee, and I worked so hard to create a new image."

"Don't bother," Todd replied, grinning back. "The one you got's not bad enough to put anyone off. Exactly."

"Oh, you! Hrriss, how are you?" and she turned to the Hrruban. "Heard you guys got drafted on that Hrrethan 'do.' "

Todd and Hrriss exchanged quick glances. How had Kelly heard of that? But men, she was an Alreldep trainee.

"Verry well," Hrriss answered, dropping his jaw. "The speeches lasted many hours. If it were not for the pleassure of having a functioning transportation grid, the people of Hrretha would most gladly have forgone the honor of having so many eminent speakers."

"Spacedep and Codep both sent representatives," Todd added. "I was a little surprised to see Varnorian there himself, instead of sending a deputy as Spacedep did."

"A good thing you went to keep them honest," Kelly said, making a face. "I've been hearing all about the two of you from my little cubbyhole in Alreldep block! You're considered to be quite a pair of heroes there."

Todd waved her words away embarrassedly.

"You must tell us all about your experriences, as soon as the Hunt is over," Hrriss said, showing his fangs in the widest Hrruban smile.

"Absolutely!" she promised them.

Kelly's mention of Alreldep brought back to Todd the full memory of his ship's passage into the interdicted zone around Hrrilnorr, and the fact that two weeks had gone by and there hadn't been the least hint that their "rescue" had been recorded, or even mentioned to the Treaty Council.

He would be interested to know if she had heard any rumors: especially one that might suggest the beacon had been planted by factions unsympathetic to the Doona Experiment. This was not the time to bring up such a sensitive topic. Riders needed their wits about them in the Hunt. Plenty of time to take her aside and get her reactions later on.

"That medical kit been renewed lately?" Todd asked her, nodding at the roll neatly strapped to the cantle.

"You bet. Mike made it up special," and Kelly gave him a wry sideways glance, "in case you fall off again!"

Todd snorted. "And when was the last time you saw me fall off?" he demanded in mock outrage.

"You have two to your credit," Hrriss said, his eyes narrowing slyly. "Did not Ken say it takes thrrree falls to make a rider?"

Todd laughed and patted his sides tenderly. "More like two hundred, friends."

The rest of Team One began to close up to the leaders. Two more old friends, Hrrin and Errala, from one of the distant Rralan villages, rode up behind and greeted them happily. The three shook hands with the Hrruban mates. Todd checked them off his list.

Places in the teams were always reserved for friends and friends of friends. The prestigious first six Hunter teams had to open further to admit high-powered guests whose inexperience sometimes tested the experience and skill of their hosts. But their presence meant a healthy contribution to the success of the Hunt and thus had to be tolerated.

Hrrubans and Humans in equal numbers joined the ride every year. Though Hrrubans required slight alterations to the standard saddle to accommodate the difference in their skeletal structure, they were keen on any opportunity to ride their beloved hrrsses. Ocelots, gifts to the Rralans from their Human friends, prowled alongside their masters' mounts, waiting for the signal to go. The spotted hunting cats were among the few animals that were fearless in the presence of snakes, and kept down other pests that troubled the settlements. The more skillful, working in teams of four or five, even brought down young snakes and killed them.

Hrrula skillfully guided his horse to join theirs, followed by the rest of Team Two. The sudden crowd caused Hrriss's two pet ocelots, Prem and Mehh, to go on guard. He swung off his mount to soothe them. Hrriss found that he did not recognize most of the Hrrubans who made up Team Two. They were undoubtedly visitors, probably from the new colony worlds. Hrrubans who lived on Rrala did not have such a wild, predatory look when discussing the Hunt, and those who still lived on Hrruba were revolted by the thought of slaying fresh meat. Though understandably excited about the pursuit and kill, Rralans were more concerned with staying alive throughout the Hunt. Hrriss calmed Prem, who seemed to have caught his agitation. The fierce little cats had been a gift from Todd and had already proved themselves in battle with the snakes. It seemed they were as eager as he was to confront them again.

Each team leader checked in with Todd as soon as he or she arrived in Assembly Square. Inessa, Todd's younger sister, hailed them from Team Six, waving a throwing stick. Hrriss poked his friend in the elbow and pointed to Inessa. They both waved. Since their older sister, Ilsa, had married and returned to Earth, Inessa and her two younger brothers, Dan and Robin, took it in turns every year to ride with the Hunt or help guard the family ranch. Hrriss, the only offspring of his parents, used to envy Todd his many siblings until he found that they regarded him as an extension of Todd.

Suddenly Todd groaned. "Will you look at that? Spare me!" He tossed his head in the direction of the Assembly Hall, to their left.

Obediently Hrriss and Kelly glanced that way. From the doorway, a young man swaggered out wearing the very latest in hunting pinks, and boots that had to have cost the equivalent of starfare between Earth and Proxima Centauri. He swung a six-foot length of polished wood between his fingers.

"Don't they ever read the advisories we send out on what kind of protective clothing to wear for rough riding?" Todd said in a low but disgusted tone.

"But, Todd, he's trying. I heard him tell me that he researched both hunting garb and polo accoutrements and decided on this compromise as being appropriate," Kelly said, her eyes brimming with devilment. "I heard him every mealtime, in fact."

"And you didn't warn him?" Todd shot her an aggrieved glance.

"What? And ruin our fun?"

"He was on the ssshuttle with you?" Hrriss asked.

"Indeed, and at my table. That, dear hearts," Kelly said, amused, sitting back in her saddle to watch their expressions, "is Jilamey Landreau, Spacedep's nephew. He's harmless."

"I'll give you any odds, Kelly dear old thing, that he's going to be trouble for whatever Team he's on," Todd said, summing up the stranger with a practiced eye, as Jilamey mounted the horse chosen for him with a modicum of expertise, though the quarterstaff proved an immediate encumbrance. "I don't like the stable he comes from."

"It is not the stable he comes from that should concern us Zodd," Hrriss assured him, his eyes glinting mischievously, "and his trouble will be in conzrolling his hrrss. He will not be in our way."

"Ah, but he said he's on Team One," Kelly replied, delighted at the shock on Todd's face.

He fumbled for the Team list in his pocket. "I've got a J. Ladrulo ... Oh, no."

"I wondered at him being on Team One," Kelly said her face full of mischief. "I thought you knew what you were doing. However, don't worry about him. I'll make him my responsibility. I owe him a couple." Now her eyes took on a gleam similar to Hrriss's, her expression bland. "For aspersions cast like bread upon the surface of our table."

"You're mixing metaphors again," Todd said, ready for the banter they always enjoyed. "Didn't they teach you anything useful at Alreldep?"

"How to manage little men like Jilamey, sweetheart," she said, giving him a coy and insincere smirk. But she sighed as Jilamey urged his animal over to Todd and Hrriss.

He threw them a jaunty salute and banged the quarterstaff painfully against his knee. The horse snorted, flicking an ear at such an unusual appendage. " 'Lo, Kelly. Didn't think I'd have the pleasure of your company so soon again, much less with Team One. Jilamey Landreau, at your service. Nearly missed my chance—shuttle was late. I've heard all about your local menace. Read up on the subject, too. I'm expecting great things of this day. I want to catch a really big snake. I'm assured that you're the best. My friends"—he threw a sly glance over his shoulder at his ship companions—"could only get on Teams Three and Four."

And why he wasn't with them, instead of complicating Team One, Kelly did not know. She'd have a small talk with the village elders later, she assured herself. Punctiliously, she introduced Todd, Hrriss, Hrrin, and Errala to Jilamey. At least he had enough manners not to gawk at the Hrrubans.

"Landreau, you say?" Todd asked with cool courtesy "Not any relation to Admiral Landreau, by any chance?"

"The Admiral's my uncle. That's why I got on your team." Jilamey grinned amiably.

"Isss zat so?" Hrriss said, taking up Todd's lead. "I find it amazing that he would permit one of his kin to take parrt in a Snake Hunt."

"Why not?" Jilamey appeared surprised. "Supposed to be the best hunting available."

"The Admiral told you that?"

"He didn't need to. Everyone knows that," Jilamey ingenuously assured them.

The three old friends exchanged glances. The boy couldn't possibly be so naive. Or was it simply that no one had ever dared tell him how his uncle was linked with the Doonan snakes? Quite possibly. The settlers had escaped Landreau's attempt to dispose of witnesses to his humiliation by driving a swarm of snakes down on the barn where he had imprisoned the colonists. He had never returned to Doona, nor would he have been welcome. It was amazing enough that his nephew had been allowed to come. However, now that Landreau was head of Spacedep, in charge of space exploration and defense, he was also not someone to antagonize. If his nephew had inveigled a place on Team One, there might be reasons not yet known to Todd and Hrriss. But it galled Todd to have to protect a Landreau from snakes. Inwardly he also winced at the comments likely being made by other teams about Team One.

"Read up on the Hunt, you say?" Todd asked.

"Everything I could find about the great snakes of Doona," Jilamey replied, grinning at everyone.

Could the fellow—Todd pegged him at the mid-twenties—really be so naive? Or was he disguising a covert assignment for his uncle with this behavior?

"Team One is only one of many, then, you realize. There are dozens of teams," and Todd gestured broadly to the various groups around the village green, awaiting the reports of Sighters. "Each team supports each other. . . ." Jilamey nodded his head as Todd made each point. ". . . and we may be called upon to break off and go to another team's assistance if they're in trouble."

"But Team One takes the most chances, doesn't it?" And Jilamey looked anxious.

"Always," Hrriss assured him. "You will have the best of sporrrt with us!" His eyes glistened.

A Sighter's craft suddenly appeared and made an almost impossible swing to land in front of the Assembly Hall in a cloud of dust. The pilot leaned out of a hastily opened window.

"We've spotted the main swarm! They're starting to come out of the hatching ground! Should be due east of here in two, three hours at the most. We've left watchers with handsets in the brush along the way."

The announcement charged the atmosphere with eager anticipation. Only the uninitiated shouted and whirled their horses in glee at the coming test of courage. Todd and Hrriss trotted their horses over to the man, demanding details. The snakes could move along with unbelievable speeds. The best way to minimize the danger to livestock and Human was to intercept the swarms as far to the north of the main settlements as possible.

Don and Jan, a husband and wife from one of the Amalgamated Worlds colonies, galloped across the village green, slowing only when near the sled.

"I was afraid we wouldn't make it," Jan panted. "We rode all the way from the Launch Center."

"Your timing's as good as ever," Todd said. The pair were good friends to Doona. "We're just getting ready to go. You haven't missed a thing."

Don and Jan had moved up steadily from the other teams over the years, and were genuine assets to Team One. A slender woman woven out of whipcord,

Jan was a fine rider who had worked with the rare horses on Earth, and also a skilled hand with lasso. Don had keen vision, and was a dead shot with a rifle. With their arrival, Team One's complement was filled. To Todd's relief, there were no more duffers assigned to them.

Team leaders made their way to preassigned positions, marked out on the maps Hrriss had distributed the night before. Transmitters of featherweight Hrruban design were now being handed out to riders. If anyone became lost or injured, he or she was to call for help immediately. No place could be guaranteed as safe from adolescent snakes.

"I don't want to carry a radio set," Jilamey complained when he was handed his unit.

"It doesn't weigh much," Kelly said, snapping hers to a belt hook.

"But I don't wear a belt with this garb. It spoils the sit of the jacket. I'm already wearing this silly safety helmet."

"Mr. Landreau," Todd said, resisting an impulse to tell the young fool simply to belt up and go home, "the transmitter is not elective wear. It could mean your life, or the safety of others." Could Landreau have deliberately planted this imbecile in the hopes that he'd be killed and the Admiral could blame Doonans? Todd shook his head. That was too farfetched. He pointed a finger at Jilamey. "When you asked to hunt, you also signed an agreement, did you not, that you would abide by our rules?" Startled, Jilamey nodded. "If the sit of your jacket means more to you than your life, and others in this team, you don't have to wear the radio." Jilamey brightened. "But you'll have to stay in one of the snake blinds until it's over."

"Not a chance!" Jilamey protested, his eyes opening wide as he finally realized that Todd meant exactly what he said. "Oh, all right. I don't see what all the fuss is, anyway." With ill grace, he slung the transmitter belt bandolero-style across his chest.

The giant reptiles of Doona made their way to spawning grounds on the plains once a year, but for some reason returned from the sea along the river. They were fearsome to behold one at a time, but when they swarmed, as they did during this season, it was a sight beyond terror. The largest ones, "Great Big Mommy Snakes" in Doonan parlance, were the stuff of campfire stories to terrify small brothers and sisters on moonless nights. The most horrifying thing about the stories was that they were true. The snakes could reach lengths of twenty meters, with maws that could ingest a full-grown horse. Their smooth-muscled bodies were as large as tree trunks and covered by tough protective scales. Fortunately the snakes were not invincible.

Biologists had arguments over whether or not the snake stench stunned smaller creatures. Or whether, after all, the snakes were smart enough to hunt upwind of their intended prey. The young snakes, the two-year-olds, making their first return trip to the plains, were the most dangerous, because they weren't canny enough to avoid trouble. The small ones were only small by comparison. Even in their second year, they measured three meters, usually more. The combination of their youthful energy and inexperience and their pangs of wild hunger made them deadly adversaries. A young snake could bring down one of the fierce mdas all by itself. Weaker animals were snapped up as tidbits.

Doonans and Rralans had the advantage of knowing their terrain, the horses they rode, and of having witnessed many Hunts. But for outworlders who arrived with more bravado than training, the objective could be fatal. The prey was tricky and very dangerous. The contest was even weighted somewhat on the side of the young snakes. After all, none of the Hunters were five meters long and muscled in every inch. Then some wit decided to add an extra fillip, awarding "coup" points for using the least technology or hardware possible in making the capture.

Every year, a few of the would-be heroes got hurt while trying to capture a young snake that was too big or too wily. Todd didn't remember who had started the newest nonsense, but it had come to be a big headache for him and the other Hunt team leaders. He sympathized belatedly with the original masters, who had been in charge when he passed the adulthood ritual himself years before. He had pulled off a highly pointed coup by using a fire-hardened lance and a garrote to finish off the snake, and carried home more eggs than anyone else that year.

Every ranch had its own defenders, well prepared with bazookas, rifles, even shoulder-mounted missiles to discourage reptiloid invasions. It was preferable to deter entry rather than kill. Some said that snakes remembered where they'd been deflected and stayed away.

The snake stench was fierce along the river embankment, where the snakes had passed on their way to the spawning ground. The Appaloosa mare rolled her eyes and twitched, but showed none of the other signs of hysteria displayed by the younger mounts. Kelly patted her neck and settled into the comfortable saddle. Kelly favored the style invented by the gauchos of old Earth, which protected rider from horse with layers of soft padding between each and the saddle frame. The fluffy sheepskin which Kelly bestrode on top of all made the contraption look heavy and ridiculous. In reality, it was lighter than most leather saddles, and held her so snugly it was almost impossible for her to fall off. She was grateful for her choice, feeling her tailbones where she had lost her saddle calluses. If she rode a day on leather now, after four years' absence, she'd be crippled for a week. Chaps, like the ones worn by Todd and most of the other Hunters, protected her legs from trees and scrub.

Fastened by her knees, she had two small crossbows, loaded with the safety catches on, and half a gross of quarrels, some of them explosive. She also had a spear with a crosspiece for protecting her hand at close quarters, and the traditional paint-capsule gun for marking troublesome snakes she couldn't reach, for the next teams to pick out.

Kelly noticed that Jilamey had an almost dainty-looking slug-throwing revolver slung on the horn as well as a number of the approved weapons and that cumbersome quarterstaff. Clicking her tongue at his naivete, Kelly smiled. Wait until he saw one of the Great Big Mommy Snakes. His pistol would do no more harm than flicking sand at a leviathan would.

They passed one of the snake blinds that lay next to the path. The reek of the citrus perfume, like citronella, was powerful enough to divert humans as well as snakes. Kelly was glad to see that the newer snake blinds were situated close to thick, climbable trees. If one of the Hunters got hurt, there was a quick haven available.

Above them, Saddle Ridge was nearly invisible through the trees. As soon as they reached a landmark rock, they turned inland away from the river path and cut through the forest into hilly grasslands. Todd was leading them up as close as possible to the dunes without breaking cover. Once the snakes finished laying their eggs, they headed in whatever direction they thought led to food on the way back to their territories. The job of the teams was to cut off their other options, riding alongside the bulk of the snake swarm, guiding it back to the sea without giving it a chance to stop.

"The safest thing," Todd reminded the guests, "is to expedite the snakes' passage. There's plenty for them to eat in the water. We try not to kill the snakes that are willing to go peacefully. We want the wild young ones that endanger other creatures. It'll be easy to pick out the rogues and mark them if we run with them. We have to keep our distance from the main group, though, or they'll just gang up on us and eat us all."

Kelly could almost have repeated his speech word for word. It was the same one he had been giving for years. She smiled impishly at his back, which he held straight in the saddle, wondering what he would do if she chimed in. She was fond of Todd, and equally fond of Hrriss. Of course it was nearly impossible to think of one without the other, they were so inseparable. A pity. She couldn't help but think that their united front was what had kept both of them single all these years.

Ahead of them, a streak of brown and gray as quick as a blink broke out of the undergrowth and showed them a patterned back. Jilamey let out a yell, and Errala jumped, making her horse dance back out of the way. The snake, a tiddler at four meters, seemed just as surprised to see them. It doubled in its own length and scooted back into the brush.

"That one is afraid of us," Hrriss said, holding up a hand to forestall pursuit. "It may already have eaten, or it has learned discretion in the last years."

"I always like a Hunt that begins with a well-fed one," Jan said grimly, calming her mount. The radio crackled into life: Teams Six and Seven were in pursuit of snakes that had left the spawning grounds in the opposite direction, but the majority were coming Team One's way.

More snakes followed the first one, but these attempted to slither past the horses without stopping. The snakes were normally solitary creatures, but at this particular moment of their life cycle, they did seem to understand safety in numbers. When pressed too closely, they split up and headed in several directions, hoping to elude pursuit. The team formed a wall with spears and flashing lights, heading off snakes and scaring them into the direction they wanted them to go. The Hunters and Beaters stationed along the way would repeat the actions, keep them moving toward the river route. Suddenly a Mommy Snake, not one of the GBMSs, but still more than respectable in size, appeared between the outcroppings of rock. It was followed by a swarm of smaller snakes that quickly outdistanced it.

Yelling into his radio, Todd wheeled his horse after them and kicked the animal to a canter. "We got some biggies on the road!"

The others followed, falling into position behind him. The team formed a cordon along the front edge of the swarm, following it downstream into the trees, keeping it contained with pain and noise. With the blunt end of spears, flashguns, whips, even brooms, they pushed, prodded, and drove the snakes back into line. The Hunters had to stay spread out, since their quarry ran anywhere between twice a man's height in length and fifteen meters long. A single snake could endanger several riders. Somewhere behind them, as the stream of reptiles advanced forward, Teams Two, Three, and Four were joining the wall of Hunters. The river acted as a natural barrier on the other side, saving manpower. Still more teams were spotted in the forests and meadows, driving stragglers that broke out between the teams where the Beaters' threshers couldn't go.

"Now we ride them into the sea," Jilamey crowed, brandishing the staff above his head like an Amerind he must have seen in the Archive Pictures.

"It is *not* that easy," Kelly yelled back, losing her composure at last. Really,

Jilamey was just begging to be killed. Or thrown. His mount really didn't like all that brandishing.

A tiddler, probably returning from its first spawning, catching the scent of the lathered mare, slithered toward her with amazing speed. Calypso saw it coming and swapped ends to buck, lashing her hind feet out at it. Kelly hung on. Calypso might be accustomed to the stink but she retaliated in proper equine fashion to the direct assault. Landreau, thinking he was being heroic, spurred his mount toward it and slammed the staff down on its nose. Abruptly his horse ran backward as the tiddler reared up, ready to lunge forward, jaws wide and eager to swallow horse and rider in one gulp.

Cursing Landreau and her horse in one breath, Kelly swung Calypso about with the strength of her legs alone and leveled one of her crossbows at the predator. The snake was all bunched to strike when Kelly discharged the bolt. She'd lost none of her marksmanship in her four years away. The quarrel struck right through the creature's forehead. Sheer momentum kept the snake moving toward its prey while Jilamey's terrified mount managed incredible speed backward until it was jarred to a halt by a tree. Then, with a squeal of fear, the horse jumped off its hocks to one side and took off in a panicked run, Jilamey clinging desperately to his saddle. Then the tiddler fell sideways, a wavy line that quickly disappeared under the mass of snakes. No doubt one of the other reptiles would stop and eat the corpse while it was still twitching. Team Two or Three would have to deal with it.

Kelly and Calypso resumed their position as they passed one of the pairs of margin Hunters, who waved them a salute with spear and flashgun. They were positioned well, on a small natural upthrust of rock overlooking the well-worn river path. The snakes disappeared from Kelly's view briefly as the Hunters looped around the far side of the ridge and the snakes followed their own old road. It was to the Hunters' advantage that their quarry preferred to slither on smooth dirt and stone rather than over the uneven floor of the jungle. Kelly guided Calypso among the huge, ridged rla trees, keeping her eye on the young snakes. Before and behind her, flashguns popped, distracting the snakes who might break out of line.

Snarling yips and growls erupted behind them, amid the sound of two horses whinnying in fear. Kelly risked a quick glance over her shoulder. One of the bigger reptiles was coming up behind them, followed by a pair of horses crashing through the undergrowth. Two of the Hrruban visitors from Team Two had earmarked a Mommy Snake and were riding it down, without regard for the organization of the Hunt or their own safety. They wore only their equipment belts and helmets, without a stitch of clothing over their furred limbs and tails to protect against the branches whipping at them.

Their quarry had slipped out of line and was now on the outside of the Hunters' cordon. The experienced riders in Team One knew that the snake was only waiting to get far enough ahead of its pursuers to turn about and strike. Hrrubans had superlatively fast reflexes, but they were slow as falling snowflakes compared with the teeth and coils of a Mommy Snake. Only experience countered speed.

The snake was tiring. The species was made for sprinting and quick striking, not long-distance runs, and it had recently laid its eggs. The Hrrubans had probably surprised it coming directly off the hot sands through the narrow gap. It was in search of a wider place where it could make a stand. Kelly didn't like the situation she could see developing. Couldn't the Hrrubans see that those meter-wide jaws could engulf one or both of them?

Todd turned his head and exchanged glances with Hrriss. The Hrruban abruptly edged his horse out of the line and slipped between and ahead of the two endangered Hunters. Kelly was sure she hadn't seen either one of the leaders lift his radio. It was this sort of instantaneous cooperation which gave them their reputation for telepathy. Todd raised his rifle to his shoulder and fired.

He was using an explosive shell. The shot went off against the ground in front of the Mommy Snake. It slid to a rapid halt in a heap of coils to see what had kicked up the dirt just as Hrriss gathered himself in his saddle and sprang.

It was an amazing leap. He landed on the back of the snake's neck. Its head went up to dislodge him, but he had sunk in his claws, the advantage Hrrubans had over Hayumans. Kelly judged the creature to be a good fifteen meters long, and the snapping teeth were as long as her hand. The Hrruban would be just a mouthful if he slipped. With one strong arm and his prehensile tail wound around the snake to hold on, Hrriss took the knife from his belt. The snake was unable to reach him with its teeth, but it had miles of muscled coils upon which it could call. It bucked and twisted, trying to dislodge him. A length of tail snapped around Hrriss's leg and squeezed. The Hrruban let out a snarl of pain and hung on. Kelly came level with him, then rode past him, looking over her shoulder in horror. She found she was riding next to Todd, who had slowed down.

"I'm going back," Todd called, wheeling his horse. "Keep the line in order."

"Right! Quick kill, Todd," Kelly replied. She turned her eyes forward. Behind her, she could hear Todd barking directions to the other two Hrrubans on how to attack the snake without further endangering Hrriss.

Jan and Don had spread out to make up for the shortage in personnel. Don was on the radio to the other teams, keeping track of the stragglers who strayed out of the cordon. He waved encouragement to Kelly, as did the other two members of Team One. Then Jilamey drew level with her, babbling something, his sweaty face red with excitement. Did he think he needed to help Hrriss and Todd? Idiot! She waved him on, to fill in the line behind Don. She lifted her radio to her ear and picked up field coordination where Todd had left off. He and Hrriss were already out of sight. They'd handle the Mommy: they were clever Hunters.

Todd galloped his horse back to where the Mommy Snake coiled and writhed, trying to dislodge Hrriss. Hrriss's now-riderless horse, cannoning between the others, had scattered the two strange Hrrubans' mounts in opposite directions, keeping them from reaching the Mommy Snake's open maw, and probably saving their lives, though the ungrateful Hunters would be unlikely to realize it.

Hrriss clung to the nape of the great reptile's neck, even though his leg had to be paining him. Repeated thrusts of his knife blade were scattering drops of ichor as the snake flung its head from side to side, trying to get rid of the agonizing pest on its back. Hrriss kept on striking powerful blows but the snake almost seemed to anticipate his targets and he hadn't hit anything vital yet. The blade bit again.

The great length of the snake coiled and writhed in fury. The two Hrrubans who were responsible for this disaster controlled their hysterical horses at a distance from the giant reptile, watching Hrriss, clearly not knowing what to do. Todd cursed. The Hunt was against killing any of the wildlife that hadn't gone rogue. Once one had gone berserk, the Doonans had no choice but to kill it to save their own lives. It was just like these senseless strangers to incite one to terminal frenzy and then sit back to watch the fun. No, that was unfair—they really didn't know what one of these snakes was capable of. But that wouldn't help his friend.

By now, Hrriss's two ocelots had joined the battle, tearing at the snake's sides to help their master. Long gouges were ripped from the skin, oozing ichor that was churning dirt into a hideously viscous mud. The snake bent its powerful neck to try and bite at the two little pests on the ground, but as it bent for one, the other would rake at it from the other side, turning its attention away.

Recognizing that he was unlikely to get a clear shot at the head of the furiously thrashing snake, Todd put up his rifle and reached for the lasso. He began whirling the rope just above Gypsy's head, keeping the noose small enough so as not to tangle in the branches above him. Despite his care the rope snagged on a bush and he had to start over.

Shouts alerted him that Team Two was closing in on them, following the next flux of snakes very near to the river path. Out of the corner of his eye, Todd could see that one of the riders had his own rope circling above his head, just shy of the canopy of leaves. Hrrula shouted to show he was ready. Hrriss ducked as low as he could go against the snake's back without flinging himself into its coils. Teeth gritted, Todd gave the signal, and both of them threw at once. As soon as the other man's noose dropped over the snake's head, he yanked back on his horse's reins, causing the animal to dig in its hooves in the soft mold and pull the rope taut. Todd pulled back, too, and the snake fought between the two lines, unable to reach either of its mounted tormentors. Struggling wildly, the snake released Hrriss's foot. The Hrruban grabbed hold of one of the ropes with a clawed hand and slashed repeatedly at the reptile's throat with his blade. It flung loops of itself forward to protect its vulnerable underjaw but not soon enough. Too much damage had been done by Hrriss's blade. Its loops lost strength and its head hung in the nooses, dying.

One of the strange Hrrubans, evidently deciding that the danger was over, rode forward and plunged his spear through one of the snake's eyes into its brain. The writhing of the coils became more frenzied, and gradually died into infinitesimal twitches. Todd let his rope drop slack and started to gather in the lengths, urging his horse forward with his knees.

The Hrruban visitor's triumphant cry echoed through the forest.

"I have killed the great one!" he crowed, flexing his claws over his head.

"The kill is Hrriss's," Todd said flatly. Hrriss was beginning to climb free. Todd swung off his horse to help him to his feet. Hrriss signalled that he was not seriously hurt, though he was favoring the leg. "If he had not acted when he did, the results might have been very serious for you."

On Hrrula's hissed orders, a Team Two rider went off into the brush to retrieve Hrriss's horse. He reappeared shortly, leading Hrriss's Rrhee, then rode off to rejoin his own team, now far ahead in the jungle. Hrriss spoke softly to calm the ocelots, mad with bloodlust who were still tearing at the twitching corpse of the snake.

"But I plunged the spear through its brain! It is dead, by my hand. I claim the kill," the visitor insisted.

Todd let his eyes meet those of the strange Hrruban. The visitor possessed a very broad back stripe, indicating that he held a position of rank in Hrruban society.

"With the greatest of respect," Todd said, dropping into full formal Hrruban which forced him to suppress the fury he felt, "there can be no doubt that the creature was already dying when you rode forward."

The broad stripe was somewhat taken aback by his host's use of the formal language. Since that was used only during events of the greatest importance, it was ingrained in the Hrruban not to disagree with the speaker without considerable forethought. Hrrula, an old ally of Todd's, waited silently nearby.

"Perhaps we will discuss the matter later," Todd said politely, gesturing to the Team Two leader. "We must complete the Hunt. Time is pressing."

"Quite right, honored guests," Hrrula said, having slathered the snake slashes and scale pinches with vrrela salve. "With your permission, Zodd Rrev, we must catch up with our team. We are needed." Before the strangers could protest, the Hrruban grabbed the rein of one of the horses and pulled it after him. The animal obediently followed the lead mount. In a moment all three of them were out of sight.

Todd mounted up again. He sent a concerned glance toward Hrriss. "There's a snake blind only a hundred meters ahead, if you need a rest."

"I am all right," Hrriss assured him. "Truly. There is no real damage. The circulation will return to the leg in a short time. It could have been worse."

"Could have been much worse," Todd said. Then, with a wicked grin, he added, "It could have been your tail!"

"Team Three leaving the spawning grounds," his radio announced. "They're moving slow this year. Vic just herded a couple of tiddlers that were trying to leave the grounds from the wrong side. Look out for 'em. They're mad."

"Fardles!" Todd put his heels to his horse. Hrriss's episode had taken only a few minutes from start to finish.

The sound of hoofbeats pounding up behind her made Kelly swivel about in concern. One, no, two horses returning. She relaxed and smiled as Todd and Hrriss passed her.

"Hrriss did it in!" Todd called. Hrriss was leaning to the right, obviously favoring his left leg. "Good kill. Mommy Snake! Fifteen and a half meters or I'll eat it. But he'd better not get a big head, or he won't get through the trees!"

"You're lucky to be alive," Kelly said to Hrriss, at the same time pulling a face at Todd. "That was a magnificent tackle! I hope those two Hrrubans realize you saved their lives."

"Those foolish ones were made to understand that by Zodd," Hrriss assured her, his tail tip lashing to one side of his saddle. The others cheered and shouted encouragement to him as he resumed his place in the line. Todd moved ahead and raised his radio on high as a signal to move out. Kelly told the other team leaders that Todd was in charge again and clipped her own box to her belt.

They were moving swiftly up on the most dangerous part of the Hunt. The team was about to leave the jungle and move out on featureless grasslands.

Without the trees to restrict them, the snakes often attempted to escape from their shepherds and go in search of landbound food. The task of keeping the swarm together the rest of the way was made more difficult by the local landowner.

Twenty-five years ago, when the Treaty allowed more Humans in, to match the Hrruban population, Codep had added four families to the original eleven in the First Village. The Boncyks were one of those four. In spite of warnings from the established colonists that the snakes used this area as a thoroughfare twice a year, Wayne claimed the fertile plain not far from the marsh for his family's holdings. On top of that disregard for local wisdom, the Boncyks compounded their problems by running herds of cattle and teams of pigs, China and Poland. Naturally the snakes, especially the hungry tiddlers, found the smell of live meat irresistible. The larger ones, with the larger hungers, would go berserk if the wind shifted to tantalize them with the odor of edibles.

To prevent wholesale slaughter, this was when the teams had to be most alert. The Hunters were already tired. Fortunately the snakes were wearing out, too, but they became more cantankerous and tricksy. Once the tantalizing Boncyk farmlands were past, the salt marshes were not far, and once the snakes reached them, they would disperse while the teams remained on guard to drive back any who might decide to return to dry land—and fat cows and pigs. When the last of the snakes were back in the salt marshes, hunting the rodents, waddlers, waders, and other such tidbits, the Hunt would be declared over and the triumphant teams would return to the village common, except for the skeleton force that remained on guard until the next morning.

Jilamey had had his eye on a pair of young adolescent snakes almost since he rejoined the run. With the bare treetops of the marsh wood in sight, he was going to have to move quickly to capture his quarries before they vanished into the fetid waters. Kelly watched him measuring the distance to the edge of the marsh.

With a now-or-never expression on his face, Landreau spurred his horse toward the pair. He had his quarterstaff well balanced in his right hand, confident that he could knock the snakes on their blunt skulls, stunning them, and secure them alive.

In theory, it was a good idea. However, it failed utterly to take into account the nature of snakes. As soon as Jilamey thumped one of the fleeing tiddlers in the back of the head with the heavy staff, it turned. As quickly as patterned lightning grounding through a rod, the snake swarmed up the quarterstaff, hissing furiously. It wrapped its wrist-thick coils around Jilamey's arm and struck at him. The long, white teeth snapped on nothing as the youth ducked and thrashed at his assailant.

Letting her crossbow dangle, Kelly drew her knife and kicked Calypso to the rescue. The snake struck again, this time penetrating flesh. With a screech that ascended into the soprano register, Jilamey warded off the snake and started clubbing the reptile over the head with the butt of his little gun, which he had grabbed in desperation. To the surprise of those observing the fracas, the snake dropped limp across the saddlebow. In the berserk frenzy of panic, Jilamey kept battering the twitching body even after the others had called to him to stop.

"Now, don't that beat all!" Don exclaimed, laughing. "That micro-sized popgun did some good, after all!"

"Well, gather him up before he slides off your lap!" Kelly ordered Jilamey, reining in next to him and expertly digging her fingers for a firm hold on the slippery scales. With her free hand, she fumbled for a snake bag and passed it over. "I don't think you remembered one of these. Cram it in and be sure you tie the neck of the sack as tight as possible. They've been known to wiggle free if they've any space."

"I did it, didn't I? I captured one!" Jilamey's red face was now suffused with incredulous triumph and his voice broke a bit on the "captured."

"If you remember to get it in the bag," Hrrin called, teeth showing under his feathery brown moustache. Although excitement made his hands shake, Jilamey managed to stuff the limply uncooperative and slithery coils of snake into the bag and securely fastened the tie. "Congratulations. You're halfway there!" Hrrin added.

Still holding the bag, Jilamey looked about him, not certain what to do with his prize. Jan took pity on him and helped him secure it to the saddle on rings embedded in the saddle tree for just such a purpose. Eyes shining, Jilamey galloped to rejoin Team One. Jan followed more sedately, an indulgent grin on her face.

Just inside the boundaries of his ranch, Wayne sat on his horse, flanked by his wife, Anne, and their eldest son. Nearby, on a pair of nervously curvetting horses, were Wayne's guests for the Hunt, a couple from the Hrruban home world. They were all armed with crossbows with explosive quarrels, ready to deal with any reptiles escaping from the cordon. The younger Boncyk hefted a bazooka on his right shoulder while his horse shifted under him, trying to balance itself against the weight. Wayne posed another problem to the teams: he was a notoriously bad shot. He had a tendency to detonate the ground right in front of a Hunter's horse more often than the snake it was pursuing. Todd's horse had been spooked by one of Wayne's bombs the year before, dumping him in the pigpens, so he kept one wary eye on the stockman as they passed him.

Kelly could feel the wind shifting as they came up the hill. That was the worst thing that could happen. Instead of a following breeze that swirled the heady snake musk around them, a new stench filled the air, as potent as snake, blindingly putrid as well as sickly sweet.

"Faugh," Kelly said, averting her head and wondering if it would do any good to jerk her scarf over her nose.

"Oh, no," Todd groaned. "Pig air!"

Not only pig was in the air but also the delectable aroma of livestock, blown directly from the Boncyk herds and teams into the noses of ravenous snakes. In a maneuver as planned as a dress parade, the snakes turned, a great river of rippling, leaf-patterned hide across the Hunters' cordon, rolling uphill toward the farm buildings. With no river, hill, or wood between the snake thoroughfare and the farm, there were no barriers to deflect the snakes' inexorable approach.

The moment the pig stink came his way, Todd called for the Sighter crafts to pick up Lures and make a drop near the marsh in an attempt to divert the main bulk of the reptiles. Then he called for any available Beaters and Hunters. The teams spread themselves out across the field to try and contain the flow and regain control. Kelly could hear the screaming farm animals, their cries reaching up the scale to pure panic. They seemed to sense their danger despite the shift of the wind. Boars might have stood and faced the reptiles, but not the gentler China and Poland pigs who were milling about their sturdy pens with no refuge from the approaching menaces. Even if the pressure of the terrified animals broke down the pen bars, they hadn't the speed to outrun snakes. The only hope of saving them was to head the snakes off again, with full firepower if need be, before they reached the pens.

"Stop them!" Boncyk called, galloping up, waving his crossbow. "My pigs!"

"Damnit, Wayne, you've been told year after year to get those pigs out of here before spawning season!" Don snapped.

"The sows are farrowing this month! I can't move them when they're birthing; they're too set in their ways."

"They're not the only ones," Don grumbled under his breath, but Kelly heard him and grinned.

The stockman and his retinue galloped after Team One, haranguing Todd all the way. Todd had one object in mind: to stand between the threatened sties and the onrush of snakes, firing to turn them away. It was unlikely that they could save all the animals, but he meant his team to try.

The wooden enclosures were too far apart and too big for the Hunters to surround. The team hauled their horses to a halt, giving them a breather as they assessed the best vantage points before the swarm arrived.

Todd and Hrriss decided that they'd best guard the narrow path between the two barns that lay between the snakes and their prey. Bottling them up in that space would make them easier to turn, with some scud bombs to halt them and give the ones behind pause. The older and bigger snakes were smart enough to sense the danger of such tight quarters and turn back to look for easier pickings in the marshes.

Wayne and his family flanked the edges of the buildings, concentrating on the reptiles who would avoid the main route and try to slip around. Still watching the way the wind blew, Kelly realized that the wind carrying the pigs' scent was blowing directly toward the worn pathway, and not back into the main mass of reptiles. If the wind shifted, they'd be surrounded in minutes. And goodbye, Boncyk Bacon.

The defiant screams of the team's horses echoed off the high walls to either side of them. The slower-moving snakes were nearly there. Kelly had never noticed before what a terrifying sound their bellies made, slithering on the dry grass. Oh, a single snake could be silent when it was sneaking up on its prey, but dozens and hundreds of them made the grass hiss beneath them.

"Don't worry about tiddlers," Todd cried. "It's the big ones that we need to turn back. They can swallow a sow whole."

"Here! I need help here!" Anne Boncyk shouted from behind the grain barn. She galloped into sight, waving an empty crossbow. "There's a mess of them sneaking around the barn!" Kelly swiveled her head. Two of the infiltrators were lying contentedly in the gravel, engulfing the bodies of their deceased comrades without a care for the crossbow quarrels sticking straight up, but half a dozen others were making straight for the farrowing pens.

With a sharp command, Hrriss sent his ocelots to Anne's rescue. Gathering their haunches, the spotted cats pounced onto the back of the two largest reptiles, four meters long, and dragged them thrashing like severed air hoses out of the pens. With a quick bite behind the flat heads, the cats dispatched their prey and went for two more. The respite gave Anne time to reload both her crossbows.

A young reptile, only about three meters long, whipped between the team's horses. Three spears jabbed for it all at once, but all missed their mark.

"Damn!" groaned Don, and shouted over his shoulder, "Anne, a three-meter coming through!"

"No, I'll take it!" Jilamey said. "I gotta get two." He wheeled his horse about and pursued the young snake.

Rolling his eyes at such bravado, Todd gestured for Kelly to follow Landreau. If the boy had been sent to embarrass Doona by getting killed in the Snake Hunt, Todd was determined the plan would fail. Jilamey had managed the first catch, somehow, but anything could happen here, with snakes all too close to valuable stock.

At first, the snake was too intent on catching its meal to realize it was being pursued. Jilamey drew his miniature gun and shot at its back. He hit it square, but the low-caliber slug just bounced off the scaly hide. But the snake felt the impact and turned to see what had hit it. Seeing Jilamey bearing down, it slowed a trifle.

Encouraged, Jilamey galloped at it, trusty quarterstaff poised above his head. "Yeee-hah!" he yelled, bringing the long stick down on the snake. It was a good, solid hit. The snake stopped dead and compressed itself into a hurt knot. Jilamey had learned a lesson during his previous misadventure. Before the snake could get a coil about the staff, he discarded it and reached for the crossbow.

He never got a chance to use it. The snake sprang around the horse's leg, lashing out with its tail to encircle a hind leg and bring the animal, and rider, down. The horse, instinctively lashing out behind, then reared and stumbled, falling across a young Mommy Snake which had broken through the cordon. The Mommy was stunned and the tiddler got mashed. Todd and Gypsy came round the corner, chasing the Mommy, Todd with his crossbow cocked. If Jilamey fell now, the Mommy would take him in one gulp.

But Jilamey's mount was an old campaigner, and once he felt his legs free, he danced backward as fast as he was able until he was stopped by the rails of the sty, where once again he reared, striking out with his front legs. The Mommy reared up, too, just as Jilamey, roaring commands at the rearing horse, slid off its rump, over the rails and straight into the sty, landing with a splat on his back in the muck.

"Augh!" the youth cried, flailing his arms and legs. "Help me! I can't get up!"

Jilamey couldn't see the danger he was still in, with the tiddler rousing from its mauling, and the Mommy equally interested in this convenient quarry. Todd shot a defensive charge under the Mommy's tail: pain and noise alarmed it enough to divert its path so that it swerved into the tiddler. A second explosive burst in front of them, and both shot away, Todd in pursuit.

Trying very hard not to laugh, Kelly swung off Calypso and, keeping a good hold on the reins, reached through the fence rails into the pen. It took an effort, but she got the young man to his unsteady feet and guided him back onto solid ground.

"You're out of the race, Master Landreau," Kelly said, trying not to take a deep breath. The sour miasma of pig excrement made her gag. Calypso kept backing away from the stench, pulling Kelly's arm nearly out of the socket "Unless you can clean up real quick someplace."

As Jilamey, disgust and horror contorting his features, tried to scrape muck off his body, Kelly managed to catch his horse and then had trouble getting the horse to approach its erstwhile rider.

"My snake? My second snake? What happened to it?" And to Kelly's surprise, he started to run back to the place of his near demise, darting about, looking for the reptile.

"That one's long gone, Jilamey."

"But what'll I do?" Jilamey looked so pathetic that Kelly nearly laughed aloud.

"What we do is get you to the nearest blind and check you for cuts. You don't want muck-infected wounds, I assure you."

"But I've got to get the second one," Jilamey insisted.

"Like that?"

He tried to approach his horse, who kept backing away snorting.

"It's not far to the nearest blind, Jilamey. We'll clean you up and maybe then the horse'll let you on him."

"But they're all going that way!" he said, dazedly looking back at the melee in the Boncyk yard. More riders were reinforcing Team One by that time, and the pigsties were well cordoned off from the snakes. "I must have my second snake."

"You're lucky you got one!" she said, beginning to lose patience. "And we've got to clean you up. Then at least you can *ride* back to town."

The prospect of walking that far clearly won his attention. So, while Kelly on Calypso led his horse, they made their way to the nearest snake blind, which was not far away, but back in the woods away from the Boncyk farmyard. As she led him, she hoped that his stench would not entice a tiddler or Mommy to investigate his delightfulness. On the way, they met the backup riders who were going out to help Todd.

"He took a fall," Kelly said, over and over again, as her friends threw her puzzled glances. "Good hunting! Good hunting!" Wish I could finish it with you, she thought. Nerd-sitting is such a nuisance. Having to sit a Landreau was close to insult in her lexicon.

Once the four spectators inside the tiny building got a whiff of Jilamey, there was no way he would be given room. Not even the heavily scented hunting box could overcome the odor clinging to the young man. There was, however, a barrel of rainwater just outside and it was the will of the many that Jilamey might have use of all of it. As there was no window on that side of the blind, he went outside and stripped off his sodden clothing. When he was safely inside the barrel, Kelly took a shovel and scooped up the stinking remains of the once sporty outfit. She left the knee boots because her brother knew how to neutralize the odor on leather. Spare clothes were donated and a sort of a towel, and pretty soon, Jilamey, smelling considerably more like a Human, was allowed back into the blind.

Then Kelly could check for wounds. Once the muck had been scraped off, she found several. Nothing major, but scrapes, one shallow cut, and many bruises, the worst of which blossomed on his left cheek and ear. If it hadn't been for the regulation helmet, he might have crushed his skull on the fence post.

"I have never had anything like that happen to me in my life," Jilamey said, over and over, as she dabbed at his injuries with disinfectant and rubbed a styptic to stop the bleeding. "I thought that snake was going to eat me!"

"You were a very handy morsel," Kelly replied, carefully smearing vrrela from her medical kit on the scrapes. She reached for one of the flasks at her belt. "But Todd doesn't allow snakes to feed on his team members. Have a drink of this."

Jilamey uncorked the mlada and took a tentative sip. He followed that taste with a more enthusiastic tot and sighed happily as the warmth of the liquor hit.

"Not too much," Kelly warned him, taking the flask away and recorking it. "It's strong."

"Strong is what I need right now," he pleaded. "One more?"

"Well . . ." Kelly studied him and decided what he'd been through was worth one more drink. His bruises would probably hurt more as they developed.

"All right," she said, pouring him another.

"Todd saved my life," Jilamey remarked thoughtfully. He sat up on the edge of that remark and winced, settling back again in the low chair. "My uncle, the Admiral, has always held a poor opinion of the Reeve family, though he never says why. Even when I asked him after I knew I was going on this Hunt. I shall tell him how wrong he is. If he had seen Todd today, he'd be ever, ever so impressed."

"Todd was only doing his duty as team leader," Kelly said carefully. She was amused as Jilamey had regained his affected manner of speech as soon as he was comfortable again. "But he is quite an impressive person."

"I agree!" Jilamey said, both hands clutching the small hammered metal cup. "It was most daring of him to sweep down like that, right in the face of the G—what did you call it?"

Kelly smiled to herself. Undoubtedly he would regale his friends endlessly about his Snake Hunt. He might even tell the truth. It certainly wouldn't hurt Todd's reputation to have the story go around. "GBMS. It stands for Great Big Mommy Snake. Nearly all of the big ones that come out for spawning are the females."

"And he drove them both off just before they could reach me. He saved my life. I admire him ever so. I know better than to believe everything my uncle has been saying about his family. He's wrong when he says that Reeve is out of his element here, and should be returned home for his own good. If the father is at all like the son, well, I've never seen anyone better suited to a wild venue." The young man chuckled self-deprecatingly. "Certainly I'm not. I know I'll only play at it the odd weekend or two." He raised his eyebrows entreatingly and extended the cup toward Kelly. She had been listening intently ever since Jilamey had mentioned his uncle.

"Oh, well, one more won't hurt you," she said, pretending reluctance, but eager to hear more. She poured the cup full. "It's all organic, you know." Any gossip about the great Landreau interested all Doonans personally. Having just returned from Earth, she was more aware than most of the tensions surrounding the upcoming Treaty Renewal, and the disagreement between the factions pro and con. "So what did your uncle think of you coming here for the Snake Hunt, Jilamey?"

chapter three

The writhing, squirming cargo was hauled back triumphantly to the center of the Human settlement. Hunters who had successfully passed their rite of passage with the capture of two snakes were congratulated and toasted with splashes of mlada, some of them directed internally. With understandable satisfaction, Todd saw the two Hrrubans who had endangered Hrriss ride back into the square, hunched over their saddlebows in pain. They had the telltale swellings or rroamal inflammation under the fur on their arms and legs. At some point on their wild ride they had passed through trees bearing the toxic vines. Because the inflammation wasn't far advanced, a quick application of vrrela would swiftly cure the agony, but Todd couldn't help but think of their suffering as a measure of justice.

The heavenly smell of cooking greeted them all. Meat was turning on spits in roasting pits, which were also filled with freshly picked corn on the cob and newly dug potatoes. The combined aromas made the returning Hunters half frantic with hunger.

"Not a bite until you clean up!" Pat Reeve shouted at her dust-covered son. Todd grinned and pointed to the carcasses of the small snakes thrown across the rump of his horse. She returned the grin and held up her joined hands over her head as a gesture of victory. The snakes' meat would be thrown into a savory stew to simmer with root vegetables and fresh herbs. Some of the traditions of Snake Hunt were a lot more delicious than others.

"Where's Mrrva?" Todd called back over the clamor. "Hrriss got his leg squeezed by a Mommy Snake."

Pat's eyes widened in concern. "She's inside," she said, gathering up the small carcasses and hurrying toward the door. "I'll warn her. You get him inside."

Hrriss protested that he was all right. "I have been pressed worse between my hrrss's body and the stable wall," he pleaded.

"Come on." Todd ignored his friend's protests, knowing that the leg had to hurt a lot more than Hrriss was letting on. He helped Hrriss off Rrhee and shepherded him toward the Hall. "If your mother doesn't kill me for neglecting you, mine will."

Once Hrriss was in the capable hands of his mother, Mrrva, Todd checked on the other members of his team.

The hunting parties, still congratulating each other, finally separated to wash and dress for the upcoming celebratory banquet. Medics took charge of the injured. There were numerous wounds and bruises due to inexperience with the vegetation of Doona/Rrala and a long horseback ride.

Nonparticipants clamored for firsthand stories and adventures from the heroes, and sympathized with the disappointed Hunters who had returned empty-handed. Todd congratulated several young friends who had passed their ritual, and checked on the various small wounds that some of his team members and friends had sustained. There had been no deaths in any team during this Hunt. The unusually hot weather had somewhat slowed the snakes' usual split-second reflexes. Todd felt they'd been extraordinarily lucky, considering how many amateurs had ridden out. He walked Gypsy and Rrhee down to the paddock to unsaddle and turn them loose, enjoying the post-Hunt atmosphere, listening to everyone comparing brags about the size of the ones that got away. Soon, he was able to work his way to his own quarters and the long-awaited and much-needed shower.

There were preparations for the usual all-out blast of a party going on in the Assembly Hall. It was the biggest building on Doona/Rrala, bar the Archives Building on the Treaty Island. It lay on the Human side of the Friendship Bridge halfway between the new construction which replaced the first Human village and the first Hrruban village. It took the place of the much smaller mess hall, which had been the chief building of the original settlement. The support beams and wide windows of the Hall were of extruded plastic, but the white walls and roof were formed of the same sealed-rla wood as the bridge. The many ornaments and statuary on and within its walls had been donated by craftspeople from both races and every village on the planet. It was surrounded by gravel walks and pathways that rambled in a pleasing knotlike pattern among gardens containing rare plants from Earth and Hrruba, proudly maintained by volunteer gardeners. During other times of the year than Snake Hunt, the entire sentient population of the planet could fit within the walls of the Assembly Hall or in its landscaped grounds, for speeches or celebrations. The Hall doubled as the social center whenever visitors came.

The five days following each Snake Hunt were designated by Doonans as New Home Week, recreating an Earth custom of reunion, but as Dot McKee, one of the senior settlers, pointed out, for their new home, instead of their old one. If at all possible, everyone returned home for New Home Week. Unless they were on exploration missions, no great effort was required of the Hrruban settlers, for every Hrruban had access to transportation grids. But the Human Rralans had to make sacrifices of time, effort, and money. Either way, both species came home some way or other. So Kelly hoped to see several of her primary-school chums back from long-term exploration missions for Spacedep and the colonizing arm of the Hrruban government. She hoped that Todd's brother, Dan, would be among them. Right now, she had to find Todd and report what Jilamey had said.

The Doona/Rrala Ad Hoc Band was tuning up in a corner of the Assembly Hall when Kelly entered. She smiled at Mrs. Lawrence, the leader of the band, and then began to circulate. The Hall had been beautifully decorated for the feast. Floating wicks burned in glass sconces containing scented oil. The sconces hung on the walls between bright festival decorations. Long tables draped with white embroidered cloths had been set up perpendicular to the head table on its dais. Kelly wandered about searching for Todd and Hrriss, and finally saw them sitting together at the opposite end of the Hall. Hrriss glanced up and caught her eye to wave her over.

"Who'd ever guess you've been chasing snakes! Give us a twirl!" Todd said. "Very pretty!" he added approvingly, as she executed a neat turn on her heel to show off her dress.

She'd brought it specially for tonight, a confection of shimmering blue and gold with a fluffy knee-length skirt. "Glad you approve, citizen," Kelly replied pertly, ducking into a graceful curtsy. "I'll have you know that this is the very latest style from Earth in evening informal—to distinguish from casual, which this most definitely is not. Notice please the wide skirt, to show an insouciant disregard for the tightness of Corridors and Aisles. The very height of fashion, or should I say width? Can I sit down or is there something else I'm supposed to do right now?"

Todd gave a snort. "We do the Hunt. Others do the food," he said. "Mother,

Mrrva, and Mrs. Hu have that in hand." He reached out and, grabbing her hand, neatly pulled her onto the bench beside them.

"Hrriss, is your leg all right?" Kelly asked, wondering if that was why the pair were so indolent in the busy Hall. She saw no bandage, though she caught the astringent odor of vrrela.

"Oh, zat!" Hrriss dismissed it with a negligent click of lightly extended claws. "It was nozzing, as I told Zodd. I am only bruised. We are sorry to have missed you on the rest of the ride," he added regretfully.

"Me, too," Kelly sighed. Despite the rain barrel, Jilamey had exuded a pong that she was afraid might cling to her and spoil this evening. "I dropped my nerd off at the medical center for a full check-over, and took a double-long shower to get the pig smell off. Did I miss anything good?"

"You left just before the best part," Todd said, grinning broadly at the memory. "We were afraid that once the mass of snakes caught up to us, they'd make short work of all Wayne's stock, but we didn't count on the sows. When the tiddlers started coming through the slats into their pens, they turned as aggressive as you could have wished. Wayne was delighted."

"Really?" Kelly wondered if Todd was teasing her, but a quick look at Hrriss confirmed that this master dissembler was telling the truth.

"They stomped the snakes flat. Hell hath no fury like a sow whose piglets are in danger," Todd chortled. "Those sharp hooves chopped lengths off the tiddlers that got through. The others turned around and fled."

"So we concentrated on the Mommy Sssnakess," Hrriss added. "By the time the Beaters arrived, we were able to get the swarm back into line. The boars were snorting war cries by the time we started to clear out of there."

Kelly applauded, laughing. "Let's have a Pig Brigade next year."

"That's what I suggested to Wayne," Todd said, grinning with malice. "Since he won't move them out of the way, we might as well get some help from them. They're as good as ocelots for chopping up tiddlers."

"Nearly as good," Hrriss corrected him mildly. Todd favored his friend with an openmouthed stare of feigned astonishment.

"Don't compare chickens and brrnas," Kelly said, playfully putting a hand between them. "I'm glad I got you two alone before everything got started," she continued in an undertone, turning so her back shielded her words. "I tried to find your father, Todd, but he's out showing some diplomats around the model stock ranches. Young Jilamey got talkative when he got mlada'd up in the snake blind. I don't think he realized what he was implying, in his chummy confidences about Uncle Landreau's opinion of the Reeve family." So she repeated Jilamey's exact words.

"Dad and me out of our element here?" Todd demanded, more indignant than insulted. He left out a harsh bark of laughter. "Earth never was *my* element!"

Kelly grinned, a sparkle in her eyes. "Well, you've won one staunch adherent in Jilamey today. Jilamey admires you tremendously for saving him from the very jaws of death. And he's going to tell his uncle how quick and clever you were."

Todd snorted. "Much weight that'll carry with Al Landreau. Candidly I was thinking that maybe the Admiral sent the kid into the Snake Hunt to get him killed and make the Reeves look worse."

"It failed, didn't it?" Hrriss said, but the tips of his claws were showing as he rattled them on his knee.

"As the Mayday failed?" Todd said softly.

"What Mayday?" Kelly asked, wondering if she'd missed something.

Todd's brows drew down over his nose. He stared off across the room, blank-faced. His hands twitched, showing the tension that he wouldn't allow his face to reveal. Kelly knew the signs. Todd was revving up to full anger even if he never let it go public.

"Landreau has absolutely no grounds to pull any of us out of the colony, no matter what his personal opinion—and grievance against us—might be."

Hrriss scowled, pulling his eyebrow whiskers together. "There were ominous undertones at the Hrrethan celebration we attended," he said. "We are all aware that pressure of some kind would increase now that the Treaty Renewal talks are so close. Two of the Hayuman speakers who were on Hrretha are here now, too, Varnorian and Rogitel. Rrev has seen them, but I think he has not spoken with them."

"At least you're aware of undercurrents," Kelly said, deciding that now was the time to reveal her own budget of suspicion and anxieties. "I caught more than that on Earth," and to give herself time to organize her thoughts, she filched nuts from one of the appetizer bowls next to her on the long table. "Jilamey's comments today merely support the innuendos. I was going to talk to Ken and Hrrestan in private, but, with the shuttle's delay, I barely arrived home in time to ride out on Hunt.

"As you two should know, Alreldep is completely pro-Doona, but I wish I could say the same for the other two space services. I feel almost endangered when I have to carry a message to Spacedep offices. Now that there are plenty of thriving colonies, there is a feeling that Doona is no longer needed. The experiment was 'interesting,' that's all. The Treaty may just as well be voided, and we can all go our separate ways."

"Has public sentiment gone that far against us?" Todd asked sadly.

"The public? No!" Kelly hurried to assure him. "They voted on allowing Doona to be colonized, and from what I can tell, none of them have changed their minds. The government agencies are what we have to worry about. To the average man or woman in, say, Air Recycling or Food Services, Doona is still the shining star, the pastoral world that opened up space travel and revitalized Earth's economy." Kelly plastered an imaginary banner on the sky with a sweep of her hand. "Even if those people're unsuited to colonization, they're making sure that their sons and daughters are taking specialized training so they'll be qualified one day. And every child who visits Alreldep on a school tour wants to be the one to find the next Doona. It's the old flatheads in Spacedep who want us to go back to square one and pretend that a cohabited colony never happened. Especially not one independent from the government of Earth and on which the Earth language is subordinated in favor of the co-inhabitor's. Having to speak Middle Hrruban when they come here is one of the things that really rankle with them." She smiled and shook her head, taken aback at her own frankness. "Listen to me go on! Do you know how long it's been since I've been able to talk like that? It's not approved for diplomats to be heard spouting judgmental statements. Unfortunately I've got no proof of opposition except gossip and the unwelcoming mien of Spacedep menials. You'd just have to trust my powers of observation, such as they are."

"How long have we been friends?" Hrriss said, speaking in the Low Hrruban of a familial group. "We have trusted you since you were able to ride a Hunt."

"Before that," Todd replied in the same vein.

Two Human women passed them, carrying a huge basket of bread between them. Hrriss looked about cautiously before replying, and glanced at Todd for permission. He and Todd had discussed the matter and decided that Kelly had to be told what had happened. With her connections in Alreldep, she'd have access to offices and ranking officials that they did not.

"Unfortunately we have perhaps precipitated an event which would ssserve Spacedep's purpose well, though we do not yet know who is responsible for engineering it."

Kelly's eyes went wide. "What happened?"

"This is confidential, you understand," Todd said, still in Low Hrruban, which would make what he said unintelligible to many. Kelly grinned at his tactic and nodded for him to continue. "On the way back from Hrretha, we received a Mayday signal, coming from an uninhabited, interdicted world," Todd went on, twisting his shoulders at their naivete. "We responded to the call, only to discover that it was coming from a beacon drone. We found no trace of radiation or ion drive to tell where the ship that dropped it came from. Anyone passing that way could have heard the Mayday, but unluckily it was us."

"The fact remains that we crossed into a forbidden zone for no purpose," Hrriss finished, his purring voice low.

"But you'd have the log record of the Mayday . . ." Kelly began.

"We nearly didn't," Todd replied sourly. "A slight malfunction . . ."

"Corrected by a kick," Hrriss said, grinning.

"In the holographic recorder," Todd finished.

"Loose circuit?" Kelly asked, even as she wondered why she was trying to find logical explanations of the malfunction.

"More likely"—Todd managed a fine approximation of an Hrruban growl—"it got *over*serviced when the Hrrethan space station insisted on being *sure* the *Albatross* was in perfect working order."

"Even though we assured them that our own people had serviced it before we started out," Hrriss added, letting one claw escape its sheath.

"So no idea who put the drone out there?" Kelly asked, knowing the answer even before Hrriss shook his head.

"There were others who would make their second warp jump at those particular coordinates," Hrriss said, "but everyone knew we were anxious to return speedily to Rrala."

"So it was set up to catch you two." Her remark was more statement than question.

"That's the most logical assumption," Todd said, "in the present circumstances, but we *have* a recording of that Mayday, which I don't think we were supposed to have."

"And you let Hrriss do all the talking, didn't you?" Kelly asked briskly, and looked relieved when both nodded. Then her shoulders sagged. "But it's just the sort of incident Spacedep would contrive, an unnecessary breach of the Treaty and by a Doonan."

"And a Hrruban!" Hrriss reminded her.

She did *not* like the inferences that even an idiot could draw, let alone an anti-Doona faction. "Who else knows about this?"

"Our fathers," Hrriss said, "Hrrestan and Rrev. It was decided to defer the matter until after the Hunt."

"Sensible. No one on Doona'd let you escape your Hunt responsibilities," Kelly said, and then to insert some levity into the conversation, "including me. And," she added more brightly, "since this is Doona, you'll be believed. It's on Earth that I wouldn't give a cracked egg for your chances. If we can only limit the incident to Doona—once the visitors have left and can't get their noses into something as juicy as an interdiction breach."

"In any case, I'm the one at fault," Todd said in his characteristic forthright manner. "I was piloting the ship, and I insisted that we respond to the Mayday, even if it meant passing an interdiction buoy. It's serious but it oughtn't to damage the Doonan Treaty."

"Hear him. He would have us suffer even before being found guilty," Hrriss said wryly, nudging Todd in the ribs with the back of his hand. "First it must be proved to the Treaty Council that we acted out of malice. If sanctity of life cannot supersede borders and barriers, then we may not call ourselves civilized."

"Well, let's not borrow trouble from tomorrow, huh?" Kelly said, cocking her head at them. "I'm not without resources, you know. Just let me know when to call in favors, and where, and you know I'll do it." Then, seeing a swarm of guests crowding into the Hall, she reverted to Standard. "It's party time, lads," she said, rising to her feet, giving her skirts a practiced flirt. "And I intend to party!"

Since by tradition and Treaty, there was no hotel, guests were assigned space in the old plastic cabins of the original village. Many visitors found them a diverting change from the usual sterile accommodations. The more prestigious were billeted with Doonan host families, and the overflow used canvas tenting shelters. However, Doonans, Hayuman and Hrruban alike, provided visitors with Friendly Native Guides to keep them company and, more important, to show them the dangerous vegetation and keep them from unexpectedly rousing the ferocious bearlike mda. Such individual contacts with those from other worlds had improved good opinions of Doona over the past twenty-five years.

This year, the Shihs, Phyllis and Hu, leader of the First Human Village, were pleased to have the honor of hosting the Fifth Speaker, the Hrruban Minister for Health and Medicine. The Hrruban's stripe was noticeably broader and his mane was whitening around his face, but he was solemnly kind to all who approached to greet him. He caught Todd's eye and smiled. They had met on Hrretha only a few weeks before. Most likely, the venerable Hrruban was still seeing the small boy dressed in mda fur with a rope tail tied around his waist instead of a grown man in normal Earth-style tunic and trousers. Responding to that memory himself, Todd straightened his tunic and squared his shoulders as the Speaker and Hu neared him.

"A fine Hunt, and, it would seem, a fine party to come," Hu Shih complimented Todd, reaching up to pat the young man on the shoulder, and nodding amiably to Hrriss. The venerable metropologist's eyes were shining as he took in the decorations and the happy crowd filling the Hall. "No Hunters with more than scrapes and bruises and"—Hu's eyes twinkled—"depressed ambitions. Very well done, indeed."

"Thank you, sir," Todd said, politely dropping into Middle Hrruban, since the Fifth Speaker was here in a social capacity. "Have you heard about the Boncyk sows?"

"Indeed we have," Hu Shih replied, his usually composed face becoming wreathed with laughter.

"The tale will return with me to Hrruba," the Fifth Speaker replied, his deep black eyes sparkling. "It is, of course, the greatest pity that the scene was not recorded, but the various narrators seem to agree on so many details that the truth will not suffer much in the retelling."

"We are considering the addition of a Sow Brigade to next year's Hunt," Todd went on, dropping his jaw in a Hrruban-style grin.

He saw Hu's start of surprise but the Fifth Speaker grumbled his throat chuckle and Hu relaxed. Todd had always been on special terms with Hrruban Speakers and could dare where protocol would have strictly forbidden such banter. Todd was not surprised when Hu deftly eased the Speaker toward the dais and the special chairs where the elders would observe the proceedings.

"I will expect a full report of their performance next year, Zodd," the Speaker said, allowing himself to be shepherded away.

The Ad Hoc Band began to play incidental music, loud enough to be heard through the low roar of conversation but not loud enough to drown it.

Todd looked around for Ali Kiachif, one of the oldest friends of the colony and its most faithful proponent. The swarthy, drink-loving old Codep captain had missed few New Home Weeks since the beginning, attending anytime he could arrange his schedule to be there. He wasn't in the Hall yet, and Todd couldn't remember having heard anyone mention that he'd arrived. Todd was a little disappointed, but he could well understand it if Kiachif wasn't able to make it back to Doona. Kiachif was a busy man these days. His rounds had grown a hundredfold since the colony's inception, and had earned him a small fleet of ships serving under him, plying the expanding spaceways, carrying cargo and passengers. Doona was still one of his favorite stops. He always claimed it rested his eyes from the sometimes horrific conditions on mining planets, which far outnumbered the agricultural planets, where people lived in miserable conditions in the stale air of domes or in the unremitting toil of prison facilities. While he never mentioned Doonan grog, everyone knew that it was more to his taste than methylated spirits cooked over a Bunsen burner.

In their festive best, everyone looked cheerfully ready to enjoy themselves to the fullest. The threat of being overrun by the great snakes had once again been averted. In the true spirit of Doona, some of the native Humans wore Hrruban dress, and some of the Hrrubans affected "Trran" trousers, skirts, or dresses. The various diplomats were attired more formally but not repressively so, while their young wards and the other guests were dressed in the latest styles from Earth or Hrruba. Evidently the fashion industries of both cultures had been stimulated by the contact, and styles had merged, mingled, and then evolved to become highly individualistic.

Oddly enough, though most Terrans still spoke in murmurs, their clothes shouted in the most vivid of shades, enhanced by additives that caused iridescence and luminosity, sometimes rather shocking to the eye. Todd felt almost conservative in the green casual trousers and darker green silk shirt sent to him by his sister Ilsa. She had gone back to Earth for higher education and had married a man she met at school. Byron worked as a consultant to Spacedep, so he was occasionally on Doona to visit the Treaty Island, as he was for the Hunt. He was a fair stickman, playing his turn with the band, bobbing his head to the rhythm as he beat the drum skins. He threw a sideways grin toward Todd.

"There's Hrringa," Kelly said, smiling at a tall, almost chestnut-maned Hrruban in crisp formal attire. "I'm glad they sent someone down to spell him at the Hrruban Center. He'd have hated to miss the fun." Todd nodded to the catman, who was serving a term as the transportation grid operator in the Hrruban consulate on Earth. Hrringa was a member of Hrriss's clan. Though his friend never made much of it, his family was of a fairly broad Stripe.

"They always do. He was on Team Ten in the Hunt, you know. Did you see much of each other?" Todd asked Kelly.

"Quite a lot. Most people on Earth don't speak the language, so I'm sort of a tie to home. So few people realize that he speaks fluent Terran: and there are always those who try to talk pidgin Hrruban with him." She rolled her eyes at such an insult to her friend. "Then there's the opposite extreme with those silly men in Amalgamated Worlds Administration treating him as some sort of sacred shaman."

Hrriss made a noise like a snort. "What do you expect from them?"

Kelly's expression turned sheepish. "I tried to wangle a ride home through the grid instead of flying out," she admitted. "Hrringa would have obliged me, I know, but they don't like us junior types to use the grid when the senior diplomats can't get access anytime they want to. They waved me off. It was no use my explaining that Hrringa and I were raised together, or that I had a right to go to Doona." She clicked her tongue regretfully. "Well, I'd better go be a good hostess. My mother said if I wasn't on the front line shaking hands . . ." She left the threat unspoken, with a broad grin to show she knew it wasn't serious. "I'll find you later, Todd. Keep your ears open."

"You, too." Todd blinked as Kelly was swallowed up immediately by the swirling crowd. He couldn't believe how fast the Hall had filled up. He looked at Hrriss, who was also looking a bit dazed.

"We were so intent, we were not paying attention," the Hrruban said. "Meanwhile, the party has created itself."

"Yeah." Todd craned his neck for one last look at the girl. "Kelly looks beautiful, doesn't she?"

"Her grace is one with her beauty," Hrriss said approvingly. "Come, Team Leader, we have other duties even as she does."

Young men and women warily carried full trays of drinks and nibble snacks past them into the main room. As the kitchen doors swung to and fro, Hrriss and Todd caught sight of Mrrva. Hrriss's mother could be seen standing over a huge simmering pot with a spoon to her lips, tasting the contents for spice. Mrrva held the Hrruban equivalent of five college degrees in physical health science, and was director of the Rralan Health Services, but she also enjoyed the simple tasks of hospitality that entertaining on Doona required. Her eyes widened when she saw her son and Todd enter.

"Go out therrre," she ordered, pointing with her spoon toward the doorway. "Why are you here? We do not need help from such as you. The Masters of the Hunt should mingle with guests, not serve like cubs and youths."

"But, Mrrva . . ." Todd began, his voice wheedling as he edged toward some of her famous pastries.

She slapped his hand with her spoon and immediately threw him a cloth to clean off the sticky liquid.

"You will be served in due courssse," Mrrva said in a tone which brooked no further discussion. She made a sound between a hiss and a growl. "When will we ever put the manners of a man and Master on you, Zodd!" Then she turned on Hrriss. "I know you have been taught. Go now and exercise the teaching."

Abashed, the two returned to the Hall. Leading the Hunt had been a pleasure. Hosting the party was a chore they would gladly have missed. The throng had swelled to hundreds in the great room. Todd passed among them, shaking hands and returning kisses. While on the one hand he was glad to see the friends that reappeared year after year, on the other, there was never any time to catch up on any details—of their success in the Hunt let alone what they'd been doing the past year—before someone else claimed attention.

He and Hrriss finally made their way to the dais and stood in front of the main table. Before the feast could officially begin, the long-awaited blooding ceremony for the successful Hunters must proceed. As Master of the Hunt and master of ceremonies, Todd was required to make a short speech of welcome to the sea of guests. He would speak in Terran, with Hrriss repeating it after him in Middle Hrruban. He had a feeling of déjà vu. It had been only a few weeks before that he stood and listened to the governor of Hrretha offer similar greetings to his guests. There had been many like events in the last few years. They were beginning to blur into one another. He began by offering his gratitude to all the people who had aided in organizing and running the Hunt, and went on from there.

"To old friends and family, I welcome you home, and to new friends and first-time visitors, I hope you'll enjoy your stay, and that you'll return to us again in the future," Todd said, winding up the necessary remarks. "I won't hold up dinner long. The cooks would throw me into the stew with the snakes!" There was a small murmur of appreciative laughter, and Todd held up a hand. "However, there are some people I'm happy to call to your attention. They've earned this moment. As I call your name, will you come up on the dais, please?"

The Hunters who had passed their initiation rite that day by capturing a brace of adolescent snakes were called up one by one, to stand shoulder-to-shoulder before the audience. Some of them were shy and directed their smiles down at their feet as Todd congratulated them on their successful passage. One among them—a young woman from the mining colony of Ellerell IV—had chosen instead to bring in eggs. She had saved all her extra pay for five years to be able to make it to Doona for Snake Hunt. When first laid, snake eggs were almost too soft to move. By the time they had hardened enough to transport, there was a real danger that they might hatch on the way in. She had brought in twelve of the soft and leathery head-sized eggs in a specially designed fluff-lined sack brought all the way from Ellerell. Her thoroughness and care impressed even the Doonan judges, who had seen a lot of inventive approaches to the problem over the last two decades. She was invested with the small gold medal from which depended two wiggly streamers. Some of the children squealed when they saw the ribbons, which looked amazingly like the tails of miniature snakes. She and the other Hunters wore their awards proudly as they were given a standing ovation.

Jilamey Landreau was called forward with the rest of the almost-successful who had captured a single snake. He shook hands with Todd and Hrriss to the accompaniment of encouraging applause from the audience.

"Thank you, Todd," the young Landreau said, clutching his medal with the single streamer. "I wish there had been a chance to take the second snake. I was so close!"

"Next year," Todd suggested. "Your first was a good capture. We can hold that snake 'on credit,' so to speak."

"Hey, you could?" the youth exclaimed, his eyes shining. Todd recognized that the Hunt craze had claimed another adherent. "Can I get the hide to take back with me? I want to use the stripe as a fashion accessory! That'll really make 'em look twice at me!"

"I'll see to it," Todd said, slightly amused at the young Landreau's naive delight. He clapped Jilamey on the shoulder encouragingly before moving on to congratulate the next participant.

The feast was then officially begun. As the Hunters, both successful and unsuccessful, sat down, Byron played a roll on the snare drum to get everyone's attention. It segued into a compelling, irregular beat on tom-tom. Clad only in their knife belts and ornamental necklaces, several young Hrrubans ran in and began a stomping, swirling dance: obviously a Snake Hunt. Two lithe female dancers, acting in tandem as if they were part of the same body, portrayed the snake. They snapped imaginary coils toward the Hunters or recoiled fearfully from their spears. It was a compelling sight, as the rear half of the snake curled herself on the floor behind the body of the other and switched her tail fitfully as the front half swayed, striking at this dancer or that with her fangs. The Hunters catapulted past the reptile to attack, missing and hitting the floor beyond. With great energy, they rolled upright to their feet like kittens and renewed their attacks on their foe.

The upright dancer was so skillful that she didn't appear to have a solid bone in her body. Her undulations had a hypnotic quality. It was a shock to the watchers when one spearman sprang forward, past the snapping jaws, and plunged the weapon into the snake's breast. The serpent gave one tremendous convulsion and subsided to the floor gracefully to quiver into stillness. When the snake had "died," a complimentary silence held the audience. Then a burst of thunderous applause awarded the dancers. They sprang up, acknowledging the praise, and then gathered to either side of the doors leading to the kitchen.

The band stayed on its dais long enough to play a fanfare to announce the arrival of a massive cauldron borne aloft on a tray by eight young men and women clad to the ears in heatproof towelling. The huge kettle of savory snake stew was presented to Todd as the Master of the Hunt. With intricately decorated ladles, Todd and Hrriss served the special guests on the dais, after which the cauldron was brought to the long sideboard. From then on, buffet style was the order and everyone served themselves from the seemingly inexhaustible supply of stew and the other viands brought out from the kitchen. Todd caught sight of Mrrva sitting down at the end of the table near Hrrestan: she had shed her apron to display gorgeous filmy robes spangled with jewels.

As the party began in earnest, toasts were offered to the Hunters and the prey. For many of the guests, the feast was a double reason for celebration. For some this would be the first time they had eaten "real," unprocessed or nonsynthetic food. For others, this was a high point of gastronomic enjoyment. It was true that every year, more real fruit, vegetables, grain, and meat were being made available to the people of Earth from its fanning colonies, but the majority of homeworld meals still came from synthesizers. Hrriss nudged Todd in the ribs and indicated a child at one of the front tables. He was suspiciously and most reluctantly taking a tiny bite of fruit from a spoon. The tot sniffed it first, not in the least willing to trust the curious substance in front of him. With much coaxing and much gesturing to others tucking into their food, the child's mother got him to accept the morsel. After a very tentative chew, the boy grabbed the spoon out of his mother's hand, finished the bowl in front of him, and reached for his mother's as well.

When all had eaten sufficiently, the party went on to its next, and inevitable, stage. The Ad Hoc Band resumed its place on the dais and started to play dancing music. A few took advantage of the music, but most sat contentedly, letting the meal settle. Gradually, drinks in hand, diners began to circulate the Hall, pausing to chat with old friends or welcome newcomers, or congratulate the new Hunters.

Todd and Hrriss excused themselves from the dais and began more protocol rounds just as the Ad Hoc Band started to play a perky song, based on an ancient Earth chantey. It was a joke among Doona/Rralans, but it had never been played at a New Home Week before. Todd guessed that Sally Lawrence, who had written the new lyrics, wanted a broader audience. He hoped that the listeners would accept it for the facetious tweak it was, and not take it seriously. Sally's eyes were twinkling as she struck a chord on her guitar and began to sing.

"My mother was a human girl from Doona Village Four
She loved a handsome Hrruban boy who lived just next door
Their love bore offspring, one, two, three
A kitten and a werecat and the third was me.

"Now my brother Hrrn and I, we were raised up quite all right
But my sister Mrrna Joan, she was different day and night
Smooth-skinned at night, by day her fur grew
She was a true Doonan through and through.

"Yo ho ho! A Rralan true
Takes the best of both as all should do."

It was a familiar tune to the locals. Some joined in the chorus, roaring a lusty "Yo ho ho!" Nearly everyone else seemed to get the joke, to judge by the shouts of approval and calls for an encore. Todd noticed that some of the Human diplomats looked annoyed, and a few of the Hrruban homeworlders looked positively ill at the thought of Hrrubans and Humans interbreeding. Todd couldn't think how to explain that the thought had never seriously crossed the mind of the songwriter.

"Maybe this is the moment to start the dancing?" Kelly said, coming up behind Todd and poking him in the side with a finger.

"I'm not very good at it," Todd said apologetically, but he gestured to the bandleader, who immediately struck a fast step.

Immediately the floor was full of couples, whirling and jigging about in circles.

"Neither am I!" Kelly seized his hand. "Let's go anyway!"

Jaw dropped in amusement, Hrriss leaned toward him. "If she promises not to step on my tail, I get the nexxxt dansss."

"It's a deal," Kelly called as she dragged Todd into the crowd.

Kelly had told a fib when she said she was a poor dancer. With her hands bunched in the folds of her skirts, she swayed and stepped with grace to the lively melody. Todd knew the steps, but he felt as awkward as a wooden mda trying to keep up with her. He was relieved when that music stopped and a slow dance began. Kelly melted into his arms, stretching up one hand to his neck. That was oddly delightful. They had grown up together, but he had never realized before that she was so much smaller than he, so delicately built—or, to be more honest, that she was a girl at all. She had just been one of the capable people he depended on, until she went away. Kelly had never balked at fences, and she could wrangle snakes or horses with the best. He could barely connect the tomboy who had grown up literally next door with the sparkling vision in his arms. Unconsciously he tightened his hold a trifle, and she rubbed her cheek against his chest. The music drifted to a halt, and Kelly turned her face up to give him a brilliant smile, her golden eyes aflame in the festival lamplight.

"Thank you," she said. "That was lovely."

Todd didn't know how to reply suitably. "Um, thank you. Isn't it Hrriss's turn now?"

"Only if I promise not to step on his tail," and Kelly's look was enigmatic but she allowed him to lead her from the floor and find Hrriss.

He stood watching for a moment as Hrriss, rather too expertly, Todd thought, spun Kelly out into the dancers, his tail wrapped around one leg, well out of the way. Not that Kelly would put a foot wrong, Todd realized.

"Hey, young Reeve," called out Captain Buckman, a former Spacedep marine. He had joined the colony on Binar 3B-IV and was now its governor. "Where can I get some mlada?"

"Allow me," and Todd located the case of mlada bottles stashed under one end of the dais draperies. As he served Buckman, he thought the man's eyes were already a little red. His breath smelled so strongly of alcohol it might ignite spontaneously. "You'd better watch your intake, sir. Too much of this stuff results in potent hangovers."

"Hmmph," said the old man, watching Todd refill his glass. "But you pour generously, boy. So this is how you impress the diplomats, hey? Is yours the last face they see before they pass out? Where's Pollux?"

"Who, sir?"

"Where's Pollux, Castor?" Buckman asked, prodding Todd in the middle. "Your twin, your inseparable pal, your other half, boy."

"Hrriss is on the dance floor," Todd replied a little stiffly. "Did you want to speak to him?"

"No, no. So the two of you aren't joined at the hip? I'll be danged. Come back and refill this in about, oh, a quarter hour, won't you?"

Todd nodded and moved on to the next group, clustered at the farthest end of the room from the band. This was an informal roundtable discussion by the Jacks of All Trades. That much-sought-after designation meant that a colonist had enough flexibility and training in such a variety of skills that he could turn a hand to any task that needed doing or problem that had to be solved. Codep preferred that there be at least one JOAT in any colony group. Both men and women could ship on in that capacity. Ken Reeve's own designation for the Doona colony project had been that of a JOAT. As an unofficial chair and host of the JOATs present, he was directing the discussion among those from several nascent colonies that had recently earned their Amalgamated Worlds status. Many of them had been born or raised on Doona. The billy-JOATs and nanny-JOATs, as they liked to call themselves, unofficially, of course, were now gleefully engaged in a loud argument about the best way to set up barrier screens against pests. Todd checked and refilled each guest's glass and picked up empty dessert plates for transport back to the kitchen. Before leaving, he exchanged winks with his father.

The band was taking a much needed break, and near the kitchen doors, Sally Lawrence was having a private discussion with Varnorian of Codep. Todd bowed over her hand as he refilled her glass.

"So why do you object to my song?" Mrs. Lawrence demanded of the Codep chairman. "On artistic principles?"

"Scarcely on that score, my dear lady," said Varnorian, loosing his not inconsiderable charm. "Your artistry is remarkable." He wasn't the friend to Doona that the late Chaminade had been, but he was at least a graceful guest. He had very pale blue eyes with dark lashes. There was something both attractive and cold about eyes like that. "My objection is purely contextual. I feel that such an idea should not have been voiced, let alone mocked. Totally unsuitable lyrics, if you could by any extension of poesy call them that."

"Mr. Varnorian, Doona's a hard world and we have developed our humor to leaven the hardships. If I care to make a joke, it's my world, and most of us got the joke."

"Forgive me, but the taste of the joke is but a little questionable in terms of the larger aberration, my dear Mrs. Lawrence," said Varnorian, and he smiled again with that facile charm. "The real aberration is Doona. The cultures here are too different, too mutually exclusive. East in East, you know, and West is West. Never the twain shall meet." He lifted his refreshed drink to her, certain he had had the last word.

"Oh, Shakespeare?" asked Mrs. Lawrence, fluttering her eyelashes at him. Todd knew as well as she that it wasn't. Everyone on Doona was more familiar with Kipling, who seemed to "know" so much about their unusual situation. She continued to sip coyly at her glass.

"No," said Varnorian patronizingly. "Not at all, madam. I believe it might be Strauss. Nineteenth century, not seventeenth."

"Really? How clever you are," Sally said, and linking arms with him, moved him out of Todd's vicinity.

"What is Ssalllee up to now?" Hrriss asked, appearing at Todd's elbow. Todd looked around for Kelly. "Oh, I left her in good hands. Is that Captain Buckman beckoning for you?"

"He's had too much mlada already," Todd said, not too pleased with matters.

"That is undoubtedly true," Hrriss agreed after a moment's consideration. "And here is someone else in even worsse condition."

Jilamey staggered up to them with a determined expression on his face. The mlada he had begged of Kelly in the snake blind was only the start of his libations, though neither Hrriss nor Todd realized that. But he had consumed considerably more with his meal, which Todd had observed. That he was still standing spoke highly of his capacity. The young man was dressed in the most precious of modern styles. His tunic had appliquéd gems arranged in a crisscross pattern at the neck to stimulate lacings, and he wore frivolous boots with knee-high tops turned over to show their long fringes, which were also jeweled. "I've been looking for you for hours, Todd, to talk about snakes."

"It's a little early to talk about next year, Jilamey," Todd said diplomatically as he touched the single ribbon on the youth's medallion.

"Next year?" Jilamey blinked at him. "Ah, yes, next year! Of course. I'll be back next year. I'm one snake up. Have a drink on that."

"No mlada, I thank you," Todd replied, smiling to defuse any insult. "I'll stay with the punch."

"Punch? On a night like this?"

"Frankly, Jilamey, I don't really like it. It leaves a taste in my mouth of something long dead. I've got fresh raspberry-apple punch here if you'd like some. Homegrown fruit."

Jilamey shuddered. "Thank you ever so, no! Mlada for me. How about you?" The youth turned to Hrriss.

"Neither do I drink," the Hrruban said, dropping his jaw in a grin. "I have felt what mlada can do. Wait until you feel your head tomorrow morning. It will seem as though a ripe melon had replaced your cranium, and that every borer worm on Rrala is trying to drill through it."

"That's enough about worms," Jilamey said, grimacing horribly. "I've seen the big kind too closely today. I almost couldn't eat the meat at supper, but it smelled so good I got over it. That pretty Kelly told me I wasn't gripping tightly enough to the saddle with my knees. I will exercise mightily, and next year, my knees will meet inside the horse before I fall off in front of a snake!"

"That's the spirit," Todd responded.

Jilamey took a steadying drink and held out his glass to be topped up. "You went through this how many years ago?"

"The first Snake Hunt on Doona—well, more of a snake drive—happened when I was six." Tactfully Todd avoided mentioning how it came about. "We've had to wrangle snakes past our farms every year since then. We had to organize it because we were losing too many head of livestock to the snakes."

"No, no," and Jilamey waved a forefinger unsteadily. "I mean the coming-of-age ritual. You caught a big one and brought it in. Pete's been telling me and my friends all about it." He swayed as he pointed over his shoulder to where Peter Ivanovich, leader of Team Three, lay sprawled in a heap of cushions, snoring.

"Right," Todd said. Something in the young Landreau's tone alerted Hrriss, who appeared suddenly behind the swaying youth. He caught Todd's eye and looked a question. Todd shook his head very slightly. "The first one was only a tiddler. Eight meters. You saw a number of those today. The second one was a real whopper. Twelve meters and a little bit over."

"I was there and saw it," Hrriss put in. "A huge creature. It provided many days of meat for the settlement, and useful skin for other purposes."

Jilamey's eyes narrowed. "I don't believe it. How did you catch something like that? It's bigger than a house!"

"Careful planning," Todd said, maneuvering Landreau toward a chair before he fell over. "This is a good time for a yarn. Let me tell you all about it." Jilamey listened carefully through to the end of Todd's narrative, and then sat up very straight. He stared his fellow Human in the eye. "You've been rehearsing your story with the others. It's a falsehood. That snake is almost as big as the one that tried to eat me. I've never heard such a load of ballast in my life. It's exactly what Pete recited to me, almost word for word."

"I give you my word of honor that the story is true," Todd replied, shrugging away Jilamey's disbelief.

"Space slag!"

Todd shrugged again. "It's too much trouble to lie."

"Twelve meters! Impossible!" Jilamey exploded.

"Well, it's still on record," Todd said, not wanting to get into an argument over what was a fact. Then he grinned at Jilamey. "I had to, you see. Hrriss caught a real big Mommy the year before. I couldn't let him get an edge on me, now could I?" Surreptitiously he winked at his friend. "I broke his record but only by a few centimeters."

"If you don't believe him," Hrriss added silkily, as Jilamey still looked skeptical, "see if you can find anyone who has heard it told differently. There are many still awake who were here when it occurred. And there is the computer link in the corner! The records are available from the Treaty Archives for anyone to read. The Hunt and its results are documented."

Muttering, Jilamey poured himself another glass from the mlada bottle which Hrriss had managed to water down. Then he took himself off.

"What a head he's going to have tomorrow!" Todd said, shaking his head sympathetically as he watched Jilamey's wavering path toward the Archive room. "He didn't contest *your* record." Loyally Todd considered that omission a slight on his best friend.

"I expect no one mentioned it to him," Hrriss said uninterestedly. "No one tells the story of the second-place Hunt. Listeners want to hear only about the first-place achievement."

Sometime later, when Jilamey came back, Todd courteously extended the jug of watered mlada.

"No, no more for me, thank you ever so. I believe I have had sufficient for this evening," he said, slurring words which were nevertheless courteous. "I must seek my quarters. How can you possibly look so . . . so hearty?" His manner abruptly turned accusing.

"Clean living," Todd said jokingly. "But I assure you that when I finally see *my* quarters, I shall not move for two days."

"Yes, well, I checked your record—just to know the facts, you see," the Terran put in quickly, with a shamed expression. "I apologize. I will never again doubt anything you tell me. Twelve point four three meters! How I wish I'd seen that fight."

"It was a good one," Todd said with quiet satisfaction.

"It must have been." Jilamey smiled with genuine good humor. "You're too much to be true, Todd Reeve, but I'd rather you beside me in the Hunt than anyone else I've ever met on any world."

"Thanks," Todd said, shaking the hand Jilamey held out to him. "It'd be an honor."

Landreau shook hands with Hrriss, too, and staggered off toward the guest accommodations.

"I could wish that another of his stripe would reassess our honor," Hrriss said.

"Let's just hope that one suddenly doesn't appear on any panel of inquiry you and I have to face," Todd replied. "He doesn't think much about Reeve honor and that's all we've got: honor."

chapter four

A loud clattering and the feel of rough hands woke Todd from a sound sleep. There were men in blue uniforms leaning over him, shouting in loud voices and shaking his shoulders. It revived an old nightmare he had had the first time he'd seen those uniforms, twenty-five years before. They were Spacedep marines, the same units that had accompanied Landreau to Doona, to round up the colonists so they could be sent back to Earth. For a moment he was six years old again, the giant snakes were being herded through the village under Landreau's order, and his family was in danger. The Hrrubans, including Hrruna, the greatest, most important of them all, were behind him. He had to hurry to save the other Humans. He raised his hand to keep the soldier from grabbing him again to hustle him away to the convoy ship. An adult arm interceded, and the marine stepped back. Todd stared at the arm. Was it his father's? No, it was his own. In a moment, reality reasserted itself, and Todd calmed down. He was grown-up and could protect himself. There was no need to assume immediately that anything was wrong. The marine was waiting a few feet away from the bed. His fellows stood in the doorway. Todd could see his mother and father just behind them. Pat looked worried, and Ken furious.

"Todd Reeve," the marine said, reading from the plastic film containing his orders. "You are instructed to accompany us to the presence of the Treaty Councillors."

"Certainly, gentlemen," Todd said, throwing off the blanket. "Allow me a moment to dress?"

Todd had gone to bed only an hour before sunrise. Once the remaining guests went home with their hosts, he and the other volunteers who could still stand had spent several hours cleaning up. The Hunters among them had had no sleep since the night before, and they were weary. Hrriss had been reeling with fatigue when he mounted up to head toward the bridge to go home. Todd was glad that he lived so close to the Assembly Hall. Much farther, and he'd be spending the night curled up where he dropped from exhaustion. He barely managed to strip off his new silk shirt and hang it up before falling into bed. His good trousers hadn't fared so well, hiking to his knees under the blanket when he thrust his legs down. He had been too exhausted to straighten them out before he dropped off to sleep. The guards waited impatiently while he splashed some water on his face and shaved quickly.

It would seem that matters had taken a turn for the worse while he slept. A marine guard meant that the Treaty violation was now being addressed. He hoped truth would be all the defense he and Hrriss would need before a panel of inquiry.

The sky still wore the pale, moist veil of early morning when Todd reached the pad where the *Albatross* stood. Hrriss was already there, standing under the chill sky between his father, Hrrestan, and Commander Rogitel, assistant director of Spacedep. Ken Reeve had wanted to accompany his son, but the marine sergeant had denied him. Todd was relieved to see that at least Hu Shih, as leader of the Human settlers, was present. The old man's clothes were rumpled, as if he had hastily grabbed the nearest to hand. He was talking in a low worried tone with a small woman wearing a long robe tagged with the insignia of a Councillor. So, Todd thought, one of the Treaty Councillors had been called away from the crucial negotiations to be present when the ship was opened. From her weary expression, she had been waiting a long time. She was a small, elderly woman with dark skin and dark gray-shot curls which clustered closely around her head. Treaty Island was not so much an island as a minor continent which lay in the southern oceans a third of the way around Doona, which made this hour midday for her. Todd could have wished it were midday here and he'd been able to get enough sleep to keep his wits about him.

Hrriss looked expressionless, which meant to his old friend that he was deeply concerned. The glance he exchanged with Todd emphasized the fact that the situation was as bad as it could be. It would have been much better for both Todd and Hrriss had they been able to approach the Treaty Council of their own volition—which they had planned to do once the Hunt was over. But, despite his feelings of foreboding at the precipitous manner, he and Hriss had the truth to support their actions. It was only that Landreau, and others, had been wait-ing for just such an incident. The presence of marines magnified the incident out of proportion.

The presence of Rogitel, one of Landreau's senior lieutenants on hand, meant that the Council had to convene an inquiry: just as Kelly had warned.

"Councillor Dupuis," Rogitel said, bowing slightly to her, "the perpetrators are now present."

"It has only just come to our attention," Councillor Dupuis said in a with-ering tone, "that this ship has violated the Treaty."

"Hrriss and I reported the incident as soon as we landed, Councillor," Todd said politely. "Accordingly, the vessel was sealed."

"The Treaty, as a condition of the Amalgamated Worlds charter, requires all ships to be inspected after out-systems flights upon landing. Postflight inspec-tion is a requirement under the law, if for no other reason than fumigation and irradiation, and inspection of the ship's log."

"Madam," Hrrestan began politely, holding up a hand to stay the marine's ac-tion, "if this is merely postflight inspection, why have the soldiers been brought here and why is this gentleman present?" The Hrruban indicated Rogitel.

"We received information that this ship did not undergo a postflight in-spection, that it has been sealed for two weeks, and may be involved in a Treaty violation," the Councillor said. She answered Hrrestan in the formal Hrruban of diplomacy, a courtesy which boded no good at all. "Naturally Commander Rog-itel as Spacedep's representative is present. The violation is alleged to involve an uninhabited satellite of a star system."

Todd felt his spirits sink to a new low. Leaving the *Albatross* sealed was no crime, and indeed, such postflight inspections were not always completed in a timely fashion. As long as the ship had been sealed, the inspectors didn't much mind. Ken and Hu Shih had been informed of the incident; they had told Hrrestan, who was scarcely likely, even under the stringent codes of honor under which Hrrubans operated, to jeopardize his only child. No one else should have had that information. Ken and Hu might have been annoyed that the two friends had told Kelly, but she'd've told no one, knowing how very seri-ous this could be. So who could have leaked that information? Clearly only those who had set the trap into which Todd and Hrriss had fallen.

"A serrious charrge this is," Hrrestan said, also in the formal tongue. He sounded calm, but his pupils were slitted to mere lines, a sure sign that the older Hrruban was deeply troubled.

"Serious, indeed," Councillor Dupuis said. "I require a deposition from the ship's crew before the ship is unsealed."

"I trust," Commander Rogitel put in so suavely that his manner alarmed Todd, "that there has been no tampering with that seal?"

"Examine it yourself, Commander Rogitel," Hu Shih said, very much on his dignity at hearing such aspersions cast.

"Hmm, it looks untouched," Rogitel said, taking a long time peeling at the seal, though he didn't touch it.

"Reeve! Hrriss!" The Councillor waved them forward to the sealed hatch. "Do you swear and affirm that you took nothing out of this ship besides articles of clothing and personal effects?" They nodded solemnly, raising their right hands simultaneously. "That the contents listed here on the landing manifest were signed by the landing supervisor at the time of disembarkation?"

"I do," Todd said with a formal bow.

"I do," Hrriss echoed with an equally formal bow.

With a gesture, the Councillor ordered the marine sergeant to break the seal. As he touched the control pad, the hatch slid back, and a whoosh of stale air made those nearest, including the Councillor, recoil. Todd thought that that was one mark on their side as he saw Dupuis recognize what that implied. Lights came up inside the *Albatross* and the sergeant stepped politely aside as the ramp extruded the few feet to the ground. The port workers swarmed aboard to do the fumigation routine. They were as quick as they were efficient and very shortly left the ship with a nod from the foreman that their task was completed.

The Councillor acknowledged this and then gestured for Todd and Hrriss to follow her into the *Albatross*. Rogitel followed them, still wearing that blandly smug expression. While he wasn't like his superior, Landreau, who blustered when angry, Rogitel was coolheaded and very quiet, a dangerously misleading trait, which tempted the unwary to talk in his presence under the delusion that he wasn't listening. Rogitel missed little, and he shared Landreau's bitter feelings about Doona. Kelly's warning about him was all too timely.

"This is a very serious matter," the Councillor said as they followed her to the cabin of the *Albatross* while the ventilation system sucked away the fumigation mist. "We have incontrovertible information, gleaned from the orbiting buoy around Hrrilnorr system, that a ship, now identified as the *Albatross*, passed through the perimeter of that system. Both of you should know," and she paused to make plain her point that they should know, "that Hrrilnorr is a proscribed system and may not be entered. *Do* you have any explanation that will justify such a violation?"

"Yes, we did enter that system, ma'am," Todd said without the slightest apology in his tone. Rogitel raised an eyebrow very slightly and sucked in his pale cheeks at such an open admission of guilt. "In response to a Mayday message broadcasting over the emergency frequency. Our log tape shows a holo of the object broadcasting that Mayday and we both felt justified, in that circumstance, to enter a proscribed system and render such aid as was needed. In view of the proscription, Hrriss, as a Hrruban citizen, answered the appeal. If you will view the log tapes, Councillor, I'm certain you will agree that our action was justified." Todd gestured for her to precede him to the cargo bay.

The Councillor pursed her thin lips, but there was an element of surprise in her manner as she moved down the short corridor, with Todd, Hriss, Rogitel, and the marines following. "Then of course I will inspect your log tapes. If you were answering a Mayday, this puts an entirely different complexion on the matter. But it would have been wiser," and she pinned them with a harsh state, "to have reported the matter sooner, rather than later."

"The Hunt, ma'am, is of great importance to Doona, and Hrriss and I were responsible for its success," Todd said, not so much in apology as in explanation.

Dupuis raised her eyebrows in an expression of disagreement of his priorities.

"What a clever explanation for breaking interdict at Hrrilnorr," Rogitel said, his eyes cold. "Have you an equally glib explanation for these?" At the commander's gesture, a marine lifted off the panel on the front of the drives cabinet, revealing a number of small packages. Rogitel tore the wrappings off one and held it up. "Would you mind telling me what this is?"

Astonished, Todd stared at the hand-sized lump. It looked like a free-form rock swirled with multiple colors, like sunshine on oil. He'd seen something like it on educational tapes in school, when they studied the biology of other alien species. "It looks . . . like a cotopoid egg case." Todd felt sick. Cotopoid egg cases were priceless and rarely available on any legitimate market, since they were artifacts of another interdicted system.

"Now, tell me how it got there, behind your engine control panel."

"I don't know," Todd said, staring disbelievingly at the equipment cabinet. "It wasn't there when I last inspected the engines."

"When you last inspected the engines. And when was that?" Rogitel asked. "Remember, you are speaking before the Treaty Councillor."

"Before we took off from Doona," Todd replied, his mind racing. When had these incriminating packages been inserted in the control panels? On Doona where a mechanic in Spacedep's pay would have had access to the *Albatross*? Or on Hrretha during that second, totally redundant "servicing"?

"And these?" the Spacedep official demanded. "What about these?" There seemed to be dozens of small artifacts shoved between the elements of the machinery. When the marines removed other panels, still more bags and bottles were revealed. Some were opened to expose objects of great value and rarity, also from interdicted systems.

Part of Todd's bewilderment reflected a droll amusement at the sheer volume of purloined valuables that Hrriss and he were supposed to have assembled. But any amusement was soon drowned by the obvious fact that a lot of trouble had gone into framing them with such a widespread cache of illegal treasures.

"I have no idea where any of this came from," Todd said in staunch repudiation as he suppressed the rising anger he felt at such long-planned treachery.

"Such a display would have taken weeks to gather. We did not," Hrriss said with stiff dignity, his tail tip twitching with indignation. He turned to the Councillor. "We answered a Mayday call. The tapes will verify this."

"Then how did those get there?" Rogitel demanded as yet another cache was discovered.

"We are not responsible for their presence on the *Albatross*," Todd said, his tone as expressionless as Hrriss's. "There were no such illegal items on board this ship when we left Doona. I oversaw the check myself."

Rogitel's heavy lids lowered over cold blue eyes. "Then where did they come aboard?" Rogitel asked in a poisonously reasonable tone.

"The Hrrethans insisted on a complimentary service of the *Albatross* while we were attending the ceremonies there," Todd said, making no accusations. "When we landed, we reported the incident to my father. The postmaster's deputy, Linc Newry, had properly affixed the seal."

"That is the lamest explanation you've yet advanced, Reeve," Rogitel said. "The seals on the hatch were intact. They were placed there not half an hour after the ship had landed, according to the portmaster's log. It would have taken far longer than half an hour for anyone to secrete all these items. Therefore, you two are the only ones capable of concealing the artifacts on this ship—sometime between your departure from Doona and your return, via the Hrrilnorr system!" Rogitel was winding himself up to a good display of outraged anger. "Councillor Dupuis, these young men, so trusted by their parents, have been using their privileged position as trusted messengers of Alreldep to pillage treasures from planets. Alreldep will be shocked at the abuse of their trust."

"I am not Alreldep," Hrriss said coldly. "I am a Hrruban, a citizen of Rrala, on whose behalf I made the journey with Todd Reeve to Hrretha. I answer to the Hrruban High Council of Speakers and to the Treaty Councillors. Not to Spacedep."

"I stand reproved," Rogitel said with noticeable sarcasm. "You shall indeed answer to the Treaty Councillors and your own High Council of Speakers."

Just then, one of the marines pulled the panel from the last cabinet, the ship's log recorder. Behind the metal sheet, some of the equipment had been moved to one side to make room for an ovoid white stone, at least a meter high. It resembled Terran alabaster, except that it had an inner illumination of its own. The Spacedep official regarded it from a safe distance.

"The very presence of such a gem," and Hrriss extended his forefinger, claw fully sheathed, at the luminous Byzanian Glow Stone, "supports our innocence. They are only found deep inside the caverns of the planet. The log will show how little time we spent in that system: far too short a span to have landed, searched, and found a Glow Stone of that quality. Further," he went on, holding up his hand, "they are why the system is proscribed. The effects of the mineral's emissions are not yet fully investigated."

"But their possible danger makes them all the more collectible," Rogitel said, an air of triumph in his stance. "Arrest them!" he ordered the marines who bracketed Hrriss and Todd, weapons drawn.

"We are innocent," Todd said, standing erect and ignoring his escort.

Hu Shih stepped forward to block the exit. "I protest, Madam Councillor. I have know these young men far too long to entertain for one moment that they are guilty of transgressing a Treaty whose terms they have scrupulously obeyed and upheld for twenty-four years. Or," and Hu Shih straightened his shoulders in denial, "jeopardize themselves and the world they hold dear by pilfering baubles."

"You call that," and Rogitel pointed at the Byzanian Glow Stone, "a bauble?"

"It is in *my* eyes," Hu Shih said in measured contempt.

"Perhaps," said Councillor Dupuis, "but this matter has gone from a minor infraction to systematic robbery and the arrest is to proceed."

"To that I must concur," Hu Shih said, bowing to her, "but an armed escort is unnecessary and insulting. I can speak with full confidence that neither Todd nor Hrriss will resist the due process of law."

Councillor Dupuis accepted his statement and gestured for the squad leader to have his men reholster their weapons.

"These . . ." and Dupuis waved at the array of incriminating evidence, "are to be impounded, identified, and placed in the highest security."

"Remove that Stone with care," Hrrestan said to the two marines who were about to lift the Byzanian Stone out of its hiding place.

"Yes," Rogitel said, stepping in front of Hrrestan and ostentatiously taking charge of the removal. "Don't touch it with your bare hands or let it touch unprotected skin. Treat it as carefully as you would radioactive substances. And it's heavy."

"What, sir?" asked one of the marines, a glazed expression on his face. He had been standing right beside the Stone since the panel had been opened. Now the light seemed to pulse, drawing every eye to it.

Shading eyes with one hand and stepping quickly around Rogitel, Hrrestan pulled the man away from the white light. The marine shook his head, looking puzzled.

"He has been affected by it already. We must all leave before the Stone's effect spreads," Hrrestan said. "The most noticeable effect it has is an interference with short-term memory."

As Hrriss and Todd dutifully proceeded with their escort, Todd caught a glimpse of Rogitel, disconnecting the flight log recorder. He carried it out of the ship cradled in his arms like a bubble made of glass.

Once the group was outside, technicians sealed the ship once more with fiberglass wafers, and Councillor Dupuis affixed her own seal. Hrriss and Todd were hustled to a shuttle which had landed while they were inside the *Albatross*.

"That Glow Stone," Hrriss murmured as they were led to seats, "affects more than men."

"Quiet there! No conversation between criminals," Rogitel said, no more the suave diplomat but the acknowledged jailor.

"Criminality has yet to be proved," Hrriss said as he was pushed into a seat while Todd was taken farther down the aisle before settled. They were advised to fasten their safety harnesses and were then studiously ignored by the marine guard.

During the entire journey to Treaty Island, no one even offered them anything to eat or drink, although Rogitel and the marines ate a light meal.

Perhaps, Todd thought, sunk in a negative mood, it was as well he and Hrriss could not speak. Rogitel would construe it as collusion to be sure their "explanations" tallied before interrogation. But Todd did not need to speak to Hrriss to know that his friend would be as puzzled as he that dozens of illegal items had been secreted on the *Albatross*, a ship used almost exclusively by themselves on official tours of duty.

And the positioning of the Byzanian Glow Stone indicated a good try at jamming the recorder. His kick must have tipped the Stone sufficiently to restore the function, but had the Stone's radiation erased the tape? Would the all-important Mayday still be recorded? Surely machinery was a little less receptive to the Glow Stone's effects than a human? And the Mayday was the only proof of their innocence right now.

Once the shuttle landed on Treaty Island, the two prisoners were hurried inside the huge Federation Center. Hrriss had only a glimpse of the high, white stone façade before they were rushed up the stairs and through a maze of identical hallways. There was no sound but the clatter of boot heels on the smooth surface of the floors. The sergeant stopped before a door, its nameplate blank and status sign registering "empty."

"You'll wait here until the Council is ready for you," the sergeant said. "Food and drink will be brought in a bit."

"That is most considerate," Hrriss said in Terran Standard. The numbness of shock had receded sufficiently to make him aware of an intense thirst and, less insistent, some hunger.

"You're a Treaty prisoner and the courtesies are observed," the sergeant said, but Hrriss could see that the man approved of his use of Terran.

Hrriss knew that the military arm of both parent governments was made up of fierce patriots who preferred their own culture in all ways. It was one of the reasons there was no standing force of any kind on Doona, the symbol of compromise. As the Treaty Organization was trying to maintain a separate but equal method of expansion in trading and colonization, each culture needed to remain independent from the other. That would make a Doonan "army" an unacceptable third force.

"Hear tell you all had some party last night," the guard said, sounding almost friendly. "What's keeping you?" he added, looking down the hall just as Todd, between his guards, reached the room. "In you go." The escort stood aside to let Todd enter. "Food and drink coming."

"Thanks, Sergeant," Todd said, and his stomach rumbled. Whether the sergeant heard that or not was irrelevant, for he closed the door firmly. Both Hrriss and Todd heard the lock mechanism whirr, and the bulb over the door lit up redly. They also heard the stamp of boots as someone stood to attention outside the room.

The two prisoners turned to view the room. No more than three meters on a side, with a long window running along the wall opposite the door. A broad table was set underneath the window, a tape reader on its surface but no tapes in it or blanks ready to be used. There were three padded chairs against the wall: a cheerless functional cubicle.

"Are they likely to listen in?" Hrriss asked.

"I doubt it," Todd said, glancing at the door. "Looks like a research room, not an interrogation facility, in spite of that tape reader." He had been listening to the sound of his voice. "It's soundproofed. Scholars insist on that as an aid to deep thought and concentration. Fardles, despite what they hauled out of cabinets and crannies on the *Albatross,* we're still only alleged Treaty breakers, not actual criminals."

"We might as well be, Zodd, with all the treasures Rogitel pulled out of hiding," Hrriss said gloomily.

"Hu Shih didn't believe we took them. Neither did your father!" Todd began to pace with some agitation. "All the way here I kept trying to remember every time we've left the *Albie* unguarded and open. Suffering snakes, Hrriss, that stuff could have been planted anytime the last few years."

"Not if proper service checks were carried out, Zodd, and you supervised the last one yourself," Hrriss reminded him.

"Yeah, so I did. Then the junk has to have been planted during that phony servicing on Hrretha. There'd've been time to platinum the hull. Furthermore," and now Todd whirled on Hrriss, pointing his index finger at his friend, "Rogitel was on Hrretha, and lurking close to us all the time. To prevent us from going back to our ship to see just what sort of servicing was being done?" When Hrriss nodded agreement with that thought, Todd continued, "Furthermore, we filed our flight plan, same as always, and, despite that short detour to Hrrilnorr system, we weren't much behind schedule landing back on Doona, were we?"

Though Hrriss recognized the validity of that logic, he knew that Todd was talking himself out of despair even as he offered the same hope to Hrriss.

"We always register flight plans," Hrriss said. "We leave and arrive on time at all destinations."

"So," and Todd stopped pacing long enough to whirl back to Hrriss, "where do they think we had time to pick up all those juicy little rarities? Cotopoids are found on only three planets in two systems, if I remember rightly, and none of them on any route we've taken recently. I can't identify half of the other stuff but," and now he sighed, "that damned Byzanian Glow Stone is genuine and there's only one place you can come by them and we were orbiting above it."

"All our flight plans are on record," Hrriss said, finding reassurance in that fact, "and they will prove our innocence. Come, stop pacing. It suggests a guilty mind."

Todd plopped down next to Hrriss and shoved the third chair a short distance away so the two of them could share it to prop their feet. Hrriss disposed his tail comfortably through the opening in the rear of his chair and composed himself.

"There's something nagging at me," Todd said after a few moments. He circled his hand in the air, trying to catch hold of an elusive thought. "Something Councillor Dupuis said, that they had received information that the *Albie* had been identified by the Hrrilnorr beacon. Isn't it a little soon for such to reach Hrruban Security? That beacon didn't dispatch a robot probe when we passed it, which is the only way that the data would get here short of a month. It shouldn't have been picked up for another few weeks even by digital rapid-transfer. That's why my father thought that the matter could be deferred until after Snake Hunt."

Hrriss yawned broadly, showing fangs, incisors, and grinders that Todd always found an impressive array. "We both know how interdict beacons operate. But there were other people using Hrrilnorr as a warp-jump coordinate. Perhaps they collected the message and reported the infraction."

"Whose side are you on?" Todd demanded, half joking. Hrriss often played devil's advocate when they had to reason through a problem. "A little too coincidental to please me, especially with the Treaty Renewal imminent."

Hrriss yawned again.

"Who else was using the Hrrilnorr connection, Hrriss?"

"I do not remember, only that some were."

"But I thought most of the top brass came by transport grid. And Rogitel is not the type to plan practical jokes. Nor is Landreau, and this thing was planned."

Hrriss was working his bottom into the padded seat, trying to make himself comfortable enough to sleep. Todd often wished he had the Hrruban propensity for sleep. Despite their generally high level of activity when awake, they could, and did, take naps anytime opportunity offered.

"I agree," Hrriss mumbled. He caught himself in the act of falling asleep. "We were promisssed food and drink. I could sleep better with a full belly. But I need sleep to make sense out of this situation. I had only an hour in my bed whenever this morning was." He sat up, suddenly anxious. "I hope my mother will feed the ocelots when evening comes. If they're not fed, they will go in search of food and raid my neighbor's ssliss coop again."

"You'll be home to feed them yourself," Todd said.

"I hope so but the ocelots do enjoy ssliss eggs."

"Don't talk about eggs. I'm starved." When Hrriss yawned even more broadly than before, Todd regarded him in disgruntlement. "And, damn your lousy furred pelt, you can sleep. I can't when I'm starving."

"Then wake me when the meal comes," Hrriss advised, and settling himself, his chin dropped to his chest; his hands, so oddly more human than the rest of him, relaxing in his lap while his tail hung slack behind him, the tip only occasionally twitching.

Todd sighed, settling back, legs stretched out in front of him, crossed at the ankles on the supporting chair, and began running over the day's happenings. *Who* had placed those incriminating items on the *Albie*? He turned to ask what Hrriss thought. Hrriss's breathing had slowed, become steady and shallow. The gentle oscillation of the tip of Hrriss's tail attracted Todd's attention. Its movement was hypnotic and soothing. As Todd watched it, his own eyes grew heavy. After a while, despite his hunger, he dozed off.

"As you can see, Madam Councillor," Rogitel continued, running the recorded flight log back to the beginning, "the so-called rescue mission to Hrrilnorr was only the last stop in a series of piracies these two young reprobates committed." Landreau's aide was able to act as prosecutor before the Treaty Council only because noncolonizable Human-claimed planets were kept under the aegis of his department. Entries in the log of the *Albatross* suggested that the ship had visited at least three in that category.

The log went through a further playback, projecting its holographic images onto a platform while sound was broadcast through wall speakers. Hu Shih, Hrrestan, Rogitel, and Ken Reeve glowered at the images while Councillor Dupuis's expression was impassive.

That morning, as soon as the marines had left with Todd in custody, Ken had persuaded Martinson, the portmaster, to let him go to Treaty Island via transport grid, for Martinson had also been called to give a deposition. Now Martinson sat nervously hunched over his folded hands. Allowing the *Albatross* to go uninspected for so long was a black mark on his record. He, too, was risking censure, even dismissal, if a crime resulted from negligence even by his subordinate, Newry.

"No fewer than eight landings are recorded between the date the scout ship left Doona and the date on which it returned here," Rogitel said. "Eight! And only the one on Hrretha legitimate. Here." He stopped the tape and rewound it. "Here is their so-called rescue, after they had passed through the perimeter of Hrrilnorr." The hologram showed the nose of the ship as it approached a distant sun. An audio signal for help crowded by static came out of the speakers. The audio monitors then erupted with the siren call of the interdict alarm, but the ship passed without stopping. Hrriss's voice could be heard responding to the Mayday message. The print update on the screen showed Hrrilnorr's identification number and location. Then the ship's nose penetrated the cloud layer of the planet's atmosphere.

"Naturally," Rogitel's insidious voice went on, "the system's buoy did not record the Mayday, since it did not exist. That could so easily be patched into the log by either conspirator. Both have the necessary qualifications."

Then the camera eye upturned for landing, to show the stern of the ship as it touched down on grassoids flattened by the exhaust from the engines.

Councillor Dupuis looked down at her notes for a long moment. Her face showed inner conflict. "This is far more serious than a simple violation. There is no choice but to make an exhaustive formal inquiry into this matter."

"I heartily concur," Ken Reeve said so emphatically that Rogitel regarded him in stunned amazement. "A formal inquiry that will clear my son and Hrriss of every one of these ridiculous accusations."

The Treaty Controller slammed his gavel down on the bench. He was the ranking Hrruban on Doona, and had been nominated to his post by the Third Speaker of the Hrruban High Council. It was a bad time for one of Third's minions to be the senior Councillor on Doona; Third had been against the joint colony from the day Humans were discovered. Ken tried to take comfort in the fact that the Controller was reputed to be a just personage who tried each case on its individual merit.

"Please be silent, Mr. Reeve. We take the log tape in evidence." He addressed the holographic recorder. "This hearing is to decide whether Todd Reeve and/or Hrriss, son of Hrrestan, have violated the Treaty of Doona, and to what degree."

Testimony was then taken from Martinson, who explained that the *Albatross* had gone unsearched two weeks ago due to extenuating circumstances. "They were Snake Hunt Masters and I know how much time and planning that takes to prevent trouble. They told the duty officer that they urgently needed to take advice on a protocol matter. Since the ship was sealed and its papers in order, Newry granted their request."

"And is this laxness typical of your administration of your post as portmaster?" Rogitel inquired acidly.

"No, Commander, it is not," the portmaster said, eyes flashing. "I've been in this job fifteen years, and I've known Todd and Hrriss all that time. I had no reason to suspect that there was anything out of the ordinary about this landing."

"Whose advice were they in such a hurry to obtain?"

"Mine," Ken spoke up, and was relieved as he succeeded in making eye contact with the Spacedep official. Ken held that contact, trying to look the disgust he felt. He had never ceased to dislike and distrust bureaucrats, and Rogitel was nearly as bad an example of the type as Landreau.

"And when were the seals on the hatch cut?" the Treaty Controller wanted to know.

"Not in my presence," Martinson said in an aggrieved tone. "My assistant, Lincoln Newry, was deputized in my absence, but in something as serious as this I should have been there! I have no idea who else was there. When I did arrive, the ship was already open, with troops pouring all over it."

Next Ken Reeve gave his evidence. Under irritated prompting from Rogitel, Ken repeated the story that Todd and Hrriss had told him two weeks before.

"I believe them," he insisted at the end. "They were genuinely distressed when they realized they'd been tricked into violating an interdicted system."

"We have asked you to draw no conclusions," the Treaty Controller said ponderously. Ken nodded, angrily swallowing the rest of his opinions, and sat down.

The Council proceeded thereafter to take evidence from the sergeant of the Spacedep marines who had searched the *Albatross*. Rogitel testified that he had received information from a confidential source, whom he declined to identify, that there might be contraband aboard the ship.

"Furthermore, I wish to put on record my disgust that two such untrustworthy men were allowed the unsupervised use of a scout ship!" he finished in a voice trembling with outrage.

"I have studied the records of the defendants, Commander Rogitel," Madam Dupuis said, sternly raising her voice above Ken's as he erupted from his chair to protest the slander, "and find absolutely no proof to support a claim of dishonesty or irresponsibility. You will kindly retract such an unsupported remark."

If Rogitel did so with an ill grace, at least he did so and it would be in the record.

"We will see"—Madam Dupuis hesitated—"the two young men now."

Ken Reeve took that as a good sign: the Councillor was by no means convinced of Rogitel's damning evidence.

Todd and Hrriss were brought in then, and sworn in as witnesses. As one, they turned to face the table. As accustomed as they were to diplomatic events, facing the full Treaty Council with little sleep and only a dry sandwich to eat was not auspicious. The holographic tape was run once more in their presence.

The first landing was shown, and the two young men were stunned.

"This can't be our log," Todd protested. "We made no landing. This must be a mistake."

"Silence!" the Treaty Controller demanded, rapping his gavel. "Continue."

Todd and Hrriss watched, incredulous, as the holographic replay continued. At each entry and departure, the ID signal repeated on-screen. There was no question that it matched the *Albatross*'s code. When the tape finished, the Treaty Controller turned to them.

"As the log shows, you visited several off-limits worlds, and took therefrom prohibited materials, and in some cases, precious and valuable items of historical worth. I must say, your thefts were nonpartisan. My notes show that some of them came from Hrruban-marked planets, and some from the Amalgamated Worlds. What can you offer as your defense?"

"Sir, something's skewed," Todd said agitatedly. "We passed into only one prohibited system, Hrrilnorr, and only to respond to a Mayday message. That much of this tape is accurate. The rest has been added. We made no entries into other interdicted zones."

"But why is there no Mayday message recorded in the alarm beacon orbiting the system?" Rogitel asked. "Such beacons are designed for that purpose, to record transmissions that originate within its range of sensitivity."

"I have no ready explanation . . . sir," Todd added after a pause. "A flaw in the mechanism? The in-system sensor malfunctioning? Plenty of buoys are damaged by space debris. But Hrriss and I heard the call for help. We diverted from our planned route to respond. All we found was that buoy, orbiting the fourth planet."

"A marker buoy, as you say," Rogitel intoned coldly. "You broke Treaty Law for an unmanned probe?"

"We did not know it was a marker buoy at the time we heard its message," Todd replied, trying to keep his voice level.

"It is what we found," Hrriss said coolly, "broadcasting the distress message." The Hrruban extended a pointed claw and replayed the section of the log.

"Mayday, Mayday," said the tape. "Anyone who is within the sound of my voice, Mayday! We require assistance. Our ship is down and damaged. Mayday!" The message began to repeat, and Hrriss shut it off. "Every pilot of whatever species must respond to such a message. As Zodd said, we could not ignore a Mayday. It would be uncivilized."

Rogitel stood up. "Please tell the council directly: where did you find the buoy?"

"We found it orbiting Hrrilnorr IV."

"The Buoy Authority lists no such installation in orbit around Hrrilnorr IV. There are no extraneous beacons orbiting in that system. There are only two assigned to it, each one AU perpendicular to the plane of the ecliptic above and below."

"There was a third one," Todd said in weary rebuttal. "The buoy was broadcasting the message for help that's recorded on our log. It still sounds genuine. We couldn't and didn't ignore it."

Dismissively Rogitel switched off the audio. "Anyone could have recorded that message in your ship's memory. The voice is broadcasting in Middle Hrruban, the language of Doona. The static could have been made by crumpling packing material near the microphone. You put it in yourself. Without correlation, the message must be accounted as false."

"I respectfully suggest that an analysis of the voice patterns of Hrriss and

Zodd be made," Hrrestan said. "Analysis will prove if one of them recorded the Mayday message."

Councillor Dupuis made a note, nodding acknowledgment of Hrrestan's suggestion.

"We didn't make that spurious recording," Todd said, turning his head to meet the eyes of the seven Council members, "and we most certainly did not collect or secrete those artifacts in the equipment cabinets."

"Simple lies to assuage your guilt," Rogitel retorted.

Todd's eyes flashed hotly. "I do not lie." He half sprang from his seat, but Hrriss pulled him down.

"Councillors, may I speak?" Hu Shih rose somewhat stiffly to his feet. "We have before us two reliable young men, considered rather more than unusually truthful by their elders and their peers. Let a full inquiry establish what is fact or fiction."

"So ordered," the Treaty Controller said, banging his gavel.

The Spacedep subdirector shrugged dismissively. "That can take months. We have before us right now recorded proof that differs greatly from their verbal accounts. Surely this is sufficient to deprive them of positions of high responsibility and trust. The flight recorder has been placed in evidence. It shows landings preceding and following their landing on Hrrilnorr. Their posted flight plan showed that they skimmed the space between the Human and Hrruban arms of the galaxy, so it is possible to have visited all these worlds in the time they were gone. In every case, they broke interdiction. In only one did they attempt to justify the falsehood with a tale of rescue. Look at the evidence"—Rogitel swept an arm to indicate the table where most of the contraband lay—"taken only this morning from the ship they alone seem to use."

"The commander forgets one detail," Hrriss said. "The flight plan we filed with portmaster Martinson is the shortest possible journey we could make between Hrretha and Rrala. There was not time for us to have landed on all these worlds and collected these things in the weeks we were gone. Especially since our log-in and log-off times were verified."

As if they had placed themselves in further jeopardy, Rogitel called up the holo again and pointed out the time/date designations. "The flight recorder says that the time was available to you. We have run it through compcheck. Though the timing is tight, you would have had the time."

"Only if we knew exactly where all these artifacts were," Hrriss protested, "with no allowance for any time to search. How could we know where they were? It would have taken months to research archaeological and geological data from the Treaty Island banks. Or are you suggesting that some of the researchers on Treaty Island are guilty of collusion and deception, too?" Hrriss asked softly.

"The matter will be investigated," was all the commander would say. He addressed the Council. "Clearly the defendants are guilty of deviating from their registered flight path. Spacedep, as the body in charge of security and defense for the Amalgamated Worlds, demands that this matter be examined as well."

"Tell me, Commander," Todd demanded, leaning across the table toward Rogitel, "just why would Hrriss and I wish to steal rarities like that? Much less something as dangerous as that Glow Stone? Where could we possibly fence our loot without being detected? Especially as we are not scheduled to take any off-planet trips in the next year?"

"We are innocent," Hrriss added, his tone more growl than speech.

Rogitel did not quite flinch, but his body inclined ever so slightly away from the Hrruban. "Machines cannot lie," Rogitel said flatly. "Only people can, and it would appear in this case, very poorly. And you"—he pointed his finger at Todd—"you admit entering the Hrrilnorr system. You have just said that you recognize the danger of a Glow Stone and that you know it is found only on Hrrilnorr IV. There are many other unscrupulous persons in this galaxy who could use the Glow Stone's peculiar properties to excellent advantage. And those"—now his finger swung to point at Hrriss—"are particularly well known to Hrrubans."

"We adjourn for due consideration," said the senior Treaty Councillor, rising to his feet to end this session. His colleagues were equally solemn. "This is a matter of unprecedented gravity."

Every face was solemn and, in some cases, sad. This was the first time in twenty-five years that there had been any infraction of the provisions of the Treaty. The ramifications were profound, and could result in punishments ranging from exile for the two defendants, up through war and/or disbandment of the colony. The negotiations among them for renewal of the Treaty had been under way for several years. All knew that the twenty-fifth anniversary would be a crucial time—a time when the Treaty could be easily swept aside. A violation of this magnitude might obliterate two and a half decades of hope and dedication.

Two of the Council, Madam Dupuis and Mrrorra, were representatives of Doona/Rrala, and were both second-wave settlers from the First Villages. They were upset and puzzled, because they knew Todd and Hrriss well. Neither could find credence in the facts that suggested these two, whose friendship had created the Decision at Doona, could willfully destroy the colony. Their interspecies friendship had been held up as a symbol for Human/Hrruban cooperation all over the galaxy.

"Therefore," the Treaty Controller said heavily, "until the inquiry has been conducted and a decision reached, the two defendants are under house arrest. They are to be kept separated at their places of residence, and interim communication denied. This matter is adjourned pending investigation." The gavel banged once more. It might have been the report of a gun. Todd and Hrriss both reacted as if it had been, startled, shocked, deeply hurt by even the mere thought of such a separation.

But they were honorable young men, and although they held each other's eyes for a long, long moment, they did not speak. Then, distressed and saddened, they turned away from each other. No solitary confinement could have been harder to bear. Especially when they needed each other's support to prove their innocence.

Ken Reeve was out of his seat a split second after the Council had filed out of the chamber. He rushed around the table to his son. Hrrestan was as quick to go to Hrriss.

"Rogitel seems to have pretty damning evidence against you, Todd," Ken said, wearily shaking his head. "But I know you've told the truth, so we'll beat this."

"What motive would we have for stealing such dumb stuff?" Todd asked his father, his hands spread in a helpless gesture of disbelief. He felt numbed by despair.

"Did either of you enter any or all of these interdicted systems?" Hrrestan asked.

"Why would we? We always come straight back to Doona, where we belong," Hrriss answered his father in the familial form of Hrruban.

"You know how we hate those damned missions, Dad," Todd added. "And one thing more, that damned beacon with its phony message had a destructive band. We were tractoring it up to the *Albie* when we saw that. Contact stuff from the look of it. Blow us and it up."

"Why didn't you mention that earlier?" Ken demanded.

"Hell, Dad, I only just remembered it," Todd said, scrubbing at his tired face with hands that nearly trembled.

Ken looked at Hrrestan. "A detail that might be useful. A convenient shot would explode the beacon."

"So it could," Hrrestan said, his tone thoughtful. "We will begin our own covert investigations. Little could we have imagined that a minor infraction of the Treaty would be subsumed by a larger and horrendous charge of piracy and smuggling. I will initiate inquiries for your defense on Hrruba."

"I've still some contacts on Earth through Sumitral," Ken said, noticeably brightening as actions became obvious. "His daughter is here on Treaty Island doing some research. I'll talk to her after I see you on your way home. I don't have all that many friends or allies on Earth, but I know we can count on that family."

"Let's just hope none of our former Corridor or Aisle neighbors get wind of this," Todd said, trying for some levity. It wrung a sad grin from Ken.

"You were never born for Earth, Todd, but you've always been a natural here on Doona," Ken said, "but I promise you, I'll holler down the doors if it'd help."

"Someone must know where that beacon came from and who put it there."

When they left the chamber, Todd and Hrriss were hustled through the bare corridors to the transport grid, which was located in another part of the building. Both were sent separately back via grid to the main continent with an escort of armed guards. The last glimpse Todd had of his best friend was Hrriss, standing too quietly between a guard lieutenant and Hrrestan. His fur seemed to have lost all its luster and his tail dragged in the dust behind him. Their eyes met, and Hrriss nodded once to him. Todd often felt that he could almost read the Hrruban's mind but there was no such feeling between them now.

The image seemed to disintegrate into mist, and then Todd was in the midst of the Hrruban village, facing the Friendship Bridge. Once he crossed it, he wouldn't be allowed back over until his innocence was proved. The thought made his feet feel heavy.

The guard accompanied him to his family ranch house, where Pat Reeve was waiting. In the living room, Kelly stood up when they came in. Todd was a little surprised to see her, until he realized that it had been many hours since he'd been taken away. She had probably come over this morning to continue the talk the three of them had been having the night before, and found he was gone.

The marine sergeant gave both women a sharp salute and then withdrew, taking his squad with him. Pat hovered for a minute, looking from Kelly to Todd, then went out toward the kitchen.

"You must be hungry. I know we are. I'll fix us all a snack."

"An armed escort? What happened?" Kelly asked, worried by the beaten expression on Todd's face.

"It's worse than I could have dreamed," Todd said. "This isn't a simple case of an interdiction infraction. Oh, no, nothing simple or easily explained like answering a Mayday call. Hrriss and I seem to have been to many planets in many interdicted systems, doing a fine job of smuggling rarities and classified items, all of which we have been secretly stashing around the *Albie*." He grinned sourly at the gasps that elicited. "We're big-time looters and purveyors of illegal artifacts, and up on charges of smuggling and contraband, using our prestigious position on Doona/Rrala to perpetrate crimes against Hrruba and Terra, and half the planets in between. That log entry we felt would clear us has had some very interesting additions." He rubbed his eyes with one hand. "I don't know how they got there. One thing is certain: neither Hrriss nor I put them there. Then Rogitel kept insisting that we falsified the Mayday signal to get into the Hrrilnorr system, to steal a Byzanian Glow Stone."

"A Glow Stone? A real one?" Kelly asked, her voice breaking with incredulity. "They've got one of those in the remote-handling research lab on Hrruba. They're considered ultra-dangerous. And," she added with a facial grimace, "they are only found on Hrrilnorr IV."

"Well, one was found in the communications cabinet," Todd said. "And whatever else it does, it deleted the short-term memory of the marine standing nearby. So Hrriss and I are not only smugglers and looters, we're stupidly dangerous pirates." His mother opened her mouth to protest and closed it, her eyes sparking with suppressed anger and resentment. "At that we got off lightly. The Councillors placed Hrriss and me under house arrest while they're investigating. We're not supposed to communicate at all." At that point, Todd's broad shoulders sagged, and he looked as dejected as a small boy, all the droll defensiveness and outrage gone. "We haven't been separated since I started wearing rope tails."

Pat Reeve could restrain herself no longer. "This whole thing is ridiculous. Why, neither you nor Hrriss have stolen so much as a . . . brrna." She spat that out after a good long hesitation as she tried to remember any other incident of petty crime. "How can they possibly accuse you and Hrriss of piracy or smuggling? *Any*one else could have done it. *Any*one on the launch pad could have access to your ship."

Todd had sunk to a chair, elbows on his knees, head in his hands, diminished more by the separation than the absurd charges. Sighing, he propped his chin on his hands and told his mother and Kelly about the additional landings and launches noted in the log, and the even stranger omissions concerning the orbiting alarm beacon. Kelly stood by him, not quite touching him, alert to any cues. When she moved toward him he caught her hand, squeezed it once, and then dropped it as if he shouldn't hold it—or her.

She was perplexed by that gesture, sensing it to be a "keep off" signal. She backed off. This was so unlike the resilient Todd she'd always known, but if he felt himself ostracized, perhaps he didn't wish her contaminated by his disgrace.

That, too, was unlike the Todd she'd always known. But then, Todd had never been under such vile suspicions before and shouldn't be now, Kelly thought in seething outrage.

"This whole affair is ridiculous," she said, dropping her hands helplessly. "It's absurd to think of you two as smugglers! The Council must all be strangers, to let Rogitel get away with an accusation like that."

"The Treaty Controller this term is one of Third Speaker's nominees," Todd said in a dull voice. "I recognized him as soon as I came into the chamber. You both know him; he'd let us get into a war if it would remove the Human threat to Hrruba."

Irritably Kelly shook her head. "Surely we have some friends on the Council. I hoped Madam Dupuis would be on your side. She used to live around here."

"She's got to go by the evidence, the same as the other Councillors," Todd pointed out. "Any way you present it, it's damning. She had no option. That log tape was tampered with! Very cleverly, by someone who knew exactly how to match holo images perfectly." He sounded more like himself and then suddenly slumped again, scrubbing at his rumpled hair. "I don't know how we can prove that. *Why* didn't I open the recording unit when the log tape jammed! I'd've found that wretched Glow Stone then and we'd've known we were being set up. That was a costly kick." A flash of Todd's usual spirit accompanied that remark. "And whaddya bet," he went on in a bitter tone, "the Hrrilnorr warning beacon will show we spent far more time in that system than we say we did."

"What about the beacons at the other planets you're supposed to have visited?" Pat asked, grasping at the possibility.

"Surely, if you're supposed to have been at so many other worlds, all of those beacons can't have been got at?"

Todd regarded his mother almost pityingly and shook his head. "This was all too well planned, Mother, for them to neglect that sort of verification. Remember, it's Spacedep involved and they have the resources to do just this sort of documentation."

"Look, Todd," Kelly began in a firm tone, being as positive as she knew how, "you two have an enviable reputation on Earth. Much better than Rogitel's. There's going to be a lot of talk when he comes up with this sort of a crazy charge. And I don't care how much evidence there is against you. *He* doesn't have as good a reputation as you and Hrriss, and Doona, have. I'll see what I can find out. I'll talk to everyone I know about this ridiculous accusation. Furthermore," and her smile was malicious, "Hrringa can start the action. He'll do it for me. And"—her voice rose in triumph now—"I'll enlist Jilamey Landreau!"

Todd gave her a frankly contemptuous look.

"Don't be so skeptical, pal," she said. "He's been following me around all afternoon in hopes of finding you. He only gave up an hour ago. He's got a superlative hangover, but he's still raving about you saving his life. I'll send the rumor about your entrapment home with him. Yes, entrapment!" For Todd had looked up with some glimmer of hope in his dull eyes. "What else would you call it? You and Hrriss were framed. To ruin the Treaty negotiations. We'll beat this, er, rap," Kelly exclaimed, her eyes flashing.

"This what?" asked Pat.

Kelly grinned. "Well, I'm studying ancient colloquialisms." She leaned over, grabbing Todd by the shoulders, and kissed his cheek. "It's okay for one of your other good friends to visit you again, isn't it?" Immediately, she regretted her choice of phrases because a shadow crossed Todd's face: the friend he most wanted to see was forbidden him.

"It's okay for you to visit, Kelly, anytime you want," Todd answered, putting as much welcome into his voice as he could. He touched his cheek where she had kissed it. "Soon, please?"

"I'd better go now. I'll be back again tomorrow, and we'll have a council meeting of our own." She started to go, but turned back a few steps from the door. "Think you should know, Todd, how many people have said how much they enjoyed Snake Hunt and the feast last night. I'm not the first to tell you that you did a good job." She gave him a wry smile and wrinkled her nose. "I won't be the last and you'll feel better when you know how many people are solidly on your side. Anyway, the Hunt was the greatest."

Todd managed to smile back. "Thanks, Kelly. That Hunt seems to have happened years ago, not just hours," he said, then rallied, sitting up and straightening his shoulders. "But it was a good one. Thanks again for all your help."

"I intend to repay that in kind," she said, grinning wickedly. "You wait and see!" She waggled her finger at him, and that brought a slight grin of remembrance for all the times he had used that gesture and spoken that phrase to her. "I gotta go now, Todd, Pat. We're expecting dozens of Home Week visitors and Mother'll shoot me if I don't put in an appearance soon."

Todd closed his eyes against the thought of the dozens of Home Week visitors his family generally entertained after the Hunt. Everything good about his life seemed to have been ripped away in a single morning: his best friend, his reputation, and his honor. He heard the front door close softly and Kelly clattering down the steps. Then he felt his mother's gentle hand on his shoulder and he patted it.

"She's a staunch friend," his mother said, then she added in a teasing tone, "and still as much the tomboy as ever."

"Not quite," Todd said, forcing himself out of despair. He looked up at his mother with a lopsided grin. "Not at the Hunt party she wasn't."

"Oh?" Pat rolled her eyes facetiously. "You noticed?"

"Of course I noticed," Todd said, hearing an edge of irritation in his tone.

Pat put up her hands to ward off an imaginary attack. "I'm not, I swear I'm not," she said. "But she *is* a staunch friend and she'll do all she can to help. She's smart. Anne says Kelly graduated second in her class, even with all the discrimination against 'colonial types.' "

"I didn't know she'd got that high," Todd said, impressed. "But why didn't she make first?"

"Oh, you," and Pat play-batted at him. "She'll call in every favor she's owed on Earth. You just wait and see."

"Oh, Mom, how did we ever get ourselves in such a mess!" He dropped his head and began digging with the heels of his hands at eyes that hadn't seen the danger. Pat dropped beside him, her arm supportively about his shoulders. "When did that stuff get hidden on the *Albie*?"

"We'll find out, son, we'll find out," his mother said. "You've always been motivated by conscience, by truth, and you've always respected the rights of others and your responsibilities to them. No one who knows you and Hrriss will believe this vile canard."

"What about those who want to? Who want to see this colony disbanded, discredited?" Todd said in a soft but caustic tone.

"We both know such people exist and they have caused this entrapment," his mother said. "But there is a way out it. The truth, and we'll shove the doubting faces into that truth. Just you believe we will!"

Todd uncovered his eyes, reddened by his rubbing and the tears he was trying to repress. "I wonder if we haven't been a little naive here on paradisiacal Doona."

"That's a possibility, but we're not too long in the tooth to protect what we've earned by hard work and fair dealings. You'll see!" She gave him a firm clap on the back, wanting him, he knew, to buck up.

"Yes, Mother, we will!" he replied with as much feeling as he could instill in his tone.

"Now, I've always found that the best way to work out a problem is to work! Since you've obviously been struck off the diplomatic lists, you can just go help Lon Adjei round up the horses for their annual injections. Since Mark Aden went off-planet, we've been a little shorthanded. Not that he was much help as a stablehand when he spent so much time mooning over Inessa. She and Robin are already out there. I'd go but we've had New Home Week callers all day long."

She gave him a second, playful thump on the back. "Go on, hon. Have a shower to clear your head."

Todd gave her a grateful glance. "That's the best idea anyone's had all day."

He went to shower and change. Wrangling horses would get him away from the house and give him something to occupy his mind. But, even as he showered, his mind kept whirling around the morning's bizarre events.

"Machines can't lie," Rogitel had said. The phrase kept running through Todd's mind. No, they couldn't lie, but they could be tampered with. But when? And how? And by whom? No face filled the void when he tried to figure out who had set a trap for them. If only he and Hrriss could sit down and think this mess through . . . The two of them could discover the answers in no time, he knew they could. They had solved countless puzzles together over the years. Not to be able to communicate with Hrriss, as he had done every day since he was six years old, made him feel empty and lost. He jerked the shower control over to cold and steeled himself to accept the chill.

After a hard day's work, Todd returned home. As the evening stretched interminably out before him, again and again, Todd found himself starting out the door to go over the bridge to the Hrruban village, as he had done nearly every day for the last quarter of a century. Quelling that urge, he sat down at the computer unit and almost typed in Hrriss's comp number. But that would be a violation. Could he send his brother Robin over the bridge with a note? Just to let Hrriss know he was thinking about him? No, not even that solace was permissible until the accusations were dismissed. No communication meant just that, and Todd had given his solemn word. He had never broken it. He and Hrriss were honor bound, and honor meant everything to them. Someone was playing on that to keep them apart. Divide and conquer. Well, Todd was determined that no one would conquer without facing a fight.

chapter five

"You'll be welcome at home for a change, my cub," Mrrva said kindly, bringing Hrriss inside as the guards withdrew from the door.

Hrriss still felt himself torn apart by the harshness of the restriction. He had never thought of himself as complacent, or smug about his reputation for honesty, but to have it so smirched and casually disregarded shocked him.

"There is considerable physical evidence against us, Mother," he said wearily. From their front window, he could see the Friendship Bridge, built so long ago by Hrrubans and Hayumans in the spirit of cooperation. Across it, not very far, lay Zodd. He forced himself to turn away. "It is false evidence, but they must believe what they see. I know only that if we were allowed to be together we could solve the mystery in half the time. We could discuss it until we understood it. It is so difficult to have a lifelong companion torn away from one's side, Mother."

Mrrva's heart went out to him. "I am sorry to learn that you and Zodd must be separated but it will be only temporary. In no time they will see that Zodd and you are innocent of any crime, and you will be together again." She guided him through the house and out through the back door. "Wait here for me, little love." She settled him under the arbor in the garden behind the house, and hastened out to the dining area to bring cool drinks for both of them. It was a fine day, and the sun warmed the colors of her sprawling flower beds. She had nearly forgotten how solitary a cub Hrriss had been. Only the explosive arrival on the scene of the lively Hayuman boy Zodd had demonstrated how lonely he had been.

"Don't dwell on the apartness," Mrrva said, urging him to take the cold drink. She had pitched her voice to intimate levels to give her words more weight. "You will only make yourself ill. Later, when you have relaxed, you shall explore the facts. For now, let yourself relax. It is so seldom I have you all to myself."

The herbal drink loosened some of the tightness in his throat. "Have I neglected my duty to you?" Hrriss asked sadly. "I offer apologies to you and Father."

"No, no! Not at all," Mrrva assured him in a purr. "We are more than proud of the way you have grown up and the way you hold yourself in honor. Since you first met, Zodd has been welcomed daily as your friend. And ours. He is nearly my second cub. The tasks which I have set you over the years have been done twice as quickly by two sets of hands instead of one." Mrrva let her jaw drop ever so slightly. "The only way in which you have perhaps slipped in your duties is in the begetting of an heir to the Stripe. Have you forgotten that you are Hrrestan's only cub? When will you choose a mate? I have waited for the matter to occur naturally to your mind." She paused, blinking solemnly.

Hrriss lowered his head, abashed. "I have not thought of a mate. My life has been so full up until now that there has been no urgency."

Mrrva gave him an understanding sideways glance. "Please to consider it now, then. I wish for your happiness, but it would increase your father's if you do not allow the Stripe to pass to another's offspring."

Hrriss flinched. He couldn't allow the line succession to die just because he was too indolent to find a mate. It would be easy, he thought, merely to mate with a willing female and produce an heir, but, without affection, such a union would be sterile. Matches based on duty were no longer common in Hrruban society, though they did still exist. But the example set by his parents, who were bound by mutual respect and admiration, was one he hoped to emulate. Hayumans chose their mates based on mutual appeal and affection. When they'd been just approaching manhood, he and Zodd had often talked about mating, but in a clinical fashion, comparing the difference imposed by the physical variations of their separate species. Once they had been able for the duties of adult males, they had both been too busy for wives and children. The time had come to review the situation. In several aspects.

Since the sordid accusations this morning, the previous tenor of his life and ways had been drastically altered. He had never imagined a different style of life.

Certainly not a life without Zodd in it every day, going out on missions, or taking care of their tasks at home, but now that he thought of it, there was an itch he hadn't bothered to scratch. Who knew how long he would be kept from acting as an emissary of Doona, and whether others would ever again consider him to fit that post. A Stripe without honor had no place in society. He must be cleared and pronounced innocent, or his life was over!

Since there was nothing more he could do that day to clear his name, Hrriss seriously considered his duty to his Stripe. Now was the time to find a suitable female. More than time. He was already much older than his father had been when he was born. It wasn't that he'd missed female companionship. He had joyfully given relief to many charming partners during their seasonal heats, vying with other young males to serve their need. No male Hrruban would touch a female without her permission, but many females had made their preference for his attentions quite blatant. Centuries of civilized behavior hadn't quite reduced that primal urge, though in these modern times, many females used contraception remedies when procreation wasn't an objective.

Hayumans were not as natural as Hrrubans about sexual matters. It seemed strange to Hrriss that a society which was so much like his own often ruthlessly repressed their natural urges and behaviors. Even when Hrruba had been reduced to crowded quarters for each den and new litters were no longer blessings, the traditional openness about sex had remained.

Mrreva left him alone in the garden with his thoughts. It was so quiet that the tiny breeze brought distant voices and the faint clatter of hooves and machinery from the property beside theirs. Turning over his mother's suggestion in his mind, Hrriss began to examine the possibilities of the females he knew. And came right up against a very important consideration: would she understand his friendship with the Hayuman? Would she like Zodd? More important, would Zodd like her?

"I suppose I shall have to trust to my own judgment alone for this," Hrriss said out loud, and laughed.

Many of the females in this and other villages had sought him as their lifemate, and tempted him to commit while in their estrous cycles. There was never anything as crass as a demand for long-term relations, only a sighing and sensuous persuasion. While the attractions were obvious, Hrriss felt there needed to be more to the perfect image than a sexual being. He wanted a woman who thought, and created, and laughed. The image which kept coming back to his mind was the lithe, cinnamon-furred snake dancer at the feast. Her delicately graceful movements repeated in his memory again and again. He remembered her name was Nrrna, a soft and pliant sound. She worked with Mrrva in the

Health Center. He wondered if she was willing. The last time she had gone though her fertile cycle, she had let him know that she would welcome him, but he had had to go off-planet then. When he returned, she had said nothing to him about what had gone on in his absence.

There was also Mrratah, a weaver whose textiles were wearable art. Last year, after Snake Hunt, they had spent a wild night together. The heavy musk in the air and the excitement of the chase had stirred him. She had been out on Hunt, too, and was as aroused as he by primal bloodlust, the beat of the dance band's drums, and the scent in the air.

Hrriss's eyelids lowered as he remembered that night, let his body sway with the rhythm in his memory. There was a high-pitched snarl that was so like the voice of Mrratah in excitation that he opened his eyes. His female ocelot, Mehh, loped out of the house past him, with the male, Prem, in determined pursuit. Mehh was young, no more than two Doonan years old. She was coming into full heat for the first time. Her attitude toward Prem was playful but firm. She intended the order of things to proceed as she pleased, not the way the male chose. That was right, according to the Hrruban way of life.

The spotted cats dodged back and forth through the bushes Mrrva had planted around the green for privacy. They were not concerned with hiding what they were doing. Simple urges moved them. Sometimes Hrriss wished that he was not a thinking being. These creatures were acting out his unspoken dream.

Mehh skidded and rolled to a halt in the grass before him. Prem followed, and tried to mount her before she was upright again. A quick blow across the nose from a paw full of razor-sharp talons let him know that Mehh was not ready yet. Prem withdrew a few paces and waited, making a soft, urgent rumbling sound low in his throat. Mehh flipped onto her belly and crept insouciantly, provocatively, into the mating position with her tail high and to the side, presenting her nether quarters to the male. She was blatant about what she wanted, and her urgent throaty growls made it certain that she wanted it now. Without hesitation, Prem was on her back, teeth gripping the female's scruff as he mounted her.

With an odd sense of detachment, Hrriss watched them. The female snarled and rolled over, driving Prem a paw's length away, and just as swiftly invited him back again with raised tail. Prem crooned, a mild sound when compared with the green fire in his eyes. Hrriss, shaking his head to break the fascination, felt a creature sympathy for Prem. Right now a relationship, wild and abandoned and fun, would take his mind off the ache in his heart and the anger in his mind. Both Nrrna and Mrratah could be extremely exciting in estrus, but they were good companions away from the mating dance as well.

His mother had made a valid point. It was more than time to seek a lifemate. While he was in this enforced separation from Todd, it might ease his loneliness to choose a mate. He would not be abandoning other aspects of his life, but filling in the parts that had too long remained empty.

Through the house, he heard a knock at the front door. Hrriss started to get up, but he heard his mother's soft footfalls emerge from the other wing and go toward the door. A short time passed, and she came out to him.

"Hrriss, I will be going out later. Pat Rrev has said that she wants the four of us, Hrrestan and me, and Pat and Rrev, to speak together this evening. She is as convinced of your innocence as your father and I."

Hrriss nodded eagerly. "Tell Zodd . . ." he began, and then swallowed the rest of his words, hanging his head and letting his hands fall limp to his sides. "I may give no message for him. It is a matter of honor."

"Poor Hrriss. He knows, my little one," Mrrva said sympathetically. "He knows."

Hrriss cleared his throat tentatively. "Mother, you know Nrrna, don't you?"

"Yes," the Hrruban woman said, clearly surprised. "She works at the Health Center in the laboratory where I conduct my research."

"Has she ever come to this house to join our evening meal?" Hrriss inquired.

He thought the pupils in his mother's eyes widened just slightly. "She has, from time to time. Her company is excellent. I shall inquire if she is free to join us."

Then she turned and left the garden in a rather abrupt fashion that made Hrriss wonder if she was displeased in any way with his suggestion.

The afternoon was fair, and the air had a fresh crispness that was far more relaxing to Todd's jangled nerves than the tropical warmth of Treaty Island. He rode Gypsy down the narrow trail that circled around the fruit orchard at the edge of the Reeve Ranch. The fruit trees were fenced in for protection, though many a clever horse stretched his neck far enough to nip ripening apples off the nearer trees. Apart from the orchard, Lon Adjei, as manager of the ranch, gave the horse herds plenty of room to graze in, but the open land made it harder to find them.

Todd was after a foursome of colts who had hightailed it this way, avoiding capture as if it was a new game invented for them to show off. He lost sight of them among the clumps of shrub and mature trees. He and Hrriss had always worked together on this sort of a detail: the Hrruban had keener eyesight and sense of smell. He could find yearlings no matter where they hid themselves.

A scented breeze shifted, and blew directly into Todd's hot face. Gratefully he took a deep breath and was nearly unseated as Gypsy slammed to a halt under him.

"What's the matter, boy?"

The gelding propped his front legs, refusing to move forward. Gypsy was a sensible animal, so if he was scared to move, he had reason. Possibly there was a small ssorasos in the woods, which Gypsy had smelled when the wind changed. When surprised, the knee-high mammal attacked like a juggernaut. Todd dismounted and sidled cautiously a few feet up the path. In front of him was a clump of red-veined plants. Todd recognized them instantly. Ssersa. It was toxic enough to humans, but absolute poison for horses. Gypsy had smelled the poisonous weed.

"Smart horse!" Todd said over his shoulder to reassure the gelding. Ssersa was nearly as bad a contact-toxin as rroamal. Most animals were wary of it while it was unripe. When it matured and dried, it lost its bitter aroma and smelled sweet and appealing. It was death for livestock, especially those of Earth origin. Ranchers assiduously cleared it from their pastures or they lost stock. The trick was to get it before it dried and left its seeds for the unwary animal. Ben Adjei, Lon's father, called ssersa "silent death." Ranch hands automatically pulled it up wherever they saw it.

The radio at his waist crackled. "Todd, where are you? I've lost sight of you and I've got two more for you to hold for their shots."

"I'm on the trail behind the apple orchard, Lon," Todd replied into the radio. The horse snuffled his ear and he pushed him gently away. "I was chasing a pair of yearlings and Lady Megan's twins. Gypsy got wind of a patch of ssersa back here. I'm uprooting it and bringing it in."

"Ssersa!" Lon's voice exclaimed. "Damn, I was sure I cleared the whole place of it. And before it could seed."

"Never mind. Probably some bird seeded it," Todd said. "Be with you as soon as I pull it up and catch those yearlings."

Pulling on the hide gloves from his belt, he yanked the plant up and beat its roots on the ground to dislodge the dirt. Then he squashed it into a ball, which he shoved into his saddle bag. The stink of ssersa sap made Gypsy restless and quite willing to move away from it.

Todd lifted the gelding into a canter. The trail was wide here and the surface firm enough to safely maintain a stiff pace. The colts were well ahead of him but, as he recalled it, there was a grassy meadow up ahead that would certainly cause them to stop and graze.

An eerie scream—like a horse in agony—made him dig his heels into

Gypsy's ribs and they galloped over the breast of the hill. Two of the colts were skittering around the pasture nervously. The third was standing over the fourth, which lay still in a patch of bracken. He whinnied shrilly.

Todd brought Gypsy to a dirt-kicking halt and was out of the saddle at a run to the young horse on the ground. The remaining twin nudged its fallen brother with its nose, puzzled by its unresponsiveness.

"No more games for this lad," Todd said sadly. He still had his gloves on, so he turned back the upper lip to see the livid magenta of the membrane. "Poisoned. Damn it. There can't be more ssersa." Fearing for the other youngsters in this meadow, he looked all around him, and then at Gypsy, who was standing calmly. Turning back to the dead animal, he opened its lips again and saw what was stuck in the colt's teeth—the twigs of dried ssersa. Sitting back on his heels, he radioed Lon.

"More ssersa?" Lon demanded disbelievingly. "Where? I cleared that meadow. I know I did." There was silence and a sigh from the speaker. "Leave it. I'll get the flyer and bring the corpse in for burning. We can't even use the hide. The toxins will poison whatever it touches. Todd, there was no mature ssersa in that field, I promise you!"

"Then where did it come from?" Todd said, aggravated. Lon was a good farm manager. If he said he'd cleared ssersa weed, he had!

He remounted Gypsy and rounded up the other two. He had to lasso the mourning colt to get him away from his dead twin but gave him a few feed pellets to make up for the insult. Whooshing the others in front of him, he kept his eyes peeled for any further sign of ssersa. It was an active seeder, like many Doonan plants: so where there was one, there'd be others.

Then, just as he herded the colts over the lip of the ridge, he spotted a burned patch in the grass on the one level place on the entire field: a patch just about the size of a small transport shuttle.

Todd got his charges back to the barn without further incident. Lon examined the three young animals and entered the control numbers in their freeze brands into a hand-held computer unit. Todd saw Robin and Inessa in the paddock, dragging one unwilling horse after another into the chute for inoculations.

"That's a hundred and forty-three," Lon said, slapping the last one on the rump as he sent it running into the corral, "counting that poor poisoned colt. I think that's all we're going to find. We've combed the landscape."

"Shouldn't there be more like a hundred sixty?" Todd asked.

"Yeah, should be," Lon said, scratching his ear with the edge of his comp. "I put in a call to Mike Solinari at the Veterinary Hospital, and the foreman on the Hu spread, just in case any of our animals have hopped the fence."

"Not bloody seventeen of 'em," Todd replied grimly.

"With that ssersa you found today, that might account for some, but we haven't even found any bodies. Not even mda will touch a ssersa carcass." Lon gave a disgusted snort. "My dad told me that if I can't hand-pull fields, I deserve to have such losses but, honest, Todd . . ."

"Didn't Hrriss and I spend"—Todd made himself continue despite the pang that the reminder of happier days gave him—"a whole week helping you? But I'll tell you something else I found—a burn-off mark on that one level spot in the big meadow."

"A shuttle burn-off?" Lon's tanned face paled. "There's been no emergency landing in that section. D'you think . . ." He stopped, not liking his own thoughts.

"Rustling does present itself as an explanation," Todd said, not wanting to believe it either, "especially if there've been no bodies found."

Since Doona's wealth was its stock, not minerals or mining, rustling was the sovereign crime and punishable by immediate transport to the nearest penal colony. To keep track of all stock, each animal was branded with freeze-dry chemicals as soon after birth as possible: a painless process that left a permanent ID, naming its ranch of origin, breeding information, and control numbers. The brand was unalterable so that it was easy to keep a record of inoculations and vaccinations throughout an animal's lifetime. It made illegitimate transfer of ownership impossible. It also made rustling—on Doona—an unprofitable occupation.

Despite rigid psychological tests devised by Lee Lawrence, the colony sociologist, sometimes unsuitable personalities slipped through. People eager enough to get off Earth were known to equivocate about their open-mindedness as regards living with aliens, or their willingness to learn and speak an alien language. Their bigotry was generally discovered soon enough to do no lasting harm and they were sent off Doona, either to Earth or to see if they would fit into a totally Human colony.

Other new settlers became overwhelmed by the responsibilities of caring for a whole, stocked ranch, let alone a house set in the midst of more uninterrupted land than anyone on Earth had ever seen. Some could not adapt to the lack of laborsaving devices which were felt to be superfluous or environmentally dangerous. Fossil fuels were avoided, and natural power, windmills, river barrages, or battery cells charged by solar panels supplied what power was required. Some settlers learned to cope, others requested transport back to familiar constrictions.

Those unwilling, or unable, to take responsibility for themselves in a pioneer society posed the worst problem. Sometimes, folk who had been told all their lives what to do couldn't adjust to making their own decisions. Or, once they realized that behavior monitors had been left behind on Earth, they began acting as if they could behave any way they wanted. And take anything they wanted. Rustlers generally emerged from that group.

"We haven't had any rustlers for years," Lon said. "And how could there have been a shuttle landing when we've got satellite controllers?"

"Have we got any newcomers from Earth who've gone possession crazy? You know that syndrome."

"How could I forget?" Lon asked grimly, spitting into the dust. "It was my father's new mares that were stolen. A guy named Hammond did it. I've a hard place in my mind for anyone named Hammond. Since then I've learned to judge people. I've a good record at picking those who won't make it through their first season."

"You helping Lee with his testing these days?"

"He has only to ask. Now, let's double-check the ones we do have so I can send in the brands of those we're missing."

Together they checked the withers of each animal that came out of the chute, entering the brand and updating the inoculation record.

"Yeah, we're seventeen shy. I'll just send the IDs on to Vet. They'll forward the list to Poldep. Once the word's out we've done that, we might just find those seventeen missing horses back in their home pastures."

Squinting at the sky, Todd shook his head. "They might not be on Doona anymore."

"Oh, come on, Todd. The security satellites would have reported any unauthorized transport in orbit," Lon said, scornful of that suggestion. "No, we'll find out where they got stashed on this planet. Might take a while, but we'll find 'em on Doona."

Todd did not argue the point now, but he was annoyed that seventeen animals were missing. Seventeen! At the current market price, that was almost half the value of a good farm. Doonan horses were a valuable commodity, not only as transportation and a constant source of fertilizer but for the end product of meat, hide, and bonemeal.

"I'll look into it, find out if the neighbors have any inexplicable losses, and I can make that report to Poldep." Even as he spoke, Todd realized he was no longer the person to make reports to Poldep.

"No, I'm farm manager. I'll make the report," Lon said, almost too quickly. "I need your help more out here in the pens," he went on, stumbling to get the words out. "You've a longer attention span than those two flibbertigibbets," he said, nodding toward Todd's two siblings.

It was obvious that the ranch foreman knew the details of Todd's house arrest, even if he had the tact not to comment on it directly. Most of the neighbors had radios, so Todd could ask his questions without leaving the ranch. But he could see that keeping his word was going to complicate life considerably.

"I'll radio them, Lon," he said quietly. "And thanks."

"The Reeves have been having a run of bad luck lately," Lon said stoutly, turning his head to spit in the dust. "I figure you don't deserve it. Count on me if you need help—off the ranch."

"Me, too!" said Robin. At eighteen Terran years of age, he was the youngest of the Reeves' five children. He and Inessa climbed out of the corral as the last of the foals galloped free. "I don't think I'm grounded. Am I?" He turned wide ingenuous eyes to his brother.

"No, it applies to me."

"And Hrriss," Inessa said in a low angry tone, then she turned to Lon. "We've put the five that need to be observed in the stable. Don't think any of 'em are contagious but they need a bit of hand feeding. So I'm through."

"Nobody is through until you put the rest of the medicines away and clean out the inoculators," Lon ordered, shouting down their protests. "And last time I looked that pen hadn't been mucked out. Hop to it!"

With affected groans, the two young Reeves shouldered the vaccination equipment and staggered dramatically toward the medical outbuilding behind the foreman's house.

"What a pair of actors," Todd observed.

"Eh," Lon said, slapping him on the back. "You and Hrriss were the same at that age." Then he ducked his head at the ill-chosen reminder and spat again in the dust.

"Hrriss?" Kelly tapped on the partition of the Hrruban's room. "Your mother said I'd find you here. Are you very busy?"

"Not too busy to see you," Hrriss said, and Kelly chuckled at his gallantry. He rose from his computer console and they brushed cheeks affectionately.

"You okay?" Kelly asked, looking him over with sisterly concern. "Do you need anything I could bring in for you?" She knew she'd be stir-crazy if she had to stay in one room too long. How she'd gotten through school on Earth without dropping out had required every ounce of self-discipline she possessed.

"I'm okay," Hrriss said, but ruined it with a sigh. "I may move about the village, you know. But it is frustrating to be restricted. I want for nothing but I will think of something to give you the pleasure of visiting me again." Then he clamped his lips so tightly that his eyeteeth were visible under the tightly drawn flesh.

"He misses you, too," Kelly said softly. "And that's not a message," she added angrily, "that's my personal opinion. I'm entitled to speak for myself."

Hrriss nodded understanding and his muzzle relaxed across his teeth.

"So, what've you been doing with yourself?" Kelly asked, hoping that she could carry on some sort of a lighthearted conversation that wouldn't constantly remind both of them of the third person who should be here and must be nameless and messageless—all for honor!

"A little research into matters of concern to my mother," Hrriss said, his eyes twinkling. "I have also been monitoring the official zranscripts of the Zreaty negotiations, and sending out correspondence to friends on other colony worlds. I hope to locate someone with contacts among the purveyors of illicit artifacts. If we could find out where the articles found on the *Albatross* were purchased, and by whom, we could prove our innocence." Hrriss felt a wash of shame every time he thought of the harsh-voiced prosecutors who dismissed his sworn word of honor as meaningless.

Kelly sensed his disquiet "That's a damned good idea, Hrriss. In fact, I'm doing a bit of research along those lines myself." Then she made fists of her hands and frowned angrily. "How anyone could be daft enough to think you and . . . to think you could be a pirate and a smuggler is beyond my comprehension. I want you to know that!"

"Thank you," Hrriss said.

"And I'll bet no one in this village believes it, either," Kelly went on, wound up by indignation.

"A Hrruban does not bring disgrace to his Stripe . . ."

Kelly rolled her eyes skyward. "You are not in disgrace, Hrriss, any more than Todd is. You're just . . . just pending investigation. You're sure I can't get you something?" she asked in a milder tone, rather surprised at her own vehemence. But the idea of an honorable person like Hrriss even thinking the word "disgrace" infuriated her.

"Nothing I can think of," Hrriss said, dropping his jaw at her energetic defense. He was as much touched as amused by it. "You have already brought me something I appreciate greatly: yourself. Will you please visit again when you may?"

"Of course," Kelly said, giving him a big hug as she turned to go. "Hang on, Hrriss. This won't last long."

Ken found Emma Sumitral in a research room in the Treaty Center. She was a tall, slim woman of thirty, with large, smoky gray eyes and dark brown hair. She had the same formal carriage as her father the Admiral, which somehow made even the casual smock she was wearing look elegant.

"I am very troubled by what you've told me," she said after Ken had detailed the seizure at the *Albatross* and the findings of the hearing. "You may count on our support. My Father will certainly want to help you, but I'm not sure what he can do. I'm not sure if there's anything I can do."

"You can help me find out who informed Rogitel that the *Albatross* was stuffed with contraband. Naturally he refused to reveal his source. The Treaty Controller doesn't know, or won't tell. The rest of the Council refuses to talk to anyone other than Hu Shih or Hrrestan. And they're probably only speaking to Hrrestan because he's head of the Hrruban contingent. I hate like poison being ignored, Emma." And Ken managed a weak smile at that defect in himself. "I've got to find out who planted that junk, especially that blasted Byzanian Glow Stone, because they admitted being near Hrrilnorr IV. But no one there believed that they'd heard a Mayday. *I* believe!"

"I personally find it very hard to believe that either Todd or Hrriss could be smugglers or pirates. But it is most unfortunate that they did not have the *Albatross* inspected as soon as they landed. Especially in view of that Mayday."

"I reported that to Hu and Hrrestan myself. You know the boys were Masters of the Hunt, that that trip to Hrretha meant they'd have to work day and night to get the Hunt organized. Newry saw no harm in sealing the ship and letting the boys get on with crucial Hunt details." He hissed out a sigh, sounding more Hrruban than Hayuman, letting his hands go limp in his lap.

"But Treaty Law had been violated," Emma reminded him in a gentle voice. She was a noted expert on the topic.

"A Mayday should be considered extenuating circumstances, Emma, not a crime. And there was no one else capable of organizing the Hunt. That could not be cancelled, and that's why I thought it was permissible for the formal inspection to be deferred. Just for two weeks." Ken raised his hands again in a pleading gesture. "You know yourself that we have to have the Snake Hunt, whether we dress it up as a tourist attraction or New Home Week or whatever. Those snakes would swarm whether or not there were any Hunters to restrict them. Hu and Hrrestan agreed with my analysis of the situation—Doona *has* to be profitable and the Snake Hunt provides a large hunk of our income. If anyone is guilty of not insisting on that inspection, it's me. I should be taking the blame."

Emma looked very grave. "Ultimately you may have to." Then, having startled him, she went on. "From what you have told me, Ken, it is not just that delay, it is also all those valuable items that were found on the *Albatross* and the tape record of landings and launches within the framework of that Hrrethan journey."

"Neither Todd nor Hrriss is untrustworthy or a pirate or smuggler."

"No, they are not the type. However, the fact that blame is being attached to those two young men may yet work in their favor. They are much admired on Earth. Their friendship is legendary. I think you could say that it epitomizes Doona in many people's minds."

"Will it? After all this has been broadcast about the galaxy?" Ken asked bitterly.

Emma looked at him sternly. "If there is any rumor, gossip, slander, or libel about this investigation before it has been completed and its report made, there will be far more trouble for the loose-mouthed than they can swallow! The boys are under house arrest, not incarcerated in a Poldep faculty. Unless they break their bond, they are safe from slander. Now, let's see what we can find." She turned to her desktop console.

She initiated a search based on the boys' names and the name of their ship, the word "Hrrilnorr," and the names of the artifacts that Ken could recall. "Now we wait."

When the computer eventually spat out a list of file names, Emma briefly scanned each one, and instead of data, found she was looking at a moiré graphic with a bunking square in the center requesting a confirmed password.

"Classified! In the last two weeks, every one of these has acquired a special clearance-password. They're locked!"

Ken swore softly. "Damn it, I'd hoped you'd be able to get through. I got the same graphics. Not a single code I knew got me any results. Do I need to start standing on desks to get cooperation?"

"Not yet . . . I hope," Emma admitted with a wicked light in her eyes. She bent over the board. "I've got Father's code-key number. They wouldn't dare classify these files too high for the head of Alreldep to access."

To Todd's surprise, his father arrived home for dinner with a very attractive woman whom he introduced as Emma Sumitral.

"How do you do, Miss Sumitral?" Todd asked stiffly, and then the name registered. "You wouldn't be related to Admiral Sumitral, would you?"

"Indeed I am, Todd Reeve," she responded, squeezing his hand warmly. "I've heard a great deal about you from my father." She had a brilliant smile that lit up her gray eyes. Then she crooked her neck to look behind him.

Suddenly his formality deserted him and he burst out laughing. "I gave up wearing that rope tail a long time ago, Miss Sumitral."

" 'Emma,' please," she said, and he gestured for her to take a seat. "My father used to regale me with stories about Doona. I was only five when the first wave of settlers left Earth for Doona, so this world has always been special to me. I always wished my father didn't work for the government so we could have come, too," she admitted. "I'm glad now that he does. His position has opened otherwise locked doors for me as a researcher, and now I believe it may help you, too."

"What?" Todd said, grasping at whatever hope was offered him.

"Todd, we'll wait until Hrrestan and Mrrva arrive. This concerns them, too, you know." Ken's expression was so concerned that Todd wondered what they could have found out that would upset his father—more than he was already.

Hrrestan and Mrrva arrived at the Reeves' house shortly before sunset. Todd greeted them courteously. He had to bite his tongue on "How's Hrriss?" Even with the parents of his friends, he would not break his given word.

Hrrestan and Mrrva nodded gravely to their son's dearest friend, their liquid eyes saying what they, too, would not say aloud. Both Hrrubans already knew Emma Sumitral.

"I've chased out the other children for the evening," Pat said, trying to set all her guests at ease. "An adult evening. Kelly ought to arrive any minute now."

Todd looked up, somewhat surprised, but Kelly hadn't smothered him with sympathy earlier and she'd scarcely do it in front of guests. "She is?"

Pat glanced at him, worried. "I thought you'd want her input. Isn't that all right?"

"Sure," Todd said hastily.

As deftly as her father would, Emma led the discussion away to other matters, and held forth on the subject of trade among the colony worlds. Todd found her not only charming but intelligent. He rather thought she and Kelly would like each other.

Kelly arrived only minutes behind the Hrrubans. They greeted each other warmly. "It's nice to see so much of you these days," she said ingenuously.

Todd couldn't help but gawk at her, for she couldn't have more plainly told him she'd visited Hrriss, too.

"Well," said Pat, surprised, "you did learn some diplomacy, after all."

Then Ken introduced her to Emma and offered drinks all round. For the first time, Todd found that the simple courtesies he usually enjoyed extending struck him as unnecessary time-wasters. Once Hrrestan and Mrrva were settled, Emma began to detail the files she had unlocked.

"It's turned out to be more than just trusting my father's opinions of you and Hrriss," she said. "I think we may have stumbled onto a very complex and highly organized smuggling operation." She waited patiently until everyone stopped demanding details. "I found some, all right. And more data from the beacons orbiting the other prohibited worlds is still coming in. So far, all of them show the identification number of the *Albatross* as having entered those systems shortly before or shortly after the ship visited Hrretha. The information is not yet complete. There are still four buoys circling interdicted systems left to be heard from, and that data will come in within the next few days."

"I can't believe that they all have the code number from the boys' ship," Pat said.

"Now, the beacons identify the *Albatross* as being the ship that crossed their barriers in each instance. The codes as you know are complex, not easy to duplicate."

"As I told you, Emma," Ken began, his anger building, "someone's gone to a lot of trouble to make it convincing."

"For a researcher like myself, there's just too *much* corroborative detail available to be coincidence or accident," Emma went on, and although Ken started to protest, Pat touched his arm, her eyes watching Emma's face. For Pat was beginning to see what Emma was driving at. "So far we have thefts committed by two young males who lack for nothing. They're psychologically normal, without any history of kleptomania or harmful pranks. Healthy in every way." Todd blushed at her frankness and she smiled gently at him. "It was necessary to take a glance at your medical profile," she said. "There's nothing in it to be ashamed of. To continue, they're respected by their community, and their future is bright if only they continue to behave as they have. This series of crimes requires a motivation."

"I know the motivation," Todd said in a flat voice that showed he was controlling his anger. "This issue would make a terrific fulcrum for the lever to pry Doona apart."

"I'm inclined to agree," Hrrestan said, nodding his head in agreement with Todd's opinion, "but if we have the motivation, can we also discover the perpetrator?"

"Landreau has to be involved in this somewhere," Todd said angrily, his eyes flashing blue fire. "Rogitel's presence at the Hrrethan affair was unnecessary. Both . . ." Todd halted then plunged, "I felt he was nearly splitting with anticipation and it couldn't have been for the inauguration of another grid facility! He was there, keeping track of . . . of us . . . on Landreau's orders. The Admiral would do anything to discredit Doona this year and to disrupt the crucial talks that are going on. A scandal like two notable citizens of Doona turning out to be pirates and smugglers could tear everything apart. Only how did it get done?"

"The opinion of the Ssspeakrrrs," Hrrestan added, "favors the idea of a conspiracy, aimed at you and our son, to discredit the Rralan Experiment. They have informed me that they are conducting their own investigations into these charges as they know that never have you or my son behaved in a dishonorable fashion. As Emma Sumitral has ssaid, there is far too much evidence against them. There are elements on Rrala who also wish this Experiment to end in disarray. These are being scrutinized. True guilt lies elsewhere but it will be discovered."

"And I," Kelly said, looking inordinately pleased with her contribution, "am handling the unofficial Terran Investigative Group. You didn't know you had one, did you, Todd?" She grinned at him. While she had admired Emma's clear-minded statements, she hadn't quite liked her tone, nor the way she had smiled at Todd. Sort of, well, proprietary and perhaps a little patronizing. Whoa! Kelly thought, yanking hard on her own mental reins. Who was acting proprietary now?

"May I remind all of you," Emma put in, "that it is essential that all investigations be done as circumspectly as possible so as not to prejudice the official one?"

Ken leaned forward toward Emma. "We must all be wary of how we proceed. But, in spite of the need for caution, I've started some inquiries through the Alreldep office, and I discover, to my relief," and he grinned at his son, "that the memory of Todd as he was has been replaced by the record of a hardworking young man."

"Which reminds me, Dad, this hardworking young man did some rounding up today with Lon. And we found out something I like even less than I like my present anomalous position. We're minus seventeen horses, mostly yearlings and two-year-olds."

"Seventeen horses gone since the last count?" Ken repeated, staring at his son hi disbelief. As if he didn't need this, too, on his plate.

"One was dead of ssersa poisoning and I helped Lon clear that field myself. There were other ssersa plants where there shouldn't be a one."

"Ssersa does not have legs to walk," Hrrestan said, shaking his head as he knew how careful the Reeves were about hand-pulling the toxic weed from all grazing areas.

"There was also this burned-out patch on the one flat space in the field," Todd went on. "Shuttle-sized, I'd say."

"Rustlers!" Ken nearly bounced from his chair with indignation.

Hrrestan hissed. "That is a most serious crime. There have been no instances of animal theft in years."

"Lon reported to Poldep. We sent a list of the brands to Michael," and Todd turned to Kelly, who was as surprised and angry as any stock rancher would be. "One or two of 'em may have jumped the fence."

"But not seventeen," Ken said, still absorbing the shock. "We'll have to hang on to some of the breeding stock, then, Todd."

"Dad, I'd ask around to see if there's anyone new here who's had a sudden embarrassment of credit. I'll just put it about that there'll be no charges pressed at Poldep if that little herd wanders home, wagging tails behind 'em."

"Could snakes have caught them?" Pat asked. "You had that breakout at the Boncyks'. What if a Mommy or two got past you?"

"None did," Todd replied flatly, frankly upset that his mother even asked such a question.

"Well, it was a possibility," she said apologetically.

"What else could go wrong?" Kelly asked, more rhetorically than expecting any answer.

"What else?" Emma asked, her expression clearly reflecting her dislike of adding to the current problems. "I think I'd better be the one to tell you. Admiral Landreau has arrived. He gridded in just before I left Treaty Island."

chapter six

Admiral Al Landreau hated Doona. Initially, when the bright blue pebble with its light cloud coverage had swum into his viewscreen, he thought it looked peaceful and pleasant. When he had been assigned to explore it for a preliminary search, it had seemed the perfect Earthlike world, class M in the old parlance, atmosphere, near-normal gravity and all, the very epitome of what Spacedep was searching for. It was full of possibilities, and the key to fame and better departmental financing for him.

Ever since the first colonists landed there, though, it had been one long headache for Spacedep and Landreau. He lay the source of all his troubles squarely upon the backs of the Reeves. A family of malcontents, by all accounts from Aisle and Corridor monitors, always disturbing civilized people with their noise and antisocial behavior. They had made a public fool of him. They, or specifically, Ken Reeve, had blamed him for not noticing their mythical cat people or the nightmarish giant snakes in time to prevent the colonization. As if there was any way he could have known about them, in spite of that ape Sumitral's insistence that the clues were all there. Reeve had made a fool of him, claimed he jeopardized the colony.

Well, the colonists had been in the wrong. They had violated the Siwannese protocol, had resisted being removed from the planet in spite of their feigned horror over that violation, and had been compounding that transgression anathema for a quarter of a century. Now was the moment to eradicate that mistake, put it behind him. He fully intended to do so. His opportunity had been handed to him, calligraphed, signed, sealed, and set under a glass bell. To make it the sweetest possible revenge, Todd Reeve, the hysterical, bilingual boy child of Ken Reeve, was to be the key to ending this quarter century of humiliation. The Treaty Council was buzzing: rumors of resignation threats already abounded. Landreau was looking forward to hearing Rogitel's full report.

There were cat people all over the building where he gridded in. Their hairy, fang-toothed faces made him shudder. The Hrrubans were an abomination against nature's plan. Cats shouldn't walk like humans. They should go on all four legs like the basically feral animals they imitated.

When the mist of transfer cleared, he was facing one of the very creatures he abhorred. The animal operating the grid center opened its mouth at him and showed its teeth, casually displaying its bestiality. The horror was that it thought it was smiling. He nodded curtly and stepped down.

It was outrageous that these Hrrubans should have stumbled on any technology as powerful as the transportation grid. While the grid was convenient, having to use it frightened him: he preferred to be in control of the mechanisms used in travel. What if the operator hadn't been well enough trained, and Landreau was trapped in the grid, neither one place nor another? Supposing someone with a grievance against him took a bribe and sent him to the wrong destination, even a fatal one? He would have preferred to have the one facility on Earth destroyed, and its operator returned to its homeworld. Wherever that was. If Landreau could only find it . . . That damned Treaty neatly blocked that aspiration. However, the cats were not fooling Admiral Al Landreau. He had long since deduced their real objective. This transport grid of theirs: a single grid, like the one on Terra, could be quickly built into a giant one, capable of moving armies. Yet the blockheads and simpering idiots in positions of power on the Amalgamated Worlds refused to see the threat inherent in the cats' technology. But he had made allies, supported causes in return for the support of his. This year would see the end to the Hrruban threat before it became a nightmare reality.

The grid operator said something in the ridiculous collection of grunts and growls that served the beast race for a language. Sounded like bad plumbing. And that was yet another insult: that Human beings were to imitate such filthy noise instead of good, clean Terran.

"Commander? I'm Nesfa Dupuis," a low voice at his elbow said in the Terran language.

Startled but relieved, Landrau turned. The speaker was a small Human woman with dark skin and glowing brown eyes. She stood next to the grid station, her hands folded quietly into her voluminous sleeves.

"Treaty Councillor," Landreau said smoothly, with a gracious nod and a quick handshake. "I want to see everything that you have on this vexing matter. When may I meet with the Council? It is important that I see them immediately."

The small woman held up a hand. "Not today, I'm sorry to inform you. We're in the midst of deep negotiation on space rights, Commander."

"Hmmph!" Landreau snorted. "Isn't such a negotiation irrelevant in the face of the crimes reported to you? You're wasting time. Might as well address yourself to immediate and germane issues. Save yourself the bother."

Landreau realized immediately that he had misjudged this one. She was a Doona colony sympathizer. Another fardling New Ager. He sighed and turned on a charm that never failed to work. "I'd like you to consider me a friend in this case, Councillor. My lifelong ambition has been to promote the improvement of the quality of life for Humanity. I'll do everything in my power to help expedite a successful conclusion to this disgraceful incident. Then the Council can continue its more important responsibilities."

"You are so cooperative, Admiral," Dupuis said aloud, her schooled expression not revealing her true feelings, but she had long since taken the Admiral's measure and was aware of some of his machinations. "The Council is, of course, grateful for any assistance in bringing this unfortunate situation to a swift conclusion. You will doubtless wish to confer with your assistant. An office has been set at your disposal near the one Commander Rogitel is using. This way, please."

The deep male voice crackled over the speaker in the airfield control tower. "Tower, this is Codep ship *Apocalypse,* on final insertion through orbit. I'll be down there in a minute."

"Can't you be more specific, Fred?" Martinson asked, clapping one hand to his headset and checking the screens which displayed telemetry from the orbiting navigation probes around Doona. "Good to hear from you. Pad eight is open for your use. Got two mechanics on duty this morning if you need any refitting. Happy landing."

The transport ship appeared as a ball of fire in the sky as the retros ignited in atmosphere and slowed the descent velocity. Below, the roof of number 8 bay was rolling open. *Apocalypse* set down expertly in the ring encircling the number on the fireproof surface of the launchpad. There was one final burst of fire and a belch of black smoke as the engines shut down. Martinson arrived alongside the *Apocalypse* in a flitter, with a fumigation team and a customs official in tow.

"Hello, Martinson. Sorry to have missed New Home Week," the burly trader said, descending from the ship as the team crowded him on its way up into the passenger compartment. "Probably cost me a lot of business, but you can only go so fast in space, eh? I've got bushels of test seed designated for the farms here. Say, what's all this?" He glanced at Newry, the customs agent, who took his manifests out of his hand and marched around to the ship's cargo hatch.

"Sorry, Fred," Martinson said. "Every ship has to be gone over with a fine-tooth comb. Orders."

"I've got my orders, too!" Horstmann boomed. He was a big man with a big voice, and pale hair buzzed short in a spaceman's clip. "Got customers waiting! You'll get your duty fees. I've never shorted you. So what's the scramble for?"

"Only takes a few minutes," said Martinson, refusing to discuss the matter. He was determined not to be caught bending the rules again.

Horstmann stood, impatiently tapping his hand on his thigh until the customs agent returned with the clipboard. "Is everything all right? I've got business to do! You can't stop the Horstmann of the *Apocalypse* from his ride forever! Ha, ha, ha!"

"All clear," Martinson said, ignoring Fred's traditional joke. Newry handed his chief the clipboard full of manifests. He nodded over his shoulder toward the flitter. From the passenger seat, the thin form of Rogitel arose and approached the trader.

"Ah! Commander," Horstmann said, extending his hand. "Nice to see you. I've got your little package for you, tapes from the governor of Zapata Three. Kept it next to my heart. Got a real fine collection of seals from a lot of places I didn't know existed . . . ?" He cocked his head, hoping to be enlightened.

"Just pass it over," Rogitel said, ignoring the query and Horstmann's extended hand.

With a shrug, Horstmann drew the package out of one of his sealed shipsuit pockets. Rogitel took the parcel, examined it briefly, and handed a credit chit to the captain.

"And thank you," Horstmann said, with overblown mock courtesy as the Spacedep official turned and walked off without another word. "Huh! What's the matter here? Doona's usually a hospitable place. Couldn't he waste an extra syllable to be polite? Some people!" The Codep captain shook his head ruefully. "Well, credits are credits." Horstmann tucked away the chit in his pouch. "Bobby! Come on! Customers are waiting!"

He walked into the Launch Center's warehouse, where stalls were set up for traveling traders across from the permanent trading booths for the Doona Co-operative of Farmers and Skillcrafters. These facilities, originally the odd table or two set up for the display and sale of merchandise, had evolved into tidy shops, complete with display cases and specialized lighting. The exchange of goods and money became comfortable and convenient for traders who didn't need to establish an on-planet trading route at every stop, and for their customers, who could browse about the wares displayed. Ali Kiachif had suggested the improvements. His ships carried trade goods from one world to another. Now the port attracted persons of both species from all over Doona, to sell their own goods and buy what traders might have on offer.

"Give me a moment to unload the merchandise, good folk!" Horstmann pleaded. "Ah, today's a good day to do business."

A couple of Hrruban ranchers from their Third Village had a string of pack ponies with them for sale. As the *Apocalypse* had suitable facilities for animal transport, Horstmann prowled around the little animals, lifting a hoof, examining teeth, before he made an opening offer.

Ken Reeve arrived at the warehouse in time to see Rogitel stalk away in the company of the portmaster.

"Hello, Horstmann," he called over the heads of the crowd.

"Well! Reeve, good to see you," Horstmann boomed, coming over to greet him. His huge hand engulfed Ken's in a companionable grasp.

"What was the commander after here? He usually doesn't grace a launchpad with his presence."

"I'd a special delivery for Ol' Skinny Shanks. Bird from Zapata Three passed it on to me for him. Since I'm not due on Terra for another couple of weeks, I could make the detour here. I got paid for it. Feels like tapes er something. Sealed up from one end to the next from places I've never visited." Then Horstmann lowered his voice. "You looking for information, eh?"

"Just curious," Ken replied, equally circumspect. "Rogitel and Landreau have been on Doona for a week, and they've stayed on Treaty Island. Not like Landreau to waste time before jumping down our throats on some damned fool petty issue."

"Hmm," Horstmann rumbled sympathetically. "Heard some spacescud I didn't like. I don't believe for a millisec that Todd'd be dealing in irreplaceables. If he was, why didn't he notify me? Everyone knows I offer the best prices on curios. What else can I tell you?"

"When is Kiachif due here next?" Ken asked.

The big trader laughed. "Soon, I hope! I'm supposed to meet him here in a few days, and I want to be on my way ASAP. Codep's got some new rulings about trading, and he wants everyone to hear them from his immortal lips. But I've got a schedule to keep."

"Having a profitable season?" Vic Solinari asked, coming over to greet Fred.

"Oh, I've made a few credits in commissions. Went through Zapata Three like wind through the trees. Almost thought they'd never seen an honest trader before." Horstmann patted his credit pouch with an air of satisfaction.

"And have they seen one now?" Vic Solinari asked, winking broadly at Ken.

"Vic! That cuts me to the quick," Fred said, his huge hands crossed dramatically over his heart. "How many times have I given you fellows the shirt off my back?" Then he made another abrupt change of mood. "In fact, I did once, when no other size I was carrying would fit one of the miners on Zlotnik. Poor devil. Gave him a pretty good deal, I might add. Say, perhaps you'll be interested in these. Zapata's doing a good line in metal chain, all grades and gauges. Bobby!" he shouted to his young son, who served as his supercargo. The boy, who was driving a loader full of merchandise, stopped when he heard his father shout. "Roll out some of that chain! I brought them a galvanizer last trip, and the results are fine. Won't ever rust. You got my personal guarantee. They're starting a line of ergonomic hand tools that I'll bring along next time. Fit the hand. Save the blisters. You'll be interested in those."

The two Hrrubans came over to discuss the ponies and ended up taking part of their price in narrow-gauge metal chain. They shook hands and Horstmann arranged with one of the Humans from First Village to have the beasts boarded until he was ready to load up and leave. Ken looked over the metalwork and other goods which Horstmann's son placed on the long tables. The trader himself passed among them, shaking hands and arranging deals quickly. Some Doonans paid in credit vouchers; others with goods, such as rough or cut gemstones or finished craftwork.

Pottery, textiles, ready-to-wear tunics and overalls were placed out by Horstmann's crew for inspection. A large, floppy bundle came out on the next skidload, and Fred pounced on it.

"Well, these have come a long way. Hey, Reeve," he called. "Here's horsehides with your ranch markings on them. Sell them, they get ridden and eaten, and the hides end up back here for craftwork. Now, that's recycling."

"My brand?" Ken asked curiously, making his way over to look. "That's my brand, all right. Where did you say these came from? Zapata? I didn't sell this many to anyone on that world. At least I don't think so."

"Well, you must have," Horstmann pointed out "I'd know the Reeve Ranch markings anywhere, and Zapatan provenance is with 'em."

Ken flipped over one hide after another. Twenty still showed his freeze mark but he couldn't remember having sold a full score of horses to Zapata Three. He'd easily recall a sale that would have fed his family for a year or more. Then he clicked his tongue on his teeth. Could he be looking at hides of animals that had gone missing? Over a period of years, there'd been a fair number of inexplicable disappearances. Some he could chalk up against hunting mdas, disease, or ssersa: a few would be a normal enough loss for any rancher. But twenty? Maybe Todd was right. Rustlers had returned to Doona and taken the animals off-world in spite of satellite surveillance.

Hides kept a long time. They could be accumulated and then sold when enough time had passed to dim memory of loss. Someone had blundered, letting the rustled hides make their way back to Doona. The general method of making profit from rustling was to take the animals to a pastoral world that wasn't yet cleared for animal residence, where colonists were desperate for breeding stock and fresh meat. Thriftily then the colonists traded cured hides to other planets for goods. Probably swapped hides for some of Zapata's new chains.

Now if he could just trace the hides back, to Zapata to the colonists and then to the men who'd sold them the animals, he could pass that information on to Poldep. Having them come back in a lump proved it was one person who'd been responsible all along, not several different gangs. That'd be a good fact to pass on to Poldep.

"Fred, who sold you these?"

"Why?" The trader squinted at him suspiciously. "Something wrong with 'em? You know damned well, Reeve, I don't deal in stolen goods and I've the Zapatan provenance."

"So you do," Ken said reasonably, "but I'd be grateful if you could give me a name."

"Truth to tell, I can't. I was shaking hands and changing credits so fast that I have no face to attach to the goods." Horstmann looked genuinely regretful. "I've checked if I'd thought it odd, but I know you sell off-world."

Ken suppressed his frustration and asked with a friendly smile, "How long will you be on Doona?"

"I've got to wait for Kiachif, 'come frost, fire, or flood,' as he says," Fred replied, grinning. "I'm supposed to take a shipment for him into the Hrruban arm, and he hasn't caught up with me yet. I got a message on the beacon that this time I'd better stay where I am. Not that I wouldn't. Don't tell him, but I'm fond of the old pirate."

"Good," Ken said. "Fred, I know you got the provenance so don't take this wrong, but I've got a feeling that these animals were stolen from me. Would you let me take the hides to check against the sales records?"

"I'd like to, Ken, I really would," Horstmann said, bobbing his head from side to side in his reluctance, "but I might be able to sell 'em. Can't sell 'em if the buyer can't see 'em, now can I? Why, my wife hear about me doing something like that, even to a good honest man like yourself, and she'd skin me and put *my* hide in with the rest."

"I understand, Fred, I really do," Ken said, hiding his exasperation. "But look, there's a computer outlet right here in the Hall. Just let me have a chance to check the brand numbers. Won't take long and these could be evidence."

At the word "evidence," Horstmann froze. Poldep investigations were the bane of any licensed trader. They meant unavoidable and unlimited delays. He narrowed an eye at Ken. "Well, so long's it's only just across the Hall. But I didn't get 'em illegal. You know we don't deal in bad merchandise."

"I know that, Fred. Thanks." Under Horstmann's baleful gaze, Ken switched on the terminal and keyed in his user code. Ken watched the trader out of the corner of his eye until he got involved in a deal and temporarily forgot about Ken and evidence.

If these were horses that had gone missing over the past few years, then he— and other ranchers who said they'd had periodic losses—might be able to break up this new spate of rustling. That is, if they could also solve how the rustlers were getting past the security satellites. Having solid evidence to show Poldep would ensure their cooperation. And prove ranchers hadn't just been careless in pulling up ssersa or keeping proper track of their stock.

Ken had to think hard to remember when he first lost track of a horse for which a carcass had never been found. Even mdas left the skull and hooves and occasionally scraps of hide and bone fragments. It had to have been five or more years ago. He called up his records for a date ten years back when the horses were rounded up for their annual checkup. Now he remembered. In late summer, one of his stallions hadn't come home, a big powerful bay who'd sired a fine few foals before he disappeared. Buster he'd been called. Ken initiated a search for that name.

The screen blanked and was replaced with the "One Moment Please" graphic. Ken twitched impatiently while the search went on. In a few minutes, the screen cleared, then filled with name, description, and freeze mark. Ken jotted the number down and started flipping through the hides, trying to find a match. He didn't.

"I'm doing this backward," he told himself. He blanked the screen and began to type in the numbers on the Zapatan hides and asked for matching data.

The program, in the way of all computer inventory programs, was painfully slow. Each query consumed several minutes, having to access data from the master mainframe on the other side of the planet. Fretfully Ken drummed his fingertips on the console and glared at the cheery graphic. When the screen changed, he pounced on the keyboard.

"There! Cuddy, two-year-old, sired by Maglev out of Corona, black and white pinto, gelded." Ken slapped the hide, pleased. "Six years ago, eh?" He hit the key to copy and print the document, then flipped Cuddy's hide over to the next one. His hand was arrested in midair as he glanced from the hide to the screen and back again. This was an Appaloosa hide, leopard Appaloosa at that, small black flecks on white. "Wait a minute! This didn't come off Cuddy." Undeniably the file said pinto, but the skin was white flecked with black.

Ken sat back in the chair with a thump. Not that a pinto could change its spots to leopard Appaloosa. He checked the brand numbers again but the figures tallied. Could Lon or Todd have entered the freeze brand to Cuddy's file? He felt a spurt of righteous anger over such sloppiness. But neither Lon nor Todd was prone to be slipshod. Not about recording the correct markings. He frowned. He didn't have many Appies. Kelly's father liked the breed. But the freeze mark was his, not Vic's. Perplexed, he turned to the next one, a bright bay with a white saddle mark shaped like a parallelogram just below the freeze brand.

The brand designated a two-year-old chestnut with no saddle mark. Could there be a glitch in the system? Could the computer be scrambling his files? He'd have remembered a leopard Appaloosa and a bright bay with such a distinctive saddle mark. These were totally unfamiliar animals. He needed a control.

He entered the markings from a horse he knew better than any other animal on Doona, his mare Socks. She was Reeve Ranch entry #1. Socks was elderly now, but still willing to go out for a ride in fine weather. Data scrolled up, and Ken went straight to the description of the animal. This one was all right. It was the mare, all the way down to her four white socks. So what was wrong with the other files?

He brought up again the first two he had tried, wondering if solar flares had interfered with the satellite transmission of data from Treaty Island Archives the first time. To his chagrin, they remained unaltered and the hides still bore marks of horses he didn't recognize.

One by one, Ken compared his records with the freeze-dry markings for each hide in the bundle. When he was through, not one of the hides matched the color description of the horse that should have worn it. It was as if someone had lifted the brands from his horses and transferred them onto someone else's, a removal that he knew was, if not impossible, then certainly achieved by a heretofore unknown process.

"You get what you want, Reeve?" Horstmann asked cheerfully, coming over in between a spate of deals to slap the other man on the back.

Ken shrugged. "Yes and no, Fred." A very clever operator was making a profit on selling rustled animals on Zapata Three and, probably, elsewhere. And with Zapatan provenances, surely there was a way of finding out who that clever person was. "When Ali Kiachif arrives, I'd like to talk with him. Had any bids on these hides?" Ken didn't want them scattered, but he also couldn't block a sale for Fred just to keep the evidence in one place.

"Well, the Hrruban in the Doona Cooperative of Farmers and Skillcrafters booth sounded interested in them."

"Look, I'll give you a deposit . . ."

"Against the price? Or just to hold 'em?"

"To hold 'em, Fred. That provenance might be forged."

"Didn't look forged to me!" Fred's eyes widened at the mere suggestion that he'd been conned.

"Nevertheless, you don't want to sell and then find out the provenance was counterfeit, if you know what I mean." Ken deliberately used Ali Kiachif's favorite phrase.

"I know what you mean: fines! Okay. Under the circumstances, Ken, I'll waive the deposit and put these damned things to one side where no one'll see 'em. That help you?"

"It surely does, Fred, and I appreciate it more than I can say." Ken smiled gratefully but he rather suspected that Horstmann might be cutting some sly deals on the side that he didn't want the senior Codep captain to know about. Normally such a favor cost a lot more than just the breath it took to ask it. "Don't forget to tell Kiachif that I need to see him."

Armed with his curious findings, Ken arranged an interview with the Poldep chief in charge of Doona's quadrant of the Amalgamated Worlds. Poldep, the enforcement arm of the Amalgamated Worlds Administration, had jurisdiction on every planet which had signed the charter. Sampson DeVeer listened politely to Ken's theory about rustlers somehow evading the security satellites, but clearly he was finding it hard to believe.

"It's a very interesting theory, Mr. Reeve," he said blandly. He was a tall man who had been called good-looking by many women behind his back, because his diffident manner kept them from approaching the man himself. He had broad shoulders and an intelligent face. His wavy hair and moustache were nearly black. "I'd need proof to proceed, you understand. Not just speculation."

"I have proof," Ken said, producing the film copies. DeVeer's casual attitude was beginning to get on his nerves. DeVeer was rumored to be anti-Doona, though he wasn't an active antagonist to the colony. He claimed he was just trying to do his job, and the presence of unknowns like the Hrrubans made it more difficult for him. "These hides have been altered in some way."

DeVeer tented his fingers, peering through them at the hard copy that Ken had spread out on his desk. "That's very unlikely, Mr. Reeve. It's more probably the records were changed. In my twenty years serving Poldep, I have never come across anyone, or anything, that can produce an undetectable alteration to the freeze-dry-process brands." His tone was unequivocal.

"Well, someone has," Ken insisted, indicating the leopard Appaloosa hide which ought to have been black and white. "I don't run Appies. But that's my freeze brand. And you know a horse has never been known to alter its hide."

"Perhaps the skin was dyed?"

"If the leopard Appie had turned black and white, I'd say that was possible, but not probable. There is also no trace of dye according to this chemical analysis of the hide." And Ken tossed that flimsy across the desk to DeVeer.

"Mr. Reeve," DeVeer said again patiently. "These are negative proofs. You have the hide of a horse that you say you never owned with a brand to an animal you did." He held up a hand to forestall an outburst. "I know that rustling has been an ongoing problem on Doona. I've investigated several cases myself. The freeze-brand system was developed to prevent rustling. I'd say it has. Now you come along, wanting to contest the validity of that excellent system. Frankly I don't think this is a case of rustling. Maybe you should look a little closer to home, where some people might have a chance to duplicate your brand on strays that they can legally sell off-world. Doesn't your son have regular access to spacegoing transport?"

Ken barely kept himself from reaching across the desk and planting his fist firmly in DeVeer's face. "Are you suggesting that Todd has rustled horses from the ranch he will one day inherit?"

"Inherit might be presumptuous, Mr. Reeve, but the opportunity is there . . . Now, now, look at this objectively, Mr. Reeve. I'm trying to clarify a perplexing set of facts. I'm not speaking with any intent to offend. Let me put it to you this way. If, for example, you had a horse, a living one, with a brand matching one of these stolen hides, I would have a lead to investigate . . . a duplication of numbers, which is a possibility. An honest error at branding time when you got to handle a lot of foals. Or if you know who had bred this leopard Appaloosa, I'd have another lead. And if you knew how these brands could be altered, which is something I've never heard of, then we really would have a cause for an immediate and intensive inquiry. As it is, we have nothing to go on but unlikely speculation and possible data base errors." He stood up, indicating the interview was over. "I assure you that, if you come to me with something concrete—even one piece of evidence—I'll be glad to listen."

Ken got most of his anger blown out of his system on his way back to the ranch. Any Poldep inspector worthy of his rank would have seen the anomalies in hides with inappropriate markings. Data base errors! Duplication of freeze-brand numbers! *That* had never happened, not in the twenty-four years he'd been breeding horses. Nor had it happened to any other rancher, Hayuman or Hrruban.

That sly dig about Todd inheriting being presumptuous. Presuming what? That Todd would be found guilty and sent to a penal colony and denied the right to inherit colonial land anywhere?

Ken made himself calm down and warned himself not to even consider such an outcome. It was dark when he reached the ranch and the lights blazed out a welcome on the flower beds Pat had labored so long to surround the house. He was glad to see Kelly had been invited over for dinner again, but he hoped Pat wouldn't be silly enough to push Todd. That lad didn't push! He stood his ground and he was doing it now with courage and fortitude. Ken was prouder than ever of his son.

The moment Ken started recounting his discovery, Pat put dinner on hold and, instead of the meal, the big round table was spread with the hard copy. Ken had talked Fred into letting him take two of the hides home and he'd stopped by the vet lab to borrow a microscope for a good look at the hide marks.

"This is a real stumper," Todd said, looking up from his turn at the microscope. He gestured for Kelly to take a turn at the eyepiece. "There's no shadow of an original freeze mark. I'd swear this one was the first one, and genuine. Only it can't be. 'Cause Cuddy was a pinto, not a leopard Appie."

"Could they have used a chemical to neutralize the original brand mark?" Pat asked, studying the printout of the descriptions of the horses whose numbers had appeared on the wrong hides.

Ken shook his head. "There's no chemical that can do that."

"A laser?" Robin asked brightly, sure he'd come up with the logical solution. "That looks like chemical burns sometimes."

"Black magic is the more likely answer," Kelly said in a gloomy tone, leaning back from the microscope. "I'd swear that was genuine and the only mark that hide had ever worn."

"You raise Appies, Kelly," Ken began.

"Yeah, but we don't sell our leopards. You know that. And if one of ours had gone missing, you know that Dad and Michael would have combed the planet to find it."

Ken knew that was true enough.

"Todd, I got a job for you," he said, placing an arm about his son's shoulder. "We've got to get all the other ranches to let us do a read-only search of missing stock and the brands they wore. If we find a missing horse wearing one of those brands," and he pointed to the lists, "we'll have some solid evidence to give DeVeer."

With a wry grin, Todd said, "The old fogey didn't suggest that your son might be using his ol' dad's legitimate brand marks to sell stock off-world, did he?"

Ken wasn't quite quick enough to mask his annoyance and dismay at Todd's droll query.

"What'll they think of next to hang on Todd's neck?" Kelly demanded indignantly. "As if you could fit one horse in the *Albatross,* let alone seventeen or twenty!"

Ken snapped his fingers. "Damn, now why didn't I think of that factor?"

"You were probably far too mad to do so," Pat said, raising her eyebrows in amusement.

"You're right about that. Now, let's get back to work. Robin, have you had a chance to find out who's missing stock?"

Robin produced a flimsy from his pocket. "And Mr. Hu said a rancher named Tobin's been complaining that some of his stock has run off."

"Let's get details on those animals, then, and not just freeze brands, but full descriptions and markings."

"Maybe Hrriss could . . ." Inessa began, and then clapped her hands over her mouth, her eyes big with regret at mentioning that name in Todd's hearing.

"You can ask him, Inessa," Todd said evenly. "You're not under any restraint. Find out if Hrruban ranches are missing horses, too. Maybe the rustling's only aimed at Hayumans."

"You can't possibly mean to imply that Hrrubans would stoop to rustling?" Kelly asked, regretting the statement the instant the words were out of her mouth.

"They'd be the last to rustle hrrsses," Todd said, whimsically using Hrriss's pronunciation. "But someone might like to make it look that way."

"Good point, Todd," Ken said. "Now let's . . ."

"Let's have dinner," Pat interjected, "before it's spoiled. The hides will keep."

After dinner, in which theory and speculation were rife, everyone went off on their designated searches. Robin took the family flitter and zoomed away to visit the Dautrish farm. Kelly went off in hers, promising to do a thorough search of the Solinari records and see if perhaps the leopard Appie had been bred by another rancher. Ken used the office system to double-check his records at source and Todd settled in at the computer terminal in his room.

He put up a mail message to the hundreds of ranches on Doona, asking permission to do a read-only on their stock files, and leaving his user number and name as the signature. Then he put a control list of the numbers and hides that his father had gone through. Before he finished that, three ranchers had flashed back permission. First he listed missing stock, by number and description. He set up a separate file to isolate description matches. When he thought of going to Main Records to obtain numbers of hides returned to Doona for leather processing, he used the ranch number, in case his was unacceptable to Treaty Island. He berated himself for the growing paranoia he sensed as a result of his house arrest, but he needed this information too badly to wish to be denied access.

He didn't dismiss the possibility that someone had made illicit use of the Reeve Ranch freeze-mark files. And although rustling had been an ongoing problem for ranchers, that sort of illegal entry smacked of a very long-term effort. Rustlers were in and out, making a quick profit from their hauls. They certainly wouldn't plan so precisely how to confuse records and an entire, viable industry. Or would they?

It was that leopard Apple hide with a blatantly Reeve brand that really baffled him. He knew he couldn't rest until he'd found where that horse had been bred and who had owned it.

As he was to discover in the next few days, lots of people had missed horses that they never traced, never found the carcass of, and had never bothered reporting. Every rancher expected to lose a few to natural calamities. But the more he looked, the more he came to realize that no ranch had lost as many over the past ten years as the Reeves.

Branding an animal with some other ranch's ID simply wasn't the sort of practical joke ranchers played on each other. Not by the dozens, certainly.

While one bay hide could look like another bay hide, swirl marks were taken when an animal was registered. Broken-color horses were far easier to identify from their birth diagrams, which plainly indicated the shapes of the darker hair.

Then a thought struck him. Maybe these weren't Doonan horses at all. At least the ones whose hides Ken had found. Maybe that was the deception: horses stolen from another planet marked with Doona brands to satisfy innocent purchasers. No wonder there was a Zapata provenance. When he discovered how many colonial worlds bred horses, with vast herds far too large to be individually marked, Todd decided he'd leave that option till last.

He'd look first for those animals which had been discovered dead. The cause of their demise would be in the records . . . and there were quite a few. All with the initials *MA* for Mark Aden, Lon Adjei's former assistant. *SS* meant ssersa poisoning, *MS* for snake, *M* for mda, *A* for accident—broken leg or some other injury which resulted in euthanasia. The unexplained disappearances, however, began to increase over the last few years.

The fact that the Reeve Ranch suffered the most losses and that the spurious hide marks were all Reeve brands as well worried Todd. Admiral Landreau was back on Doona. Any example of incompetence, any whiff of dishonesty that could be charged against the Reeves, could be seized on and used by Landreau and others to try and get them deported, could work against the welfare of the entire colony. This was too precarious a time for him to be trapped by a home arrest, out of circulation, out of action when he was most needed. Anger suffused Todd. Ever since he set foot on Doona, he had defended the ideal it exemplified—harmonious cohabitation. He knew to the marrow of his bones, the cells of his blood, the lungs that breathed clear Doonan air, that Hrriss felt an equal dedication.

Why had he decided that they had to answer that Mayday? He answered himself. Because, being who he was, reared as he was, he could have done nothing else. And someone very clever had counted on that! He couldn't quite see Admiral Landreau being so psychologically astute. Rogitel, now, he might. But Todd had had little intercourse with the commander—only that one meeting on Hrretha. Not really time enough in desultory formal responses for even a trained psychologist to have taken that kind of measure of anyone.

Another file for a missing horse recalled him to the task at hand and he punched the print button. The stack of films beside him was growing.

He'd had to make a joke out of DeVeer suspecting him of doing the smuggling for profit. And yet, with all those valuables found on the *Albatross*, it wouldn't be so hard for someone else to accept that possibility. But for anyone to think that he, Todd Reeve, or Hrriss, son of Hrrestan, Hrruban leader of Rrala, would sully all they had lived for, worked for . . . that was very hard to swallow. The beautiful dream that was Doona was inexorably slipping away from his grasp, deny it though he might. Ilsa had never understood his passion for Doona. And really, neither did Robin or Inessa, but they had never lived under the restraints of Earth society, so they'd no idea what they'd lose. He wished for the millionth time that he could talk to Hrriss. If it wasn't for the support of his family, the often stumbling reassurances of old friends, the wisdom of Hrruvula, his counsel and Kelly's daily visits, he would find that unendurable.

The cheery "One Moment Please" graphic appeared on the screen again.

Todd felt another rush of hot rage, which he fought to dispel. It didn't do any good to tear himself up, but he was frustrated and angry. Instead of being out there, offering support for the ongoing Treaty talks which would cement permanent relations between Earth and Hrruba, ensuring Doona's continuance, Todd was being used as a pawn to break the colony and the alliance. Every time he answered one charge or began to solve one problem, another cropped up to claim his attention. It was curious, because everything seemed centered on him or his father. And that incontrovertibly led to Admiral Al Landreau as the most likely origin of this complex conspiracy. He had no proof nor the freedom of movement to secure any.

Why did animosity consume Landreau to the point where his revenge on the Reeves, father and son, embraced Doona, and all the good that had been achieved over a quarter of a century?

Todd searched his memory of those early days on Doona. Of course, he had arrived after Ken and the other ten colonists had struggled through an unbelievably long and cold winter to build homes for their families when the ship arrived in the springtime. Eleven men, placed alone on a supposedly uninhabited planet, had to make all the decisions of socialization and civilization that would frame a new world. They courageously faced physical hazards and the incredible moral obligation. When Ken had discovered the Hrruban village, they had been ready to leave in obedience to the prohibitions which had been hammered into their heads almost from birth: cohabitation with another species could only result in the destruction of the other species. But the Hrrubans were no gentle, vulnerable, sensitive ephemerals.

Circumstances had swept the Terrans along at a furious pace, and they had found themselves cohabiting, with no way to adhere to their decision to leave Doona. Todd grinned, wishing he had been more aware when his father had lost his temper at the various bureaucrats who had blamed the colonists for the untenable situation. Once the mutual benefits of this trial cohabitation had been understood, Alreldep, with Admiral Sumitral, and Codep had accepted with fair grace. But Landreau, the Spacedep representative, never forgot and showed no hint of forgiveness.

Todd took a break from the computer and got up to stretch. He raised his arms over his head and heard the crack as muscles protested being forced to remain too long in the same position. At some point, his mother had quietly left a pitcher of juice, some buttered bread, and the final wedge of the dinner pie on a tray on the worktop. Gratefully he poured a glass of juice and, with the pie in one hand, walked to the window. He was thankful every day for the abundance of real and tasty food. He still remembered the metallic taste of childhood meals, the sameness of each supposedly nutritious meal. He had always felt hungry.

He pushed open the window and leaned his elbows on the frame. The sun was starting to drop behind the trees over the river at the bottom of the pasture. He wished he could be out and doing, back at his job, able to visit his friends. Even when he was a small boy, he had hated confinement. Never mind that his prison was the many acres of his father's ranch: his freedom of movement had been severely curtailed and he was unused to that. It was, however, better than a genuine incarceration in a four-by-four-meter cell. The only times he had been allowed to leave the ranch over the last two weeks had been to appear on Treaty Island, for more questioning. Each time, he had hoped for a glimpse of Hrriss, but their visits didn't coincide. The prosecutors were being careful to keep them strictly apart.

The incriminating evidence of illegal artifacts found on the *Albatross* was quite enough to convict them of criminal activities inconsonant with the positions of trust both he and Hrriss had held. With Landreau and Rogitel briefing their attorneys, this could call into question the success of the Doona Experiment of Cohabitation. That would be a rather farfetched allegation, since one Hayuman and one Hrruban were involved, not two members of the same species working against the interests of the other.

Their defense attorney was Hrruvula, a brilliant Hrruban advocate of the same Stripe as First Speaker but young enough to be light-furred, a shade that the horseman in Todd named buckskin. His stripe, while still narrow, was a dark accent to his fine hide. His Standard was as fluent as a native-born Terran and indeed he had assiduously studied both the language and the legal systems of Earth as well as those of his home planet. He had one assistant, the physical opposite of his tall muscular self, a diminutive dark-haired, dark-complected Terran named Sue Bailey, a name Todd thought inordinately appropriate for a legal clerk. During all the sessions Todd had attended, she said little, rarely glancing up from the square portable over which her fingers flew in taking down their conversations.

Hrruvula made no bones about the fact that the evidence—tape and objects, and most especially the Byzanian Glow Stone—damned Todd and Hrriss. Todd suggested that Poldep had not investigated any of the anomalies or made any attempt to question other suspects.

"When they have you and Hrriss, with your fingers in the till as it were," Hrruvula said, revealing a fine understanding of old Terran metaphors that would delight Kelly, "they have no motivation to look for anyone else. But you two have no motive that I have been able to discover. You both have the reputation of indisputable honor and dedicated responsibility. You both have a splendid future on Doona, and only fools, which neither of you are, would jeopardize such a future so near to its real inauguration: the renegotiation of the Treaty of Doona."

"Have you discovered anyone else with such motive?"

Hrruvula lifted his shoulders. "As you suggested, Admiral Landreau's public animosity toward Doona as well as his frequent assertions that he would 'get the Reeves' have been verified. Documentation has been provided by many eminent personages. But there is no proof . . ."

"There has to be . . ." Todd had interrupted.

Hrruvula held up his first digit, claw tip showing. His jaw had dropped slightly and his eyes sparkled. "Yet." Then Hrruvula had asked if they had any more information about the hides.

The Treaty Council members sat looking austere and troubled, facing Commander Landreau over the Council table. The head of Spacedep was flanked by Rogitel, his assistant, and by Varnorian of Codep, who looked bored by the whole proceeding. Landreau sat hunched slightly over his clasped hands, like a moody predator bird, as he reiterated the charges against Todd Reeve and Hrriss.

Todd and Hrriss were not present for this introductory session. They were, naturally, represented by Hrruvula, with Sue Bailey tapping quiet fingers on her keys. With a Poldep officer on guard, the illicit artifacts were displayed, the Glow Stone in a heavy plastic case. Sampson DeVeer was also present, seated next to the recording secretary at the foot of the table.

"The accused, Todd Reeve and Hrriss, both colonists of this planet, have been granted numerous unusual privileges," Landreau began. "Among them, exclusive use of a scout-class spaceship and almost unlimited access to the Archives and other records."

"These 'privileges' were warranted by their extra-planetary duties which they have faultlessly executed to the benefit of their native planets and their adopted world," Hrruvula replied. "They were elected unanimously to fulfill the position of travelling emissaries for Doona/Rrala."

"Yes, and see how they reward the trust put in them," Landreau spat out. "Illegal invasion of space, piracy, smuggling!"

"We are by no means convinced, Admiral Landreau," Madam Dupuis said in a stern tone, "that the defendants are guilty of piracy and smuggling. They have both separately maintained that neither of them placed the artifacts on the *Albatross*, nor could the one have done so without the other's knowledge."

"But their own log claims otherwise." Landreau made his voice sound reasonable, even saddened by the clandestine activities of Todd and Hrriss. "I am not at all satisfied by the so-called confessions that your interview extracted from the, er, defendants."

"My clients would be happy, in fact delighted, to answer these allegations under oath," Hrruvula replied.

"How good is the word of such deceitful parties?"

"Objection!" Hrruvula said, shooting to his feet.

"Sustained," Madam Dupuis said, shooting a repressive look at Landreau.

The Admiral took a deep breath and, with a fixed smile, continued. "Oaths in a case such as this are not good enough," Landreau said, and began enumerating his reasons. "They claim there was a robot beacon orbiting Hrrilnorr IV. Admiralty Records emphatically proves that no such beacon ever existed. *On* the off chance that a rogue beacon from some other system or passing vessel had entered the system and been drawn to Hrrilnorr IV, a scout was dispatched to search. No trace of any mechanical devices was found except the ones assigned to that system. But," and now he waggled his finger, "an astonishing assortment of illegal objects *and* that Byzanian Glow Stone were unquestionably found secreted aboard the *Albatross,* and those two . . . young men"—his tone made that designation an insult—"deny any knowledge of them." He paused dramatically. "I insist on guaranteed veracity. They must submit to interrogation—by qualified technicians, of course—under querastrin."

An agitated murmur rumbled through the Council chamber, although Hrruvula, whom Landreau was watching, appeared unmoved by such a drastic course. Querastrin was by no means a new truth drug, but it was a harsh one. It stripped the person under its influence of both privacy and dignity. Suicides following querastrin interrogation were frequent: more often in the cases of those proved innocent under such a drug than those convicted of crimes they had denied.

Hrruvula fixed his deceptively mild green gaze on Landreau and allowed the pupils to slowly contract. Landreau shuddered inwardly.

"But why should it be needed in this instance, Admiral?" the counsel asked. "Querastrin seems rather an extreme measure. Both Terran and Hrruban courts permit suspects of all but the most bizarre crimes to retain their dignity and give evidence under oath. My clients, on the occasion of the inspection in Councillor Dupuis's presence and separately during every interrogatory session, have explained the circumstances of their entry into the Hrrilnorr system. Their account has not varied in any particular during any repetition."

"But their 'account' does not tally with the physical evidence supporting their arrest. The future of an entire colony is at stake here, don't you understand that?" Landreau asked plaintively, meeting every Councillor's eyes in turn. "Does that not count against the well-being of two single citizens? As a Human, I am appalled that one of my kind invaded a sector which you Hrrubans claimed as your own territory. A deliberate and premeditated abrogation of a specific Treaty clause, and that is the least of their acts against the Treaty. Surely you must wish such unscrupulous persons removed from this society to prevent them tainting the minds of your young folk who have, I am told, become accustomed to following the lead of . . . these two young men. Doona does not need such role models." Landreau allowed his dismay to be clearly seen.

The Treaty Controller nodded slowly as if agreeing with that assertion of opprobrium. Landreau's eyes narrowed slightly and the hint of a smile pulled at his thin lips. The common good was a sensible tack to take in ramming home his points. A nice wedge, neatly driven in to make these idiots reexamine their values.

Hrruvula dismissed that with a wave of his hand. "Who are we to consider to have tainted whom, Commander?" he asked.

"*Cui bono*, Counsellor," Landreau said. "Who profits from the crimes? In the testimony given to this august body, the suspects failed curiously to address several interesting items which I have uncovered. Then, too, I have recently come into possession of evidence, just brought to my attention, on another matter entirely. The government of Zapata Three felt obliged to submit this directly to me. This includes not only these financial records," and Landreau extended a sheaf of flimsies for the court steward to present to the Councillors, "but a description of a male, one point nine meters tall, with dark brown hair and blue eyes, calling himself Rikard Baliff, the named depositor. This so-called Rikard Baliff has had a most lucrative and active account for the last ten years. The date of the first deposit, by chance, happens to be only two months after that scout, *Albatross,* was assigned to Todd Reeve and Hrriss, son of Hrrestan. The most recent deposit was made only three weeks ago."

"I fail to see the relevance of these documents," Hrruvula remarked with a slight, exasperated sigh of boredom.

"It's obvious enough to me, to any thoughtful person," Landreau replied, piqued. "Young Mr. Reeve has been building a stake himself, should the Doona Experiment fail. A new life, with a new name—financed, in part, we may now surmise on this new evidence—by the sale of horses bearing Reeve Ranch freeze marks as well as the rare artifacts found on the *Albatross.* I have depositions," and he fluttered more sheets for the steward to hand over to the Councillors, "that this Rikard Baliff was always accompanied by a Hrruban. Plainly the two have been in collusion for a long time."

Madam Dupuis disguised her anger only by a great effort of will. Despite this new and most unsettling evidence, she could not imagine Todd Reeve as a conniving rustler and smuggler any more than she could see Hrriss being led around by the nose as an accomplice in such a nefarious undertaking. Why, Todd would have been barely twenty-one at the time he allegedly started this galaxy-wide enterprise. Furthermore, someone in those ten years would surely have recognized Todd and Hrriss at some point during their visits to Zapata and commented on it. Especially if Todd and Hrriss were at the same time representing the colony at an official function. She eased from one buttock to another, compelled by her oath as a Treaty Councillor to hear out this remarkable fabrication of Landreau's and fretting the way evidence upon evidence was being piled up.

When Landreau began to read from the documents, as if the Councillors were too infirm to do so for themselves, she interrupted him. "Have you any witnesses who can testify to the presence of Todd Reeve and Hrriss on Zapata to conduct these transactions?"

"Only scan the frequency of deposits, Madam Dupuis, and you will see"— Landreau's smile broadened—"that the dates match the times—on List B-2— when Reeve and his Hrruban partner were logged off Doona on official visits."

Madam Dupuis turned to her colleagues. "I would like to see their flight plans and log records for the past ten years."

"That is List B-3, Madam Dupuis," Rogitel said helpfully.

"It would seem that they have become deft at altering the *Albatross* log to delete unauthorized landings at Zapata, and on other worlds," Landreau said.

"If I may interject a word here," Rogitel said, "since the assistant sealed the *Albatross* immediately upon its landing four weeks ago, they did not have time to alter the log on that journey. The need to do so would account for why they were so insistent on postponing the obligatory inspection of their craft until such time when they could return and delete the incriminating portions."

One of the Treaty Councillors rattled the deposit sheet. "A lot of credit's flowed through this account. Where did the withdrawals go?"

"Why, to purchase illegal and smuggled items, sir," Landreau said as if any fool could have deduced that. "And undoubtedly to secure silence from any who might inform on their clandestine activities."

"Frankly, Admiral, I find that allegation harder to believe than any other evidence you have presented to this court," Madam Dupuis said. "Both young men have worked ceaselessly to ensure that the Doona Experiment continues."

"Ah!" and Landreau raised his hand, his face alight. "That is why their duplicity is so monstrous. Especially where the Reeve family is concerned, for it is well known that they would not be welcome back on Earth. Therefore, seizing an opportunity to be sure that he and his family would live in comfort somewhere else, Todd Reeve used his position and privilege to accumulate the necessary credits."

Hrruvula managed a chuckle and in a very human gesture, covered his eyes as if unable to maintain the dignity such a hearing required.

"Your humor is ill timed, sir," Landreau said, stiffly drawing his body to its full height in the chair, "for all of you must remember that ten years ago, demonstrations occurred on both Hrruba and Terra demanding that the Siwannese Noncohabitation Principle be upheld and the Doona colony abandoned as a violation." Then he gave Hrruvula a smug glance of satisfaction for that unequivocal fact.

"Those demonstrations subsided and an inquiry proved that the agitation had not been spontaneous as claimed but had indeed been subsidized by unidentified conservatives from both planets."

"That is on record," Madam Dupuis said. "More to the point, at no time during the period were any colonists permitted off-planet."

"Exactly, Madam Dupuis!" Landreau shot to his feet in triumph. "And shortly thereafter Reeve and Hrriss began their 'goodwill' appearances."

"To dispel any lasting doubt as to the validity of the Doona/Rrala Experiment," Hrruvula said.

"And just look how that privilege has been abused by Reeve and Hrriss!" Landreau exclaimed. "To smuggle and steal in order to provide an alternate lifestyle in case the Doonan Experiment should not prove successful at the end of the Treaty period. The Reeve family has a well-documented history of dissidence and anarchy."

"That is libel Admiral," Hrruvula said. "They are self-motivated, hardworking, disciplined colonists with achievements any Stripe would be proud to acknowledge. And do!"

"I insist that the defendants submit to interrogation under querastrin," Landreau said, his face flushed, his eyes flashing, and his manner uncompromising. "That is the only way in which the truth of the past ten years can be unraveled."

"I protest the need for any such extreme measure!" Hrruvula was on his feet.

The Treaty Controller gave a sharp rap of his gavel.

"That may not be necessary," he said, though his phrasing caused other Councillors to regard him in surprise. "The defendants will be interrogated in court in the normal manner as to the violation of the interdiction of Hrrilnorr and their possession of illegal objects found secreted on the ship solely used by them. The defense attorney is to have time to review the new evidence presented to this court today and prepare a defense."

Madam Dupuis regarded the Controller in a fixed stare, for he intimated that he didn't believe there could be a defense adequate to clear the charges. She noticed that Hrruvula was quick to catch the innuendo.

"If those proceedings prove inconclusive," the Controller went on, "time enough to administer querastrin."

Landreau covered his jubilation. He had become worried at the Controller's silence, for it had taken a long time for his colleagues to place that nominee of the bigoted Third Speaker in the senior position. He had to deal with Hrrubans, to be sure, to effect that end, but at least they had been Hrrubans who felt as he did—that the Doonan Experiment should be disbanded. He tossed Hrruvula a challenging look. Just let that cat try to discredit the evidence that had been so carefully obtained. Just let him try!

And after discrediting the Reeves, such sterling examples of Doonan colonials, he was quite willing to start an interspecies war to depopulate Doona. Those plans needed only a few more little twitches to provide ample excuse for the protective preemptive strike he felt was necessary against the danger of a Hrruban invasion of Earth. Soon that twenty-five-year-old mistake would be exonerated.

The gavel startled him out of his reverie.

"Due notice of the trial date will be forthcoming," declared the Controller. "This session is adjourned."

Admiral Landreau sprang to his feet as the Councillors filed out, well pleased with the events. He failed to notice either their thoughtful expressions or the bland expression of Hrruvula.

"Well, that's a horse of a different color, if you get what I mean," Ali Kiachif said, startling Ken, who had been disconsolately stroking the leopard Appie hide. "I thought so when I shipped it. Alive, alert, and akicking, it was. Freddie lad told me you were looking for me. I've got another sled or two of your hides, myself, if you were interested in having them. Chance of a drink for a dry man? Some of your pussycat punch around, if you know what I'm talking about, eh? That mlada's a powerful temptation."

Ken looked from the hide on the table to the merchantman's friendly face. "Sure thing, Ali," and he swung out of his chair to get bottle and glass from the cupboard, "but are you saying that you remember this one horse in particular, out of all the hundreds you've carried?"

The captain lifted his shoulders expressively. "Thousands, Reeve, thousands!" He knocked back the generous tot Ken had poured. "Horses are what Doona ships the most of. But that leopardie Applousa was a real looker."

"Leopard Appaloosa," Ken corrected automatically.

"Don't see many of them, if you know what I mean. Er, I'm a bit dry."

As automatically, Ken splashed an even more generous portion and set the bottle down in front of the wiry old spacefarer.

"Tell me all you remember, Captain, please! I'm going half crazy trying to find out where the horse which wore this hide came from. My records come up blank and we're having to cross-check it against every animal ever bred here."

Ali Kiachif had been lowering the level of mlada in the glass slowly but steadily as Ken spoke. Now, wiping his wild whiskers with the back of his hand, he sighed with relief. "Ah, that cuts the spacedust and sifts the sand, with a vengeance. I remember perfectly because one, the unusual hide on the beast, and two, it was the first time I'd seen an animal with your freeze mark being exported. Looked like a nice animal so I couldn't understand why you'd sell it on. I take a fairly friendly interest in your family, from far away back. Got another reason to remember yon spotted laddie because I was taking your stablehand, young Mr. Aden, out into the great beyond with it! He was going to one of the new places to ply his trade." Kiachif scratched his beard. "Though I can't rightly remember what that trade was. He had a lot of tricky toys and equipment with him, but it was all his. He had a manifest, money, the works. A lot of money, I was thinking, for a young lad who never did anything but manage horses all his life. He was off to a grand start with all those gadgets wherever he was going."

"Now, that's the best thing I've heard in weeks, Ali," Ken said, but his smile was grim. "And it—partially—explains who knew so much about my ranch and freeze IDs."

"But that Appie laddie wasn't rustled. He was sold proper by that Aden feller."

"Who's part of a conspiracy to frame me and my son."

"What's that?" Ali Kiachif paused, hand on the bottle neck.

"I never bred a leopard Appaloosa, Ali. The Solinaris do. Those are, undeniably, my ranch markings but they should be on a two-year-old pinto."

"Well, I can swear that they're on the hide of the animal I loaded. That animal!" And Ali stabbed a stubby stained finger at the hide in front of him.

"You'd be willing to swear to that?"

"In front of anyone and as often as need be. But it's not one hide that's got your drive revving."

"No. So far I've found nineteen other hides, provenanced from Zapata, that don't tally with any horse I ever bred and marked, Poldep is saying it's Todd who's been rustling from his own father, amassing a fat credit account offworld." Ken could feel the frustrated anger building inside him again just having to repeat the foul accusations. "And there're more rumors that Hrriss is either coming along for the ride or sharing the take." At the astonished and dis-believing expression on Ali Kiachif's face, he reined in.

Ali did not. He poured a quick tot to steady himself, for his face had turned an apoplectic red.

"Not those boys!" he said, pounding his fist on the table, a separate bang for each word. "Charge anyone else from any planet anywhere in Terran space or even Hrruban space and I might agree, but not Todd and Hrriss."

"The Council and Poldep do not share your faith in their honesty. And damn it all"—the boost which Kiachif's instant defense had given Ken dissolved as quickly—"the facts, the evidence are against them."

"Facts! Facts? Evidence?" Ali narrowed his eyes, the shrewd trader, not the spirits-guzzling reprobate. "Facts can be altered, even evidence can be counter-feit to suit needs. But I'm a man who's dealt with all kinds, all over this arm of the Milky Way," and he waved expansively, "and I've never been wrong judging a man in my life. And I'm not wrong about that lad of yours who wore a rope tail to look like his best buddy. Anyone else, of any creed, color, conformation, or character, might do the dirty on his own dad so we'll have to find out who did!" Ali waggled his stained finger at Ken. "And by fire, frost, and every ounce of faith in this old bod, we'll prove it."

His wrath was so great he began to choke on the accumulated spittle in his mouth and Ken had to pound him on the back. Still strangling, Ali Kiachif held up his glass for a refill.

As she had promised, Kelly brought the ranch files to Hrriss's house. He came out to meet her.

"I thought I recognized the distinctive beat of Calypso's pace," he said warmly, greeting her. "Nothing's wrong, is it?"

"Not with Todd," she assured him, dismounting and throwing the mare's reins over the rail at the door. "But we got another small problem. Ken Reeve thought maybe you could help on the Hrruban end of things. Give you some-thing to do."

"Constructive work is always welcome," Hrriss said, gesturing for her to pre-cede him. "What is the task?"

Kelly outlined the story of the mismarked and unidentifiable hides. Hrriss scowled deeply, grasping the implications immediately.

"Zo, now we are alzo rustlers!"

To her surprise, Kelly actually saw the hair of Hrriss's stripe rise in resent-ment.

"Ken Reeve saw a leopard Appaloosa hide in a bundle Fred Horstmann brought in. The puzzle is that the Reeves don't raise leopard Appies. We do. But the freeze mark was a Reeve Ranch that was put on a two-year-old pinto."

"Neither pintos nor leopards change their spots," Hrriss said thoughtfully. "Had the freeze mark been altered in any way?"

"No. Ken had the hide analyzed and we've all had a look at it through a microscope. Dad doesn't show a record of any missing leopard Appies. But we need to know if any Hrruban rancher might be missing one."

"What good would that do? A freeze mark cannot be altered."

"But a duplicate number could be put on another stolen animal, couldn't it?"

"Ah, that is a different matter. And no reliable trader would export animals which did not bear the brand of a reliable rancher."

"Todd's already working on a read-only scan of Hayuman ranches but it takes so long on this antiquated computer net that if you could handle the Hrruban end of things . . ."

"Of course," Hrriss said, patting her knee to reassure her. "I will begin at once."

"I would like to help in any way I can," said a soft voice as a female Hrruban slipped into the room. "I have computer skills."

Kelly tried hard not to gawk at the unexpected presence of a female in Hrriss's company. "I'm so sorry. How very rude of me not to ask if you were already occupied, Hrriss." She started to rise but Hrriss gently pushed her back down on the divan.

"I am Nrrna," she said, coming straight to Kelly and holding out her hand. She had a short, fluffy dark beige pelt, evidence of her youthfulness, but her stripe was broad and dark, suggesting she came from a very good family. She wore a braided cloth in aqua shade, looped in decorative swags from her shoulders, waist, and ankles that offset her delicate form and beauty.

"I remember you," Kelly said, cordially gripping the slender hand, for Nrrna's face markings were familiar. She glanced at Hrriss and saw the glowing look in his eyes, not the least bit fraternal. Nrrna returned his glance in the manner of one who has developed considerable rapport. "We took a language class in High Hrruban, though I admit it's been years. Aren't you working for the Health Services these days?"

"Yes," Nrrna replied with shy friendliness, sidling slightly closer to Hrriss. "I heard of your academic success from my parents. Yours must be very proud."

Hrriss moved imperceptibly closer to the dainty female. "Nrrna and I will become lifemates this season," he said, looking proud and self-conscious at the same time.

"You will? Lifemates? Oh! Oh, I'm so happy for you!" Kelly leaped up to seize Hrriss and rub cheeks with him again, then turned to offer both hands to Nrrna, squeezing the delicate bones very gently.

Considering how Hrrubans mated, Hrriss was likely using the word "season" advisedly. Nrrna would know her cycle, and was planning carefully so they would have time for a joining ceremony before estrus began. Kelly felt that her face was cracking with her delighted smile.

"So this is the research into matters of interest to your mother, Hrriss! How wonderful! May you have every joy!" She snapped her jaws closed before she said what was in her mind, and didn't know where to look in her dismay.

Hrriss reached for her hand and pressed it between his. "When Zodd and I are able to resume our association, Nrrna and I will tell him together."

Kelly sighed. "Your news would cheer him up, but I can quite imagine how his knowing such a private arrangement could be construed. I may pop out in spots of anticipation but I won't mention it. That's one thing I've learned at Alreldep—how to know and not know. Just please let me be there when you do break the news. I want to see him really smile, from deep down," and she touched her diaphragm, "instead of just his lips."

"You have my word . . ."

"Which is worth a lot, believe me," Kelly said, her tone suddenly fierce.

Hrriss nodded solemnly and his eyes glowed at the strength of her conviction. Once again he took her hands but this time to seal their agreement.

"Well, I do feel better, Hrriss, I really do."

"And these records? Have you arrived at any style to conduct the search?"

"I have," Kelly said, and opened the packet "It's such a boring job, takes forever, but if you can both help . . ."

"Nrrna, your parents may not wish you to involve yourself in an investigation of this nature."

"Locating missing hrrsses?" She raised her delicately marked brows at him, her emerald eyes wide with surprise. "It is to help the friend of your heart, Hrriss. And I am my own person. I may make my own decisions." Now she gave Hrriss a certain look that caught Kelly's breath. Undeniably the twinge of regret she felt at seeing such unselfconscious love was partly jealousy for what they already shared.

Hrriss turned back to Kelly, his jaw lightly parted and a mischievous glint in his eyes. "You see, she will have her way if she knows the rightness of the path."

"Are you and Zodd not on the same path?" Nrrna asked. "Hrriss has told me how much you are trying to help revoke those ignoble accusations."

"Ah, yes, well, Nrrna, that's another matter."

Nrrna's delicate laugh came out a soft purr. "It is so easy to tell when bare-skins are embarrassed. Oh, I do not mean to offend with that term . . ."

"We are bareskins and I take no offense from such as you, Nrrna. Never," Kelly said. "And I blush far too easily for my own good."

"Especially when Zodd is the subject," Hrriss said, cocking his head to join in the teasing. Then he turned to Nrrna. "Hayuman females do not have your advantage."

"I wish I did," Kelly said with complete exasperation. "I don't mind telling you two—and talking about Todd is not a violation of that stupid ban you two are under—but I love the guy and he doesn't seem to see me as anything more than his 'trusted Hunt second' and the girl next door."

Hrriss regarded her with eyes that glowed now with a slightly different but equally tender regard than the one he gave Nrrna.

"He danced more with you than with anyone else, Kelly," he said. "And he kept his eyes on you wherever you were. And if he was not aware of it, he did not look at you as a trusted Hunt second."

"And I know he's annoyed because Pat and Ken keep inviting me over for dinner and I don't think he wants me to come. When I only want like blazes to help any way I can."

"Ah, but you do not know Zodd as I do, Kelly."

"No, I don't. That's why I'm asking you, and I really shouldn't belabor you with personal problems right now, but you do know him."

"Right now Zodd would be careful to shield you, as I tried to shield Nrrna," and he looked lovingly at her.

"Who refuses to be shielded," Nrrna said on a purr, "just as Kelly does."

"I most certainly am capable of taking care of myself," Kelly said vehemently. "Oh, Todd and that damned awkward sense of honor of his! Well, he wouldn't be Todd without it."

Hrriss contented himself with a nod. "Be yourself. Be helpful, be cheerful. And now let us all be helpful and see what we can learn." He glided across the room to the computer station and flicked it on with just the nail of his first finger. Sitting down, he logged on his user number. "I shall begin with Hrrula's ranch. He mourns every time one of his hrrsses goes missing. It is a personal affront to his care of them. I will drop a note to obtain permission."

Nrrna and Kelly watched while the data base brought up the user message board. Hrriss had his fingers poised over the keyboard when the screen cleared to show the last user number accessing the file.

"I cannot continue," Hrriss said, his voice sad and reluctant. "That is Zodd's number at the bottom."

"But if he's not on the net now, surely . . ."

"Not now. The time indicates that he logged off thirty minutes ago."

"Then go ahead."

"I cannot. It might be construed as an infringement of our oath not to contact each other. What if it was suggested that he left messages in a file for me to find and erase?"

"Sometimes . . ." Kelly raised hands above her head in pique, then lowered them, accepting such a scrupulous interpretation of their restriction. "You're becoming as paranoid over this as Todd."

"Thank you," Hrriss said solemnly. "In that context, it is a compliment."

Kelly rolled her head and threw up her hands again, this time turning to Nrrna for guidance. "Well, then, Nrrna. It's up to us. We'll investigate on our own, won't we?" Nrrna nodded enthusiastically. "So move out of that chair and let either me or Nrrna log on. Get you out of the room so you cannot be tempted, scaredy cat," and Kelly made shooing gestures with her hands at Hrriss. "If you're so concerned about our involvement, we may or may not tell you what we learn. Your place or mine, Nrrna?"

"Stay here!" Hrriss said, his tone just short of pleading. "I will not look." And he went to sit on the pillows farthest from the computer station.

"You can be in the same room with us while we're jeopardizing our reputations in helping you?" Kelly said teasingly.

"You both do us honor," Hrriss said gravely, and picked up a tape viewer, turning his head away. "But please tell me when you have located that leopard Appaloosa hide."

chapter seven

Kelly found Ali Kiachif in the pub of the Launch Center, weaving to a circle of his captains a story of derring-do during an ion storm in which he and one of his men had rescued the ship, getting the cargo and everyone on board to their destination with nary a scratch. The Codep captain's talk was punctuated with alliterative triads and circumlocutory references, but he had a knack for making a story come to life. When the others drifted apart to discuss the merits (and veracity) of his tale, Kelly approached him.

"Captain Kiachif?"

The spacer looked up. "What may I do for you, little lady?"

"My name's Kelly Solinari. I'm a friend of Todd Reeve."

"That's something we have in common," he said kindly. "Come and commune, with a cup of cheer?"

"No, thank you," Kelly said, declining the offer of a drink. "I don't really feel very cheery. His father said that you offered to help clear him of these accusations against him."

"I've been of that mind, if you understand me."

Kelly dropped her voice to a discreet whisper. "It is Admiral Landreau, isn't it, who hates Todd and his father enough to frame them?"

"Hates 'em lock, stock, and block. Always has since they made a fool of him.

Only he made more of a fool of himself. They didn't have to help much, if you see what I mean," Kiachif said. Having spoken his mind in as guarded voice as she had used, he took a deep drink and let out a sigh of satisfaction as he put the glass down.

"You don't happen to remember any other distinctive horses wearing Reeve markings?"

Kiachif screwed up his face. "I remember that one, like I told Ken. But perfect pat and plain, Miss Kelly, I didn't think much of that incident. You see, that Aden feller, their manager, was doing the shipping, so it seemed natural that all the horses had Reeve Ranch marks. That leopard-spotted one just stood out so much among the bays and browns."

"But it did have a Reeve brand on it, then?"

"Yup, it surely did."

"But how could it have?" Kelly's voice went squeaky as she tried to keep it low and couldn't repress her outrage.

"Well, now, the freeze brand is not supposed to be alterable. Technique's practically perfect. But nothing's perfect."

"Oh, don't tell me someone has a system for altering brand marks! Can you think of the havoc that'll cause?"

"Nope, don't want to think about it. I want to think how I can prove Todd Reeve never rustled nothing in his life, never stole nothing, never fiddled with log tapes or deviated from his registered flight plans. I want to think how ships been getting through one of the most secure security systems in the galaxy. That's what I want to think about. And this helps." He lifted his empty glass and signaled a passing barman. "Bring the bottle!"

When the bottle had been brought he inspected the cap with a narrowed eye before he broke the seal and filled his glass. Kelly was somewhat astounded by his capacity but she kept her expression polite.

"Can't be one of the Codeps. I got them under my thumb," and he held it up, flat and broad and stained, "if you know what I mean. They know all better'n accept stolen goods 'cause it makes me mad and besides that makes it look like the government's condoning theft. Fred Horstmann was some upset about that bundle of hides but I calmed him down. That Zapata provenance checked out genuine. So we got to go back further in this rustling-business, hide-marking, moneymaking nonsense. I do remember"—Kiachif paused thoughtfully—"carrying a feller back to Earth. He'd done his prison term. Knew all about lasers did Askell Klonski. A weasely little wart, if my memory doesn't mislead me. Claimed he could change a tattoo of a wanton, winking woman so she was blinking with the other eye and you'd never know it hadn't been that way to start."

Kelly smothered a laugh, for his words conjured up an indescribable vision. Kiachif held up his hand.

"He'd be just the sort to deftly do the deed, if you know what I mean. Now, I don't know if he was bragging or not. Those types do. He'd served his sentence, but he didn't learn it, if you understand me. The guards in the galley said he was a genius in laser techniques. Served as a trustee his last years on the Rock because he was the only one who could fix the alarm system. He was so good no slips, skips, or blips went undetected. No escapes at all during his tenure. Shortened his sentence slightly, where it shouldn't have ended at all, if you follow me. If I hadn't had orders signed by Varnorian himself, I doubt I would have carried him anywhere."

"Where is he now?" Kelly asked eagerly.

Kiachif massaged his whiskers. "Still on Earth, so I hear. No decent colony would have him. He was pushed in on a snooty section of Corridor and Aisle, to the infinite consternation of his neighbors. They say he's 'not our type, dear.' " Kiachif did a humorous imitation of a proud matron looking down her nose at Kelly. "Spending a lot of money, too. I'd like to know where he got it. With his record, the chances that it was hardly honest are high."

"Hmm," Kelly said thoughtfully. "Any chance of contacting him soon?"

Kiachif nodded his head up and down, refilling his glass again. "Strangest part is that that man was released just about ten years ago."

"Oh!"

"That's what I said. Ten years ago. Not so long before I saw that leopardy horse."

The moon played hide-and-seek with the clouds as the two girls sneaked down toward the transportation grid on the Hrruban side. A thin spot of light penetrated the clouds, striking the ground in front of them, and they ducked behind the bushes. Kelly hoped there were no small nocturnal predators abroad, not when they didn't wish to draw attention to themselves. Night critters all had mean bites.

"You do know how to set the grid, don't you?" Kelly asked Nrrna in a tone barely above a whisper.

"I do, but, Kelly," Nrrna replied, "you know this is highly illegal."

"So is what they're doing to Todd and Hrriss," was Kelly's whispered reply. "Time's running out. Ali Kiachif thinks he knows the man who could have used a laser to change animal brands and he's on Earth, so that's where I've got to go and fast. If we can just cast doubt on one of those phony charges against Todd and Hrriss, we might be able to prove that a conspiracy exists. If we can't, who knows what will happen to them—or to Doona."

Nrrna sighed. "I know, I know. But you must be very careful. If it was discovered that I assisted you to grid back . . ."

Kelly brought her face very close to Nrrna's. "I'd never tell who helped me, Nrrna. Anyway, who's going to know, if we keep to the schedule you worked out? I'll get to the medical supply warehouse on Earth. You just make sure you're here to rescue me when the pallet comes, all right?" She squeezed Nrrna's hand for confidence.

"A female shouldn't be so fearless," Nrrna said.

"Where did you get the idea I was fearless?" Kelly demanded. "I'm terrified but that doesn't keep me from doing it, because it's the only way I can help Todd." She took three deep breaths. This was worse than watching Big Mommies heading toward you. "And it's your way of helping Hrriss. So let's get it done. 'To she who dares falls the prize,'" she muttered to herself before she beckoned for Nrrna to lead the way.

When they reached the grid, there was no one in sight. Kelly didn't at all like using the Hrruban grid: it made her nauseous. Nevertheless she jumped lightly to the platform, turned to stand inside the pillars, and held on to them for support until her knuckles hurt. Silently she begged Nrrna to hurry as the slender Hrruban bent over the controls. The grid beneath her shoes started to vibrate. She barely had time to register that effect before the misting clouded her immediate vicinity.

"Good luck," came Nrrna's soft voice, and lingered as Doona dissolved around her friend.

Kelly materialized inside the transport chamber on Earth. Nrrna had carefully chosen a time when Hrringa was unlikely to be on duty. The only light was the circular glow of the clock calendar facing the grid. It was not quite dawn here on Earth. As Nrrna had suggested, a time when security guards of any species are likely to be less alert. So all those excuses she thought up for Hrringa could be forgotten. None of them had sounded very convincing anyway. So the first hurdle was over. Now to proceed without getting apprehended on Earth when she wasn't supposed to be here. If she was caught, her career as a diplomat might be over before it had properly begun.

She swallowed hard, trying to open her throat. Fortunately she knew the floor plan of the Hrruban Center. It was in the middle of the Alreldep block, part of the Space Services cube. Once she got out of the building, she should have no problem finding her way around, but there might be sensors and alarms designed to detect body heat or movement. She couldn't remember much about the security measures in the Alreldep block, but there was generally much more fuss about getting in than getting out. If she was caught in the Hrruban Center, it would be obvious that she'd had a Hrruban accomplice, because no Human knew how to operate a Hrruban grid. And, undoubtedly, Nrrna would come forward to share the blame.

Gingerly she moved off the grid, expecting any moment for lights to flash and alarms to shriek. She stepped onto the floor below the platform, her body tense, until she realized she had broken no security circuits. She took a deep breath of relief.

She took a second and a third, forcing herself to calm down so she could think logically how to proceed now. Pending the end of her holiday and her return for a permanent assignment, Kelly's privileges in the Alreldep computers had been suspended. Therefore, she needed someone else's help in finding Ali Kiachif's clever parolee. She knew several people who had the necessary skills, and clearance, to find that file in the central computer complex. But first she had to contact them. She didn't dare use the Hrruban Center's communications units. Hrringa shouldn't have to answer questions about why calls were made from his office in the middle of the night. A public facility would be much more sensible, if farther from her present position.

Her luck seemed to be holding, for the center must have been designed to accommodate visitors appearing through the grid at times without benefit of operator on this end. As her eyes grew accustomed to the dark, she could see a double line of tiny low-intensity lights set into the floor leading away from the grid. Cautiously Kelly followed them to the door. She tried the handle, hoping that she hadn't come all this way only to be locked in the Hrruban Center all night long. As the handle moved without hindrance, she murmured a thanksgiving. It probably locked on the outside. It swung easily and silently open.

No alarms sounded and no lights came on. For all her apprehension, she had accomplished the transit without problems. In no time, she found an exit Aisle and was shortly in the main Corridor of Alreldep block and in the main swim of foot traffic without drawing any attention. Now to find a communications kiosk.

The hour may have favored her undetected arrival on Earth, but this was the time when late-shift workers were abroad, and a certain dangerous element of society crept out of their lairs, dens, and hiding places to catch the unwary for what they might have of value about their persons. Proper citizens were too afraid of Aisle and Corridor gossip to report assaults or robberies, so the petty criminals were bold as well as vicious. Kelly was Doonan bred as well as born, and trained to take care of herself, but she didn't want to be noticed. To deflect a would-be assailant would be easy but it would certainly identify her as a most unordinary pedestrian.

Cautiously she kept glancing right and left. No monitors were in view. The gray passage with its moving conveyor belts carried scattered traffic. It wasn't elbow-to-elbow as it was at major shift change times, though there seemed to be as many as Doona had hosted for the Snake Hunt. As she watched all the dutiful citizens in their dull muddy clothing, one mumbled an apology under his breath and his fellow passengers moved aside so he could get off without touching them.

Kelly stepped carefully onto the far edge of the belt, keeping her head down so that no one would look closely at her. She concentrated on walking in the short mincing steps she had learned to use in her years on Earth. She adjusted her usual stride, hunched her shoulders, let her arms hang listlessly at her sides, and pretended disinterest in those she passed on the faster belt. It wasn't as hard as she had feared. The greater gravity of Earth made her muscles work harder at keeping the same pace. The one precaution she had taken before leaving Doona was to alter the vibrant shade of her hair with a dulling brown rinse. It would wash right out, but she'd recognized the wisdom of that artifice. She hadn't had time to search for her old student tunics but she'd worn the dullest, grungiest clothes she owned. Even these were a little bright in comparison with the garments of shift workers at five o'clock in the morning. However, she wasn't going to be on the beltway very long and no one was paying any attention to her. She remembered to take shallower, grudging breaths, just like everyone else. That way she also avoided "tasting" some of the stink of an overcrowded city. Had the air got worse in the short time since she'd left? Or was it the shocking change from breathing the exhilarating air of Doona?

As soon as she spotted a communications kiosk, she muttered the appropriate apologies and stepped off. Her fellow riders carried past her without ever looking up. Monitors might be watching: they always were even if Earth was less restrictive than it had been a quarter century earlier. Controls remained in place to handle the offenses, both real and imagined, of the multiple billions of Humans who lived in such restricted space.

The booth provided her with complete privacy once she shut the door and activated the "engaged" signal. Now it was decision time. Which of her former friends could she positively rely on? Who was well enough placed to get the information she needed? There were rewards available to those who turned in miscreants. Returning without leave was only a misdemeanor but she didn't want to risk even that. One by one, Kelly considered a list of her fellow university students. Cara Martinek was a supply clerk in the Spacedep offices. She couldn't inquire about a former felon with impunity. Jane Kaufenberg worked as a senior researcher at the Amalgamated Worlds Library. Unfortunately Jane probably wouldn't have the necessary clearances to access Alreldep and Spacedep records. She was also rather prissy and would very likely balk at the thought of making an illegal data search. Dalkey Petersham? He was bright, and had graduated first in his class from his Section Academy before attending the university. Kelly hesitated to approach him, even though they had once worked together on a class project—or perhaps because they had worked together. Dalkey was good, but his after-school thoughts went in one direction only, and Kelly had always told him no. Still, he did work for Landreau, in the right department, and he might even have heard office gossip.

Kelly checked her reflection in the viewscreen. With her fingers, she swiped her hair into place. It was a little earlier than was decent to make a comunit call, but she remembered that Dalkey worked first shift. He should already be awake.

The unit in Dalkey's apartment answered after the first blink. Kelly plastered on a big smile as the camera changed to live. "Dalkey! Hi!"

"Kelly!" She was right Dalkey was up and dressed. He was still rail-thin, and his hair was brusquely chopped into the bureaucrat's unbecoming clip. He wasn't bad-looking, but there had always been something too smooth about him that turned her off. Trying to be impartial, she had to admit that there was never anyone so obviously born to wear a narrow-necked suit. "Are you back on Earth?"

"I am," Kelly said, and let out a deep breath. Once she uttered the next phrases, she was committed. "Can I come over and talk to you? I'm not far from your Aisle. I've got a favor to ask."

Dalkey looked surprised but pleased. "Sure. I've got thirty before I've got to punch in. Come and have breakfast."

Kelly paid a credit into the kiosk and accepted a receipt chit from the slot so the door would open. Then she retraced her steps to the Corridor. Dalkey lived one more Aisle over, and down to the right several hundred meters on the same level as the Hrruban Center. Several times along the way, she had to force herself to slow down and remember to bow her head like native Terrans. People were beginning to notice her. Kelly bit her lip and concentrated on the appropriate mincing steps, though it was permissible to move slightly faster in an Aisle. She couldn't take any chance that a sharp-eyed monitor might become suspicious and whisk her off the Aisle into Poldep headquarters.

Dalkey was waiting right inside the door of his apartment. He lived in a block of flats occupied mainly by government employees in the Space Services. With an elaborate bow, he escorted her inside.

"Welcome back, Kelly. May I hope that you're back on Earth for a long stay?"

"Actually not," she said, glancing around. The room was a typical bachelor pad. The Residential and Housing Administration allowed the minimum amount of space for single people. The place was sparsely furnished, the walls one of the neutral colors permitted, but it held one surprise: a very colorful tapestry in the Doonan style which brightened the room immensely. Kelly didn't recognize the weaver, but it was an excellent piece of work. In her eyes, that upgraded Dalkey a notch above the usual run of bureaucrats. "Thank you for the invitation to breakfast. Can you really spare the calories?"

"Sure can," Dalkey said, waving her to a seat. "I have more than I need. I keep some of the excess on credit for times when friends drop in, such as now." He programmed two breakfast meals out of the food machine and smiled at her as the characteristic whirring began behind the panel.

Synth-food! Kelly smiled bravely back, wondering if she could keep from gagging. The moment she left for Doona weeks ago, she had gladly put the horrors of synthesized food behind her.

The hatch opened to reveal two plates. Several different grayish or pale tan masses were arranged on each.

"Here we are," Dalkey said cheerfully, as if conferring a real treat, as he brought the steaming plates over to the table and placed one before her. "Go right ahead." He slid into the chair opposite her and began on his own food.

From long experience Kelly remembered which lump was supposed to simulate eggs, and that the next was a milled, grain colloid, but the last one's origin she had never been able to figure out. Certainly it could never have been meat, and it wasn't sweet enough to be fruit. She knew that only because the saccharine dessert lump that followed the midday meal was supposed to be fruit.

Dutifully Kelly picked up her fork and started to eat. With the first mouthful the flavor, or lack of it, brought back memories of four long years of makebelieve comestibles. She reminded herself that billions of Terrans started every single day with this food. It was healthy, contained every vitamin and mineral necessary for life, and was easily digested. It was still disgusting. She thought she was doing fairly well at disguising her distaste until a tiny chuckle brought her attention back up to Dalkey. He was watching her with an impish gleam in his eyes. He waggled his fork at her plate.

"Not what you got used to on holiday, is it, colony girl?"

"Well"—Kelly laughed self-deprecatingly, putting her fork down—"when you grow up eating real food, it's hard to adjust to a synthetic substitute. If you hadn't been born here, you'd know what I mean." The inadvertent use of Kiachif's favorite bridging phrase reminded her of her errand. "Look, I'd be happy to send you some fruit and things from Doona, so you can find out what you've been missing."

"From the look of you, plenty," Dalkey said, raising an eyebrow. "You don't need to finish the meal, if you can't stand it."

Gratefully Kelly got up to put the dish into the hatch. As she turned back to the table, she found Dalkey standing over her. She started around him, but he pinned her against the wall, his hands on her shoulders.

"So," Dalkey said, lowering his eyelashes seductively. "Come on. Out with it. You didn't come back here just so I can look into your beautiful eyes, although I'm always happy to have that opportunity. What's the favor you need?"

Kelly squeezed back against the synthesizer hatch so there was a few centimeters breathing room between them. The expectant expression on his face alarmed her. She had spent all that time worrying whether anyone would notice her on the street when she should have been figuring out how to fend off Dalkey's advances. He was taller than she was and thin; even his neck was thin. He needed more muscle on him. She could probably knock him down with just a good hefty push. Which wouldn't get her the favor she needed, and she didn't need a wrestling match. Resolutely, so he might realize she had other things on her mind, she folded her arms over her chest.

"All right, here it is," she blurted. "I need to find a man, housed somewhere in the blueblood Corridors. He was released from a prison planet about ten years ago. He was an expert in laser technology and he's been given some kind of annuity. I need to know why. The safety of two of my dearest friends is at stake, not to mention the continuation of the Doona colony."

He gave her a measuring look. "And in return?" he asked, running the back of his hand down her cheek. "Surely you're not going to offer me a silly case of Doona oranges for performing an illegal act with such broad-reaching consequences? Spacedep frowns on people trying to penetrate the privacy files of a former convict. I could be exiled to a mining planet, and so could you for asking. Hard labor."

Kelly nearly asked him what he did want, and realized that she didn't have to. She decided to tell him the truth, and trust to his discretion.

"Dalkey, two friends of me and my family are being framed for crimes that there's no way they could have, or would have, committed. I have it on very good authority that this man might know something about the method that was used to incriminate them. He's the right kind of expert, and he seems to have more money than someone recently paroled ought to have. It's also very odd that a man who faced a life sentence should be paroled, at just about the time we have now discovered a conspiracy was evolved to discredit my friends. He could be an essential party to that conspiracy. I always thought of you as a person with a fine sense of justice. I'm appealing to that now." And she looked Dalkey straight in the eye.

"You've got me interested, I'll say that much. Too many criminals get loose and there've been gangs that have done serious damage. So what sort of crimes are your friends supposed to have committed?"

"Horse rustling, theft of antiquities, possession of stolen goods, and breaking prohibitions set by the Treaty of Doona," Kelly replied, still keeping eye contact. "No matter what you decide, please keep this confidential."

"You just bet I will," Dalkey said with a weak laugh. "As a colonial, couldn't you have fallen for small-time offenders? I'm sure not in your class." He stepped back then, still shaking his head as he let his arms fall to his sides. Kelly gulped in relief and flushed with embarrassment.

Dalkey winked at her consternation. "You don't have to look so surprised. I may not be the man you thought I was, but I'm not the one you were afraid I was either. Ah, ah, ah, don't deny it!" He shook a finger under her nose. "On the other hand, if you're feeling grateful later on, I wouldn't refuse."

He gestured for her to sit on his couch, an old piece Kelly remembered from his student digs and a lot more comfortable than it looked.

"Now, suppose you acquaint me with all the details you've got about this mysteriously paroled felon," he said. "I don't suppose you've got a name?"

"Captain Kiachif knew him as Askell Klonski."

"He'd change his name first thing," Dalkey said, "to shield his real identity. Or maybe that was the name he changed to. Never mind. What else do you know?"

While Kelly talked, he made notes by hand on an old piece of film. "Best not to enter anything on a computer, even for immediate printout and erasure. You never know when the government monitors might choose to check for employee subversion."

Kelly was impressed by his caution. "You surprise me, Dalkey. Thank you."

"Oh, it's not such a surprise. I'm not quite the perfect cog in the machine yet. You know, I've always been attracted to you, partly because you come from Doona. You seemed so much freer than most of the other girls. A pity that freedom didn't extend to the sensual pleasures." Kelly eyed him warily, wondering if he was going to make a grope. He pursed his lips, amused by her. "I'll help you because it's one way for me to get back at the upper-up bureaucrats. There are dirty tricks being played on other people, not just your friends, and I'm getting sick of them. Are all the government services as dirty as Spacedep?" He made a face.

Kelly hurried to reassure him. "No, they're not. Alreldep isn't, otherwise I wouldn't be staying with it. Sumitral's a straightforward man, and he attracts people of a similar stripe."

"Stripe?" Dalkey asked.

"That's a Doonan compliment. You should transfer to his service. Or," Kelly said, laying a hand on Dalkey's arm, "opt for Doona the next time you hear of a residency opening. I'm a citizen. I can sponsor you if you want to come. You could work in the Treaty Center. You've got the right kind of training."

"You'd do that for me? Just like that?" Dalkey asked, snapping his fingers. Kelly nodded. "Yes, I believe you would, colony girl." Then he grinned wryly. "So it's to my advantage to help your friends clear themselves, thus keeping the Doona Experiment going. Fair deal. Look, you'd be safest staying here in my apartment while I get the data crunching. What monitors don't see, they can't report. I don't share with anyone, so you wouldn't be disturbed. If you don't feel comfortable," and Dalkey eyed her for a long moment, "I've some friends who work in Residence Administration and maybe they can let you crash somewhere. It may take a couple of days to snoop into the right files."

"A few days? I don't have that much time, Dalkey. I've got to go back to Doona tomorrow, no matter what. I don't mind sleeping on the couch either: it's not that uncomfortable."

"No, you'll sleep in the bed," Dalkey insisted. She opened her mouth to protest, and he clicked his tongue chidingly. "Ah, ah, ah, there you go again. I can sleep on the couch. Especially if my courtesy gets me out of Spacedep. Oops, five to the starting clock. I'd better go and sign in. I'll see you after shift."

Kelly's conscience stung her as Dalkey saluted her rakishly and stepped out of the door. She'd had to revise her opinion of him upward. During their years at school, she had never had the courage to brave her way past his cool façade: an impenetrable barrier to the self-effacing colonial girl she'd been. She was sorry now that she'd been so reserved that she'd missed the chance to know someone who could have been a good friend.

The time passed with maddening slowness. Kelly tried to sleep but the walls seemed to close in on her. They weren't that far apart. She was very tense during the first few hours, afraid that a friend of Dalkey's might decide to visit him. Then she reminded herself that everyone would know Dalkey was at work. She didn't dare use any of the electronics, for fear of alerting the residence monitors, who would also know that no one should be in the Petersham flat. So she didn't, for fear she might be apprehended as a burglar, taken into custody, and have to explain why she was on Earth when she wasn't supposed to be. She'd be incarcerated on Earth: never see Doona—or Todd—again. Years of claustrophobia and synth-food! She paced out the dimensions of both of the small rooms over and over again. The apartment was about three times the size of her student studio flat. It astonished her to recall that she had actually existed for four years in a box that was smaller than Calypso's stable.

Dalkey had only a few nonfilm books on his shelf. One of them was an antiquated economy text. Another was an old, old copy of a novel about a great lover of the fifteenth century. She smiled, wondering if Dalkey considered himself a latter-day Casanova. For lack of better occupation, she began to read.

"Kelly?" a voice prodded her softly. "Shift's over."

To Kelly's drowsing unconscious, the voice was unfamiliar. Alarmed, she shook herself out of a sound sleep and sat up. Dalkey Petersham was looking down at her, smiling. She remembered then where she was: on his couch in his apartment on Earth. The swashbuckler novel was open upside down on her stomach.

"I want you to look at this," Dalkey said, nudging her over so he could sit down. "Behold the product of many hours of furtive work. I hope you appreciate this. Lucky today wasn't a busy day." He handed her a film printout of a residence document. "I'm glad you didn't want the names and addresses of a whole host of people. It took forever just to get this data. The system hasn't been debugged since ice covered the Earth. I lived in fear while the computer was processing. I wanted to climb through the screen and bang its little chips together. You're right by the way. There is such a man who knows lasers. He is a former felon, by the name of Lesder Boronov. His name's been changed to Askell Klonski, and he does live in a fancy part of town."

"Oh, Dalkey, you're amazing!" Kelly said, devouring the closely typed sheet. "How did you find him?"

"Strange to say, he was in the Spacedep file index, bold as brass. It required a little special jimmying, because it was restricted under the Spacedep privacy seal, but I managed to push my way in."

"Spacedep?" Kelly asked, staring at him. "Why?"

Dalkey raised his hands helplessly. "Who knows? But only Landreau himself, Commander Rogitel, and a couple of other top brass normally have access to that index. See where it says that he's been retained for 'special services.' Special services covers a multitude of bureaucratic sins."

"I could cite a few right now. You didn't have the same sort of luck about his financial records?"

"I couldn't get more than a credit balance," Dalkey said with a rueful expression. "My supervisor came by, saw the kind of screen I had up, and said if I was doing my personal banking on Spacedep time I might as well go officially on break. He watched me the rest of the afternoon, but I had all I could access without generating suspicion. He got a fine big credit balance, that Boronov!"

Kelly agreed. "But did he make it the way I think he did . . . ?"

"Which is?"

"I don't want to say it for fear I'm wrong," Kelly said, not wishing to cross her luck at this juncture. "What are those other printouts?"

"More research," Dalkey told her with considerable satisfaction. "While I was in the index, I got curious. Do you know that there isn't just our laser friend here under the seal? There are several people, all listed as performing special, unspecified services, and getting paid hefty hunks of credit. I got to the initial screen, showing their profiles. There wasn't time to get more, but I'll look into it when I have half a chance. Rather a lot of them are out on early remission."

Kelly's eyes widened. "So Klonski-Boronov isn't an isolated case. They've got a fileful of dirty tricksters."

"All on file," Dalkey said, disgusted. "More than I feel comfortable knowing about, too. Makes me more fed up with Spacedep. Codep's no better. I contacted one of my pals at lunch. He ran a similar check for me in the Codep index. He found something like this there, too, before he got caught accessing forbidden files. As soon as you're safely off Earth, I'll bring him to the attention of Amalgamated Worlds Administration as a whistle-blower. They'll have to take his statement as a public document, so he doesn't unexpectedly get shipped off to a mining colony."

"I didn't intend for anyone to get in trouble," Kelly said, concerned. But she held tightly on to the film printout Dalkey had given her. It wasn't full proof, but here in her hands was the beginning of what she needed to clear Todd and Hrriss.

"Not your fault," Dalkey stated promptly. "There's more than one of us sick of the corruption. Before they took him away, he managed to get his printout to me. They're trying to trace down what he was doing and who he saw afterward, but I'll wait till you're clear. They have their dirty secrets, but you are my clean one."

"I'll keep faith with you, Dalkey," said Kelly, "as soon as ever I can. But these," and she shook the printouts, "mean that Todd was right. Landreau is involved and using Spacedep facilities. I can't take the chance that I'll get caught before I can get these to an official source. I don't like mines either."

She had Dalkey make a call to the Poldep office from a public kiosk, requesting a confidential appointment on matters concerning the Doona Experiment. Kelly prepared to leave as the hour approached. She was surprised to find that she wasn't as nervous as she had been when she arrived through the grid. In fact, she was almost looking forward to her meeting with a Poldep official.

"As soon as I get more data, I'll send it out to you," Dalkey promised. "Meanwhile, you watch out for yourself."

"I want to thank you, Dalkey," Kelly said, kissing him on the cheek. "You've been a gem."

"Just don't forget your promise to sponsor me to Doona," Dalkey said. "I'm going to be counting on it." He grinned ingenuously. "If I get caught, I'll need somewhere to go. Come back if you can or need to. And good luck."

It was not unheard-of for informants to request informal meetings with Poldep. Many cases would never have been solved if ordinary citizens, taking advantage of anonymity to protect themselves and their families, couldn't come forward with incriminating information and data. Few did it with malice, for Poldep could turn an entirely different face toward the prankster. Dalkey had assured Kelly that Poldep wouldn't pry into her true identity, for that would defeat the purpose of anonymity. Kelly hoped that the immunity extended to no curiosity on how she had travelled to Earth.

The Poldep offices differed from those of the other government services only by the color of their uniforms: black. Even the entry operators, and the officers, bailiffs, and investigators swarming in and out of the main entrance wore black. The color was ominous and off-putting, but she supposed that was intentional.

The big man behind the desk in the little room was not unfamiliar, but he did not appear to recognize her: the hair dye had been a very smart idea. True, she had only seen him from a distance in the halls of Alreldep and once on Doona. They hadn't actually met. DeVeer made the rounds of his beat periodically in a small, fast-moving scout ship. He had a reputation for being straightforward and honest. Firmly she overcame her feelings of nervousness and gave him her hand. The Poldep captain shook it.

"I'm Sampson DeVeer, miss. What name are you using?"

So the anonymity was genuine. "I don't know how much you have to know about me to believe what I'm going to tell you," Kelly said, stalling.

DeVeer gave her a brief smile. "I find the facts often speak for themselves. How about a pseudonym for the time being? That's not incriminating."

"All right," Kelly said boldly, "call me Miss Green." That was stupid, she admonished herself, but apt. She was green enough in more than name. Imagine blurting out a name so close to her own. But she didn't really care. Kelly was surprised how calm she felt now that she was facing the Poldep man. She recognized that she was riding the high of success when she had expected none. She was surprising herself. She'd been a dutiful child, a good student, an obedient second on Snake Hunt, and a biddable employee of Alreldep. But now, for her friends' sake, she was discovering a lot about what she could dare and do.

"What can I do for you, Miss Green?" DeVeer asked.

"You're familiar with the situation on Doona?" she asked. His eyebrows lowered, and she went on quickly. "I know there's lots of situations, but I mean the one concerning the Reeve Ranch. And the son, Todd. He's being accused of horse rustling, smuggling, and entering restricted zones. And you've got to believe me when I tell you that he wouldn't do any of those things. He's innocent."

"Ah, yes," DeVeer said, tenting his fingertips. "I know the circumstances. In fact, I recently had an interview with his father. He had hides bearing freeze marks for his ranch on animals he never owned. The hides had been recycled from Zapata Three with a genuine provenance. Yet he claims the brands have to have been altered."

"They were! I think I know how it was done," Kelly blurted. "I mean, I believe I know who could have done it."

DeVeer's expression didn't change, but his moustache twitched. "Tell me more," he said.

She produced the first of her film prints and put it before him. "This man was paroled from a labor colony and returned to Earth. He's a laser expert and innovator. His name was Lesder Boronov, but he's called Askell Klonski now."

"What makes you think that he involved himself in stock theft? Name changes are not illegal."

"He might not be involved directly, but he came into a lot of money when he was released," Kelly said. She produced the printout of Klonski's credit balance.

DeVeer read over both films carefully and made notes on a pad as he scanned. He glanced at her from under beetled brows. "May I ask where you got these screens?"

"The one about Boronov is from Spacedep sealed files. I . . . would like to protect my sources but they are reliable. I expect Poldep would be able to check the information. You can see that Klonski has been paid sums for 'special services.' Now"—Kelly swallowed, because she was diving forward into conjecture—"what services could a laser expert do to earn that much money?"

"The matter could be legitimate."

"Then wouldn't he be listed in Spacedep's regular contractor file?" Kelly asked. "Why hide him under the privacy seal? And he's not the only one." She showed him Dalkey's other printouts. "These men are all ex-felons, all received early paroles, and they're all under similar privacy seals."

DeVeer didn't insist that she identify her sources, which was an immense relief to her. She hoped that he thought that she herself was the Spacedep employee who had pulled the files. He read the third set of films with the same focused attention he had read the other two. Partway through the first page, he pulled over his computer terminal. He spent some minutes entering data and looking from the screen to the printouts. Then he became engrossed, fingers stabbing at function keys, tapping out new requests. Kelly sat with her hands clutched in her lap, her eyes pinned on the Poldep investigator.

"Interesting," he said, looking up at her after nearly an hour. He leaned back in his chair, tented his fingertips together again, and fixed his keen gaze on Kelly.

Kelly leaned across the table. "Then you believe me? Can you find out if Klonski does have a way to alter the freeze-dry brands?"

The chief investigator smiled thinly under his moustache. "I'll try to help you, Miss Green, but I have only your suspicion, based on hearsay, that this Klonski might—just might—be involved in illegal activities. Even if he admitted to developing such a process, that wouldn't automatically clear your friends. They could have made use of his 'special services' as easily as anyone else. In fact, some of that large sum in his credit account could have been paid in by them."

"But they didn't. They didn't!" In her frustration, Kelly banged her fists on his desk. "Why would he be in the Spacedep files if that bunch didn't use his 'special services'? And you surely don't think they'd let him take outside contracts!" DeVeer smiled at that remark. "This is the first real evidence to support my friends' innocence. Won't you help me prove it? Please! There's really a lot at stake!"

DeVeer tapped his fingertips together. "Yes, I will have to initiate an investigation. Not necessarily on your friends' behalf, for some of those charges do not lie in my jurisdiction. But rustling does. The problem of stock theft has recently trebled. New worlds are desperate for all kinds of stock, not just horses. Every animal must be marked and records kept of inoculations to prevent the spread of disease, and to be sure that livestock is protected against any indigenous problems on their destination planet. But if the marks can be skillfully altered, then our very complex disease control system has been bypassed. That can't be allowed to happen, especially on an increasingly larger scale. One of my priorities is putting an end to illicit traffic in livestock."

"Then Doona isn't the only planet to have trouble with rustlers?" Kelly asked.

"Unfortunately, it isn't. But you may just have brought me the tip I've needed."

He smiled at her, and his face changed from an austere mask to that of a warm and charming man. "If this Klonski has an illegal means of altering brand marks, I can help you clear your friends at least of that charge. And Klonski is on parole?" DeVeer sat up and entered the identification number from the film into his computer console. "Yes, he is. The creation of a process used for illegal purposes is a parole violation. That can land him right back on a penal colony world, with or without Spacedep approval. I see he's due for a meeting with his parole officer, should have met with her yesterday. Didn't show. That gives me the right to have a few words with him." DeVeer stood up, indicating the interview was at an end.

"May I come along?" Kelly pleaded. The chief considered the question for a long moment.

"It is not necessary for an anonymous accuser to face the defendant prior to a hearing. In fact, it could be dangerous."

"Look, Mr. DeVeer," Kelly began earnestly, "I've risked a lot to lay this information before you. It might even be dangerous for me to go back out into Aisle and Corridor if anyone guesses where I've gone. If I'm with you, I'm safe."

"I could arrange for protective custody for you . . ."

"Mr. DeVeer, I only feel safe in your presence," she said firmly.

He considered her argument. "It is certainly not regular procedure."

"There's been nothing regular about this whole mess," Kelly replied tartly. "I trust you, Mr. DeVeer. I can be discreet but I'd rather be in your company."

"Would Klonski recognize you? No? That's as well. But there is another aspect you must consider, Miss Green, in this compulsion of yours to stay under my protective wing. Suppose he describes you to his contacts at Spacedep?"

"Let him," Kelly said, sticking her chin up and shoving her shoulders back resolutely.

He handed her a black tunic. "Lift your right hand"—she did—"now swear that you will obey me as your superior," which she did. He fastened a plain bar to the collar tab. "There! You are now a deputy under my direct orders." They left the office together.

The address on Klonski's file was in a block which had been occupied from before living memory by clans calling themselves the First Families. The living spaces bordered on the spacious homes of distant memory and were located in the widest Aisles Kelly had ever seen: Aisles with plants in the malls. Security devices and operatives strode slowly but alertly up and down. She was startled to see several men and women in poorer dress hurrying along between the buildings. Security didn't seem to notice them, and then Kelly realized they were undoubtedly menials, serving in the fine apartments of the wealthy and powerful families. The genuine residents of the houses swept by in much fancier dress, reminiscent of Jilamey Landreau's posh togs.

Kelly and DeVeer made their way as unobtrusively as possible to the address given for their quarry. The Poldep officer pushed a doorbell, and they waited.

"Askell Klonski, also known as Lesder Boronov?" DeVeer asked as the door edged open a crack.

"Who wants to know?" demanded a short, scrawny man through the gap. Kelly recognized him as quickly from Captain Kiachif's description of a warty weasel as from DeVeer's updated file photo.

"Poldep," DeVeer said, flashing his identification. "May we come in?"

"You can state your business first," Klonski said pugnaciously. "I've got nothing to hide from my neighbors."

"You did not keep your appointment yesterday with your parole officer, Mr. Klonski," DeVeer said, keeping his voice low. Klonski wavered for a moment and then flung the door open wide.

"I'm not a well man," and he coughed a few times to prove it. "She knows. She don't hassle me."

"A few moments of your time is all that's required, Mr. Klonski," DeVeer said smoothly.

"Well, if that's all, you can come in," he said, his eyes shifting warily from one to the other of his unwelcome guests.

Klonski's apartment was of the size intended for the use of high-ranking families with two legal children. The main room was palatial compared to Dalkey's, but it had been furnished in a totally haphazard fashion: the furnishings and decorations were obviously expensive but were placed in awkward groupings or hung without care or taste. If Klonski had intended to impress his neighbors with his wealth, he certainly had achieved that aim. Kelly glanced at a brilliant pink couch draped with a handwoven teal and red throw, and shuddered at the effect.

Klonski might be wearing expensive clothing but it could not camouflage his small stature, and the color only emphasized his gritty complexion. The padded tunic did not disguise, much less improve, his narrow chest. So he gave the impression of being held prisoner inside his clothes. The style was practically a parody of what his neighbors wore with elegance.

"I'm respectable now," the man insisted. "Gone straight and square. I'm not supposed to be bothered with parole matters. I call her up when I remember. Give me the usual blab, then you've done your duty and you can leave."

DeVeer drew himself up to his own impressive height and loomed over the little man. "Askell Klonski, not only have you violated the terms of your parole with your nonappearance, but you seem to have violated it much more seriously. We'd like you to come down to Poldep with us and to answer a few questions."

"What about? I haven't done anything wrong."

"That is what we need to determine," DeVeer said.

Klonski eyed them. "You're on a fishing trip, Officer," he said, grinning maliciously. "You haven't got a thing that could make me go anywhere with you. You're from them, out there." He jerked his thumbs toward the apartments on either side of his. "They want me to leave, but I won't. I like it here, see, and I've got a long, long lease. All paid up through the year double-dot."

"Yes, we have that data in our files. But there are other discrepancies in your record that are currently of interest to Poldep."

"Yeah? What, for instance? Ask me anything you want . . . right here." The former felon hitched himself up into a huge, thronelike chair.

"On a routine investigation of your case," DeVeer went on, ignoring the sneering voice, "it would appear that the robbery for which you were incarcerated involved a death."

"It was an accident!" Klonski said agitatedly. "He shouldn't oughta have been there in the first place. That's all in my testimony."

"The laws are explicit in the case of death, whether accidental homicide or premeditated murder. Especially murder. You were rocketed up without the possibility of parole. So how, Askell, were you allowed back on Earth at all?"

"I was given clemency for being a sick man." Klonski essayed a few dry rasping coughs, then he looked up, his expression far more genuinely indignant. "Hey, those records were supposed to be sealed!"

"To Poldep?" DeVeer asked scornfully. "Well, they might remain sealed to the public at large, or they might not. That's up to me—and up to you. I think Poldep might ignore that anomaly if you will help us with our inquiries in another matter. Come down to my office to talk."

There was evidently something in those records which Klonski didn't want made public. Or was there someone he didn't want to know that his file had been opened? He was on his feet and standing by the door, exhibiting a marvelous agility for a man ill to dying from a cough.

"You call for a private copter, then, hear? I don't want to be seen talking to no Poldep inspector." He straightened his tunic as they stepped outside. "I got some standards."

As soon as they had arrived, Klonski made himself comfortable in a chair in DeVeer's office. When the computer recorder was turned on, he took the oath to give a true statement. (Not, Kelly thought, that the truth was likely to mean much to a man like Klonski.)

"So I'm sworn in. Let's get this over with."

DeVeer began austerely, "You're known to have unusual laser skills. We have reason to believe that you have perfected a means to alter or undo freeze-dry chemical brands on the skin of herd animals."

"*What?*" Klonski bounced up and down in his chair in amazement and began to howl with laughter, rolling from side to side, until the tears streamed down his warty face. "That is the most ridiculous thing I ever heard a Poldep say! Ohhhoo, hhahaha!" He was off again in paroxysms of mirth.

With hands lightly clasped on his desk, DeVeer regarded Klonski patiently while he enjoyed his amusement at their expense. Getting madder every moment because she knew this little weasel was a key find, Kelly wanted to box his ears or kick shins or do something to stop him laughing with such abandon. She saw her hope disappearing to the sound of his cackles. They merged into a genuine coughing fit. DeVeer poured a glass of water and passed it on to Klonski, no emotion whatever on his face.

"Me? Rustling?" Klonski demanded when he finally caught his breath. "Waste my time and know-how changing freeze marks? Mind you, that's beyond even me."

"It made a starting point," DeVeer said, not the least bit disconcerted. "A man must keep his skills up or lose them. Right?"

"Ri . . ." Klonski began, and then realized he was being indiscreet. He pressed his lips together.

"However," DeVeer continued, "you do have laser skills and we do believe that a laser technique had to be used to alter freeze marks. Therefore, if you do not wish to be charged with aiding and abetting the theft of livestock and the illegal transportation of animals, you might just clear up the point of what you are doing with your special skills."

"Now, wait a minute . . ." Klonski began, no longer so arrogant.

"You know the drill, my man. Rustling's grand larceny, and between unauthorized planets, it carries a double penalty. There'd be no possibility of parole for an offense of this magnitude." He pulled his console to him and began typing. "We'll just enter you for a preliminary, based on those unusual deposits in your credit account." DeVeer peered at Klonski from under his thick eyebrows.

"You'd never trace the source of those deposits," Klonski said with a sneer, his confidence somewhat revived.

"Really?" DeVeer asked cheerfully. "Anything on a computer tape, no matter which mainframe, can be opened for inspection—especially when a major crime is involved."

"They told me no one could crack their codes!" Klonski was mutinous with fear.

"They?" DeVeer asked softly. "You forget that Poldep has extraordinary powers to investigate any department, given sufficient cause. Rustling is an excellent example." He turned back to his keyboard.

"Stop!" Klonski cried. DeVeer's face was immutable stone. "I never rustled nothing, nor helped no rustlers."

DeVeer pushed the keyboard slightly to one side, folded his arms on his chest, and gazed at Klonski. "I'm waiting."

"I need a deal from Poldep."

"Our budget is exceedingly tight this quarter."

"I don't need credit. I need immunity. I want an undetectable change of identity and location." He paused as DeVeer nodded solemnly. "I didn't help rustlers, and I sure didn't change freeze marks, 'cause you can't. But I'll tell you what I did do. Is that enough to deal?"

"I can't say until I know," DeVeer said. "I may just consider your information sufficient to return you to your current quarters with the parole violation forgotten."

"I gotta have security." Klonski was so insistent about that point that Kelly's hopes began to rise again.

"Security you'll get for cooperating with Poldep."

"Okay," but Klonski's expression indicated he was still dubious. DeVeer just waited while Kelly found it hard to restrain herself from jumping up and shaking the truth out of the weasel. He gave a nervous cough and then said, "What I did do was a little patching and splicing of log tapes. Nothing that looked illegal."

"For that kind of credit?" DeVeer allowed his face to register disbelief.

"And . . ." Klonski hesitated, his eyes darting from DeVeer to Kelly. She tried to look encouraging. "And . . . I showed 'em how to neutralize security systems."

"Really?" DeVeer's response was mild, but Kelly had to grip the arms of the chair to keep from jumping up in exultation. "I thought your specialty was improving such systems."

Feeling slightly more confident, Klonski grinned, showing badly discolored and jagged teeth. "Improve, disimprove. Same techniques needed."

"Who?"

"You think I'm stupid, Polly? No blinding way do I name names. You find 'em yourself with all your extraordinary powers." He leered smugly. "We made a deal. And I don't say nothing more. I got rights, too, you know."

"However, for a new location, new name, and the right to retain the credits in your account, you might nod your head if I drop a familiar name or two?"

Klonski was not too pleased to be probed so deeply but he didn't deny further assistance. DeVeer pulled over a flimsy.

"Your file indicates that you worked for Spacedep before your . . . first prison term," the Poldep inspector said conversationally. Klonski gave a sharp nod of his head and darted a glance at Kelly. "You were in Research and Development, is that correct?" Klonski did not hesitate to nod, since that was known fact. "Wasn't old Bert Landreau in charge of R&D?"

Kelly hoped that DeVeer noticed the shuttered look that altered Klonski's expression.

"Isn't his son an Admiral now?" DeVeer went on in that deceptively casual fashion. This time Klonski's head moved as if physically restricted. "I think that about covers it, Klonski," DeVeer said more briskly. "You'll be moved in the morning to similar quarters in a different sector. New ID will be issued and Klonski/Boronov will be listed as deceased, cause of death, a fatal respiratory condition. Does that suit you?"

Klonski's nod was enthusiastic.

"I'll have you returned in an ambulance to your current residence. Tomorrow a reputable firm of undertakers will arrive and your 'corpse' will be removed for the benefit of any observers." DeVeer pressed a button on his communit and a uniformed constable appeared in the door. "Medical escort is to be provided for this person, Constable. Do you wish a guard?"

Klonski snorted in his arrogance. "No one could get in my place!" Then he clamped his mouth shut, shooting a quick glance at the rigidly attentive constable.

"Use the discreet exit from the block, Constable."

"Very good, sir. This way, sir," and the constable gestured courteously for Klonski to follow him.

"We got a deal, Polly," Klonski said, turning in the door and jabbing his finger at DeVeer, who nodded acknowledgment.

The door hissed shut behind him and Kelly bounced out of the chair in her elation.

"He admitted it. Those log tapes were altered. Todd and Hrriss *are* innocent."

"Do calm yourself, Miss Green," DeVeer said, flicking off the recorder. "This is only the beginning of what is going to be a very difficult investigation."

"But he said he altered log tapes and tinkered with security systems. Don't you see what that means?"

"I see what you wish it to mean, but the wish is not always parent to the proof. However, such statements do cast doubt on the authenticity of the logs in question. Nor did he give us any inkling as to which security systems he has adjusted."

"But don't you see? It has to be the Doona/Rrala satellites. That would explain how rustlers could get in and out with livestock and be undetected!"

"Oh, I take that point, Miss Green. But it doesn't solve the matter of mis-marked hides, does it?"

"No, it doesn't," Kelly said, and then started to giggle, covering her mouth with her hand and shooting an anxious look at DeVeer. "Klonski was so indignant to be taken for a rustler!"

"I have discovered, Miss Green, that there is a certain form of honor among thieves."

"Well, then, honest men ought not to be discredited, should they?"

DeVeer regarded her kindly after that vehement declaration. "No, they should not. I shall consider it my prime obligation and most urgent priority to assist you in clearing the good reputations of those two young persons. *But,*" and he held up his hand warningly when Kelly exclaimed her joy aloud, "to prove that Klonski did, in fact, use his skill on the tapes in question and on the Doonan security satellites is going to take time."

"We don't have time," Kelly said in a despairing wail. "The Councillors will bring Todd and Hrriss to trial any day now. And then there's the Treaty negotiations . . . The charges against Todd and Hrriss were planned to coincide with this critical period. My home is at stake, Inspector DeVeer."

"So you are a Doonan colonial?"

Kelly sighed for her indiscretion.

Not unkindly, he smiled. "Doona must fall or stand on its own merits, but clearly the odds against it have been staked by what does appear to be a genuine conspiracy. Personally I have had doubts about the Experiment, but I was old enough to experience the repercussions of the Siwanna Tragedy, so perhaps I'm not entirely without prejudice. But I try to overcome what I know to have been early conditioning. I think it's a mistake to mix two such advanced races."

"But that's the best kind to mix," Kelly exclaimed. "Equal intelligence and parallel societies with similar aims and mutual respect."

"But Hrrubans are much more powerful than we smaller Humans. And their technology more advanced."

"Not in the same direction ours is. So we've learned from each other . . ."

"They have not granted us that transportation system of theirs . . ."

"And we have not given them the right to build our more sophisticated spaceship engines, so I think we're even on the question of space travel."

"You argue well, Miss Green."

"I've specialized knowledge to back up my arguments, Mr. DeVeer."

"I trust that events will conspire to let us continue. I have never met a more devoted adherent of the Experiment. But, in my estimation, the appalling Si-wanna Tragedy has not been diminished by the short period of Doona's success." He brought himself up short. "You remind me of my daughter. She argues for her causes with all her heart, too. And you've risked much to lay your case before me." He rose to his feet, signalling an end to their discussion.

"I'd risk a lot more!" Kelly got to her feet and shrugged out of Poldep black. "Can you let me know how your investigations progress? Or do you no longer consider me your special deputy?"

"That deputization will be in force for the remainder of your stay on Earth, but I'd prefer that you didn't wander into a situation where I have to notice you officially. I'll be in touch with the communications number that made your appointment with me. And by the way," he said, "next time, please obtain permission to visit Earth. If you have a legitimate reason, or an invitation, there isn't any problem."

Kelly smiled. "You are thorough."

"I like to think that I am, Miss . . . ah, Green." He actually winked at her and she wondered if he had discovered her real identity but thought better about asking. "The amnesty policy is scrupulously maintained."

"Can that cover my 'sources of information,' too?"

DeVeer frowned slightly, then his face cleared. "You did mention that there's someone about to whistle-blow, didn't you? We'll see that your friends are protected if at all possible. I expect there'll be a great deal of housecleaning before this matter is concluded. An official privacy seal is not meant to conceal capital crimes such as grand larceny and security tampering." DeVeer took her hand. "I am grateful to you for your information. Poldep does need the help of all honest citizens, otherwise where would we be? Thank you, Miss Green."

Kelly grinned at him, positive that he did know who she really was. "Thank you, sir."

She spent the night curled up on Dalkey's hard mattress, dreaming of snaking tapes with matched ends that then split apart to reattach themselves to other loose ends, and satellite spheres with the face of Askell Klonski, and each wart on his face another capped sensor.

The medical supply warehouse was in a section of Corridor and Aisle that Kelly had never visited before. She had to descend on a packed elevator through several levels, through the newer, smaller residences of Labor workers, and then pattered off the elevator into the manufacturing zone. Her fellow passengers, mostly maintenance workers for the Air Recycling Service, marched past her in a single mass, almost as if they were stuck together from being squeezed in the elevator.

The noise control standards had evidently been waived for this level, and so had the air purification ordinances. Hooting and wailing from machinery battled with the deafening thrum of turbines and the cumulative babble of Human voices. This Corridor was full of unrelieved gray and black buildings. They looked clean enough—no graffiti, no layers of dirt or filth—but they left her with the feeling that if she touched anything her fingers would come away filmed with soot.

Kelly found the address Nrrna had written down for her and slipped past the great open doors. Inside was the largest single room she had yet seen on Earth. The raftered ceiling loomed the full height of the level. Hundreds of men and women in drab bodysuits and heavy gloves passed her in pursuit of their various tasks. Pallet loaders, large, small, and staggeringly huge, rolled around the floor, picking up crates and packages from teetering stacks of merchandise. The scale of the warehouse amazed her. The entire Doona Launch Center could fit in the middle of this vast facility, and leave room for its normal day's operation on every side, and this facility only forwarded medical supplies to outer worlds.

Stinking of hot oil, the forklifts trundled great bales of goods into giant freight elevators, for conveyance to the lower levels for distribution, or to the surface, where they could be loaded into spaceships. Neither of these two destinations was appropriate for Kelly. She needed to find where a particular small delivery was being prepared. The Hrruban Center grid was only a few meters square.

She had fitted herself out with a clipboard and a small parcel, wrapped under Dalkey's instruction and sealed with a Spacedep logo they had cut out from a discarded film copy. The box was filled with food from his synthesizer. After two unappetizing meals of the stuff at Dalkey's flat, she hoped she wouldn't have to eat it, but who knew how long it would be before she could be rescued from the container? Nrrna might have to wait for solitude to open the crate.

"Is this the shipment for Doona?" Kelly asked in a bored tone, consulting her clipboard. "I've got a parcel to add to it. Spacedep," she added with a nice touch of apathy.

The man glanced up at her with equal disinterest. "Nope. Try dock sixteen."

"Is this the shipment for Doona?" Kelly inquired at dock sixteen.

"It is." The short woman directing the lowering of boxes from one side of the dock onto a pallet glanced back over her shoulder at the tall mousy-haired girl. "Why?"

Kelly's heart gave a little jolt within her. "I, uh, have a package to go on it. Spacedep."

"There's nothing in my manifest from Spacedep for Doona," the woman said, tapping the clipboard she held under her arm.

Kelly pretended disgust. "Well, it was handed over to me this morning to make sure it got aboard."

The woman stopped and flipped open the clipboard. It was full of neat documents, all sealed at the bottom by the departments of authorization. "Codep; Healthdep; Healthdep, that's not here yet; Alreldep; Healthdep . . ." She turned each one over until she came to the last one. "No, nothing from Spacedep. You must have the wrong order." The woman looked up, but her querist was gone. Shrugging, the woman turned back to her bales.

While the woman's attention was focused on the documentation, Kelly had slipped away and squeezed between two large boxes. One of the crates heading for Doona was only half full. Nrrna had arranged for Healthdep on Earth to send just enough sterile gloves to fill half a standard case but too many to be crated in a smaller container. Nrrna and Kelly calculated that there should be enough room for her to fit. Kelly began to look at labels to find the Healthdep shipment. She found it by the logo—a cross and crescent in a circle—marked on a blue crate. She tapped out the security code on the small comp, wriggled into the crate, and pulled the lid down over her, hearing the whirr as the cover locked itself again. Now all she had to do was try to make herself comfortable, and she would be home in hours.

The muffled sounds around her crate got louder, so she had a bit of warning before the box rose into the air and swung wildly from side to side. One of the cranes was doing the transfer. Kelly had the terrifying sensation of flying through the air, followed by a bump that tossed packages of the flimsy gloves all around her. The plastic envelopes stuck to her clothes, hair, and face. She peeled them off, and cupped her hands over her face to keep from being suffocated by the flying packages. As soon as the case was fastened down on the pallet, the gloves settled. She burrowed her way into the packages until only her head and her shoulders were jammed against the side of the box, her feet propped against the lower end and her knees under her chin. Not the most comfortable of positions and she tried to make herself believe that claustrophobia was a small price to pay for the success of her illegal voyage.

The crate jerked again as it started to move sideways, bumping Kelly's head. The whole pallet must be on its way to the Hrruban Center. She could hear the squeak of unoiled wheels as it was pushed onto the transportation grid which rattled under her buttocks. She had little room in which to relieve cramped muscles and half wished that she'd asked Inspector DeVeer to arrange legitimate transport for her back to Doona. But that would have required too many explanations and too much time by ordinary Human spaceship. However uncomfortable, at least this trip would be instantaneous.

Through the sides of the crate, she could hear the low rumble of Hrringa's voice, asking for the cargo manifests. She hoped he didn't have to search each package before sending it. No, she merely heard the telltale beeping of the bomb detector as it was swept over the bales, and then it trundled sideways again. Kelly hoped her bale wouldn't be sent somewhere else in error. All she could do now was wait and try not to worry.

At least she didn't see the transfer mist or feel nauseated by the dislocation amid her padding of glove packets.

chapter eight

Nrrna waited at the transport station. She was trying to appear calm, but she could not control the nervous twitching of her tail tip, a giveaway to anyone watching her. She was no longer of an age where she could have held her tail between her hands to subdue its reaction to her mood.

The Hrruban male who was in charge of the transport grid had passed a few pleasantries with her, but he had to keep his attention on his job, and not on the very attractive female hovering nearby. The timetable on transmissions and receptions was very tight. Two sendings could not be received on the grid at the same time. If one overlapped another, he had to put it on hold until the first one was entirely received.

"The medical shipment is not due from Earth for another thirty minutes," he said once again.

"I know that," Nrrna said, dropping her jaw in an appealing smile to belie her nervousness. "It is very important that I take delivery as soon as possible. There's quite a lot of fur flying over letting the supply of sterile gloves get so low."

"Hmm," grunted the technician, unimpressed. Everyone was always in a hurry. His tail began to switch impatiently.

The Treaty Controller, clad in his magnificent red robes, appeared out of a corridor and addressed the technician, who stood to attention. Nrrna slipped into the shadows of the terminal to keep from being noticed. "Hasn't the transmission from Hrruba arrived yet?" the Controller asked.

The operator made the proper bow to such an important Hrruban. "No, honored sir. It is scheduled to arrive in three dots. You do not have long to wait. I could have notified you if you had called me."

"Hmm," the Treaty Controller growled his dissatisfaction. His eyelids lowered halfway over glaring green. "I was informed that it would be here at half past the tenth hour."

The grid operator courteously gestured to the display of quartz timers, synchronized with grid transporter terminals in the other spheres of Hrruban autonomy. "That time approaches rapidly, honored sir," he said, his voice hoarse.

The Controller turned away from the nervous young Hrruban and noticed Nrrna. To distract the grid operator, she had put on some of her most attractive ornaments, and a spicy cologne which approximated the pheromones of mating. She had not counted on anyone else coming along, especially not the Treaty Controller. At once she assumed a position both humble and hardworking, hoping he would look away. To her horror, she saw his nostrils flare as he scented her.

"Rrrmmm," he purred, moving toward her. "And who is this? What is your name, lovely one?"

Flustered, she murmured her name, and was gently asked to repeat it. "Nrrna."

"Nrrna. A soft name for a soft pelt. I find you most attractive, Nrrna." He rubbed his hand along the length of her arm. Offended by the familiarity of the contact, she moved her arm, trying not to give deliberate insult. After all, she was wearing a provocative scent.

"You honor me, sir, but I am already promised."

"Surely no single male will be sufficient to relieve one as young and feminine as you, Nrrna," the Controller said, pitching his voice intimately. "I would be the one honored if you would choose to favor me with your company."

Nrrna looked to the grid operator for assistance, but he had folded his ears tight to his head in an effort not to overhear. Which was only discreet of him, Nrrna had to admit. Why had she chosen such an alluring scent? She really had left herself open to offers. The operator she could have teased, but it would be most unwise of her to lead on the Treaty Controller.

"Please, sir, I am promised as lifemate." She hadn't wanted to admit that yet. Particularly not to this old male. She edged away. He sidled closer to her, and she could feel the heat of his body against hers and the rising scent of his sensual response to her condition. "I am not yet at full cycle," she added as coolly as she could. Indeed she was a few weeks away from her season and sexual activity would be distasteful. He had no right to be harassing her.

"Really?" and the Controller looked genuinely surprised. "I think perhaps you have misjudged your readiness, soft Nrrna," the Controller suggested in a low voice. "My quarters are most comfortable." He was a much older male, with persuasive ways that should overwhelm such a young and obviously inexperienced female.

She shifted away from him, revolted by his manner. Any decent male would have desisted, but this old stoker obviously didn't recognize a genuine denial.

"The transmission from Earth," the operator announced.

With the agility of her youth, Nrrna sprang toward the pallet in a graceful leap that took the Controller totally by surprise. With her own hands, she helped the operator roll the crate off the transport grid to make room for the next transmission.

However, the Controller, not to be done out of his prize, followed her. Ignoring him, she opened the top crate, which did not contain Kelly, and began to inventory the materials very slowly, checking each box several times as she marked it off on her list.

"One box of size 00 sutures, one box of size 0 sutures, four cases of plas-skin . . ."

"You haven't answered my question yet, Nrrna," the Treaty Controller pressed.

She gave him a smile. "All thought of personal indulgence must give way to duty, honored sir." She paused to give him the most courteous and coolest of bows. "You must forgive my diligence but it is my first position and I cannot discredit my Stripe with less than my closest attention. Everything must be inventoried before it can be transported to the village center." She began her count over, glancing from the clipboard to the pallet with an anxious expression. "One box of size 00 sutures, one box of size 0 sutures . . ."

"I thought you needed to get this to the medical center as quickly as you could," complained the operator, wondering that the pretty female was silly enough to ignore a Controller.

"As soon as it is counted," Nrrna said firmly. "Earth must be notified promptly if the count is short." Once again, she began at the top of her list. Just as the Treaty Controller moved in to pursue her, the grid bell rang.

"Honored sir, the transmission from Hrruba!"

On the grid platform a cluster of small boxes appeared. The Treaty Controller bent over them and straightened up with an exclamation of self-satisfaction, one of the document cases clutched in his hands. "Yes, this will ensure the number of days is finite." He glanced at Nrrna, who was still pantomiming a diligent inventory and walked over to her. "Silly stripe," he said in a voice low enough to reach her ears only, "you would do better to accept my protection and virility so that I can provide well for you when you have to return to Hrruba. It is not too late to reconsider."

"My Stripe has a long tradition of honoring its promises," Nrrna said with a swift sideways glance toward him before returning to her inventory check. Halfway between checking off a film tape for educating small children about bacteria control and reaching for the next film in the stack, she heard an annoyed snort, and the Treaty Controller swept away, holding the small document box. She sighed with relief.

"My goods are all accounted for," she told the grid operator. "Will you transport me and this shipment now to First Village?"

The gesture with which the irritated technician directed her onto the platform showed that he would be very glad indeed to get rid of her. For her sake, he had nearly had to annoy the Treaty Controller. No male, not even a Treaty Controller, should persist when a female has made her disinterest so plain. He would be glad to see the last of both of them and the end of a possible disgraceful incident.

The moment that the village coalesced around Nrrna, she shoved the crate off the grid and tapped the code to open it. Kelly exploded up in the midst of a snowstorm of plastic packets. They were plastered all over her like wet leaves.

"Oh, my poor neck," she groaned. "This was such a good idea but neither of us counted on sweat and plastic suffocation. I hope I don't offend your nose."

"I am so glad you are all right," Nrrna said, trying hard to keep her nostrils from flaring at the reek of the Hayuman. She couldn't help her current odoriferousness and Nrrna helped Kelly out "I would not have left you in it so long, but that wretched ol' cat"—and Kelly blinked at such an epithet coming from the gentle and polite Nrrna—"of a Controller was revoltingly offensive!" Nrrna almost spat in outrage and Kelly could see every single hair of her stripe was standing up.

Nrrna began to pick the static-charged packets off Kelly's hair and clothes. Each time she tried to put a pile down, they seemed to spring back to adhere to her fur. When Kelly tried to help, it only made matters worse. The packets merely transferred themselves from Nrrna to Kelly. Frustration gave way to laughter and then Nrrna thought of moistening her hands, and when that seemed to help, Kelly wet hers and they began to divest themselves of their unusual decorations.

"I heard him, the old tomcat," Kelly said, grinning at Nrrna. "But he's a persistent bugger, isn't he? I thought males didn't bother females without permission."

"It's partly my fault," Nrrna said. "I used too much of a provocative scent."

"Not to get his attention, I'll warrant."

Nrrna wrinkled her nose. "The operator was too well mannered to pursue me, but it kept him interested until white muzzle interfered."

"All's well that ends well. But remind me not to ride in a crate again," Kelly said when the last of the gloves were stuffed back into their container, and the top was clamped down again. "I also caught that bit about you reconsidering him so he could provide for you when you had to return to Hrruba. What's happened since I left here?"

"Nothing," Nrrna said, but she was as worried about his phraseology as Kelly was. Possibly more than Kelly was, for she had lived on Rrala all her life and the quarters of her clan on Hrruba were very crowded.

"What was he waiting to collect? Did you see?"

"A document box. Well covered with Third Speaker seals, that much I did notice."

"Neither the Treaty Controller nor Third Speaker is a supporter of the colony. Strikes me as odd that that Stripe should be in control with Treaty Renewal approaching. I wonder what kind of documents were in that box."

"I don't know how we'd find out, but I'd better complete this shipment without any more delay." Nrrna spoke into a radio unit which was hooked to her belt, contacting the Health Center's operator. "They will send a flitter for the shipment. Now, did you have any luck on Terra?"

"I sure did, Nrrna. We've got a Poldep inspector on our side, willing to look into certain oddities that came to light. I want to tell the Reeves, but I'll meet you later at Hrriss's so I only have to tell this twice, but tell him I got good news." She was stretching and working her arms and legs to relieve the kinks. "I never could have found out so much without your help, Nrrna. You've been a star! See you soon."

With a final wave, Kelly jogged off toward the Friendship Bridge on her way to collect Calypso and make her way to the Reeve Ranch.

Todd took one look at her and yelled, "What did you do to your hair?"

"My hair?" she shrieked back at him, hand to her head before she remembered the rinse. "I couldn't go back to Earth in my own hair and expect to be unnoticed!"

"To *Earth?*" he roared, white-faced with shock. When he had finished bawling her out for the risks she had taken, she got just as angry right back at him for not letting her deliver her good news.

"In the first place, I was never in danger, Todd Reeve. In the second place, I got more information than I ever thought I'd get, and thirdly, we got Inspector DeVeer actively pursuing an investigation on our behalf."

"Is that Kelly Solinari with you, Todd?" Pat called, and rushed into the room, her expression both anxious and relieved. "Young woman, where have you been? Your family's been worried sick about you. And what have you done to your hair?"

"It washes out and I left my parents a note to say I'd be away a few days. Didn't they get it?"

At the moment, Ken Reeve came bursting into the room. "Robin was right. It was Calypso tearing up the road. Where have you been? And what did you do to your hair?"

"I *dyed it*! And if you'll all drop out of panic mode, I'll tell you why I dyed it and where I've been and what I've been doing," Kelly yelled back, glaring at all of them. Then she turned less aggressively to Pat. "That is, if I can have a drink to soothe my throat after all the shouting I have to do in this house to get listened to."

It was Todd who provided the juice and then sat down at the table, where she began the recital of her inquiries.

"Nrrna helped?" Todd interrupted as she began. Then, "How well did you know this Dalkey? Can you trust him?"

"I probably shouldn't have mentioned his name," Kelly said tartly, "but I trust you not to repeat it. And not to get stupid about me approaching the only one I felt could help us. And he's still helping us, or rather Inspector DeVeer is."

"Cool it, Todd," Ken said in an aside. "Continue, Kelly."

She did but was aware that Todd was uncharacteristically morose until she got to the part about DeVeer taking her with him to interrogate Klonski.

"You see, we were all working on the wrong assumption," she said, looking at Ken, "that the brands had been altered somehow. Even Kiachif thought Klonski might be able to do that but he didn't. In fact, he burst out laughing at the very notion that he was being accused of rustling." The others didn't quite seem to see the humor in that, so she continued. "He did much worse . . . all to incriminate you," and now she turned her gaze to Todd to see the dawning of hope in his eyes. "Klonski altered the log tapes . . . By the way, which of you handed them over to Rogitel?"

"Neither of us did. He removed them from the unit himself," Todd said.

"Well, then, that's when he switched them."

Todd opened his mouth to protest. "You know, you're right. He bundled the log box into a plastic sack and carried it off in a proprietary fashion. I didn't think about it till now and I was certainly too shocked at all he was flinging at Hrriss and me to think his manner odd."

Kelly nodded. "It had to be Rogitel substituting the altered tapes and at that moment, since the ship had been properly sealed. I wonder where your real log went."

"Into the nearest vat of acid," Todd said with a deep sigh.

"Possibly not," Ken suggested thoughtfully. "Go on, Kelly. What else did Klonski do?"

Her eyes glowed. "This is sort of the best part. He altered satellite security modes."

"He what?" Ken lifted off his chair and Todd stared at her as if she had suddenly changed shape.

"Don't know how, do know why," she went on.

"To let the rustlers in and out," Ken continued, throwing both arms in the air at such an obvious explanation.

"Klonski was rather proud of that. And DeVeer has it all on tape!" Kelly said, grinning broadly.

"Is DeVeer really on our side, Kelly?" Ken asked, his expression grim.

"I think so, sir," Kelly replied. "He admitted he doesn't really like the Doona Experiment. He was alive when the Siwanna Tragedy occurred but he also admitted that colored his opinions. But," and she waggled her finger at all three Reeves, "he's out to crush the rustling because too many uninoculated animals are being transported illegally. And he said the incidents of rustling had increased all out of proportion. He couldn't figure out why."

"I brought the illegal hides to him . . ."

"And I've been squaring my eyeballs trying to match missing horses to those hides with duplicate Reeve marks."

Ken brought his fist down on the table so smartly that it startled everyone else. "Okay, we've had the wrong end of the stick. Kiachif gave me a clue in reporting Mark Aden helping to load that leopard Appie for export. He was also about the height you are now, Todd, dark-haired and blue eyes, and to Zapatans that description also fits you. Let's assume that Mark rustled while he worked for me. So he probably stashed unmarked foals, born in the pastures, in some blind canyon. He had the run of our ranch as well as our neighbors'. He could have picked up unbranded foals from all over. Every breeder expects a few mares to abort in a year or lose their foals to mdas before we round 'em up for branding. But just one or two from fifty or so ranches, and that'd make a nice ship-

ment off-world. Especially if someone is turning off the satellite tape—or however your Klonski rigged the system, and your rustler's away with no one the
wiser."

"Spacedep is involved up to its armpits," Kelly said, "and I think Inspector
DeVeer is going to prove it. Which reminds me, I promised my friend Dalkey
that I'd sponsor him to Doona."

"You did?" Todd gave her the queerest look she'd ever seen on his face.

"How else can we repay him for the help he's given?"

"If there is a Doona for him to come to," Todd said in a bleak tone. "Neither
Hrriss nor I is cleared . . ."

"You will be!" Kelly said emphatically.

"Kelly, this family can never properly repay you," Pat said, tears of relief in
her eyes. She dabbed at them with the edge of the dish towel she had had in her
hand when she heard Kelly arrive.

"We're neighbors, aren't we?" Kelly replied, struggling not to get too senti-
mental. Wanting very much to hear Todd commend her. "And it's Hrriss and
Todd who've been jeopardized. I don't let my friends get done over. How much
more time do we have before the trial?" She looked at Ken Reeve because she
couldn't look at Todd, who still faced that ordeal unless lots of things fell into
place in the next few days.

"We've not yet been informed," Ken said in a taut voice. Then his face broke
into a relieved smile and he leaned forward with his elbows on the table. "Look,
we can't do much about the satellite . . ."

"Kiachif?" Todd asked, also leaning forward, his expression alert even if he
wouldn't look at Kelly next to him.

"Possibly," Ken said, "and I don't know how we'd locate the genuine log
tape . . ."

"Emma Sumitral?" Pat suggested, her eyes brighter with hope than with
tears.

"I can ask, but now we concentrate our efforts on finding where stolen livestock could have been hidden."

"Tadpole in a tangle of tiddlers," Todd said, "but there'd have to be water,
good grass, some sort of shelter . . ."

"Well off all known trails, especially snake ones," Kelly added. "But every
rancher'll help now."

"They've all been helping . . ." And Todd inadvertently turned his head
toward her. Kelly held her breath, not wanting to turn away from the look in his
eyes, keen again and as intense as they got when he was thinking rapidly, as he
did on a Snake Hunt, examining and rejecting alternatives. He was her buoyant,

marvelous, alive Todd again. He lifted his body from the chair in a lithe movement. "I'll send out a revised message, for mares that ought to have foaled and didn't come in with foal at foot. Let's see how many come up missing on that data!"

"No, son," and Ken grabbed Todd's arm as he passed. "You'll saddle up Gypsy and go out hunting for likely places to stash livestock. Pat, you send out a blanket message to all ranches to be on the lookout for such storage spots, and also query folks about barren mares. Kelly, will you ask your father and brothers to help?"

"I'll go there first, but I promised Nrrna that I'd come over and give Hrriss the good news as soon as I'd told you." She dared look at Todd again.

"You were nearer Hrriss if you came in on the village grid," he said.

Kelly cocked her head at him, thought she wanted to shake him out of his stasis. Couldn't he see what her priority was? She planted her fists at her belt so she wouldn't do something drastic in front of his parents. "I've got my priorities in order, Todd Reeve. Hrriss doesn't ranch horses." With that she pushed past him and out of the house, down the steps, and vaulted to Calypso's back before she thought what she was doing.

"Hey . . . Kelly?" Todd's plaintive, puzzled call followed her down the track.

When he went back into the house, he saw the amused expressions on his parents' faces. "What'd I do to upset her?"

"For a bright man, you can be as dense as two planks," his mother said, and took herself back to the kitchen.

Todd looked at his father, who was making strangled noises.

"I think, son, it's more what you didn't do that's upset her. And you should get your priorities right. But not now. Now we got some rustler pens to find. You'll have time to apologize to Kelly later."

"Apologize?"

Ken turned his son around and shoved him toward the door. "Saddle my horse when you're tacking Gypsy. Tell Lon what we're going to look for and let's get going!" Ken's voice raised to a triumphant shout as Todd pitched forward and out the door from his father's hefty push.

What he should apologize to Kelly for bothered him as soon as he set off in the southeasterly direction his father had appointed him to search so that he could stay within the Reeve Ranch limits for more klicks than if he went west or north.

Perhaps he ought to have been more effusive in his thanks, but he'd been so scared that Kelly had done something stupid—which she had, only it worked out right—or been abducted—which was not really a possibility, but in his anxiety he had imagined all kinds of gory fates. She really had come up a heroine to smuggle herself back to Earth on a Hrruban grid . . . he ground his teeth, knowing that she had faced a sentence of life on a penal world if she'd been caught. Why hadn't she gone to one of those girlfriends she'd told him about? Who was this Dalkey Petersham? Why would she sponsor a Terran to Doona, a Terran working in Spacedep? It was analogous to inviting Jilamey Landreau to a weekend at her family's lake cabin.

And this DeVeer Polly! Who hadn't really listened to his father when he reported hides that didn't match their records. They had got the wrong end of that stick, all right. Stupid not to have tumbled to the duplications. Kiachif once again to the rescue. Only then did Todd become aware that Gypsy's gallop was slowing. Gently he eased the gray to a more sedate pace. No sense taking his frustration out on his horse. He gave Gypsy's neck several affectionate slaps to reassure and kneed him toward the nearest height. It commanded a good view over to the next range of hills. As he reined Gypsy in, he looked out over the land, peaceful and greening up well. More mares would be foaling . . .

An odd noise attracted both him and Gypsy at the same time, the horse pricking his ears and turning his head to the right. An echo it was, a bass echo, too loud for a nearby mda. The sound gathered intensity, and suddenly, out of the fold of the hills before him, he saw the pointed snout of a shuttle angling upward. It pulled up above the hills, its engines roaring, thrusters blazing.

Todd sent Gypsy down the hill at a gallop while he grabbed for his radio and called the ranch.

"Mom! Notify Martinson at once. A shuttle just illegally lifted off our property. I'm going to see if there are any traces of stock near the launch burn."

"What? Are you sure, Todd?"

"Mom! Don't argue. Tell Martinson to monitor the tracking satellites. They can catch him as he leaves the atmosphere."

Despite the clip at which he pushed Gypsy, it took him nearly an hour to reach the launch spot. What he saw there made him weep, but it was also incontrovertible truth that someone had been rustling Reeve livestock. Concealed in a fold of the hill, where trees formed a screen, a paddock had been fenced, the posts and rails so well disguised by shrubs, some of them rroamal, that Ken, or Todd, or Lon could have ridden by here every day and never noticed the setup. They wouldn't have looked past the rroamal to the glade, for horses avoided that plant as carefully as Humans did. Water had been piped into a big barrel, fitted with a stopcock. Dung dotted the little glade, enough for twenty or so horses, just the number to make a nice profit for the rustler's efforts. But not all the horses had been loaded and that's what upset Todd the most. Three yearlings, well grown, freeze-marked with the Reeve brand, lay on the ground. One had a broken neck—probably caused fighting to resist being loaded, for the rope burns on head and neck were obvious. The other two had broken legs. The nails that had been driven between their eyes into their skulls had not been removed. Todd shuddered. Circling the corral, Todd also found the bleach marks that freeze-brand chemicals made when carelessly spilled.

His radio bleeped.

"Todd?" It was Lon.

"They caught 'em?"

"Nothing, Todd," and Lon's voice sounded as savage as Todd felt. "Linc Newry says there was no alarm from the orbiters."

"But that's impossible. I saw it launch. There has to be traces of that!"

"I'll patch Linc through to you," Lon said, and Todd was too enraged to bother to hold the handset from his ear to avoid the high-pitch squeal as the patch to the Launch Center was made.

"I know you think you saw something, Todd," Newry said apologetically but firmly. "But no ships took off Doona today at all and none were scheduled to land."

"Linc, I know what I saw! I know what I see about me right now—three dead yearlings with nails driven through their skulls because one had a broken neck and two had broken legs. Check your readouts, will ya? Check your equipment . . ." Todd almost suggested that Linc check for tampering but that would be premature. He knew Linc Newry too well to suspect the man was in league with Doona's detractors, but this was the time to stand pat and let someone with clout, like DeVeer, handle that end of the business.

"Todd, I'm serious. Nothing came through the atmosphere. All readings are normal. But you can be sure I'll keep my eyes peeled to the gauges. Could be they only up-and-overed. Maybe they had another rendezvous but they won't leave Doona without my seeing 'em tonight."

"You're probably right. They up-and-overed. Thanks, Linc. Over and out!" He held the radio away from his ear as the connection ended, then dialed Lon again.

"Ouch," Lon said. "I didn't disconnect. I heard what he said, Todd, and I heard what you said. Fardling bastards! When I get my hands on 'em . . . Give me your whereabouts. We'll join you to film the evidence. Got any idea whose they were rustling?"

"The one with the broken neck is a leopard Appaloosa," Todd said, his shoulders sagging at the irony.

*   *   *

Uncharacteristically loud voices echoed in the Council room of the Speakers of Hrruba. Third Speaker raised his voice to be heard above them all. He was getting old, but fury gave his throat the power to shout down his opponents who were arguing over his tirade against Rrala. Only the banging of the gavel of First Speaker Hrruna put an end to the snarling and growls.

"That is enough," First Speaker said in a very soft voice. "Third Speaker, will you give substance to your demand that Rrala be disbanded?"

"You have all read the report from the Treaty Controller," Third said, raking his fellow administrators with a glare which stopped short just before it fell on First Speaker. "One of our most prominent young diplomats is involved in a disgraceful situation, in which he is accused of capital crimes, in violation both of the Treaty of Rrala and of Hrruban Law. Hrrss theft! Robbery from interdicted worlds! He has been corrupted by his Hayuman companion. I have been getting full reports from my representatives on Rrala, and none of it is good news. It would seem that this is not an isolated case. Honorable, honest citizens are being lured into a life of crime by these animals who walk like Hrrubans! Rrala must be closed to Hayumans, or all of society will suffer!"

"Surely responsibility for reporting the actions on Rrala falls to Second Speaker for External Affairs," Hrruna said, indicating Hrrto, seated to his right. The First Speaker's mane had gone entirely white, but his eyes were as keen as ever. "I have already had his report, and it gives me the same information you offer."

"This information affects Internal Affairs," Third Speaker said doggedly. "Now that the date draws near for Treaty Renewal, when the Hayumans hope to have it extended, there is a chance to painlessly end these harmful influences before they do more ill unto the youth of Hrruba. I have been besieged by special interest groups here on Hrruba. This young Hrruban, Hrriss, has been implicated in crimes committed solely to profit a Hayuman. We cannot support corruption of this kind. It is an ill example for our young people. We must withdraw our support for the continuation of the Treaty."

There was more shouting, and the First Speaker applied his gavel to its stand. "I have heard also from Hrruvula, counsel for the accused. He is adamant that his clients are innocent of the charges brought against them and must be allowed to clear their names. I find that I agree with him. Hrriss and Zodd have always acted in honor before."

"A ruse! Never did trust bareskins." Seventh Speaker for Management was the newest member of the Council, and of the narrowest stripe. As a result, he tried harder than any of the others to follow a clear mandate from his constituency rather than make risky decisions on his own. He was diligent and the trade figures continued to rise. So much so, in fact, that the higher the balance from the benefits of trading under the Treaty conditions, the more certain he was that the Hayumans were stealing profit from Hrruban interests. "They will destroy us."

"I disagree," said the Fifth Speaker for Health and Medicine. "I have close associations with many Hayuman practitioners in my specialty. They have provided us with knowledge and techniques we could not have developed on our own. They have done nothing but improve our standards. You cannot deny that mental outlook and physical health have been on the upswing since the Rrala Experiment began. Rrala has moved steadily out of what could have been a terminal situation in the younger generations, in the main due to interaction with another speaking, thinking race. Why," he said, trying to lighten the mood, "if only for the fresh food alone, the Rralan Experiment should not be ended— certainly not because of a situation involving one single Hayuman."

"He is representative of his race," Third Speaker raged, unamused. He pounded on the table and pointed a claw at First Speaker. "The one you considered to be most honorable, above all other Hayumans. Here, honor is at stake. What is cohabitation without trust? We were warned from the beginning of this unnatural colony, by this Zodd's own father, that one day Hayumans might try to take what is ours. What is more precious than honor?"

"Honor certainly is at stake," Second Speaker Hrrto agreed. "The honor of a Hrruban as well as a Hayuman. And Hrruban honor requires us to wait for the results of their trial before we condemn an entire society. That would be honorable behavior on our part."

There was more shouting, which First Speaker silenced by banging the gavel.

"Very well, we will put it to the vote," Hrruna said. "Those in favor of allowing Hrriss, son of Hrrestan, and Zodd Rrev to be proved innocent, vote aye."

Third Speaker held up a hand to stay the voting. "As a rider to this resolution, let us set a time period in which their honor must be proved. A significant date approaches: Treaty Renewal Day. If these two have not expunged the stain on their honor by that day, we must vote against renewal, for the sake of our youth. Those on Rrala will not be penalized, for other planets have been opened," he added, "and they can make homes there, safe from Hayuman influence."

No one spoke to debate that rider, though several faces reflected dismay.

"Very well, the rider is allowed," Hrruna said reluctantly, then called for the vote. It was overwhelmingly in favor of the motion. Satisfied, Hrruna nodded. His eyes were bleak as he addressed Third. "You may so notify the Treaty Controller of our decision."

Third Speaker bowed. Probably to hide his true feelings, Hrruna thought sadly.

The Launch Center bar was the perfect place to hold meetings, Ali Kiachif thought as he entered the place. It had small nooks and obscure corners where private conversations could be held—and the proprietor debugged his rooms at random intervals. Kiachif had most opportunely made a gap in his schedule for a long stopover at Doona; originally to discuss new rulings and profit principles with the captains who answered to him. He had acquired a second purpose which he diligently pursued, leading almost every conversation to topics that might help Ken Reeve and his boy.

"Well, look at you," a man said, blinking, as his eyes became accustomed to the gloom in the bar. "If I'd known you were already here, Kiachif, I'd have gone to the Centauris instead."

"What for?" asked Kiachif airily, shaking hands with Captain Feyder. "We've been there already, with all the best the colony worlds have to offer. Tell 'em, never compel 'em, and you sell 'em, that's my motto." The friendly rivalry between the independent merchant Rog Feyder and Ali Kiachif had gone on for years. Feyder sat down, and Kiachif signalled to the barman to bring bottles for them both.

"I've got a shipment of unrefined sugar for Doona. Special order. Just unloading." Feyder let Kiachif fill his glass, waited till Ali had filled his own, and then raised it courteously to his old rival. "Your health."

"Yours! Hear unrefined sugar used to make damned fine spirituous potables."

"Did it? Well, we make sure the customers get what they order, don't we? Though sometimes you wonder why they pay the freight charges."

"Oh?" Kiachif had long since learned the art of subtle prompting.

"Sugar's the most ordinary thing I have on board. The damnedest things are getting shipped these days."

"That they are," Kiachif agreed. "Last season, I carried a copper sculpture fifteen meters long to one of the outer agri-worlds from Doona. A commissioned work by the governor to commemorate ten years of the colony, engraved with the name of every colonist and his accomplishments. It was a pain up the afterburners to handle, but orders are orders! I hate to see what he'll ask for when twenty-five rolls around, like Doona's is."

"Aye, I wanted to come back for the big celebration, but I should be worlds away by then," Feyder said. "I'm just here on turnabout, starting me route over from the topside. No, when I say strange, I mean the epitome of strange, not ordinary strange. Listen to this one. Got a meteorite puncture on my way in from the outer worlds. After we sealed it up, I found a container cracked open in that bay, with the meteorite smack in the middle like a ball through a glass window. Splintered the whole damned thing into pieces. D'you know what had been inside?"

"Not an idea."

"A beacon. An orbital drone beacon," said Feyder, slapping his leg. "No assignment code. No idea where it came from. We checked its memory, and it was hollering Mayday like a pack of banshees. Did you ever hear such a thing in your life?"

"By all that's white, bright, and right," Ali said, holding on to his excitement, "that surely is a strange thing to report. Never heard its like in all my years in space. And it didn't have no ID number, you say?"

Feyder was not at all taken in by Kiachif's idle curiosity and gave him a long sly look. "Now I can't rightly remember."

"We could both take a look," Kiachif said.

"So you can see what else I'm hauling and cross-ship me? Try another one, Kiachif."

"Surely there must be a little favor I could do for you, Rog ol' boy!"

Feyder regarded him speculatively. "Well, now, there's the matter of the Eighth Sector."

"Oh?" and the single sound dove and swooped up again while Kiachif's eyes went round as ball bearings.

"Hell, Ali, you gotta leave some routes open for the independents."

"That's true enough," Kiachif said, scratching the stubble on his chin. "I don't want to appear greedy, or restrict free trade . . . You don't happen to have it still on board, do you?" He winked at Feyder.

"Happen I do. But you don't get a look at it. That amadan portmaster's gone all rules and regs on honest traders and he sealed my hatch when I told him that I was only here to refuel and get a drink or two. I can't unseal till I reach Earth, my next port o' call."

"Earth, huh? Is that where your funny gizmo's going?"

Feyder drained his glass, which Kiachif promptly refilled. "Yup, going to Earth. Spacedep's the address on the manifest."

"Is that so?"

"It is."

"That's the queerest sort of cargo to carry, I do agree. A beacon with no point of origin, screaming a Mayday, if you get what I mean."

"Do you mean to let us have some routes in Eighth, then?"

Kiachif affected hurt innocence. "Of course, I do. Soon's you can give me the beacon's ID. Give you my word," and he held up his right, bargain-making hand in promise.

Just then some of Feyder's gangers entered the bar and Kiachif had a chance to slip away to find Feyder's supercargo, who was an old friend, and called in a favor he had with that man. "When you get to Earth, just make certain you order that box opened in front of the inspectors because it was 'damaged in transit.' "

"Why?" the super wanted to know.

"I'm not going to tell you why, what, or wherefore," Kiachif insisted, fending off the man's questions. "That would be suborning the witness, if you know what I mean. I just need an official inquiry into the contents of that container! And let me know who picks it up. That's important, too."

He left the Launch Center, looking for Ken.

Only Pat was at the farm, just getting up from the computer and looking so sick to heart. Kiachif thought he'd better let her talk her worry out of her system. And a drink'd help that process.

"They should be back fairly soon, Ali," she said, still distracted and worried.

"Now, Patricia, why don't you get me a little drink and tell me all about it?"

"Ali, you haven't changed in twenty-four years," she said, but she looked at him, not around him, and he chuckled.

"Why should I?"

"I know what you mean," she capped his jovial question with his own words. "Perhaps a drink's not a bad idea what with everything that's happened today."

"You look wore out, Patricia. You sit. I'll get the bottle. Know where you keep it."

"That doesn't surprise me," she murmured, low enough so he wouldn't hear her out in the kitchen. But his low chuckle suggested that he had. He was back in no time with the bottle of mlada and two glasses. "Oh, that's too much for me, Ali."

"Not a bit of it. You're paler'n a milk stone and this'll put heart in you. Your health!"

They touched glasses and she watched in fascination as half the large tumbler disappeared down his throat while a sip was all she could swallow. Still, as it slid down, she felt its warmth easing the tension in her body.

"Now, what's been happening here today?"

So she told him, including a summary of Kelly's activities on Earth, DeVeer's assistance, and Klonski's admissions.

"Knew that feller was involved in all this. Shoulda known he'd be put to better use than changing freeze marks. Hmmm. And Todd saw the shuttle blasting off and it didn't register at the Launch Center?" Kiachif frowned deeply. "That do sort of point to the fact that Doona's security satellites might have felt the touch of Klonski's little talented digits."

Pat frowned in the act of sipping the mlada. "Linc Newry—whom we've no reason to distrust—thought maybe the shuttle up-and-overed. He promised to keep a close watch on all the orbital monitors."

"Huh! If one's been tampered with, they all have. That your men coming back now?" he asked. Ears sharp enough to hear air escaping from a pinhole caught the thud of horses' hooves and wagon wheels. Two wagons, he thought.

Pat hurried to throw open the door.

"Ali!" Ken swung his leg over the pommel and, throwing his reins to Robin with an admonition to rub Sockertwo down well, charged up the steps to greet the spacefarer. "Glad to see you. Got some questions . . ."

"Got some answers, but not necessary to your questions. Hi there, ropy," Ali added, shaking Todd's hand as he joined his father on the porch. "Need a drink? Made your wife join me in a glass and you both look like you need a swig er two to set you right before we start jawing."

Ken and Todd instantly saw the merits of that suggestion. They'd had a bad time in that hidden corral. Vic Solinari and Ben Adjei had sledded over to verify their findings. Vic had taken blood and tissue samples from the little leopard Appie—he was positive it had been foaled by his spotted mare—and Ben had done the same with the other two. One bore so many of his sire's physical traits that it was easy to identify it as having come from the Hrrel Ranch. The other, a chestnut filly, had no distinguishing marks to give clues to her origin. Ben Adjei would freeze all three carcasses in case they were needed as evidence. They had made the most careful sweep, section by section, to find any more clues. The only one they did find was a half-empty sack of ssersa seed, which proved that the rustlers must have been responsible for the proliferation of that weed on previously cleared pasturelands.

Halfway through their recital, Pat slipped from the kitchen, having been distressed enough by the details to feel that preparing food was a better occupation for her.

With a tray full of steaming bowls of stew and bread rolls as well as a fresh bottle of mlada, she returned in time to hear why Ali Kiachif had sought them out.

"I've found me a new occupation," Ali began, sipping at a freshly filled glass. "You might say I've taken to reading the future, if you know what I mean," and he winked at Robin and Inessa, who had joined those in the living room once their evening stable chores had been completed. Lon had come in, too. "If I was to say, for example, that someone in the docks on Earth is going to open a container in four days, and make an official note that he found inside it a homeless beacon drone calling Mayday, would you believe me?"

Todd and Robin let out a wild, joyous war cry. Ken pounded the old merchant on the back. "How did you discover that, you old pirate?"

"Never mind," Kiachif said, much gratified by the reaction to his news. He tapped his lips. "I have my sources, if you understand me. But I'll say that the probe's code number will be ARB-546-08, and see if it isn't."

"I'd better let Poldep know," Ken said, starting toward the computer.

Hastily Kiachif put a hand on his arm. "Easy on the retros, mate. It'll be reported to them by the appropriate authorities. It might seem as if you know something about it as you shouldn't, if you know what I mean. Just concentrate on what's near, dear, and here, and everything will work out all right. They'll soon have proof that these boys passed through into Hrrilnorr space for good and sound reasons." He winked solemnly and took another long pull on his drink. " 'Sides, Patricia's been telling me a thing or two that falls pleasantly upon the ears. It's all coming together, if you get what I mean, all coming neatly together."

"Finding that shuttle beacon'll really clear us, Dad," Todd said, his whole being revitalized. "How will we ever thank you for locating it, Captain Kiachif?"

"Well, laddie, there's such things as hidden profits. I get what you need, you keep this planet viable, and I cart off the excess and sell it. You plant it, I transplant it. Neither of us loses that way! Better get going. Can't trust those gangers of mine. Might get randy drunk er something."

A few days later, Hrruvula notified them that information about the nameless beacon had been received by Poldep and passed on to the Treaty Council. An audience with the Council was arranged immediately to plead for their release.

Rogitel appeared, representing Spacedep, followed by Varnorian of Codep, who thudded heavily into a chair and gazed without much interest at the ceiling. Sampson DeVeer, having tendered an official copy of the supercargo's report, represented the Poldep arm of interplanetary government. Ken and Hrrestan slipped in when the boys' attorney was admitted. They ignored indignant, outraged, and pointed glances in their direction; Hrrestan patiently, Ken stubbornly.

Although DeVeer also handed copies to each of the individual Councillors, they seemed to read as if spelling out each syllable in whichever language the document had been rendered.

Hrruvula finally cleared his throat several times and gained the Controller's signal to proceed.

"As you have all had time to read and absorb the significance of the document so kindly brought by Inspector DeVeer, it is apparent, honored ones, that my clients have told the truth from the very beginning." Hrruvula noted the glowers from Rogitel and Varnorian. "I am certain we are all relieved that two such fine young men have been cleared."

"On this one point," the Treaty Controller snapped out, "not on the other crimes of which they still stand accused. They must be adjudged guilty or innocent on all." The Treaty Controller was adamant in his particularity. "More than just a simple matter of truth or falsehood is involved here. It pivots on the trust of one race for another in all matters concerning Rrala."

"Is that just rhetoric," Ken asked Hrrestan in an undertone, "or is he issuing a challenge?"

"It would seem so," the village elder said. "Hrruvula tells me that he has heard of a resolution passed in the Hrruban Council of Speakers that will require it to withhold approval of the Treaty if our sons are proved guilty of the charges laid against them."

Ken felt as if the floor had dropped out from under him. "That's ridiculous!" he exclaimed, his voice rising. He hastily recalled where he was. "Holding up the Treaty for a pack of trumped-up allegations? What happened to 'innocent before being proved guilty'?"

"Silence, please!" Treaty Controller banged on the table with his gavel.

Ken glanced up and received the chairman's full glare. He forced himself to subside and sit quietly beside Hrrestan. Hrruvula resumed speaking.

"If one accusation has been proved spurious, honored Council members," the attorney said, bowing gracefully so that his long red robes swayed, "and the characters of the two young men must speak for them somewhat . . ."

"Granted," Councillor Dupuis spoke up from her end of the dais. Councillor Mrrorra nodded her agreement, too.

". . . Does that not cast significant doubt on the other incidents?" The Hrruban paused, hands extended to the board, appealingly.

"One piece of proof doesn't negate the other charges ipso facto," Rogitel said with dry contempt. His grasp of the formal court language was by no means as complete or subtly shaded as Hrruvula's, but his diction was exact. "They will have to prove their innocence on each and every count and I doubt that lies within their abilities. There is still massive evidence on the charge of illegal purchase and smuggling of controlled artifacts."

The Treaty Controller polled his Council, and the result, to Ken's dismay, was a majority requiring a total acquittal. "The Council agrees. Innocence must be proved in regards to each of the remaining charges."

"Then let them prove their innocence together," Hrravula said in a rich, rolling purr. "Keeping them apart was perhaps an acceptable remedy when their probity was at issue. It no longer is. Therefore, I feel that the separation of these two friends of the heart perpetrates an unnecessary cruelty. They both must be proved innocent so let them both work to prove it. That is not an unreasonable," and Hrruvula's cultivated voice rolled out the word syllable by syllable, and rolled out the next word, "request to make." His voice rose slightly, not quite a question, but certainly subtly insinuating that it was too pretty a contingency to be denied. Now he made deliberate eye contact with the Treaty Controller. "There is much at stake as you, honored Controller, know."

The Controller seemed somewhat taken aback that anyone else knew about the Speakers' decision, and he stared at the tall and elegant attorney.

"We can't release them from house arrest," Rogitel protested vehemently. "If they are allowed loose, who can tell what they'll do next. Spacedep does not recommend giving that pair the freedom of the planet."

"Honored Council members, may I speak?" Sampson DeVeer rose impressively to his feet and gazed down upon Rogitel. "Poldep disagrees with Spacedep. I agree with honored counsel that to be fair the house arrest should indeed be lifted. I have only so many hands and eyes at my disposal. I would be grateful for the additional help, which I assure Spacedep I will direct most carefully." DeVeer bowed toward Rogitel, who sat staring up at him in barely concealed consternation. Ken could almost hear the wheels twirling in that machinelike brain of his. "They will be released, as it were, into my cognizance. I will know where they are at all times."

Ken and Hrrestan could have cheered for DeVeer when he sat down, but that would have annoyed the already tried Treaty Controller further.

"I cannot condone their release for any reason whatsoever," Rogitel said flatly.

"Nor I," said Varnorian, after being pointedly nudged by his companion.

"But you do not have to. You have no actual authority in these cases," DeVeer said gently. "Though you are frequently asked for advice, all misdemeanors and certainly grand larceny fall within Poldep jurisdiction. In my opinion, Codep and Spacedep are grossly overstepping their authority by attempting to investigate crimes or act as a judicial body where one is suspected." He raised his voice. "I held my tongue before this, but in light of proof represented by the beacon and other data I have recently been shown, I urgently request the Treaty council to release Todd Reeve and Hrriss, son of Hrrestan, from a home arrest which I understand neither has violated in any particular. Rather this body should applaud their humanity in answering a Mayday signal, knowing that it was an infraction of the Treaty they have both upheld and promoted."

"He should have been a barrister," Hrravula murmured in an aside to Ken. "What a presence!"

The Treaty Controller found himself outnumbered by his own Council, who were overwhelmingly in favor of DeVeer's proposal.

"We have spent enough of our valuable time on this case," an elderly Hrruban member argued. Treaty Controller had always suspected that Second Speaker Hrrto had seen to his nomination to the Council. "Our time is limited. We should turn our attention to the matters which truly concern us and I suggest respectfully that we have the chamber cleared so that we may proceed."

Treaty Controller had no choice but to agree. He referred to the printed agenda on the table before him. "Very well. The Council will reconsider this matter four weeks from today. The allegations against the defendants and their proof for and against their guilt will be discussed before the final vote on Treaty Renewal. So moved." He banged the small hammer.

"Seconded," Madam Dupuis trumpeted. The gavel fell again. "You are excused, gentles."

Ken almost danced out of the austere chamber and he could see the violent switchings of Hrrestan's tail as he walked beside him. When the doors had closed behind Hrruvula, Ken and Hrrestan could no longer contain their roars of triumph and were shushed by Hrruvula as well as the bailiff. Ken's stride quickened to a jog, and he flat-handed open one side of the heavy door of the Treaty Building, Hrrestan doing the same to his leaf, until they were out in the open and able to cheer as loudly as they chose. Hayuman and Hrruban made for the transport grid, Hrrestan telling the startled operator to send them to the Friendship Bridge.

Once there, Ken looked at his old friend, his eyes dancing. "Shall we see which of us gets to his son first?"

Hrriss's swifter feet made the reunion just barely on the Human side of the Friendship Bridge. He and Todd slammed into each other's arms, pounding each other on the back and talking at the same time. Hrriss felt something slapping him in the legs. After a startled downward glance, he started to howl with laughter until his tear ducts overflowed.

"So, my Zodd, while we have been apart, you have grown a new tail," he said, when he could catch his breath between snorts of laughter.

"What better way to celebrate our reuniting," Todd replied, grinning until his jaw ached but not far from tears of joy himself. "It proved a talisman once before and I felt we needed all the luck we could cobble up."

With the practice of many childhood years, Todd reached for the length of rope, carefully frayed at the end to resemble the tufted tip of the Hrruban caudal appendage. Then with a decisive gesture, he hauled it loose from his belt. "I couldn't miss a real tail more than I have missed you, friend of my heart."

"I have missed you, too," Hrriss said, giving Todd a rib-crushing hug. "Half of my life was severed from my heart, my mind, my soul. Twenty-four years we have been friends, and these last weeks have seemed far longer than those we have enjoyed together."

"We don't do as well apart as we do together," Todd said with a rueful grin. One arm about Hrriss's shoulders and he felt twice the man who'd slumped about the house and ranch, unable to concentrate, like a machine idling . . . "Whoa there!" And his hand dug into Hrriss's forearm to stop him.

Surprised, Hrriss stopped and regarded the sparkling in Todd's blue eyes and noticed the wicked grin shaping his hairless lips.

"What thought has occurred to my friend now that his brain is engaged again?"

Todd slapped a hand to his forehead. "I haven't been thinking. And it only just dawned on . . ." He turned, gripping Hrriss by both shoulders. "Okay, so they know we weren't lying about the Mayday: they found the bloody beacon, but there's other incontrovertible evidence that the *Albie* couldn't have made all those stops, and not one of us, not even Captain Ali, thought of it."

Hrriss racked his brain, shaking his head. "I do not know what you mean. Spare me more suspense, Zodd."

"The engines of the *Albie* . . . and us!" Todd's grin got broader and his eyes were so bright that Hrriss thought they would pop from his head. He fanned his fingers at his friend. "C'mon, c'mon. What effect would all that warp-jump travel have on an engine? What effect would so many warp jumps have on the crew of a ship making them?"

Hrriss's jaw dropped to his chest and his tail began to lash. "Of course! Proof that we weren't where that tape said we were has always been in front of our faces."

"*In* our faces, if you please. That sort of travel would have left us trembling wrecks. How many jumps were we supposed to have made? Nine? We're pretty fit guys, but we'd've been dragging for days after so many transfers. And the engines? They'd've been dry as old snakeskins and badly in need of realignment. Wowwee!" Todd ripped off a wild yell that echoed across the village green. "C'mon. Race you to Hu's. His is the nearest console and we want him to hear this, too."

Since their meeting on the bridge had been more on the Hayuman side than the Hrruban, their few steps brought them to the Hayuman lands.

"Rrrace me?" Hrriss demanded. "We rrrace but together, Zodd. Together!" Hrriss was so full of joy he could have run to Hrruba and back without benefit of the grid, but now he lifted his thighs to push off, Todd beside him, the friends heading toward the low bungalow that housed Hu Shih and his wife, Phyllis.

She saw the pair thundering down the path toward her house and called over her shoulder at Hu.

"Todd and Hrriss are coming at a stampede pace, Hu. Oh, dear, you don't think any more has happened, do you?"

Her husband, his age showing only in his slower movements, patted her hand as he peered out the window.

"Something good, to judge by the elation on their faces." And Hu felt the better for seeing that as well as seeing them together again. That had been such a miserable thing to do to those boys. Young men, he corrected himself.

"Mrs. Shih, good morning. Good morning, sir," Todd said, his bows as jerky as his breath from running. "Please, sir, can we use your comunit? We urgently need to contact Captain Kiachif."

Hrriss had said nothing but he was bowing and grinning his jaw off its hinges and Hu stepped aside, gesturing toward the alcove which constituted his home office and held the communications equipment.

"You'd better hear this, too, sir. Don't know why we didn't think of it sooner than this."

"You boys have always operated as a team," Phyllis said, her indignant expression showing her poor opinion of the separation.

Todd raised Captain Kiachif's ship only to be informed that the captain was asleep.

"Look, Todd Reeve here. Hrriss and I have to speak to him. I know he's probably hung over. Put a cup of malak in his hand and ask him to please come speak to me. It's urgent or you'd better believe I wouldn't bother Captain Ali so early."

Todd flung a grin over his shoulder, for it was close to midday. Hrriss chuckled, and even Hu smiled.

"That man!" Phyllis muttered, for she had never understood how anyone could consume so much hard spirits and be allowed to command a ship, much less a whole fleet of them.

"This better be good, young feller me lad," came a growl that was barely recognizable as a voice.

"Drink the malak, Captain Ali, while you listen," Todd said. He explained his theory in crisp sentences and was rewarded by a string of curses.

"Plain as the nose on my face, which has always been very plain to see," Kiachif replied, his voice rougher with chagrin than with overindulgence. "Look, laddie, this is something we don't leave to just one engineer. And that ship of yours is under Martinson's seal, isn't it? So we gotta have an order to see the condition of those engines. They ain't been touched, have they? . . . No, good! Ha! Better 'n' better. Them's as they were left but how d'you prove you and Hrriss weren't space-shattered?"

"And start organizing the Snake Hunt the very next morning?"

"Everyone saw you then?"

"Hrriss and I had day-long conferences and there'd be tapes on the whole day . . . that day and the next thirteen!"

"Ha! Best way to wake up of a morning, laddie. Good news sure sets a man up, if you know what I mean. I'll just get the DeVeer feller. He seems to know beans from bran and brawn. Leave it with me, laddie."

"Of course, of course, of course," Hu muttered to himself, past chagrin that he hadn't thought of that factor: that no one, trying to clear the boys these past weeks, had thought of it.

"Don't fret, Mr. Shih," Todd said, grinning, "Hrriss and I just thought of it ourselves! You'd have to make a lot of warp jumps to know what it does to your circadian rhythms . . . or be an engineer to know what that kind of punishment does to your engines!"

"Or the skin of the ship," Hrriss added. "The *Albatrrrosss* is remarkably unpitted and bright."

"Thanks for the use of the com, sir. We'd best be going. Got a lot more to sort out today."

"Have some . . ." Phyllis's offer of lunch trailed off as the two young men were out the door, leaping off the top of the steps and making for the village corral. Spare horses were always available for emergency use.

Hu took a deep breath. "I feel better than I have since . . ."

"Since Todd Reeve came out of the mist leading the First Speaker?" his wife teased.

He nodded, his smile nostalgic.

Todd and Hrriss didn't bother with saddles. They used bridles only because they didn't recognize any of the horses standing hipshot in the bright noonday sun. They set off at the easy ground-covering lope most Doonan-bred horses were trained to use, kind to both horse and rider.

Pat and Inessa came out onto the porch the moment they heard the horses.

Ken, Robin, and Lon jogged up from the barn, warned by shrieks of welcome from the two females.

"Oh, it's so good to see you, Hrriss," Pat said, pulling his head down to rub his muzzle affectionately, squeezing his hand, for he was too massive now for her to embrace.

Inessa bounced about, clapping her hands and hooting like a hunting urfa, a habit her mother deplored, but this day was too special for reprimands.

Pat was babbling about the feast they must have to celebrate the reunion, that Mrrva and Hrrestan were coming, and . . .

"Kelly and Nrrna," Inessa said, "and half the Solinaris and most of the Adjeis, and Hrrula because that filly they killed was his."

The men arrived and they welcomed Hrriss with much back-thumping and handshaking, while Ken went so far as to rub cheeks with the young Hrruban.

"You've had no lunch!" Pat declared, suddenly noticing their hot faces, the sweat on Todd's and the dust on Hrriss's. "Get washed up this instant. Inessa, come with me."

"Dad, got some real good news for you," Todd said, interrupting the general tumult and launching into what he had asked Captain Kiachif to do.

Ken stared, as drop-jawed as a Hrruban, as he assimilated the information. Then he swung about, banging his fist against the nearest wall in self-abnegation.

"Why didn't one of us think of that aspect?"

"Calm down, Dad," Todd said, grabbing his father's fist. "You haven't warp-jumped half as much as Hrriss and me, and you haven't logged in enough space-time to know how it disorients you. You know we didn't come into your office that day shagged."

Ken shook his head from side to side, still blaming himself for not seeing so plain a verification that they could not have been plucking items from so many different systems during that controversial Hrrethan flight.

Todd gave his father a clout with his fist. "Stop it, Dad, no time for recriminations now. If Captain Ali gets an independent, and well-witnessed, overhaul of the *Albie*'s engines, and we get statements from everyone who saw us working all hours of the day to organize the Hunt, that still only proves we couldn't have made those side trips. It doesn't prove who did. And that . . ." Todd glanced at Hrriss as he began spacing his words in an implacable tone, "is . . . what . . . we . . . have . . . to . . . find . . . out!"

"You're right about that, son," Ken said. "From the way the Treaty Controller was handling the hearing, not to mention the smug look on Rogitel's face and that sycophant Varnorian, proof that you didn't smuggle is not as important as documentation of who *did*."

"Right. Then let's figure out how to go about getting the proof." Todd pulled his father to the dining room table at which so many happier conferences had been held, snagged a chair back, and guided his father to sit. He and Hrriss sat down in the same instant beside each other while a grinning Lon Adjei and Robin joined them.

"By any chance do we have holos of those items we're supposed to have stolen?" Todd asked.

"Hrruvula should have been given copies of all the evidence against you," Ken said.

"Rrrobinn," Hrriss said, "please brrring us the star maps and the handcomp. We must calculate prrrecisssely."

"Kelly's good at that," Robin said. "And she'd want to help." He didn't glance in his brother's direction but there was a twinkle in his eye.

"Both Kelly and Nrrna will be here shortly," Pat said, bustling in with platters piled with sandwiches.

"We owe those girls a lot," Todd said, reaching for a sandwich. The appetite which had deserted him during his separation from Hrriss had returned, doubled.

"Well, don't tell me," his mother said archly. "Tell them!"

Astonished at her tone, Todd watched her leave the room. Then shook himself.

"We've also got to find out who could have possibly assembled such a variety of items, how much they'd cost on the black market—I figure Kiachif might know—"

"And I will inquirre of Hrruban sssourrrces for those which came from ourrr interdicted planets . . ." Hrriss was making notes, too.

"Any word from Linc Newry about launches?" Todd asked, remembering another detail.

Ken shook his head. "But all the ranchers are looking for burn-offs and other illicit corrals. Those hides aren't as important . . ."

"Oh, yes, they are, Dad," Todd replied. "Every single element has to be sifted, sorted, and sewed up."

"Could Kiachifisms be contagious?" Robin asked, his face screwed up in a grin.

Rogitel did not move from his seat when Reeve and his feline friends left the Council chamber so noisily. The bailiff closed the door and returned to his post. Once order had been restored, Poldep Officer DeVeer took up where he had left off, deferring to the Spacedep official.

"If Spacedep has any further objections, I hope it will inform Poldep," De-Veer suggested politely. "We would be happy to cooperate in any interdepartmental inquiries."

Rogitel was already considering the ramifications of the Poldep official's words. He wondered what other data Reeve had uncovered that caused Poldep to intervene on their behalf. There might be a leak in Spacedep's own offices. Internal security checks must be promptly initiated. "None at this time. Spacedep is grateful for Poldep's interest."

"Then, honored Council members, and gentlemen, I must take my leave. There is much to do in the next four weeks." DeVeer left the chamber. It seemed larger without him there. Rogitel felt less pressured. Beside him, Varnorian had fallen asleep.

"I would not wish it to be understood that the department is unwilling to cooperate," the Spacedep subchief said, addressing the board. "Admiral Landreau will be happy to assist in any way he can to fulfill all our wishes." He met the Treaty Controller's eye, and the Hrruban nodded almost imperceptibly. Landreau was correct. The Controller was willing to form a détente to prevent the renewal of the Treaty of Doona. Little did Treaty Controller realize that his actions would displace his fellow animals and leave the entire planet in the possession of its rightful owners, the Human race.

"I am convinced that we both want the same thing," the Controller said. He will help me, the Treaty Controller thought. And then he and his bareskin cohorts will be expelled, leaving only Hrrubans here on Rrala. The unnatural colony would be disbanded. He and Rogitel smiled at each other companionably over the conference table.

chapter nine

Captain Horstmann found DeVeer and whisked him off to Portmaster Martinson's office, where that official was in a state of dithering shock. For one thing, he had every spacefaring captain and every chief engineer of the many ships on landing pads in his facility crowding his office and the adjacent hall.

"Make way! I got 'im," Horstmann bawled, and bellies were sucked in, toes splayed, to allow the passage of two more large men. "Special delivery! Live cargo!"

"Now, will you tell me what this is all about?" DeVeer demanded, for he was unused to being manhandled without explanation, and his temper, exacerbated by the hearing, was becoming shorter with every passing second.

"They say . . . the engines will show wear and tear," Martinson said, gulping in anxiety and waving his hands about. "But I can't let them in unless I have proper authorization. They absolutely refused to let me contact Spacedep or Codep . . ." He flinched as bass and baritone rumbles reinforced that prohibition. "Inspector DeVeer, I can accept your authorization to unseal the *Albatross*?" It was more entreaty than query.

"It's like this, Inspector," and a swarthy, hook-nosed wiry man with a stubbled chin, bleary-eyed, stepped forward. He wasn't a large man, but he exuded an air of authority that DeVeer related to immediately, accepting him as spokesman for this crowd. "Ya see, Todd and Hrriss are supposed to have made these nine warp jumps in the *Albie* on their way back from that Hrrethan do. They say they didn't. The engines in a ship that has been tightly sealed since that Spacedep chair pilot charged 'em with all that piracy will show to this impartial"—and a long stained hand waved at the crowd silently listening—"jury of experts just how much wear and tear those engines took since their last service." He hauled flimsies which DeVeer recognized as maintenance records. "We got these from Martinson here and the Hrrethan Space Authority, dated, sealed, and all legal-like, as proof of the most recent service checks the aforementioned *Albatross* had. You sign the authorization. We all take a look, write up official reports, and I'd bet you credits to cookies, we'll all discover—not to our amazement but what we all know without having to check—that those engines'll prove those boys didn't take no nine warp jumps in that vessel like they're accused of doing. Whaddaya say?"

DeVeer had had to concentrate to follow the rapid-fire explanation in a hot cramped space. It took him a moment to absorb the points.

"It will not prove who did, o' course," the captain went on before DeVeer could respond, "but those engines will prove those boys didn't! Hear you got word the Mayday beacon turned up, if you know what I mean?" The captain winked. "By the way, I'm Ali Kiachif, skipper of the *White Lightning,*" and he offered DeVeer his hand.

Absently DeVeer accepted and the slender fingers were as strong as his own though the hand was half the size of his.

"I believe that could prove a profitable investigation, Captain Kiachif." DeVeer turned to Martinson, who was wiping the sweat from his face, looking haggard and harassed. "Can you supply me with the proper documents, Mr. Martinson?"

"All made out, ready for your John-Cock on the dotted line," Kiachef said, wiping out a second sheaf of official-issue flimsy and spreading it out on the one clear portion of Martinson's desk.

Writing implements were offered by eight or nine different obliging hands. DeVeer, for once feeling completely overwhelmed, twitched the nearest one free and poised it over the quintuplicate form. He was far too experienced an executive to sign what he had not scanned, but he was a speed-reader. The form had been filled in properly, and when he actually started to sign, a deafening cheer resounded from office and corridor.

"You must of course be present during the unsealing and the investigation, Inspector," Kiachif said, seizing the form and separating its sheets, crumbling the first one, which he fired at Martinson, shoving a second into DeVeer's hand, and, waving the rest over his head, pushed his way out of the office while the cheers still echoed. Realizing that DeVeer was not on his heels, he paused and beckoned urgently for him to follow.

Several hours later, the truth of Captain Kiachif's allegation was proved beyond question. In all particulars, the engines were in excellent running order, no wear, tear, or abuse visible: rather no more than was consonant with a journey to and from Hrretha, and this was verified not only by the Hrrethan Space Authority maintenance check but by nine fully qualified warp-drive engineers and nine fully qualified space captains of impeccable integrity. In order to prove their qualifications and allegations, DeVeer learned more about the workings of warp-drive engines, fuel capacities, gauges, the pitting of ship skins from forced warp jumps, and the condition of lubricants, greases, flux levels, and rocket tube encrustations than he would ever again need. He fully appreciated why Martinson had looked so fraught: he felt rather wrung out himself.

"Ah, Inspector, I see you are in need of sustenance," Kiachif said, folding away the sheaf of formal declarations from captains and engineers. "Lads, we can't let this fine gentleman suffer a moment longer."

DeVeer had no option but to accompany the jovial group to the pub. He also had no memory of how he got back to the accommodations he had been assigned on the Treaty Island. Some thoughtful soul—possibly Ali Kiachif—had left a small vial and a brief note where he could not fail to see it the moment his eyes could focus. "Drink this!" the note said. He did and rather more quickly than he thought possible, his condition improved.

Others had celebrated during that evening of which DeVeer had few lucid memories. For immediately upon finishing the scrupulous inspection of the *Albatross*, Ali Kiachif had informed the Reeve family.

"Don't fret too much about the smuggling charge either," Kiachif said. "Got friends working on that, too, if you know what I mean. It'll take a bit more time 'cause we've more to check."

"Ali, you must be calling in favors by the container load," Ken said, immensely grateful.

"Give a little, take a lot's been my motto for decades, Reeve. And, like I say, we all got a lot at stake, same's you Doonans. You keep on tracking down livestock. That's where your expertise lies. I'll keep on prodding, poking, and producing where mine'll do us good. Have a drink on me, you hear me?" Kiachif hadn't waited for an answer and Ken was staring at a crackling handset.

As everyone had heard Kiachif's inimitable voice on the radio, cheers rose from around the dining table. Kelly and Nrrna executed a triumphant dance routine before careening into a table.

"One by one, the charges are being dismissed," Hrrestan said while Mrrva nodded as if she had expected no other outcome.

"Down to two—identifying who purchased the artifacts and who's playing Todd and Hrriss off-planet," Ken said.

"No, three," Todd said. "We've got to find out how the security satellites have been fixed."

"Is not Inspector DeVeer investigating that?" Hrrestan asked.

Ken and Todd both frowned, increasing the resemblance between them so much that Pat, Kelly, and Inessa grinned.

"DeVeer would need Spacedep authority to check the satellites," Ken said, shaking his head over the improbability of assistance from that source.

"Would he?" Hrrestan asked, stroking his chin. "Would he not have authority over Martinson?"

"He must have some, to get clearance for Ali to check the *Albatross* engines," Ken replied, but he wasn't all that certain that DeVeer might not press the issue. "But Linc Newry's got a separate authority and reports only to Spacedep."

"The inspector wants to help us," Kelly said. "And he practically got Klonski to admit that he had."

"You didn't mention that," Todd said bluntly.

"Well," and she shook her spread hand to indicate uncertainty, "Klonski is known to have done that sort of security tinkering—Inspector DeVeer established that—so why else was Spacedep paying him, and putting him in their restricted 'special services' category?"

"We still need more documented evidence of who's behind what we may now call a well-planned and long-standing conspiracy," Ken said, addressing everyone but looking at Hrrestan.

"I think they overdid the evidence bit," Pat said. "They might have made one charge stick but so many?"

"Ah, but that is where they have been clever, not stupid, Pat," Hrrestan said. "They have created a variety of charges, none of which can be ignored by one or the other of those departments of yourrs and ourrs that are involved. Rrala is to be torn apart by debates on which allegations are true and which might be specious. The fact that would, I fear, become lost in the morasss of true, half true, and false, is that our sons never committed any of the crimes of which they stand charged. But by the time they can be cleared of all counts, any hope of renewing the Treaty would be lost and the colony forced to decamp."

Nrrna shuddered and drew closer to Hrriss.

"But I'm positive Landreau is behind all of this," Ken said. "He's hated me and Todd since the first time you all disappeared and left us looking like first-class liars."

Hrrestan and Mrrva bowed their heads. "We had no choice."

"Oh, I know that, Hrrestan," Ken said, dismissing any implication of blame. "But it was Todd who kept us here because Hrrubans would not leave a small child in a dangerous forest. And it was Todd who brought First Speaker here, and Al Landreau has never forgiven him or me for that humiliation."

Kelly and Hrriss grinned during Todd's obvious discomfort at that summary, but Nrrna was curious, not knowing all the historic details from that period.

Hrrestan sighed. "If only Third Speaker's associate were not Treaty Controller this period . . ."

"Another piece of deft planning on Landreau's part. I gotta give him credit for that," Ken said with a hint of grudging admiration.

"Trrrue, for with another Hrruban as Controller, we would be able to lay before First Speaker the framework of this conspiracy . . ."

"Would First Speaker not be aware of that already, Hrrestan?" Mrrva asked, her hand lightly on her mate's thigh. "We know the pressures that are being exerted in the Speakers Council."

"This time," Hrrestan said, "there is no child with a tail of rope to capture the hearts and minds of our people and swing a vote in favor of a Treaty of Cohabitation."

"I know this might sound silly," Kelly began tentatively, "and forgive me if this question offends, but it's something that has never been addressed in Alreldep either: if the Treaty breaks down, which of us gets to stay on Doona? Or do we both leave, lock, stock, and block?" She tried to make a joke of it.

When everyone stared at her, she began to flush and ended up with her head down.

"No, no, Kelly," Todd said, "that's a very good question indeed. In fact, that might actually be the crux of the matter."

Kelly looked up, eyes shining and face alight with his genuine approval.

"Indeed, Kelly, that is a question which has not been asked," Hrrestan said, "and one we should have considered long before now. Have we all been looking at the forest without seeing the trees?" He leaned forward, elbows on his knees, his eyes slitting with the intensity of his thought. "You and I, Ken, like our sons, wish the Rralan Experiment to succeed. We both know in our minds that there are Hrrubans and Hayumans who do not wish that. If the Treaty is not renewed, each sees this planet as a prize for the taking. As you once confided in me, Ken, twenty-four years ago on a hilltop, Hayumans get greedy. Well, so do Hrrubans. There is indeed much more at stake than just this planet and which species gains control of it." Hrrestan paused, unwilling to follow that line of discussion to its obvious conclusion.

"An interspecies war?" Todd exclaimed, horrified.

Nrrna gave a frightened yip and clung to Hrriss's arm. Kelly and Pat Reeve turned pale.

"I could go back to Alreldep," Kelly said earnestly. "I may be only a junior but if I could present any proof whatsoever that this is what's going down on Doona . . ." Kelly's voice failed her as the permutations of a struggle between Hayumans and Hrrubans sank in. "Oh, no! We can't let that happen!" she said in a whisper.

Todd jumped to his feet, glaring about him. "You just bet we won't." His words rang in the frightened silence.

"By all that's holy, we won't," Ken added, rising from his chair.

"We will not!" Hrrestan and Hrriss spoke at the same moment, springing to their feet.

"Rralans forever!" Kelly shouted in Middle Hrruban, jumping up and down, fists clenched.

Todd grinned at her, proud of her for using that language, and more moved than he could say by her offer to help, by returning to Earth and the Alreldep job he knew she must hate. But, then, she was as Doonan—no, Rralan—as he.

"All right, now then, folks," Ken said, rubbing his hands together as he would before taking on any difficult task. "We've got more to do than we thought. But we've got help. I don't think we'd better let tonight's conclusions loose on the planet. There's enough panic and crazy-minded speculation as it is, with rustling and false accusations and suchlike just before Treaty Renewal. So, while we're knocking down the accusations against the boys, we'll see if we can also find any clues that might show us that the scope of the conspiracy goes beyond Landreau and—" He looked at Hrrestan.

"And Third Speaker," the Hrruban added for him.

"Too bad we can't use their techniques against them," Kelly said, "and start finding the tadpoles in their ponds. Get that Treaty Controller impeached or something."

"Oh!" Nrrna's little cry of surprise focused attention on her.

"Yes, Nrrna?" Hrriss prompted, and that was when Todd really began to notice how tender his friend was toward the pretty female and how often she seemed to rely on him for reassurance.

"The Treaty Controller," and she bowed her head slightly, keeping her eyes averted from Kelly's sudden grin of comprehension, "received delivery of a document box the day Kelly returned. It must have been very important for him not to send an assistant or secretary."

Kelly snapped her fingers. "I've got a memory like a sieve. I got a coded comp-line message today from Dalkey Petersham. He was very cagey even in code. He's got something he needs to get to me and he doesn't trust the comp-mail lines."

"Did he say what?" Todd asked, aware of an unusual uneasiness with a guy comp-lining Kelly all the time. But that was silly. They needed help from whatever quarter it came.

"What I got from the code was that, as a very junior official, he was supposed to check over and delete some ancient accounting tapes. They were for the Spacedep slush fund. There seemed to be large financial disbursements about ten years ago from that fund and all of them were paid to accounts off-Earth. He thought they might be useful to me, but he won't send it comp-line and wants to know how he can get it to us in . . . as they say . . . a rapid irregular fashion."

"Isn't Captain Feyder back on Earth?" Todd asked.

"Been and gone, according to Kiachif," Ken replied. "He'd done us all the favor we can ask of him with that Mayday beacon."

"We could get in another medical shipment," Kelly said, glancing sideways at Nrrna.

Her eyes went into slits of anxiety. "Oh, no. I was in trouble over the gloves when they saw how many packets had been trampled on. My superior was going to send a harsh message to our office on Terra. So I told them that I had opened the box outside, to take inventory, and a wind had come up and scattered them."

"The wind was named Kelly," the redhead said, giggling at the memory of the trouble she and Nrrna had had to get the static-charged packets back into the carton. "I even found one inside my tunic."

"The count was off so I had to say that some had blown away," Nrrna dropped her jaw and purred her pretty laugh.

"You've got a resourceful female here, Hrriss," Kelly said. "And you nearly wouldn't let her help."

"I shall not again be so foolish as to interfere with her good plans," he said, pulling a solemn face that made Kelly laugh.

Todd looked from Kelly to Hrriss and Nrrna, and then at Hrrestan and Mrrva, who seemed quietly pleased about the behavior of Nrrna and their son.

"Hey, friend, did you forget to tell me something this morning?" Todd asked.

"Nrrna and I plan to be lifemates," Hrriss said, his eyes glowing as he glanced down at Nrrna. "The joining is due to take place about the time of Treaty Renewal."

Todd dropped his jaw, so like a Hrruban that Kelly smothered her giggles. "Oh, really? Well, you didn't waste any time while I was gone, did you?" But his eyes were glowing with pleasure and approval. "Why, you old tomcat, you? Congratulations!" He gave Hrriss a hearty punch on the arm and took one of Nrrna's hands, lifting it to touch his forehead in the Hrruban gesture of well-wishing and congratulation. "To think you went out and did that that by yourself," he said, unable to leave off teasing Hrriss. He could see that Hrrestan and Mrrva were delighted and his parents seemed to have known. He felt a little silly that he hadn't twigged to it.

"We plan a celebratory feast on the occasion," Hrriss said, "and we would be honored if you would stand as master of ceremonies."

"The honor is mine," Todd said, falling back into his chair and letting out a hoot of relieved laughter. "Well, I feel lots better. I admit I wondered why Nrrna was suddenly so much a part of the investigation. I thought she was a friend Kelly had brought in to help her."

"Of all the . . ." Kelly jumped to her feet and ran out of the room.

"What got her so uptight?" Todd inquired of everyone in the room.

"Kelly has been helping *you*, you numskull," his mother said with a weary sigh of exasperation for her son's obtuseness. "She's the main reason you and Hrriss have been reunited."

"I know she's been helping me," Todd said, still perplexed.

"Then do not sit like a mda in warm mud contemplating its toes," Hrriss said. He rose and gave Todd a shove toward the door. "I have had the opportunity to make plain to her my gratitude. It is time that you adequately express your own. Do it suitably in the style of Hayumans, but do it now!"

Half stumbling onto the porch because Hrriss had put considerable strength into that push, Todd corrected himself and looked about for Kelly. Twilight made it difficult to see, but he spotted Calypso's hide and saw the mare moving before he realized Kelly was astride her.

"Kelly! Kellllleeee! Wait a minute!"

He knew she had seen him, for he saw her white face turned in his direction, but she cantered off anyhow. Piqued, Todd took the nearest horse from the tie rail, Robin's fleet racer Fargo, and started after her.

Todd was just gaining on the cantering Calypso when Kelly realized that she was being pursued, and kicked the mare into a gallop.

"Kelly! Pull up!" Todd yelled angrily.

She bent low in the saddle and urged Calypso faster.

Todd had half a mind to pull up right then and there. He hadn't meant to insult her. Didn't she know him well enough by now to know he liked her? Why, she was as moody as a Hrruban female in estrus.

In shocked surprise, Todd almost pulled up Fargo as he suddenly understood what he'd been too self-involved, first in the Hunt and then in clearing his name, to recognize. His heart seemed to expand in a peculiarly painful but marvelous way . . . as it had when he had embraced Hrriss on the bridge . . . but not quite the same way. Stunned by the intensity of his feelings for Kelly, he clapped his heels into Fargo's sides and sped after his girl.

For Kelly was, and she had proved her love for him over and over again, only he'd been dense as two planks not to realize that his former friend and willing cohort had turned into a lovely girl, who could wear frilly wide skirts imported specially from Earth to look her best at the Hunt dance. For stupid him! Why she bothered with such a lunkhead he couldn't understand, but he had to catch up with her and see if he couldn't set matters straight between them.

A girl who had ridden between his home and Hrriss's doing her best to say to each what they weren't permitted to say to each other. And she had even gone to the extreme of dyeing her gorgeous red hair, risked her safety on Earth's slideways and sleazy Aisles, bearded inspectors with purloined documentation and . . . And he hadn't the sense to realize what any Hrruban male would have known—that Kelly wanted him just as much as Nrrna wanted Hrriss.

Now he exercised his wits and saw the turn off the main road that would give him the jump on their head start.

He drove the bay up the hill and down, hauling him to a dead stop across the narrow trail. Calypso was travelling at such a speed that she did a stiff-legged stop to avoid crashing into Fargo. Kelly, who'd been looking over her shoulder, came tumbling out of the saddle, right into Todd's arms. He caught her before she could slide out of his grasp and pulled her sideways across the low pommel.

"Gotcha! Fair and square," he said, grinning because it had been a close thing. But he hadn't been about to let Kelly go now he realized how much she meant to him. And before she could say or do anything to put him off his intended action, he kissed her hard.

The shock that coursed through his body at the touch of their lips was totally unexpected. Briefly he held her off so he could see her face, see if she could possibly be feeling the same way he did about that kiss. But her eyes were closed and there was an incredibly dreamy look about her face. So he gathered her to him more tenderly and found that their second kiss was even sweeter than the first and so he didn't break it off in any hurry at all. Especially when he felt her arms clasping him, one around his ribs and the other pressing at the nape of his neck so he couldn't have released her even if he'd wanted to.

The feel of Kelly in his arms was something magical. Much better than dancing with her had been, so he pressed her as close to him as he could. Until he felt Fargo—who was not up to the weight of the pair of them—buckle a bit on the forehand.

"Robin'll kill us if we lame Fargo," she murmured. "But Calypso could carry us both a long time."

"I think we'll rest both horses after that mad race," he said, managing to dismount with her still in his arms. Then he clipped an arm under her knees and carried her to the nearest clear patch of grass. "I love you, Kelly Solinari. Will you forgive me for being dumb blind stupid iggerant not to realize how precious you are to me?"

"I might, but it could take a long time—like forever," she replied in a lilting voice.

Sometime later, Fargo decided that he'd make his way back to his stable. Calypso had better manners. She wouldn't leave her rider and grazed contentedly until she was needed again.

chapter ten

The next morning, the two young couples composed a carefully worded message to Dalkey, containing instructions on where to hide the information he wanted to send. They posted it signed with Kelly's key-code. Couched in the chatty phrases about their years together in college was the fact that several pallets of medical supplies were being transported to Doona in two days. Dalkey swiftly responded with an ardent note, the tone of which made Todd frown and Kelly blush.

"But it sounds genuine, Toddy," Kelly said soothingly. Then she giggled. "You're here and he's parsecs away. Don't be silly. Besides, he does say that he understands the instructions and I get the impression that he accessed more data than he originally promised."

Todd apologized for acting silly, but the truth was, they were all nervous. Something could delay the shipment, or Dalkey might be seen where he had no reasonable explanation to be. Both Nrrna and Kelly arranged to be on hand to receive the supplies. This time Nrrna did not wear any scent.

The grid operator flinched when he recognized Nrrna appearing on the platform from First Village. He still found her attractive, though not as strongly, and especially not when she was accompanied by a Hayuman female. He only hoped that the Treaty Controller was not expecting another shipment, but a quick glance at the manifest told him he didn't need to worry about that tonight.

Kelly was relieved that the operator seemed too busy to chat them up. She and Nrrna managed a desultory conversation while they waited, but they were so keyed up they'd forget what the other had just said. Kelly kept imagining problems: What if the envelope didn't come or got torn loose in the transfer? What if Dalkey got caught? They needed to have genuine, hard documentation. Well, maybe if Dalkey didn't come through for them, they might have some luck with the documents that the Treaty Controller had personally awaited. Anything that pleased an associate of Third Speaker was likely to be bad for Doona.

When the suspense became so great that Kelly was prepared to dive right through the pillars and drag the shipment up from Earth, the air thickened over the gridwork and the pallets materialized. She and Nrrna let out sighs of relief.

"Will you check it now so I may clear the grid?" the operator asked.

"That's why we're here," she said, handing a sheaf of papers from her clipboard to Kelly and peremptorily gesturing her to go to the back of the grid.

They'd planned this so Kelly would be screened from the operator and could feel under the pallet for the envelope. Then she thought of a better stratagem than blind groping.

She let her clipboard drop. "Ooops," she said gaily, and, in attempting to pick it up, kicked it under the pallet. "Wouldn't you know?" she said with cheerful self-disgust. She got down, peering under the shipment, trying to see Dalkey's envelope. He'd been instructed to use a gray one which wouldn't be so readily visible to anyone casually glancing under the plastic pallet. She shook her wrist so the small torch would fall out of her sleeve where she'd hidden it and played its dim beam around, but she saw absolutely nothing, not even cobwebs.

"Does your friend need help rising?" the operator asked rather irritably.

"Probably," Nrrna said in intimate pitch, trying to stall. "Her balance is very poor. Hayumans have weak inner ears."

"I had noticed that their ears are abnormally small," he said, and came round to help Kelly to her feet. She feigned momentary weakness before she met Nrrna's eyes over the boxes and gave a shake to her head.

"Thank you, sir," she said to the operator, reaching out suddenly to grab his arm, swaying in a fashion that alarmed him. "My balance is none too good."

That had given Nrrna sufficient time to look underneath on her side. But she shook her head, too.

"Is this all we're supposed to get today?" Nrrna asked, checking over the number of boxes on her board. "I am missing several cartons."

He leaned over to examine her list. "No, you do not have all. Those sizes have to be broken down into two shipments. Second lot will come through in"—he paused to check his own schedule—"two hours. A shipment of ore from one of the mining worlds is due in next. Come back."

"Very well," Nrrna said, masking her relief in a cool response, "I will accompany this lot to the Health Center. Will you stay on the island and wait for the rest?" she asked Kelly.

"Oh, I don't mind. I've got a few things I can do while I wait. See you in the village." Kelly threw a good-luck gesture to Nrrna.

Once the characteristic mist rose around the crates and Nrrna, whisking them from sight, Kelly left the reception area. As she departed, she heard the operator's audible sigh of relief.

She'd been to the Treaty Island often enough to know the general layout, which was another reason why she had the best chance of accomplishing her second, and possibly more important, errand. But she stopped for a long moment to reread the inaugural plaque outside the main administration building.

"This Treaty Center was constructed in the fourth year of the Colony by the people of Hrruba, Earth, and Doona/Rrala in the spirit of cooperation represented by the Treaty of Doona."

Kelly felt a tingle of pride and renewed determination that the colony world, the turning point in the histories of both civilizations, would not become a future battleground. She knew where the Councillors' quarters were but she didn't want to blunder into the Controller's rooms if he was present. From the look of so many lights in the low Administration Building, there might be late meetings that would solve that problem.

She strode right up to the information desk where two Humans and a Hrruban, wearing official guide badges, were drinking malak.

"I've a message for the Treaty Controller," she said brightly, addressing all three.

One of the Humans peered at a list on the desk. "He should still be in the Council chamber. They've got an all-day session. Back the way you came and around the corner to the right at the T-junction."

"Oh! But I was told to take it to him at his personal quarters, sir."

The guide exchanged a glance with the other two. "Well, they'd be due for a break soon." He pointed out the glass door facing the desk. "Across the courtyard there, and along the garden walk. Treaty Controller's apartment is the last on the right."

"Thank you so much," Kelly said, and followed the directions, swinging her arms and striding off as if she hadn't a care in the world.

Several blocks on the left of the Administration Building housed visitors to the island, mostly researchers there to consult the ever-increasing Archives. To the right were the residences assigned to members of the Treaty Council. Each species, Hayuman and Hrruban, sent three delegates to the Council. Of those three, one was chosen from the species' homeworld, one from Doona/Rrala, and the third could be from either of those or from a colony world. The seventh member, the Treaty Controller, was nominated every three years in turn from the Hayuman or Hrruban side. Most frequently the Councillors were justiciars by profession.

The seven apartments were actually small detached houses abutting the formal garden and maintained by Treaty staff. Kelly followed the row to the end and found the modest home of the Treaty Councillor. Swallowing her nervousness, she slipped through the gate and approached the door, which was shaded by a stand of fringed palms. It wasn't just the tropical sun that was making Kelly sweat. She had no idea what excuse she could give if the Controller should find her here.

Following the spirit of openness and trust fostered on Doona, nothing was locked. Doors had fastenings and fences with strong latches to keep animals from wandering in or out. Irreplaceables and valuables were locked up safely out of sight, but few residences on Treaty Island were ever secured. She hoped the Treaty Controller, not known for his acceptance of Doonan traditions, followed the local custom.

The door opened without resistance.

"Sir?" she called out tentatively. There was no answer, and indeed, as she stepped inside, the apartment had the silence of an uninhabited space. Gently she pushed the door almost shut. She ought to hear footsteps on the shell-lined walk.

The Treaty Controller lived in style. The fine green carpet was deep and soft, and took footprints all too easily. Her sandals made smaller impressions in it than slender Hrruban feet would. Would the nap spring up to erase her inward path? Or would he notice? His furnishings were lavishly decorated and suited to Hrruban anatomy. Not a single Hayuman-style chair or stool. The walls were hung with warmly colored Hrruban tapestries. All manner of Rralan-made crafts were displayed in wall niches and on small stone-topped pedestals, presents from Hrruban villages on the planet. Grudgingly she admitted that the old tom had good taste, but the furnishings also afforded numerous hiding places for the document box she sought.

As the tapestries were fastened to the wall from rods on a picture rail, she could look beneath them and tap the bright orange-dyed rla wall for hollow places. She found nothing and was examining the walls in the sleeping chamber when she heard the front door swing open and bounce against its hinges.

She froze and listened, hearing with great relief the sighing of a breeze. She tiptoed back to the door and peered around the corner, trying to keep out of sight. Someone stared right at her. Shocked and still in a half-crouch, Kelly stared back. But it wasn't the Treaty Controller. It was a small, coffee-skinned Hayuman with gray hair twisted into a coronet on her head. A Councillor's robe was slung casually over one arm.

"Who . . . who are you?" Kelly asked meekly.

"I was going to ask you the very same question, girl," the woman replied in a stern voice. "I thought the wind had blown the door open but I see he has a snooper going through his possessions. A thief on Treaty Island itself! Disgraceful! Give me your name this instant and your business here."

"Please, Madam Dupuis," for Kelly recognized her, "I'm not stealing anything. I'm Kelly Solinari of First Hayuman Village and I'm trying to help Todd Reeve."

"In the Controller's bedroom?" Madam Dupuis's eyebrows rose in amused query. "He doesn't like Hayumans, you know."

"Don't I just!" Sensing a sympathetic relaxation of the Councillor's disapproval, Kelly decided the truth would do her more good than any invention. So she summarized her illegal return to Earth and approaching Inspector DeVeer for assistance, and how she had overheard mention of a very special document box from Hrruba anxiously awaited by the Treaty Controller. "We've got Todd and Hrriss cleared of one charge," and Madam Dupuis nodded, so Kelly didn't bother to explain other matters of which the Councillor would have more intimate knowledge than she did. "But it's more than just an attempt to ruin the Treaty, Madam Dupuis. We think it's a conspiracy between certain Hayuman and Hrruban elements that might lead"—this was the hardest part to say aloud—"might lead to an interspecies war . . ." Madam Dupuis's hand went to her throat and her complexion paled noticeably. "A war that is meant to leave only one species on Doona and only one dominant species in the known galaxy."

Madam Dupuis regarded her for a very long moment with eyes dulled with sorrow.

"I fear you may be right, Kelly Solinari, though I have not had the courage to admit it to myself. I have always known that our current Controller was one of Third Speaker's nominees, but he has, until recently, been scrupulously fair in his judgments during our negotiations." She bowed her head for a long moment, her hand idly stroking her robe. "I have suspected a subtle alteration in his mien. You don't live for twelve years in close contact with someone, even of another species, and not notice"—her fingers flickered—"little things. I've wondered about his much-vaunted impartiality, but then," and she gave Kelly a rueful grin, "mine has been slipping somewhat, too. With all of my heart I want Doona to remain as it is." Her manner altered abruptly. "It is extraordinary behavior for a born and bred Doonan to break and enter, but if you can keep it to yourself and can find what you seek, I shall forget I've seen you."

"You will?" Kelly couldn't believe her escape.

"Hmm," Madam Dupuis murmured in an absent fashion. "I just came over to shut his door. I had noticed that the wind must have blown it ajar. Surprising how strong the breeze can be when the temperature starts to fall at this time of day." She started back to the door then turned, hand on the knob. "Have you found what you're looking for?"

Kelly shook her head. "I only just got here."

"Then for the sake of us all, find it," she said in a voice of command. "I'd help you myself because I believe you have seen the true reason behind all this maneuvering. I've got a boondoggle that I've been waiting to raise before the copies of the Treaty are written up. A Human outpost on Hrruba, similar to the facility Hrringa occupies on Earth. I want to see equal treatment for our species, but it's a sticking point I haven't been able to maneuver that old tomcat past. That should make a good long point to argue. I will make certain that you have an hour to search, but that is all I can hope to extend the argument. His patience isn't infinite. Will that suffice?"

"It will have to," Kelly said, her tone expressing her intense gratitude for understanding and assistance.

Just as Madam Dupuis was about to close the door behind her, she added, "If you need a haven, my office is on the first floor above the commissary." Then she closed the door firmly behind her.

The first thing Kelly did was to look about the sleeping quarters for a hiding place for herself. The heavy curtains would do and they gave onto a small shrub-lined yard but the bushes would be nothing for her to scale.

His closets yielded nothing except that the Controller was a fastidious person, for everything was neatly hung and arranged in outfits for lounging, public appearances, and ceremonial receptions. Nothing among the films and flimsies in his desk looked like official documents or reports. She read Hrruban, High, Low, and Middle, but a quick scan told her there was nothing incriminating in the drawers.

The communications unit was like any other on Doona or Earth, with no place for concealment in, on, or under the console. Brushing her hands on her legs to dry nervous perspiration, she started on the other furnishings.

She was halfway through her hour's dispensation when she found her prize.

The document box was hidden underneath the last drawer in the bedroom bureau. The Treaty Controller had sawn out and removed half of the supporting board under the drawer, leaving a large hiding place accessible without turning the heavy chest over. Kelly drew the box out and rested it on her knees.

It was a very ordinary document box, like any other used for conveying official papers back and forth between offices. Kelly had seen, and handled, dozens like it at Alreldep. She hefted it: light, couldn't be much inside. But then she didn't need much, only the right sort of document.

She examined the lock and here the resemblance to ordinary courier boxes ended. It was fitted with a custom lock intended to discourage unauthorized entry. The lock was flat, but a glance inside the keyhole with her tiny torch showed that it was made to accept a key with multiple wards each as narrow as a strand of hair. Box in hand, she looked about the room for something she could use to manipulate the lock. She found a straight pin but it was no use. She didn't dare try to force the box or break it open and her time was nearly up.

She started to put the box back into its place of concealment, but stopped when she noticed the remains of an official seal on the untied tapes that dangled from the sides of the container. It reminded her of something, and the memory tickled at the back of her mind. She had seen a seal used by the High Council of Speakers of Hrruba. This one was a lot like it but not as complex. Using the point of a pin and an old scrap of film she found in a wastebin, she copied down as much of the seal as she could.

Madam Dupuis's gift of an uninterrupted hour was definitely over. Not daring to try the lock any longer lest she be caught there fiddling with it when the Treaty Controller returned, Kelly put the box away and replaced the drawer.

On her knees, she backed out of the room, fluffing up the woolly carpet with her hands. At the door, she stopped, and tried to remember if there was anything she had left open or out of place. No, she had been thorough, if unsuccessful.

"There," she said. "I hope he doesn't check for fingerprints."

Striding with as much nonchalance as she could, Kelly made her way to the research quarters where she knew Hrruvula was quartered for the hearings. Without explaining her presence or her occupation the past hour, she showed him her drawing of the seal. He gave her a startled glance and peered at it closely. When she opened her mouth to explain, he held up his hand, his eyes dark and inscrutable.

"You are not my client, Kelly Solinari, so anything you might wish to impart to me would not be done under the cloak of confidentiality," he said, still studying the scrap of film. "You have not been here. We have not talked of anything, especially about a replica of the private insignia of the Third Speaker."

He handed it back to her, gestured politely for her to exit as quickly as she had entered, and turned his back on her.

She left Hrruvula's office at a trot, heading for the transport grid. So that was it! The Treaty Controller was, against all the precepts of his current position, actively collaborating with his sponsor to prevent the renewal of the Treaty! She hoped the evidence Dalkey had found was indeed on the next shipment. There wouldn't be another medical shipment for weeks, and by then Doona might be just a memory. The thought scared her so much she ran all the way back to the grid station.

The grid operator transferred Kelly and the remaining pallet directly to the transport station in First Village. She all but fell off the platform into Todd's waiting arms and let him sustain the embrace to restore her self-confidence. Hrriss watched the salutation with glowing eyes, Nrrna beside him, delicate hands nervously clasped together.

"It's here," Kelly said excitedly, thrusting the dark gray envelope into their hands. "He came through. I just love Dalkey. He did it."

Todd eagerly opened the packet which contained a sheaf of printouts, folded neatly in half. To the top a note in Dalkey's precise, impersonal hand-writing was attached, which Todd read aloud. "None of these account numbers Earth-based. Good luck. D." Todd's fingers fumbled as he opened the sheets and glanced quickly through them. "He's done it. We've got it!"

Hrriss hissed softly. "This will take time to decipher," Hrriss said, reading over Todd's shoulder. "First it must be determined which numeric prefixes per-tain to which worlds."

"A lot of money changed hands," Todd said, and whistled at the size of sep-arate amounts. "I don't think it'll be that hard with so many good minds"—he grinned about him—"focused on the job. Look. The numbers repeat. Some of these accounts have had several deposits. With what we already know, we ought to be able to figure out which worlds are involved. We can start by checking the amounts against what we've got in Klonski's."

"Shouldn't we take this right to Poldep?" Kelly asked.

"Call me paranoid if you want, Kelly, but I want to decipher this for our-selves first before we show it to anyone else."

"Yeah, if they turned out to be legitimate supply payments," Kelly said with a grimace, "we'd damage our cause. We can't afford to do that! And"—her voice strengthened and her eyes flashed up at him—"you're not paranoid—not any more than you have reason to be."

Todd grinned down at her, really enjoying their newfound intimacy. "These could turn out to be quite legitimate remittances to free-lancers on infrequent invoices."

"I think Dalkey would know if that's what they were," Kelly said, slightly defensive. Dalkey had taken risks to get these to her, and he wasn't stupid. "But you're right. Let's divvy them up among us so it'll go faster."

"All for one and one for all," Nrrna startled Todd and Kelly by saying. Seeing their surprise, she smiled in pleasure at the effect. "I found that quote in one of your Earth classics."

Todd grinned. "I think a more appropriate quote might be 'If we don't hang together, we will most assuredly hang separately.' Any luck on the other half of Project Infiltrate?" he asked Kelly, his arm still lightly about her shoulders.

Kelly rolled her eyes over that little escapade and then gave her friends a quick summary.

"Madam Dupuis is on our side?" Todd exclaimed when she had finished. "That's a real plus." Then he shook his head. "It's just tough luck that you couldn't get inside the document box, but the seal's incriminating. The Treaty Controller is supposed to be impartial. He certainly shouldn't be receiving documents from Third Speaker. No wonder he collected the shipment himself. Let's get cracking on what we do have."

They quickly determined that what Dalkey had sent was the complete printout of all transactions within the slush fund account for a period of fifteen years, ending two years before the present date. Once decoded, it might provide the hard documentation they needed.

"Three eight one is the prefix for Zapata Three," Todd said, referring to the printout that had been presented to the Treaty Council by Landreau. "So shall we assume that this first number is the account opened by 'Rikard Baliff'?" He compared the dates with missions he and Hrriss had been on: those which Rogitel had intimated had included nefarious side trips. "Well, whaddya know? Every single transaction date matches with one of our trips, Hrriss."

The Hrruban hissed softly between his teeth. "Someone has most scrupulously kept track of our journeys. But that could be anyone on Rrala. We made no secret of our departures and of our estimated time of return."

"And told their Zapatan contact just when to make lodgments," Kelly said, seething at the complicity and the way it had been turned against her friends. "Isn't that a second Zapatan account?" and she tapped her stylus on another 381 listing. "Is that our rustler being paid off? It's too neat to be mere coincidence, especially when all the figures match all that incriminating junk Rogitel was waffling on about. Sure looks like a connection between Spacedep and that rustler to me. Let's take it to Inspector DeVeer."

Todd grinned at her for her enthusiasm. "Not yet," he said, ticking off the entries they had identified. "I'd rather find out where all these other entries fit in." He held up his index finger. "One correlation is not sufficient. We present the entire package and they have to believe us. Someone has gone to a lot of trouble to make us look as guilty as possible. We have to shoot down all the br-rnas in the flock."

Rogitel left the official chamber as soon as the Treaty Council adjourned for the day and transferred by grid back to Earth. Without a word to Hrringa in the Hrruban Center, he made his way swiftly out of the Alreldep block and directly to Landreau's office at Spacedep. The secretary silently admitted him to the director's small private office.

He stood vector-straight before Landreau's desk while his superior finished a comp call.

"I have information from our contact in the Archives," Rogitel reported as soon as Landreau had completed the call. "Inquiries are being made through to Zapata and several of the other worlds where the Reeve accounts are being maintained. They are in possession of specific deposit information, so they must have a source, within Spacedep, providing them with data from our records."

"So that is what's going on," Landreau said, his face suffusing with anger. He began scrolling through his console, his finger hard on the key. "A report came to my notice a few days back but I couldn't see why I should be bothered with minor infractions. Here it is!" And he gestured for Rogitel to scan it. "Trivial matters must never be ignored: even something so insignificant as a junior making copies of old screens. Take this Dalkey Petersham into custody, for illegal copying of official documents. Find out who he's been working for, if he's sent on the documents and to whom. Take his brain apart if you need to. Use querastrin if you must. But get a full confession from him." Landreau sprang out of his seat, pacing up and down, his stocky body quivering with fury.

"A confession under duress, sir? That's not altogether prudent. Nor can we obtain permission to use the truth drug on him for copying old, declassified accounting records. Wouldn't it be wiser, Admiral, to leave him in place and watch him? If he thinks he has gotten away with this first foray, he'll feel bolder about repeating his success. If you catch him in the process of committing a crime, you have far more latitude in extracting information from him."

"I don't like it," Landreau said, sitting down again, and flicking his fingers at the damning report on the screen. "I don't like it in the least." He pressed hard on the scroll key, stopping it and rewinding to position a new document, bearing the Poldep seal. "Reeve has had the damnedest luck. Couldn't you have done something to keep that beacon from being discovered?"

"Admiral, we had to get it out of the way as fast as possible and that meant using the most accessible transport, a merchant ship. Safe enough under most circumstances."

"But it wasn't! And that Mayday has removed one of our weapons against the Reeves. How did they find that shipment, Rogitel? That beacon should never have seen the light of day and it surfaces . . . plainly marked to Spacedep."

"Freak accident, sir," Rogitel replied calmly. He had often discovered that the calmer he remained, the sooner the Admiral's rages cooled. "Meteorite hole penetrated the hull and the carton, setting off the Mayday. I interviewed the captain himself. He was eager to talk about it. He appears to have been 'dining out' on it. Fortunately I was able to cancel the pickup and the crate remains unclaimed. If someone inquires, we say that it could well be an attempt on the part of the Reeves to implicate Spacedep to clear themselves of complicity."

"Good thinking, Rogitel, good thinking," and Landreau began to relax, even to smile. "But we'd better find out if there's any connection between this Petersham clerk and Doona. They can't slip out of any other charges or our plans will be ruined." He rattled his fingers on the desktop. "And I've an unsettling report from Varnorian's contacts in Codep. A Dr. Walter Tylanio from Prueba V was hired for a special job by someone from Doona." Landreau's eyes narrowed. "The only laser technology that Doona has is in its security satellites."

Rogitel could well appreciate how serious that could be, but he didn't know how anyone had discovered Klonski. Surely not the Petersham clerk. Maybe he had better acquire a vial of querastrin from his sources. Then an angry thump brought his attention right back to Landreau.

"I want Doona to be totally discredited. I want our plans to succeed in every particular, and for that to happen, the Doonan Experiment has to fail. Fail! Be wiped clean of its contaminated Humans and especially those misbegotten animals."

"Sir, calm yourself," Rogitel said, leaning across the desk toward his superior. "Your plans will succeed. While it's too late for subtlety, it's not too late," and he paused to smile reassuringly at Landreau, "to remove the primary cause of the entire problem."

"What?" Landreau said, staring fiercely up at his subordinate.

"Really quite simple. Remove the Reeves from Doona. I think they are at the bottom of much unfavorable publicity about Doona. Surely they should report—in person—to their Codep superiors here on Earth."

Landreau's ruddy face slowly broke into a smile. "See to it," he ordered. "Varnorian will oblige. Get them here and get them eliminated!"

*   *   *

Admiral Landreau was the epitome of regret and sorrow when he informed the Amalgamated Worlds Congress of the dreadful situation which existed on Doona when so much was at stake in the renewal of the Treaty. He stood in the beam of a pinpoint spotlight, addressing the half-seen figures illuminated by twelve identical cones of light in the vast chamber. In the blackness between was the faint peeping sound of the court reporter's machine.

"The Reeves are threatening the very safety of your design to form a Federation of Sentient Planets. Their activities destroy the very integrity and credibility of the Amalgamated Worlds and our dream for a united galaxy! Once the models of probity and dedication, both father and son have conspired to seize Doona for their own, and, had it not been for the discovery of their heinous infractions of the most basic Treaty stipulations, they might have succeeded in their scheming."

"Treaty Councillors are supposed to deal with such infractions, aren't they?" one of the panel inquired.

"Not when the crimes have such far-reaching consequences. No, honored sirs, this matter goes far beyond the Doonan system. It has most certainly raised awkward questions in the Hrruban Speakers Council and the Treaty Council as well!" Landreau shook his head sadly to add that detail. "I am deeply concerned that the Hrrubans will feel obliged to alter their opinions of us all, if these deplorable men remain in so public a position on Doona. The least that will happen is for the Hrrubans to pull out of the Federation or, worse, decide that we Humans must be rigorously schooled in their ways. They will undoubtedly impede our reach for the stars, cut short our explorations, confine us to the few planets we already own. Since Todd Reeve has not, cannot be cleared of his alleged crimes, I call for the removal of the Reeves from Doona to Earth for being detrimental to the renewal of the Treaty of Doona. I am sure your counterpart on Hrruba will also withdraw their, er, embarrassment from the colony, for that young male causes his people great sorrow. You must surely understand why we cannot have people of questionable integrity involved in high-level positions in the colony at this critical time. Remove the Reeves from Doona and let that situation resolve itself without further detriment."

There was a lot of muttering among the panel as Landreau's suggestion was discussed. He waited patiently, knowing that he had presented a valid and timely argument. He was rather pleased by his eloquence and the way he had deftly emphasized the salient points.

Landreau was even more pleased when the prevailing sentiment favored his solution. He had also counted on the fact that trade agreements had been drawn up and were awaiting the renewal of the Treaty before Hrruban ratification. That factor had probably contributed to the necessity of removing such controversial persons.

"You have made a plain case of a disgraceful situation," the chairman said. "At such a critical stage, nothing may be permitted to jeopardize the Treaty Renewal. Bailiff, give orders for Ken Reeve and his son Todd to be immediately brought to Earth to appear before this panel. Make the necessary representations to the Hrruban Center for the use of grid transportation of these two." Then the chairman inclined his head toward Landreau. "You may, of course, be present at the hearing, Admiral."

"Gladly," Landreau said. "I wish to further the cause of justice in every way within my power."

With some effort he restrained his elation. He must now make arrangements so that when that pair arrived, the Hrrubans on duty at that wretched grid would be those who would deliver the Reeves into his keeping. Soon, soon, he thought, rubbing his hands together in smug anticipation, he would be rid of Ken Reeve and that hyperactive son of his forever. Then his most ambitious plan could be initiated. Instead of the panel of inquiry meeting them, there would be an entirely different kind of reception committee awaiting the Reeves. Landreau smiled.

"My eyes will be ruined reading this small print," Todd said, briefly knuckling his eye sockets as he wearily turned over another one of Dalkey's printouts. "Some of these entries date back from when we were kids. Have you found anything relevant?" he asked Hrriss, who was as diligently examining his share of the packet. He paused, stretching his arms above his head to release the tension across his shoulders.

"They may be old but we have decided that the conspiracy against us was very carefully put into motion long before there was any reason to suspect one," Hrriss replied, but he also took a moment to stretch cramped muscles. "These entries," and he tapped a claw tip on the sheets, "are all from Darwin II-MF-4, a very remote colony world, not yet qualified for full status."

"Could be a place to ship stolen livestock," Todd said. He bent to his task again, stylus poised to cross off an entry, as he peered at the next line. "Whoa! Here's an account number right here on Doona!"

"Whose?" Hrriss asked. Todd swung around to the computer and instituted a name search. Madam Dupuis had arranged for them to use Archival records to match numbers with names, providing they limited their inquiries to that.

"Dunno yet. The last payment in these records is two years old. The person it belongs to might have left Doona in the interim." He drummed his nails irritably on the tabletop, waiting for the data to appear. When the screen scrolled up in answer to his query, Todd just stared at it, his face turning into a cold mask. Without a word, he rose, snatched up the printout, and started for the door.

"Whose number is it? Zodd? Where are you going?"

Todd kept walking. "To the Launch Center."

"Why?" the Hrruban demanded.

"To skin a snake."

Hrriss glanced at the name on the screen and hurried after his friend. "Lincoln Newry! How very convenient!"

"Todd!" Lincoln Newry said pleasantly as they marched into the circle of light cast by the single spot set into the ceiling. Martinson's assistant had his feet up on a desk in the Launch Center office, watching the tape of an entertainment program on the comunit screen while keeping half an eye on his scopes. "Hrriss! Nice to see you both. We don't get many visitors way out here. It's lonely in the evenings. Can I offer you something to drink? Nice warm night for this time of year."

"Your boss isn't here?" Todd asked expressionlessly. "I'd like him to hear what I've got to say."

"Nope," said Newry gaily. "He's gallivanting around the galaxy with old Kiachif. Some people have all the fun, I get to mind the store while he's gone."

Todd nodded. "How convenient, but that does fit another piece into the puzzle. We'd no reason to suspect either you or Martinson."

"Suspect? Me or Martinson? Of what?"

"Of helping Doona's enemies."

"Ah, c'mon, now, Todd. You're imagining weeds into snakes," Newry said in a soothing tone, but Todd noticed a wariness in his eyes despite his rallying words.

"Someone knew when and where Hrriss and I went on the *Albatross*, knew our flight plans and where we'd warp-jump. Someone also had to be here, in this office," and Todd had Newry's complete attention now, "to let rustlers lift from the surface. Whaddya want to bet that we can prove that every time a heist was made, you, Linc Newry, just happened to be on duty?"

With an incredulous laugh, Newry shook his head. "No way, son . . ."

"I'm not your son," Todd said, his face hard and implacable with suppressed anger. Hrriss had never seen him so furious. He moved to the balls of his feet in readiness. "And you know a ship launched the other night and somehow you can turn the security satellites off so they don't record either launches or landings of rustier shuttles."

"Hold on, hold on, there!" Newry said, raising his hands to pacify Todd and shooting Hrriss an indignant look that suggested Hrriss should calm his friend down. "You can't run around accusing people of doing this or that just to clear yourselves."

"I think I can," Todd said in an icy certain voice. "I figured it out. If Martinson's not here, you're the one who creates legitimate documentation for export shipments from Doona. You mind the shop, as you said yourself. And no one could have missed that atmospheric insertion the other night. You were probably looking at its trail as you assured me that no one had blasted off-planet with a load of horses rustled from Dad's ranch."

Newry was still waving his hands and shaking his head incredulously at Todd's accusations.

"You can look at my records. You'll find there was no insertion that night, Todd!" Newry turned to Hrriss, hands open to emphasize his innocence and disbelief.

"Oh, I believe we'll find no blips on the security satellites. That I do believe, Newry," Todd said, and then smiled. "Ever heard of a man named Askell Klonski?"

Newry shook his head, his reaction genuine.

"Or maybe you knew him better as Lesder Boronov?"

The change in Linc Newry was dramatic despite the man's attempt to cover that momentary lapse.

Seeing that Newry was rattled, Todd sat on the edge of the desk, folding his arms on his chest, his gaze never leaving Newry's face.

"Boronov is a genius with security systems. How'd he fix Doona's? D'you use a code so the satellite recorders blank? Or maybe just a convenient function key that isn't supposed to be programmed at all? Ah, yes, so it is a function key!" He twisted so he could reach the console that Newry had pushed to one side of the desk, making circles with his index finger over the ranks of spare keys. "Now . . . eeny meeny tipsy teeny . . ." he said in a singsong voice.

"Enough!" Newry cried, sinking dispiritedly back into his chair and burying his anguished face in his hands. "How'd you know about Boronov?"

"Amazing the things you can learn when you've been falsely accused, Newry. So what's your story? Martinson in on this with you?"

Newry shook his head from side to side. "No, he never knew a thing about it. He's too damned honest. And he gets paid what he's worth."

"Spacedep pays well," Todd said, his voice now a soothing coaxing one.

Newry looked up at him, his expression sour. "Not at my level. And nothing to make up for hours of sitting here night after night, day after day, doing double shifts when Martinson's away. I'd only two more years to go. What I got for pressing a key now and then would be far more than that ridiculous pension Spacedep pays you. I wanted enough to buy into Doona. I saw my chance and I took it. And I was nearly there. So nearly there!" He buried his face in his hands again and his shoulders began to shake.

Todd looked away from the broken man, moved by contempt as well as pity.

"Who is the rustler, Newry?" Hrriss asked.

"You haven't figured it all out, then, have you?" Newry's muffled voice was bitter.

"Cooperation could mitigate your guilt," Hrriss added gently. "You can repair some of the damage you have caused."

Newry kept shaking his head in the cradle of his hands. "You're so smart, Reeve, you should know who it is."

Todd racked his brain. Who "it" is? Newry couldn't mean Landreau. He meant someone much nearer, someone who knew enough about the management of their ranch and . . . "Mark Aden?" He could scarcely believe that the young assistant manager whom he had so admired as a youngster could have turned against the people who had trusted him and encouraged him to learn as much as he could so he'd be able to start up his own spread on Doona. "Why would Mark turn on us? Dad paid him well. He gave him excellent references when he said he wanted to leave us. No one really wanted him to leave."

"That's not the way he told it," Newry said, his voice blurred by his hands. "That sister of yours thought herself too good for a ranch manager."

"Inessa?" Todd remembered that his sister had been infatuated with Mark Aden at one point, although she hadn't been unduly upset when Mark had suddenly decided to leave. But Todd did remember that Mark had a vindictive streak in him: he never forgot a grudge and he'd wait months to pay back an imagined slight that anyone else would have forgotten. Only Mark Aden would have been vindictive enough to sow ssersa in pastures used by horses. "He manages the rustling operation by himself? He didn't have the kind of money that would buy him any kind of a space vehicle. Certainly not one large enough to make rustling pay."

"Did he not perhaps have assistance from those who have been adding to your pension fund?" Hrriss asked Newry, pulling on his shoulders to make him look up.

Slowly Newry raised his head, and then his eyes began to widen, his whole face brightened, and a smile of unexpected salvation parted his lips.

"Todd Reeve?" a stern voice said.

In a swift move, Todd was off the desk and looking into the shadows beyond the console, trying to locate the newcomer.

Rogitel emerged from the darkness, Todd's father behind him, Spacedep marines flanking him.

"You are always found in the most incriminating situations. Harassing a Spacedep employee, were you?" Rogitel let out a patient sigh. "You will come with me. Now."

"With you, Commander? Dad?"

Todd stared at the lack of expression on his father's face. "But Dad . . ." Todd began before taking his cue. "Linc was explaining to us how the security satellites record incoming and outgoing traffic." It might sound lame but it covered the surreptitious sign he made to Hrriss. Just let Hrriss get free. "Weren't you, Linc?" And let Linc prefer to keep silent about the last few moments in front of one of his Spacedep superiors. Commander Rogitel dealt harshly with failures . . . and probably drastically with informers.

"That's right, Commander," Newry said in a drawl that almost disguised the tremors in his voice.

"Let's go, Reeve," Rogitel said, motioning to one of the marines. "You have to report in an hour to the transport station." He caught sight of Hrriss, edging farther into the shadows. "You! You've no business in a Spacedep installation. Out of here!"

Todd had the satisfaction of hearing Hrriss's low and menacing growl as he swung around the marines and out the door.

Ken shot Rogitel a furious glare for his uncalled-for incivility to the Hrruban, but the commander paid no notice as he took his place in front of the detail.

"I've some things for you in the one bag we were allowed," Ken murmured to his son. "I don't think we'll be gone long for all the precipitousness of our departure."

"What's up, then?"

"We're to appear before a panel of the Amalgamated Worlds in their Terran offices."

Todd was seething to tell his father what he and Hrriss had got out of Newry. More pieces had fallen into place, pieces he never would have considered as part of the conspiracy. And yet they fit!

They had no chance to talk on the way to the Treaty Island, not with Rogitel looking so smug and well pleased with himself. At the grid, though, Todd began to worry. The Treaty Controller and two strange male Hrrubans wearing sidearms awaited their arrival.

"Send them to Earth," Rogitel ordered the grid operator.

The Hrruban glanced nervously at the Treaty Controller, who nodded, and the Hrruban had no option but to manipulate the controls. Todd watched the bright room around him dissolve and vanish. In a moment, the features of their destination started to coalesce around him. He could see the posts of the transport station becoming solid at the four corners of the grid, and the blank walls of a corridor beyond them.

As soon as the Reeves had fully materialized, they were attacked from behind.

chapter eleven

In high spirits, Ali Kiachif tapped at the door of the Reeve residence. He and the other two men had debarked so hastily from the *White Lightning* they were still in shipsuits.

"Now, this will just take a minute," the Codep captain assured his two companions. "Hello-oo?" he called out, and rapped with his knuckles on the window. "Reeve, are you home? Ah, hello, Patricia. Surprised to see me so soon? Rank has its privileges, I always say. I brought someone by for your husband to meet. May I introduce Dr. Walter Tylanio? He's the best laser expert in the whole galaxy. What he don't know about 'em, no one does, if you see what I mean. Martinson you know." The tall, bearded man behind Kiachif bowed.

"How do you do?" Pat asked. Her daughter Inessa and Kelly were crowded behind her in the doorway. The merchant tipped them a little wink. Their faces fell when they didn't see the figures they expected.

"Good afternoon, Mrs. Reeve," Martinson said impatiently. "Kiachif, I have to get back to my office."

"Patience, patience," Kiachif said chidingly. "Surely you can give the man one moment to crow over all of you who thought so ill of him. *Honi soit qui mal y pense*, if you know what I mean."

"Neither Todd nor Ken is here, Captain," Pat said, her anxiety increasing because she thought it just possible that the captain might know where they were. "They were supposed to see an Amalgamated Worlds panel."

Kiachif clicked his tongue. "That's bad luck. I guessed he'd want to see my smiling face, soon's my expert here had a chance to unreel that doctored log tape that was on the *Albatross*."

"Come in, come in," Kelly said, usurping Pat's prerogative, but Hrriss had told her and Nrrna all about Newry. And if this expert was so good, maybe he could figure out which function key controlled the security satellite bypass and how Klonski-Boronov had managed to scramble supposedly tamperproof chips.

"Martinson here," Kiachif said, stepping lightly inside and peering about as if he hoped Ken and Todd were only hiding in their own home, "wouldn't let me bring the tape to Tylanio, so I brought the mountain to the prophet." He caught Kelly's grin. "Well, I alter to suit m'purpose, girl, if you get my drift. Martinson kept his word of honor like the fine upstanding man he is, and the log was never out of his sight for a moment. So we have returned with the news and Martinson maybe has returned to Doona a wiser man."

"What did you find, Dr. Tylanio?" Pat asked, absently gesturing for them to be seated. She signalled for Inessa to get refreshments.

"To give you the tall, small, and all of it," Kiachif said, still dominating the conversation, "the log was some messed with." Dr. Tylanio, who apparently took no umbrage from Kiachif's ebullience, nodded agreement.

Martinson cleared his throat and shot a quelling look at Kiachif. "Let the expert explain, Captain. I thought that's why you insisted he return with us."

"The tapes had clearly been extensively altered, Mrs. Reeve," Dr. Tylanio said. He had a pleasant tenor voice and spoke in the measured phrases of a born lecturer. "It was apparent from the tape that it was not recording anything on its homeward-bound journey: certainly not when they paused outside the Hrrilnorr system. Internal recordings were being taped. I would guess that the VU and transmitter had been tampered with."

"But that doesn't prove it was altered by an outsider," Martinson said, obviously unsettled by Tylanio's report.

"It does to me," Kiachif said, accepting a glass from Inessa. "And there's more. Oh, how I wish Todd and Ken were here right now. Walt says the box was only diddled once. That puts paid to that Spacedep stringy bean's charge that the boys had been wiping the memory clean every time they were ex-Doona while committing all those piracies and smugglings."

"That's right, Mrs. Reeve," Tylanio said. "The alteration could only have been made before or after their latest mission. Since the ship was sealed, that would mean it would have to have been done before. The inserted material was masterfully done, very carefully filmed to present such a single continuous record of multiple warp jumps and atmospheric insertions and launches. The most masterful piece of logging I've ever seen."

"But couldn't it have been substituted for the real log?" Kelly asked diffidently, for they had figured out how such a switch could have been made.

"Now, how could that possibly have been done, young woman?" Martinson demanded, irate. "I was present the entire time. I saw Commander Rogitel remove the log box myself, package it very carefully, and carry it off the ship. No one could have substituted this . . . this . . ."

Kiachif was waving a finger under Martinson's nose. "That lassie has made a very good point, Martinson, so don't get hot under your collar, which you aren't wearing, but you're getting riled."

"Commander Rogitel . . ." Martinson began again with greater indignation, but Kiachif's crow of exultation totally disconcerted him.

"I wouldn't trust an Amalgamated Bond, sealed, signed, secured, if that Spacedep stringy bean gave it me. Ah, no," Kiachif said. "I'll bet my *White Lightning* herself that that's when a switch occurred. Found the real log, lassie?"

Kelly shook her head. "We only figured out how and when the other day." She wanted desperately to get Dr. Tylanio and Kiachif to herself to tell them about Newry, which she couldn't quite do in front of Martinson. For all that she knew Martinson was respected and seemed straight as a die, she wasn't going to take any chances. Especially as he seemed to think Commander Rogitel was such an upright type.

"So when d' you expect your men back, Patricia?" Kiachif asked easily.

"I don't know, Ali," she said, and began to wring her hands. "They should have been back the next day. And now there's this awful rumor that they never appeared before the panel at all. That they've . . . they've skipped out of an untenable situation." Pat blurted the slander out and then began to weep. Kelly put her arm around her protectively.

"Never!" Kiachif said in a voice that would have been heard from stem to stern of the *White Lightning* through closed safety hatches.

"Commander Rogitel escorted them," Kelly said in a caustic voice, her eyes on the captain. "With marines. I heard," and while she couldn't mention Madam Dupuis, she was certainly the most reliable source, "that two strange and armed Hrrubans took over from the marines when they got on the grid."

"Did they, now?" Kiachif's eyes went wide. "Now, that's a nasty turn-up. And I'll tell you one thing." He swerved toward Martinson, his long stained finger almost in the man's nostrils. "I don't want to hear one more word from anyone that Ken Reeve, or Todd, skipped out of any obligation—to Doona, to Amalgamated Worlds, even to ol' Terra! You see that gets put about right smart, Martinson. I've known Ken Reeve a quarter century. He's run *at* a lot of stuff *I'd* never be caught charging, but he's done it and won out over odds that would have pipped plenty on this planet. If he didn't show up when and where he was supposed to, then he was prevented, if you understand me. Now, you dry those tears, Patricia Reeve, and stand up proud for your man and that fine son of yours," he said, somewhat awkwardly but kindly patting her shoulder. "Your man is a fighter. Your boy, too. They'll be back, sure enough, before you've any more time to miss them."

"Thank you, Ali," Pat said gratefully. "You know him in ways I don't. You've given me new hope. And so have you, Dr. Tylanio. You were so good to come all this way for us."

The laser expert took an envelope from his pocket. "This is a copy of my report, signed and sworn to by an accredited Amalgamated Worlds notary. Your son and your husband will doubtless find this useful. I will, of course, be happy to testify in person to the authenticity of my investigations." Tylanio handed it to Pat and bowed. With Martinson at his side, he left the room.

"You see, signed, sealed, and sworn to. Proof positive of no perjury, Patricia," Kiachif said in a low voice. He gave her one more squeeze and started for the door.

With the pretext of courtesy, Kelly followed him, touching his arm and bending close to his ear. "I gotta see you, Captain, and preferably before that expert leaves the planet." Kiachif gave an almost imperceptible nod of acknowledgment, not so much as altering his stride as he continued on out of the house. Then she turned back to Pat, Inessa and Robin comforting her, and said in her normal tone, "I'd better get on home now but I'll be back tomorrow."

She clattered down the steps, whipped Calypso's reins free from the rail as the men piled into the flitter. As it took off, it wallowed from side to side and she grinned. Trust Kiachif. Which she did.

Kelly had been looking over the last charges against the boys that still had to be cleared before Treaty Renewal Day. And the valuables and interdictables they were supposed to have stolen and secreted on the *Albie* would be the hardest part. Having Dr. Tylanio's proof that the log tape had been altered, or even a carefully edited one substituted, was a real relief. If only they could somehow prove that Commander Rogitel had switched the doctored tape for the genuine log record . . . He'd had more opportunity than anyone else. And reason.

But if the tapes of alleged visits to collect valuable artifacts, including the

Byzanian Glow Stone, were adjudged a simulation, then they hadn't been where they were accused of stealing things. They hadn't stolen anything. As Todd and Hrriss maintained, all that junk had been planted on the *Albatross* and that had to have been done while the *Albie* was on the pad at Hrretha. Rogitel had been there.

But where were Todd and his father? Thank goodness, Captain Ali had soothed Patricia Reeve on that score. Maybe the word that they were detained would get out and Robin wouldn't be sporting black eyes for defending the family honor. She knew Hrriss was lying low. Which was smart of him. Rogitel might not have considered the young Hrruban dangerous when he shooed him out of the Launch Center, but Newry knew different. Why hadn't Todd come out with an accusation right then? In front of the marines. Surely they could be made to testify . . . or could they?

A tiny noise penetrated her cogitations. Looking up from her desk, she nearly fell off her chair at the face grinning outside her window.

"You scared me to death, Captain Ali," she whispered hoarsely at him.

"Your manner did suggest a need for caution, lassie."

It wasn't the first time Kelly had crawled through that window, and taking the captain's hand, she ran with him to the deep shadows of the barn where no one was likely to look for them.

"You hit the nail on the head with Klonski, you know," she said, "though I daren't even get in touch with Inspector DeVeer right now."

"And which nailhead would that be, lassie?" Kiachif asked. "Though Tylanio agrees privately with me that the work on the tape is exactly the sort of thing Klonski would do so well."

"You also said he was a genius at fixing security systems." Kiachif nodded, his eyes glinting in the dark. "And Dalkey's records show he got paid several huge hunks of credit. I think some of it went to pay for him hobbling Doona's security satellites."

"Oh-ho-ho! I've been away too long."

"You have. Todd and Hrriss found payments to a Doonan account . . . and it belongs to Lincoln Newry."

"Martinson's assistant?" The whites of Kiachif's eyes, for once, Kelly noted, without bloodshot cobwebs, were visible in the shadow. "No wonder you wouldn't speak out in his presence. Does Patricia know?"

Kelly shook her head. "She's got enough to fret over right now. 'Sides, I didn't think it would cheer her up."

"Not a mite nor a moment, if her men are missing. Go on."

"Hrriss said Todd broke Newry down into admitting that he'd been letting the rustlers in and out of Doona, only when he was on duty. The ship Todd saw the other night was probably registering on Linc's screens while he was denying an atmospheric insertion."

"But the beacons . . ."

"Klonski's fixed them. Hrriss said there's an unprogrammed function key on the launch board that interferes with satellite recording. Furthermore, Linc Newry can authorize export documentation . . . like for Reeve freeze-marked livestock going off-planet to unknown destinations. And the rustler is Mark Aden."

"That young lad? Hmmm, isn't often someone fools Ali Kiachif." The captain frowned. "The nerve of him, making me transport rustled animals! And all that scud about making a new life."

"Apparently he's made a very profitable one," Kelly said drolly. "At the Reeves' expense."

"But they always treated him well. He even said so."

"Inessa didn't," Kelly said. "She had a flirt with him but she gave up on him because he always wanted her to get her father to help him get a ranch of his own. He was a funny guy, never forgave a hasty word or a silly joke on him. Hrriss thinks he's the one seeded the ssersa. Todd found a half-empty sack of it by the corral he found. It'd be just the sort of rotten trick Mark Aden would do, to make Inessa sorry she ditched him."

"Fascinating, lassie, fascinating. I think Dr. Tylanio has one more job before I return him to the quiet rectangles of his hall of learning."

And between one breath and another, Captain Ali Kiachif disappeared. That night Kelly slept well for the first time since Todd and Ken had been hauled off to Earth.

The very next morning, Kelly had a call from a frantic Nrrna.

"Kelly, they are hunting Hrriss." The girl was sputtering so badly that Kelly at first didn't understand the import of her words.

"Hunting? Hrriss?"

"The Treaty Controller has demanded his presence immediately on the Island. He sent four of the Third Speaker's special force for Hrriss."

"So where's Hrriss?"

"He has made himself scarce. Hrrestan told him that is what he must do. Oh, Kelly, I am so frightened."

"Don't be," Kelly said as firmly as she could. "I've got official confirmation that the *Albie* log tape was a fraud. Tampered with, fixed, altered. And that means that neither Todd nor Hrriss was where they're charged with being, so they couldn't have stolen those things. And illegal possession of those artifacts is really the last charge against them. And we'll soon have proof, too, of what Todd and Hrriss discovered talking to Linc Newry."

"But what good does all this proof do when Zodd is missing and Hrriss is, too?"

"A good point that, Nrrna," Kelly said. "You just keep your cool, friend. It's up to us now."

She stopped by the Reeves', just in the crazy hope that Todd and his father had returned home. They hadn't and the gloom that hung over the ranch house was depressing. Kelly did ask to have a copy of Dr. Tylanio's document.

"To keep with all the rest of the evidence, Mrs. Reeve," she said in an offhanded manner.

"You've got all these mysterious sources, Kelly," Inessa accused Kelly, her face and eyes showing the strain that affected the entire family. "Why can't you find out about Dad and Todd?"

Kelly suppressed her annoyance with the girl whose flirtation with Mark Aden was having such a long-range effect. Then, generously, Kelly reminded herself that Inessa had been just a kid at the time. Perhaps this would all sort itself out and Inessa would never realize that her childish infatuation was part of this dreadful affair.

Kelly left for Nrrna's house in First Village. She had all the proof they had so painstakingly gathered, including Hrriss's summary of Newry's disclosures. Surely that was enough! Surely Nrrna would see how terribly urgent it was that they stop messing with underlings and go to the top!

"Go to Hrruba? To First Speaker?" Nrrna's voice broke into a startled squeak and Kelly shushed her.

On her way into First Village, Kelly'd noticed some strangely accoutred Hrrubans milling around the clearing in the center: the biggest specimens of their species she'd ever seen. Deciding they were not in First Village for census taking, she ducked around, taking a narrow little track to the fenced-in pasture where the village horses grazed. Unsaddling Calypso, Kelly turned her out and lugging saddle and the bulging pouches, finally reached Nrrna's house, entering by the back flap.

"We should have gone to First Speaker in the beginning, as Todd wanted to," she said, a trifle annoyed with Nrrna's timidity.

"Oh, Kelly, no! I dare not!" Nrrna said. "It is absolutely forbidden to convey Hayumans to Hrruba."

"Now! But Todd's been there and he thought seeing Hrruna was his best chance."

"Todd went to Hrruba before the Treaty was written and the Treaty has a clause utterly prohibiting visits from Hayumans. Todd was held in high honor by the Council of Speakers . . ."

Kelly flicked her eyebrows up in disgust. "Was held."

"He is honorable. He would say that he must obey that prohibition."

"Yes, but no one has specifically prohibited me and, where Todd is concerned, honor can go out the window for all the good it's done him lately!" Kelly scowled fiercely. "Look, both Todd and his father are missing. Some nasty minds say they've done a flit because there's too much evidence against them."

Nrrna was shaking her head now in staunch disagreement.

"Right. So something's happened to them. And it's up to you and me to get them released. *Before* the Treaty gets sighed. So we go to Hrruba and sort things out."

"We can't do that."

"Why not? You know how to work the grid controls. You sent me to Earth."

"But that was different," Nrrna replied, aghast at Kelly's daring plan. "You are of Terran stock. It is not forbidden under the Treaty for you to travel to your homeworld. It would be as impossible for me to send you to Hrruba as it would be for me to go to Earth."

"You'd be with me. I'd be your guest, as Todd was the guest of Hrrestan and Mrrva twenty-odd years ago. And it's for the same important reason. To save both our planets." She paused, watching Nrrna shake her head, her eyes mournfully big as she struggled with her principles—her honor. "This is the time to dare all. All for one and one for all."

Nrrna smiled wanly at Kelly's joke, but it took two hours of solid persuasion to get the Hrruban to see that Kelly's daring plan was the only option open. Kelly ruefully insisted that this scheme also went against everything she had been brought up to believe sacred and binding. But sometimes one had to make exceptions. As Hrrestan and Mrrva, and Hrrula, had made an exception of the six-year-old Todd.

Nrrna still experienced pangs of deep guilt over telling Dalkey when the medical shipment was being sent out.

"This is the time for stouthearted females to save their menfolk, Nrrna. Or didn't you see those Hrruban heavies prowling around the village center?"

"What?"

"Go have a look," Kelly said. "They're Third Speaker's or I don't know my Hrruban insignias. And they're armed."

As a terrified Nrrna sidled cautiously out the back flap, Kelly decided that if this wouldn't persuade the female, she'd have to think of some other plan. Only nothing, absolutely nothing, would come to mind.

When Nrrna returned, she was shivering and the fur along her entire stripe stood up.

"They are very powerful males. They are dangerous. They look for Hrriss." She took Kelly by the hand. "We must go to First Speaker. Such males should not be on Rrala. They should not be in our village."

There wasn't time to wait until dark, for males might take to searching the houses and Kelly didn't think they'd like finding a Hayuman in a Hrruban village right then. She covered her bright hair with an edge of a sleeping fur and wrapped herself in Nrrna's big winter cloak, the all-important dossier clutched to her chest with one arm.

"We don't have to go to the Treaty Island grid to get to Hrruba, do we?" Kelly asked, suddenly realizing that her mad scheme had a few large holes in it.

"No, we can reach Hrruba from here," Nrrna reassured her. For once the little female had made up her mind, she was capable of as much cool resolution as Kelly. "Until the Island grid was established, all shipping and travel were done through the village grids. It is only to satisfy the Controller of what is being sent in and out of Rrala that all goods now go first to the Island."

"Where are we likely to find the First Speaker?"

"First we will go to the Executive Cube which houses the Speakers' chambers. Someone there will direct us to First Speaker Hrruna." Nrrna was pressing the appropriate codes into the transport controls. She gestured for Kelly to step up onto the grid. "If they do not arrest us first."

Their first bit of good luck was that they arrived late in the Hrruban night. No one was immediately visible, although they heard the rumble of several voices issuing from a side corridor. Together they raced down the nearest aisle until they spotted a curtained alcove. They dove behind this and sank to the floor, their knees cocked so that they would not disturb the fall of the draperies.

When light began to filter through the soot-covered window, Nrrna carefully crept out to find out where she might find the First Speaker's quarters. She returned to Kelly, who had been fearful of discovery, that at any moment, a functionary would arrive to pull back the curtains.

"The Council is not in session today," Nrrna whispered to Kelly. "The First Speaker has expressed a wish to be alone in his retreat." Kelly's hopes crashed about her. Nrrna gave her hand a little pat, her eyes gleaming. "The chief of the Council chamber told me how beautiful was the First Speaker's retreat and I do not think he realized that he also told me exactly where it is. We must go swiftly while there are not too many using the slidewalks." Then she wrinkled her nose.

"Even in that cloak, Kelly, you do not stand or walk or even smell like a Hrruban."

"It's too late to worry about a minor detail like that," Kelly said, nervousness making her snappish. "What about me limping and crouching over like I'm ancient or hurt?"

"That is a very good idea, Kelly," and Nrrna nodded approvingly. "I am your dutiful daughter, taking you to see the beauties of the countryside. It is fortuitous that the fur you took is a white pelt. Here."

Nrrna made some rapid adjustments with her delicate hands, and, although Kelly felt she was more in danger of suffocation than discovery, she let Nrrna's strong hands guide her as she settled into a limping gait which she felt suggested advanced age and decrepitude.

With corridors and aisles separating blocklike buildings many levels deep, Hrruba was not unlike Earth, which surprised Kelly, though she managed only a few glimpses behind the folds of the pelt. They rode a slow-moving beltway to a remote section of the capital city of Hrruba. Around them, Hrruban workers, clad in tool belts or robes to denote profession and status, passed them on every side. The only differences between the Human workers of Earth and the Hrrubans were the preponderance of bright colors in the latter's dress, the inborn grace with which they moved, and the scent. Scent, not smell, for although it was just as strong as the odors of Earth's passages, it was different.

"Do not speak if anyone bumps you," Nrrna whispered. "Your Hrruban is good, but your accent would inform anyone that you are from a colony."

"I couldn't talk if I wanted to. Is it much farther?" Kelly murmured. Her right hip was protesting the unnatural gait, and she ached to stretch her back up.

Nrrna peered at the lettering on the block they were passing, and her pupils contracted to slits in the strong light. "Not very far. We are nearing the passageway. We must get off as soon as we see a lift. First Speaker lives on the top floor."

Hrruna's retreat was in a well-soundproofed block of the Hrruban residential complex. To the surprise of both Kelly and Nrrna, no one guarded the entrance or any of the lifts. Though only one, Nrrna discovered, went as far as the twenty-second story. When the lift stopped, the door slid back and, to their utter consternation, the First Speaker faced them. Later Kelly would remember that a green light blinked above the lift, informing the First Speaker that someone was coming to his retreat.

"By the first mother, what brings such a lovely young one to the door of such an old man? Is this your mother who comes to entreat me? Or to protect her cub?" He beckoned them to leave the protection of the lift.

Once they had moved on into the first of the boxlike rooms that comprised the retreat, Kelly opened her hood. Hrruna's eyes widened with surprise and the barest trace of amusement.

"Not an aged and grieving mother, but a redheaded Hayuman. I have heard that such hair color is possible but never have I seen it." His wise eyes twinkled at her.

What surprised her most was his voice, clear and musical, and young! She could not believe that the greatest Hrruban of all would sound so young. She had met some of the other Speakers who came to New Home Weeks or other celebrations of importance on Rrala, but First rarely left Hrruba. He had been old when the Treaty was first signed, but, in the intervening years, he seemed to have changed little from his image in the old tapes. His mane was as white as snow, and the fur on his face and chest was faded, too, making a striking setting for the characteristic bright green eyes of his kind. First's eyes, under fluffy frontal crests which served the catlike race for eyebrows, were kindly and wise. Kelly felt quite shy under his scrutiny, but she knew immediately that she could trust him. So she fell to her knees, threw back her cloak, and deposited the precious pouch of documents on the floor before him.

As Nrrna appeared to be speechless, Kelly began in her best High Hrruban. "My name is Kelly Solinari. This is Nrrna, daughter of Urrda. We came from Rrala seeking an audience with you. We apologize most profoundly for disturbing you in the privacy of your retreat but we had no option save an appeal directly at your feet."

The old Hrruban's jaw dropped with pleasure. "That sort of posture is all very well for formal occasions, young Kelly Solinari," he said, responding in Middle Hrruban, "but this is not an official visit or I should have been informed of it by the appropriate underling. Please, raise yourself and walk as a Hayuman should, tall and proud. And be welcome in my home."

This was evidently the dayroom, furnished in a fashion similar to that of the Treaty Controller's apartments on Doona. A translucent panel gave onto a terrace, open to the sky and surrounded on all sides by high walls. The rarefied air had the chill of the mountains, though none could be distinguished because of the walls. If Hrruba was anything like Earth, many of its original heights had been terraformed into plateaus, to provide solid building bases for residences and factories. All the view Hrruna had was an unending plain of buildings. No wonder the Hrrubans were as desperate as the Terrans to find suitable colony worlds on which to expand.

Someone (and quite likely, Kelly thought, Hrruna) had filled this little space with colorful flowering plants from the hydroponics laboratories deep inside his planet, and from the wild plains of Rrala. The effect was the equivalent of a miniature Square Mile park. Overhead, though neither heard nor seen, a force-screen kept out the choking pollution that stained the air above a sickly gray. The atmosphere inside the conservatory was sweet with the scent of the plants.

Hrruna beckoned to the girls to sit down in the garden. Kelly hadn't been born yet when he accompanied Todd back to Doona to save the Human colonists from deportation, and to negotiate the Treaty of Doona. She had no idea how he would receive the information she had for him now.

"So what is it that makes two lovely young ladies risk safety and freedom to visit an old man?" Hrruna asked. He glanced warmly at Nrrna, who was made somewhat uncomfortable by his openly ardent expression.

With a deep breath, Kelly began. She had rehearsed what she would say to Hrruna, if they got to him. "It is of the greatest importance to us, sir, that the Treaty of Rrala is renewed in two days. To cohabit and cooperate with your people on that world a joy to all us Hayumans is," Kelly said. Despite Hrruna's use of Middle Hrruban, she couldn't switch from what she had so carefully memorized. And she was certain she had the right rhythm, the pitch and inflection to say what was needed in High Hrruban, which was as difficult as singing opera. "There may be a difficulty to the Renewal of the Treaty. We come to you to prevent that difficulty. The First Speaker Hrruna is the only personage to prevent rapidly approaching disaster."

"You are perhaps a friend of the young Zodd?" Hrruna asked in his kind young-sounding voice. "I seem to have had several visits from and on the behalf of that young man. What is it this time? And do not worry about the form of address. We speak as friends."

With great relief, Kelly lapsed into the more familiar idiom to relate the events of the past several weeks. When appropriate, she handed him the relevant documentation. He read through Hrriss's translations, sheet by sheet. Although not all Dalkey's lists had been done in Hrruban, there was more than enough in Hrruban script to show First Speaker sufficient proof of illegal payments out of Spacedep funds. That is, if he chose to believe that neither Todd nor Hrriss was guilty.

The First Speaker was skilled at posing questions in a natural progression, making the conversation a comfortable chat instead of a headlong plea for help. Kelly hardly felt she was speaking to him of planet-shaking matters in which the safety of her friends and her home was at stake. He considered everything she told him with a gentle gravity, nodding as she pointed out items that had seemed to Todd to be the most important.

"Why are you emissaries of Zodd?" Hrruna asked at last, his jaw dropping in a smile. "Why did he not come himself?"

"He and his father have disappeared. They are not the sort of people who run from trouble," Kelly said, once again feeling her crushing worry for Todd's safety.

"Neither son nor father is craven or thin-striped," Hrruna said encouragingly.

"We're afraid they've been abducted."

Saying that aloud in Hrruna's presence made it sound so horribly true that Kelly burst into tears. She was exhausted and worried. Nrrna sat beside her, holding her hand and muttering soothing phrases. Hrruna offered her a small glass of clear water and she sipped it, determined to control herself. This was no time to show weakness. The water helped. Then she could tell Hrruna what Todd and Hrriss had learned at the Launch Center, what Kiachif had discovered about the incriminating tapes, and if the tapes had been falsified, that neither Todd nor Hrriss could have stolen anything they were accused of stealing, including that awful Byzanian Glow Stone.

"But Mr. Reeve was taken from his house, and Todd from the Launch Center, by Commander Rogitel. They were taken by aircraft to the Treaty Island to go by the grid to speak before the Amalgamated Worlds panel and they never got there." Kelly forced back tears. "They wanted to clear their reputations. But they didn't even get that chance!" And then she stuck her fists against her mouth so she wouldn't disgrace herself with more tears.

"I do not like what you have told me," Hrruna said, his voice suddenly sounding very old.

"It is the truth, most honored Speaker," Nrrna said, speaking for the first time.

Kelly hiccupped back her sobs. "You're the only one we know who can demand an investigation into their disappearance. No one on Earth even cares what happens to them!" she added bitterly.

"Please, please, most honored First Speaker, help us! Help Rrala!" Nrrna's voice was low but so sweetly imploring that Hrruna leaned down to pat her cheek.

"I must assist you," Hrruna said, his voice kindly but firm. "I have known much of what you related, but you have also brought me the proofs which were withheld, or falsified, or conveniently misplaced." Hrruna chuckled, a series of throaty grunts. "I was truly unable to interfere until now. The continuation of the Rralan colony is far more important to me, as Hrruna, and as First Speaker, than I am willing to let any of my colleagues realize. If, however, I tried to interfere, that would give leave to others who are less altruistic to meddle in their own fashions and for their own reasons, which would not be as benevolent as mine. So I sheathe my claws to give others no excuse to sharpen theirs. They are compelled to show restraint, or suffer censure. A subtle means to an end but sometimes a more potent weapon than it first appears. When reputation and honor are more important than life, it becomes a greater lever." He sighed. "Perhaps not long enough a lever, for it does not appear to have unbalanced Rrala's greatest foes. I have been watching this contest from a distance. The players are not only fearful Hayumans. Some are very powerfully connected Hrruban xeno-phobes, including ones living on Rrala, who are trying to abort the Treaty."

"You know all this?" Kelly asked, and then bit her tongue for such impudence. "I beg your pardon, honored sir," she said humbly. She hadn't learned quite enough at Alreldep. She really had no business dealing at such a level.

First Speaker took no offense. "I have my sources," he said. "Young Hrrula has not been idle throughout all this, reporting directly to me. He is intelligent and most discreet. I value his observations enormously. He is devoted to Rrala, as well as to his world of birth. If you had asked him, he might have been able to bring you directly to me. Hrrestan knows of my trust in Hrrula."

Kelly and Nrrna looked at one another in amazement. "I didn't know that. Neither of us knew that. And with Hrriss gone . . ." She broke off.

"Exceptions have been made before now," Hrruna said enigmatically. "But someone has lowered himself to the dishonorable practice of kidnapping. I see the ramifications of that clearly. If Zodd and Hrriss do not appear in court with the proofs you have shown me, they are guilty by default. One more tool has been used by the hands of those without honor who would see Rrala fail. The involvement of Admiral Landreau, Commander Rogitel, and Codep Varnorian is known. The dishonorable Hrruban is not."

"It's the Treaty Controller working under Third Speaker's orders," Kelly said, and then closed her eyes because now she had to admit to her own dishonorable sins. "I, um, I sneaked into Treaty Controller's rooms to look for that document box Nrrna and I knew he had received and which he was so fussed about. Well, we had to know what he meant by the days being numbered," she said, defending herself, but Hrruna merely looked amused. "I couldn't unlock it, but it had been sealed by Third Speaker's personal sigil."

"There is no crime in his receiving such a package," Hrruna reminded them. "Third is his sponsor, after all."

"Yes, but why did he feel it necessary to hide that case in a specially made place at the bottom of a chest instead of putting it in the safe in his office or in the Archives? If the documents were innocuous, why didn't they arrive in a courier pouch?"

"You took out all the drawers in his bureau?" Hrruna asked, chuckling merrily. Kelly turned red. "I am not judging your actions, child. But I do see the point of your suspicions. Third may indeed be involved in this conspiracy. It is not beyond him when he feels thwarted. Yes, I am sure he is not uninvolved. Rrala is a nightmare to him. If the Treaty is not renewed, he would be unimaginably relieved."

"Please, honored sir. Don't let them scuttle the Treaty! Surely you can keep Treaty Controller from listening to the pessimists on Hrruba?" Kelly begged.

"Rralans are no threat to Hrruban society," Nrrna said. "We want to live our own life in peace."

Hrruna nodded his approval. "I think it would be best if Rrala continued as it is, I agree. But there are those who feel that once we unleash the ocelot, we will cease to be master of the hunt, and one day may even become prey. An all-Hrruban colony will behave as any Hrrubans will anywhere else. When you add in the Hayuman factor, behavior becomes more uncertain. I prefer to trust, but others cannot. It is not in their natures. I must not interfere in the negotiations or decisions of the Council, or it would not be a genuine agreement. It would be forced. But I will see what I can do to keep others from meddling so deeply."

With some difficulty, First Speaker rose stiffly to his feet. "A line of inquiry will be initiated immediately, even though I said I would spend my day in private. I hope, pretty one," he addressed Nrrna, "that you will stay, so we can get to know one another better. Though I am old, I would be entirely at your assistance, should you care to remain with me."

Nrrna shot Kelly a black-pupiled look of entreaty and the fur stood up on the backs of her forearms and on her tail. Such an invitation from the First Speaker was a high honor and Nrrna could not think of how to answer in a polite but negative way. It had been one thing for her to vie with other females for Hrriss's notice, but to diplomatically extricate herself from the attention of another, more assertive male, especially one of the broadest Stripe on Hrruba was more than she could handle. Kelly had noticed how fascinated Hrruna was with Nrrna's dainty beauty and realized it was now her turn to rescue her friend before Nrrna really panicked.

"O most honorable First Speaker, how we wish we could stay, both of us." Kelly ignored the glance he flicked at her that suggested the Hayuman had not been included in his invitation. She rose to her feet. "But we will be missed and awkward questions might arise from our disappearance—especially as we are known to be the promised mates of Todd and Hrriss."

Giving Kelly a long and somewhat amused look, Hrruna shook his head. "I suggest both of you remain with me, for safety's sake, my dear Hayuman. A tactful message will be sent to Hrrula to settle disquiet in both your houses. But should any whisper fall upon the breezes near Treaty Island that you have come to the First Speaker, you would be in mortal danger if you returned to Rrala."

"Oh," Kelly said in a very small voice. She sat down again and exchanged looks of alarm with Nrrna. Put in that light, neither of them was eager to go. Hrruna's jaw dropped as he watched the byplay between them.

"I was preparing food when the lift light flashed that visitors were on their way to me. Come, we will eat together, for we will need our strength. You may even assist me. Then we will set to work, for there is more to be done than I thought and I will need your assistance."

"That's what we came to get," Kelly said, and grinned broadly at him. Nrrna even managed a soft purr.

Hrriss had found a safe haven with the Reeve family, keeping out of sight in the house and trying to piece together from them what Kelly and Nrrna might have learned that had sent them into hiding, too. According to his betrothed's mother, Kelly had arrived to see Nrrna. She had left Calypso in the village pasture and her saddle was still in Nrrna's room. Marva had been busy with her tasks, somewhat worried by the strangers in the village center, and when she had gone to call the girls to eat at midday, they were gone. No one had seen them since.

"I've called all the nearby ranches and no one has seen either Kelly or Nrrna," Pat Reeve told Hrriss. "Did you have any luck?"

Hrriss had contacted every Hrruban he knew to be trustworthy, and some had set out discreet search groups to the farms around Nrrna's home village and some of the ranches where Nrrna had friends, but no one remembered seeing the girls.

"If she left Calypso, she's not anywhere a horse could go," Pat said. She was past worry, and into numbness, but she could still sense others' pain. Hrriss had only just been reunited with Todd after a traumatic separation, and now he had more troubles to concern him. Hrruvula had told Pat discreetly that if she saw either Todd or Hrriss, they must be prepared to appear before the Councillors or be judged guilty by default. He devoutly hoped that one or both would appear at the appointed time.

Robin came home from school with another black eye and many scratches and bruises.

"They're saying my brother's too much of a coward and he's flitted. They say Hrriss has run, too, which proves both of them are guilty as sin!" Robin was nearly in tears and refused to let his mother or his sister touch his injuries. "And I can't even tell 'em you haven't run. And they won't listen when I tell 'em my brother wouldn't! It's not fair. They weren't saying such things about Todd and you and Kelly at the Snake Hunt, and that wasn't that long ago." Robin didn't quite succumb to tears in front of Hrriss but it was touch and go.

"There are as many whom you have not seen today who do not believe that of either of us, Robin," Hrriss said. "Hrrula is one. Vic Solinari is another. And Lon Adjei."

"And Captain Ali Kiachif!" And, light-footed as ever, the spacefarer stood in the doorway.

Hearing his voice, Pat ran out from the kitchen. "Any news?"

"If you call no news good news, Patricia, then I've plenty of good tidings," the swarthy spacer said, shaking his head. "I've been listening in among my captains. No one reports transshipping any mystery guests off this planet in the dead of night, or knowing anyone who did. Any package that looks big enough to hold an unwilling prisoner, or one past caring, if you understand and forgive me, has been opened, turned over, and shaken. There's no trace of either of your men, either heading toward Earth or going in the exact opposite direction." Kiachif grimaced apologetically. "I've been on to Murphy, the supercargo at Main Station, Earth. No one's come by to claim that beacon yet. I'm still hoping someone might so I can tie a can to his tail. No offense meant, Hrriss."

"None zaken, Captain. I have sent more messages to our friends on Earth," Hrriss said. "My father was there when they left to Zreaty Island. We have so little time left, but I believe they are on Earth."

"Earth's a damned big place to find two Humans, laddie," Kiachif said grimly. "I'd have more luck searching space."

The radio buzzed and Pat grabbed up the handset, her face wild with her desperate hope for good news.

"Yes, Vic? . . . They are? But where? . . . You don't know? Then how can you be sure. . . . Oh, Hrrula . . . Well, yes, I do trust him as you do . . . Yes, yes, I understand. Oh, I think I do understand!" There was a glow on her worn face when she turned to the rest of the room. "Vic Solinari has had a message from Hrrula. Kelly is safe, and Nrrna." Pat reached out to grip Hrriss's arm reassuringly.

"Where did they get to, then?" Kiachif asked.

"Hrruna would only say that they are in the safest place they could possibly be. We're not to worry about them."

Hrriss threw his head up, his shoulders back, and his eyes began to gleam. "Zzoo! Zat Kelly," and his laughter was a loud purr of mixed satisfaction and surprise.

"Where are they, Hrriss?" Pat asked, giving his arm a shake as she peered up into his face.

"With the best friend we could have right now."

"I think I get what you mean, m'lad," Kiachif said, and winked.

Dalkey Petersham straightened his narrow collar before answering his comlink line's signal. Six hundred hours was an odd time for a call, but fortunately he was already up and dressed. Kelly again? She was always turning up at odd times. Dalkey switched on the unit. The screen displayed the face of a man he'd never seen before, but he certainly recognized the uniform: Poldep. Dalkey gulped. He knew he was being watched in the office now, but pretended he didn't. Partly because he really didn't want to be under observation. That only resulted in unpleasantness sooner or later. Fortunately he'd sent all he could to Kelly without breaking into the current data banks, so perhaps they'd stop watching him if he went strictly about his proper business. He still didn't know how Kelly had talked him into stripping those old files, but Kelly had a way with her. And it had been fun, delving into files, showing how cleverly he could penetrate massive files and extract just the information he needed. If only someone else would realize that Dalkey Petersham had untapped potential. But why was a Poldep inspector calling him at this hour? Spacedep had their own—and Dalkey gulped again—disciplinary branch. Then he remembered that Kelly had gone to Poldep, so this call might have more to do with Kelly Solinari than Dalkey Petersham.

"This is Sampson DeVeer," the moustachioed man said. "This is the communications number left by a young woman who has been assisting me in one of my inquiries. A Miss Green."

Kelly! Then he had lulled suspicion in his office. Relieved, Dalkey wondered if he should try to look dashing and piratical, suitable for the acquaintance of a police informant, or as harmless as possible. Harmless seemed more sensible. You lived longer if no one felt threatened by you. He let his shoulders hunch forward a little bit and tried to look clerkish. "Yes, sir?"

"I have received a request from another quarter to locate one of the subjects concerned in that investigation," DeVeer said obscurely. He waited, and Dalkey realized that he wanted Dalkey to prove he knew what the officer was talking about.

"That wouldn't be a member of the Reeve family, would it?" Dalkey asked, and DeVeer nodded. "Has that party been found?"

"Ahem, how did you know the party was missing?" DeVeer asked.

"Mrs. Reeve inquired by way of comp-line if by any chance one of her relatives had been in touch with me," Dalkey replied, thinking there was no harm in that. "She doesn't think they got as far as here."

The man sighed gently and smoothed his moustache with a fingertip. "That is a possibility which this office has been investigating. We thought you might help."

"If I should hear from either of them, I will contact you immediately." Dalkey felt that was safe to say.

"Please be sure to."

There was something ominous about that phrasing but the call was disconnected.

Hrringa didn't often leave the Hrruban Center. Hayumans should be accustomed to Hrrubans by now, but he was always conscious of stares, discreet, indirect observations. Nor could he tell if this was mere curiosity, bad manners, or outright hostility. The last seemed unlikely, judging by what he had observed of *Them*. Their lack of expression bothered him most, for he could not tell, as he could of any Hrruban countenance, what they felt: their eyes black dots in the center of oblong white orbs. Without another of his kind to keep him company, he often felt himself a hostage on Earth. Should something go very wrong with the Treaty, he might be eliminated by a tribe of these expressionless white-eyed folk, even if physically he was larger than most, and certainly stronger. That he might be faced with death on this posting had been subtly suggested to him in his original briefing. He had been chosen from the young applicants of many distinguished stripes because of his calm nature, excellent bearing, and diplomatic training.

"The Zreaty is at a crucial stage, as I am certain you are awarrre," Hrringa said to Rogitel when he was finally admitted to the Spacedep subchief's office. With Terran officials, he spoke Terran. "I have juzt been approached by an official of yrrr Poldep. He asks is it possible zat I wass given the wrrong date and hourr for the arrival of the Rrevs? I was zold to expect zem. Zey have not come. I waited all that night for zeir appearrance, and set the alarrrms so that I would be awakened zereafter by the activation of the grrid."

"Alarms?" Rogitel asked. His face remained still, but he felt agitated. He had been waiting for a report from the men he had hired to wait for the Reeves outside Alreldep block, and was concerned at the delay. This was a snag he had not anticipated, that the Reeves had failed to appear inside the Hrruban Center.

The Hrruban's tail lashed once in dismay. "Yes, motion alarrms. I do not usually set zem because no otherrs of my species are perrmitted on Arrth, and the only Hayuman outpost with a grid is Rrala, so I do not see much trraffic. There is no need to arrise in the off-shifts to rreceive a nonsentient shipment, the most frrquent use of the grrid."

"True." Rogitel wasted few words, especially ones that might be misconstrued.

"The alarrms are very sensizive. Nothing set zem off, not yesterday, and not zoday. I tessted zem mysself just beforre I came to be certain that they were in worrking orrder and zey are. Zo I must ask you, onorred sir, has something happened to delay the Rrevs? Surrely if they were summoned by the court, zey would have come? Zey are known to be honorrrable men. Am I in error?"

"You are not," the commander said. "The Amalgamated Worlds court was waiting for them." Rogitel stood up and nodded curtly to the Hrruban. "Thank you for coming to see me, honored sir. I will look into the matter, and bring it to the attention of my superior."

Hrringa bowed and left.

Within the hour, Admiral Landreau appeared in the Hrruban Center and demanded instantaneous transport to Doona. He was upset. He had been expecting to hear in bloody detail how Rogitel's hired toughs disposed of the Reeves and found out that the damned nuisances had not even reached Earth! Rogitel was in trouble, for not verifying that the prisoners had not been taken into custody by his hirelings and disposed of as arranged. There was only the one fast way back to Earth—by the Hrruban Center's grid. Had someone tipped off the Reeves as to the reception awaiting them?

Landreau had thoroughly enjoyed listening to the furor among the Doonan colonists, caused by the midnight summons of the Reeves to appear before the Amalgamated Worlds panel. What had happened? Rogitel had seen them safely to the Treaty Island grid. They had been transferred by that abominable mechanism, but the men waiting outside the Hrruban Center swore blind that neither Reeve had left the block. None of the corner monitors at each angle of the building recorded anyone passing, in either direction. Could the rumormongers on Doona be correct? The cowards had done a flit? Unless, and Landreau considered this possibility, they had been in cahoots with the grid operator on Doona and got themselves transported to some village where they were no doubt lying low until after the Treaty was ratified.

Landreau swore under his breath. Damned cats couldn't be trusted to do even the simplest things: like key in a proper grid destination. The wretched felines had been a thorn in his side all along. If those Reeves were hidden somewhere on Doona, he'd find them if it was the last thing that he ever did in his life.

He continued muttering to himself while Hrringa hastened to set the controls for transmission to Treaty Island. The engulfing smoke rose around him and blotted out the Hrruban's expressionless cat face.

Landreau grunted in relief as he recognized the Treaty Island facility and strode off the platform. Yes, that was what had happened. The bedamned grid operator had redirected the Reeves somewhere on Doona. Why hadn't Rogitel checked the settings? Or had the Treaty Controller do so? Slack discipline, that! You had to do everything yourself to see it done properly. Landreau wheeled, confronting the grid operator directly.

"What is your name?" he demanded of the astonished Hrruban. All grid operators understood Standard. Had to.

"Hrrenya," the Hrruban replied, surprised.

"Who is your superior?"

"Zreaty Conttrollerr," the catman answered, backing away from Landreau and blinking his eyes. "He is seniorr diplomaz on Rrala."

"You were on duty three nights back? When the Treaty Controller and Commander Rogitel brought the Reeves here? D'you know the Reeves?" The Hrruban nodded quickly. "Where did you send them?"

"To Arrth as I was inzructed, honorred sir."

"You didn't!" Landreau shouted. "You didn't! They never arrived on Earth. Where *did* you send them? Someplace right here on Doona. Isn't that right?"

Landreau's rising voice had attracted attention. Out of a nearby corridor, three of the Treaty Councillors hurried toward the grid, the Controller among them. The grid operator tried to keep his dignity, tried to remain calm, but the Hayuman's face was growing very red and, without fur to cover it, it was a terrifying sight. Grid operators were not trained in diplomatic matters, so Hrrenya was intensely relieved to see assistance near at hand.

"Admiral Landreau," the Treaty Controller snapped out in Hrruban. "Why are you berating our operator? You should report any insubordination or impudence to me."

"Where are Ken and Todd Reeve?" Landreau turned on the Controller as perhaps the genuinely guilty party in this absurd miscarriage. He stubbornly kept to his own language, too enraged to exercise any courtesy until he had the answers he had come to find.

"What?" the Controller demanded, as stubbornly replying in Hrruban. "Are they not on Terra? You demanded their presence there three days ago. I myself witnessed their departure."

"What do you mean, they're not here? Your drone there," and Landreau swung an arm toward the grid operator, whose tail was between his legs in fear, "sent them somewhere here on Doona instead of back to Earth so they could answer for their crimes. They are my prisoners. I demand that the Reeves be produced and sent immediately to stand trial."

"You demand?" the Hrruban snarled, the points of his teeth exposed. Treaty Controller flew into a rage. "You have dishonored our people who live on Rrala, by using these Humans, whom you have yourself misplaced, to commit foul crimes against the Treaty which you pretend to support. If you cannot find them on your planet, then that is no fault of ours. Seek to set your own tribe in order without falsely accusing those of another."

Landreau's momentum came to a dead halt. The Treaty Controller's anger was too genuine to have been faked. Landreau was a fair judge of knowing truth from lie and the Treaty Controller obviously told the truth—or what he thought was the truth. If the Reeves had transported, why hadn't Rogitel's men detained them? Or did that fur-faced Hrringa assist them and send them out of the Hrruban Center a secret way? He'd never been too happy with the secrecy shielding the Hrruban Center from outside interference.

"Naturally you would defend your employee," Landreau began, trying another tack. "How do you know that he was not got at? Bribed? Those men should have been sent to Earth to answer for their offenses. They did not arrive. They are still on Doona!"

Treaty Controller drew himself up indignantly, looking down with great condescension on the stocky smaller Human. "We have more important matters to debate than the whereabouts of two troublesome Hayumans. If the young Reeve does not appear at his trial, he is by default guilty and so is his partner in crime. We are constrained to continue for the next two days to work out details which may, indeed, be irrelevant. But we are by honor bound to continue."

He swept magnificently away, though the other Councillors did not immediately follow. The small woman who had met the Admiral on his last visit, Madam Dupuis, gazed at him steadily, as if she was trying to read his mind. Did she know something of his secret plans?

"You have no jurisdiction to search Doona, Admiral," she said in a cold expressionless voice. "Go back to Earth. Where you belong." She signalled to the grid operator, repeating her order in her fluent Hrruban and waited, arms folded, to see that her order was obeyed.

Uncomfortable on many counts, Landreau had to step back on the grid and hope that the presence of Madam Dupuis meant that the grid operator would explicitly follow his orders.

When Ken tried to move, his head hurt, and his wrists were pressed against the small of his back. His hands were numb. He tried to turn over and pull them apart to restore circulation, but he couldn't move. He opened his eyes to the unencouraging sight of a dull gray wall. Squirming, he tried to free his hands, but they were tied by a taut binding that allowed no slack he could use to free them. He turned his head in a quick survey. There wasn't much light, but sufficient to see Todd's limp body on a flat plank of wood similar to the one under him.

"Todd?" Ken said, trying his voice.

Todd was on a flat plank of a bed that was identical to his own. As Ken's eyes grew accustomed to the dim light, he saw the bruises on the boy's face, blood on his nose, cheeks, and chin, but old blood, dried. Torn clothes revealed bloody scratches and more discoloring bruises. But at least the blood was clotted and dried. Todd was breathing heavily through his mouth, not surprising, for his nose was probably broken. At least he was breathing. Ken remembered the two of them standing back-to-back, fighting for their lives against too numerous assailants.

When the transport mist had cleared after their departure from Treaty Island, Ken had been struck across the back with something hard, like a bar. The force of the blow had dropped him to his knees. Gasping with pain and surprise, Ken struggled to his feet to defend himself against the attacking Hrrubans. Demanding that they identify themselves and repeating his own name brought no answer save for grunts at the punches he landed wherever he could. Ken Reeve had wrestled a few steers in his day and, bigger though the Hrrubans were, they only had two legs. With a well-aimed kick, he forced one attacker to his knees, kicking the sheath knife out of his hand and ducking the claws that swiped at him as the Hrruban sprang up.

Then the prehensile tail wrapped around Ken's waist like a snake. Their caudal appendages weren't really very strong. They were made for holding, not subduing. Ken jerked an elbow down hard over the joint between two of the small bones under the fur. The Hrruban let out a wail of pain and whipped his tail out of reach. But then someone jumped Ken from behind, trying to throttle him. He kicked out at another who leaped at him in a frontal attack, catching him in the throat, snapping the fringed jaw shut, and knocking him unconscious.

Another Hrruban merely lifted both Ken's legs off the ground while the one behind him forced his hands together. Ken knew from sounds beyond him that Todd had been acquitting himself well against such overwhelming numbers of assailants. As Ken waited bravely for his neck to be broken, he felt only that his hands and legs were being tied tightly. So they weren't trying to kill him, just capture him. He looked toward Todd, struggling in the hands of three Hrrubans. One thing was certain with so many Hrrubans around: they were not on Earth. Had they been diverted to Hrruba?

Though Todd had the height and heft of his attackers, he couldn't quite fight free. Years of riding and hard work had given him the strength of a mule, and the Hrrubans couldn't pull him down. While Todd was still on his feet, Ken had hope, and filling his lungs, he started to yell at the top of his voice in Hrruban.

"Help! Someone! Help us! We are being denied honorable treatment!"

Todd added his voice, shouting in High Hrruban for the Speakers. Whether or not they were on Hrruba, such a cry should raise an alarm nearby. Their yelling upset their assailants. The one behind Ken began to clout him across the mouth to silence him. Ken writhed, trying to evade the blows with his bound arms. Suddenly he heard Todd's shouts end abruptly. Then a pair of fists caught him on the point of his chin, and that was the end of his fight.

Now Ken squirmed and rolled until he got himself into a sitting position. The sound of a throat being cleared told him that the two of them were not alone in their small, gray prison. Ken glanced over to the far corner of the room. Two Hrrubans in the harness of official guards sat in chairs beyond the end of the small chamber, closed off to the corridor by a wall of bars. Ken peered at them. They were both of a very narrow Stripe. They looked unmarked, so they were unlikely to be part of the gang that had attacked them. The narrow Stripes wore only bare harnesses, giving Ken no idea of where they were and which faction had captured them. However, he could rule out Earth because of the presence of so many Hrrubans, though the corridors beyond the chamber reminded him of Earth. They could have been taken to any one of several dozen Hrruban-settled worlds.

"Todd? Wake up, son!" Ken whispered. He eased himself slowly along the bench until he was sitting opposite Todd's head. Neither of the guards moved, either to help him or to make him lie down again. Trussed up as he was, guards were no more than a formality. His movement had been noticed and the Hrrubans muttered between them in Low Hrruban.

Todd stirred, and his eyes opened. Ken noticed that his chin was dark with stubble. They had been unconscious a long time, perhaps even a day. Todd started to sit up, and winced at the pain of his bruised muscles. "Where are we, Dad?"

"I don't know, Todd," Ken said. He caught Todd's eye and then looked significantly toward the barred wall. "But it sure isn't Earth."

Todd turned his head and opened his mouth but Ken intervened.

"No, son, don't. Don't speak Hrruban. Just before you woke up, one of them said to the other, 'They're a lot more docile than Third said they'd be.' "

"Oh?" Todd raised his eyebrows at that indiscretion.

"This pair obviously don't know we understand their language." Ken smiled grimly. "If we keep listening, we may hear something even more valuable. Here, move toward me and I'll see if I can't undo your bindings. Hey, untie us, would you?" he asked the guards loudly in Terran. The two Hrrubans stared at Ken without saying a word and then went back to their own conversation.

"I don't think they understand Terran," Ken said with satisfaction.

"So does Third plan to kill us?" Todd asked with commendable detachment.

"I think not or they'd have done so during the fight on the grid," Ken said grimly. "No, they want us alive and I'd give anything to know why."

"So I can't appear at that trial and Hrriss and I are judged guilty by my default?" Todd suggested.

"Could be, son, since it was Third Speaker who made your innocence a sticking point for Treaty Renewal."

Both kept working surreptitiously to release their hands. If the guards thought them docile, so much the better for the success of their efforts to free themselves.

Plainly bored by a long stretch, the two guards leaned together and began to speak. They didn't bother to lower their voices, believing that their bareskin prisoners did not understand Hrruban. Their conversation was less than complimentary about the cravens they had no real need to guard. When one said that the bareskins would be easy to subdue, after all, Ken and Todd redoubled their efforts to free themselves.

Todd got his hands loose first. He stifled an inadvertent gasp as blood rushed to his fingers, causing excruciating pain. As soon as they worked again, he moved closer to his father and unbound him. They'd have to be very careful getting their legs free. Perhaps if they pretended to sleep . . . It was when Todd shifted cautiously onto one side that he realized what had been taken from him.

"Dad! They've taken it."

"What?"

"All the documents we were going to show the panel, to prove me innocent, to prove Landreau's conspiracy."

Ken's groan was genuine. In Third Speaker's possession, those documents were pure gelignite! He closed his eyes, knowing total defeat of all he'd strived to build, all he hoped for the future of the Doona/Rrala Experiment. He couldn't look at Todd, but the boy's soft anguished moan told him that Todd understood the scope of the disaster.

chapter twelve

On the dais of the assembly hall, elders from all ten villages of Doona waited for the huge crowd of colonists to come to order. The transportation grid on the Hrruban side of the Friendship Bridge had been busy all day, bringing in anyone and everyone from all over the planet who wanted to help organize the celebration for Treaty Renewal Day. Carts and flitters full of food and decorations lined the paths outside and spilled over into the garden. Children caught the mood of excitement from their parents, who whispered among themselves about the upcoming great event.

"Please!" Hrrestan shouted over the din. "We have much to do before tomorrow. May we have your attention, please?"

"I'm glad I lived to see this day," said Hu Shih, smiling through his spectacles at his friends, both Human and Hrruban. "The celebration tomorrow will be both a tribute to all the hard work we have put in and an acknowledgment of the cooperation between our races."

"If there is any celebration to look forward to," Anne Boncyk said sourly, from just in front of the dais. She had been passing on the whispers she heard to anyone who'd listen that Ken Reeve and his son Todd had disappeared rather than appear in court to defend allegations against them. "They're probably headed for one of the outer worlds where they have all that money hidden away," she confided out loud to Randall McKee.

But she picked the wrong target for such a statement.

"You know better than that, Anne," Randall replied, rising to the defense of both Reeves.

"Yes, indeed," and Vic Solinari joined McKee, facing down the woman's gossip. "There'll be a bloody damned good explanation for their disappearance, just you wait and see."

"I'll wait but I don't think I'll see," she replied tauntingly. "Those Reeves never could run things right."

"Confound it, Anne Boncyk," and now Ben Adjei confronted the small woman, "if you mean how they run the Snake Hunt, I've told you three times for every pig you own, Anne, if you'd have chosen a different homestead than the one you did, the snakes wouldn't come anywhere near your spread."

"They're supposed to make sure all livestock is safe all along the way," Anne retorted, getting angrier.

"Those reptiles have been sliding up and back between the dunes and the marshes along that stretch since before your acres had even surfaced out of the sea. I showed you a dozen better sites when you came here. You'd be better off if you moved."

"I might not have a choice, thanks to those Perfect Twins you all think so much of." Anne sniffed, turning away from the burly veterinarian and looking around to make sure Hrriss was not within earshot. "What I've heard is, if they're judged guilty, then the Treaty won't be renewed. All along, you thought they were such saints, and look what they're doing to us!"

"Todd and Hrriss are innocent," Vic Solinari said. "Most of the charges against them have been proved bogus. You know that as well as anyone else here, Anne Boncyk, so stop acting the maggot."

"If they're so innocent, why isn't Todd here to stand beside Hrriss and prove it? Because if they don't, we're off Doona! The Hrrubans will confiscate our homes, our stock, everything we've worked for."

"Hrrubans do not intend to confiscate Hayuman homes," said Hrrula, stepping through the crowd around them. "I, Hrrula, know that Zodd Rrev is innocent."

"Well, we're not sure of that," a Human woman cried out.

"Yet your system of justice, like ours, clearly states that one is innocent until proved guilty. If, after knowing how hard both Todd and Hrriss have worked to make this colony succeed, you think they are guilty, then this great Experiment is already over."

There was a moment's stunned silence as Hrrula's words condemned many for their lack of faith. Hrriss, standing well back in the crowd, lowered his head in shame. He had endured much calumny and heard his dearest friend slandered. Nothing he had said, or proved with the precious documents they had worked so hard to gather, would change the minds of many of these distressed folk, Hrruban and Hayuman, when they realized that all their hard work could be swept away at any moment by the dissolution of the Treaty and the Doona/Rrala Experiment.

"No, the Experiment has not failed," cried Hu Shih, struggling to the dais. "Not if we, Hayuman and Hrruban alike, present a unified front. We must be of one mind now, more than ever, putting aside petty questions of innocence or guilt. The Colonial Department and the Speakers will have to realize that we, Hayumans and Hrrubans, are sincere and dedicated to the principles of the Decision at Doona and the Cohabitation Treaty."

"Well said, well said!" Clapping his hands above his head in Hayuman fashion, Hrrestan jumped to the dais to stand beside the slender little Hu Shih. "This colony is a state of mind as well as a place for both species to live and prosper. It was founded on hope. Let us keep that hope alive. Now! Let us hope that our faith in those young men is vindicated as I know it will be!" And to the surprise of everyone listening, Hrrestan threw his head back and uttered an ancient Hrruban challenge.

It had barely died away when others repeated the challenge, Hrrubans with their uncanny howl and Hayumans with wild ululating cheers.

"Okay, folks," and Vic Solinari leaped to the dais. "No one's called off the ceremonies so let's make sure they start on time. Senior dignitaries from Earth and Hrruba are due in shortly. Let's show them as united a front as we did twenty-five years ago. They didn't believe us then, and we made them. Let's revive that spirit and show 'em now, today! We're here to stay, Hrrubans and Hayumans, equal and together." He waited through long seconds of renewed cheers and then held up his hands for silence. "We got a lot of work to do now, everybody, so let's hop to it. First Village has sent rails of brrnas for roasting, Wayne Boncyk's given us four of his boars to roast. Norris has donated a hundredweight of those special sausages he makes, Phyllis here has ssliss eggs by the cartload, and I dunno how many women have been baking. Let's get organized, folks!"

He sprang down from the dais, genially pushing one group one way, another toward the doors, gesturing at the fire pits that were already glowing.

"We have the crop of our berry harvest to offer," called out Hrrmova of the Third Hrruban Village. "A bounty of blackberries and drroilanas."

"The Launch Bar will donate beer, mlada, and wine," the owner called. "If any spacers come wanting a drink, they'll have to find me here. I don't want to miss a minute of the celebration."

"That's the spirit," Vic Solinari cheered him. "Hrrestan, where should I put my two hundred kilos of good aged urfa cheese?"

"We shall find a place, my friend," the Hrruban said, "for I know that many Hrrubans are particularly fond of that commodity."

"And the hunters of First Village," Hu Shih said, "have made a record catch of the hatchlings. Snake stew must be on the menu."

"We're doing all this for nothing!" Martinson of the Launch Center shouted, pushing through a crowd which had recovered its hope. "We'll all be off this planet before that food can be cooked, much less served."

But his warning elicited more jeers than agreement.

"You may leave now, if that is how you feel, Martinson," Hrrestan replied, letting his eyes slit as he looked at the portmaster. He didn't show the irritation he felt at this attempt to puncture the delicate mood of optimism that was beginning to build. "Go if you do not share our hopes. We will not miss you." And resolutely he turned away.

Martinson stared after him, looked around the room, but others had turned away, too. He stamped out of the Hall, cursing fools and fatheads and men who wouldn't face reality.

Soon even the most pessimistic caught the growing spirit of hope and resolve. There was a lot to be done, however the events of the next day turned out. After all, twenty-five years ago, there had been less hope for those who remembered that fateful day. Was it wrong to expect a second miracle?

Hrrestan hoped that he sounded more convinced than he felt. If some worked only because it was something to do, that was better than doing nothing. And so the preparations for the feast began, Hrrubans and Hayumans working side by side.

The next day dawned, for better or for worse. Pat forced herself out of bed and set about kneading bread dough which had risen during the night. She put the loaf pans on the sun porch to rise again. Deftly she put fancy touches on each, spread glazes on some and sprinkled seed on others. For someone who had never baked a loaf of bread before she came to Doona, over time Pat had mastered the skill until she had pride in it. If she worked, she didn't think about how frightened she was. Once again she was alone on Doona without Ken: she hadn't liked it the first time it had happened twenty-five years ago and she didn't like it now. He should be here with her. Where was he? Where was Todd? And where were Kelly and Nrrna? Safe, they said, but where *was* safe these days? Kelly had given her so much support, ever since Todd had woken up to what everyone else had seen—that he and Kelly were so well suited to each other. The bread made, she had only to wait until it was ready to bake. Only to wait? That was the hardest part of all. Wait for what?

The handle of the front door rattled, and Pat flew to answer it. On the doorstep was her daughter Ilsa, and her two small daughters.

"Oh, sweetheart," Pat gasped. "I'd almost forgotten you were coming."

Ilsa put down her bags and threw her arms around her mother.

"Happy Treaty Renewal Day, Mom," she said happily, embracing Pat and then stood back at her expression. "If it is. What's wrong?"

Pat bent to cuddle her two small granddaughters, four and seven they were now.

"How would you two like to help me make bread?" she asked, diverting them as well as herself. "Wash your hands now," and when they had, she showed them how to shape spare scraps of dough into little loaves and left them to it.

With them happily occupied, she explained to Ilsa what had been happening since their last contact.

Ilsa listened quietly and thoughtfully to the most recent troubles. Knowing her brother's sense of honor, Ilsa had expected Todd to have cleared up all that nonsense about smuggling and stealing and things. She kept to herself her anxiety when she learned of the disappearance of both her father and brother.

"Why didn't you comp-line me, Mother? If Dad and Todd are on Earth, we could have gone to Poldep to instigate a search for them."

"I didn't want to worry you, dear," Pat replied, knowing that she hadn't considered her gentle daughter could be much help in such circumstances. "Every minute I expect them back, to walk in that door and explain where they've been. And there's no time left now. Nothing they could do even if they do make it back today."

"Now, now, Mother, I'll just make us a nice cup of tea and think what to do."

When the baking was done, the two women put the still-steaming loaves and buns in the flitter and went to the Assembly Hall kitchen. The room was uncomfortably silent. The previous day's ebullience had dissipated when dawn brought no sign of the missing Reeves. Preparations for the feast were proceeding, but the mood was of people performing chores by rote or by sheer and dogged obstinacy, with none of the laughter and joking and excitement that should infect such a task on a day of such historic importance.

Those who would cling to their hope and faith until the bitter end of all expectation tried to resist the spread of despair. Some of the faces were stunned and incredulous, others resentful. A few doomsayers murmured to any who would listen that there was no way to avoid or escape the inexorable end of this sad day.

Hrrula, Hrrestan, Mrrva, the Solinaris, and the Shihs moved constantly about the work parties, encouraging, complimenting, urging people to greater efforts. The preparations continued in spite of the general depression. It looked like it would be a magnificent feast, in the very best tradition of Doona. Even if it did turn out to be the last one, the condemned would eat heartily.

"You always present food so beautifully, Miranda," Pat told one of the young women who had just been carving Doona blossoms out of root vegetables. Smiling, the girl glanced up at the compliment and her smile turned to a sneer as she swiftly moved away.

Pat felt as if she had been slapped. She glanced up and met the eyes of one of the Hrruban males who were helping trim roasts, and he too turned his head, without changing expression. Pat cast wildly about for Ilsa and found she'd watched the whole thing. The young woman's eyes were full of shocked hurt. Pat was embarrassed that her daughter had to be witness to her mother's humiliation. It was so obvious that people unconsciously blamed Todd, and Ken, for their predicament.

"Pat, I'd appreciate your help outside," Dr. Kate Moody said, wrapping an arm around her shoulders and escorting her firmly to the door. Once they were hidden behind a cultivated hedge which separated the rear of the kitchen from plain view, Pat let go and sobbed bitterly on Kate's shoulder.

"You've been a model of fortitude, Pat, don't spoil it now," the colony pediatrician murmured to her, patting her on the back. "This isn't a personal rejection of you, you know. Everyone's tense, frustrated. I don't have a notion what happened to Ken or Todd but I'm damned sure they'd be here if they could! And I keep hoping any minute now they'll come striding over that bridge and set everything straight. Mind you, they may be cutting their timing a bit close, but they'll come."

"If I could believe that . . ." Pat wiped her eyes with the doctor's handkerchief and let out a sigh. She wanted that very scene to take place, and soon. She looked over at the bridge, hoping against hope that Ken and Todd would materialize from the grid. "I can't blame people, Kate. If . . . We'll all lose our homes and everything we've worked for and we really don't belong anywhere now but Doona. And why is it that both Todd and Hrriss have to be at the hearing? Hrriss has almost all the evidence. Why, that Mayday beacon being found on Earth, and Dr. Tylanio proving the log tape was doctored beyond recognition. That proves that the boys didn't steal those things because they weren't even near those planets, just as they've always said." Pat had to stop to blow her nose. "And if Hrriss is innocent, then Todd is, too. Or that's what Hrruvula assured me. And that's how he's going to present the documentation we have!"

Kate smiled at her. "Well, you're a lot more generous with the fools than I'd be. Come on back inside. There's a lot left to be done, and we need you. I know they've got almost all the evidence, but they may hang us all on the specific wording of the Speakers' resolution. Both boys and all charges dismissed. No one could ever keep either Ken or Todd down for long. And you know it." Kate lifted Pat's chin and smiled at her. "So hold your head up and shame the devil."

Pat managed a weak laugh. "My grandmother used to say that. If I just knew that they were both . . . okay . . ." She couldn't bring herself to use any other word. "I feel so lost without them."

"Well, you're not lost, and you're not alone. You have all of us. Let's see if I can remind these doubting fainthearts of that."

Kate pushed through the door and escorted Pat back to the cake-decorating station. With a firm hand, she sat her down on a stool and put tools in front of her. To the others who glanced at them in surprise, the pediatrician stated in a loud voice:

"Now let's get something straight, you gaggle of gossiping grannies. No, you're acting like pre-teens, and I've the right to kick sense into that age group. You know where to lay the blame for all the anxiety we're experiencing, and it isn't on Pat Reeve's shoulders. It's because her husband and her son haven't turned up. Do you know them so little after twenty-five years that you'd honestly believe they'd leave us in a lurch?

"Well, I don't, and there're plenty of others who agree with me. Someone, or some group of ones, made sure Ken and Todd never made it to Earth. 'Cause there's no way they'd go unnoticed there! Not those big-striding, proud-walking men. Can you imagine them mincy-mincing," and she mimicked the short polite stride of the Terran natives, drawing a giggle from some quarters, "along Corridors and Aisles without being noticed? We know they're not on Doona because where we Hayumans haven't looked, we Hrrubans have! And any of us silly enough to believe that there aren't some Hayumans and Hrrubans who'd both prefer never to set eyes on the Reeves again better take the next shuttle out of here."

"We'll have to anyhow, won't we, if the Reeves don't show up?" a woman murmured.

"Well, I got hopes on that score, too. We've got Hrruvula, no narrow-stripe mince-stepped poseur either, to present the documentation that has been assembled. And if Hrriss can be proved innocent, then ipso facto, Todd Reeve is. And that ought to be good enough for everyone here and good enough to sway the Councillors. *And*, I don't want to hear another sour word from anyone." She clapped her hands vigorously. "We got a lot to do. Let's do it. And with a few smiles to make the work go quicker."

Few could argue with her facts or the good sense for which Kate Moody had always been noted. Flagging hopes revived again and soon a few smiles appeared on faces. Several people deliberately came up to Pat, giving her affectionate squeezes on her forearm or apologizing for their unkindness. Instead of seeking for something or someone new to blame, long glances passed between friends who were fearful that they would never see one another again. Work resumed at a more energetic pace with the renewed sense of solidarity.

Old Abe Dautrish, carefully decanting wines of his own recipes from herbs and local berries, spoke in reminiscence. "Remember that first winter? Ten months of misery. Living in one miserable plastic hut until we could get the others up. Remember what that was like? Who'd believe we could come so far?"

"And together," said Lee Lawrence, smacking Hrrula on the back.

"All was bezzer when we became frriends," a Hrruban woman said, with dropped jaw.

"We'll fight this," Phyllis Shih stated, whipping a bowlful of eggs with a vengeance. "They can't throw us out of here. This is our home. We'll take the appeal to the Amalgamated Worlds court ourselves if we need to."

"That's the old Doona spirit," Kate Moody said with satisfaction. She winked at Pat.

All the preparations were complete by midafternoon. The First Village's hunters, following Hrriss, returned with dozens of young snakes and a few wild fowl for the stewpot. Carcasses of dozens of urfas, pigs, and cows rotated over coals in the many roasting pits downwind of the kitchen.

The transportation grid was brought over the bridge from the Hrruban side and laid in front of the Assembly Hall's big double doors. Its posts had been draped with floral streamers. Not long thereafter, diplomats of both races began to appear and were escorted into the Hall with much attendant dignity.

The weather was cheerful and bright. Doona's long winter would arrive within two months, but there was no early chill which the organizers feared might mar the celebration. Some colonists from warmer climates shivered a little in the autumnal air. Every settlement, including Treaty Island, had lobbied to hold the celebration, but the honor was eventually returned to First Village, where the original accord had been signed twenty-five years before.

Depressing any misgivings, the population of the planet turned out in its best. All the Hrrubans wore the formal red robes: the males in heavy, opaque garments that fell to the tips of shiny black boots; the females in filmier garments of jewel-spangled gauze. The Humans wore monochromatic tunics with touches of white, and beautifully cut but simple ankle-length gowns. There was none of the cheerful cross-cultural dressing that was usually prevalent at most other big events. Today's garments unexpectedly became a restatement of racial identity.

Hrriss stood tall beside his father just below the dais inside the Hall, hiding his emotions. In a few moments, he must present evidence to prove his and Todd's innocence of the crimes of which they were accused. On the basis of that proof or lack of it, the Treaty Controller might refuse to ratify the Treaty, and the colony would be dissolved.

What Hrriss had not been able to tell anyone was that the carefully gathered documentation had vanished from the Rrev home at about the same time Kelly had. He had worked night and day to duplicate the evidence from the files still remaining in his home. Dr. Tylanio had supplied him with a copy of his report on the tape's alteration. He had the latter half of the Spacedep slush fund dispersals which Dalkey had procured but not the more important entries. Tylanio had gone off with Kiachif and so the expert was not available to present direct testimony to the Councillors. To be sure, the Mayday beacon had been discovered but the Speakers' resolution required a total clearance of all charges—and Zodd's presence! Would Hrruvula be able to make what they did have sufficient to clear all those charges even in the face of Zodd's nonappearance?

One by one, the high-ranking officials of Earth emerged from the grid, some looking puzzled and taken aback by the process of transportation which they were experiencing for the first time. Most of them, nervous about suddenly being bereft of walls and ceilings around them, walked as quickly into the Hall as dignity permitted, without so much as a quick glance around at the beauties of the village green.

The settlers clustered in and around the building, their bows and smiles becoming more and more mechanical as time went on. Sampson DeVeer of Poldep, wearing the dress uniform of black with silver touches, emerged from the chest-high fog, accompanied by a slim, pale man wearing a plain uniform.

"My heart isn't in this," Lee Lawrence muttered, feeling the strain of smiling when he hadn't any reason to do so.

"I am still determined to put the best face on the day," Hu Shih said. Then he arranged his most benevolent smile on his face as he stepped forward to introduce the newly arrived Treaty Island Archivist to the other village elders.

"Perhaps the Treaty Council will still take what is best for Doona into account," Abe Dautrish said quietly to Lee. "They shouldn't pay too much attention to overworld councils, since we are supposed to be independent of both governments. We have proved ourselves capable and worthy of self-governance."

"After all the accusations of the last few days, can you genuinely say that?" Lawrence asked.

"I want to," the old man said humbly. "I keep it closely in mind. Ah, here is Admiral Sumitral and his daughter."

"Good day, my friends," Sumitral said, mounting the ramp with quick strides and taking Hu Shih's hand. Age had done nothing to bow his proud carriage, but he bore the same heavy expression of concern that troubled the Doonan elders. He was still the greatest friend Doona had in the Terran government. "You know my daughter, Emma?" The tall girl smiled and nodded to each of them, then took her place among the colonists in the audience.

"Hrrestan, it is good to see you," Sumitral said, turning to the younger Hrruban. "Hrriss, have you had any word from Todd?"

"No, sirr," Hrriss said.

"It looks very bad that they haven't returned yet," Sumitral said. "Where could they have gone? And why? The Amalgamated Worlds court was well disposed to give men a fair hearing on the basis of their achievements."

Hrriss burned with shame. "They would come if they could," he insisted.

Sumitral eyed him curiously. "Do you know where they went?"

"No. But they would have returned if they could. Of that I am certain. They are held somewhere against their will." He placed his hand on his heart, his upper lip, and his forehead to emphasize his stated belief.

"I fear you may be right. Neither has ever betrayed an ounce of cowardice. Defection does not fit their characters," Sumitral declared. "You have searched Rrala?" Hrriss nodded. "I alerted all Alreldep offices. Can none of you Hrrubans search your own planet? They have to be somewhere."

"If they are alive," Hrriss murmured, for he had denied that possibility as long as he could.

Then he saw the slender frame of Admiral Sumitral stiffen. A hand touched his arm in apology and Sumitral moved toward Hu Shih.

"Come, Hu," the Admiral said as he urged the man toward the platform where a small, thin, clean-shaven Terran in a white tunic descended from the grid. "May I introduce you to the representative of the Amalgamated Worlds Congress? Hrrestan, I am pleased to make you known to Dorem Naruti, of the AWC." He continued to make introductions among the village elders.

At a signal from the Hrruban grid operator, Sumitral took his place beside the other Terran delegates. Third Speaker appeared from the mist surrounding the transport grid and, looking neither left nor right at those who bowed courteously to him, marched majestically into the Hall. The glow of triumph in his eyes was absolutely indecent. Many Rralans, seeing that look, growled quietly under their breath at his lack of restraint and the implications for them.

The rumors of dissolution spread from Rralans to Hayuman friends and neighbors. Hrriss fielded glares and blatant animosity from longtime acquaintances. Who was holding the Rrevs captive? No, which of the known antagonists to the Treaty had succeeded in denying the Rrevs the dignity of facing their enemies and confounding them?

As if in answer to his thoughts, Admiral Landreau in gleaming dress whites and an almost garish display of medals materialized on the grid. A moment earlier and he might have tread on Third's tail. The Admiral was accompanied by Rogitel and two other aides. Landreau had arranged his features in an expression of pious serenity which would fool no one on Rrala, certainly not Hrriss. His demeanor added more discouragement to Hrriss's depressed morale. Why didn't Zodd appear, through the grid or out of the underbrush, with his document case in his hands, to wipe the smugness from the faces of Third and Landreau?

At last, Second Speaker Hrrto made his way from the grid through the hanging garlands of flowers to the platform. With his arrival, the complement of delegates from both sides was complete. Only the Treaty Council was yet to arrive before the ceremony would begin.

As the assembly of settlers held its collective breath, the Council appeared, clustered together on the grid behind the Treaty Controller, magnificent in flowing red robes. On his breast hung a medallion of two intertwined gold suns, studded with sapphires mined and cut from native crystals. It represented the interweaving on Doona of Human and Hrruban cultures. The light reflected from the jewel vanished abruptly as soon as the Treaty Controller stepped inside the Assembly Hall. Immediately behind the Council came two clerks, one Human and one Hrruban, each of whom carried a large leather-bound and gem-studded book.

Solemnly the Council ascended to the dais. Each member bowed to the assembled dignitaries. The Treaty Controller was the last to do so. He made an especially deep obeisance to Third Speaker, who returned a curt nod. The clerks moved silently to lay the huge books side by side on the table in the center of the stage. Without further hesitation, the Treaty Controller held up one hand.

"Hrriss, son of Hrrestan and Mrrva, stand forth! Zodd Rrev, son of Ken and Patrricia, stand forth!" he intoned. The purrs and growls of High Hrruban had never sounded so severe.

Hrriss stepped forward, holding his spine straight, and willing his tail to refrain from twitching with his inner turmoil. Hrruvula, clad in his official professional garments, joined Hrriss.

"Sir, Zodd Rrev has been unavoidably detained," Hrriss said. "I speak for us both."

The Treaty Controller's tail twitched once from side to side behind him. "Both of the accused must face this Council. Have you, perhaps, a document of the ill-health of your codefendant?" At that moment, Hrriss was very certain who had detained Zodd and his father. His heart sank but he raised his chin just enough to show that he knew the sordid game the Controller was playing out. "Be that as it may, you and your absent accomplice stand accused of crimes which violate the laws of the Hrruban League, the laws of the Amalgamated Worlds, and the Treaty of Doona. These are serious crimes, which shake the very fabric of trust which made the Treaty possible twenty-five years ago. What proof can you present to attest to your innocence?"

"There is documentation," Hrruvula said, stepping forward and pulling one flimsy after another from his case, "to prove that the Mayday beacon was heard by Zodd Rrev and Hrriss, son of Hrrestan, said beacon being found among cargo shipped to Earth and designated to be delivered to a minor office connected with Space Department. And here is a declaration from a noted laser expert stating that the log tapes of the *Albatross* had been skillfully tampered with to show landings and launchings never made by the *Albatross*, as further testified to the signatories of the documents that the condition of its engines, rocket tubes, and other equipment showed no sign of the abuse such a hegira would have done to said equipment. I have these documents stating the health and energy of both defendants, who would have suffered even more physical deterioration than engines, rocket tubes, and other equipment from a medical condition known as journey lag, which is known to affect unwary travellers making as many different landings and launchings as the defendants are alleged to have done." Hrruvula paused for breath. "Also available are documents," and the attorney spread the Spacedep slush fund flimsies, "that prove that deposits ostensively made into an account purported to have been initiated by a Terran of Zodd Rrev's general description in fact tally with sums and deposits from a slush fund. There is a signed and attested declaration by an ex-criminal known as Askell Klonski . . ."

"You overwhelm us," said the Treaty Controller with broad sarcasm.

Hrruvula bowed. "Even as my clients were overwhelmed with evidence which we have conclusively proved to be a massive conspiracy to discredit Zodd Rrev, Hrriss, and in their names the integrity of the entire population of this lovely planet." Hrruvula took another breath. "With such overwhelming evidence to sustain my clients' plea of innocence, these charges must, in all conscience, be dismissed and their reputations and honors returned to them." He bowed low in deep respect toward the other members of the Council, but noticeably not in the Controller's direction.

Behind Hrruvula, an entire planet's population held its breath.

Third Speaker's eyes narrowed and glittered. He stepped forward. "You have defended your clients well, Hrruvula," and the attorney executed another courteous bow. "But it was clearly stated, and so resolved by the Council of Speakers, that both young men must be present to clear their names. One is clearly not present. The reason for his absence is immaterial. The conditions of that resolution have not been met. Therefore the Council of Speakers must withhold ratification of a permanent Treaty of Rrala."

There was a silence that nothing in the Hall disturbed. Third Speaker, his manner patronizing and smug, turned to Second Speaker Hrrto. Second Speaker seemed to rise with great difficulty, his shoulders slumped beneath the weight of his robes.

"It was so resolved and must be maintained." He sat down heavily, head bent, arms limp at his sides.

"No!" a woman wailed from the depths of the crowd. "No. That's not fair. Not fair at all! They were innocent."

"You can't use that as an out, Third Speaker!" a Hrruban called.

Dorem Naruti of the Amalgamated Worlds Congress rose then, holding up his arms for silence. "It was resolved. In honor we must abide. Our Congress is constrained to comply with that resolution, much as it pains me to do so. The Congress cannot sanction the colony any longer. We would be glad and proud to trade with the Hrruban League under a new treaty, but the Decision at Doona must be considered annulled. The Cohabitation Principle is herewith invoked."

Protests were yelled from all directions then until Dorem Naruti, not wishing to be a target for anyone's frustration, took refuge behind Third Speaker.

Landreau was all but jumping up and down in jubilation. He, Rogitel, and their assistants kept calling for silence, for order, for good manners. But it was Admiral Sumitral whose amazing voice was heard above the babel and restored order.

"Dear friends, Hrruban and Hayuman, we are all persons of honorable intent. Having entered into an honorable agreement, we must indeed recognize the commitment we undertook twenty-five years ago, and abide by this very, very painful conclusion to what has been an experiment of cohabitation of . . ." He paused, craning his neck to see through the open doors of the Hall. His attentiveness, the surprise that began to wreathe his features with new hope, caused everyone to turn to discover what he saw.

The grid was misted, indicating a transportation, and as it cleared, three figures became visible: a bent figure in ornate red robes supported on either side by two others, one tall, straight, and proud, one slender, delicate, and equally proud. The central personage could only be First Speaker Hrruna! His companions, dressed in diaphanous red gauze spangled with gems, were Nrrna and Kelly.

Hrriss felt joy nearly bursting his heart. The girls had reached him, after all, and with the remaining evidence that Hriss had felt lost forever. A reverent silence settled on the green and the Hall as if noise was snuffed out like a candle flame. Everyone watched the aged Hrruban walk into the Hall and slowly toward the dais, leaning heavily on the arms of the two girls.

He looked kindly at the colonists and gave an especial smile to Hrriss, who was gawking like a cub at the First Speaker.

"This is an occasion for which I have waited long," First Speaker said in High Hrruban, mounting the ramp to touch hands with Sumitral.

"Sir," Sumitral said, replying in the same tongue, "we did not think to expect you."

"Your accent has improved so very much over the last years, Admirrrl. You no longer need your young translator," Hrruna said, dropping his jaw in a smile and glancing around at the crowd. "But I miss his presence. He has been a joy to me. Where is my young friend? Where is Zodd?"

With a surprising swiftness that belied his age, he rounded on Treaty Controller, and his tone, no longer kindly or gentle, rang with conviction. The Controller was so startled, he backed up a pace.

Hrruna's eyes narrowed to fierce slits, though his clear voice was calm and even-toned. "I believe that you know precisely where Zodd and his father, Rrev, are to be found," Hrruna said. "You are to produce them instantly, or your Stripe will be forever dishonored. If harm has come to two Hayumans of indisputable integrity and honor, you and your immediate family will be transported to the most primitive mining colony in the galaxy, and allowed only the most meager of rations."

Hrriss listened with awe. Few of the settlers could understand Hrruna's speech, but they could easily see the effect it had on the Treaty Controller. From a haughty administrator, he was reduced to snivelling like a cub, protesting that his actions had been taken in the best interests of Hrruba.

"The return of the Rrevs at this point would have made it impossible to avoid the ratification of the Treaty," the Controller babbled. "I meant no harm to them. They are unhurt. They would have been returned to Earth with everyone else of their species."

"You kidnapped my friend?" Hrriss demanded in a snarl. He felt the savage blood of his ancestors coursing through his veins and forgot his upbringing, the position he held as a scion of a civilized race. Claws and teeth bared, he gathered himself to leap and strike, as he had leaped at the Momma Snake. Without a moment's hesitation, Hrrestan knocked his feet out from under him, and signalled to several others to drag his infuriated son away from the cowering Treaty Controller.

"Produce the Rrevs, father and son!" Hrruna commanded, his eyes ablaze with green fury. Cringing, the Treaty Controller signalled to his grid operator in the audience, who ran to the transporter. Making a few deft adjustments to the controls, the operator stepped onto the platform and vanished. In a few moments, the Hrruban reappeared, no longer alone. With him were two very large Hrruban males in guard harness, and Ken and Todd, clothes torn, faces empurpled here and there with bruises and long scratches, but alive and smiling as they recognized their destination.

"Come here, my friends," Hrruna beckoned them. His voice, soft again, nevertheless penetrated the ringing cheers that reverberated inside and outside the Hall at this much-longed-for reappearance.

Together Todd and his father marched smartly up the steps and into the Hall. When Todd saw who occupied the dais, he smiled in amazement and, shaking his head, continued through the parting crowd. When Hrrubans and Hayumans alike reached out to slap his back or grab his hand, Todd became aware of the deficiencies of his appearance in such a gathering. Still walking forward, he brushed at the dirt on his tunic and combed back his hair with his fingers. Ken, similarly embarrassed, straightened tunic and hair. Crying with relief, Pat ignored protocol and pushed through the crowd to embrace husband and son just as they reached the foot of the dais.

"It is good to have you back," Hrruna said, as if Todd and his father had only been off on some minor errand. With Pat between them, they climbed the ramp to the dais. The old Hrruban signalled for Hrrestan to release his son. In two leaps, Hrriss was beside his dear friend, wrapping his tail firmly around Todd's nearer thigh. "This silly cub"—Hrruna pointed to the Treaty Controller—"is not the only dishonorable one among Hrrubans to sow discord on Rrala."

"The discord was not solely Hrruban," Ken said. "And during our incarceration, our guards spoke freely, not being aware that we bareskins understood what they said."

"Whatever is pertinent to sustain the Treaty and this colony must be related so that all may hear," Hrruna said at his most austere, "although I am aware of much that has happened of late, of false accusations and tamperings and alterings that would have greatly strained my patience had they not been delivered by such charming couriers."

Todd had not failed to notice that his Kelly and Hrriss's Nrrna were

Hrruna's attendants. Kelly was grinning at him with a total lack of discretion, which gladdened his heart immensely, but at least Nrrna had cast her eyes down modestly despite Hrriss's attempts to make eye contact.

Then Todd saw Hrruna's peremptory gesture to Ken. "Be so good as to explain what you overheard, Rrev."

"While it was the Treaty Controller who had our destination altered from Earth and our appointment with the AWC panel, he received his orders from another, high in the Speakers Council," Ken said. "In good plain Low Hrruban, they mentioned his name frequently: the Third Speaker for Internal Affairs." Ken looked pleasantly at Third Speaker. "We can repeat what was said in our presence . . ."

"Lies!" Third Speaker hissed. "All lies. These Hayumans mean to dishonor me."

Hrruna gestured for those on the dais to move aside so that he could confront Third face-to-face. His eyes had narrowed to implacable slits, and the hem of his heavy robes flicked with the lashing of his tail.

"I will believe the words of Rrev and Zodd even over those of my own Stripe," Hrruna said in an ominously calm tone. "Deceit is not in them. Any dishonor on your stripe has been brought there by you. You have forsaken the objectivity necessary to just administration, Third. You have sought to interfere in a matter which is outside your commission. You were also one who insisted that Rrala would stand or fall on its own merit. You have not abided by your own decree. I invite you to resign your post."

Third opened and closed his mouth a couple of times, but at last nodded curtly at Hrruna.

"Very well," Third Speaker said, his own eyes closed to vindictive slits. "I tender my resignation."

"I accept it, effective now! But we have waited long enough to discover whether Rrala may continue. In view of what you have heard in these past minutes, do the Treaty Council and the representative of the Amalgamated Worlds Congress wish to alter their decision?" Hrruna asked pleasantly, turning firmly away from the dismissed Speaker. "I surely see no bar to the continuation of this colony nor to the ratification of the Treaty Renewal so anxiously awaited by us all. What say you?"

Madam Dupuis smiled as she stepped forward, assuming the position of Controller. She bowed with great reverence to the First Speaker. "Most honored of persons," she said in perfect High Hrruban, "the Council must indeed overturn the recent verdict, and clear the defendants of all charges against them, including nonappearance."

Dorem Naruti was jittering with relief at being able to rescind the verdict he had been forced, by the previous circumstances, to announce.

"Then let us adjourn all this formal talk and harangue and let the festivities begin," said Hrruna, dropping into Middle language and leaning toward Nrrna in a paternal fashion. "The smell of roasted meat is making this old belly rumble."

Few heard that comment, for cheers had erupted as he ordered the festivities to begin. Colonists of both species were hugging each other, weeping or purring in an excess of relief after the dramatic scenes that had first dashed then restored their hopes.

Robin and Inessa were shrieking for their father and brother to come down so they could be suitably welcomed. Ilsa was trying to calm them down but she was smiling and crying at the same time, upsetting her daughters, who began to fret, too.

"We should take an official vote, you know," Sumitral said, looking out over the jigging, whirling mass of colonists.

"Oh, don't be so hidebound," Madam Dupuis told him, waving at the jubilation below them. "That's the loudest, most unanimous 'aye' I've ever witnessed."

"I'd agree to that," Dorem Naruti said, beaming from ear to ear. "I've never seen anything quite so official as this! Must be something in the air here, I think."

Sumitral chuckled. "Then we shall record that the vote was unanimous. And I'm hungry, too. Naruti, they have the most delicious little birds here, covered with a sweet spice, that simply melts in your mouth. You really must try some, mustn't he, Nesfa dear friend?"

"Indeed, and although the suggestion might seem bizarre, the snake stew they make is exceedingly tasty. We shall tell you what to sample first, Dorem, if you will accompany us."

While they were settling the voting issue, First Speaker's escorts had guided him to his place at the Treaty table set in exactly the same place it had rested twenty-five years before, under the trees that clustered just beyond the Hall. Hrruna gestured for Naruti to be seated to his right and Sumitral to his left. Both senior diplomats, with the precision of long practice, sat down at the same moment. The gemmed and tooled volumes containing the Treaty of Doona were opened before them.

"There's a lot of work, many years of negotiation in the document," Madam Dupuis said, "but it is as fair as it could be made."

"A thing of beauty, outside as well as inside, these are," Naruti said in flawlessly inflected High Hrruban. "As handsome as the ideals they represent."

Hrruna's jaw dropped in pleasure. "So they are," First Speaker agreed.

Each signed one, and the volumes were exchanged. One by one, the Treaty Councillors stood by to affix their signatures to the documents. Hrrestan placed heavy seals on the signature pages and closed the books. Bowing, he presented one to each of the principals.

Sumitral looked to Hrruna for permission to speak and it was graciously given with a nod of the dignified and graying head.

"The Treaty of Doona/Rrala is now officially extended indefinitely. May I extend the congratulations of my service to Hrrubans and Hayumans alike!" His last syllables were drowned out by wild cheering.

When the noise began to abate, Todd approached the Treaty table. Someone had found him a decent tunic to replace his torn one, and he'd been able to wash his face and comb his hair so that he looked considerably more presentable.

"May I be permitted to speak?" Todd asked in High Hrruban, executing a deeply reverent bow to the First Speaker.

"Pray listen to the first Hayuman ambassador to the Hrruban people," Hrruna said, his voice carrying over excited conversations and laughter, and immediately silence prevailed again.

Sumitral, leaning across to Hrruna, chuckled. "And that was a day! About a meter tall, dressed in mda skins with a rope tail hanging behind and the dignity of a dozen judges for all he was six years old. He and Hrriss have done great service for Alreldep since then. I hope they'll continue to do so."

Todd glanced at Hrriss, who nodded, jaw dropped humorously. "As long as we can, sir."

With Hrriss beside him, Todd stood forward to address his friends and neighbors. "I feel like I got thrown from a bucking stallion into a compost heap, so I hope you'll forgive my appearance." The assembled settlers chuckled. "I've dreamed of this day since I was a small boy. I was afraid for a while that the day wouldn't come, and then I feared I wouldn't be able to be here. Now"—he grinned, throwing an arm around Hrriss's shoulders—"all we have dreamed of has happened. Doona is now a permanent reality. As long as we live, we can live here together.

"Today is not just a continuation of Doona but the start of a brand-new era for Hrrubans and Hayumans. From the trust that has been built here, both species can spread out, can make new homes on new planets together and separately." He smiled around at all the faces, bare and furred. "Honored folk, Doona has taught us all the most important lesson: that we both can make friends, firm friends, trusted friends, of each other and of other species. The Siwannese example must never be forgotten, but it mustn't stop us from keeping an open mind and extending an open hand. The generations that will be born on this planet," and with that he sent a glowing look at Kelly, "will meet others, strong in the practice of Cohabitation. So long as they remember what we have all learned here, the stars beckon. Long live Doona/Rrala!" Todd shot his fist toward the sky and Hrriss's joined it in the next second.

When other arms tired of holding fists aloft and throats turned hoarse with cheering, Hrruna turned plaintively to Sumitral. "Now do you think we can eat?"

Totally reunited and in the best of harmonious spirits, the entire population of Doona and its guests began the long-awaited feast. Platters of food poured out of the kitchen to tables inside and outside the Hall. Beer, wine, mlada, and even wild-berry juices flowed to every cup as friend toasted friend and the success of the Doona Experiment was drunk to over and over again. The members of the Doona/Rrala Ad Hoc Band rarely got time for more than a few mouthfuls of food, so much in demand was celebratory dance music.

Hrriss tried repeatedly to extract Nrrna from attendance on the First Speaker, but he couldn't get any nearer her than Todd could get to Kelly. If it hadn't been Hrruna who monopolized the attentions of their promised ladies, the two friends would have snagged them away at the very first opportunity, but Hrruna seemed to require that they serve him the various delicacies prepared by the colonists' best cooks.

"Damn it, Hrriss, I'm the one who was on short rations. Couldn't Kelly come feed me?"

"I'm doing my best, Todd," his sister Ilsa said, her knees buckling under the laden tray she was bringing them.

"Urfa steak *and* snake stew?" he said, salivating. "Sis, you know how to treat a brother."

"When he remembers to come home to eat," Ilsa tossed at him as she went away to see to the needs of her children. Todd stared after her.

"Marriage has done her good," he muttered to Hrriss, and dug into the stew. "I never thought I'd eat any of this again." Then he had to swallow without truly savoring the fine flavor, for Sampson DeVeer approached their table.

"You cut that mighty fine," DeVeer said, and then drew up the young man in the plain uniform hovering beside him. "You might like to meet my companion, Reeve. Dalkey Petersham."

"Really?" And Todd realized in one second that the man he had feared as a rival to Kelly's affection was no real competition. So he pumped the young man's hand energetically. "We owe you a lot, Dalkey, for putting out your neck for people you didn't know. Come, sit down."

"Well, I did know Kelly and I sure discovered a lot of real creative accounting. Which . . ."

"Which what?" Todd prompted, gesturing for Dalkey to fill a plate from the food on the freshly filled tray.

"Which actually lost me my job."

"You haven't really lost a job, Dalkey," Todd said, "you've just been transferred. An accountant who could uncover that Spacedep slush fund is just the sort of fellow we need to set up a system here on Doona that can't be diddled."

After Dalkey had expressed his deep appreciation of the offer and accepted with considerable alacrity, Todd turned to DeVeer.

"Which reminds me. Just before Dad and I got kidnapped, Hrriss and I got Linc Newry to admit he'd been falsifying export documents and disarming Doona's security satellites to let rustlers in and out. What's happened to him?"

"He gave himself up," DeVeer said with a note of satisfaction in his voice, "after I had a most interesting chat with a Dr. Walter Tylanio. Once he was in custody, Newry gave me more information which led me to the real rustler."

"You got Mark Aden?" Todd's eyes flashed, remembering the score he had to settle with that bastard for his vindictive use of ssersa.

"He is under arrest on Zapata Three, awaiting transport back to Earth for trial. It would seem that he kept a computer file of the layout of each ranch on Doona and the best secluded spots to secrete the livestock pens. He's the one who planted the artifacts on your ship while you were occupied by your mission on Hrretha. He did so with Spacedep credentials to pass by Hrrethan security guards. Newry was the one who switched log tapes."

"I always thought Rogitel had done it when his men were busy hauling artifacts out of the *Albie*'s panels," Todd said.

"No, I have Newry's confession." DeVeer nodded at the grim looks that Todd and Hrriss exchanged. "It couldn't have been Rogitel. He did the shopping for the artifacts with the illicit traders on Hrretha. Remember, Newry had asked you to give him your flight plans nearly two weeks before your actual departure. So he sent them to Klonski, who's rather proud of the way he handled that assignment. Took him thirty-six hours of intensive work. He shipped it back to Newry in an authorized Spacedep courier run and put it in the *Albatross* before you launched. Klonski had left gaps for your legitimate stops, triggered by signals from the beacons orbiting Doona and Hrretha. Aden is the one who made the insertions into the interdicted systems in a ship with identification codes altered to match yours."

Todd let out a long sigh. "So we're cleared of everything? Then why was the Treaty so nearly cancelled?"

"Third Speaker had also rigged that resolution so that your presence was absolutely essential to the Renewal of the Treaty."

"And Hrruna waited until he knew he had Third right where he needed him," Todd said thoughtfully. "It was close!"

DeVeer nodded. "However, you both might like to accompany . . . that is, if you can leave off eating that delicious food for a short time?" he asked them. "You rather deserve to be in on this. I've one more criminal to bring to book."

Todd and Hrriss hastily dashed their fingers into bowls set on all the tables to cleanse hands. DeVeer led them to the head table where they waited respectfully until Sumitral and Naruti concluded their conversation with Second Speaker Hrrto. When Ken and Hrrestan were beckoned by DeVeer to join them, the group advanced on Landreau and Rogitel who were seated as inconspicuously as possible for men in brilliant white uniforms. They were the only two ignoring both the food and the merrymaking going on around them.

"Well, what do you want?" Landreau asked sourly, glaring at the Reeves. "You have everything you claim you value. This abominable colony has a permanent charter, and your so-called honor is restored."

"Admiral Allen Landreau?" DeVeer said formally. "As an inspector of Poldep and in the presence of a representative of Amalgamated Worlds Congress and a senior officer of Spacedep, I arrest you on the following charges: conspiracy, fraud, misuse of public funds, attempted kidnapping, suborning of witnesses, aiding and abetting grand larceny and felony theft, aiding and abetting violation of Treaty Law, and conduct unbecoming a senior officer of the Space Department."

"Have you quite finished with this fairy tale?" Landreau snapped. "I am about to return to Earth and pressing duties there—unlike other officials who seem to have infinite time to play."

"This is scarcely a laughing matter, Landreau," Sumitral said.

"Don't attempt to instruct me," the head of Spacedep growled, his face turning red. "You're my equal, not my superior. You don't outrank me in any way. In fact, Spacedep is a larger department than Alreldep and takes precedence over yours. If we didn't exist, there would be no aliens for your department to relate to, not the Siwannese, not your tame pussycat people!"

"Sir," DeVeer said, "I must suggest that you not make any more statements until you have engaged a counsel for your defense. We have impounded your records, and I am obliged to remind you that anything you say now can and may be used in evidence against you."

"Read me—Admiral Landreau—my rights?" Landreau shouted.

Nearby Doonans turned to look. Once they identified Landreau, they continued to stare.

"How dare you even question a senior official of the government, when these damned Reeves are the real troublemakers?" He flung a contemptuous hand in Todd's direction before he planted a fingertip in the middle of the Poldep chief's black tunic and pushed, "You, a jumped-up little Aisle constable, have the unmitigated gall to interfere with Spacedep, to access Spacedep files, to snoop into my department! I have a good mind—I have—!" Landreau suddenly clutched at his chest. His eyes protruded in DeVeer's direction and then rolled up into his head as he slid to the floor.

"Get a doctor!" Todd shouted, dropping to his knees beside the man. Rogitel knelt down and bent his head to Landreau's chest.

"His heart has stopped," Rogitel said, his voice more expressionless than ever.

"He doesn't get out of it this easily," Todd said, and flattened a hand over Landreau's sternum. He hit it a short rap with the other fist and then started cardiopulmonary resuscitation.

Mike Solinari was beside them in a moment. "Dr. Moody is coming." He looked at Landreau. "I don't think anything can be done, Todd. Look at all that blood in his face. I think he had an apoplexy."

"What?" Rogitel demanded. "Can't you revive him?"

"Not from that sort of a fit," the young veterinarian said, exhibiting only a clinical detachment. "He burst a blood vessel. Embolism. Instantly fatal. People with high blood pressure are prone to it. Probably had it coming for years."

"You can say that again," said a new voice, and Ali Kiachif pushed his way to the group looking down at the Admiral's prone body. "No one had it coming to him longer, stronger, or wronger than he did, if you know what I mean." He pulled at Todd's shoulder. "You might as well stop that, laddie. It won't do him a bit of good. Don't waste any more breath on him. I know a deader when I see one."

Kate Moody arrived a moment later and confirmed young Solinari's and Kiachif's diagnoses. "There's nothing I can do for him. Here, some of you help me get him out of here. We'll take him to the Health Center. My skimmer's outside."

"Commander Rogitel," DeVeer said, laying a hand on the assistant's arm and bringing him to his feet. "If you are not going to indulge in a medical emergency of your own, I have a list of charges that have been laid against you. Will you come with me now?"

Rogitel rose silently. DeVeer turned back to the Reeves. "Oh, and save me some punch, won't you?" he asked with a twinkle in his eye. "I'll be back as soon as I shut this fellow up." He marched his prisoner away toward the grid, accompanied by Hrrula to operate the controls.

"I don't believe he's dead," said Todd, watching the stretcher team leave the Hall with their burden. Someone had spread a tablecloth over Landreau's body before they carried it away.

"Believe it," Kiachif said firmly, slapping him on the shoulder. "Well, that's that, if you know what I mean. The end of all your troubles, trials, and tribulations. Well, this set! Third's gone, Landreau's sputtered his last, and the Treaty's signed. Nothing to stand in the way of you living happily ever after, is there?"

Todd and Hrriss exchanged meaningful glances. "Now that you mention it, no," Todd said, "particularly the 'happily ever after' bit. C'mon, Hrriss, Hrruna's had our girls far too long."

"We owe you so much, sir, for coming in when you did," Hu Shih was saying to First Speaker Hrruna as Todd and Hrriss approached.

"If it is not an imposition, honored sir," Hrriss asked Hrruna politely, "I would like to dance with my betrothed." He reached out a hand to Nrrna.

Nrrna glanced appealingly at the First Speaker, who patted the female's hand. "Yes, of course. Such a charming young lady. You are most fortunate, young Hrriss."

"You are so kind, sir," Nrrna said, lowering her eyelids prettily at First Speaker.

"And when is the joining to be?" Hrruna asked.

"Soon!" Hrriss said emphatically.

"Very soon," Nrrna agreed, looking lovingly at Hrriss. "Possibly tomorrow."

The old man sighed as the couple slipped through the crowd. "Ah, if I was thirty years younger! But it is always the lady's choice, isn't it? I must say, he is a fine young cub."

"I couldn't agree more," Second Speaker Hrrto said, watching the couple swirl gracefully onto the dance floor. "He is one of the hopes for Hrruba's future."

"Kelly?" Todd asked, bowing to her. "May I have the honor of this dance."

"May I, sir?" Kelly asked Hrruna sweetly.

"Yes, do. Enjoy yourselves, young ones!" Hrruna said, jaw dropped. "Ah, youth."

"That's a very pretty dress you have on," Todd said as with a firm hand he guided Kelly out among the dancers.

"Almost have on," Kelly grimaced, tugging at the filmy swags of cloth and settling them more securely across her nicely developed chest. "Red's not really my color."

"I think you can wear any color," Todd said with genuine gallantry.

"But I'm really not sure I should be dancing with you," she said, with such a firm arm around his neck and such a firm grip on his other hand that he stared at her in surprise. "For one thing, you're not really suitably dressed for the occasion."

"Kelly, that's not fair . . ." he began, and then saw the merry devilment in her sparkling eyes. "All right, I'll bite, how should I be dressed?"

Suddenly she took the lead from him and danced him over to a window ledge.

"You're not wearing tails," she said, waving a coil of rope in front of him that she must have somehow secreted on the ledge. "Imagine you forgetting an old Rraladoonian custom like that!"

Enchanted by his lover's gesture, he let her tie the rope around his waist and proceed to tie the other end around hers, completely ruining the line of her gown.

"Hey, that's not how to make a rope tail!" he said, laughing.

"No, it's to keep you from going off somewhere without taking me with you!" Now she backed him into the curtains of the window and whirled a length around him, before she pulled his head down to hers and kissed him long and lovingly. Not at all surprising, especially since he had never hoped to see her again, he responded passionately. Kiachif had been right—there was nothing at all to stop them living happily ever after.

"Friends, feasting, and fine firewater," Ali Kiachif said, carefully enunciating each word to Ken Reeve, swigging the last of the mlada from his glass. "That's the elements that make the best parties, if you know what I mean! No, don't take that bottle away, Reeve," he implored Ken as he swept dirty dishes off the table in front of him so he could prop up his elbows. "Pour me another portion, if you please."

"Nothing left in it, Kiachif." Ken upended the crock to show that it was empty. "See?"

Kiachif looked mournfully at the bottom of his glass. "You couldn't find another bottle somewhere nearby, could you? I always thought you were a merry mate of mine."

From long experience, Ken judged the old captain was only a few minutes from falling asleep when the power of the mlada hit. "Oh, I suppose there's one more in the kitchen. You wait here, Kiachif, and I'll see if I can't find it."

"That's fine, fair, and friendly of you," he said with satisfaction, and propped himself up to wait, tapping his fingers to the slow dance music and watching the couples swaying rhythmically. Ken went into the kitchen and peeped out through the door until he saw the old spacefarer sag over onto folded arms at the table. It had only taken a moment when he wasn't moving or talking for the liquor to relax him completely.

"Hrrestan, give me a hand, will you?" Ken asked, getting under one of Kiachif's arms and heaving upward. "We'd better put him to bed."

"With pleasurrre, my friend," the Hrruban said, taking the other arm. Together, they hoisted the Codep captain upright and started to walk him toward the guest cabins at the far side of the common.

Kiachif woke up partway there and glanced at each of his escorts in turn from under his bushy brows. "That's what I like to see," he said, nodding approvingly. "Cooperation between happy Human and Hrruban. Long may it continue."

Ken and Hrrestan got Kiachif onto the bunk in one of the rooms and considerately pulled his boots off. "So long as we can help it," Ken said, glancing at his old friend, as they lowered the lights in the cabin behind them, "it always will."

They left the old pilot snoring and went out together to rejoin the celebration.

Treaty at Doona

chapter one

Through the void the small blue-white star twinkled enticingly, promising light and heat in generous measure. Those aboard the massive, matte-black spaceship approaching that star system on an elliptical angle had been drawn to investigate it by the various communication signals emanating from the third planet of that star. The planet, a blue and green globe around which three pocked moons circled, was also ringed by orbiting drones and several spaceships of considerably less mass than the newcomer. Such vehicles were considered by the passengers of the enormous spaceship to be as worthy of investigation as the broadcasts, for both phenomena indicated the presence of sentient beings and advanced technology.

The visiting vessel, which had no insignia or identifiable markings on its kilometer-long, irregularly cylindrical hull, sailed boldly toward this so-intriguing star system. Even as those aboard contained their initial elation of discovery and began to record this event, sensors at the system perimeter were spotted, their messages and internal composition examined by probes, the mechanisms briefly prevented from performing the function for which they had been designed. Excitement grew to a feverish pitch as specialists and consultants eagerly inspected the diagrams of the sophisticated warning systems. Everything pointed to the amazing fact that the inhabitants of this star system had created and nurtured a civilization sufficiently advanced to be worth the strangers' complete and immediate attention.

At the door of the Council Chamber, Todd Reeve, Human colony leader of Doonarrala, bowed and shook hands with arriving delegates, hopefully dissembling his most uneasy and ambivalent feelings about this wretched conference. He'd never imagined the idea of turning the Treaty Island subcontinent into a free trade and spaceport facility would come this far. The slim margin by which the colony referendum had passed vindicated his position, but the "yeas" had barely outnumbered the "nays," and the measure had passed. So he had been forced to take the next step—this meeting of Hrruban and Hayuman officials.

Beside him in the receiving line was his best friend, Hrriss, their twenty-seven-year friendship badly strained by their current, disparate views on the subject of a free port. Todd found it very hard to understand how Hrriss should pursue a course which, so obviously to Todd, abrogated both the Decision and Treaty by which this unusual mixed colony had been promulgated.

Right now, being greeted by smiles and affability, none of the delegates would have suspected that the almost legendary friendship of Hayuman and Hrruban was under considerable stress. For the first time, they had agreed to disagree.

The visiting delegates entered the room one by one, exchanging pleasantries with each of the Doonarralan dignitaries. Todd was impatient to get past the preliminaries and plunge into the problem, which might relieve the tension that twisted his nerves and tightened his neck and shoulders. His wife, Kelly, had done her best to knead out the worst of the kinks, silently supporting her husband throughout his campaign to defeat the proposal. Despite their mutual respect and deep attachment to this planet and all it stood for, Todd wasn't sure if Kelly totally agreed with him on this matter. She'd said all the proper things and had accompanied him and his father on their trips to all the Villages where the pros and cons were argued in open debate. But somehow, the feeling niggled at him that she was not as dead set against a free-trade port as he was.

Todd's father, Ken Reeve, had worked tirelessly for a "nay" verdict on the referendum, for the situation represented his worst nightmare come true for Doona: an insidious expansion that defeated the initial purpose of the colony—for both species. Doona could cease to be the pastoral paradise it was if suddenly plunged into rapid commercial development.

Somehow, Todd must make that fear so real to the delegates that today's conference would be the end of the matter. Otherwise, he might be forced to resign his position as the Hayuman colony leader, since he could not wholeheartedly accept such a change in Doonarrala.

The fact that the idea for a trade and spaceport facility originated with the Hrruban half of the colony did nothing to placate Todd's anxieties. The original premise, hammered into the Decision—and later the Treaty—would, he argued, be invalidated if part of the planet were to be commercialized. Ironic that this whole wretched idea had come from his suggestion that they name the western subcontinent "The Hrrunatan" after the late First Speaker, as a mark of the respect and love in which all Doonarralans, Hayuman and Hrruban, had held Hrruna.

Todd and the old First Speaker had had a most unusual relationship, despite their differences of species, culture, and age. It was therefore doubly ironic that what had been meant as a sincere tribute to Hrruna was rebounding against those he had so subtly protected during the colony's early stages.

Todd almost welcomed the discomfort of the formal, tailored tunic which rubbed his neck raw as the receiving line continued. It kept distracting him from his troubles. His thick black hair was newly cut and neatly brushed and he knew he looked well in the formal tunic, despite its constriction. He had good shoulders, a deep chest, and was tall, even for a Hayuman. Todd had never stood on ceremony but, as Kelly had said at their mostly silent breakfast, ceremony could be used to advantage. As he hoped to use it today. That didn't keep his collar from binding his neck.

He took some consolation in seeing that Hrriss was likewise chafed by Hrruban ceremonial gear, surreptitiously tugging at the jewelled straps that crisscrossed his tawny-furred torso under the loose red robe he wore for such a formal occasion. On other, less-charged occasions Hrriss would have glanced up at Todd, a hand-span taller than he, and rolled his large green eyes ceilingward, flattening back his tufted ears to express his discomfort. But today they were opponents—still friendly, still hoping for a way out of the dilemma which obsessed both—so their normal exchanges were constrained.

Beyond Hrriss was his father, Hrrestan, Hrruban co-leader with Todd, who was as staunchly in favor of the proposed alteration of Doonarrala's function as Todd and his father were opposed to it.

The veteran diplomat was currently chatting to the Hrruban Space Arm representative, Prrid. An old Stripe, the Senior Space Commandant stood with his hands clasped behind him, rocking back and forth, his tail tip held at a relaxed angle. Beside him, his aide, a mature and seasoned explorer, Mrrunda, stood on one foot and then the other, trying not to appear impatient for the proceedings to begin. He seemed to feel exactly the way Todd did. For all the times when, as a small boy, Todd had wished for a tail, he was glad now that he didn't have one, for it would have been lashing nervously. On the other hand,

Hrrestan's caudal appendage was curved slightly, showing that he was at ease. The rest of the Hrruban Space Arm party were already standing near the conference table: three more officers, each with pouches stuffed with documentation.

"Admiral Barnstable," Todd said, calling himself to order as he greeted a tall, white-haired man in uniform who resembled the very portrait of an ancient sea captain. In a face of weather-beaten red, surprising in a man who had never been out on the seas of any planet, he had sharp blue eyes with which he now studied Todd. Hoping he passed muster, Todd smiled and bowed.

"Welcome to the Treaty Island of Doonarrala, sir. May I present Leader Hrrestan, Senior Commandant Prrid, and his aide, Captain Mrrunda?"

Everett Cabot Barnstable, representing Spacedep, was one of the more important delegates to the conference. There had been a lot of jockeying to see who would head the military Arm of Amalgamated Worlds, with its huge budget, resources, and manpower. Barnstable, possessed of a strong conservative bent and vast support on Earth, had finally succeeded. His predecessor, Admiral Landreau, had been no friend to Doonarrala. Barnstable was known as a decision-maker, a good administrator and negotiator. Todd felt Barnstable, though not entirely perfect, was a significant improvement over Landreau. At least, Doonarrala had had no trouble from Spacedep since he had been in charge—until now. Barnstable wasn't so reactionary as to favor Human Separatism, but he was sure to support the inauguration of a base on the subcontinent; a base that would be as useful to the Hayuman Space Arm as to the Hrruban. Another point that Todd had tried to emphasize in his contentions was that Spacedep had no right on Doonarrala; had always meant trouble to the community. And now they wanted to invite Spacedep *in?*

Barnstable accorded his Hrruban opposite numbers a sharp, respectful half-bow, eyeing them as keenly as they did him. Then he gave an odd, convulsive shudder and frowned. "Confound it, I can't believe it's safe for a body to shift planets so fast. Ten minutes ago I stood on a grid on Earth, and then I was decanted on Doona."

"It saves time," Prrid said, lifting his upper lip in a toothy Hrruban grin.

Todd was relieved to see that Barnstable was familiar with the awesome sight of a Hrruban smile.

"I imagine you do not favor further grid installations on Doonarrala," Todd said to Prrid, seizing the opportunity for some subtle indirection.

Prrid's unexpectedly orange eyes regarded him, the pupil slits narrowed to a thin line.

"Zat will depend, Leader Rrrev. Zat will depend."

"Come now, Reeve," Admiral Barnstable said, turning jocular. "Surely you won't stand in the way of progress."

"If I were certain it was progress . . ." Todd let his comment trail off. So Spacedep was, as he anticipated, eager to obtain a legitimate position on Doonarrala.

"Now, Todd," Jilamey Landreau said, appearing at Todd's elbow, a-jingle with the tiny bells sewn in patterns on his stylish motley-colored attire. "It's not like you to resist any change which improves this planet. The more grids, the merrier, what? Think of how many more people would come to the Snake Hunts," he added, grinning mischievously. Then he turned to the Senior Commandant and his aide, his round face ingenuous. "Todd saved my life on my first Snake Hunt, you know. By the way, Admiral, Commandant, I represent the Grid . . ."

"Save it till later, Jilamey," Todd said, grabbing his friend by the elbow and pushing him away from the military group.

"Oh, I can take a hint . . ." Jilamey said with mock dismay, marching off into the conference room with an agitated jingling of his tiny bells.

Todd sighed to himself: it would seem that all his erstwhile friends were aligned against him. But Jilamey was "Grid" mad. If civilians of either planet could have had matter transmitters, Jilamey Landreau would have been first in the queue. Perhaps it was as well that the Hrrubans were so paranoid about sharing their technology.

To benefit from a trade and spaceport installation, the Hrrubans would have to put down grid facilities, probably the largest feasible one—similar in size to the one they had originally used to transport their "village" in the earliest days of the Doonan colonization.

Todd couldn't really blame the Hrrubans for wanting a free trade port. Their lack of large cargo vessels had weighed heavily against Hrruban traders expanding their territories. Of course, there were grids transporting goods among Hrruban home and colony worlds, but there still didn't seem to be much metal-bearing ore available on Hrruban worlds for more than small two- or three-man exploration vessels. Those were hardly large enough for cost-efficient intersystem trade. Spacedep had persisted in its restrictions on the sale of Hayuman spacecraft to Hrruban merchants. On the day that the Hrrubans released information and/or licensed grid matter transmitters to Hayumans, Spacedep would lift its embargo on vessel transfers.

"Yo there, Reeve," said Fred Horstmann, a stout man with fair hair and a flamboyant gold-trimmed tunic, an independent trader affiliated with Codep's leading administrator and negotiator, Captain Ali Kiachif. That wily old skipper was already holding court at the near edge of the great oval table. Ali had not changed in all the years Todd had known him, except for a little more gray in his hair and beard.

Some of the lesser lights chatted quietly at the other end of the table. Lorena Kaldon, with scarlet-dyed hair and a firm, pointed chin, was a banker from one of the major Amalgamated Worlds institutions. Her presence suggested that the project was favored by the money markets, and Todd's spirits sank even further. Damn it! Were they that certain this wretched facility would be approved? Her opposite number, Hrrouf, a financier from Hrruba, soon arrived with a pale-pelted female named Nrrena, whose limp air was belied by her scarred ears and forearms. Both were moderately broad Stripes, indicating that they were of good family.

Closely following them was Hrrin, a Rraladoonan from the Third Hrruban Village, who represented Hrruban independent traders and was an old friend of Todd's and Hrriss'. The stripe down his back and tail was narrower than Hrriss', and his leonine mane was much darker. Hrrin had kept his opinions to himself, so he might indeed side with Todd.

Barnstable and the two Hrruban Space Arm delegates moved straight for the conference table, to check their places.

Old Ali Kiachif caught Todd's eye and winked as he rose to take Barnstable's outstretched hand. It was too early in the day for a drink, but Todd could have sworn that the bulge in the old spacer's tunic pocket was a flask. It probably contained mlada, the Hrruban native liquor and Kiachif's favorite tipple in this lane of space. Though Kiachif had made port only a short hour before the conference was due to start, that was time enough for him to acquire "needful" supplies. Drunk or sober, the old man's mind was sharp, never missing the chance to turn an advantage his own way, occasionally even supporting the good of Doonarrala to his own detriment. But would Ali prove an ally or antagonist? He had every reason to want better shipping facilities on Doonarrala but he certainly wouldn't want to give up his edge on interstellar trade. Todd sighed.

Last to arrive, undoubtedly by design, was Hrrto, Second Speaker for External Affairs, currently the most senior administrator from Hrrestan's homeworld of Hrruba. This was the first time any of the Speakers had visited Doonarrala since the First Speaker, Hrruna, had "joined the Ancestral Stripes."

Todd knew that Hrrto, who had not always been a strong supporter of the Rrala Experiment, was under considerable pressure to make his mark at this conference. Rumor had it that he was on the short list of nominees for the post of First Speaker. He would be caught between his desire to win on his own merits and the necessity to compare favorably with his late superior in wisdom and probity. Comparisons were always odious, and even a Second Speaker from a well-regarded Stripe would not be exempt from them. The election was not far off, a fact that Todd knew would make Hrrto eager to conclude the conference as soon as possible so he could devote his time and energy to domestic matters.

Beside Hrrto, but one pace behind him, walked a female Hrruban in plain black robes: Hrrto's aide, Mllaba. Her hot yellow-green eyes showed Todd that her deference was deliberate, but not entirely out of respect for her employer. Todd found her a curious individual. Hrriss told him that Mllaba had abstained from cub-bearing and even companionship, in her drive to advance a political career. She came from a very broad Stripe, equal in rank on Hrruba to Hrrestan himself.

Hrrto turned first to Hrrestan and Hrriss, favoring his fellow Hrrubans with his first words, then came to face Todd.

"Speaker Hrrto," Todd said in High Formal Hrruban, bowing deeply. "You honor us with your presence."

"Zodd Rrev, I greet you," Hrrto said cordially, bowing slightly. Todd realized with a shock how much older Hrrto seemed. His tawny mane was almost all silver, and he moved with greater care, as if his formal red robes weighed heavily on his shoulders. "My assistant, Mllaba."

"Honored," Todd said.

"It is I who am honrrred," Mllaba replied in a low, throaty voice.

"Now that all the delegates are assembled," Todd said, "let us begin." He nodded at an attendant, who shut the heavy folding doors of the conference room.

Hrrestan politely led Second Speaker to his designated place and bowed him into it, before taking his own seat. Hrrin leaped up to move a chair from the row against the wall for Mllaba. She said nothing, but her tail twitched once before she draped it demurely to one side instead of sticking it through the gap in the chair back intended for the Hrruban caudal appendage.

As Todd took his seat he appreciated the irony that he now presided over proceedings in this chamber where he and Hrriss had once been on trial for their honor and more. The ultimate stake that day had been nothing less than the continued existence of their shared world, Doona/Rrala. In Todd's estimation, today's deliberations were no less critical. Doubly ironic was the fact that this was also his first chairmanship as Human colony leader, and he wanted it— against all odds—to fail!

He glanced around the table, meeting the eyes of friends and acquaintances, forcing a smile which he hoped would not appear inane or false.

"Friends," said Todd. "As co-host of this conclave, I welcome you all to this vital conference. I have to tell you that I am completely opposed to the formation of a spaceport and commercial facility on the Hrrunatan subcontinent." There was a murmur of surprise at his bald statement. "I feel strongly, as does my father and our former leader, Hu Shih, that such an installation is in direct conflict with the Decision made on Doonarrala thirty-three years ago.

"That Decision was ratified in a Treaty nine years ago, setting this planet aside as a peaceful, co-existent colony, specifically limited to an agrarian economy. To install an interstellar complex—even at the distance of the subcontinent—violates both Decision and Treaty. In light of this prejudice, I turn the meeting over to my co-leader, Hrrestan." He nodded to Hrrestan at the head of the table and sat down amidst a buzz of muted comments.

With great dignity, Hrrestan rose, nodding to Todd and holding up his hands, claws sheathed, to still the murmuring.

"There are many *good* reasons why the establishment of a *separate* and autonomous spaceport facility on the Hrrunatan subcontinent would benefit both our species. With the appropriate safeguards, ensuring the integrity of the work here"—he waved his hand to include the Treaty Island—"and what has been so successful on the main continent of Doonarrala, many of us feel that there would be no conflict, certainly no abrogation of either Decision or Treaty in having a free trade port. We must ensure"—he paused to accord Todd a respectful bow—"that all reservations and apprehensions are discussed and set to rest."

"With respect," Jilamey said, standing up and bowing to Hrrestan, motions which set off his minute bells. "I really do believe that this planet is ideally suited for three separate and diverse installations. Certainly it would be much easier to conduct trade in this sector of the galaxy, expediting"—he turned to the Hrrubans—"our allies' participation, at the moment seriously hampered by a lack of cargo transport." Sweeping the table with a glance, Jilamey managed to subtly criticize both Admiral Barnstable's Spacedep for its refusal to sell Hrrubans larger vessels that could handle the potential volume of trade, and the Hrrubans for refusing to reciprocate by releasing more of their matter transporters. "I will not, of course, at this point, mention the crucial need for more grids."

"Thank you for not mentioning that, Jilamey," Todd said, glaring at him to keep off a topic that made Barnstable, Prrid, and the Second Speaker all bristle with irritation.

Hrrestan let the claws on his right hand unsheathe so he could drum them warningly. Shrugging, Jilamey subsided, but there was the faintest smile on his lips.

"Speaker Hrrto," Hrrestan said, "are you willing to comment on the pro-posed trade center?"

The Second Speaker, absently smoothing the lapels of his ceremonial robe, rose to his feet. Mllaba, beside him, sat stiffly erect, ears slightly aslant to catch every word her superior uttered.

"Hrruban trade and commerce would significantly benefit from such a fa-cility," Hrrto began, switching his thick hands to a firm and oratorial hold on the lapels. "Due to certain constraints"—he flicked his left ear and pointedly did not glance in the Admiral's direction—"only a bare trickle of Hrruban goods, some urgently sought on Hayuman worlds, manages to reach their destination. Ze cost is prohibitive, and subject to priorities which make deliveries uncertain. A universal marketplace would certainly improve industry on Hrruba and open up immense possibilities for further, mutually productive manufacturing. Hav-ing discussed this possibility with Hrruban officials in all areas of business man-agement"—he held one hand out to Mllaba for a sheaf of notes which he then brandished as proof of his efforts—"ze majority would be quite amenable to such a project. With, of course"—he held up the notes—"safeguards to protect ze existing colony and ze Treaty Island from any commercial contamination."

"How large a trade grid will Hrruba install?" Jilamey asked, all but physically pouncing on Hrrto, who recoiled.

"Zat subject has certainly not been discussed as yet, Mr. Landreau," Hrrto said repressively as Hrrestan simultaneously called for order, glaring at the un-repentant Jilamey.

"What I'd like to know," Tanarey Smith said, his voice overriding others wishing to be heard, "is whether or not the construction of such an installation will be joint?" His expression suggested that it had better be.

"That question is premature, Mr. Smith," Hrrestan said. "The matter to be discussed is the advisability of such an installation in the first instance, not who will build it."

"Ze Speakers must be assured zat regulations will follow zose already in force—" Hrrto began.

"Aw," Ali Kiachif interrupted, "let's not start that old keep-the-home-world-sacred stuff."

"Hell's bells," added Fred Horstmann, "there isn't a space captain worth his salt, Hayuman or Hrruban, who hasn't a fair idea where each homeworld has to be." He caught Hrrto's outraged expression. "Well, you only have to narrow the options available, Speaker."

"Don't we know each other well enough now, after thirty-something years," Tanarey Smith began, "to forget this nonsense about homeworld integrity?"

"No!" Second Speaker Hrrto leaped to his feet, the fur on his back bristling. "Homeworld integrity is not nonsense. It is ze most vital point of agreement between our two races and may not, must not be abrogated. Never be abrogated."

"So is the Treaty!" Todd couldn't restrain himself from saying in a tone just short of a shout.

"The Treaty stipulates," Barnstable said, raising his own voice to top Todd's, "the conditions on which the Doonarrala colony is promulgated. It says absolutely nothing about that subcontinent nor the use to which it can be put. The Treaty specifies only the main continent known as Doonarrala, and the Treaty Island, where observers are permitted and where any disputes are settled. This isn't an abrogation. It's an expansion."

"Well now, I shouldn't want to see anything violate the Treaty," Kiachif said, somehow inserting himself into the discussion. "I seen it start and don't intend to see it finish. How about a space station?" And he looked appealingly at Todd. Though Todd hadn't expected such a suggestion, he welcomed it.

The delegates, all speaking at once, responded excitedly. "Space station?" "Landside free port?" "Now, wait a minute!" "I thought the matter under discussion was the use of The Hrrunat!"

Appalled, Speaker Hrrto listened to the babble, his increasing outrage at such lack of courtesy demonstrated by the lashing of his tail.

"SILENCE!" Todd belted the word out in such a roar that there was silence, as much from surprise as to wait until ears stopped ringing. "You will all be heard in order. In order, I repeat. We may all know each other very well, but that is no reason to dispense with formality."

Even Mllaba regarded him with respect, and Second Speaker was mollified.

"Hrrestan . . ." Todd said, turning the meeting over once more to its chairman.

Having thrown out the suggestion of a space station, Ali Kiachif was acknowledged by Hrrestan to give particulars. He was listened to politely but when he had finished, five people vied to follow him.

Discreetly, Hrrestan acknowledged Hrrin, who spoke about the benefits to the burgeoning agrarian economy which could not profitably market its surplus beyond those few traders who regularly reprovisioned at the present small, and totally inadequate, space base. More people could be accommodated at a land base than a space station; therefore the agronomy of Doonarrala would certainly benefit more from a facility at The Hrrunat.

Lorena rose to support a space facility where the integrity of the colony would not be at risk. But, as she was speaking for bankers who would profit from either venture, she chose to fall on the side of the more expensive installation. Hrrouf, in terser language but with a thick accent, appeared to corroborate her statements on the Hrruban behalf.

Fred Horstmann wanted to be heard on the matter of the frail safety of a space station, whereas a land port wasn't half as vulnerable and furthermore could simultaneously accommodate far more vessels and cargo at a considerably lower cost.

"Costs could be reduced even further with the use of the bigger grids," Jilamey interjected, causing the Admiral and the Hrruban commandant to erupt in protest.

"Jilamey!" Todd said again, using his penetrating voice to cut through the rising level of peripheral conversations. "One more word about grid and you are O-U-T. Out!"

Jilamey's unrepentant shrug was on the order of it-never-hurts-to-try.

"I don't like gridding around," Barnstable snapped out, his crisp voice ringing in the big chamber, "and a big one wouldn't be any easier to endure than a small one. Brr! At least with a ship, you know where you are and how you got there." One of his ice-white brows lowered slightly as he turned in Second Speaker's direction. "But I would like to take this occasion, face to face, to ask the Honorable Senior Commandant Prrid and the Honored Second Speaker why the Hrrubans won't trust us with grid technology."

Hrrto's eyes gleamed, and the fur at the back of his neck bristled. Todd prepared to stand up and dive in.

"All I am prepared to say is zat it is not a question of trust, Admiral," Prrid replied. Second Speaker merely bowed to second that comment and turned his head resolutely from Barnstable.

"But will you say whether or not—if this project goes through—there would be a large grid at a free trade port?" Jilamey asked.

"No more will be discussed about ze grrrids," Second Speaker said with such finality that Jilamey subsided. "We discuss ze advisability of a free trade spaceport on Ze Hrrunat."

"Then let us get down to the nitty-gritty," Ali Kiachif said. "The size of the place, its organization. Will it be jointly administered?"

"Of course!" Mrrunda said emphatically.

Ali grinned at him. "Of course!"

Hrrto grumbled out a growl, shifting himself to face the old captain. "Hrruban trade has been at a disadvantage zat would be remedied by such a facility. I am instructed to make suitable arrangements."

So, Todd thought to himself, no reprieve was forthcoming from the Hrruban side. How was he going to delay the matter? A glance at the massive old-fashioned, long case clock in the corner of the room gave him the excuse he needed.

"Let us adjourn for lunch before we deal with details," Todd suggested, glancing about the table. "There's a splendid sampling of the local dishes, both Hrruban and Hayuman, for your pleasure. If you will follow me?"

Not every one of the delegates was pleased at such an interruption, but Barnstable was clearly in favor of a meal. The alacrity with which Second Speaker rose from his chair did much to sway other Hrrubans to follow his example. Hrrouf immediately sought Lorena Kaldon for a few private words as they followed Todd.

The wide marble hallways of the Federation Center were peopled by tour groups and employees hurrying to and fro. But these stood aside to allow the distinguished delegates to move freely toward the dining area. As they neared the facility, delightful aromas wafted out into the hallway. Todd took a lungful and began to relax a little. Hrriss' jaw dropped open in a contented smile. The anticipation of food was having much the same effect on the others.

"Friends, welcome!" a warm voice greeted them from inside the doors. "I'm your hostess, Kelly Reeve. Please, come in and make yourselves at home." She repeated her greeting in excellent High Hrruban, bowing low toward Hrrto.

Her coifed red hair ablaze in the room's pendant lights, Kelly Solinari Reeve beckoned them inside. She was a tall woman, whose graceful athletic figure was enhanced by the wheat-colored dress and short jacket she wore. As if caught in the act of making last-minute preparations, she set down the earthenware pitcher she was holding on the edge of a long table laid for a feast and advanced to the doorway, beaming.

"Mrs. Reeve, this is a pleasant surprise," Tanarey Smith said, bowing over Kelly's hand.

Ali Kiachif sprang forward to greet her. "A fine day, a fair lassie, and food fit for a Pharaoh. How are you, lass?"

"Wonderful, Ali," Kelly said, returning the old spacer's embrace with a kiss on his grizzled cheek. "How good to see you! And Jilamey! We're so glad you got here. I was very surprised to see no one but Barrington on the landing pad two days ago. We didn't know what became of you." Barrington, Jilamey's "gentleman's gentleman," accompanied him on almost every trip the young businessman made. He was a combination of amanuensis, mother hen, and genie from the lamp, to judge by Jilamey's accounts of his silent miracles of organization.

"Well, surprise," Jilamey said sheepishly. "I got a ride on the grid with Admiral Barnstable, hands across the water—or the void, so to speak." He winked at the Admiral, who ignored the cheeky familiarity. "I sent Old Patience-is-a-Virtue on by himself to breathe ship air and mind my parcels. He's marvelous. So I was able to stay home and tweak a few more deals before I came up. Grids are wonderful. You only grow lovelier, Kelly." He seized one of her hands to kiss.

"Well, your house is ready. I was up there only yesterday to check on it."

"I am in your debt," Jilamey said expansively.

The nephew of the late Admiral Landreau had bought a large house high on a hilltop southwest of the original First Villages, and equipped it via Codep transport ship with all manner of modern doodads, including private vehicles not specifically mentioned nor barred by the Doona charter. As for horses, he owned a few, but except for the weeks he was on-planet, they boarded in stables owned by friends. Except for the ambassadorial residences on Treaty Island, his was the only permanent home on Doonarrala owned by a nonresident. But then, Jilamey was an exception to many rules.

"Well, sit down and eat," Kelly said, waving him to a seat. The table was laid with individual place settings, but the platters and bowls of food were intended to be passed from guest to guest. "How have you been?"

"I'm surviving," young Landreau replied happily. "How are the Alley Cats? And Hrriss's cubs? I'm looking forward to seeing them."

"And they can't wait to see you," Kelly assured him. "They all send their love. Nrrna is minding all the children while I play hostess."

"I've got a baby present for—what's her name? Hrrunna?"

"You're so good with them," Kelly said, shaking her head. "You should have some of your own." She caught herself and threw him a little shrug of apology.

"Not me." Jilamey laughed, without a trace of discomfort. "I'm much more definitely uncle material. Besides, I couldn't spoil yours so well if I had my own tagging along behind me."

"How is my youngest grandchild?" Hrrestan asked fondly, his voice dropping into intimate mode, as he stopped to rub cheeks with Kelly.

"Growing," Kelly said with a grin. "She follows everything with her eyes now, and that tail of hers is positively prehensile. When she doesn't want you to stop patting her back, she holds on."

"Hrrunna is named for our dear First Speaker," Hrrestan explained to Hrrto. "She was born a mere four days after he joined the Ancestral Stripes."

"A most touching sentiment," Hrrto said, with a mere suggestion of a drop-jawed smile. "It is good to know those so far away from the homeworld would recall him and pay such a tribute. We of the High Council all regret the loss of our senior statesman."

To Todd and Hrriss, Hrrto's regret didn't ring entirely true. Hrriss shook his head, recalling that Second was enmeshed at present in a difficult contest to win the vacant speakership for himself, which likely overshadowed any real feelings he might have.

Kelly burst in to dispel the uncomfortable silence. "Well, come along, everyone. I hope you enjoy everything. Don't stand on ceremony. I'm sure you're famished." She came up to Todd and lifted her face for a kiss.

"How's it been going?" she asked in a hasty whisper as the others moved about the table to find the place cards with their names.

"From whose viewpoint?" Todd asked ironically. Kelly gave him a quick, worried look as he tucked her arm in his and escorted her up the length of the room. "Ali tried to help by suggesting a space station. Jilamey's doing his best to irritate Hrrto and Barnstable with his constant nudging about grids. But—" She sighed as he conceded, "the majority see it as a way to improve their credit position one way or another! Even Hrrin sees the spaceport as profitable to the agricultural community."

"Oh? A new outlet for surplus. Hmm. Well, it would be. Ooops, sorry, love."

Smoothly, Kelly ducked away from him toward the Second Speaker.

"Ah, gracious sir," she said in her impeccable High Hrruban, "we have the urfa pie you so much enjoyed the last time you favored us with your presence," and she steered him toward his place and began serving him.

Then she turned her bright smile on Tanarey Smith, who beamed under her charm.

Soon everyone was seated, with filled plates and glasses, looking all too pleased with the morning's meeting. Despite the fact that the menu included two of Todd's personal favorites, he could find no appetite and pushed the food about on his plate.

He could hear snatches of conversations and shook his head because, without exception, everyone favored the instant establishment of a spaceport on The Hrrunat. The instanter, the better, and why wasn't this suggested years ago?

Because Hu Shih and Hrruna had squashed that snake any time it came out of its lair.

Why wasn't I able to? Todd thought in miserable isolation. *Dad and Hu Shih are as certain as I am that such an installation abrogates both Decision and Treaty. Why am I unable to convince the others?* He sighed deeply, noting Kelly's anxious gaze on him. He smiled at her, though it was a feeble attempt, and pushed a forkful into his mouth. The food was almost cold but he chewed it anyway. *I must not be the leader everyone thought I was, if I cannot protect the community from an evil I perceive as encroachment.*

The jingle of Jilamey's bells broke through his thoughts, and he saw the enthusiastic entrepreneur bumping up and down on his chair as he explained, with many gestures as well as body language, some point he was trying to make.

Maybe, thought Todd, *I was foolish to stop Jilamey yattering away about the grids. Maybe if I let him irritate Hrrto, Prrid, and that bunch sufficiently, they'll leave in a huff. Todd, my friend, think with your head, not your heart. There're more ways to deflect a snake than ramming a boulder up its maw.*

He brightened considerably as he turned over the possibilities for sowing discord. Certainly, if he insisted on discussing grids, he'd disorganize the meeting so that nothing could be accomplished but a venting of temper. He'd have to be subtle, which had never been his best suit, but so much was at stake.

Just then a stray phrase from Lorena Kaldon caught his attention.

"Once again, I want to know if this project will be open for tenders?" She looked agitated. "And who will make the final decision?"

"Why, obviously, that must be decided by the villages," Todd said, smiling affably as if he'd been following the discussion all along.

"In this instance," Barnstable began, joining in with a verbal pounce, "since the matter concerns more than the villages, the parent worlds must have a voice."

Todd lifted one eyebrow and gave Hrriss a long look, which Hrriss shrugged off. That annoyed Todd even more. Was Hrriss blind that he didn't see how eager Spacedep was to get a legal foothold on Doonarrala?

"Parochial attitudes must give way to interstellar requirements," Tanarey Smith said, and Lorena nodded hearty agreement.

"Yes, but with both Earth and Hrruba complaining about costs already, where is the money coming from?" Todd asked.

"This project will interest independent financial sources . . ." Lorena began.

"Don't you worry about the financing," Tanarey said.

"All right, I won't," Todd said, "but how does the facility manage itself once it's built?"

"Tariff, of course," Fred Horstmann said, regarding Todd with surprise, as if that source was too obvious.

"Which includes a yearly rental?" Hrrestan asked in a bland tone. Even Todd regarded his co-leader with surprise at that nicely landed bombshell. Hrrestan dropped his jaw in a smile. "You did not think that we Rraladoonans would let you have a whole subcontinent rent-free from us, did you? A percentage of the annual income . . ."

Todd covered his eyes and bent his head so no one would see his grin. Maybe Hrrestan wasn't totally lost to common sense in this matter. In Todd's mind, however, a hefty addition to the colony's coffers did not quite compensate for the violation of the Treaty. As it was, Hrrestan's remarks effectively silenced everyone—except for the jingling bells of Jilamey's suit as, first he sank back in his chair, then abruptly sat up to cause more chiming.

"Of course," the young entrepreneur said, beaming at his sudden inspiration, "Doonarrala must benefit from the project. But I think it's only a matter of working out an acceptable figure. Think of all that has already been worked out here on Treaty Island so harmoniously." He gave his arm a hearty shake, grinning at the effect on those seated around the table.

In the small reception room on board the cruiser which was describing a temporary orbit just outside the range of Doona's most distant moon, a smartly uniformed Spacedep rating awaited the passenger of an admiralty scout ship that had just arrived. The esteemed visitor, a stocky man in his early forties with a commander's insignia on his uniform, had a broad spread of shoulders, a strongly drawn jaw, and sharp, brown eyes that made the rating quail inwardly when they momentarily met hers. There was something almost cold about him. His square, handsome face was unlined except for the disapproving indentations framing his molded mouth. The rating waited at attention while the visitor cleared decontam and slipped out of his pressure suit. The glassteel doors slid open one at a time, allowing him to enter the atmosphere lock, and finally to admit him to the lounge.

"Welcome aboard, Commander," the rating said, firing off a perfect salute. "The captain awaits you in her office. I'm to take you to her." Frozen like a waxwork, she held the pose, waiting for the guest's reply.

"Thank you," Commander Jon Greene said, returning the salute promptly, but not too promptly.

The rating relaxed subtly, as if the precise timing was what she had expected, and Greene smiled inwardly. Without a single glance back at the scout ship now being swarmed over by a crowd of technicians for its courtesy checkup, he strode off behind his guide.

Greene surveyed the various work stations they passed, glancing first at the hands and then at the eyes of the crew working at them. Each person, as Greene met his or her eyes, straightened up involuntarily, and went back to the task at hand with renewed energy. As Admiral Barnstable's personal assistant, Greene represented Spacedep command in the flesh, and expected efficiency and the stiff-backed respect of subordinate officers.

Greene himself had come up through the ranks. By virtue of sheer efficiency and drive, he became indispensable to his various superiors, working his way up to a position of trust where he was empowered to carry out tasks that required strategy and thought. By making his commanders look their best, he acquired a vicarious importance.

In time, he had managed to ingratiate himself with the new head of Spacedep, Admiral Barnstable. Greene was an ambitious man, and hoped to go higher still in time. Who knew what might await him in the future? The chairmanship of Spacedep? A seat on the Amalgamated Worlds Admin Council?

The Admiral was presently on Doona for the purpose of attending a conference to carve a Spacedep niche in the proposed spaceport and negotiate other details of interaction between the two races. The Admiral was an adequate administrator, and spoke only passable Middle Hrruban, but he was a better negotiator than anyone in the Spacedep hierarchy. Greene knew his own talents would be employed there, as an adjunct delegate, speaking for the rights of those governed by the Amalgamated Worlds Council, to facilitate Barnstable's agenda. Greene himself was not anti-Hrruban except where the goals of the Hrrubans interfered with what was properly due to Humanity.

Barnstable recognized Greene's talents, and made use of them on missions like this one. It was ostensibly a courtesy call, allowing Greene to visit the captain of the Spacedep cruiser, which was passing through Doonan space, for the purpose of asking her to join him at the negotiations. His visit had a sub rosa purpose: the Admiral suspected that Hrruban warships would also be in the area, maintaining a discreet distance from the planet, and Greene's primary mission was to find out what they were doing. If they were behaving in a suspicious manner, the Admiral wanted to be informed as soon as possible so that he could take appropriate measures. Barnstable wasn't an isolationist, but he firmly believed that good fences made good neighbors.

Greene and his escort passed into the rear of the bridge area and skirted the main dais, heading toward an alcove facing it on the left. The officers of the current watch on the bridge glanced up only briefly at the visitor and his escort. No inefficiency here. Greene nodded approval. Overt curiosity in a fleet officer was a fault.

The metal door slid away into a recess as he approached it. The rating stopped at the threshold to announce him. Beyond the door was a utilitarian metal desk behind which sat a short, muscular woman with ice-blond hair and direct brown eyes that arrested Greene on the threshold. She looked up from her desk monitor as the young rating performed the introductions. Greene felt a tingle at the back of his spine as she summed him up with a glance. A most attractive woman and, by her expression, not unpleased by what she saw. By her record, she was also a successful, intelligent officer, on track for flag rank. A good person to get to know. He smiled.

"Captain Grace Castleton, I bring you greetings from Admiral Barnstable," Greene began very formally, approaching her. "I am Jon Greene."

Castleton stuck a hand out over the desk, clasped Greene's, then released it and indicated that he should sit down. Her deep eyes were frank and full of concern.

"Good to see you, Commander. That's quick work! We only just heard the Alert."

"Alert?" Greene gawked blankly, and the captain frowned at him.

"Yes, Alert! You've come about that orbiting monstrosity out there, haven't you?" Castleton swivelled her miniature viewscreen toward him. On it was the image of a hovering hulk. Shock hit Greene in the pit of the stomach. The odd-shaped vessel was huge. "The system perimeter alarms went wild! Can you make anything of it?"

The outline, a long, irregular cylinder like a tree trunk, was somewhat familiar to him, but he couldn't place it. Greene made a point of familiarizing himself with all makes of spaceships—naval, civil, and private. And he had seen one like this recently, too. He concentrated on plucking the circumstances out of his memory.

"Not the usual design of Hrruban warships, is it?" he murmured, struggling to grasp the elusive recall. With a deft tapping, he brought up the computer telemetry statistics and studied the image, trying to identify it.

"Can't be Hrruban," Castleton snapped immediately. "Furthermore, the ship doesn't answer any communication signal we've thrown at it, and I know all the Hrruban codes. It's heading for a high orbit around Doona. We've our weapons trained on it, though it hasn't offered any overt threat. But then, how could it?" And her grin was ironic. "It's not carrying any heavy armament."

"None at all?" Greene demanded. "Ridiculous."

"Look there." She pointed at another shape on the screen, so far in the background that it could have been painted on the starry backdrop. Statistics, expressed in hot yellow numbers, inscribed themselves on the screen around it. "See? There's the biggest registered Hrruban ship, armed to the nines, right where the Admiral thought it'd be. That one set off my weapons sensors all right. High-grade radiation, well-shielded but still detectable. Bastard's not supposed to be there, but I guess they don't trust us completely either, with one of their High Council members down there. The way they're hanging off the stranger, they don't know where it came from, either."

As if in corroboration of Castleton's assertion, the intercom rang through. "The commander of the Hrruban ship," a voice said.

"Put him through."

The images faded, to be replaced by the face of a middle-aged Hrruban. "Zis is Captain Hrrrv. Your other ship refuses to answer our hails."

"Captain Castleton here. It's not one of ours. Can't you identify it for us?" she asked pointedly.

"One cannot identify what one has never seen beforrre!" the Hrruban said, snapping his jaw shut.

"Then, something new? A Doonan dreadnought built in secret? It would be within their philosophy to build a ship without guns," Greene murmured softly, knowing he was not in the intercom's audio range. The instant he realized that Captain Castleton had heard it and was glaring at him, he gave her a facile smile as if he'd meant to be facetious. Castleton was not stupid and, while she couldn't express political opinions, from her expression it looked as though she might entertain pro-Doona leanings.

"I doubt that very much," she said drily. "Doona has no heavy-metals resource to produce a ship that big, much less a space dock that could construct one."

"Then where is it from?" Greene asked. His inner agitation increased.

Of all the possibilities he could have anticipated in coming to Doona for this conference, the incursion of another alien race was not one of them. Another race of aliens becoming involved in the already complicated political dance between the Humans and Hrrubans would not please Admiral Barnstable. A new variable in the equation would be the last thing he wanted. And the faint familiarity Greene felt for the ship on the screen plagued him.

"I'd sure like to know," the captain replied, staring at the screen, "but I'm rather short on answers, and I've initiated all the approved procedures for contact. Captain Hrrrv, shall we pool our readings?"

"You have obtained some, Captain?"

"I'm seeing the same thing you are, Captain." Castleton shook her head slowly from side to side. "Science Officer, have you anything to report?"

"Proceeding with routine scans, sir." Even over the intercom, his voice held little expectation of success.

The outline of the massive ship, Greene decided, attracted the eye. It was such a peculiar shape. A central tube pierced through an almost globular center section. From the upper and lower parts of the tube, smaller clusters sprouted, almost like tumors in a tree. It looked harmless, but then so did a land mine, he mused.

"We have life-form readings, sir," the science officer reported. "But, sir," he added, "I think there must be something wrong with our instrumentation or the stranger is somehow scrambling them."

"How so, mister?" Castleton asked.

"Too big. Neither Humans nor Hrrubans grow 'em that size, sir."

"Captain Hrrrv, do your life-form readings concur with ours?" Castleton asked. "Patch readings through to Captain Hrrrv."

The next moment, Hrrrv nodded solemnly.

"Let us report the presence of zis vehicle and its anomalies to our superiors immediately. Over and out." As soon as the Hrruban's image had faded, Castleton called for her communications officer. "Get Admiral Barnstable on the horn." She frowned as Greene raised a hand for her attention. "Belay that. Yes, Commander?"

"He's in the middle of a conference with a number of civilian officials, Captain."

"Noted, Greene," she said crisply, but she smiled to take the sting out of her brusque reply. "Use Command Code, Barnet."

"Admiral Barnstable," the Treaty Island aide said in a low voice, bending down to the Admiral. "Message from Captain Castleton, Command Code."

The old man looked around for the audio pickup. "Can you pipe it in here, son? Don't care to leave present company even for a Command Code!" He gave a snort. "Whatever is up Castleton's nose now?"

"Admiral?" A woman's voice, sounding agitated, echoed from the satellite feed. The pickup was audible only to those nearest the Admiral.

"Yes, Captain. Nice to hear from you. Something go wrong between you and my envoy?"

"There's a matter of extreme importance . . ."

"Well, Grace, spit it out," the Admiral ordered.

Her words pinged crisply from the speaker. "There's an intruder, a huge ship beginning entry into distant orbit around Doonarrala. I've never seen anything like it in space before. It's seven times the size of Spacedep's largest flagship! Captain Hrrrv can't identify her, either. I'd appreciate it if you'd come upstairs and take a look, sir."

With this information, those who heard erupted into surprised protest and consternation. In a few seconds, everyone knew the substance of the message. Second Speaker glared nervously around him, as if expecting the intruder to appear in the room. A young Hrruban wearing the single bandolier belt of a Treaty Island employee ran into the room and slid to a kneeling position on the polished wooden floor beside Hrrestan. The aide began to whisper urgently in the leader's ear. Hrrestan's eyes narrowed, and he rose to address the gathering.

"That was confirmation, my frrriends, if we needed it. An unknown ship of great size entered our system over three hours ago, and it has made full orbit. Ze space centers are on rrrred alert. Until we know more, I think we may consider zat we are being invaded."

"Why do we have to assume," Todd asked in a low, angry voice as he and Hrriss ran for the nearest comlink terminal in the corner of the room, "that we're being invaded just because it's a strange ship."

"Because it's big," Hrriss murmured, inserting his sleek body into the chair before Todd could, "and no one recognizes it." His long fingers flew over the keys, his partly bared claws clacking. Using an entry code, Hrriss hooked directly into the computer net used by the three Doonan space centers. Panting, Ali Kiachif peered over his shoulder.

"That," Todd exclaimed with awed respect as the scan started, "is truly one big mother!"

Castleton hadn't exaggerated: the stranger was approximately 7.4 times the size of a Spacedep flagship, and of no configuration Todd had ever seen before.

"Do we classify zis scan?" Hrriss asked, his talons flexing slightly in and out over the keys.

"Let's just hope that we're not too late," Todd said, "and that someone isn't linking into the net right now. We don't need a panic. Classify it, need-to-know clearance only."

"Just what I was about to suggest," Admiral Barnstable said, dropping a hand on Todd's shoulder.

"Hrrestan?" Todd looked up from the screen to his co-leader. Barnstable might suggest but he was outside his jurisdiction right now. Hrrestan nodded agreement, and pulled Barnstable back a little way.

"Ze knowledge will become common soon enough," Hrrestan said with a little sigh of regret. "It is for ze leaders to preparrre others to receive it. In ze meantime, we will be gearrring ourrselves frrr whatever may follow."

"And if the intruder is hostile! Who will protect us?" other delegates demanded. Kelly stood, watching, her arms wrapped around herself but showing no sign of fear.

"Zere is no need to assume ze worrst," Hrriss said resolutely, echoing Todd's feelings, "before all facts are known, is zere?"

"We don't have to assume," Todd added, supporting Hrriss, "that a stranger, any stranger, comes only with hostile intent."

"That big?" Tanarey exclaimed. "What else could it have?"

"I've got a fully armed ship on alert upstairs," Barnstable was saying at the same time. "It's ready in case of any emergency."

"We don't know if we have an emergency yet, Admiral," Todd said. "We have a visitor, not a proven enemy. Hell, it isn't shooting at us, is it?"

"Enough of this," Barnstable said firmly. "I want to see this mystery visitor"—he shot Todd a sardonic look—"with my own eyes. I'm going up to the *Hamilton* immediately. As head of Spacedep, I need to be where I can make informed decisions as soon as sensor data are received and analyzed."

"As planetary administrator," Todd said instantly, "I need to be on hand for any decisions that affect Doonarrala."

Barnstable gave him a long, measuring look, then nodded his head sharply once.

"Zis surprise arrival affects more zan just Rraladoona," Hrrto said promptly. "I must be present, as well."

"I go, too," said Hrriss, glancing at Todd, who nodded agreement. Their estrangement over the spaceport was momentarily forgotten in this new crisis.

"I must accompany the Speaker," Mllaba said, glaring at Hrriss as if he had usurped some perogative of hers.

"Hrrubans on a Spacedep military ship?" Barnstable said with sudden pompous suspicion.

"Zese are exzraordinary circumstances," Second Speaker said urgently, his tense stance suggesting he would brook no refusal. "I wish to see what you see when you see it. We will coordinaze wiz ze Hrruban ship from zere."

"Dammit, very well! Come along! But let's get a move on!" the Admiral barked.

"We don't know that anything's wrong, love," Todd whispered to Kelly as he gave her a quick farewell hug. "Don't panic when there's no need."

Kelly let her head rest briefly on his shoulder, as if memorizing his touch and scent, then pushed herself firmly away. "I'll wait with Nrrna and the kids."

"Thata girl," Todd said almost flippantly. "Don't I always come back to you?"

Nearly giving way to the very panic he had mentioned, she caught herself in time and said, "Just don't take any unnecessary chances."

"Me? Never!" He gave her his most charismatic grin and then turned back to the emergency before him. "Ali, I believe that the Admiral's shuttle is already on the *Hamilton*. Can you get us another one?"

"No tussle, trouble, or toil there," the Codep captain said, cheerfully, "providing we don't get shot out of space on the way. Follow me, all."

chapter two

Kiachif took the skiff off in a fast-climbing orbit, cleaving the atmosphere. Crowded into its forward cabin behind Kiachif and Hrriss in the pilot's couches were Barnstable, Todd, Second Speaker and his assistant Mllaba, Hrrestan, Barnstable's personal aide-de-camp, and Jilamey Landreau, who squeezed on board through the closing airlock before he could be stopped. Rather than waste any more time, he was allowed to remain.

Below them, the vivid blue of the Doonan sky glowed, illuminating the nearside of vessels hovering in local space above. Communication satellites, merchant ships, and beacons went by unheeded. As soon as the skiff attained its first looping orbit, the unknown ship came into view, watched cautiously at a prudent distance by the Spacedep and Hrruban Space Arm vessels. The invader had made no overt movements, either hostile or friendly. It just hung there in space, circling the planet at a distance. Everyone stared in turn at the screens and the forward port, as if to make certain what they saw on the screen existed in real space.

"Where did that large leviathanic liner come from?" Ali Kiachif demanded. His eyes gleamed. "I'd powerful like to take her for a test spin, make no mistake about that. Wonder what fuel she runs on?"

"Brr! It looks dangerous," Jilamey exclaimed. "All those bits and pieces sticking out. Surely that's not good design." The visitor plunged into the nightside of Doonarrala, making itself a sinister shadow against the stars.

"Isn't that a breakaway orbit?" Kiachif asked, checking his sensors. "Is she doing a spit, split and flit if anyone so much as says 'boo' to her?"

Todd scrutinized the outlines of the ship as it reached dayside again. The vessel was slowing down.

"Seems to be settling into a stationary orbit, Ali," he said. Details were hard to pick out on the black hull. He could see nothing at all that he could identify as weaponry, nor did the skiff's monitors register any telltale radiation glow. "They look like they mean to stay awhile," he added very softly.

Hrriss, beside him, was the only one to hear that comment. "I know what I wish zey are doing here," the cat man said wistfully.

"Me, too," Todd agreed, smiling slightly. Once again, he and Hrriss were in the minority. He was positive that most of the others were reacting with various degrees of xenophobia. Had neither race learned anything from the Doona Experiment? Or were they two the only ones who understood the true significance of this unique colony? Bearing in mind the result of his father's initial encounter with two small Hrrubans over thirty years ago, Todd believed a show of friendship might once again prove more useful than overt hostility. The very fact that this skiff contained persons from two races, observing a possible confrontation with a third, surely meant some good had been achieved by the Decision at Doona. His grin for Hrriss broadened. "Well, if wishes were hrrrses . . ." he murmured in a very good imitation of Hrriss.

"It is a terrifying giant," Mllaba said, exhaling with a hiss as she shivered.

The skiff caught up with the leviathan, passed underneath, and shot out in front Kiachif turned the craft out of an ascension trajectory and headed for the Spacedep cruiser.

Captain Castleton was waiting for them at the docking bay. Todd had met her once before, two years back, at a Treaty Day observance. He didn't know much about her, except that she was a good dancer. Her crew considered her a tartar because she expected honesty and tireless dedication from everyone who served under her. She appeared unruffled and calm, saluting the Admiral smartly before holding out a firm hand to each of the others.

"Welcome on board the *Hamilton*, gentlemen, madam," she said. Mllaba shook her hand gravely.

"Grace, I'm glad to see you," Barnstable said at his heartiest. "We've just had a good look at your mystery guest. Damned if I know what it is. Any new info?" The Admiral turned to acknowledge another uniformed figure in the bay with a lift of his thick white eyebrows. "Ah, Jon, there you are. My aide, Jon Greene," he said to the others. "I'll want your reading on this ASAP, Greene."

"Of course, sir," Greene said, stepping forward. "My report is waiting for you."

Todd decided the aide was about his own age but a hand-span shorter, compact and trim in his dark blue uniform. Greene glanced at the civilians behind his CO, meeting Todd's eyes, then focusing, as if identifying him. Greene's look of concentration faded abruptly, dismissing the civilians as unimportant, and he returned his gaze to his superior. Todd felt a swift flush of irritation at being so negligently dismissed.

Castleton went on. "Sir, I've invited Captain Hrrrv of the Hrruban vessel to take part in this conference."

Barnstable nodded. "Good. In the ready room?"

"This way, Admiral," Castleton said, indicating the portside corridor.

It was then that Todd saw the two Humans in dark blue uniforms with security flashes on their shoulders. They peeled away from the group waiting behind the sliding doors and fell in behind the Hrrubans as they went down the blue-gray corridor. As everyone filed out of the bay, more of the ratings took positions behind the other Hrrubans. It was not very subtly done and Todd could see that Second's spine was stiff under his red robe. Mllaba's tail switched angrily back and forth. After so many years since the Decision at Doonarrala, it was infuriating to see that there was still such blatant evidence of distrust.

"Blast it out of space," the Hrruban captain suggested, his fangs clicking together with a sound of finality. He waved an imperious hand at the image hanging on the large screen. Hrrrv bore a broad, dark stripe down the middle of his gold-furred back, sure indication of his clan's high position on Hrruba. Both cruisers were now matching the stranger's orbit, but with one fourth the curve of the great blue planet between them for safety. The Hrruban's ship was just barely visible in the corner of the viewscreen. "I do not like its appearance," Hrrrv said, "I think it means us no good." He walked up and down one side of the ready room, switching his tail irritably.

"Captain Castleton, when the ship did not answer any standard hailing messages, did you try any other methods of communication?" Todd asked, exasperated by the military mind.

Grace Castleton regarded him with surprise. "I tried all known codes . . . on all frequencies available to my equipment." Her tone and look implied that she had the very best, state-of-the-art equipment. "Oh, I see what you're driving at," she said after a moment, her face lightening.

"Thank goodness someone does," Todd said, throwing up his hands in gratitude.

"And just what is that?" Admiral Barnstable demanded, annoyed.

"Sir, how can they communicate with us if there isn't a common language? Or symbols or even a medium of communication. My father had the advantage of being face to face with two members of another species."

"And how do you propose to emulate your father, then?" Barnstable asked.

"By going to meet them."

Barnstable's eyes protruded and his face flushed with either surprise or anger, but Todd kept his ingenuous smile in place. "Worked before," he said.

"That's why we ended up learning Hrruban," Jilamey broke in. When he saw Barnstable, Castleton, and Greene giving him a concerted cold glance, he demanded, "What was wrong with that? We learned it. I think Todd's got the right approach. Go meet 'em and find out what they want. It doesn't do us any good to sit here in space with that big thing looming over us, neither side making a move. Their ship may be bigger, but"—he waggled his finger around the room—"we got more. They could be the ones scared stiff to do anything, you know. Make the wrong move and get blasted out of space."

Todd rubbed at his mouth, trying to make his lips behave. Jilamey was making exactly the point that Todd wanted to.

"Landreau's talking sense," Ali Kiachif said. "Don't know why I didn't see it that way myself, since I've traded with some mighty odd folk, using signs and trying to savvy their grants, groans, and gargles."

"D'you mean to say," Castleton asked Todd, leaning forward across the table, "that you're willing to approach them?"

"If you'll let us have a tender, Captain," Todd said equably.

"But . . . but that could be a vanguard!" Barnstable protested.

"A vanguard? That big?" Kiachif asked incredulously. "If that's Baby, I don't want to meet Papa, if you get my drift."

"An unarmed baby," Todd said, seizing the initiative again. "Unarmed. I'm more than willing to go . . ."

"I'll go with you," Hrriss said.

"I wouldn't mind the trip myself. Be sort of fun," Jilamey said, grinning in his eagerness.

"Now see here," Barnstable began, trying to regain control. "That is not standard procedure."

"I didn't realize there was a standard procedure for encountering large unknown spacecraft, Admiral," Todd said. He stood up. "If you'll be good enough to assign us a shuttle to make first contact, Captain Castleton . . ."

"Dammit, young man," and Barnstable thumped the table with both fists, "nothing's been decided."

"I know," Todd said, gesturing to Hrriss and Jilamey. "That's why I decided to do something on my own initiative as co-leader of the planet, which I do not honestly believe is in any danger from this visitor. But the sooner we establish communications, the sooner we learn exactly why they are in our space and what they want."

"They'll want to blast you to motes if you're foolhardy enough to approach them," Barnstable said.

"With what, Admiral?" Todd asked, feeling the tide of aggravation rising in his blood. "You've established—at least you say you have"—he glanced for confirmation at Castleton and Hrrrv—"that the ship is unarmed . . ."

Barnstable waved that consideration away. "You can't know what kind of weapons they might have. The whole ship, in that peculiar configuration, might act as an amplifier for some kind of huge energy beam! Who knows what those bulges on the surface are for?"

"I'm willing to take that risk, Admiral," Todd said, adding grimly, "I've also considered that they might have biological armament which doesn't require high-powered delivery systems. But I prefer to believe that they're friendly; only waiting for an invitation from us. Enemies barge in; friends wait for invitations."

"Good point, Todd," Kiachif said, grinning broadly. " 'Enemies barge in; friends wait for invitations.' Great notion."

A notion which did not appear to amuse many of those present. Hrrto's expression was unreadable, though his tail tip twitched. Mllaba's was extremely active.

"Admiral, remember that thirty-four years ago," Todd went on earnestly, "Humans discovered that we were not alone in the galaxy, that there was another sentient race with whom we could be friends," and he nodded solemnly at Hrrto, who looked pleased, and grinned at Hrriss and Hrrestan, dropping his glance lastly on Mllaba, who sniffed back at him. "The presence of a sophisticated spaceship that big means that whoever is aboard is not only sentient but of an intelligent and advanced civilization. The fact that they haven't opened fire or made any threatening moves against us, I take to mean that they are not aggressive. I'm willing to test that belief."

"So am I," Hrriss said.

"Me, too," Jilamey piped up, grinning in an inane fashion.

"So, do we have a shuttle, Admiral?" Todd was becoming more and more irked at the specious delays. He wouldn't call them cowardly, but certainly close to it.

Grace Castleton flicked a glance at Admiral Barnstable.

"You can use my skiff, Reeve," Ali Kiachif said then, with a glance of veiled contempt at the naval officers. "Glad to oblige . . ."

Barnstable was on his feet, so was Hrrrv.

"Now see here, Reeve, that's encroaching on military prerogatives . . ."

"It's our planet down there, Barnstable. C'mon, Ali, you can pilot while this lot dithers."

Grace Castleton slid in front of Todd before he had taken a full step. "Stow that, Reeve. I take your point, and I'm sure the Admiral does, too, even if your method is high-handed . . . especially while you're on board my ship." She gave him a wry grin. "You've volunteered to test the intentions of our . . ."

"Visitor?" Todd suggested in an edged tone.

She nodded. "Visitor. But Spacedep is responsible for the safety of all its citizens, and Captain Hrrrv for his nationals."

Todd gave her full marks for remembering the Hrruban presence, naval and diplomatic. "That is true, but as these are aliens, whatever form they take, the approach falls in the province of Alreldep, of which I'm a representative."

"Out of the question," Barnstable said firmly. "Alien Relations or no. Until these beings, whatever they are, are proven harmless, it is still a Spacedep matter. I concur that logic suggests that, Reeve lead a first-contact team . . ."

"And the elder Reeve," Todd said. "He has, after all, had more experience than anyone else in successful first contacts."

"Your father?"

"The very one."

"Humph. Well—" Barnstable cleared his throat. "Makes sense."

"I'll lead the armed guard," Greene said, taking a step forward.

"There'll be no armed guard," Todd and Hrriss said in unison.

Barnstable bristled but Hrrestan's eyes flashed. "A show of arms is unnecessary. And might even be considered an insult. A friend advances with open hands."

"It worked before," Todd said, exchanging glances with Hrriss. Out of the corner of his eye then, Todd caught a look of intense disgust on Greene's face. Here was one man who didn't hold with the pacific approach. And probably one who might be a borderline xenophobe. "I think we've discussed this matter long enough. Too long a delay might jeopardize good relations. They'll have seen the skiff arriving. Captain, may I get in touch with my father on Doonarrala?"

As Grace Castleton bent to the terminal to instruct the commofficer, Todd saw the resolute glint in Greene's eyes. That man's middle name might be "trouble," he thought: he had a skeptical and suspicious air about him. Then the line to the surface of Doonarrala was open.

Ken Reeve was delighted to be asked. "I wondered what the lines were humming so hot and heavy for," he said, his image beaming an ear-to-ear smile at them from the screen. "I knew the perimeter alarms went off because I was jawing with Martinson at the Space Center up here between the First Villages. It was too late for the shush order when it followed. The gossips hanging around in port spread it all over town in jig time. Everyone's speculating on who's come calling."

Barnstable looked grim. "I was afraid of that. What's the response?"

"Not exactly what you'd think by your reaction, Admiral," Ken said with a grin. "Doonans are more inclined to think that outsiders who don't come in shooting are minded to be friendly. We know we're not the only ones out there, and I for one am happy for a chance to be one of the first to meet these new friends."

"They aren't friends yet," Greene reminded him sharply. Ken glanced over Barnstable's shoulder at the commander, his black eyebrows mounting into his hairline.

"Nor yet enemies," Ken replied quickly. "How can I get up to you?"

"I'll send a shuttle for you," Barnstable said, cutting Ken off and putting an end to the argument. "In the meantime, this is still a security matter. Please consider this as top secret. You may not inform anyone where you are going or what you'll be doing."

"Right you are. I'll be ready," said Ken cheerfully, and signed off.

"I'll go get him," Kiachif said, rising from his seat. "My skiff's faster'n any naval shuttle and I want another look, leer, and laying of a lens on that big ship. See if I can't get any more on her, if you get my meaning. Back in a ten-count." The Codep captain nodded to Castleton and the Admiral, and left the room.

"Until Dad arrives and we can proceed with a first contact," Todd said, once the door shut behind Kiachif, "we must not make any moves which the . . . visitors could consider antagonistic or hostile. No more scans, no probes, no drones. They could think that latter two were weapons."

"Let's not be overcautious, Mr. Reeve," Captain Castleton said, studying the image of the ship in the holoscreen. "Their range of power fluctuations alone invites closer investigation. Surely if they're the advanced beings you speculate they are, they'd expect us to try and uncover any information about them that we could, short of intrusive hardware."

"Who knows what they'd consider intrusive?" Todd asked. "Beings more sensitive than our two races might find probe scan painful. Do I have to remind anyone here of the Siwannah Tragedy? No. Well, then. You've already done enough remote scans." He didn't add "for all the good it did."

"I would feel better if I had more on them than the long-range data my passive telemetry picked up," Castleton said. "To quote an ancient Earth philosopher, 'It is a mistake to theorize in advance of facts.' "

Jon Greene was beginning to find the endless beating of the air dull and purposeless. The Doonarralans—wasn't that a word?—babbled against logical research that would help guarantee safety for their own people, not to mention the ships orbiting around their planet. Any part of that huge ship out there could conceal weapons. It didn't make sense to remain uninformed when useful data could be picked up as easily as vacuuming space dust. He wished he could recall under what circumstances he had seen that sort of vessel before. Castleton looked annoyed, and rightly so, with civilians usurping the appropriate naval roles in this sort of contact.

Barnstable gave him a glance and pushed his clipboard across the table to him. Greene picked it up and read the note the Admiral had discreetly added amidst the leviathan's readings. "Send probe." Greene erased the words and entered a random jotting of his own. He stood up.

"Permission to be excused, sir?" Greene asked, coming to attention.

Barnstable glanced up briefly from the discussion, and waved a hand. "Go ahead, son. I'll call you if I need you."

"Aye, sir. Captain, may I see you outside?"

Castleton looked surprised, but followed him out of the room. Greene escorted her a few meters from the door and automatically checked the corridor before he spoke.

"Sir, the Admiral asks if you will authorize launching a telemetry probe at the intruder."

Castleton looked down at her feet a moment before her shoulders relaxed a degree from their tight set. When she tipped her head up again, she wore an expression of relieved approval.

"Reeve's overcautious, Greene. Personally, I'd feel better with more data about that leviathan on hand. The distance scanners aren't giving us much to go on. This way." He followed her to a waiting 'vator car. "Level four," she said.

On an impulse, Greene stood closer to her than necessary in the small chamber and was surprised and pleased that Castleton didn't seem to mind. He was even more encouraged when she returned his smile.

*   *   *

A Gringg in the cargo-bay operations room of the gigantic spaceship watched on a viewscreen as a tiny metallic cylinder floated casually in the direction of the bow of their ship. He leaned lazily over and touched the key of the intercom with a long claw.

"Captain?" He knew he would find her in the bathing room. "The others have begun to acknowledge us. They are sending something toward our ship. I estimate it will be here within the hour. It is very small and does not seem to be armed. Shall I take it aboard?"

Splashing echoed in the background, and the sounds of other Gringg conversing provided a pleasant hum; then the smooth, rich voice of the captain came out of the speaker. "Do, please, and inform me when you have it. I'll come down to examine it."

"Captain? Ken Reeve is here," the bosun informed Grace Castleton, "with Captain Kiachif."

"Show them in."

Conversation around the ready room table halted as the bosun stood to one side to allow the two men to enter.

Grace Castleton would have known Reeve anywhere as Todd's father. Both men were rangy and taller than average, with big shoulders and long arms, and both had a cap of smooth black hair cut straight across the forehead over decidedly stubborn features. Ken's hair was somewhat thinner, and there was more gray in it than in Todd's. Lines had been graven by time in his fair-skinned face, but he exuded the same boyish enthusiasm that his son did. With a new adventure arising, years fell away. He might have been the same youthful jack-of-all-trades who had landed on Doona with a handful of tyro colonists more than thirty years ago.

"Hello, friends! Speaker Hrrto, Admiral Barnstable," Ken said, coming over to clasp hands and bow respectfully to the Hrrubans. He pounded companionably on his son's shoulder.

Ken slid into the empty seat beside Hrrestan.

"Well, anything happen while Kiachif and I were on our way up?" He looked around the table, which bore the remains of a recent light meal. "He's filled me in on the discussion. We're still going to make the contact?"

"We'll have to, Dad; they're not making any move," Todd said. "Captain, could we have a rerun of the tapes for my father?"

"I was about to suggest that," she replied and toggled the board for the replay.

Watching the tape with keen eyes, Ken whistled softly as he read the telemetry codes around the image of the ship.

"So we know very little about our friends over there." Ken heard a soft snort but couldn't tell who had it come from. "Not friends?"

"That has yet to be established," Barnstable said in a neutral voice.

"By me," Ken said with a grin.

"By us, Dad," and Todd indicated the other volunteers of the first-contact group.

"Can it be established if they're oxygen-breathers?" Ken asked.

"We'll need to know how to dress for our meeting."

"Can't even establish that, Dad," Todd replied.

"Just like you to volunteer for a blind mission," Ken said in a mock-disgusted tone.

"Begging the captain's pardon," Commander Greene said, watching the codes change on the main viewscreen. "There's data coming through right now."

"Put it up, Commander Greene," said Captain Castleton.

"More data?" Todd asked, startled even as he scanned the new readings. "Where did you get it?"

"From a robot probe," Greene said.

"What?" Todd demanded, sitting angrily upright. "Who authorized the launch?" He stared accusingly at Greene.

"I did," Barnstable replied, his face reddening at Todd's imperious tone. "For the safety of all of us, including our Hrruban allies, I felt it was vital we obtain more information."

"Admiral," Todd said in a restrained tone, "I specifically requested that there be no more probes, drones, or even scans until we were ready to proceed with the first contact."

Barnstable narrowed his eyes to glare at Todd. "Until proven otherwise, this is a Spacedep matter, young man. I am acting in the interest of safety for all the sentient beings on this ship. I don't need your permission to proceed."

"This is Doonan space," Todd said. It made him furious that this bureaucrat would take a unilateral action that might endanger the whole mission. Hrrestan, who hated the high-handedness of Spacedep, would back him up.

"We must not show distrust," Hrriss agreed.

"We do not know if those aboard that vessel arrre worthy of trust," Hrrto reminded him sharply.

"Nor do we know they are not, Speaker," Hrrestan said with equal asperity.

"In any case," Castleton said, raising her voice to put an end to the argument, "the probe only transmitted readings for a short time. They stopped the moment the ship took the probe aboard."

Todd struggled to control his vexation. "It probably stopped sending readings because they disabled it, thinking it might be a bomb."

"If they have not by now discovered its . . . benign"—Greene drawled the adjective, staring at Todd—"purpose, then they're by no means as sophisticated a species as you like to think them." Greene was rather pleased with that shot at the officious Doonarralan. He felt malicious glee at Todd's surprise.

Todd knew he'd been outmaneuvered there, but a soft touch on the back of his arm came as a quiet warning from Ken not to pursue the point. His father, better than anyone else in the galaxy, knew how hard it was to control the infamous Reeve temper, and how much damage it could do when let loose. Normally Todd was in control, but the combination of Spacedep's xenophobia and the unknown potential orbiting his beloved home planet was enough to put him at his worst. He reminded himself that he was one step away from a great adventure, equal to that when his father spotted the first Hrrubans near the earliest settlement over thirty years ago. These narrow-minded people did not, could not, understand the sheer joy of reaching out to another race, joining the far, cold reaches of the galaxy together in friendship. He had to be on that ship first, no matter what. It was a longing as strong as love. He glanced back and nodded at Ken to show he was under control.

"Let's see what the probe did transmit," Castleton said, settling down once more behind the table.

Greene pulled open the hatch over one of the inset consoles. He punched in a code. The view changed to a much closer image of the great ship, which steadily filled more and more of the screen. An overlay of white characters sprang up, constantly changing as the readings altered.

"We deployed a Mark 24-M probe with advanced sensors," Greene calmly announced. "As you can see from the metallurgical report, the alien defense shields are very strong. Most of the inner core of the ship resonates as a power plant. It's well insulated, with main conduits running down the pith of that central pillar. There are power fluctuations that build up from half a megawatt to over five gigawatts. My estimate is that the strangers are prepared to attack with some sort of electrical weapon."

"So far, your assumption about their intentions is speculation," Ken said. "The ship masses heavy. What's in it?"

Greene pointed to the relevant data. "Mostly water."

"Water? You mean H_2O? What kind of beings are there inside?"

"Big. Look at the readings. There's one weighing two hundred thirty kilos."

"Individuals?" Ken asked, amazed. Greene nodded.

Jilamey whistled. "They're as big as Momma Snakes."

"That'd explain the power requirements, if you follow me," Kiachif said. "Maintaining mass gravity for massive beasties."

"Or for quick power-ups on the weapons systems," Greene added.

Todd shook his head in vehement denial.

On the screen, a circular opening appeared in the side of the ship, gleaming silver against the blackness. The little probe's eye moved into it, giving an impression of a vast entry area and a quick view of some kind of computer console, and then the screen went blank.

"That's all there is. As you can see, once it entered the ship, it stopped sending," Greene said. "There is no visual of the inhabitants."

Barnstable rewound the report and started it from the beginning. Stroking his chin, he studied the screen closely. "Wonder what they're using all that water for? Ballast? Weapon storage?"

"Nonssenssse!" said Hrrestan, hissing his sibilants. "This is all speculation. In any case, it isn't a destroyer of any kind. There's no armament to speak of aboard. No irradiation patterns which to me would indicate dangerrrous or powerrrful orrrdnance."

Castleton scratched her cheek thoughtfully. "I'm just as glad they haven't returned our compliment. The *Hamilton's* considered a peaceful ship, but we do have small lasers and missiles. I wonder if they've scanned us telemetrically."

"We prrrove we arre peaceful by ze composition of our landing prrrty," Hrriss said.

"All I hope is they don't think the probe was some kind of threat," Todd said grimly.

"Wish I knew what sort of survival equipment we need," Ken mused aloud.

"May I suggest," Ali Kiachif spoke up helpfully, "the fullest rig and gear the *Hamilton* has to offer?"

Capturing the small unit proved to be no trouble at all, for which the technician was grateful. Like all Gringg, he hated to expend unnecessary effort on any task. The captain, a magnificent female of their species, entered the cargo bay accompanied by her small son, a curious lad of eight Revolutions, and the chief engineer, a female of many Revolutions and much experience. The three of them sat down in a semicircle on the floor near the console. The technician retrieved the little device, hoisting it lightly by one arm. He set it down on the floor and settled opposite the captain.

"I have decontaminated it, but you will be pleased to know that I found no dangerous organic substances on it or within. It makes a noise," the technician pointed out, indicating the subspace receiver on his console. "I believe it to be a message of some sort."

"How kind!" the Gringg captain declared. "Ghollarrgh, I am so relieved to find that these people did not attack us upon sight. Homeworld will be pleased. We must try to answer it, an unprovoking message. They must see us as being completely peaceful. Match the frequency, and we will attempt to translate. Grrala"—she turned to the engineer—"you should try to construct a similar device so that we may send them our compliments in return."

"In time, Captain." The engineer yawned. "In good time. Now, may we see how this little toy works?"

Eager to please, the technician began to display the workings of the ship-sent device.

Aboard the *Hamilton,* the shuttle was being made ready for departure. Todd and Ken were fitted out with tough transparent pressure suits. An attempt was made to find one which would accommodate Hrriss' tail, but nothing could be adapted in the short time allowed. In the end, Hrriss decided to simply stuff the caudal appendage down one pant leg and be done with the problem.

"I'm satisfied," Todd said, fastening the last seal on his suit. "The three of us should be able to handle any situation that comes up—or get out fast if it looks chancy."

"I want some personnel from Spacedep to accompany you," Admiral Barnstable insisted. "This is still a matter under my jurisdiction, whether or not I go along with your interpretation. I've got a couple of volunteers out of Castleton's crew, one from xeno and one from medical. And I'm sending my assistant to be my eyes and ears: Commander Greene."

Todd suppressed his reaction to that unwelcome news. The last thing he needed was the inclusion of a xenophobic Spacedep regular, but he conceded with as good a grace as he could manage. "All right. Have them suit up and meet us in the launch bay."

"Hrruba must also send an observer," said Second Speaker, after a quick conference with Mllaba.

"We've already got a Hrruban in the party," Barnstable said, glowering at Second. "Hrriss."

"I am willing to go," Mllaba announced. "I intend to go," she added.

Todd caught Hrriss' gesture of ears-back, and shook his head. "Six is more than enough for a first-contact team," he said carefully. "More could be considered hostile. In fact, six might be considered too many."

"Will you not trust me, Speaker?" Hrriss asked softly in High Hrruban, seeking to smooth things over before the argument put an end to the mission. "I will uphold Hrruban honor."

Hrrto studied the younger male, who gazed at him earnestly. He grunted. "It is not a matter of trust, Hrriss. I did but think to give you the support of another among all these Hayumans."

"One of them is my brother," Hrriss said, "as well you know."

Hrrto, forgetting his argument with the Hayuman admiral, dropped his jaw in a smile. "I have known this for many years, young Hrriss. Very well, a Hrruban and a half-Hrruban. I simply did not wish Hrruba to be disadvantaged."

"None shall see it that way. They shall believe that only one Hrruban—and a half—is needed to balance out any number of Hayumans," Hrriss said innocently. Behind Second Speaker, he could see Todd and Ken grinning at his quip. They were the only ones who understood the brief conversation.

"I believe it may be so," Second Speaker replied at last. He retired, with Mllaba and Hrrestan, to the reception room beyond the blast doors. Ken gave them a thumbs-up.

"I'd like to go," Jilamey spoke up unexpectedly. "As an independent observer. On behalf of Earth."

Just how much High Hrruban did Jilamey Landreau understand? Todd wondered.

Barnstable glared at Jilamey. Although the young man's uncle was no longer head of Spacedep, the name Landreau was a prestigious one on the human homeworld. Barnstable looked for a moment as if he were about to say no, until he took a closer look at the obstinate expression on the younger man's face. Jilamey himself was not without influence on the Amalgamated Worlds Council. If the Admiral refused him permission, there could be endless small roadblocks for funding in the future, and unfavorable reports in the press about his administration. If he agreed, it might conceivably work out to Spacedep's advantage. In spite of his flamboyant wardrobe and occasionally foolish mien, Jilamey was known for his shrewd and observant mind.

"You're on your own, Mr. Landreau," Barnstable said at last. "Bear in mind that you're vulnerable while on alien ground, and we cannot adequately protect you. But . . . I'll allow it."

"Great! I'm ever so pleased you see it my way." Jilamey patted the Admiral companionably on the back. It was cheek and Jilamey knew it, but Barnstable suffered it expressionlessly. "Now, where can I get a suit?"

*   *   *

"You guys act like you have nothing to lose," the xeno technician said as he suited up in the landing bay, listening to Todd, Ken, Hrriss, and Jilamey all eagerly speculating on what they might find aboard the alien ship.

Like all men raised on Earth, Commander Frill had a soft voice that was currently afflicted with a quaver of fear. His quiet manner of speaking prompted the creation of his nickname, Frail, which he was not. Frill was tall, a bare centimeter shorter than Todd Reeve, with thick, solid arms and a burly chest. He was an All-Spacedep champion wrestler. Neither he nor the medic assigned to the mission seemed to share the sense of exhilaration the Doonarralans felt.

"Wrong, friend," Ken said. "I have everything to gain!" He grinned with unaffected delight at the challenge he was about to face. "My batting average's pretty good in first contact, you know. Lighten up. You're making history. And it could be fun!"

"Fun, he says," the medic observed, checking his gear. Ensign Lauder had been volunteered by his section chief, an honor he clearly would have foregone if he could have thought up a valid pretext. A slender, brown-skinned man with narrow shoulders, Lauder was to run scans, with permission, on who or whatever they met. The rebreather unit on his back was cycling at twice normal speed. He was very young.

"Hey, easy does it," Ken said, laying a kindly hand on the medic's shoulder. "If you want to back out now, no blame'll be attached."

"No, sir!" the medic said, gulping. "I'm no coward." With an effort, he brought himself under control. His respiration slowed, and his face went from flushed ocher to a more normal tawny shade.

"No one said you were, son." Ken smiled.

"If there are no more delays?" Greene asked with a touch of rhetorical sarcasm.

Todd nodded as if the question had been serious and put his clear plastic helmet on his head. Grommets around the neck bolted to the bubble with a final-sounding snap.

"We arrre waiting for you," Hrriss said. His pupils had narrowed to thin slits, and his ears lay slightly back to avoid contact with the headgear.

"Let's go," Todd said.

The shuttle left the lock and dipped slightly below the edge of the bay before the engines engaged fully. Todd felt his insignificant as they left the big ship behind them. Frill, who was flying the craft, nudged the controls to pilot a wide-angle route toward the stranger, approaching with the sun at their back to get the best view.

The leviathan lay before them, huge and black. Todd admired the shape, wondering what sort of naval architects had designed it and why this shape was chosen. Hrriss' eyes glittered in the lights from the console. He must be wondering the same things, Todd decided. What purpose was seized by the irregular bulges along the length of the central core? Ali Kiachif had speculated that the ship had substantial artificial gravity, undoubtedly to help maintain the muscle tone of the massive inhabitants that Commander Greene's probe had revealed. As they drew nearer, Todd was flatly amazed at the incredible size of the vessel. Beside it, they were a pinpoint, a dust mote. Behind him, Commander Frill let out a low moan, and was quickly reprimanded by a shake of the head from Greene.

Todd recognized a thrill of terror underneath his enthusiasm and anticipation. Was this how his father had felt thirty-four years before, when he got his first glimpse of a nonhuman, sentient life form? What if, after all his proud and confident words, the creatures inside this gigantic ship were unfriendly? And what if the "visitors" mistook the purpose of the shuttle and shot at it now that it was getting so close? What if they refused to allow the Doonarralan ship aboard? Well, that only meant his assumptions had been wrong. But he hated to think that Admiral Barnstable and Captain Hrrrv could be right.

As they got closer, more detail became apparent to their unaugmented vision. The surface of the alien ship was not actually black, but a matte-charcoal color that probably repelled certain wavelengths of radiation or light. Spotlights dotted the hull here and there, mostly marking out the place where antenna arrays or access hatches lay. These features were only now visible, Todd noticed. The matte coating provided unusually good camouflage of such details.

The shuttle circled a third of the way around the big ship's central "trunk" until they found what seemed to be an airlock lens, the same one that the probe had approached and entered. Triangular panels pivoted slightly to the left, forming an irislike opening. As Frill resolutely piloted the craft toward the aperture, Todd had the eerie sensation of being swallowed, ingested in one insignificant bite. Smoothly, the tiny shuttle sailed through the enormous circular hatch.

From each of the shuttle ports the passengers stared at the size of the chamber into which they were moving. The landing bay was a virtual cathedral, with shining, metallic walls, at least one hundred meters long—and high. Several craft rested in dry dock inside. Each was at least equal in size to a Spacedep passenger ship. The largest was as big as the administration building that contained Todd's office in the Human First Village. At the far end of the bay was a set of double doors both tall and broad, made of a translucent gray material. Behind a clear window set high in the left wall the party could see a vast console with rounded viewscreens glowing blue. The maintenance equipment and freight-loaders were made for bodies a good deal bigger than any Human or Hrruban. Beside a low console not far from the landing deck Todd noticed a man-sized device with the Spacedep insignia: the missing probe. It was still signalling feebly, its colored lights drowned by the brilliant illumination in the bay. The strangest thing about the control console was that there was no sign of a chair. What were these 230-kilo creatures, giant snails? Frill set the craft down on a lighted circle in the shadow of a ship twice the size of an Alreldep scout. The shuttle touched down with a hollow boom.

"Amazing," Hrriss said, voicing the thought in everyone's mind. "Ourrr hosts must be immenssse."

"Seems like," Jilamey murmured, his mouth hanging open. Ken Reeve just looked around him and grinned in pure joy.

While the party surveyed their surroundings, the airlock wheeled shut behind them, and hissing sounds arose. Greene felt a surge of panic. He was beginning to remember where he'd seen this ship before. It had been on a tape sent to Spacedep by an exploration team. He couldn't recall any details yet, but he associated the memory with violent death. For once, he hoped he didn't remember too many details.

Formless shadows passed back and forth behind the gray glass doors. As soon as the hissing stopped, the medical man checked his sensors. All the passengers checked their suit telemetry.

"G-force is zero point five over Earth normal. What's the atmosphere? Can we breathe in here, Lauder?" Greene asked, his voice hollow in the bubble helmet.

"It's a nitrox mix, plenty of oxygen," Lauder said, carefully reading the sensors in the control panel. "Reads like a class-M combination. I mean, I'd call it safe if we came across it on a planet."

"No trace elements?" Ken asked.

"Some," the medical man admitted, checking his instruments. "Nothing noxious in any concentration. No bacteria known to be harmful to Humans or Hrrubans, at least in this section. I won't give the atmosphere a hundred percent clearance, though, simply because I haven't run a lab analysis on it yet. Keep using the rebreathers."

"So ordered," Greene said with a sharp nod.

"Let's go," Todd said.

Frill released the hatch and he climbed out. The ambient temperature in the bay seemed slightly cool. Ken put part of the chill down to the room's having just been open to vacuum, and his trembling to excitement. The bay was already warming up.

Lauder stepped cautiously onto the deck and avoided the lighted circle. He bent over his scanner. "I wonder if this is what our hosts breathe or if they just made it up for us?"

Hrriss followed the tech. "I wonder where they are," he said, craning his neck to look up at the high ceiling.

A roar sounded over an unseen intercom, startling them all with unintelligible syllables. The shadows behind the door grew denser, darker, larger, giving an impression of vast size.

"That sounds like the overture," Todd said facetiously. "Here come the players."

chapter three

At the end of the hall, the gray glass doors parted and slid soundlessly into the walls. Todd and the others waited, mouths agape, as their hosts entered the landing bay. For all their height and girth, they made little sound when they moved.

"Stars!" whispered Frail, his voice sounding hollow through the sides of his plastic helmet. "Mother always said I'd meet someone bigger'n me."

The first of the aliens to enter, a bulky creature covered except for its face and the pads of its forepaws with thick, long fur of light honey-brown, stood just over two meters in height. Its face had a square muzzle with a black, leathery nose, black-fleshed lips, and two deep-set, eyes the color of red wine protected by thick, smooth-skinned eyelids fringed at the edges with more honey hair. Todd was amazed to see that its facial features were arranged in the same way as a Human's or a Hrruban's.

Its shoulders sloped from a thick neck toward a huge rib cage, and downward over a powerful lower body supported by very short but thick legs. It wore a pouch-laden belt and ornately decorated collar cut from a scaly hide of some kind. Todd thought it resembled snakeskin—but what a snake! If the size of the scales was any clue, it had been equivalent to a Great Big Momma Snake. The alien blinked at the visitors curiously before standing aside to make way for the two other aliens. The being behind it, identical in appearance but black-brown in color, was nearly two and a half meters tall. It too wore a collar, this one more elaborate than the first alien's, consisting of woven strips punched and stamped with complex designs. From one side of the collar depended a loop of decorated hide that circled the upper part of the big alien's arm. Todd wondered if the attachment might serve some specific purpose, concealing miniaturized devices, or was it a mark of rank, or both?

The third alien, of the same dark brown as the tallest being, but with a white patch on the throat that covered part of its chest like a bib, was just over one meter high and wore only a simple belt and collar of scaly leather.

With plenty of hairy fur to protect them from weather, the aliens had as little need for clothing as the smoother-coated Hrrubans. The three moved forward with commendable grace, until they were within ten meters of the party. Then they stopped in a line facing the landing party, regarding their visitors with calm, wine-colored eyes.

At first, Todd was taken aback by their sheer size. These creatures were terrifying, as if animal giants out of a children's story book had come to life. With that thought, their appearance struck Todd as hilariously funny. He felt a childish urge to break into giggles.

"It's the Three Bears!" he whispered under his breath to Hrriss. "I sure hope they don't want me to tell them a story."

"I do not undrrrstand," Hrriss whispered. Inside his helmet, his ears were laid back tight against his round skull.

"Earth fairy tale. They look just like bears, creatures that were found on Earth up to the last century—ugh! Tell you later." He stopped talking as Ken elbowed him in the ribs.

"Shush! You notice? They don't want to appear aggressive," Ken said. He smiled widely at the beings, and let the set of his shoulders hang loosely. "They're waiting for us to close the distance."

"Wait a minute," Greene protested, grabbing Ken's arm. "Consider the size of them!"

"They're friendly," Ken said, calmly taking the man's hand away. "They've brought one of their young along to show us they mean us no harm—in fact, that they trust us. You'd never bring a baby where you intend to be the aggressor, nor where you expect threats."

"That's a baby?" the medic asked, agog.

"It must be," Ken assured them. "Look at the way it's acting."

Todd understood completely what his father meant. The small alien was more awkward than the large ones, and kept looking up at the tallest one for reassurance. "That's his—or her—cub."

"Well, I don't know . . ." Frill murmured, unsure. He swallowed nervously. The medical man stood with his mouth hanging open while his telemetry gear went wild making recordings.

"Keep your mind on the job," Greene said peevishly. "Come along!"

"Yes, Commander," the two navy men replied. The group moved closer to the aliens, and stopped three meters away as the medic faltered once more. The three creatures watched them calmly, waiting.

Ken steeled himself. "I feel inferior, inhibited, and intimidated, as Kiachif would say if he was here. The sheer size of them! One of us has got to take action." He swallowed, and put a hand on Todd's arm. "Well, as the first and most successful xenolinguist in Earth history, we'll see what sense I can make out of whatever noise they make. Wish me luck, boys."

"You can do it, Dad," Todd said firmly. He clasped his father's arm, imparting confidence.

"Find out everything you can about them," Greene added. "Tell them as little as possible about us."

Todd shook his head pityingly at Greene. The man had absolutely no idea how long it took to establish the most superficial linguistic exchange.

Ken opened his arms wide in a gesture he hoped projected friendly intent, and walked right up to the furred trio.

"Greetings, and welcome to the skies of Doonarrala," he said, speaking as cheerfully and enthusiastically as he could, though his heart was pounding in his throat. "We come in peace. We hope you do, too."

Echoing his gesture, the three aliens opened their upper limbs and stretched their flexible muzzles up and back so that their teeth were showing: sharp, white stalactites almost as long as a human hand.

"Fardles! Now, those are fangs!" Jilamey whispered. His face was pale but his eyes glittered in fascination.

"We must be very careful, Captain," the Gringg linguist said, glancing upward at her. He was nervous about the possibility of disease, though he had been assured by the ship's physician that an alien species was unlikely to carry germs that could infect them. Still, he, like all the others aboard, were volunteers. If it cost their lives to discover the truth about this species, so be it. The linguist swept the hold with one more nervous glance, to reassure himself that there was nothing there to discourage these small interesting beings. "One of them approaches. Remember there is certain knowledge we must not reveal yet."

"I know what to do. Is it a female or a male, Eonneh?" Captain

Grzzeearoghh asked, looking Ken up and down curiously. "These creatures are all so skeletal! And so small and weak!"

"It is difficult to know. But since some of them wear garments under those protective shells and some do not, that is clearly the demarcation. The unclad one's body configuration slightly resembles our males, so that must make the tall ones female."

"So they have a female linguist or first speaker," Grzzeearoghh noted. "How interesting. We shall have to converse much on the divisions of labor among gender once we have established communication. But she moves like a Gringg, slowly and carefully. I am glad. I find hurry so disconcerting." The captain raised her head and called out a command that made the aliens at the other end of the hall jump. "Rrawrum? Have you sent the message notifying Homeworld that we have been contacted and are carefully following procedure?"

"I am getting it done now, Captain." Rrawrum's voice echoed overhead in the cargo bay, a little loudly to Grzzeearoghh's thinking. She would have to ask the technician to correct the sound level when she had a moment. It was making their visitors nervous. Every care must be taken to put them at their ease. The strangers should have no cause to view them as a threat. *My cub should help to reassure these small aliens,* the captain thought.

"Tell them also that we are beginning contact."

"As you wish, Captain."

"Mama," Weddeerogh interrupted, as Ken stopped a meter away. "What is she doing?"

"She is identifying herself, I think," the Captain said, patting her cub on the head. "A pity their voices are so soft. I was not paying attention!"

Ken activated the recording unit at his side and put his hands to his chest. "My name is Ken Reeve. Ken Reeve." He extended one hand slowly toward the largest "bear," and pointed. "And you?" He gave the words the strongest interrogative tone he could.

The massive head swung toward him, and the rubbery lips receded behind the teeth again in a passable reflection of the Human's smile. Ken was impressed by the flexibility of the aliens' faces, and their ability to imitate expressions. Todd was right: they did possess a superficial resemblance to Earth bears. Their coloring, shape, and musculature were very much like that of the ancient species Ursa. They seemed to be made for defense, armed with heavy claws and a thick, loose skin. And they were so unconsciously powerful. If they proved to be unfriendly, they could tear him apart without trouble. The likeness to bears was not exact, of course. These beings had tails about the length and thickness of his forearm, covered with shaggy hair. What purpose did the appendages serve? Balance? Defense?

He studied the faces closely. They had been growling among themselves. He had clearly heard distinguishable syllables, some of them repeated. The creatures had long, agile tongues, suitable for pronouncing the complexities of a well-developed language. It was disconcerting to stand next to beings who made him feel so insignificantly small, like a child among giants.

The aliens must have sensed his discomfiture, for all three rolled back off their feet and onto their tailbones. It was a graceful gesture, ending with the body being braced solidly with hunched-up rear legs and outspread tail. Their lower limbs were short in comparison to the length of the body, but they were heavy and solid, made for balance, not speed.

"I am Ken Reeve," he said again, pointing to himself as he hunkered down in his best approximation of their new posture. He wondered if he should ask Hrriss to display his tail. "And you?" He extended his hand toward them.

The largest of the aliens roared again, and waved a thick claw at him, turning it palm down and drawing it from the floor up to its head. Seeing that he didn't understand, it levelled out the claw at its eye, and drew an invisible line out toward Ken.

"What are they doing, Dad?" Todd demanded.

He smiled, delighted. "Oh, I get you. You're trying to equalize things. They want me to remain standing up, so that we're all at eye level," he said over his shoulder. "Ken Reeve," he indicated once more to the aliens.

"Grzzeearoghh," the largest replied slowly and carefully in its basso profundo voice. It sounded like the revving of an engine.

"Errizz-eer-oh?" Ken repeated uncertainly, trying to duplicate the growl.

"Grzzeearoghh," the large one said complacently, wrapping its forepaws over its belly.

The gesture made it look even more like the holos of Earth bears, and Todd suppressed a chuckle. Hrriss shuddered, his ears halfway back.

"Their voices make me uncomfortable," he said in Low Hrruban. "Do they always speak at such volume? Spoken so loudly, the deep notes reverberate harshly on my ear bones." He shook his head as if to relieve the pressure. "Hrrubans do not raise their voices unless they wish to attract attention or if they are angry. Could we have made them angry?"

"How could we? I don't think they're upset, or they wouldn't be looking so comfortable," Todd said. "And with the size of those rib cages, I'd be surprised if they spoke in soprano voices."

Ken tried the alien's multisyllabic name over and over again, until the large one smiled at him. "I think I've got it, chaps," he called. "Meet Grzzeearoghh. Looks like he's in charge here."

Todd and Hrriss cheered. The aliens looked surprised but not displeased at the noise, regarding their visitors with polite curiosity. Beside Todd, the Spacedep men seemed to be making themselves as insignificant as possible, except Greene, who stood boldly pointing his recorder at the aliens. Jilamey was taking in the whole situation with awed joy.

"We're communicating already! It's too fascinating!"

Grinning at Landreau's genuine enthusiasm, Ken pointed at the medium bear. "Who?"

While he was learning the complexities of pronouncing "Eonneh," the cub rolled off its haunches and waddled toward him.

"Look out!" shrieked Lauder, backing away. The young medic's face was pale.

"What for?" Ken asked, breaking off his language lesson. "Hi, there, fella," he said as the cub bent to sniff his shoes. While he waited patiently, the cub ran its shiny black nose up his suit leg, sneezing briefly as the acrid stench of the transparent plastic tickled its nasal passages. But it continued its olfactory examination, shoving its nose into Ken's armpit and down his arm to his gloved hand. It sneezed again. Ken threw a shrug back toward his party. The cub meant him no harm. It was only curious, like any youngster. When they all unsuited, the bears were likely to get a few aromatic surprises.

The cub threw both of its heavy upper paws up onto Ken's shoulders and dragged his face down so that it could look at him. It seemed puzzled by the helmet. Ken rapped on the plastic bell with a fist, then waggled his head back and forth inside, trying to show that it was an artificial covering. The cub let out a series of pleased grunts that sounded like stentorian giggles, and let go of him. Ken hunkered down and extended his hand. The youngster sniffed it and squealed. He noticed that the black nostrils of the other two were twitching, but more discreetly. Scent must be important to them; a fact worth noting. The trouble was that humans did not smell like plastic suiting.

"You're a real sweet little critter. What's your name?" Ken asked the delighted cub. "Ken Reeve," he said, carefully enunciating the two syllables as he pointed to himself. "You?" he asked, pointing to the cub.

"Weddeerogh," said the youngster in an unexpected baritone, then scooted shyly back behind the largest alien.

"Aw," Jilamey said. "Acts just like a kid, too."

"I guess," Frill said, finding his voice at last. "If you like kids that big."

"Gringg," the biggest one said suddenly, indicating itself and the two others. "Gringg."

"Gringg?" Ken asked. "Grr-ing?"

"Reh." The big alien tilted its head to one side and let out a short grunt. Ken fancied it gave him a look of approval.

"Hayuman," he said, pointing to himself. "Hayuman."

"Ayoomnnn."

"Good." He walked over to stand beside Hrriss. "Hrruban."

The red eyes followed him carefully. "Rrrrrooobvvnnn," Grzzeearoghh said, growling the *r*'s rather than rolling them as a Hrruban would.

"Close," Ken said approvingly. "Good for you, little fellah. And we're all Doonarralans." He gave the leader a big nod and a smile, which it copied, as he indicated Todd, Hrriss, and himself. "Well, now we know what we all are. Let's start on things." He knelt down, and patted the floor. "What do you call this?" Ken asked the big bear. "We call it *rllama*. Rllama."

"What are you doing, teaching it Hrruban?" Frill demanded, indignant. "You should teach it Terran."

"One language at a time," Ken warned him. "We need a lingua franca, and both of *our* peoples speak Middle Hrruban. The Gringg can learn the niceties of Terran and High Hrruban once they've mastered this one. Now pipe down, unless you want to do this for me?"

"No, I sure don't," Frill said quickly, backing off.

"Urrrlllah. Ma," the alien intoned.

"We're making progress. Rllama," Ken said, rolling the *r,* and keeping his mouth wide open so it could see the way he rolled his tongue. The little one watched him from the shelter of its parent's body, trying to match his facial expressions and rolling its long tongue. Ken laughed.

"Do you know, I think I'm the first sentient alien they've ever encountered."

"How can you make an assumption like that, Reeve?" Greene demanded. He looked slightly sick.

"This all seems to be new to them," Ken replied. "They're not acting as if they're anticipating what I'm going to do. And I think they're enjoying it."

"Weddeerogh, you have no need to be shy," Grzzeearoghh said, turning her head over her shoulder to beam at her offspring. "This is becoming most interesting. Will you go and get writing materials for us? Now we are starting to work with vocabulary, I don't want to miss anything. This is a very important moment in Gringg history."

"Yes, Mama," the cub said, with one more peek at Ken. "What funny hands she has, with no claws. I do not like the smell of that stuff she wears. I would like to smell her. I hope her own skin smells better."

"She wears a protective covering, showing concern for our health and hers. I admire that," Grzzeearoghh said. "I did not know what to expect from another race, certainly not such scrupulous consideration. And we know we must act with caution. Now, please go."

"Yes, Mama." On all fours, the cub scurried toward the doors, which opened and closed behind him.

"Rllama," the strange female said.

"Rrrllahma," Grzzeearoghh intoned. Her pronunciation seemed to delight the visitor. "I do believe we are getting somewhere. Good! I wish the female's friends were more calm. One of the females and the male seem quite at home, but I think those others may faint. And that female with its limb stuck out holding the little device seems most uncomfortable."

"I must confess to a certain amount of nervousness, too, Captain," Eonneh admitted. "They are a feeble-looking race, are they not? No fur to speak of. I am almost afraid to move for fear of hurting them. We have all been shown how important it is to give the appearance of being no threat to any new race we encounter. And such amazing dimorphism between sexes. You'd think they were almost separate species. When the male speaks, his voice is so shrill it hurts my ears."

"Here it is, Mama," Weddeerogh said, galloping in through the blast doors with a tablet and stylus in his paw.

"Good, dear. Give it to Eonneh. Write this down, Eonneh. Their word for floor is 'rrrllama.' "

The Gringg male put the pad of thin but solid tiles down between his feet and hooked the two loops of the stylus over the first and second claws of his right upper paw. He sounded out the word to himself carefully before beginning to inscribe it. In Gringg culture, writing anything down with a living hand made it official. Gringg males made the best record-keepers, poets, librarians, even artists; they also mastered the theoretical sciences to forward development. Eonneh was unusually skilled in all the arts, and was considered a credit to his gender, though he was too modest to allow such compliments to his face. The females, larger by ten to thirty percent, organized, and exercised the practical arts, such as all forms of engineering, and tended to take the lead in exploration. In Eonneh's opinion, Grzzeearoghh was an excellent captain, and was handling the situation perfectly. The World Congress which chose her as their envoy to any possible sentients had made the best possible choice.

As the alien female looked on with interest, Eonneh made the characters for a short growl, followed by a lingual extension, then a nasal hum. The accents that went above and below the characters indicated the subordinate vowel sounds.

*   *   *

"I'm enjoying this," Ken said, coming close to the scribe for a good look at what Eonneh was doing. "Their written language is beautiful: a minor work of art if this is any sample. Nothing from even ancient Terran civilizations comes close to it." Showing his camera first to the two adult Gringg, he walked around and pointed it down at the pad to record the scribe's work. "I think he's trying to get it down in a phonetic fashion. That's what I'd do. Well—" He snapped another shot. "This is their attempt at 'floor.'"

"Can you tell how they phoneticize, Dad?" Todd asked.

"Hardly," Ken said with a laugh. "Not after just one word. It's going to take a while to get anywhere useful."

"Don't worry," Hrriss assured him. "Our hosts have settled in for the linguistic siege."

Eonneh scribed busily at the big pad, with Jilamey behind him to watch how the handscript was made. The pen contained free-flowing ink that the scribe carefully controlled to make thick and thin strokes on the smooth surface of the tile. Landreau was clearly impressed by the skill required, for each pictograph was complex and beautiful.

"What's that?" he asked, pointing down at the character that Eonneh was patiently drawing. "Er, how do you say it? *Aaah? Bbbb?*"

"Vv."

"And that little one?" Jilamey moved his finger to a mark like an accent that went over the top right corner of the squarish character.

"Ooo," Eonneh said carefully, glancing up over his shoulder at the Ayoomnnn.

"Really? This must be the way you spell 'Hrruban,'" Jilamey replied. "And that?" He indicated another mark, this time set below and to the side of one of the elaborate pictographs.

"Hhhh."

"That's not a vowel," he protested.

"That's an aspirate," Ken said, coming over to look. "So the different notations are divided into hard consonant sounds and vowels? Good job, Landreau."

"Huh?" Jilamey frowned in query.

"Is it all like this?" Ken said to Grzzeearoghh, pantomiming the handwritten panel onto the nearest round screen.

"Be careful, Reeve," Greene called. He felt down his hip for his side arm, and remembered with regret that it had been left behind on the *Hamilton*. If these gigantic aliens got out of control, he had nothing but his skills at unarmed combat with which to protect the Human of the party.

The captain rose to her full height and padded over to the console. "The skinny Ayoomnnn female is both intelligent and curious," she told Eonneh. "See this, Genhh Rhev," she said, pulling up a textfile on the screen.

Ken, recognizing the slightly mangled pronunciation of his name, followed her to the console. As he watched, fascinated, the computer laid down lines of the complicated characters first, followed by the small marks above and below the lines. As Grzzeearoghh sounded it out slowly to him, he realized his guess was right.

"They're going to be a little confused by written Terran," Ken noted. "If they're used to aspirates and vowels as separate notation, it's going to take them a while to get used to seeing the characters all the same size and on the same line. It'll be interesting to see how quickly they cope with such a difference."

"It's primitive," Greene said dismissively. "Inscribing information by hand is slow and inefficient. Technology like this must be a fluke."

"Oh, I don't think so, Commander," Jilamey said from his post behind Eonneh. "Even on Earth, the ancient art of calligraphy is still practiced and held in esteem. It seems perfectly normal to me. I spend a lot of time in the Artists' Corridor, where there's a good deal of reverence for the old forms."

Greene snorted. "You can't attribute Human characteristics to aliens who may turn out to be dangerously barbaric."

"I wish this could go faster," Ken said, sighing, as he studied the round screen. "It could take us an age to put together a working vocabulary." He went over a number of items in the bay, asking for the aliens' words, and giving them the Middle Hrruban equivalents.

"And what's this?" he asked, pointing at the Spacedep shuttle.

"Va'arrel," said Grzzeearoghh.

"Va'arrel?"

"Reh."

"Good," Ken said. "Well, what do you call the big ship?" He gestured in a wide circle, indicating the vessel around them. The big alien followed his hand with its eyes.

"Va'arrel," the Gringg repeated.

"This is the same? Va'arrel?" Ken pointed at the shuttle. "Va'arrel?" He circled his arm.

Grzzeearoghh seemed to be listening carefully for something, and was mildly disappointed not to hear it. The alien shook its large head from side to side. "Va'arrel."

"But that's what I said," Ken insisted. "What am I missing? Va'arrel," he said again, pointing to the shuttle. The alien sat back with paws folded. "Va'arrel."

"Morra," the Gringg corrected him. "Va'arrel."

"There is no difference," Frill complained.

"Wait a second," Ken said. "I thought I got a sense of something there. It's possible I'm not capable of hearing the difference between two similar sounding words, and yet there is one, isn't there, old fellow?"

The dark-red eyes were sympathetic but encouraging. Ken grinned. "Your voices go so far down I wonder if you're dropping past the registers that we Hayumans can hear. Or perhaps it's a somatic element I'm missing. Of course, I could just plain be pronouncing it wrong. Only practice will help with that. Let's collect some more examples of Gringg speech to take home with us."

To speed things up, Todd and Hrriss volunteered to work with the other Gringg to teach one another vocabulary, leaving them with plenty of data when the Doona party finally left.

Ken, with the loudest voice, found himself talking to Grizz, as he nicknamed the Gringg captain. The big alien approved the shorter form with a dropped jaw and a discernible twinkle in its eye. In its slightly nasal voice, the elder Reeve's name came out as *Genhh*.

Eonneh, Hrriss, and Dodh, as the Gringg pronounced Todd's name, were already working out the pronunciation of more words, and writing them down on the pad. Frill, who was beginning to become interested in spite of his initial apprehensions, hung over their shoulders, kibitzing. The navy medic, still nervous but growing bolder, circled around. Greene maintained his distance, making the occasional comment into his recorder, still prepared to defend himself if necessary. Jilamey hunkered down on the floor in front of the cub, with his knees akimbo.

"Hi there, little guy. I'm Jilamey."

"Chilmeh!" the cub echoed happily, and reached out to push the Human's knee companionably. Jilamey pushed back, and found himself rolling over the floor in the crowing Gringg's powerful embrace. His helmet hit the ground with a clonk.

Greene ran after them and interposed himself, on guard, between the alien and the Human. The largest of the Gringg tensed, watching carefully.

"Be careful, Landreau," Greene cautioned the younger man, who lay gasping and breathless with laughter on the deck. With one arm, he pulled Landreau to his feet. "You have no idea what your actions may mean to these aliens."

"Aw, he's playing, Commander," Landreau said. The cub's tail swished from side to side like that of a large dog, and Jilamey ruffled the fur between its ears.

"It'll think you're a child, too."

Jilamey pouted. "Oh, don't ascribe Hayuman assumptions to him, Commander. We're learning a lot about each other, aren't we?" he said to Weddeerogh, who blinked shyly at Greene.

"I'd like to bring some of these fellows home with us," Ken said to the navy medic, "but I'm afraid they might not survive on Doona. We don't know anything about their physiognomy, nor they ours. What are your impressions?"

"I wish I could get some samples of skin, blood, and hair," Lauder replied. "I could tell you a lot more if I could do microscopic analyses."

"When we can speak a little more of their language, we'll ask," Ken said. "It's presumptuous to try before they can understand just exactly what we want. And why." He turned to Frill, whose attention seemed to be wandering. "How about you? Any ideas?"

"Sorry, sir," Frill said, reddening slightly. "My stomach's rumbling. I, uh, couldn't eat before we left. Hope they don't misconstrue the sound."

Ken smacked him on the back. "Good idea. Food! We'll offer them some of our rations, let them analyze them, see if our food's safe for their insides. There's got to be emergency packs in the shuttle."

"There should be, Dad," Todd said, "if it was stocked according to regulations."

"Naturally the shuttle was prepared according to regulations," Frill said, regarding father and son with horror. "You're not proposing to give them our food, are you?"

"Why not?" Ken asked reasonably. "It will give them an idea if our biosphere is compatible with theirs. They appear to be carnivorous, with those teeth—maybe even omnivorous. Be interesting to see if their comestibles are at all similar to ours."

During this discussion the Gringg withdrew to have a conference of their own.

"Our visitors seem willing both to teach and learn," Grizz said thoughtfully. "I feel it is safe to risk the second step. Move slowly and give them no cause for suspicion."

"As you wish, Captain," Eonneh replied, watching Genhh Rheu expostulating with the rest of her party. "I'll go get what is required." Grizz shouldered him companionably as he left the room.

"Go quickly, my mate. If this works out as we hope, you'll have plenty of material for an epic poem, with yourself as the hero!"

Todd, Hrriss, and Commander Frill went back to the shuttle. According to Spacedep regs, emergency gear, including "rations ready to eat," or RRE's, were always kept in a locker beneath the co-pilot's couch. The ring latches securing the cubby door were frequently stiff, but a quick twist and tug by the powerful Frill opened the door without trouble.

"Don't give it all to them," Frill asked, eyeing the RRE's as Todd stacked them into a heap. "Leave me one, won't you?"

"You won't faint dead away on us, will you, Frail?" Todd grinned, and got an answering smile from the Spacedep officer.

"Not now," Frill answered, a little sheepishly. "Not as long as I get something to eat."

"Don't worry," Todd said with complete understanding. "I'm a big feeder myself. You can be the one to taste it in front of them so they can see that we warrant this food as safe." Willingly, Frill picked out his favorite from the sealed packs, and split up the rest to carry between himself and Hrriss.

"Todd," Ken called as they emerged from the shuttle. "Our friends here had the same idea."

Todd grinned. Piled high between Ken and Grizz was a quantity of wrapped and unwrapped goods. Eonneh and another medium-sized bear, whose coat was colored a dark, dusty cocoa, had Ensign Lauder by the console, showing him a program that displayed changing views of complex designs that Todd couldn't distinguish from where he stood. As he closed the distance, he imagined that he recognized the designs.

"You know, if those were on our computers," he suggested, "I'd think they were molecular diagrams. But of what?"

"The proteins, or whatever's in these goods?" Ken asked. He pantomimed to Grizz, pointing to the items on the floor and back again at the screen. "Is that the substance of this?" The big ursine roared softly, a triumphant sound. "I guess that's what he said."

"Reh!" Grizz acknowledged, crossing huge paws across his chest once more.

"How about it?" Todd asked Lauder. "Would a molecule like that be safe for Hayumans and Hrrubans to eat?"

"No doubt about it," Lauder replied, showing him his pad screen. "It's a common protein chain. The others are complex carbohydrates, pretty similar to stuff we eat. It's strange, because their digestive systems are very different from either of our two races."

Greene frowned. "In what way?"

"More efficient, I'd say. My scans, though I can't absolutely warrant the accuracy on alien biosystems, pick up a kind of 'afterburner' below the stomach, just after the pyloric valve. Well, that's what it'd be on one of us. For their size, I bet one of them doesn't eat much more than one of us does."

"Speak for yourself," muttered Frill, disconcerted.

Todd slapped him on the back and escorted him to the Gringg leader. "Now, Commander, you want to demonstrate the purity and deliciousness of one of our RRE's for our hosts here?" he asked. Collecting a nod from Frill, he and Hrriss placed their armloads of packages in front of Grizz, next to the heaps of Gringg offerings. "These are examples of our food. We're giving them to you for your examination. First, we'll eat a sample." He accompanied his speech with pantomime, which he hoped was comprehensible to the aliens.

As the Gringg watched with interest, Frill eagerly tore open the pressed-plastic packet, then looked dismayed as the difficulty became obvious.

"The helmet," he said, glancing at Todd for help. "How'm I going to eat wearing a helmet?"

Todd and Hrriss looked at each other and then at Ken.

"Well, one of us is going to unseal sooner or later," Todd said. He attacked the grommets around the base of his helmet, twisting the fastenings loose.

Greene sprang forward and grabbed his wrist. "What do you think you're doing, Reeve? Attempting suicide? If you choose to take foolish risks, I can recommend to Lauder here that we have you brought back to the cruiser in restraints to wait until a psychiatrist sees you."

"I never take foolish risks," Todd said. He shook off the man's hand. "The ensign here has already told us that if he encountered an atmosphere like this one planetside, he'd consider it safe. Isn't that right, Ensign?"

Lauder, not eager to get into the middle of a battle between a renowned planetary leader and a formidable ranking officer, quickly nodded his head. Encouraged by Todd's friendly smile, he added very timidly, "I'd think we were lucky, too, if the air on the *Hamilton* was this fresh, Commander." The medic swallowed hard as Greene turned his stare upon him, but he didn't recant.

"Therefore I consider the odds very much in my favor." Todd unfastened the plastic bubble and took it off. In the same instant, Hrriss removed his own headgear, and both took a deep breath. There was a murmur of approval from the Gringg. Todd almost choked with nervousness as the warm air hit his lungs. The two of them waited, watching each other for signs of anoxia, wondering if they had made a mistake, each ready to slap the helmets back on.

One minute, two minutes, passed. There was no sound in the landing bay except for a mechanized hum deep in the heart of the giant ship. Todd could almost hear the sweat trickling down his back. It was hard to believe that only a couple of hours ago he had been sitting at the head of a tableful of voracious and self-seeking delegates who intended to ruin a special part of his planet to satisfy trade requirements. If he guessed wrong, if the data that the young medic had been carefully monitoring was incorrect, he could be about to die. Todd felt with every nerve-ending the touch of moving air on his skin. It was pleasantly warm. His lungs dragged it in and pushed it out. It took more of an effort than breathing usually did, but he was in a slightly heavier gravity than what he was used to. He was consciously tasting each breath for poisons, but there was only the cloying smell of recycled air and a musky, not unpleasant aroma, probably exuded by the Gringg.

He felt lightheaded. What was it they said? That after five minutes without oxygen one became irreversibly brain dead? Everyone was looking at them, expecting a reaction of some kind. Hrriss's nostrils twitched, and his ears swivelled forward expectantly. Todd suddenly realized that he was holding his breath. If there'd been enough oxygen to sustain him for the last five minutes, the next breath should be fine, too. With a halfhearted laugh, he let go and sucked in a deep lungful of air. Nothing adverse had happened. He was alive. Hrriss was alive. They and the Gringg breathed the same sort of air.

"It's all right." Todd nodded at his friend, and they fell into one another's arms. "Go ahead, Frill," Todd said, as he and Hrriss pounded each other on the back in relief. Ken Reeve was smiling. "Lauder is right. Our atmospheres are at least compatible."

"So they could live on our worlds, if they disposed of us," Greene said, his eyes cold.

"Enough of that, Greene!" Todd said firmly. "There are no indications whatsoever that these creatures are aggressive. On the contrary, in fact! May Commander Frill assist me now with a food demonstration?"

Grudgingly, Greene gave the order. Frill saluted and began to undo the helmet fastenings.

Watching Todd and Hrriss all the while, the big Spacedep officer lifted off his helmet and put it on the floor beside him. He, too, took a few tentative breaths before relaxing.

"It's real air!" he said simply, a grin spreading over his big face.

"This'll cause speculation among the scientists," Ken said. "Are all spacefaring races oxygen-breathers? Or do oxy-breathers tend to be pacific? There's a theory in there someplace." He took off his helmet, then peeled off his gloves. The baby Gringg toddled toward him again, this time chortling joyfully to itself that Genhh now exuded a totally different, and much more preferable scent— one compounded of many subtle smells. Ken was sniffed over from toe to crotch to pate.

With no hesitation, Jilamey removed his helmet. Timidly, with a glance at Greene for permission, Lauder opened his a crack, testing the air against what was in his rebreathers. Only Greene remained sealed in his protective gear, like a disapproving robot glaring at the others.

The Gringg, too, seemed to be happy with the removals, grunting low, pleased sounds to themselves, though only the littlest one made tactile, and nasal, contact.

As the Gringg watched with considerable interest, Frill consumed an RRE. He tore mouthfuls away from the bar of compressed protein, chewed, and swallowed them. The carbohydrate wafer crunched loudly in the metal-walled room, and the packet of fruit conserve went down with a slurp or two.

"Uh, see?" the officer said, twisting the packets into a little ball and tucking them into the empty box, a little uncomfortable to have his greed witnessed by such a crowd. "That's good food. Not as good as fresh, but okay."

"O-kaayy," Grizz echoed the word.

Todd thought that the big alien understood. It signalled to Eonneh, who undid one of the sausage-shaped packets and ate the contents, patting his chest to indicate satisfaction when he had finished. Todd caught a whiff of his scent. Not too bad, he thought. It smelled a little like smoked snake.

"Here, try this one," Todd said, pushing aside containers of tuna fish, Doona snake, bean curd, turkey, and cheese, to open one of his favorites. It was popcorn, in a self-heating hemispherical container. Cautioning the Gringg not to touch, he pulled the seal. The disk-shaped base started to glow. In a few seconds, the whole unit began to shake. Weddeerogh jumped, letting out a squeal of surprise, then hunkering down, getting as close as it dared to the twitching and bulging package. Todd grinned. Popcorn was not only food, but entertainment. Grizz watched more calmly while the silver dome unit expanded one pop at a time, until it had reached four times its original size. A small red spot appeared on the top of the dome, signalling that it was through cooking. Todd burst open the thin covering and took a handful of popcorn.

"See? This is really good." He ate it piece by piece, crunching each between his teeth with obvious satisfaction.

"Goo-ood." Using its long claws, the Gringg picked up a single puffed kernel and looked at it, a giant examining a grain of sand. Then it indicated to Ken that he should take the other Gringg rations, and sat, continuing to study the fluffy morsel of corn.

"Great," Ken exclaimed, collecting the bundles and putting some of them in his equipment pouch. Lauder, his hands shaking slightly, picked up an armload of the supplies and stowed them in his equipment carryall. "Thank you, Grizz. We'll be happy to take these. Soon as we have a good close look, we'll know if it's safe for you to come back with us." He bowed to Grizz and nodded to the others. "Thank you for letting us visit. We'd better get back, boys. The Admiral and the others will be going spare wondering what happened to keep us so long."

"One more thing," Greene said quickly, planting a hand on Ken's shoulder.

"Tell them they've got to keep their ship in this orbit. If they move, we'll consider that an act of hostility, and we will attack."

"Now, how do you expect me to explain that to them?" Ken demanded, fed up with the Spacedep commander acting the eternal wet blanket. "I don't even know how to say 'how are you?' much less 'stay put.' "

"Oh, draw them a picture," Jilamey said impatiently. He knelt down beside Eonneh and held out a hand toward the Gringg's two-finger stylus. "Can I borrow that?"

Surprised, the honey-colored alien put the drawing implement in his hand and pushed the tablet toward him. Jilamey whistled at the weight of the instrument, then fitted his fingers into the twinned loops. He drew a little circle on his hand with the point, and smiled up at Greene.

"Now, what kind of orbit do you want them to stay in?"

Glancing at the Admiral's aide for permission, Commander Frill slumped down beside Jilamey, and looked up at the Gringg captain. "Draw Doona there," he said to Jilamey, indicating the center of a blank tablet page. "Now, draw a big circle around it, far out, beyond the moons—better draw in the moons—and put their ship on the big circle. Boy, this is undignified," he complained, looking up at Ken.

"Go on," Ken encouraged him. "You're doing fine."

"Well," Frill said, showing the tablet to Grizz. "This," he said, following the circle around the planet, "is good. Uh—This"—he took the stylus from Jilamey and drew a tangential line leading away from the circle with an arrow—"er, is bad." He crossed out the line. "This is bad, too." Red to the ears, he drew in another tangent, this one leading inward toward Doonarrala, and crossed it out. "Do you understand? Stay on this orbit." His finger traced the circle around and around.

"Reh!" Grizz said, following his gesture. "Orrrbitttt. Nggh yaahrr mmm-monnya." The Gringg showed a mouthful of long white teeth and black gums to indicate comprehension.

"Well done, Frill. Satisfied?" Ken asked Greene. "Again, Captain Grizz, our compliments. Until we meet again?" He bowed and turned away. Together, the party walked back toward the Spacedep shuttle.

For big creatures, the Gringg could move surprisingly fast. Eonneh and the strange bear who had brought in the Gringg rations waddled swiftly past them, and stood by the shuttle. The party stared at them, their initial fears returning.

"Now what is this?" Greene demanded, stopping at a distance from the ship. He felt again for his side arm and cursed Todd Reeve's insistence on coming unarmed. "Are they preventing us from leaving? Are we prisoners?"

"Eonneh gerrvah," the light-brown Gringg said, and indicated its companion. "Ghotyakh gerrvah aui'd." The other, its rubbery mouth drawn back in the imitation of a human smile, waved at them and set a gentle paw down on the top of the shuttle.

"Quite the opposite," Ken suggested, eyeing this gesture with amusement. Ghotyakh must be an engineer, if he pats spaceships like ponies. "I think they want to come with us as emissaries."

"Impossible!" Greene was alarmed at the thought of Gringg loose on a Spacedep ship, or amuck in the colony itself.

"Not at all." Ken glanced back at Grizz, who raised a giant snout in their direction. The intelligent, red-brown eyes were calm. "They're showing that they trust us."

"They could die from exposure to toxins or bacteria on Doona."

Ken shook his head. "Obviously, Commander, they're willing to take that chance. That's something they need to learn from us, too: if both species can exist in the same biosphere. And I get the impression that if we don't take them, we don't leave."

Jilamey blinked. "Who do we leave behind as volunteers? As our ambassadors?"

Ken grinned pointedly at his son. "Any volunteers?"

"Hrriss and I will stay," Todd said quickly, barely beating out Hrriss' call to remain.

"We are the logical choices," the Hrruban agreed. "We already serve the diplomatic arm for both Hrruba and Earrth, as well as Doonarrala."

"Wish I had your background in languages, Dad," Todd said, "but I think we'll get along."

"I have all the faith in the galaxy in you two," Ken said, and his eyes twinkled. "Good luck."

Hrriss and Todd shook hands in turn with Ken, Jilamey, and the two Spacedep officers. Greene continued to look disapproving.

"You should return to the cruiser with us."

"Not a good idea," Todd said promptly. "The Gringg have trusted us with two of their people. They might take it amiss if we don't reciprocate. Remember, it's their initiative."

"We shouldn't take them aboard, not until the Admiral has cleared such an important decision."

"Spacedep isn't involved in this aspect of the encounter, Commander. Alreldep is!" Todd told him. "Hrriss and I are Alien Relations. Report that to the Admiral."

*   *   *

"Two of our new friends are staying with us," Grizz said contentedly, watching Dodh and Rrss stand by as the other Ayoomnnns entered their fragile little vessel. "We have much to ask them. Go in peace," she called.

"Errrrungh!" The cub called out his farewell to his new friends before the shuttle door closed.

"Goodbye!" Ken called back, waving.

The cub let out squeals of glee. "Errrrungh! Gggbyyy!"

Just then the comunit in Todd's helmet began to crackle. Todd picked it up and held it close enough to hear any message.

"Frill here, Reeve. If you can hear me, nod." Todd obediently nodded. "We'll keep sending on our way back to the *Hamilton*. Give some answer as long as you hear us. Okay?" Todd nodded. "If we can't stay in touch, we'll come back for you in twenty-four hours!"

Todd nodded vigorously, relieved.

The last sight Ken had of his son and the Hrruban who was nearly his second son was the two of them disappearing behind the gray glass doors with the dark-furred aliens. For a moment Ken was afraid, wondering if he had made a mistake leaving them behind.

It was a tight fit in the cabin with the two huge Gringg each spreading across two couches intended for one Human-size body. They were muttering excitedly to one another, their intelligent eyes scrutinizing all elements of the interior of the shuttle. Ken smiled to himself. The Gringg captain was probably having the same misgivings about sending two of his people with them.

"Good luck, son," he said quietly as Frill lifted off the little shuttle from the launch circle.

chapter four

Commander Frill got a certain amount of perverse pleasure opening a communications channel to the hovering Spacedep flagship and giving his message.

"Exploration shuttle returning at 1815 hours shiptime with two aliens aboard. Please inform the Admiral we will be with you by 1847. Frill out." That'll bring 'em running, he thought.

Out of the corner of his eye, Frill could see the colonist in the co-pilot's chair grinning like a fool. Frill had to admit he felt the same elation. They'd gone out on a dangerous mission and had returned not only intact, but in the company of two members of a new species. Although at first the assignment had made him nervous, Frill was grateful that Castleton had selected him. The aliens'd be well worth getting to know. For all his xeno training, he'd never had contact with any other species—apart from the Hrrubans, of course—that was sentient, let alone so eager to cooperate. Humanity deliberately avoided contact with intelligent extraterrestrials, lest such encounters result in a disaster like the Siwannese Tragedy. Despite his excitement, Frill was grateful that two of the smaller specimens had been sent. The giant ones were going to take a lot of getting used to.

The two Gringg were silent until the shuttle was inside the *Hamilton's* landing-bay doors, then began quietly muttering between themselves. Commenting on the differences? Frill wondered. The Spacedep bay walls were enam-elled a spanking-clean white and stencilled with the Spacedep logo, and every-thing was smaller. A lot smaller. When he considered the size of the Gringg themselves, the volume of their ship wasn't so extraordinary. They needed a lot of head and elbow room.

Personnel in the Spacedep shuttle bay were fully clad in protective suits, and the board was showing full Red Alert. Frill thought that was rather overdoing se-curity measures. If he had reported that they were under duress, or had given the covert danger code, it would have been appropriate. He had to remind him-self that he had just spent a few hours on an alien vessel, and that those who re-mained aboard ship had no idea what the visiting party had experienced. He grinned again.

Setting down the shuttle smoothly, Frill began to switch off systems and run over the cross-check list, ably assisted by Ken Reeve.

Outside the small ship, a security force had been deployed. Marines, armed with powerful slug-throwing and laser weapons, hurried into a line surround-ing the craft and knelt, waiting for the aliens to emerge. Behind the glass doors separating the bay from the waiting lounge stood Admiral Barnstable, Captain Castleton, and other interested parties.

Ken Reeve emerged first, grinning, followed by the Gringg. Frill had a good look at the reactions: the marines, to a man, recoiled and tightened their hands on their weapons as the huge bearlike beings hunched to get through the portal and then stood up and stretched to relieve the cramp they had endured on the small shuttle.

"They're friendly and they are not armed," Ken Reeve said, raising his arms, elbows out and away from his body as he maneuvered himself between Eonneh and the nearest marines. The Gringg followed suit.

"They're very friendly," Frill added in a bellow, grinning as broadly as he could to reinforce his words.

Castleton's voice echoed over the P.A. system. "Security, assemble at a safe distance. Await further orders."

"Yes, sir," replied the lieutenant in charge.

He signalled to his men, who re-formed in a close group beyond the shut-tle. Frill felt his face redden.

"Captain," Ken Reeve said, frowning with annoyance at such overt hostility, "aren't you being a bit paranoid? They've shown no signs of aggression at any time."

"This is a security vessel, Mr. Reeve," the captain said in sharp tones.

"So it is," Ken retorted sarcastically. "I'd forgotten."

"There are definite procedures for this sort of thing, you know," Frill added, with a glance of apology at Reeve.

"Don't apologize for doing your duty," Greene snapped. He marched toward the decontamination booth.

Following Commander Greene, the party went through one by one. Ken and Frill stayed behind with the Gringg to reassure them as best they could, by smiling and trying to appear totally relaxed, that this was customary procedure. Neither of the two emissaries seemed dismayed, ignoring the actinic lights and the fans that fluffed up their fur. Ken admired their phlegmatic behavior in a totally foreign environment. Certainly there had been no similar procedures on the Gringg ship.

Barnstable was waiting as Greene, then Jilamey, followed by Lauder, emerged from the launch bay. The Spacedep chairman was containing himself with difficulty. Behind him, Castleton couldn't keep her eyes off the massive figures now passing through decontamination. Greene saluted and made directly for a computer terminal and began to enter codes.

"Whew, aren't they big mamas?" Ali Kiachif breathed.

"My son?" Hrrestan asked of Jilamey, the fur at the nape of his neck erect with fear. "He did not rrturn with you?"

"He's fine, Hrrestan. Stayed on board the visitors' vessel with Todd," Jilamey said soothingly. "They've volunteered"—he wrinkled his nose and grinned—"to be our ambassadors to the Gringg. These are our new friends. The gold one's Eonneh, and the other's Ghotyakh."

"Amazing crrreatures," Hrrestan said, gazing up at the two Gringg with wide eyes.

Snapping off the computer terminal, Greene marched up to his superior officers and saluted. His face was pale.

"Sirs, I must see you immediately," he said.

"Commander, how could you so mislead me as to the size of these . . . these . . . things?" Barnstable demanded.

"They aren't things," Jilamey retorted indignantly. "They're Gringg . . . and intelligent folk."

Barnstable brushed that observation aside. "This is a Spacedep vessel . . ."

"Currently assisting Alreldep," Ken said, bracing the Admiral, "in establishing friendly communication with a new species."

Barnstable glared fiercely at Greene. "When I sent you along as a Spacedep representative, Commander, this was exactly the kind of lamebrained, irresponsible behavior I expected you to counter."

"In point of fact, Admiral, encouraging this . . . delegation is not irresponsible." Greene aimed a very significant look at Barnstable. "They are, as you see, larger than any of us."

Barnstable cleared his throat. "Yes, there's that." He began to reconsider his position as Eonneh approached, passing close to him as he entered the lounge. "Did you . . . ah . . . manage to establish communications?"

"No, sir. We've exchanged a few words, nothing more. The rest was accomplished through a primitive sign language, and demonstrations." Greene shot a jaundiced glance at Ken Reeve. "Then they wouldn't allow us to reboard the shuttle unless we brought them"—he cocked his thumb at the Gringg—"with us." He glared again at Reeve.

"Well, what do we do with them?"

Greene flapped one hand indecisively. "Whatever one does with a new species . . . sir. They came voluntarily. Just as young Reeve and Hrriss remained. Sir, permission to speak to you privately concerning the Gringg. It is urgent."

"Watch it there, Greene," Jilamey said in a firm and angry voice. "The Gringg may not understand our spoken language, but your body language is sending hostility signals. Lighten up."

That made the two Spacedep men pause and glance suspiciously at the aliens.

"We have to know what we're dealing with," Barnstable said.

"I don't know about you, Admiral," Castleton said, "but the size of them makes me nervous."

Ghotyakh waddled in and began to exchange quiet murmurs with Eonneh.

"We'll keep them here long enough to run tests," the Admiral said.

Emerging just then from decontam, Ken heard the last sentence.

"Hold everything, Admiral," he began, noticing Jilamey's agitation. "If there's going to be any testing done, physicians affiliated with Treaty Island or Alreldep and Hrruban Alien Relations should administer the tests. Spacedep isn't involved."

"I agrrrree," Second Speaker put in, taking a step forward. He seemed much put out by the huge aliens' appearance and was maintaining a discreet distance. The one with the light-colored pelt leaned his way, sniffing. Affronted, Second clutched his robe tighter around himself. Undaunted, the alien turned its huge head toward Mllaba and snuffed at her. "You cannot sequester such data."

"You may perform your own examinations when we have finished," Barnstable said stiffly.

"You're not getting the message, are you, Admiral?" Ken said, stiff with indignation. "These aren't lab animals. They're sentient beings from a highly sophisticated culture and they're here as envoys, not creatures to be dissected. Get that straight now, once and for all. They are to be treated with honor and respect!" He let out a breath—"Because that's how we hope they're treating our emissaries."

"Surely," Kiachif put in silkily, "you don't want unwelcome, untested, and unauthorized aliens aboard your flagship any longer than you have to? I'll take 'em off your hands right smart."

"Since Spacedep may have to clean up after you Alreldeps mess up this first contact . . ." Greene began.

"I didn't mess up first contact before, did I?" Ken said in a voice that was cold with threat. "Ali, we accept your offer of transport here and now."

"Just a living minute, Kiachif," the Admiral began, clearly determined to keep the aliens aboard where he would have control of their disposition. "Castleton, escort these . . . these creatures to suitable quarters."

The captain stared at the aliens, and turned to her commanding officer.

"With all respect, Admiral," she said, "we haven't any quarters big enough for them outside of this lounge"—she gestured about her—"or the wardroom, which cannot be secured. . . ."

"Dammit!" Ken Reeve said in an exasperated roar. "The Gringg are not subject to Spacedep authority. They are Alreldep's. They're coming down to Doonarrala with us. And that's that!" His bellow made everyone look at him in surprise. The Gringg rumbled and shifted their big feet.

"Now look what you've done," Jilamey said, glaring accusingly at Barnstable and Castleton. Making reassuring sounds and waving his hands in placatory gestures, he went up to Eonneh and Ghotyakh, who blinked rapidly but made no move.

"Relax, lassie, they don't have any weapons," Kiachif said to Castleton, who had instinctively reached for her side arm.

"Just claws and teeth," she replied, but she dropped her hand to her side. Greene seemed poised to move between her and the Gringg if she so much as gestured.

"They look so dangerrrrous," Mllaba murmured, still standing closer to Second Speaker than protocol allowed.

"Then we mustn't upset them, must we?" Kiachif said, rather enjoying the navy's alarm.

"Especially at the outset of what should develop into mutual respect and harmony," Ken said in a disgusted tone. "Now, let's get these good . . . creatures," and he made the term far more a title than Barnstable had, "down to an environment that is not bristling with hostility and weapons."

With ill grace, Barnstable finally agreed.

"The Kiachif vessel has leave to depart," Captain Castleton said into her comunit to the bridge.

"Captain, will you also make contact with Admiral Sumitral at Alreldep?" Hrrestan asked, then turned politely to Second Speaker. "Sir, you will wish to inform the Hrruban Council of this development."

"The Terran Council will hear of this," Barnstable said.

"Along with the rest of civilized space," Ken said, shedding all trace of his previous aggressiveness now that the navy had acquiesced.

"Sometimes, Hrrestan, you exceed your authority," Second Speaker remarked in a taut voice.

Even as Hrrestan bowed low in apology, he wished that the old First Speaker were still alive, with his wisdom and forbearance available to help them through this tense situation.

"I thought you would not wish to be seen in the same light as that Hayuman admiral," Hrrestan said meekly.

Hrrto regarded him through slitted eyes, and his tail switched just once. He pulled his nails through his muzzle whiskers and then dropped his jaw ever so slightly.

"A point, Hrrestan. A point."

"Shall I also give permission for Sumitral to use the grid for conveyance to Doonarrala? Alreldep has always been the most intelligent branch of the Hayuman authorities."

Hrrto considered the question for a moment, then with a flick of half-bared claws signalled his assent. It would do him no harm in his campaign for the First Speakership to be seen to side with the Alreldep, always the nemesis of the conservative element of Hrruba in vying for influence on Rrala and in the lanes of space.

Hrrestan turned to Castleton and swept her a graceful bow. "Please let it be known in the Federazhon Building that we request the most immediate prrresence of Admiral Sumitral in the First Village complex. I am most grrrateful for your assistance."

"This way, folks," Kiachif said, gesturing broadly toward the bay in which his shuttle was docked.

"I'm to be kept posted, do you hear me?" Barnstable shouted as Ken and the others swept toward the connecting link.

The security force drew back, hands convulsively closing on their weapons as they swung through.

"This way, gentlebears," Jilamey said, skipping in front to lead the way. "Next stop, a fine little planet that I'm sure you'll adore."

*   *   *

After a quick huddle with Captain Castleton and Admiral Barnstable, Greene followed the Second Speaker and the still apprehensive Mllaba as they started to leave the bay.

"A moment, Honored sir," he said in good Middle Hrruban, laying a hand on Hrrto's robed arm, "of your most valuable time."

"For what reason?" Second Speaker asked stiffly, glancing down at the offensive hand. Beside him, Mllaba let out a hissing breath.

"I beg your pardon." Greene snatched his hand back, bowing apologetically. "Honored Speaker," he went on in a humble tone, though Hrrto recognized in the Hayuman a warrior's bearing that showed he bent the knee to no one, "please let the shuttle depart without you. Admiral Barnstable and Captain Castleton wish a few words with you. About this new species. It will delay your return to Doonarrala only a few moments."

"Very well," Second said, without inflection or expression. Greene nodded to the captain, who lifted her communication unit.

"The shuttle may depart now," she said. The blast doors closed before anyone on board the small ship could question the absence of the Hrrubans.

The Hayuman glanced toward the brilliant light of the shuttle's exhaust port, fast disappearing over the curve of the planet. Second Speaker followed Greene's gaze, then directed a curious stare at him.

"The Admiral thought that perhaps you are not so sanguine about the nature of these new beasts." The brown eyes searched the slitted green feline ones. "Perhaps you, too, believe that more caution should be exercised in regard to these Gringg."

"Perhaps," Second said, very cautiously. "But why should you share these thoughts with me?"

Greene moved closer to him, into uncomfortable proximity. Though he was shorter than the Hrruban, he seemed to loom.

"Because, Honored sir, you have power and influence here and on your own homeworld, and you are known for your sagacity in their use," the Hayuman said in a low voice. "The arrival of these beasts complicates the equation that already exists between Hrruban and Hayuman and interrupts proceedings that have long been on the agenda. Should this be allowed to occur? And at this critical point? There is more to this than meets the eye. Admiral Barnstable and the captain beg a few moments to discuss their views with you. Nothing official, or binding, certainly. Merely a friendly chat."

"You interest me, Commandrrr," Second said, his pupils narrowing. He stepped away from the Hayuman, restoring his breathing space. He found the commander almost more threatening than the Gringg. "Very well, so long as it is understood that this is only a small chat."

Kelly Reeve fidgeted. When Todd and his party had departed to investigate the strange spaceship, Hrrestan's assistant had addressed the remainder of the delegates left in the dining room.

"Honorred frriends, we must postpone frrthrr deliberations until the others have retrrrned. We have zaken measurres to ensurre yrrr comfort while you are here, and we will keep you inforrrmed about the ship orbiting above us. Please do not dizcuss what you have hearrrd with anyone who does not have ze proprrr classificazhon. Securizy is vital."

The financier from Hrruba was the only one to voice a protest. "Our time is valuable. Zis interruption must not interferre with ourr negotiations," he said.

"We have not a choice," his assistant replied. "We may not continue in ze absence of ze honorred Second Speaker and half our membrrrs."

Putting aside her nervousness, Kelly smiled at the Hrruban executive. "Perhaps you would care to return with me to my village? I would be delighted to make welcome one who is so invaluable to the High Council."

"Zank you, no. I will remain on ze Zreaty Island until ze Speaker returns. I have calls to make zo ze homewrrrld," the banker said in cold, if polite, refusal. The delegates dispersed, muttering, to their guest quarters. Seeing she could do nothing else to help, Kelly transported back to the Hrruban First Village, to Nrrna and the children.

It was still early morning on this side of Doonarrala. Children, not yet summoned by the school bell, raced around the green of the sunlit common. Worried about Todd, Kelly forced herself to smile at the serene picture they made.

"Mizzis Rrev," a Hrruban youngster shouted. "Where are Alison and Alec? Zey will be late zo school! It iz almoz time!" A crowd of children carrying books and tapes ran past them, heading toward the Friendship Bridge.

"They're not coming today, Zhrrel," Kelly said, fighting to keep from letting concern show on her face. "They're at Mrrva's, with me and Nrrna. Will you tell Hrromede I'll call him to explain?"

"Yes, Mizzis Rrev," Zhrrel said, turning almost on his tail and racing for the bridge as the bell began to toll. "Aiee! I'm laze!"

Mrrva, lithe and graceful in spite of her sixty years, hurried to put Kelly at ease, and would not let her speak until they were all seated comfortably in the garden with hot morning drinks. Perhaps in spite of her importance as the head of

Doonarrala medical services she prized her reputation as a genial hostess, and she was as fond of Kelly as she was of her son's mate.

Nrrna appeared in the doorway, with her two younger children in tow. She was a soft-furred female with pretty green eyes and pointed cheekbones that made her look very young.

"Gelli, whateverrr is wrrrong?" she said in her soft voice.

She held the children close while Kelly told as much as she could and still be discreet. Ourrh, only a year older than his newborn sister, silently watched the faces of the adults with no comprehension of what had upset those who loved and protected him. Solemnly, he nestled close to his mother's chest and put one arm around the baby. Knowing that all the villages would have learned of the strange ship's presence, Kelly could, and did, describe its awesome size and appearance.

"Then they just piled into Ali Kiachif's shuttle to go take a look at it. Sometimes, Todd Reeve is enough to drive a woman to mlada!" Kelly finished, letting righteous ire dissipate some of her inner fears. "But, best of all, the pair of them went off together, Nrrna. Just like always."

The estrangement between the two best friends over the matter of the spaceport had been of great concern to their wives, and other discerning friends. It had seemed incredible that any matter could have strained the deep bond shared by Todd and Hrriss. There had been tension even on the Double Bar Gemini Ranch, which Todd and Hrriss owned in partnership. Even the children had become aware of some stress between the two adult males, though for the most part they continued their games and running in and out of the two ranch houses as always.

"If these aliens have brought about a reunion," Mrrva said in Low Hrruban, "then they are thrice welcome in *this* house. So don't fear, Gelli," she added, patting Kelly's knee, "Hrriss and Zodd are resourceful. And never more so than when they face a mutual challenge. I have earnestly wished to help, you know." She tilted her head to gaze into Kelly's eyes.

"I know you have, Mrrva." Kelly smiled and grasped the slender furred arm. "It's just so utterly . . . weird that those two could ever find something to quarrel about." She closed her lips then, for she had to be loyal to Todd's principles even if, in her innermost thoughts, she didn't *see* why he so disapproved of the spaceport. Trade would expand, and the Doonarrala economy would improve enormously. A spaceport would make it so much easier for everyone. "I just hope we don't have to wait too long to hear what that infamous pair are up to now." She brushed away a vagrant tear because they *were* once more up to something!

"The most difficult part will be for you, waiting until they return! You are both welcome to stay here, since they must come through the village grid from the Zreaty Island."

"Thank you, Mrrva," Kelly said. As long as Todd and Hrriss were together, perhaps they'd also find a way past this spaceport difficulty, too. "It'll be like old times," she added, making her smile as genuine as possible.

Outside the house, she could hear the yells and hoots of her twins and Mrrva's two oldest children. They were accustomed to their fathers jetting off on special trips or being involved in colony business at Treaty Island. As Kelly had also been busy with the Treaty Island business, she had left her pair with Nrrna and Mrrva in First Village. So, totally unconcerned and giving their all to this extra day of leisure, they raced around Mrrva's front garden, playing out their notions of what was going on. Kelly sat on the stoop watching them, reassured by their carefree presence.

Her twin children were tall for their eight Standard years, and skinny as a pair of saplings. Early muscular development and plenty of exercise gave Alec and Alison such innate grace of movement that they resembled a pair of young Hrrubans, hence their nickname, the Alley Cats. Alec had his mother's red hair, but had inherited intense blue eyes from Todd. Alison was a more exotic combination, with shining black hair and eyes with golden, black-rimmed hazel irises. Except that they were obviously male and female, the twins' faces were extraordinarily similar in feature and form, though Alison's was slightly rounder than her brother's. Often friends would remark on how glad they were that they had different color hair, for in a losing battle to keep their locks from being eternally tangled messes, Kelly had clipped both heads short.

Also eight years old, Hrruna was slight and very shy like her mother, Nrrna. Hrrunival was a chunky six-year-old with wise eyes. He was the youngest of the four on the lawn, but tended to be the ringleader in games and feats of daring. The children had, of course, heard of the appearance of the strange spaceship in orbit.

"Zoddandhrriss will burrrst into ze alien vesssel," Hrrunival said, punctuating his phrases with zooming motions of his hands, "and drrrag out ze aliens and say 'What are you? Where do you come from?' " He was wild with excitement, dancing around on light toes. His elder sister, Hrruna, grabbed him by both ears to hold him still. He spat and batted at her.

"Then they will find out everything there is to know about the aliens," Alison said, calmly releasing Hrrunival from his sister's grasp and fluffing up the fur between the offended aural appendages. The Hrruban boy's eyes slitted pleasurably at Alison's fussing, and he wrinkled his nose at Hrruna. Unconcerned, the female pirouetted and did a boneless somersault, to land lightly on her feet again.

"And what happens then?" Kelly asked, distracted from her dark mood by the children's fancies.

"They'll make friends with them," Alec said, triumphantly spinning toward his mother, clapping his hands like cymbals, "like in the story where they brought all the Rralans together. Don't you think that would be nice, Mommy?"

"Yeah!" exclaimed Hrrunival.

Kelly sighed. The story of how Doonarrala was founded had become almost a legend, with "Toddandhrriss" the boy heroes whose names were always spoken together until they became an indistinguishable mass of syllables. She hadn't been born when that happened, but if Todd as a youngster was anything like eight-year-old Alec today, it was no mystery how he had insinuated, or rather, cannoned himself into the midst of a delicate situation that could have had disastrous repercussions for both races. The unexpectedly deep bonding between the young Todd, so out of phase with Earth social protocol, and Hrriss, had surprised and touched both Hayumans and Hrrubans. It was this friendship, and Todd's determination to enjoy it without adult-conceived hindrances, that had been the cornerstone for amicable co-existence between the two species. Which had resulted in the Decision at Doona.

The true adventure gave the children of Doonarrala heroes of their own age to admire and emulate. It also prompted the occasional outbreak of rope tails attached to the trousers of Human youngsters. If being the sons and daughters of legends made things a little tougher for the Alley Cats and Nrrna's brood, they never acknowledged the problem. Possibly their peers never connected the Todd and Hrriss of the stories with the two very accessible adult males, fathers of their friends, who played with them daily and who led the annual Snake Hunts. Those occupations, Kelly reminded herself, were adventurous enough for eight- and six-year-olds.

In the meanwhile, two hours had stretched into five, and five into nine. Worrying about Todd, Kelly ate a lunch and dinner she didn't taste. She tried to tell herself that the long delay was because things were going well, not because there'd been problems. Problems one usually heard as soon as they occurred. But she couldn't completely discount her nagging premonition of trouble, however nebulous it was.

After the early evening meal, Mrrva retired into the back garden to leave the two younger women alone. Nrrna dandled baby Hrrunna on her lap, playing with the small cub's perfect little hands and feet. The baby's fur was light gold with a mahogany-brown stripe down her back, a contrast to her mother's tawnier pelt. The cub fussed a little, and opened a little pink mouth to emit a weak, mewling sound. Nrrna, reclining on her side to expose the four gentle swellings nearly hidden in her fur, put Hrrunna to a nipple. The child began to suck, settling its little rounded ears back at an absurd oblique angle: a peaceful tableau, if not for the presentiment of danger plaguing Kelly.

Unable to sit still, she thought of calling the Federation Center again to see if they'd had any word from Todd and the others. Arms crossed over her chest to keep her fingers from twitching, she paced over to the console, wondering if it was too soon after her last call.

"What time is it, Nrrna?" she asked, tightening her fingers on her arms.

Nrrna shifted to her other side and nestled Hrrunna in the crook of her other arm so she could look at her wrist chronometer. "Only half past six."

"Hmm," Kelly mused. "That means it's nine-thirty on Treaty Island. Do you think there's anyone in the Space Center office?"

"There was not half an hourrr ago, Gelli. Why do you not try to relax?" Nrrna settled the nursing cub, peering at the concentrated little face with its tight-shut, shell-like eyelids.

"I don't see how you can stay so calm!" Kelly said. "Hrriss and Todd could be in great danger."

Nrrna let out the low, musical growl that was a Hrruban laugh. "I must stay calm or this tiny one gets gas through my milk," she said. "It is an exercise in self-control. I myself do not think of danger to Zodd or Hrriss! You could go to the Treaty Island?"

"What good would that do?" Kelly grumbled, pacing to the window at the opposite side of the room. "No. I'm not going."

"I am glad you do not," Nrrna said, jaw dropped in a gentle smile. "I prefer that we are together and not alone."

Kelly glanced down affectionately at the Hrruban woman. "Me, too. I guess that's why I didn't stay this morning. I'd get that 'useless female' reaction and be acidly asked what I thought I could do about anything. That lot at Treaty don't worry about people; they worry about treaties and agendas and . . . things! Besides, it'd be unfair to leave my two monsters here! Look at them out there!"

The Alley Cats were in the midst of a rough and tumble with Hrruna, Hrrunival, Ourrh, and a group of the neighborhood youngsters, freed for evening games until darkness. As Kelly watched, Alison was pulled to the ground by a couple of Hrruban cubs, and shrieked happily, coming up dusty to drag her friends over with her.

"Where do they get the energy?" Mrrva asked with a sigh as she walked up and gazed at their spirited racings.

"It's not fair, is it?" Kelly said, shaking her head. "Ooops, there goes Alison's shirt. Well, it was an old one," she added. "Once they knew they weren't going to school today, I had to fight the two of them into clothes, and now they're half-naked anyhow. 'If Hrruna and Hrrunival don't have to wear anything but belts, then why can't we?' " Kelly piped, in a flawless imitation of Alec at his most difficult. Nrrna chuckled again. The baby squirmed and let go of the nipple, licking her tiny chops. Her mother repositioned her, and with eyes still closed, she placed her head on her front paws and went to sleep.

"Take joy in the differences, that is what I think they should do," Nrrna said in Low Hrruban.

"Try telling them that," Kelly said wryly, then shouted out the window at the children. "You're playing too rough! Look out for Heeranh's nose! Augh!" she exclaimed, and started pacing again. "I don't know where they get the idea that they're indestructible."

"From their fathers, no doubt," Nrrna said. Hrrunna twitched in her sleep, and gave a squeaky little moan, which brought a loving smile from her dam. Nrrna glanced up at Kelly, who was biting her own thumb. "They will be all right, you know that, Gelli. They always are when they are working together."

"I guess so." Kelly paced back to the window, glanced out, and recoiled in shock.

"Mrrva!" she shrieked. "Get the snake rifle!"

The Gringg stepped off the grid in the midst of the Hrruban First Village and looked around them with great interest. First they had been landed on this new world in full dark; now they had entered twilight. They were glad to be able to see where they now were.

More Rroobvnnns had met them in the orbiting ship, including one very quick-moving male clad in black, and many more Ayoomnnns. From the ship, they had been transferred to a larger shuttle, flown by an engaging Ayoomnnn with black-and-gray hair who showed his teeth frequently and spoke in a poetic cadence. Once this vehicle had reached the surface of the planet, they had been ushered into a large white-stone cube of a building and down a corridor which echoed when one trod on the floor. The Gringg had obediently followed their guide to a small platform with pillars at each corner. When they stood upon it, the room became misty. Suddenly, they found themselves here. Eonneh was impressed. This form of transport was much more effortless than any he had previously encountered. The Gringg had much to learn from the Rroobvnnns.

A second group of four emerged from the mist. Genhh gestured to Eonneh and Ghotyakh to be patient and wait.

By some of the scents, the Gringg decided that the Rroobvnnn Rreshtanh lived here. The smell of the green groundcover and some of the flowers had been in his fur.

To one side, a high escarpment bounded the valley in which they stood, which was rich with trees and flora. Like the life forms they had seen so far, even the trees seemed less substantial here than on the Gringg world. But it was a beautiful place, and the air smelled good. In the distance, they could scent the musky odors of wildlife. One creature, which they guessed must be a service animal, unlike the Ayoomnnns or Rroobvnnns, stood tethered, calmly eating long strands of yellow herbage. It had not noticed them, but many more Hrrubans had. They were coming out of the little houses, staring and pointing at the Gringg. Most of them did not react with fear, but with interest. Eonneh found that to be heartening. Much more reassuring than the emotions he had perceived on the large orbiting ship.

The Rroobvnnn Rreshtanh was much honored here. Most of the Hrrubans spoke to him before circling around to look at the two aliens. Eonneh returned their gazes for a while; then, because there was little variation between one tawny-gold face and another, he became more interested in the scenery. There was much greater variation in color among the Ayoomnnns.

"Act as if there was nothing unusual in the way we were just transported," Eonneh said to Ghotyakh. "Though we have only seen a small part of this world, I am relieved that we seem to have been taken into the living places of these people. Even in the place where we first stopped we have seen nothing of the weapons carried by the guards on the ship. Accept anything they do with padded claws. Let us be sure not to frighten them."

"Observe the shapes of the domiciles, Eonneh," Ghotyakh said, turning a slow circle. "Square roofs, as had that building into which we were first taken. Everything is built using flat planes, and nearly all of them above ground. Curious."

"It is so. They do not build as we do, in echo of the natural shelters of the motherworld." Eonneh stared at one dwelling. "I would guess they have better ventilation than our homes. Perhaps their seasonal changes are not as drastic as ours. A very pleasant place." His tail wagged slowly. "I shall enjoy our time here."

The gesture seemed to interest his hosts. Genhh had no caudal appendage, as Eonneh had already observed. The angry male in black, who appeared to be subordinate to the male wearing an ornate red robe, both of whom had remained behind in the ship, had long, flexible tails that switched back and forth all the time.

"What interesting creatures these are," Ghotyakh said, glancing at the

Rroobvnnns. "There is so much variation among the members of one sex. And do you notice that all the males seem to live on one side of this place and the females on the other? Look how many Ayoomnnns are coming from that direction. None live here."

"Reh. It is most curious. Is there water about? I'm thirsty, but a swim is even more necessary."

"I hear some running over there," Ghotyakh said, peering in the direction from which the Ayoomnnns were coming. "There is a bridge." Curious to see a Doonarralan river, the two ambled toward the sound.

A shout from behind reminded them that they were not alone.

"Oh, I apologize, Genhh," Eonneh said politely, turning to the Ayomnnn female. Her thin, nearly hairless skin was reddened from the effort of running. Eonneh noted again how small and weak the creatures of this world were. The tall being showed her teeth, and spoke. The Gringg listened, catching a word here and there, but comprehending more from the accompanying gestures.

"We will follow where you go," Eonneh said agreeably.

"They speak so quietly, Eonneh! I will be so glad when we work out what it is they are saying," Ghotyakh said. "They give every indication that they wish to learn our words, although it is also clear they want us to learn their language. I am glad we at least are no longer being watched by Ayomnnns carrying weapons, but this is in its own way a threat."

"I, too, still worry that they do not trust us. It is vital that they see us as harmless. Let us continue to shield our reactions and walk among them to reassure the small ones. If Grzzeearoghh commands that to speak their language is the best thing for Gringg to do, we shall do so, as we will deal with whatever else befalls us," Eonneh replied, following Ken into the heart of the Hrruban village. "For myself it is worth the risk. I am delighted to learn an alien language. It is easy to master other Gringg dialects, for they are all based upon the one mother language. This—this is genuinely different, and challenging. I have been waiting for a chance like this all my life."

The Gringg, gliding along in the midst of their escort, seemed fascinated by their surroundings. Ken pointed out objects, attaching names to each, but they paid scant attention to him. They did seem to be taking everything in with all their senses. Occasionally, Eonneh or Ghotyakh stopped to touch a tree or the wall of a house, feeling its substance with the sensitive pads of their handpaws.

A crowd of Hrrubans had gathered, and as word spread of the visitors' presence, Hayumans came over the Friendship Bridge to watch—at a respectful distance, having noted the aliens' size, teeth, and claws. The Gringg noted them placidly, and went on.

"What are these monsters? They look like giant mda!" demanded Anne Boncyk, riding up on a skittish horse. She was a dainty woman with a decided chin and large, fringed brown eyes.

"Our latest visitors," Ken said affably. At times, one didn't know which way Anne would jump. "They call themselves Gringg. Their ship is in orbit around Doonarrala."

The horse stretched out its neck to sniff at the Gringg. It sneezed once, but didn't shy away. Anne looked surprised.

"What about that? I'd've thought he'd be off across the compound," she said. "They don't scare him. Good lad!" And she gave her mount an affectionate slap on the neck.

"I find," Jilamey said mischievously, "that horses do not tend to judge by appearances."

"All ze children are still here," Hrrestan noted, sorting out the whirlwind of small bodies that whisked back and forth across his front garden. "Our sons' mates are waiting together." The older Hrruban paused. "You are certain that Zodd and Hrriss are safe?"

"Have you ever known a situation where they were at a loss?" Ken said lightly. "Except for that dratted spaceport issue. Seriously, old friend, I wouldn't have left them if I felt them to be endangered. I have a gut-strong reaction that these fellows are peaceful. Otherwise, they wouldn't send the captain's own archivist with us, and that's what I judge Eonneh here to be." Then he grinned, poking Hrrestan in the ribs. "Let's see what the grandkids think of our new friends! If I remember rightly, Todd trusted you on sight and he's never been righter."

"You'rrre not inzending to let zese strangers near childrrren, are you?" Hirro, Hrrestan's nearest neighbor, was shocked.

"The advantage is on the kids' side, Hirro," Ken said patiently. "This is open ground, and you must know how fast Hayuman children can move if they have to."

"Who are zey?" Hrrula, one of Ken's oldest friends, shouldered his way up to walk beside Ken. The Hrruban's big green eyes were shining.

"Gringg," Ken said, grinning.

" 'We arrre not alone,' " Hrrula quoted, dropping his jaw so far it nearly dislocated. "Mrrrvelous!"

The Gringg, largely ignoring their escort, caught sight of the cluster of children. Eonneh's ears seemed to perk up when Hrruna let out a shriek of mock fear, and ran away from her brother, who was stretching out a hand to tag her. Her tail, streaming out behind, whisked out of the way just as he was about to grab it. Fascinated, Eonneh and Ghotyakh moved closer to watch.

"Beep-beep!" shrieked Hrrunival, poking his sister in the belly when she twisted around to avoid running into a rosebush. "Now you have to say that!"

The other children dodged away from the Hrruban female, who finally caught Alec up against the pillar supporting Hrrestan's porch.

"Beep-beep!" she cried, and changed the symbol by tugging Alec's ear lobe. "Mrow!"

"Uh-oh!" Alec yelled, and ran around trying to catch someone else to be It.

"Uh-uh!" Alison cried, as Alec made a dive for Hrrunival. "No fair grabbing tails!" The pudgy Hrruban boy rolled away just in time and ran behind Alison.

The Gringg stood entranced by the children, ignoring the adults' efforts to move them along. Eonneh let out pleased little mutters at seeing younglings at play.

Suddenly Alec caught sight of the Gringg. "Look at them!" he shouted, standing stock-still and pointing. "Are they bears, Granddad?"

"What are bears?" Hrruna asked, swivelling and then standing as rigid as her friend.

"Earth animals, and these are not really bears," Ken explained, "but close."

All the children had paused in their noisy game of symbol tag and turned to look. They stared wide-eyed at the Gringg, who stared back. Shock held the children immobile for a moment. Hrrunival was the first to recover. Nose a-twitch and tail straight out in defiance of his own uncertainty, he squared his small shoulders.

"Who are you?" he demanded, walking up to Eonneh. The child wasn't quite as high as the Gringg's hip, but size wasn't going to deter him. The Alley Cats and Hrruna, holding Ourrh firmly by the hand, followed in close support. The baby's tail wrapped and unwrapped around one hind leg and his yellow-green eyes were huge, the pupils outspread across the irises.

"Totally unafraid," Frill muttered, watching this exchange. "What do you think of that?"

"Amazing," said Jilamey. "Unless you know Ken's family."

"Doonan children," Ken said, shaking his head. "They don't even know they're supposed to be afraid."

"Mrrva, hurry! Where's that rifle?" Kelly shouted again, as the children, aware of the beasts staring at them, stopped their play.

"Why?" Hrriss' mother came running, her tail lashing. "Where's the peril?"

The baby woke, crying. Nrrna snatched her up, holding her protectively to her chest.

"There are two absolutely gigantic mda out there looming over the children!" Kelly exclaimed. "They might attack at any minute. The kids are just standing there, frozen. Oh, my babies!" She followed Mrrva's pointing finger toward a closet, and was on her knees loading shells into the chambers of Hrrestan's powerful snake gun. "Call my brother at the animal hospital. Call the colony buildings. See if there's anyone in Animal Control!"

Nrrna ran for the commlink.

There was a rap on the door behind them. "Anyone home?" Ken called, then pushed the door open, aware of agitated movement within. "Oh no, Kelly! No, wait!"

She looked up at the sudden appearance of her father-in-law, her hands moving as if of their own volition. "Ken! Where's Todd? There are two huge mda out there! They never come so close to villages. These must be killers. I have to protect the children." She snapped the gun shut.

"They're not mda! They're our new friends. They're from the strange ship." He put one hand on the rifle barrel and deftly relieved her of it.

"From the ship? The one that came in out of nowhere?" Kelly swallowed hard, trying to grasp his statement as he unloaded the heavy-bore rifle. Behind him, Nrrna, green eyes huge, still clutched her baby.

"These fellows are peaceful. Their ship isn't even armed." Ken grinned reassuringly. Had all Kelly's training in Alreldep gone down the drain since her marriage? He smiled more broadly before he said, "Todd and Hrriss are staying aboard their ship. In exchange, we've got a couple of visitors. They really are friends, Kelly, Nrrna."

"Friends?" Kelly repeated, her voice sounding unsteady even to her. Her hands were shaking, and she didn't seem able to focus. "And you left Todd and Hrriss on board that immense ship?"

"They volunteered, but I wouldn't have agreed, dear, if I didn't truly believe it's the right way to deal with this unexpected situation. After all"—he winked at her as he helped her to her feet—"your father-in-law's had some practice in this sort of 'unexpected' encounter." Not quite certain, Kelly gave him a shallow grin. "So come on out and meet the Gringg. Even mda'd stay away from something that sizable!"

"Are you bears?" Alec wanted to know, confronting Eonneh, not too close, but close enough so that he could see the Gringg's furry features. "Why are you wearing belts? That's a very beautiful belt. I didn't think bears wore belts like Hrrubans. They have pockets in their belts, too. What have you got in your belt pockets?"

Eonneh was delighted that this red-topped Ayoomnnn seemed unafraid of him. It appeared to be asking about his belt, for the slender little finger was pointing at his chest. But courtesy came first. "Eonneh," he said, pointing at himself.

"Honey?" Alison asked, joining her brother in a semiprotective fashion. "Is that your name? Honey?"

"Reh. Ghotyakh," Eonneh said, indicating his companion.

"I can't say that!" Alec said. "It sounds like gargling."

"Don't be stupid, Alley, it sounds like Kodiak," Alison said. "That's a kind of bear. I guess they must be bears."

"But what are bears?" Hrrunival wanted to know.

"They're an Earth animal," Alec said, somewhat pompously. "Mommy read us about them in a storybook."

"I thought there were only Hayumans on Earrth," Hrrunival said. "Hrruba has no ozzer animals."

"Well, Earth did and does," Alec informed him condescendingly. "You've seen the pictures in the book."

"They're Gringg," Jilamey said, coming over to kneel beside the children. Following his example, Eonneh, renamed Honey, rolled back on his mighty haunches, bringing him closer to their level. "They've come to Doonarrala from their own world to meet us."

"You do not have any assurrrance of zese fine senziments," an older Hrruban male snapped. Ken recognized him as Trrengo, a relative newcomer to Rrala.

"I think we do," Alec said, suddenly turning an incredibly adult expression on Trrengo. "Uncle Jilamey says we shouldn't be afraid. He doesn't lie to us. You're friendly, aren't you?" He held out a hand to Ghotyakh, who engulfed it completely in his vast paw.

"Wait, don't let him touch you!" cried one of the Human colonists, Bob Lawrence.

"He's okay," Alec said, shaking hands solemnly. Alison followed suit, putting her hand into Ghotyakh's other paw.

"Just like their father," mumbled Macy McKee, patting his wife's hand where it rested, on his arm. "I remember the first time Todd brought us a passel of Hrrubans to meet—" He broke off and looked about in surprise. "And hey, these fellows don't make me sneeze!"

"By analogy that should prove that these fellows are dangerous," Lawrence said sardonically.

"What a bizarre way to distinguish friend from foe," said Dr. Kate Moody in her caustic way as she pushed past her neighbors. "Allergies apart, they're sure not acting hostile. And the Alley Cats aren't the least bit skeered. Nor young

Hrrunival. Look at them hunkering down to get level with your kids. Evening, Ken," she said cheerfully as he approached. "Back to your old habits, huh, finding aliens. Well, a man has to keep his skills honed or lose 'em. By any chance, are these the patients I was told to examine? I don't see any wounded lying about. Of course, the fellow on the Spacedep cruiser wasn't sure if they were a job for Ben Adjei, as head veterinarian, or for me, so we both came. And I'm glad we did! The size of 'em! Well-grown lads!"

Ken had brought Kelly, Mrrva, and Nrrna, still clutching her baby, all three women somewhat hesitant. "Come on, ladies, let me make you known to the Gringg. This is Eonneh. Go on! Introduce yourself. Tell him your name. I need more recordings of his responses to get more of their inflections."

Kelly glanced at Ken to make sure he was serious. With one hand he urged her forward, showing the recording device in the palm of the other.

"Kelly," she said, turning her thumb to her chest. "I'm Kelly." Then she turned her thumb to the smaller of the two Gringg and raised her eyebrows quizzically. "Your name?"

"Gelli," Eonneh repeated carefully, thumping his furry chest with an immense fist. "Eonneh. Eonneh."

"Honey!" the children chorused, delighted with such a name.

Ken made the rest of the introductions, laying his hand on each child's head and saying the name. Then he turned to see which of the neighbors were willing. Most of those who were, he noted with amusement, were members of the original Doonan colony or those who had arrived just after the Decision. Hrrula was delighted by the Gringg, especially the way they sniffed, very politely, at each person they met. The others, mostly recent arrivals, watched cautiously from a discreet distance.

The children had none of their parents' reserve. They were eager to meet Honey and Kodiak, as they'd been renamed. The Gringg tried to pronounce each new name, causing some of the kids to muffle their giggles in their hands. Made bold by their curiosity, more children came out of the surrounding houses and came forward timidly to see the visitors, then retreated, loud with relief, having experienced nothing more terrifying than a handshake.

"Come on, Nrrna," Ken said, urging the shy Hrruban forward. "They're really very friendly."

Still clasping Hrrunna, Nrrna slowly approached Honey and Kodiak. When she got close enough, she stood on tiptoe, her tail balancing out behind her, and looked deeply into their wine-red eyes. Both Gringg saw the sleeping cub and exchanged wide-eyed glances. Kodiak urged Honey forward, almost prodding him toward Nrrna. Very cautiously, as if afraid to frighten her or disturb the sleeper, Honey crept forward, eyes always on the curled-up infant. He hunched his shoulders and extended his neck, twisting his head from side to side, all attention focused on little Hrrunna. Then, ever so slowly, Honey held out his huge paws and gave a single, soft interrogative grunt. As one in a trance, Nrraa held the sleeping cub toward him and slipped her into his great furry paws, where the little Hrruban was cradled with tender care. Nrrna ignored the gasps around them.

Hirro even went so far as to leap forward, as if to snatch the cub from Honey, but, as if she hadn't even seen his movement, Nrrna stepped in his path.

"I trust you," she told the Gringg in the Middle Hrruban most of the onlookers would understand, her voice clear and strong in the sudden silence. "There is no harm in you that I can sense. You do come as friends."

The aliens were obviously entranced with Hrrunna, and ignored everything else. Ken could barely contain his delight in Nrrna's actions and words. In the hush that fell on the crowd, he could plainly hear the tiny whirr that meant someone was recording this on film, too, for which he was very grateful. He'd been so concerned with getting Gringg sounds down, he'd forgot to attend to a visual account.

Now Honey let out a tiny coo, the softest sound Ken had heard a Gringg make. The baby opened her eyes and briefly stared up at him, then stretched her pliant body across Honey's broad palms. The coo seemed to soothe her eyes shut. She let out a little sigh, and went back to sleep, curling her tiny tail about her. Honey's coo turned into soft melodic sounds, hovering just above audible level.

Ken turned up the gain on his recorder, hoping to get every note. Maybe it wasn't a Gringg lullaby, just Honey murmuring under his breath, but the tableau the Gringg presented was an effective one as far as a crowd-pleaser went, for soft looks were exchanged, and people definitely relaxed. Against their original intent, the settlers were being persuaded of the Gringg's pacifism by the gentleness shown a cub. Even the skeptics, with the exception of Hirro, regarded the large Gringg with less obvious apprehension.

"Music," Ken murmured to Kelly. "If that's what we're hearing now, is one more common language. I wonder what their reaction will be to Terran classics."

"Wagner? Mahler? Mtxainah? Hrnatn?" asked Kelly dubiously. "I can't help but be prejudiced *toward* a race that genuinely likes our young," she added, listening while Eonneh and Ghotyakh continued nimbly bass notes in soft harmony. She swept away a red wisp of hair from her sweaty forehead. "Whew! I thought they were mda! Just as furry, but much nicer."

Commander Frill seemed equally charmed by Hrrunna, too. He hung over Honey's arm, admiring the cub.

"This is the tiniest Hrruban I've ever seen. She's beautiful," he told Nrrna. "How old is she?"

"Born within the month," Nrrna said proudly.

"The youngest ambassador in the galaxy," said someone behind Ken. He turned to see Admiral Afroza Sumitral, his gray eyes alight, waiting beside Ben Adjei.

"You got here quickly," Ken said, shaking hands with his old friend.

"Not quickly enough, I see," Sumitral replied, half chidingly. "Once again the legitimate function of interplanetary diplomats has been usurped by the children of Doona. I wonder that we don't just induct the whole colony into Alreldep. Will you make me known to your friends here? Everyone else seems to have met them."

Laughing, Ken made a sweeping bow, from Sumitral toward the Gringg. "Introduce yourself. That's what we've done."

"And now," Kate Moody said when Sumitral had completed the formality, "if we've all finished becoming acquainted, I'd like to take a professional look at these two bruisers here. Ken, can we sort of maneuver them toward the Medical Center?"

"I am puzzled, Ghotyakh," Eonneh said, following the new Ayoomnnns through the village. "That Rroobvnnn with the small cub was at first very reserved with us. When we gave it back, it made suckling motions toward him as if looking for the source of milk. Could he, in fact, be a she?"

"A distinct possibility," Ghotyakh agreed. "We may be in error in our original assumptions. Previously I thought all the ones with tails were the males. Have we erred?"

"We must not be hasty in this. The appearance of the first Rroobvnnn we met closely matched our generative configuration. Perhaps they change after they have borne young?"

"Oh, I see!" Ghotyakh exclaimed, his roar of comprehension alarming some of the Ayoomnnns. "Our first visitor must have been a heifer. We must ask Genhh for the truth of this. I would not want to bring back specious data to Grzzeearoghh."

chapter five

Castleton escorted Admiral Barnstable and his party back to her ready room. The two Hrrubans were very nervous, and kept looking back at the escort of security guards that followed. She regretted the necessity of upsetting them, but regulations were regulations, and anyone on board who was not Spacedep had to be accompanied at all times. At least the rules allowed for the safe passage of visitors. Thank heavens Admiral Barnstable was more moderate than his predecessor.

The Admiral waited to speak until they were all seated and had been served refreshments.

"Good," he said when the door was quietly shut. "This room has been secured?" and when Castleton nodded, he continued. "We must address the matter of the Gringg. Now that we have some data to analyze, we can consider whether or not we are being rushed into intimacy with a potentially hostile race by overanxious individuals."

"I find zem most zrreatening," Mllaba said firmly. "Zey seemed so complezely unafrraid when zey boarded zis ship for ze first time. I felt as if zey had previous intimazhons of what zey would encounzer here."

"Too confident," Barnstable agreed, nodding. "That suggests a very sophisticated culture. Accustomed to dealing with alien species. You didn't sense any probes, did you, Grace?"

"None at all, Admiral," Castleton replied. "I would have said they made no attempt whatsoever to scan us. I find them interested and curious, but not overtly hostile."

"I am not so surrre," Hrrto said. He was torn. On the one hand, it was important to establish good relations with an obviously sophisticated new sentient race. On the other, he realized that it was foolhardy to rush into such relationships, without having a firm understanding of mutual intentions. So far, the Gringg had made the Hrrubans and Hayumans come to them, thereby giving them what the Hayumans called "home court advantage." It would not look well to the Hrruban High Council to appear in a subordinate position. Such loss of face could be fatal to Second's hopes in an election year.

There were many candidates standing to take over the now-vacant First Speakership which Hrrto felt he had to win. In his opinion, very few of the nominees had either the experience or acumen for the office. The prime Speakership should not be allowed to fall into the hands of some dilettante or partisan who might involve the Council in irrelevancies to please his supporters: someone with no standards or appreciation of true Hrrubanism. He felt himself to be the best possible choice. Having been Speaker for External Affairs for more than forty years, he understood what could happen to their carefully maintained civilization if Hrruba was badly led, and he was determined not to allow that to happen. If he was seen to be in the wrong in such a sensitive matter as dealing with the Gringg, his popularity, and his reputation, would plummet. Public opinion was fickle.

"In my opinion," he went on when he realized that a polite silence prevailed in expectation of his next words, "caution is indicated. I would like more data as soon as possible. Should we not be hearing from ze medical examiner on Rrala about now?"

"I doubt there could be any comprehensive results so soon," the captain said. "Laboratory work takes time."

"Yes, of course," Hrrto replied, fingering his robes.

Across the room from the Second Speaker, Jon Greene was busy over a hooded monitor, his fingers flicking swiftly over the controls. Grace Castleton eyed him, wondering what he was seeing that gave him such a worried expression. Mllaba flexed and stretched the claws of one hand along the tabletop.

"Well?" she said at last and with some impatience in her tone. "Do we go? Or stay? You must not waste more of the Speaker's most valuable time."

"Sirs, ma'am, Captain, the wait is worth it, I assure you," Greene said, straightening up, "for I have finally found what I've been searching for. Now, this is the tape made while we were aboard the Gringg ship." He manipulated the controls, and the holoscreen displayed a still frame of the Gringg landing bay. One by one, the landing party entered the frame. Castleton drew in a sharp breath as she realized the scale of the big chamber. At its far end, the Gringg entered the room and began to interact with Ken Reeve.

Second Speaker's tail lashed in surprise as the largest Gringg spoke, its roar rattling the tympanum in the speaker unit. Greene allowed the tape to run for a short time, then sped it up so the action was telescoped into a few minutes. The Hrrubans watched in silence, then turned questioningly to Greene.

"Zo, we zee the ftrrst meeting of these creatures. Zey show intelligence and caution in zeir approach. No less did we," Hrrto said, as impatient as Mllaba. "What of it?"

"That it was only Ken Reeve's impression that they have never met sentient beings before. Just wait, sir," Greene said. The commander froze the last frame of the three Gringg waving to the team as the shuttle-lifted off, then blanked the screen.

"Now, this is a tape sent to Spacedep by an exploration team less than a month ago. It is coded classified, but Admiral Barnstable has given permission to allow you to see it. I feel it is vital to our understanding of the current situation."

Everyone drew shocked breaths when the new tape showed an uncompromising picture of a planetary landscape brutally torn and burned by conflict. Wrecked hulks of buildings of an unfamiliar architecture had been sliced in two with some potent destructive weapon. Battered shafts that did resemble known weaponry littered broad open spaces that must once have been graceful avenues. Castleton peered at the screen, looking desperately for signs of living creatures. A series of scenes of stark, dead forests and the stumps of shattered cities flashed past without relief. Nothing living interrupted the bleak landscape. Of the residents, only a few skeletal remains could be found, and those were darkened and twisted: by radiation, the captain thought, somewhat familiar with the look of such deaths. Nothing moved except ashy debris swept around by the wind that howled eerily. The statistics overlaying the image showed readings of heavy radiation. The changing symbols also showed that biological and chemical weapons, and an unknown energy weapon of great force had been deployed.

"This planet is in the Fingal system," Greene said, narrating. "Spacedep interdicted it as soon as they received the exploration team's initial report. No life forms higher than deep-sea algae remain on a world that, to judge by the artifacts left behind, had an advanced civilization. Estimates are that it would take over two thousand years for radiation levels to drop sufficiently to allow Humans to live there."

The image faded, to be replaced by that of an orbiting spaceship. Hrrto caught his breath as he realized it was identical to the one currently circling Rraladoona. It seemed subtly different, and as the exploration team's camera drew closer, he could see that this ship was derelict, its hull riddled with jagged rents caused by explosive charges and the neater, milled holes of laser bolts. The image, now recorded by a handheld unit, moved through darkened corridors, the white glare of its lights resting momentarily on the occasional floating corpse. Hrrto's tail twitched in surprise. There was no doubt about the identity of the dead. They were Gringg.

"It would seem that Ken Reeve's assumption was wrong. The Gringg have met other sentient species before," Greene said. His eyes met Castleton's. "And they destroyed them. The population of an entire planet, wiped out."

The captain felt a cold finger trace down her spine. She shuddered. Greene moved his gaze from Castleton to Barnstable.

"In the light of that"—he gestured toward the screen—"this hail-fellow-well-met attitude toward the Gringg has gotten a trifle out of control. Hasn't it, Admiral?"

The Admiral shifted in his seat. "Damned straight. It's turning into a regular circus animal act already."

"Perrhaps too much openessss was ssshown," Second agreed, edgily, "but zince it iss shown, what is to be done about ze steps Rrev hass already taken?" And he gestured toward Rraladoona.

Barnstable brought his big fist down emphatically on the tabletop. "Get in touch with him immediately and require him to show some restraint, that's what. Don't show so much damned much hayseed cordiality until we've got a tap on what they're really here for. This dumb show of theirs, so polite and open, could mask invasion procedures," and he waved his hand at the screen and the devastation it still portrayed. "They could be softening us up so that our defenses are down when their main fleet comes powering in."

"With all due respect, sir, the Gringg have done nothing—here—to arouse suspicions of their intent," Captain Castleton said with some restraint. Even a ship's captain practiced tact in dealing with an admiral. Greene's evidence was upsetting but incitement made her twice as cautious. "Their ship sent no probes. They waited until we made contact. To me that shows peaceful intent. Envoys have been exchanged—which I feel is a mark of amazing trust on their part, considering we're two species to their one. So far all those envoys have seen are the insides of a shuttle and the reception area of this ship. Right now, they're on an agriculturally based colony world, not one of our homeworlds which are not in the least bit endangered." She grinned to relieve the tension, for the Admiral was scowling even if he was listening to what she said. "Not that we know where the other's homeworld is," and she inclined her head in a courteous bow to Hrrto. "How can their mere presence on Doonarrala constitute a *serious* threat? Surely they are more vulnerable than we. Their vessel's not armed."

Greene cut in. "We don't know that they're completely without armament, sir. When you consider the devastation of the Fingal planet, they might have some new weapon we can't identify."

"Zat is true enough," Captain Hrrrv said thoughtfully. "All we know iss zat zey have no nuclear weapons or what we consider usssual orrrdnance."

Finding an ally, Greene continued forcefully. "Other weapons with less sophisticated delivery systems might be concealed aboard: powerful incendiaries composed of unknown substances and not easily detectable. I suspect whatever that ship used on Fingal Three could be easily hidden in that mass of water in the central globe of the ship. They are a new race. We don't know what they are capable of. All we do know is that they can destroy a planet. Since we have no direct verbal contact, I feel it is necessary to limit what they are allowed to see, and establish verbal communications as quickly as possible."

"They ought to be allowed the benefit of the doubt," Castleton said, appealing to Barnstable. "How long ago was the war in the Fingal system? Have the usual tests been done to discover how long that ship has been floating in space? How do we know that isn't a Gringg world and those were the defenders and not the aggressors?"

Greene shot her a dire look which she ignored. "The point is, Captain, that ship was armed, and Ordnance is still trying to puzzle out their weapons systems."

"Has Admiral Sumitral been briefed on the Fingal Three discovery?" Castleton asked.

"How could he be when the matter's been classified? He's Alreldep anyhow, not naval, for all his title," Barnstable said, then waved his hand to dismiss that consideration. "The fact remains that a ship of indisputable Gringg design was discovered in orbit around Fingal Three—call it circumstantial evidence, if you wish, Grace—which has been absolutely wasted. That's enough to give me pause to consider very carefully how to proceed with the Gringg. I trust"—he looked around the table, nodding politely to Hrrto and Captain Hrrrv—"that you all realize that this meeting is not to be discussed at all? Good. You'll remain on Yellow Alert, Captain Castleton. Second Speaker, I'd appreciate your giving the same orders to your ships. Forewarned is forearmed!"

Castleton could not fault those orders as she sat staring at the frozen frame on the screen. Her initial impulse was to trust the Gringg, but intellectually she understood very well the need to remain on guard until both sides were satisfied of the other's peaceful intent. The Amalgamated Worlds had been at peace for centuries. The very thought of an interstellar war chilled her. She felt a warm touch at the back of her hand, and looked up to find Jon Greene watching her with his brows drawn upward, asking a silent question. His molded lips curved at the corner in a small smile of confidence. She nodded at him, returning the smile in spite of her worry. The expression in his eyes became warmer. Despite their obvious differences of opinion, she was inexplicably attracted to this man. But she was now on Alert status and there was no time for any private life.

"Of coursse, all waits upon being able to speak to each otherrr," Hrrto said.

"At least the most experienced man we've got is in charge of that," Grace Castleton said, finding relief in the fact.

"Sumitral?" Barnstable asked. "Has he arrived?"

"Not that we've been informed, Admiral," Grace said, "but I meant Reeve."

Barnstable gave a little grunt. "I heard that he learned Hrruban first." Then he remembered the presence of Hrrubans in the room, and smoothly went on. "Which was only logical at the time, of course."

"I hope he's the right man to do the initial work," Greene said, looking concerned. "Some people get so wound up in their own specialty that they fail to see the broader view."

"Rrev has proved his competence on several levels," Hrrto said, surprising himself as well as Mllaba. "He prrotects, as alwayss, Rraladoona." He dropped his jaw in a slight smile.

"Of course, Second Speaker," Greene said quickly, "but I found his manner of taking charge of the first contact a shade officious."

"He was asked to do so," Castleton reminded him. "After all, he expedited them to the planet, which protected the technology on the *Hamilton* from their scrutiny."

"Aye," Hrrrv agreed. "It waz wise to rrremove zem from zis vessel at once."

"Zo, Admirral," Second said, folding his arms across his chest. "We wait?"

"I'll instruct Sumitral," Barnstable said decisively, "to find out as soon as possible—using whatever methods, signs, sketches, are needed—what part of the galaxy they come from, and how they found their way here."

"Zat, surely, can wait, Admirrral," Mllaba said smoothly. "Ze threat is here, now, not wherever ze Gringg home system iss."

"But the Gringg fleet?" Barnstable held on to his concern.

"No evidence zat zere is any. Nothing is detectable in ze near reaches of space," Captain Hrrrv said.

Castleton confirmed it. "I've checked with my telemetry officer. He agrees. They came in alone."

"Each one of them is an eight-hundred-pound warrior!" Barnstable barked. "They're a potential danger to Humanity!"

"And to Hrrubankind as well," Hrrto added.

"And from that tape," Greene added, "it doesn't look as if it takes more than a single ship to decimate a planet."

Mllaba was thoughtful. "Now what we really need is furzzer support for our position of caution. Ze Doonarralans will go on zeir merry way, never suspecting zat zey are set up frrr destruczhon until ze bomb falls on zeir heads. We require prrrsons of influence, who can prevail upon zem to move with greazzer care. What about zis Hayuman Landreau? Can we gain his support to suggest a more cautious approach to ze Rralan administration?"

Greene shook his head. "No, he's like a child with a new toy where the Gringg are concerned. In fact, he treats them rather like playmates. He's frivolous."

"Son, never call a Landreau frivolous," Barnstable warned him darkly. "His family has considerable influence on Earth and elsewhere. I'd prefer to have him with us than against us."

Second spoke up. "I shall endeavrrr to inform ze Hrruban High Council zat a wary approach is a wise one. Most of zem are conservative, and I do not zink zere will be protest. Perhaps more pressure can be brought to bear on ze Doonarralans from ze two home governments?"

"Direct intervention would be better," Barnstable said. "We need reinforcements, to have a physical presence. Trouble is we can't get them here quickly enough. It will take weeks for ships to arrive from Earth or any of the colonies where some of our potential allies reside. We must be ready for any eventuality!"

"In zis I can help," Second said, "at least with regard to transportation. I will auzorize use of ze grid for ze specific purrpose of supporrt in zis possible crisis. A wise Stripe moves cautiously zrough a strrange forest."

"Honored Speaker," Mllaba began, "it would be wiser still to be sure zat ze grid operazors on duty are ones known to us, and zrrussworzy. Zey must not disclose who auzorized zis movement wizout your specific prrrmission."

"Discretion widens a Stripe," Second replied, nodding acceptance.

"I'd feel a lot happier if we had some sort of military backup, just in case the Gringg slough off the charm and turn on the heat," Barnstable said.

"Sir," Castleton said, an odd expression on her face, "need I remind you that we have a full marine complement on board the *Hamilton!* Not to mention the fact that her crew have won every single martial arts competition the fleet has put on over the past five years?"

The Admiral grimaced and raised a conciliatory hand. "Now, Grace, medals for exhibition affairs are not quite the same thing as military experience. . . ."

"Who's had that in God knows how many years?" she asked, pursing her lips.

The Admiral's face reddened, a sharp contrast to his mane of white hair. "Grace, don't overstep yourself. I'm in charge of the safety of this sector, and dammit, I'll protect it any way I can. I allowed Reeve to take those aliens to the surface of a peaceful colony and I'll make damned certain peace is maintained there."

"Yes, sir," Grace Castleton said. "But may I still counsel moderation?"

"I've taken your counsel, and now hear mine. We're on yellow alert, and I mean alert! We're going to be ready for any thing—" Barnstable paused, closed his eyes briefly, suddenly remembering that there were Hrrubans right there with him, so he hastily altered what he'd been going to say. "What I mean is, those Gringgs are naturally armored, those fangs, their talons; their forearms have the reach of any among us. Why, that thick furry hide of theirs could probably turn away slugs."

Mllaba put in silkily, "Perhaps permeability of zeir skin and skin tension can be one of ze tests performed by your medical technician."

"Good suggestion. Maybe. In the meantime, Speaker Hrrto, I'll take advantage of your offer to use the Treaty Island grid. And, bear in mind, please, that if those Gringg make a move before we're ready for them, one of those grid operators must reach Earth alive to let them know what went on here."

Hrrto nodded. "I will remain on Rrala," he said, well aware that the Hayumans might have thought he'd chosen the easy way out by grid. The Gringg terrified him, but he was in acute terror of losing face by fleeing.

"As you wish," the Admiral said, rising. "I'll get in touch with a few people, transfer them up here for a little conference." He turned to Greene. "Put the connections through yourself, lad. I want a stop put to this chummy foolishness, stat!"

"Admiral," Castleton said, also rising, "shouldn't we inform the planetary administration of our discovery?"

"Indeed we should not, sir," Greene said suddenly. He was still smarting from Todd Reeve's off-hand treatment of him while on board the Gringg vessel, and his flamboyant disregard of safety in embracing the aliens. "I'd recommend against it. For security reasons alone. We certainly don't want the grids jammed with people insisting that their department has to have representatives here, too. The necessary departments have already been informed and are present. No more information should be broadcast." And when eventually the Amalgamated Worlds knew, Greene thought with satisfaction, Todd Reeve would be disgraced, even removed from planetary office as a danger to Humanity.

The passengers aboard the Spacedep shuttle were silent on the way down to the surface of Doonarrala. Admiral Barnstable sat making notes on his clipboard, pausing occasionally to call up data from its small memory bank. Second Speaker, unaccustomed to travelling in Hayuman spaceships, stared over the shoulder of the pilot, reading the control panel as if reluctant to trust the Hayuman female's expertise.

Mllaba glanced occasionally at the Hayuman who was her opposite number. Greene was attempting to meet her eyes. She wondered what he wanted. It was unusual for a Hayuman to remain silent; normally they chattered away, regardless of the gravity of a situation. Perhaps this male was different.

It was the middle of the night on the Treaty Island Center. The cleaning staff, busy with brooms and a floor polisher, paid no attention to the mixed group on its way to the grid. Mllaba took her place behind the controls.

"Ze Firrrst Village grid," Hrrto said to Mllaba, as he walked between the upright pillars, and assumed a dignified pose. The female's claws clattered swiftly on the keyboard. Second Speaker vanished slowly in the rising mists. Barnstable looked uncomfortable and wary as he strode up onto the dais and squared his shoulders.

"Bring me back in four hours," the Admiral directed. Mllaba inclined her head.

"I, too, must return to my homeworld to report to the Council," Mllaba said to Greene, when the Admiral had been dispatched. "May I assist you to travel somewhere first?"

The Hayuman seemed in no hurry. "No, thank you. I've waited because I wanted to talk to you alone," Greene said, his warm brown eyes meeting her yellow-green ones directly. She could feel the power of his personality being brought to bear upon her. "You have no reason to trust me, and I don't trust you," he continued disarmingly, "but we could help one another to our mutual benefit."

"How?" Mllaba asked politely.

Greene turned and gestured to a bench facing the grid station. Mllaba shook her head, so Greene sat down alone. He drew up one knee and wrapped both hands around it nonchalantly. The arrogance of the pose put Mllaba on guard. She slipped her hands protectively into her robe sleeves and stood stiffly before him, waiting.

"I know that election for the Speakership is imminent," Greene said, gazing up at her. "If Speaker Hrrto were to gain that honor, a new Speaker for External Affairs would be appointed."

If Mllaba was surprised to learn that a Spacedep officer was conversant with the intricacies of Hrruban government, she did not show it outwardly. Inside, she felt a prickle of excitement. Greene spoke to the carefully tended ember of ambition she bore within her. She concentrated on keeping her tail tip from flicking back and forth.

"And should I display more zan usual competence in zis most difficult and dangerous affair," Mllaba said, "I should be ze favored candidate. Is zat your idea?"

Greene nodded, grinning. "I, too, am trying to stay on what we call a 'fast track.' I'm a risk-taker. I was sent to these talks partly to get me away from Spacedep HQ, and out of the line of promotion. So far, the Admiral is getting all the glory here, but I'd like a little of it to drop on me. If we work together to save Doonarrala, as well as Earth and Hrruba, from the Gringg menace, both you and I would gain favor in the eyes of our superiors. Wouldn't you agree?"

"And you in the eyes of ze attractive Hayuman captain?" Mllaba asked, and complimented herself on making a telling stroke. The naked skin of the Hayuman's face flushed red. Had he thought the signals going back and forth between him and Castleton were invisible to the others in the room?

"I'll tell you why Admiral Barnstable has really gone back to Earth," Greene said, changing the subject. "He is ordering the Human defense fleet to Doonarrala. Only he has the authority to do so. From its current position, it'll take thirty days for the fleet to get here. Then, if the situation warrants, the Admiral could declare martial law."

Mllaba nodded. "Hrruba should prepare a similar defense fleet," she said. *Second Speaker is not acting as decisively in this matter as he should be,* she thought. Hrruba ought to have been the first to take such steps, not Earth. He should have issued such an order. She resolved to bring it up to the Council in his name. "And so you and I will cooperrrate and share knowledge?" she asked. "Only because zis is a crrrisis, and zat is what is best for our own species, you understand."

"Of course," Greene agreed gravely. He stood up and put out his right hand to her, thumb upward. Mllaba stared at it for a moment before offering her own in the same position. He clasped her hand strongly, then released it. Hayuman customs were so strange! She tucked her hands primly back into her sleeves, and Greene stepped away. He respected her; that was good. She intended to maintain the upper hand in this relationship. He needed her cooperation far more than she needed his.

Mllaba set the grid controls for a thirty-second delay, and stepped onto the dais between the pillars. "I will return in four hours," she said. As the mists rose around her, she watched the Hayuman turn and stride away toward the landing pad.

The procession into the Human First Village had taken on the aspect of a parade. Hordes of children, led by Kelly's and Nrrna's youngsters, danced around and around the cluster of adults walking with the Gringg. When they reached the doors of the Doonarralan Medical Center, Dr. Kate herded the Gringg, Ken, Lauder, Frill, Sumitral, and Hrrestan inside. Almost as an afterthought, she pointed at Jilamey Landreau.

"You, mind the children! I need Nrrna and Kelly as lab assistants. Okay with you?"

"Anything to help," Jilamey agreed cheerfully, and was promptly dragged away by Alec and Alison, demanding to hear all about the Gringg ship.

To the adults outside, Kate said, "Go on with you. We'll give you the news when we have any." She smiled, scattering them with a wave of her hands as if they were chickens. When the door had closed, she turned around and let out a deep sigh. "Well! Welcome to you folks," she said, inclining her head to the Gringg. "And welcome to you," she said to the naval officers. "Who's my lab partner today?"

Lauder raised a timid hand. "I am, ma'am. Ensign Mauro Lauder."

"Just Kate, all right?" She smiled at the young officer. "I'll call you Mauro. Everyone this way, please?" She led them to her office and pointed toward the waiting room. "The rest of you stay here. I'm going to take this bruiser first." She laid a hand on Ghotyakh's furry arm. "Be good and you get a lollipop."

The door to the examining room shut behind them. Ken looked around at the wooden-walled waiting area, remembering how many times he'd sat here with a sick child or a farm-related injury his wife, Pat, hadn't been able to mend.

"Now, Reeve," Sumitral said, beaming, "tell me all about the confrontation."

Ken recounted their adventure without benefit of the tapes he and the others had made, but he didn't think he left out any important details or observations. Sumitral, who believed that the mark of a good diplomat was to be a good listener, nodded occasionally as Ken talked, only interrupting once in a while to clarify a point.

"Very interesting," Sumitral said. "Very, very interesting. I want to see those tapes as soon as we're through here. Thanks to Hrruban technology, I got here a lot faster this time."

"I think we need you more this time than we ever did with the Hrrubans," Ken said.

Sumitral's eyes twinkled. "I'm good for show and to wrap things up nicely."

"Much more than that, sir," Ken said, protesting such modesty.

"I don't have your fine honesty and instinct, Ken, which incidentally I respect immensely. Anyway, you've more experience in first contact than anyone else here. And, with creatures as large as the Gringg, I'd really feel easier when we establish a communication medium! I don't want misunderstandings of any kind with folks that big." He grinned.

But the Gringg were not without ways of making themselves understood.

"Genhh?" Eonneh asked, then paused, as if puzzled how to make his question clear.

Ken sat up straighter. "Go ahead, Honey. What?"

"Rrss. Rroobvnnn?"

"Sure is," Ken said. "Er, yes." Eonneh cupped his forepaws together, the way he had while holding the Hrruban cub, then drew them to his breast.

"Nrrna. Rroobvnnn?"

"Yep. I mean, reh," Ken replied.

"This is fascinating," Sumitral said, studying Eonneh closely. "What's he trying to ask?"

"I don't know yet," Ken said. "Vocabulary's very limited."

"Rroobvnnn, Rrss? Genhh, Ayoomnnn?"

"Reh," said Ken.

"Gelli, Rroobvnnn?"

"Ah . . . ah . . . morra. No. Ayoomnnn."

"Morra," said Eonneh, disbelievingly. He made the sign for baby again. "Gelli. Morra Ayoomnnn?"

"Reh, Ayoomnnn, Kelly," Ken said. "She's my daughter-in-law."

"Nrrna morra Rroobvnnn."

"Reh, Rroobvnnn." Ken nodded firmly.

"What's the problem?" demanded Sumitral, exasperated to be on the fringe of understanding.

"I'm not positive, but I'm beginning to get the drift," Ken said with a wry smile.

They went through the pantomime several times, with Hrrestan and Frill attempting to guess what explanation Eonneh was trying to elicit. Eonneh took hold of his own tail and held up the end.

"Rroobvnnn, shrra. Nrrna, shrra. Nrrna," and he made the baby sign again. "Morra?"

Ken fell back in his chair and burst into loud hoots of laughter. "Oh, I get you now! Oh, no!" He clutched his sides and beat his feet on the floor.

The noise brought Kate Moody running out into the waiting room. "What's the matter?" she demanded. Lauder, Nrrna, and Kelly were right behind her.

"It's hilarious," Ken gasped, coming up for air. "They think 'Hrruban' is the word for male, and 'Hayuman' is the word for female. Or maybe the other way around." When the others looked puzzled, he sprang the other half of the joke. "They think we're one species!"

"How could they think that?" Lauder asked, appalled as well as slightly indignant.

"Why shouldn't they? We arrive together on their ship, so we are together. They see us living together here on the surface. Why shouldn't they think we're the same species? They thought the Hrrubans were males and Hayumans females. The sight of Nrrna with a baby who's obviously hers knocked their assumption into a tailspin!"

Sumitral grinned at Ken's inadvertent witticism, his gray eyes alight. "So we are a species more than usually dimorphic?"

"They thought I was a girl?" Lauder demanded huffily. "I don't think that's funny."

"Well, I wouldn't take it to heart, lad. You'd be a good-looking girl—if you were one, which you're not," Kate suggested mildly. "But, under the circumstances, I think the Gringg copped on to the error of their assumption pretty quick."

Noticing how politely Eonneh and Ghotyakh waited for some explanation of his unusual behavior, Ken shook his head. "I haven't got the words to explain laughter yet. Much less how to explain that we're two species, male and female each, from two different worlds."

"Watch it, Reeve," Frill said. "That's strategic information."

"It might be if either of us knew exactly where the other's homeworld is," Ken said in mild disgust. "Lighten up, Frill. A basic explanation won't give away any more than our kids get in primary school."

"We can't base a solid future relationship on deceptions," Sumitral said more mildly. "Can you help us with the gender explanation, Dr. Moody?"

Kate grinned. "Sure can. Take the bull by the horns, so to speak. While Lauder and I are taking samples, we'll show them tapes on Hayuman and Hrruban reproduction and birth. They'll get the idea."

Kate ran the tapes used for sex education in the Middle School, all the while taking blood, skin, and hair samples from her unprotesting subjects. Honey and Kodiak watched the tapes with every indication of understanding what they were seeing. They muttered—"A little like embarrassed twelve year olds," Kate said later—and growled furiously between themselves.

"I'm running a CAT scan on each of them. They seemed very interested in everything, the equipment and procedures. They're both very intelligent. By the way," Kate said with a grin, "they're male. What we'd classify as male. Both of them."

"How do you know?"

"I got them to give me urine samples. There's no way that a baby could be born through that orifice, and there's nothing else appropriate. I did a very careful physical examination. No womb, but very substantial generative organs. We went through some pantomime to confirm it. But that big captain on the tape, the one you keep calling Grizz, and referring to as he? She's female! All of her, and that squat one's her second-born cub. Honey's the sire."

"So they are dimorphic with regard to size, but the other way round to our two species," Ken said, nodding.

"Right. There's precedent for this configuration, living on Earth at this minute. The males are tercels, an old word meaning a third smaller, Terran birds of prey. The large birds, falcons, are the females."

"Well, I'm glad we got that figured without making a serious gaffe. It doesn't matter what gender one is, so long as we don't mistake one for t'other," Ken said.

Eonneh, emerging from his turn in the ring-shaped scanner, sought out Genhh and Frrrill and the new Ayoomnnn. They were sitting in the wooden room, speaking softly to each other. He sat down beside them.

"I am terribly sorry for mistaking your gender," Eonneh said in his own language, pantomiming disgrace, which involved drawing an invisible line from his bowed forehead to the floor. "You are larger than others of your species, so we thought you were female. We didn't realize you were males of two different species of alien."

"What's he saying?" Frill asked, mystified.

"I think he's trying to apologize," Ken said. "It's okay, you know," he said, putting a hand on the Gringg's upper limb. The fur was smooth but thick, like horsehair. "It's no insult to be thought female, or male, for that matter. I know you're trying to learn all about us, but who said you had to get it all right first crack?"

"Nereh?" Eonneh understood his forgiveness, but missed the colloquialism.

Sumitral sighed. "We have got to make some sort of device so we can start understanding one another."

"We've got one problem," Kate said, leaning out the door. "I can't get this lad into the X-ray. He's too big! It's only made for Hayumans and Hrrubans. We're going to have to take him over to Ben Adjei's unit at the Animal Hospital for a peep at his insides."

While Kate Moody continued physical examinations, Lauder made use of an unused biochemistry lab to start work on the Gringg tissue samples and food-stuffs. Nrrna, who worked in the bio-lab, prepared samples for the centrifuge and electron microscope.

"I'm a duffer at chemistry," Kelly informed them. "My training is in diplomacy. I'll wash glass, or whatever you need me to do."

"One thing I'll need," Lauder said, very tentatively, "and I'm not sure I should ask you, is a volunteer to taste the foodstuffs if they test out as safe."

"Ouch," said Kelly, wrinkling her nose. Nrrna looked alarmed. "Well, if you promise me I won't die of it, I'll try anything."

"Oh, you won't be the only guinea pig at the table," Lauder said with a shrug. "We need to try at least one of the Gringg on Doonan food. Once we've got results on the tissue, I'll know what we can offer them and what we shouldn't."

"That's good," Kelly said cheerfully. "I do hate to eat alone."

"Them?" Kate replied, when asked about the Gringg's gastrointestinal system. "They can handle anything that isn't moving too fast. I did a whole-body sonogram on Ghotyakh as long as I had him over at the vet clinic. He watched everything I did, and I got the impression he doesn't like to go to doctors of his own species! That digestive pouch you detected below the stomach is one tough little organ. I wouldn't try them on concrete, but there's not much shy of that they can't eat. My husband, Ezra, went home to get some supplies. We may as well all dine together."

In the Federation Center, Jon Greene waited before the transport grid. Only moments before the four-hour time limit, the mists arose on the grid platform and the form of Mllaba took on shape and substance. Greene stepped forward to greet her.

"Did you meet with success?" he asked. The glare of her yellow-green eyes warned him not to get too close. He stopped short and gestured a fine bow as she left the dais.

"I have accomplished ze firrst of my goals," Mllaba said, settling her black robes back on her narrow shoulders. "Others from Hrruba will be following me very shortly to aid in slowing down ze Gringg agenda. As frrr ze second, it awaits ze Speaker's own presence to be set in motion. But I have laid ze groundwork well," she added with a degree of smugness. The two of them discussed plans for a few moments, then Greene glanced at his wrist chronometer.

"Now," he said.

The Hrruban put her clawed fingers on the controls. The air over the grid thickened, gradually revealing a crowd of Hayumans exclaiming to one another at the novelty of transporting by grid. Barnstable was at their head. Greene recognized two of the men and one of the women as members of the Humanity First! movement. Another was a prominent journalist with a talent for rabble-rousing. Three others were minor politicians and animal-rights activists. Greene grinned. The Admiral hadn't missed a trick.

As soon as he was aware of where he was, Barnstable looked around. "No unauthorized personnel present. Good. My thanks, Mllaba, for our safe transport. Greene, I'll want a report from you in an hour's time."

"Aye, sir," Greene said, saluting.

"Your allies from ze Hrruban homeworld await you at the meeting point, Admimral," Mllaba said. "Ze Speaker is with them."

"Good. To the First Villages, then," Barnstable said, nodding at the Hrruban female. Mllaba's claws clattered quickly over the controls. She had just enough time to join the party on the platform before it vanished.

Unnoticed by the others, three men in mufti slipped off the rear of the platform and waited until the mists cleared.

"Bouros, Gallup, Walters," Greene barked. The three men stiffened to attention. "Follow me." The commander led them out of the building into the night.

"Quit staring at me," Kelly complained, turning aggrieved hazel eyes on Ensign Lauder. "If I feel my insides curling up, I'll tell you."

"Sorry, ma'am. I'm just curious as to what's going on with you." The young medic blushed and went back to his plate.

Kelly grinned. "I'm just fine. In fact, some of this is pretty good." She turned to her dinner partner, Ghotyakh, and pointed at a sausage-shaped mass. "What do you call that?"

"Raghia," Kodiak said. "Neehar, ar . . ." He made his four fingers into the legs of some animal and walked them in a lumbering gait across the table.

"Meat of some ruminant?" Ken decided. "We'll have to get him to draw us a picture later. These fellows have fantastic skill."

Sumitral took another helping of stew. "It's clear that it is an important part of his job, even class station, to be able to write and draw well. I'd say that they're at the top of their grade, by the way, though I observe that Ghotyakh defers to Eonneh."

"I think if they're organized like us, Eonneh must be Grizz's special aide as well as mate," Ken agreed.

Eonneh nodded, showing his teeth, having caught the gist of Ken's statement. He and Ghotyakh were making significant inroads on the pot of stew. When Kate's daughter Rachel had arrived with dinner, the Gringg's agile noses went into full twitch. They waited, looking wistful, while Kate did a quick test to make sure there was nothing in the meal that would disagree with them, and howled with joy when she led them to the table to be served.

"By the way, Lauder," Kate said, "you were wrong about one of them eating as little as one of us. That was Kodiak's sixth bowlful."

Lauder grinned lopsidedly. "I could eat the same, myself. This is delicious. You don't get meals this good shipside."

"My very thought," Sumitral said placidly.

"Go on with you," Kate said. "It's all last year's dried snake meat."

"No, it's terrific," Lauder insisted.

"Do not let Dr. Kate ovrrwhelm you with hrrr modesty," Hrrestan said, his jaw dropped in a genial grin. "Hrrr cooking has been praised widely by all, including my mate, Mrrva."

"Well, that one's a winner," Kelly said, marking the packet of raghia with a plus sign. "Alison would like it: tasty with a flavor rather like urfa." With businesslike fingers, she pushed it to one side and opened another packet. She was taking only small portions from each of the Gringg rations, to leave room for as many samples as possible. The next was a chopped vegetable in a messy red sauce. She spooned a little of it onto her tasting plate and took a mouthful. Her face wrinkled up, and she choked.

"What's the mazzer?" Nrrna demanded.

Hrrestan rose to his feet in alarm. "Shall I get the szomach pump?"

Lauder was out of his chair and beside Kelly in a moment. She waved them away. Her face had turned red.

"Salty," she gasped, gesturing at the water pitcher. Kate handed her full glass over and then he filled Kelly's.

"So that's what they use to keep up their electrolyte balance," Kate said briskly. "You might like to know, Ensign, that unlike Earth animals, they have sweat glands here and there under that great pelt. Suggests to me that they evolved from animal with less body hair. And they have a tremendous lung capacity, more than four times ours, plus a layer of fat beneath the skin that ranges from three to five centimeters. Now what does that suggest to you?"

"Nozzing," said Hrrestan, shaking his head.

"They're swimmers," Ken guessed, playing with a piece of bread.

"That'd be my summation," Kate said with satisfaction. "Seems to me as if they must have evolved from something more like otters than bears. It would certainly explain the tail."

"Hmm," said Kelly, taking another packet. This one contained dried brown kernels shaped rather like Brussels sprouts, and coated with a fine tan powder. She crunched one tentatively between her teeth, and smiled with pleasure. "Um, these are great. Gringg candy," she said, offering some to Ken, who reached out to take it.

"Ah-ah-ah!" Kate scolded, putting a hand between them. "No one else gets to try anything until you, my dear, have gone twenty-four hours without a reaction."

Kelly gulped. "I guess I didn't realize what a serious job this was going to be."

"I'm sorry," Kate said kindly. "I'm sure everything'll be all right, but if you're going to run a proper experiment, control is essential."

"Oh, well." Kelly sighed, and opened another packet. "And what do you call this?" she inquired of the Gringg.

Commander Frill entered, his nose twitching almost as much as one of the Gringg's.

"Something smells wonderful," he said. He was holding an armful of tapes and a couple of small pieces of equipment.

"Sit down and have some," Kate invited him. "There's stew, tenderfoot chili, creamed potatoes, mixed veg, and plenty left if you can beat the Gringg to it. Your friend Lauder here was just saying that this compares favorably to ship food."

"Thank you, ma'am," Frill said with alacrity, sitting down next to Ken. He helped himself generously from the stewpot and tore a huge section from the loaf beside it. "I don't know when I last had a home-cooked meal." Between bites and exclamations of pleasure, Frill explained what he had found.

"One of the engineers at the computer control in town let me use the equipment," he said, "to listen to these tapes. I think I've found the problem," he went on, setting down the equipment: a hand-recorder, a speaker, and a paired unit with glass-fronted screens. Across the upper screen was a flat green line. The lower showed stepped levels in green light. He started the recorder, and they heard Grizz repeating words after Ken. "Here, watch the screens carefully. Now, this is Gringg conversation." On the oscilloscope, the green line etched peaks above and below the center line as the sound level rose and fell. The frequency monitor below showed peaks and valleys, too, but more peaks than valleys when Ken's voice was heard, with just the opposite whenever the Gringg spoke.

"Interesting," Ken said, peering at the numbers beside the levels on the frequency monitor. "That would explain why I couldn't approximate some of their pronunciations. Their voices dip down into subsonics."

"How low do they go?"

Frill checked his printout. "Thirteen to fifteen cycles, sir."

"We Hrrubans would merely feel zose lowest tones," Hrrestan commented.

"Ah," Sumitral said. "So the words go below the range of Hayuman and even Hrruban hearing."

"It would also explain why we felt nervous, sir," Frill explained. "Some of these low tones provoke fear responses."

Sumitral nodded. "That guides us toward what we'll need to make coherent contact with the Gringg."

"If I can ask a favor, Admiral?" Kate Moody said, standing up to dish out more food.

"I'll grant it if I can," Sumitral replied, watching her heap potatoes onto his plate.

Kate strove to keep her voice light. "Don't forget the little people who helped make this meeting possible, will you? The citizens of Doonarrala are wildly interested in helping to learn whatever they can about the Gringg, and want a chance to help. They're not afraid of challenges or they wouldn't be here. Don't shut them out."

"Madam, I don't discount the input from those who have helped so far, especially the children, to whom the Gringg seem very attached," Sumitral acknowledged. "And I'd be a fool to push aside volunteer staff who are so eager to be included, so long as they acknowledge that I'm in charge of this mission."

"Oh, I don't think they'll mind that," Kate said. "It's being left out that they'd hate."

"This is Doonarrala," Kelly said, indicating herself and Nrrna. "We take pride in getting to know others on equal terms. That's what our husbands are doing right now on the Gringg ship, and on behalf of Alien Relations, over the twitching frame of Admiral Barnstable, I might add."

"Cooperation made Doonarrala what it is today. I'm all for extending the principle," Sumitral said, smiling up at her.

"Good, because cooperation is going to start with someone else cleaning up after this meal," Kate said with a broad grin. "Rachel, organize a few volunteers from those outside, will you? Then we can get on with the tests."

"I must go," Nrrna said. "It is nearly time for Hrrunna's meal. I must find Jilamey and ze children."

Sumitral rose and helped her out of her chair. "You take good care of that small ambassador," he told her.

"Zank you, I shall," she said, beaming shyly at the ambassador from Alreldep.

"Make sure the Cats get to bed on time," Kelly called. "Jilamey will let them stay up till all hours, and they are not to stay out of school on Uncle's say-so."

Hrrestan yawned, slurring his words out of pure exhaustion. "I frrr one am wearry. I am adjuzzed to Zreaty Island time, and we started earrly wiz ze confrrnce zis morning."

Unexpectedly, Nrrna was in the doorway again. She gestured behind her.

"Zese people wrrr waiting outside ze drrr." She did not have a chance to move aside, for she was pushed in by the crowd of Hayumans and Hrrubans who forced their way into the room. To Ken, their uniformly stony expressions gave them the aspect of a mob, not yet touched off, but potentially dangerous.

At their head were Barnstable and Second Speaker. Sumitral, standing beside the table, crossed his arms and waited calmly, while the mob organized itself around the perimeter of the big room, keeping wary eyes on the Gringg but patently determined to be in earshot. Hrrestan rose and stood beside the Alreldep ambassador.

"Well, Ev, how are you?" Sumitral asked.

Barnstable ignored the courtesy. "These people wanted to have a word with the colony leaders about this situation."

"And precisely which sizuazhon is zat?" Hrrestan asked, his tone relaxed but his eyes moving warily over the faces.

"The interruption of our spaceport conference by these . . . things," protested Lorena Kaldon, jerking her hand at the Gringg. "I came here to talk construction, mortgages, and interest rates, not alien invasions. My time is valuable, as is that of my colleagues here."

"We must do what we came to do!" added a Hrruban whom Hrrestan remembered as being a crony of the now-retired Third Speaker, a notorious reactionary. "Send zem back where zey came from. I oppose negotiations wiz zese aliens."

"They're called the Gringg," Sumitral said, a pleasant smile on his face. Eonneh and Ghotyakh, recognizing that word, rose to their feet and turned to face the newcomers. Both Kaldon and the Hrruban, suddenly obliged to crane their necks up, stepped as far back as they could.

Swallowing, Kaldon continued, but her voice was considerably less contentious. "We came so far, planned so long for this conference. It has to continue. You must understand our positions."

"No one planned to have zuch an interruption, Delegate Kaldon, but ze conference cannot resume at this time," Hrrestan said, "and, as co-leader of

Doonarrala, I muss ask your indulgence in zis matter. Surely you should recognize zat zeir appearrrnce has altered everything. For ze time being, all discuzhons about ze spaceport must be deferrrred while we learn more about ze new arrivals."

"But we've been working for months to make our bids on the construction of a spaceport," she protested indignantly. "We can't just call a halt and continue as before simply because of . . . hairy monsters. They aren't interfering with the spaceport project. Why can't we go ahead with it?"

"Now, my dear Ms. Kaldon," Sumitral said, stepping forward, "that wouldn't be wise. And indeed, the hold may be for a very short time. But look at the arrival of the Gringg from a different angle: you are witnessing an incident of immense international significance. It isn't given to many to be the first to see, and meet, an entirely new species of star traveller. And I put this to you, as well: once we have established communications, why we may even have to construct a larger spaceport. For, frankly, I suspect that their main objective in seeking other civilized or inhabited planets is to initiate trade." He pointedly ignored a growl of protest from Barnstable's direction. "Were I you, I would believe myself lucky to be in on the ground floor for those you represent. I'm sure they'll be delighted to learn of the possibility of even more customers at the space facility."

Kaldon regarded Sumitral with no little amazement, and obviously considered his advice.

"Admirral," Second Speaker said, stepping forward, "are you not prezuming too much? How can you speak of trade when zeir objectives are not known. Nor can zey be until we can speak to zem! And even zen, such matters must be carefully prrsented to our respective goverrrments for sober, mature reflection . . . not decided out of hand herre on Rraladoona."

"I speak as Alreldep's representative, who is always ready and willing to speak to inhabitants of our galaxy no matter what form they appear in or from what quarter of the Milky Way," Sumitral replied with great dignity and a gentle smile for the Second Speaker's querulous attitude.

"Msss Kaldon, zere is also ze unassailable fact," Hrrestan added, "that my co-leader, Rrev, has had to absent himself from our prrroceedings, so zey could not, in any case, continue without him."

Barnstable now beckoned imperiously to Hrrestan, Sumitral, and Ken Reeve to move to one side, away from Kaldon's group.

"See here, now, my friends," he said, scowling deeply and glaring from one face to another, "I can't approve of all this good-folks-at-home routine. These Gringg are an unknown quantity . . . and don't give me that they-came-in-friendship-unarmed guff, Reeve. How can you be absolutely positive these creatures are so pacific?"

"Suffer little children, Barnstable," Ken replied, more amused than irritated by the Admiral's attitude. "But then you didn't see, as everyone here did, how the Gringg."

Barnstable cut him off abruptly. "It's just not good tactics to be open with an unknown quantity."

"Do I have to remind you that it worked before, Admiral? Didn't it, Hrrestan!" And now Ken included his oldest Hrruban friend.

The Hrruban co-leader, whose tail had begun to lash in short hard twitches, relaxed and dropped his lower jaw slowly.

"We were not quite as formidable in appearance as these. Is zat what alarmss you, Amirral?"

"What alarms me is a basic disregard for caution. I don't want these good folk unnecessarily alarmed."

"They 'don't' look so alarmed," laughed Kate Moody, joining them. "And how'd they all get in here? Place is crowded with strangers."

"She's right about that," Ken murmured to Hrrestan, who also began looking at the curious faces of those backed against the wall.

"Now, that is not the issue," said Barnstable darkly, not liking Kate's interruption at all. "You really are most unwise to allow such broad contact between the Gringg and the rest of the Doonarralan population. As the official head of the organization charged with the protection of this sector, I want all data kept secure and the Gringg out of public contact until we know more about them. We have nothing but their physical presence to go on as yet, and that bothers me."

"Oh, but we got plenty of physical *data* on them," Kate said jovially. "I've got enough test results to satisfy anyone—" She gave Barnstable a jaundiced glare. "And even more reassuring empirical stuff. Gringg like snake stew. And beans give them gas."

There were a few chuckles from the back of the crowd. Barnstable turned around to glare at the group. "And what about the safety of these aliens? They could come to harm in this environment," he protested, trying another angle.

"They're pretty sturdy," Kate replied. "Not much could hurt them. I haven't found a single allergen or toxin that their tissues react to, not even rroamal. They've got functioning immune systems, ticking away beautifully right now, and they don't react to anything we do. I also can't find anything in their systems that bugs us, except for the odd irritant, and that can be inoculated against.

They're strong, the air is good for them, and our gravity is at least twenty percent less than they're used to fighting. They'd be almost super strong here."

That appeared to upset Barnstable further. "In that case, you are exposing an entire population to danger from accidents incurred during casual contact. I can't allow it. Remove them at once."

"You do not have jurisdiction here," Hrrestan said, his eyes flashing.

Sumitral was calm, almost apologetic. "This is an Alreldep matter, Ev, and you know that."

Barnstable could not refute it, but he hated to relinquish command to another authority.

"You will keep me in the loop, of course," he said, not without a measure of sarcasm.

"But, of course, Ev."

"Dad?" Robin Reeve poked his nose around the door and peered into the room. "Ah, there you are, Dad!" Reeve's son seemed to have an energy level befitting a man younger than his early twenties, and the poise of one much older. "Have I interrupted anything critical? Mom sent me to ask you when you're coming home and if you're bringing guests. Them?" he asked. Robin's eyes gleamed in keen anticipation of such a happening. "They're just as big as advertised. I was out on the range when they arrived."

"You zee?" Mllaba hissed. "It has alrready ze aspect of a vreakshow!"

"Not at all," Robin said cheerfully. "We always turn out for visitors. Whew! Wouldn't they be something on Snake Hunt? Can they hang around that long? Hunt's only six weeks away!"

Barnstable frowned. "They must certainly be off-planet when the Hunt takes place."

"Why?" Robin regarded Barnstable equably. "Everyone else wants to join in! At least these Gringg wouldn't need to be protected! For that matter, maybe we ought to protect our snakes from them! Let's ask Todd and Hrriss to invite them officially."

"What I should like to know—" said a new voice, belonging to a woman who stepped out of the crowd that had been politely, but avidly, listening to what they could hear of the discussions. She had a pinched mouth set in a plump pink face and wore rather dowdy clothing, neither travel nor leisure wear. "—is how you dare continue to hunt those poor snakes? Much less show such brutality to . . . to individuals who could only misconstrue the barbarism you exhibit."

"Barbarism?" Robin exclaimed as other Doonarralans started to protest. "Hell, lady, you've never seen what those snakes do to *our* domestic animals. A

blow from a Big Momma Snake's tail can break the back of a cow or horse . . .
then the snake eats the poor critter whole and sits there digesting it for weeks.
Who's being brutal?"

The woman had turned quite pale, but she wasn't one to give up easily.
"Then it is imperative that you not expose outsiders to such dangers. Why, I believe that some of the larger snakes grow as long as twenty meters." She regarded
the Gringg, who were not twenty meters in any dimension.

"Those big ones are usually too canny to cause trouble," Ken said, striving
to remain polite. "Have we met, ma'am? I haven't seen you at any of the Village
Socials, and I make it a point to get acquainted with all our visitors from Earth."

"I . . . I've just arrived," the woman said, clearly flustered.

Barnstable felt that it was a good time to retreat. "We intend to remain on
hand throughout your investigation, of course."

"Of course," Sumitral agreed, and Hrrestan nodded.

As soon as Barnstable and his cronies withdrew, Ken made for the communications console at the side of the room. In a few moments, he returned to the
group.

"I've just spoken to Martinson at the Space Center and to Hammer at Treaty
Island. No one fitting her description has arrived on the last couple of ships
from Earth."

"Then how'd she get here?" Kelly demanded.

"The grid?" Ken said, a light dawning. "I think I'm beginning to smell a conspiracy."

"I zink you arrre right, my old frrrnd," Hrrestan said. "Both Spacedep and
Second Speaker, I do so dislike inzerference from outside."

"And you can put it down to Spacedep's distrust of the Gringg," Ken said,
aggrieved. "Present company excepted," he said to Frill, who gave a sheepish
shrug.

"Second Speaker has also shown discomfort wherrrre our new friends are
concerned," Hrrestan said thoughtfully. "It would be well to be preparrred
against such azzacks in days to come."

"The best defense is progress," Sumitral said. "We're having a fine time chatting with these fellows,"—he smiled at the Gringg, who had remained silent
throughout the confrontation—"but it's too slow. We require some kind of device to speed our understanding of one another. I'd also like to know how they
found us."

"I can ask the communications center to help me get to work on a . . . a
voder," Frill volunteered. He turned to Hrrestan. "That is, sir, if you'll give me
the necessary authority?"

Hrrestan was openly pleased that a Spacedep officer deferred to the local authorities without argument. Ken was glad, because he was getting to like the burly commander.

"Grrranted, gladly," the Hrruban replied. "In ze meantime, it seems we must continue with drrawing of pictures to obtain informazhon."

"How will you describe light-years in pictographs?" Sumitral asked blandly as he settled down with an artist's block between Ghotyakh and Eonneh at Kate's laboratory table.

chapter six

Todd had felt a pang watching his father and the others enter the shuttle. He hoped that Barnstable wouldn't try to hold the Gringg on board the navy vessel. He wanted them safely on the surface of Doonarrala, where folk were sympathetic to aliens. He particularly wanted the Gringg out of the vicinity of Greene and Barnstable. But his father would take charge. After all, the matter was clearly an Alreldep problem.

But would his father wait for Admiral Sumitral to back him up? Of course he would! Todd derided his lack of faith in his father's common good sense. He also wished he could be in two places at once—to see the reactions of Doonarralans to the Gringg.

Best of all, he and Hrriss were in this venture together and he wished they could just forget—forever—all that nonsense about the spaceport on the Hrrunatan. But he couldn't, could he? Well, he could for the duration of the task at hand.

Then Grizz touched his arm and indicated that Todd and Hrriss should follow him into the long, high-ceilinged, semi-oval corridor from the landing bay toward the central core of the ship. Immediately, Todd applied himself to the task at hand—perception and observation, absorbing what he saw and felt as if all his pores had eyes and ears and noses. So, the bay itself was situated in one of those "knots in the tree-bole" he had observed from space. The walls were smooth, a silver metal—steel?—equipped with rows of hand- and toe-holds at two points in the parabolic arc of the ceiling, no doubt to cope in zero-grav.

"For no grrrav?" Hrriss asked, pointing.

"They'd have to turn off the artificial gravity from time to time," Todd said. "If they turned gravity off, we'd be in a right difficult case trying to get our feet from one of those holds to another. Look at the size of 'em and the distance between!"

"I am glad zese are peaceable creazures," Hrriss said fervently.

They stopped in a corridor that was split around a central pillar in which were set more gray glass doors. Grizz hulked between them and the pillar, indicating that they should wait. The captain poked a claw into a hole in the door plate, and it slid open. Grizz took one Doonan by each hand and directed them to look carefully up and down inside.

Against the far wall, narrow white platforms with transparent back panels slid endlessly upward until the perspective shrank the shaft down to a pinpoint. The bottom of the lift shaft was much closer. Todd could see the platforms were an endless loop: up on one side, down on the other. He and Hrriss grinned at Grizz to show that they understood the principle involved.

"Reh," Todd said.

Grizz roared approvingly and stepped onto an ascending platform. Together, Todd and Hrriss stepped onto the next one, which could easily accommodate two Humans. But the baby bear, Weddeerogh, also leaped aboard, landing in a heap of fur at their feet. They laughed and helped him up.

"Do you feel a strong grrrvitic pull behind us?" Hrriss asked, swaying back and forth to test it.

"Yes," Todd replied, watching columns of gray glass doors sink into sight and out again past his feet. "I'd say there's a spiralling core inside this central pillar. It's compelling me to lean back against the wall. I guess that's how they keep from having accidents in this shaft. It must go up for three hundred meters." He let the pressure drag him backward, and he put a heel against the upper flat of the panel. "Look at this!" He inched upward until it appeared that he was standing several centimeters above the floor.

Weddeerogh snorted his baritone laugh and threw himself at the wall, back first. He adhered at eye level with Todd, then deliberately inched himself around until his toes were in the air. The Doonans joined in the merriment, experimenting with the increased gravity. Hrriss found that he could squat perpendicularly to the wall.

"But it causes trrrible pressure in my head and neck," he said.

A roar from above caused Weddeerogh to wiggle right side up once more and urge his two friends to do so as well. The next set of doors they were approaching were open, and Grizz was waiting for them. Weddeerogh made a flying leap and landed in a shoulder roll on the floor. Todd and Hrriss circumspectly hopped from platform to floor.

This corridor was not as lofty as the lower level, and had only one set of handholds, running up the exact center of the ceiling. The Doonans followed the captain along, taking in as much new input as they could with quick looks inside the various rooms that opened off the broad hallway.

The Gringg medic was black and white with a kind expression in her light red eyes. Todd still couldn't easily distinguish between the sexes, but for the sake of argument decided to call this one female. There were beautifully rendered anatomy charts on the wall, showing skeletal, muscular, and circulatory systems for two genders. The black and white bear seemed to fit the female mold, as, to the Doonarralans' surprise, did Grizz.

"Wait until the scientists at home get a look at these," Todd said.

While he was studying the charts and trying to remember significant details, the medic prompted him to sit up on a raised platform, produced a device with a small drum at the end, and put it to Todd's belly.

"My heart's up here," he said, tapping himself on the chest. The medic grunted, and moved the diaphragm upward. She let out a pleased noise when the heartbeat registered in her device. That seemed to be what she was looking for. Todd counted his own pulse as she listened. It was faster than normal, probably due to the increased gravity of the ship.

The medical examination went very much like the one that the Gringg were probably being put through by Kate Moody, with the medic, whom Todd and Hrriss decided to call Panda, signing when and where she was about to take yet another tissue sample.

Panda seemed a little puzzled when Todd automatically pulled off his shirt but left his trousers in place. She plucked at the heavy denim with a claw and crooned a question.

"I always say you Hayumans put too much emphassiss on clothes," Hrriss said with a grin, as he unself-consciously pulled aside the decorative loincloth he wore.

"I don't have a furry hide, cat man," Todd replied in an undertone. "Stark naked suits you, but I'm getting goose bumps and how'll I explain them?"

Actually, the room was warm enough for comfort, but Todd still felt chilly. He pretended total indifference when Grizz and Weddeerogh, as well as Panda, leaned in to have a good stare at all his parts. The Gringg stepped back to have a conference, during which they looked from one to the other of their visitors with increasing agitation.

The argument ended seemingly without resolution. Panda resumed her examination, and Grizz sat back on the floor to watch. The medic handled them both very gently as she went carefully over their entire bodies, then guided them to a host of strange, Gringg-sized machines.

"X-ray? CAT scans? EEG's?" Todd asked.

"You must ask zem when we can understand one anozzer," Hrriss said. "Zere is somezing very wrong zat happens to me when zey speak. Do you feel uncomfortable, too?"

"Without clothes, of course I do," Todd said.

Hrriss gave his head a little shake. "I don't mean physical; I mean in the nerves of the ear and the mind."

"That's a relief, Hrriss. I was putting the agitation down to nerves, but if you're getting the same sort of unsettling nudge, it must be more than that."

When Todd emerged from the last machine, Panda drew him back to the table and handed him a cup.

"Oh, no," he said. The Gringg looked at him expectantly. Panda indicated the cup, and made a gentle arc with one claw, pointing to the interior. "No. I don't think I could."

"Go ahead. I have done it. Why do you have so much zrouble producing waste wazzer?" asked Hrriss, amused.

"Doing it under these circumstances—with them watching the whole process, is slightly inhibiting," Todd said, annoyed with himself, Hrriss, and the whole affair. He turned his back and shortly was able to provide a sample. Panda and Grizz spoke in a crisp dialogue, their bass voices sounding excited. He hoped that they weren't amused by his behavior. When he passed the specimen to Panda, he noticed that Hrriss was now holding his ears.

"Are you all right?"

The Hrruban's forehead was drawn in long furrows of gold plush. "It is somezing about ze way zey talk. It is loud, but I am used to loud speech. We who live on Doonarrala have always used louder voices zan on Hrruba. Ze Gringg are not just loud but grating."

"Subsonics," Todd said, snapping his fingers. "That could very well mean that they're not hearing everything *we* say, either. I'd sure like to see an analysis of their hearing range."

He gestured toward his ears, and made faces so that the Gringg could understand that sound was causing him discomfort. Panda took a small scope from one of her pouches and looked in his ears. She grunted, puzzled.

"That didn't work, Hrriss. Aha!" he exclaimed, pointing at his friend. "Your voice is higher than mine."

"So?" Hrriss asked.

"Talk in the highest register you can. Go up through falsetto. If their range is too low for us, chances are ours is too high for them."

Obediently, Hrriss began to hum in his own tenor range, then climbed gradually, a breath at a time, into a piercing shriek. Long before he topped the highest note he could reach, the Gringg were holding their ears. At the top of the range, they were looking at him closely. Grizz folded her thumb and forefinger together in imitation of a mouth and opened it to show she didn't hear anything.

"That's it," Todd said. "Up at that end they're only seeing your mouth move."

Enlightened at last, Panda put the two Doonarralans onto a frequency generator and tested their ranges of hearing. Hrriss was capable of hearing a few cycles lower than Todd, but the lowest tones to which the machine was set were inaudible to both. They could only feel the cycles that Grizz indicated she was still hearing.

"Zat one could shake my bones apart," Hrriss cried, much agitated, waggling his hands for them to stop it.

Grizz called for another scribe. When Grrala arrived, slow of movement but bright of eye, they were gestured to a table.

"We'd better call this one Koala, so we don't mistake her with Grizz," Todd suggested in a low voice.

Panda motioned Todd and Hrriss to sit at the table as Koala set up some kind of aural transponder and demonstrated how it worked.

Using the settings on what Todd identified as a frequency generator, he demonstrated which tones he and Hrriss could hear, and which ones were painful. The Gringg did the same, and the scribe noted them down busily. The engineer, with a device like a round-screened pocket computer in her great paws, was clearly busy drafting a design.

"Now I think we're getting somewhere," Todd said happily. "This thing should translate the tones they speak in to the ones we can hear, and vice versa."

"Zat will help mightily," Hrriss agreed. "I do not zink we should miss any of zeir tonal qualities. We need to hear all to understand."

After a while, Koala signalled that she had enough to work on. She and the scribe excused themselves and went off.

"Now, the question is, how long will it take them to whip up a frequency voder?" Todd said, grinning at Hrriss. As he moved on the table, his bare skin slid and he gave an exclamation. "Great snakes! I don't need to stay in the buff any longer!"

The Gringg watched him dress no less closely than they'd watched him disrobe. He winked at Weddeerogh, who squealed. Then Grizz stood up and stretched, allowing the visitors a splendid look at her fine, strong frame. Refreshed, she addressed the two Doonarralans.

"Dodh, Rrss, kwaadchhs?"

"Quadicks?" Todd asked, struggling to match her pronunciation.

"Kwaadchhs," Grizz repeated and, obviously demonstrating, moved her great arms in broad arcs, starting at her breastbone and pushing outward.

"Could she mean swimming?" Hrriss asked, turning to Todd in surprise. Todd shrugged, grinning for Hrriss to answer. "Yes, we swim."

"Rehmeh," Grizz replied, and ushered them back to the elevator platforms.

"Swimming?" Todd muttered to Hrriss as they ascended another level.

When they followed her lead and stepped off in what must be the center of the ship, they could even smell the water. Even knowing that the probe had shown a mysteriously large quantity of water in the center of the Gringg ship, neither Todd nor Hrriss were prepared for what they saw.

"Swimming," muttered Hrriss in mild shock as they passed the transparent doors that led into the most astonishing room.

Instead of weaponry or generators of any kind, the water-filled center of the ship turned out to contain a swimming pool, vast and deep. The central pillar containing the elevator system pierced straight through the heart of it, but also supported several levels above the water, on which a few Gringg lounged while dozens of others swam and sported in the pool.

"This is absolutely spectacular!" Todd exclaimed, astounded, letting his face reflect his opinion. He bowed and grinned broadly at Grizz, who seemed pleased by his reaction. "That is some pool."

"More a lake," Hrriss said, staring about him at the sheer size, and shaking his head at the quantity of water put to such use.

"Greene'll never believe this is what the water was for. Though what sort of a weapon requires water . . ." Todd trailed off, shaking his head.

"I zink he would prefer anozzer explanation," Hrriss said. "He is not a man to appreciate gracious living. Ah, but I can!"

"And look at the range of colors in the Gringg," Todd added, nudging Hrriss. "Pied, patched, white, brown, black, tan, gold. See the black fellow there with a white shirt-front and chin and white boots? My sister Inessa had a cat who looked just like him, remember?" Then he craned his head about, able to take in more details now that the first shock of the space-lake had passed.

The room was, indeed, remarkable. A full, curved ceiling of a soft blue that arched benignly over the lakelet had been made to appear a natural sky. Hidden ventilators provided soothing breezes and the occasional surprise gust that made the water's surface skip and quiver. Except for the toroid shape and the fact there was an elevator shaft running through it, it was hard to believe that the immense pool was situated in the heart of a space-going craft. The elegant homes of the very rich on Earth had once had such amenities, or so his father had told Todd, before living space on the planet became so constricted that such luxuries had been prohibited. Man-made lakes on the few resort areas were out-of-doors, and few would have been as large as this one. Todd wondered how close this approximated the living style of Gringg on their homeworld. He knelt to dip his fingers in the water and taste it.

"It's fresh, with only a slightly chemical taste," he said to Hrriss. From his pouch, Hrriss took a little bottle and filled it for later analysis.

Having enjoyed their reaction, Grizz now took off her collar, shoulder piece and belt, placed them on a rack filled with other such accouterments, and slid into the water. Beckoning with a long, slow wave of her arm, she signalled them to join her. Todd started to strip and was distracted by the workmanship of Grizz's adornments. He picked up the collar and felt the material. It was smooth and supple like leather, though thin as vinyl.

"Is this snakeskin?" he asked, showing the way a snake moved.

"Morra," said Grizz, and molded her face around a gaping mouth. She submerged, and Todd leaned close to the edge to see her. She opened and closed her mouth, using exaggerated motions of her lower jaw, and flapped her hands alongside her jowls for gills.

"Oh," Todd cried, enlightened, as she surfaced. "Fish. They must be whoppers!" He sketched a fish of great size with his hands.

"Reh, reh," Grizz said, adding another length to Todd's. He whistled.

"Oh, the one that got away," he said.

Squealing, Weddeerogh bounced off the side and landed belly-first in the water, splashing everyone. One of the adults swam quickly toward him, only its head and the line of a dark-brown-furred spine and rudderlike tail showing above the water. The cub paddled noisily toward his dam, but his pursuer caught up with him. As he made cries of mock distress, the larger Gringg picked him up, lifted him bodily out of the water, and tossed him. Weddeerogh laughed aloud all the way down.

The resultant splash caught Todd and Hrriss full in the chest. "Agh!" Todd cried. "I'm soaked."

"Zen come in alrreddy," Hrriss said, teasing his friend. "You can get no wezzer zen you arrre." He undid his belt and threw it across Grizz's, and jumped in near Weddeerogh.

"Here I come," Todd said, hopping out of his shoes and hastily pulling off his clothes. "Damned nuisance. If I'd known I was going swimming . . ." Stripped again, he stood poised on the side of the pool. Then, as the Gringg audience watched with interest, he leaped up and cut a beautiful arc, entering the water with scarcely a ripple.

When he surfaced, halfway across the pool, the Gringg applauded him, batting the water noisily with their palms.

"Very prezzy," Hrriss said. "I didn't know zat was possible in zis grravity. I zink zey have not seen diving of zis sorrt."

"No," Todd said, surveying his companions. "They're not really built for swan dives and jackknifing are they?"

At Grizz's encouragement, Todd demonstrated more Hayuman-style dives, using the highest of the pillar islands to do a half-gainer. The Gringg were impressed, calling out their approval to him in loud, gruff voices.

When he was worn out, he pulled himself onto a nearby level and lay back listening to a youthful male with a stringed musical instrument gutturally rendering songs requested by the other Gringg. Todd asked to see the instrument, which was not unlike a guitar.

"But far heavier," he told Hrriss. He bent his fingers around the long stem as well as he could. They didn't reach the fretting, so he laid the instrument in his lap as if it were a dulcimer and tried to make chords. The resultant sounds were harmonious, but nearly inaudible. "These strings are heavier than baling wire. It's more like playing tent spikes."

The doors swung open. Koala, followed by the scribe, padded into the swimming room carrying a crescent-shaped solid in one hand and, in the other, a device not unlike Todd's recorder, with a slot intended to take the moon-shaped piece. The two Gringg settled down beside Todd and showed him diagrams on the reader's round screen.

"That was quick," Hrriss said.

"Let's hope it works," Todd replied. With a little stretch of imagination, Todd began to recognize the complex molecular structure of proteins.

Koala pointed to one. "Ayoomnnn."

"Yes, if you say so," Todd agreed with a grin. "And that's Hrruban, right?" He put his finger on the other pattern.

"Reh," Koala said, and put a claw to a control on the viewer. The two patterns moved toward and then overlay one another. Atoms stuck out to either side of the chain, and Koala seemed puzzled.

"Hayuman and Hrruban," Todd explained, pointing to himself and Hrriss.

The two Gringg conferred, and finally it fell to the scribe to draw pictures. With care, he sketched Todd and Hrriss, then began to draw in lines around them.

"The quality of artwork is magnificent for such quick drawings," Todd said. "Jilamey could make millions for this fellow in the Artists' Corridor on Earth."

"And on Hrruba," Hrriss added.

The scribe's sketch complete, he turned it toward them.

"It's a family tree," Todd realized. The scribe dashed small symbols between the images of the two of them, pointing at one, then another, and asking for clarification.

"He's not sure if we are siblings or . . . mated?" Hrriss turned with twinkling eyes to his friend, dropping his jaw in amusement.

"Uh, no," Todd said, shaking both hands and head vehemently at the misunderstanding. With the scribe's permission he took the tablet and stylus. While Koala watched closely, Todd drew two different family trees and peopled them with figures not much more detailed than stick figures, but clearly male and female of each species: one with tails, one without.

"You are not as good an artist as he is," Hrriss said.

"Agreed, but let's hope they get the message, and see the difference." He patted his work to show it was finished and pushed the drawing to the scribe. "We're two separate species! See—tails, no tails!"

The revised drawing prompted another spate of conversation. The scribe depicted a planet with figures of Todd and Hrriss standing on top of it.

"Ah. I presume he now wonders how we came to be on one planet," Todd said. "How do I explain?" So he drew Earth, marking out the Western Hemisphere continents, then its moon and sun, added a creditable spaceship and a line leading it to Doona, depicting its distinctive continental masses. Then Hrriss took over the double-looped pen from Todd, and sketched Hrruba and its satellites, and a dotted line for a Hrruban ship's journey to Doona. Todd jammed a forefinger onto Earth and held out his hand to Hrriss, who shook it, while with his free hand he pointed to his homeworld. Then they looked to see if the Gringg had understood the pantomime.

The Gringg passed the drawing back and forth, mumbling in rapid bass notes with such intensity that Todd felt his ears itching, and Hrriss could not keep his tail still. When the sketch had done a complete circuit, the Gringg smiled and nodded their acknowledgment to the two friends.

"Wish one of us could draw better," Todd said.

"Scrawl or not, zey seem to understand," Hrriss said, but his tail tip kept twitching.

"Two races sharing a world in peace," said Grzzeearoghh with a blissful sigh. "How wonderful! These are species I want to cultivate assiduously. We must learn from them how they contrived to co-exist so successfully. That harmony must explain why they are so willing to accept our peaceful intentions. Perhaps they cannot conceive that we might intend them harm. I hope this is so, for it will make our job much easier. This will be of great interest to all on the home-world. Now, let us show our guests the entire ship so that they know there is nothing hidden on it to harm them or their mutual world."

They led the Doonarralans on an exhaustive tour of the ship, from the living quarters to the galley to the cargo holds, and finally to the bridge. Soon, the small beings began to tire.

"Mama, perhaps they want to take a nap," Weddeerogh suggested when Rrss yawned and attempted to conceal the gesture.

Just then, however, Grzzeearoghh received a signal from Grrala. "First we will return to the infirmary, for Grrala has something she wants them to see," she told her son.

"I'd say they deliberately trotted us up and down this ship to prove that they're not hiding anything. I feel as if we haven't missed a corridor or a single level," Todd said wearily. "Certainly nothing resembled a weapons system anywhere. They didn't even stop you when you opened that triangular hatch."

Hrriss wrinkled his nose. "No one is in danger from a compost heap. 'Rhaddencch,' Grizz called it. Zey seemed to let us go where we wanted to go. But it is so big a ship; to really explore would take weeks. Now, zat bridge was interesting, was it not? So vrrry casual."

Todd gave a soft snort. "Did you notice the configuration of the switches, toggles, and buttons? No way either of us could manage that sort of control board . . . not unless we could grow foot-long fingers and treble our handspans."

"Zat does not worrrry me as much as ze absence of couches," Hrriss said thoughtfully. "How do zey absorb ze g-force in takeoff and landing wizzout padded couches of some zort?"

"Maybe there's cushioning fat under their fur." Todd suggested and bent over to rub his thighs. "Their normal g-force is enough to make my muscles ache."

Hrriss gave a snort. "It wasn't ze diving you did?"

"Come to think of it, I haven't done much diving lately. But I know the difference between gravity-ache and muscle strain."

When Grizz guided them back to Panda's office, Koala and Ursa, another engineer, had several small devices to show them. Ursa strapped one about her massive throat and offered Todd another one.

"How do I operate it?" Todd asked. Out of the device resting against his larynx, his words came out in a basso profundo that made him jump. "Was that me?" he asked, and the device repeated it.

"Dodh?" Ursa began. Her voice, instead of being a deep, chocolate baritone, had been raised to a pleasant tenor range.

"Zat is much better," Hrriss said.

"Promising," Todd agreed. He turned to Ursa. "Say 'v va'arrel.' " He encouraged her comprehension of what he wanted by zooming his hand around like the shuttle. Ursa glanced at Grizz for permission.

"Vamarrel," the Gringg said, sounding faintly ridiculous in soprano.

"Aha!" Todd said. "See, we were missing something. Now say the word for the big ship." He gestured all around him. "Va'arrel?"

"Vasharrel," Ursa piped.

"Wonderful! We're on our way."

Ursa signed to Todd to take off the device collar and pass it to Hrriss. The Hrruban fastened the band, and tried a couple of words. "Spaceship, food, wazzer, rllama . . ."

The Gringg voder repeated much of what he was saying in a deep bass, but skipped parts of the higher tones. Wielding a tool that was a cross between a laser and a screwdriver, Ursa attempted unsuccessfully to adjust the tympanum to encompass all of Hrriss' vocal tones. She grunted and raised her paws palm up to show helplessness.

"Not perfect yet," Todd said sympathetically. "The waveband it uses is too narrow. We'll just have to wait until we get back down to Doonarrala. Better still, we could make use of Spacedep's engineers. The *Hamilton's* still floating along behind us. The Admiral was hinting none too subtly that they wanted to be involved. Let's get one of their technicians over here."

With a little tinkering and a lot of luck, Todd was able to adjust the Gringg communication system to the frequencies monitored by Spacedep. The communications officer, Rrawrum, maneuvered up and down the band until Todd heard static, and gestured for him to fine-tune onto that narrow wavelength.

"Hello? The *Hamilton?* This is Todd Reeve. Repeat, this is Todd Reeve."

"Where are you transmitting from?" demanded the voice of the communications tech. "You're interrupting a secured signal."

"Sorry," Todd apologized. "I wasn't intending to break in on anything. I don't know the field strength of this transmitter. I'm aboard the Gringg ship. I need to speak with Captain Castleton."

"The captain's not available at present, sir."

"Then, Admiral Barnstable? The matter I have to bring up with him is pretty important."

"Not available either, sir."

"Strange," Todd said, frowning at Hrriss. "I wonder where they went?"

"I'm not at liberty to divulge that, sir," the Spacedep comtech said.

"Uh-huh. How about Commander Greene?"

After a short pause, Greene came on the line. Todd described the situation and told him what they needed.

"Wouldn't construction of a translation device be their problem? Surely they've had to deal with the other species they've encountered," Greene said slyly.

Todd sighed. Greene had been his last option for help. "I doubt it, Commander."

"Really? A virgin species. Ripe for the plucking?" Greene asked acidly.

"Certainly ready to, and helpful in forming a meaningful relationship," Todd said, trying not to let the other man's sour tones annoy him. "A frame of mind I doubt you've ever experienced. At that, Greene, I'd expected that a man of your caliber and ambition would be able to catch the moment and run with it."

"What do you mean by that, Reeve?"

"Spacedep wants answers about the Gringg, don't they? They don't want them secondhand, do they?"

"No," and the reply was grudging.

Todd grinned. "So send us a communications technician who can help us refine a translator. They've whipped up a voder but it doesn't compensate for under- and overtones . . . and they're necessary to establish communications. Get a two-way exchange going and we'll find out what the Gringg are really saying."

"Will we?"

"As an Alreldep representative, I'm asking you, a Spacedep officer, to provide assistance. You know, the sort of addition that looks so good on a code sheet. Or are you unable to function without direct orders from Barnstable?"

"I can't order Castleton's officers to suit you, or Alreldep," Greene said in a sort of a snarl. Then he paused. "If someone volunteers . . ."

"Yes, a volunteer is the answer," Todd said, trying to keep the irony out of his voice.

"Not that I think anyone in their right mind—" Greene began and then briefly shut off the channel. He returned shortly. "You're in luck, Reeve. There's a sucker on every ship."

"I knew I could count on you, Greene," Todd said cheerfully. "Send him across. And don't worry. We'll vouch for your reluctance to send a man into danger. Reeve out!"

"This thing's pretty good," Lieutenant Cardiff, junior grade, said as he examined the Gringg prototype voder, running a sonic probe over the exposed interior of the device. He'd brought two heavy tool kits with him. And Commander Jon Greene.

Neither Todd nor Hrriss were surprised that Greene had accompanied the signals officer. The Gringg had courteously retired from the bay once the little ship was safely docked in their massive vessel.

"Sound reproducer of some sort, huh? First, what is it supposed to do when it's alive and well and working right?"

Todd explained the difference between Gringg voices and theirs. He had acknowledged Greene's presence but had to ignore the suspicious and cynical expression on his face, determined not to be provoked by Greene's open antagonism.

"Yeah, well, they were nearly there, I think. This resonator, here, is really brilliant. Should handle any decibel range. It looks like something they mass-produce, by the way. This plastic core looks prefabbed and the chips are probably standard for all their audio equipment. But I think these relays are too cumbersome; that's why you can't fine-tune. Think I can alter that to suit the purpose." He grimaced, and settled his probe on one of the baffles. "This one'll poop out on you after a few too many high notes."

"Can you remedy the problems?" Todd asked.

"Oh, I'm a master fixit," Cardiff said easily, and grinned at Todd and Hrriss. He had very white teeth in a face as dark as Grizz's fur, and a mat of silky, silver hair which he continually raked upward with the fingers of both hands. He seemed to be one of those enthusiastic people whose vocation was also his avocation, and was more interested in a challenging job than the wherefores of it. "Got some tricks of my own, I have. I'll just tinker with these relays—here and here—strengthen this baffle, and put in a more sophisticated tuner. Odd how there're only a few ways of doing some jobs? Sound's one of 'em. These guys have some mighty slick gadgetry."

Cardiff frowned slightly, turning the voder from side to side, re-examining its components. "But why leave it as just a frequency modulator? I can add a memory chip so it uses terms in the languages as soon as we have equivalents, build up the usable vocabulary. I've got some multiprogrammable blank chips here that'd do the job stellar! That way, all three races get used to hearing one another's tongues."

"Zat would be much more useful," Hrriss said approvingly.

"Sure thing," the tech said. "You know, they're trying to build something like this on the surface, too. Or so I heard from Commander Frill. He was looking for a decent resonator. I ought to turn him on to this one."

"Well, pool your knowledge, Lieutenant," Todd replied. "No use in redundancy."

"Nossir."

"Cardiff can't work here," Greene said irritably, looking about contemptuously. "There's no work space in this . . . barn."

"Since you've now seen what needs to be done," Todd said, ignoring Greene, "the Gringg have set up a place where you can be comfortable. They stayed out of the way on purpose"—he flicked a glance at the commander—"first to let you examine the voder without distraction, and two, so I can reassure you how hospitable they've been. Three, so I can warn you that they're big, Cardiff, really big."

"I figured they must be, from the size of their ship," Cardiff said affably. "Won't bother me."

"Well, you have nothing to fear from them."

"Nothing to fear?" Greene said, his lip curled derisively. "With claws that could gut a space shuttle."

"Which, I remind you, Greene, they haven't done. Keep your xenophobia to yourself," Todd replied in a harsh voice.

Greene raised a taunting eyebrow, his expression supercilious.

"I'm ready, sir, I think," the tech said, slinging one huge tool case to his bony shoulder and nodding for someone to pick up the big padded one that held his inventory of chips. Todd hefted it. "Lead me to 'em."

Through pictures and pantomime, Todd had managed to convey to Grizz the need of work space for the technician. She and Panda had shown him one not too far from the shuttle bay, one level up on the belt elevator, and a short dogleg. It was yet another mark of Gringg tact that they met no Gringg on their way to the workroom. That Todd hadn't expected, but it pleased him very much. Hrriss, too, grinned as he followed behind the others while Greene kept glancing apprehensively up corridors and around corners. The belt elevator had surprised both Greene and Cardiff, though they were familiar with such mechanical lifts.

"What are they like, these Gringg?" Cardiff said, listening to his voice echoing back from the high, smooth ceilings. "I was hoping for a glance, you know."

Todd indicated the door to the workroom allocated to them and opened it. "See for yourself."

Cardiff lifted one foot, froze, and stared into the huge room. "Holy fardling afterburners!"

Grinning, Todd gave Cardiff a little shove in the back so that he moved on. Nevertheless, as he himself entered, he had to admit it was an impressive scene. Grizz and Weddeerogh sat beside Chief Engineer Koala, who was working over a low table, tweaking the components of the second voder. Her scribe, and Rrawrum, the communications officer, lounged around. At the appearance of the Human, all of them turned toward the door and smiled.

"Great gods! What a set of cutlery!" Cardiff declared, his eyes focused on the long claws the Gringg had extended in her work. His ebony-dark face had an ashy tint to it, and his already wild hair seemed to stand out further. "D'you suppose they file their nails like screwdrivers? Do I gotta work with all of them? They're big enough to cramp my style, I think."

"The silvery one over there's the engineer," Todd said with a chuckle, pointing out Koala. She waved a gigantic paw, and Todd could see the technician's eyes riveted to the length of claw displayed.

"You all right?" Todd asked, bracing the man's shoulders with a sturdy arm.

Gamely, Cardiff gulped. "Even with you warning me, I didn't quite appreciate . . . Hell, I've seen a stuffed bear in the museum and I just thought you meant they'd be a *little*—but whew!" He whistled softly.

"Get on with it," Greene muttered.

"Button up, Greene," Todd said in a fierce undertone.

Greene glared back with a hatred which he now made no effort to hide, but he said nothing. He could contain himself now, in anticipation of the total humiliation of Todd Reeve in the not-too-distant future. The Gringg had never met another species, had they? When Reeve found out the truth . . . When he could not retreat from his untenable position . . . When they had all the proof they needed . . .

Meanwhile he watched as the lanky technician was urged forward to be introduced to the Gringg. Greene momentarily sympathized with the reluctance evident in every line of the man's body, but then, Cardiff had volunteered. Greene contented himself with a smile and settled himself on a low counter, while Cardiff eased himself down on the floor with Koala and the scribe, and put the voder he'd examined on the table beside the other.

"Now, this is a good piece of work," Cardiff said, removing the resonator chip from the heart of the device and brandishing it at Koala.

"The word for good is *rehmeh*," Todd told him, squatting down alongside. Hrriss joined him, leaving Greene by himself, glaring at the roomful of absorbed Gringg.

"Right," Cardiff said, grinning. "Rehmeh, this. Not rehmeh, that. Downright cow patties, that. What you need is a couple of these transformers; a different microphone assembly, something with real range, but solid, too; and a new power supply." He rummaged in the big tool case. "I've got the very thing—somewhere in here."

The language of engineering had intrinsic universality. Circuitry symbols might be different, but the way to diagram a circuit was surprisingly similar. In no time, Cardiff and Koala were communicating easily through the sketches, augmented by nods, smiles, frowns, grunts, and much gesticulation, oblivious to all else. Cardiff's long, thin fingers assembled components, using hot-tipped tools and minute pliers as Koala made suggestions by pointing and making hand signals.

"Where's my soldering iron?" Cardiff cried, pawing through his case. "I'm sure I packed it. Oh, never mind. I can use the laser tool."

"Rehmeh," Koala said, at last, giving the Hayuman technician a rubbery-lipped smile of approval.

"Right," said Cardiff, straightening up. "Let's teach these things to talk." He had made use of the original casings, but shuffled components from both worlds. Out of the kit, he pulled a frequency monitor, and ran the dial up and down the cycles. "This will compress the greater range of Hrruban tones into the range the Gringg can hear, and match Human stuff as well. It'll also translate any one of the ranges into any one of the other, depending on who it's set to be worn by. This switch has three settings."

"Aha," said Todd. "Now we're getting somewhere."

Cardiff strapped one of the voders onto his neck. "You want them to learn Middle Hrruban first?" He ignored Greene's belated protest. "Sensible notion, since so many of us can get along in that. So that's what we're going to record into the memory."

Todd began to recite the words for which he already had the Gringg translations. Grizz recorded the translations in her booming voice when Cardiff pointed to her. Back and forth they went, putting more and more into memory, slowly expanding a Gringg/Middle Hrruban glossary. Todd suggested the words for body parts, things in the lab, male, female, baby, and any verb he could think of for which he could express the concept. Grizz responded.

"Right. We've got a good starting vocabulary," the technician said happily. "Go ahead, try it."

Todd cleared his throat. "I'm Todd, not Dodh." His voice came out as a deep bass, but with more inflection than he'd had through Koala's preliminary model. "Todd. Todd Reeve."

"Todd," the Gringg all repeated one by one. "Todd Reeve."

"See?" Todd said with satisfaction. "Supersonics—at least super to them— are dropping out as subsonics are for us."

Hrriss took the other voder, and let Cardiff tune it to him.

"I am Hrriss, and my people are called Hrrubans." His voice was repro- duced, but matching his *h*'s and *s*'s without dropping out any of the hissing.

"Hrrissss. Hrrrroobans," the Gringg intoned.

"Piece of cake," Todd said, spreading his hands happily.

"Peess of kkayyk," the Gringg echoed, showing their massive teeth in a grin.

"Don't encourage them to smile," Cardiff said with a twitch of his lean shoulders. "It reminds me of K.P."

"Well done," Hrriss praised him. "Well done by you, too," he told Koala, who grunted at the compliment.

"Well, let's take these things away and replicate 'em," Todd said. "Because of the tone differences, anyone who ever wants to talk with the Gringg will have to use one. That means dozens, if not hundreds, of copies. I'll see what inventory we've got and what we can manufacture in a hurry. Maybe even arrange a license to grid stuff in."

"Happy to help, if I can," Cardiff offered. "This was fun! Usually, I'm bent fixing electronics blown up by the visiting brass. No offense to you, Comman- der Greene." The three visitors looked around.

"Wherre did he go?" Hrriss asked, springing to his feet.

Todd glanced at the Gringg and raised his hands questioningly. Grizz cocked her head, and addressed a question to the others. No one had seen the other Hayuman leave.

"Wait," Todd said. "Where's Weddeerogh?"

Grizz moved faster then than Todd had yet seen. In a moment, she was on her feet beside a crescent-shaped device on the wall. She fitted a claw into a hole and spoke into a slotted grille on the side. "Ahrgha, geerh vnamshola Hayuman, parghhen va Weddeerogh. Ahrgha, meena lorrangh." Todd and Hrriss could hear her voice echoing in the hallway.

The announcement, if it was an order to bring back any Hayuman found to be wandering the halls with Grizz's cub, was redundant. Two strange Gringg, one male and one female, appeared in the doorway with a struggling Greene between them. Weddeerogh loped in behind the party, and rolled onto his haunches beside his mother. Grizz's eyes were hot with anger, but her voice sounded calm when she turned to Todd with a question.

"Geerh rhaddencch?"

"No, I mean, morra, that won't be necessary," Todd said, standing up to pinion Greene by the arm. The Gringg male moved away to make room for the tall Hayuman. "I'm taking him out of here now."

"What did she say?" Greene asked.

"She said, should she take you and throw you in the compost heap," Todd said, trying to master his fury. "What are you trying to do? Ruin the good work that's been done today, sneaking off for a private pry around this ship? You could have asked and Grizz would have seen you had the guided tour. This your idea? Or Barnstable's?"

Greene gave him a look of total contempt. Only the place and company kept Todd's anger in check. One day he was going to square off against Greene!

"Captain Grizz," Todd said formally, switching on the voder as he turned toward her. "We have truly enjoyed our visit aboard the vasharrel." Grizz murmured approvingly at his correctly enunciated words. "We'll be speaking again with you soon. May we be guided back to our vamarrel?"

"Reh," Grizz said, allowing a glint of humor into her eyes. Weddeerogh trotted up to nose Todd's hand, then over to Hrriss, and back to his mother.

"See you soon, little guy," Todd said warmly. "All packed up, Cardiff?"

"Lug this, will you?"

"I'll take it," Greene said unexpectedly, stepping forward to sweep the tool kit out of Todd's grasp.

"As you will," Cardiff said amiably, then turned. "See you again, Koala," and he tipped a salute to the Gringg engineer, who waved one large silver paw in response.

They both paused by Greene, and Todd gave a curt nod of his head for the commander to precede him.

"I'm sure you know the way to the shuttle bay, Commander," Todd said with barely concealed sarcasm. "Or didn't you get that far before they hauled you back for poking about?"

Greene said nothing as he expertly caught the next descending platform of the belt elevator. To Todd that meant he'd gone this far. Had he gone up or down?

"As you pointed out, Reeve, it's catching the moment and running with it."

"Even at the expense of violating good will?"

"Good will?" Greene snorted explosively. "Yes, good will! I'll show you some good will one of these days—" He broke off. Now was not the time to let anger overset good judgment. He took a deep breath and refused the bait.

Their guide hopped off the platform and Greene followed, knocking the tool kit against the wall as he slightly misjudged his momentum. Its flap bounced open, and a small, rodlike device fell out.

"Hey, there's my soldering iron," Cardiff said, diving for it before it dropped off the platform. He straightened up to tuck it back into the carryall, and stopped, looking curiously at the remaining contents of the bag. "Shooting stars, what's that? I never packed that."

"What?" Todd asked. A growl from the corridor suggested their guide was waiting.

Todd held up one hand to the Gringg before he grabbed for the tool-kit strap, to summarily lift it off Greene's shoulder. Greene twisted away but Hrriss barred his way.

"Hey, what's the matter?" Cardiff wanted to know.

"I want to see what's in there that you didn't pack, Cardiff," Todd said and jerked at the shoulder strap.

Greene struggled hard, but with a powerful yank, Hrriss stripped the bag from his shoulder while Todd deflected the commander's blows. The powerfully built aide had an excellent repertoire of hand-to-hand combat dirty tricks, but Todd had been wrestling snakes every year since he was ten. When Greene kicked, Todd hooked his feet out from under him and sat on him while Hrriss continued his inspection of the tool kit.

The Gringg guide came back to see what was holding his party up, and growled a question.

"Morra," Todd said grimly, keeping his weight on Greene's back. "What's in it, Hrriss?"

"It looks like a small bomb," Hrriss whispered angrily. "I do not know what zis sssmall device on top is."

Cardiff took a quick look. "Remote control receiver," he said, his face expressionless. "No fuse, just need a radio signal to set it off."

Todd closed his eyes against the arrogance of a man like Greene, too ready to destroy what he couldn't understand. Though he wanted to close his fingers tightly about Greene's neck, instead he hauled the commander upright by handful of his tunic.

"So that's what you intended, skiving off like that? To plant this bomb. When were you going to blow the ship? While Hrriss and I were still on it?

Or when Barnstable gave the orders?" His fingers clenched and unclenched in the tough fabric of Greene's uniform. Though his eyes did not narrow in fear, the commander watched him warily, offering no resistance to the mauling. "No wonder you let Cardiff come. I should have been suspicious the moment I saw you in the shuttle with him. When, Greene? When was this to be set off?"

"A fail-safe, Reeve, just a fail-safe," Greene said, grating the words out, adding, when Todd relaxed his grip slightly, "Should the Gringg suddenly turn hostile."

Disgusted, Todd pushed him out at arm's length and let go. Greene staggered back against the corridor wall before recovering himself. He then straightened his tunic with careful gestures and smoothed back his hair with nerveless fingers.

"Do marines require their officers to be paranoid?" Todd demanded.

"Paranoid, hell, Reeve! Marines protect! Which is more than you're doing," Greene replied in a low, angry voice and strode down the corridor toward the waiting Gringg.

The two Doonarralans hurried to bracket him, making certain he took no further detours across the huge bay to the shuttle. Silently, Cardiff paced ahead of them, eager to get into the shuttle and out of the way before the others boarded it. Hrriss managed the Gringg words for thanks and pulled the shuttle door closed. The small ship waited until the bay doors opened and slowly left the Gringg ship.

"If you'd planted that bomb and the Gringg found it, Greene, all the strides toward understanding that we've made today would have been neutralized."

"Why would they look for something, Reeve? Answer me that! They have such peaceful intent, and you are so honorable, why would they look for anything? But, why won't *you* look at matters from another perspective. What if all their compliance is a cover?" Greene demanded in a hard voice. "What if the Gringg are hiding something from us?"

"Hrriss and I were taken over the whole ship, and looked wherever we wished with no hindrance or supervision," Todd replied, still fuming at the appalling brush with near disaster. "They trust us. We must return that trust, and that means you keep your little gadgets off their premises."

"That little gadget might have saved more lives—" the commander began, and stopped before he blurted out why he had reason to be concerned.

"For the last time, Greene, this isn't your business. This is Alien Relations business, and in the interests of Amalgamated Worlds and this invaluable alien contact, I'll have you denied further access to the Gringg. This time, my father and I have the authority to keep the brass and bureaucracy right out of the loop so we can get on with unarmed diplomacy!"

It was with trepidation that Second Speaker returned to Hrruba to bring his news to the High Council. He had gotten no satisfaction from the confrontation engineered by the Hayuman Admiral. Between the medical examinations and the invention of a communication device, things had gotten totally out of hand. The stakes were far too high. In the presence of these immense aliens, Hrrto felt reduced to insignificance, although he was of large stature among his own kind. Beings should not be made in such massive forms, should not be allowed to grow to such abnormal proportions. They must not be permitted to come to Hrruba to dwarf even the largest of his people. He hoped that more of the Hayuman contingent felt that way than the Doonarralans did. After all, so many of them were shorter than the average Hrruban. Which reminded him that he had not felt any physical or aural intimidation when he had encountered the Hayumans for the first time, certainly not the unnerving sort he experienced in the company of the Gringg. He did not understand why others were not over-whelmed by the Gringg's presence. Even young Hrriss, whom he trusted as a true Hrruban, had taken to these furry giants as if they were veritable beings of honor, integrity, and value.

Mllaba seemed to feel that the coming of the Gringg could be a great advantage to him in the upcoming election. He was at a loss to know how he could possibly present such hulks as advantageous, though Mllaba was usually shrewd in seeing possibilities and potentials. Still, he had been there at the beginning and that did give him an advantage from which to speak. If he could build on that, with Mllaba's assistance, he might indeed enhance his bid for the Speakership. He need only be calm—and pretend to know more than he actually did. Mllaba was up to something, he knew, and she would inform him when her maneuvers were complete.

As Hrrto entered the impressive, dark-panelled Council Meeting Room, his tail gave a single twitch. The place had not felt the same since the death of Hrruna. It had turned into a cold, unfriendly place, with whispering shadows.

Hrrto took his place in the second seat, beside the head of the table, facing Third Speaker for Internal Affairs, a moderate Hrruban named Rrolm. The First Speaker's place was, of course, respectfully empty, draped with blue and red. In the center of the seat was the precious blue stone given as a gift of peace to Hrruna by the Hayuman settlers in the very first days of Rraladoona. On his deathbed, Hrruna had directed that the stone should be displayed in the Council Chamber until a successor was chosen. To him who assumed the office would pass ownership of the stone, to remind him that peace with one's neighbor was as valuable and vital as clean air or pure water. Yes, Hrrto thought, peace and trust were necessary, but in good time, when the Gringg had proved, beyond the shadow of a doubt, their pacificism.

"Be confident, sir," Mllaba whispered from her place, a seat rolled deferentially back from the table, suitable for one who was not part of the Council. "Contain this situation firmly. It will be the key to the election. Your rivals do not have such a good opportunity to display leadership as you do right now with your ultimate connection in the Gringg incident. Fifth Speaker backs Third now, but the few outside candidates have little chance of assuming the post. Be firm. Be confident. You have the advantage."

"I know the tone and stand to take, Mllaba," Hrrto said, with some irritation, and flattened his tail against the chair leg, hidden by his robes. At times her attitude bordered on the officious, and she was not in contention for any Speakership.

Word had already spread over Hrruba that intervention by an alien presence had put a halt to the spaceport talks. The delegates, not held to temporary residence on Rraladoona as were their Hayuman counterparts, had come home full of tales about the giant Gringg. Mllaba's initial report had made a strong impression on the Council. The Speakers were eager to hear more from Hrrto.

So Second Speaker first explained the circumstances of the Gringg's advent, then signalled to Mllaba to ran the tape of the huge aliens who had visited Rraladoona as emissaries.

As Eonneh and Ghotyakh appeared on the screen, gasps ranged around the table, then modulated into murmurs of discomfort when the Gringg spoke.

"What horrible sounds they make!" Fourth Speaker said. "Barbaric garble! Threatening in sound and appearance. So monstrous. Bare-skinned Hayumans were peculiar enough to behold, but these are at the other extreme!"

"Alreldep, which agency you already know includes several prominent Hrrubans of good Stripe," Hrrto said, rising to his feet as the tape ended, "maintains that these Gringg wish to establish peaceful relations with both Hrrubans and Hayumans. They are to learn Middle Hrruban," he said with a smug smile, intimating that this was a concession he himself had managed. "We must, of course, wait until sufficient understanding of language allows us to communicate to purpose."

"Peaceful relations?" Rrolm asked. "How can we be sure of that?"

"Of course their ship was thoroughly scanned and probed," Hrrto went on "No weaponry of any sort was discovered, that is true. Alrelddep sent envoys who were treated courteously, and no show of force or violence occurred . . . "

He let his voice dwindle ominously. "We have little hard data, except the results of physical examinations done by the Hayuman medical team on Rraladoona. Alreldep does tend"—he paused solemnly—"toward optimism." He gave a diffident shrug. "On the other hand, Spacedep has given me reason to suspect that the Gringg assurances of good faith and their appearance of defenselessness—as far as their vessel goes—could very well be false. Until we are absolutely certain of their intentions toward us, Hrruba and Hrrubans, we should keep the Gringg contained in the Rraladoona sphere, but prepare ourselves for all eventualities."

"I do not think we wish a close association with these huge creatures," Sixth Speaker said, assuming the speech-making posture he had lately adopted, evidently believing that it gave his listeners more confidence in his ponderous opinions. "Once again the Hayumans have forced an untenable situation upon our peaceful citizens. I must tell you that there is great anxiety among those with whom I have spoken at length when word of this new incursion was brought to me."

"I second that, Sixth," Third Speaker said brusquely and turned to Second. "Have you any action to propose at this time, Second?"

Hrrto smiled, for matters were proceeding well if Third deferred to him to act. Although that could be a trap. Still . . .

"Surely, Third," he said with a smooth growl to his tone, "that is obvious. The fleet must be"—he let one talon extrude slightly from his right hand—"discreetly mobilized. Held on alert, undetectable behind the Rraladoonan moons. I have been assured that there will be those on the planet who will turn a blind eye to the occasional anomaly on the surveillance screens. And, should it become necessary"—he paused again significantly—"the Hrruban fleet will be able to move with surprise and great speed."

The others reacted with varying degrees of approval or censure, muttering among themselves.

"You are convinced of threat?" Third asked, over the hubbub.

"The prudent Stripe is prepared for any eventuality. In the case of large, unexpected visitors, mouthing peace, prudence is only . . . ah . . . politic. To be frank"—and now Second turned confidential, addressing his remarks directly to Third across the table from him—"I would fell less threat, actually, if their ship had shown some armament. With none . . ." He lifted his shoulders, leaving the anxiety for others to enlarge. With the fleet in place, Hrrubans on the planet are supported. And our allies can turn to us for immediate assistance in case this situation turns ugly. And it very well could!"

"How? From what source? If the alien ship has been probed as weaponless?" Fifth asked doubtfully.

Second bowed his head, miming reluctant silence. "This is, of course, to be kept among us. Spacedep offered me incontrovertible truth of the possibility that the aliens are by no means as pacific and genuine as they would have us believe. But such information is classified. Suffice it for you to know that my eyes have seen, and my shoulders bear the heavy burden for you all. For the safety and sanity of Rrala, it must remain so."

"The Speaker did observe to me," Mllaba said, standing up, "that while Hayumans have weapons capable of destroying a planet, they have shown a moral code which prevents them from I doing so. These Gringg, on the other hand, seem cultured and peaceful, but the evidence, which I, too, was shown, suggests they have two sides to their nature. The one we have not seen is vicious and ruthless."

The timbre of her voice only emphasized Second's less emotional narration.

"Yes, well, no one has answered me on the matter of the spaceport facility," said the Seventh Speaker for Management, slightly testy. "What's happened to it? There has been so much preparation, so many negotiations and hard work. Surely . . ."

Mllaba bowed to him. She enjoyed being able to speak freely before the entire Council. "It has been postponed indefinitely, Honored sir. The arrival of the Gringg is considered a priority of utmost urgency, and the conference co-leader is intimately involved in the negotiations. There is no surety right now that the facility will be discussed in the near future."

Sixth Speaker cleared his throat. "Do we yet know what part of the galaxy they came from? And, if they have come so peacefully, might they not have come for trade? That is why we—and the Hayumans—took to the stars: to find new sources of metals and foodstuffs and new planets on which to settle."

Mllaba realized with annoyance that Sixth was not convinced of the deadliness of the Gringg threat, nor was Fifth Speaker. Fifth saw the Gringg as potential allies and customers, and Sixth was more concerned with the inability to shift Hrrubans goods anywhere and the current recession due to that inability.

Hrrto rose and immediately Mllaba seated herself.

"The Gringg claim their discovery of Rraladoona was an accident," he said. "When they visited the First Village, they managed to convey to Ken Rrev that their instrumentation discovered an ion trail which they followed to the Rraladoonan system. They were encouraged to enter the system when they also found the marker buoys and realized that the third planet was not only inhabited but obviously using sophisticated technology. Their level of technical expertise is high. I cannot say whether it is similar to ours or to the Hayumans."

"To be fair," Second continued, planting his hands on the table, "the public face that the Gringg show is one of thoughtful, creative civilization. Their standard of artwork and music is high, and they have been quick to comprehend symbolic communication. They may have much to offer us—not only trade goods, but cultural gifts."

"This suggests an understanding of technology and tenacity of purpose," said Fifth Speaker, combing his chin mane with thoughtful claws. "These Gringg could be useful and worthwhile allies."

"If they are not planning to destroy us," Seventh said in alarm.

"I don't like it," snarled Sixth. "They could be a threat to Hrruban independence and individual development. There are already too many outsiders with influence on the Hrruban way of life."

"I feel it necessary that the Hrrubans take the lead in all discussions," Hrrto said primly.

"It may be more important than ever for you to *manage* such discussions," said Fifth Speaker, his green eyes wide with alarm. "I have heard something from our returning delegates which troubles me greatly. Is it true that the Hayumans are becoming more insistent in their demands to share our grid technology?"

"Yes," Mllaba said, rising gracefully to her feet. "But the Speaker stated without equivocation that such a thing was impossible. The Hayumans were not pleased by his adamant position."

"You did not admit to them why we could not share that technology, did you?"

Hrrto was genuinely insulted. He controlled his voice, but his tail lashed once under his flowing red robes. "Of course I did not. If the Honored Speaker will recall, I voted in favor of the proposition to make details of grid technology and construction available only to Hrrubans of the homeworld. I am only too aware that our supply of the element purralinium which makes the grids possible will only last for a hundred years at the present rate of use. Expanding the network of planets in our Explorations Arm and colony worlds will deplete it faster."

"We may find more," Seventh argued.

"How? Without better ships we are unlikely to find other asteroid belts where novas have collided and the minerals have formed into purralinium. The Hayumans are our only source of those ships, but they demand access to grid technology in exchange for spaceship technology. They will hold firm on that point," Second finished with genuine regret.

"How they dare! They go too far," Sixth said.

"They are curious," Second explained wearily. "Hayumans wish to know how everything operates. I must admit that many of the arguments put forth by the delegate Landreau make sense. As we know from many decades of use, grids save time and lives."

"Has no more purralinium been found?" Fifth asked Sixth Speaker.

Sixth stood up. "Plenty has been discovered, as the Honored Speaker may know from reading his texts. But never with the key trace elements which comprise the compound needed. I think we must curtail the establishment of any but the most urgent additions to our transport network. Research is, naturally, on-going to find alternatives, but we must face the fact that we have a finite quantity of material which is not renewable. We would do well to accelerate alternative power sources."

"We cannot!" said Third Speaker, looking panicky. "We've thrown all our support into grid research. We haven't the funds to advance new research into space technology. If the Hayumans remain on a hard line of negotiation, we are lost. In a short era, we will be circumscribed on every side by Hayumans and possibly by these, these Gringg. Something must be done!"

Fifth Speaker smiled grimly. "I heard through some sources who live on Rraladoona that the Gringg were not surprised by the grids when they first used them. Is it possible they might also have discovered matter transmission?"

Hrrto dropped his jaw and waved both hands dismissively. "The chances of their discovering matter transmission are exceedingly slim, Honored sirs, especially"—and now he drew himself up—"since the Hayumans have been unable to duplicate our process no matter how hard they have tried."

"Yet you imply that the Gringg have searched many worlds," Sixth said. "Might they not have found purralinium somewhere in their travels? We must discover what they have seen during their explorations. We must ignore no opportunity to replenish our supplies. Especially if we must use a third of our dwindling resources to erect an efficient grid in the spaceport facility. Never must the Hayumans discover how important purralinium is to us or how little we have left." Sixth Speaker was all but babbling in his urgency. "We cannot fall from our present prominence and become vulnerable to either the Hayumans or these Gringg creatures."

"Sixth, do not exercise yourself," Second said kindly, for the old Stripe was spitting in his agitation. "After all, the Hayumans have treated fairly with us. The delay on the spaceport is actually due to Zodd Rrev's contention that a spaceport is an infraction of both the Decision and Treaty." Second smiled benignly. "Despite their desire to share our technology, I do not see Hrruba made vulnerable to Hayumans."

"It is recorded that those who live on Rraladoona have always conducted themselves with honor toward Hrruba," Fifth agreed, "but there are too many on the Hayuman homeworld who are willing to take advantage of us. We must protect ourselves, or our culture will be swallowed up and lost, as our natural resources—nay, even as the surface of our planet was—by our own carelessness. The spaceport is essential if we are to maintain the precarious balance of trade. In the matter of the Gringg, you must ensure that any concession from them that the Hayumans receive, so also do we Hrrubans."

There was a murmur of agreement. Second realized he needed to walk carefully if he wished to be successful. Fifth was a determined and intelligent rival for Hrruna's place. And yet he judged that he had not done so ill in this meeting. Mllaba seemed to be very pleased.

"I concur," he said. "Steps shall be taken to establish Hrruba's preeminence. And its safety."

chapter seven

Over the course of the next weeks, Hrrestan took over as many duties from Todd in their joint management of the colony as he could.

"Todd can get his tongue round ze new worrds bezzer zan I," was Hrrestan's comment, "for all my dam said I was borrrn grrowling."

So, except for brief consultations now and then between the colonial co-leaders, Todd was free to spend long hours with Ken and Hrriss as they parsed and rehearsed Gringg sounds, memorized what vocabulary had been exchanged, and figured out the probable syntactical forms. As often as he could, however, Hrrestan dropped in, earnestly trying to refine those phrases he could enunciate properly.

Kelly and Nrrna kept pots of coffee available and the herbal teas that Hrrestan preferred, feeding them whenever the women could get their attention long enough, and reminding them that a good night's sleep would do wonders for concentration. Finally Kelly laid down a law.

"No Gringg at mealtimes," she said firmly on the evening when Alec had tried to emulate his father's tones and inadvertently regurgitated his last mouthful. "Give it a *rest!*"

Surprised by Alec's mishap, Todd offered sheepish apologies for his behavior and refrained from practicing the deep gutturals at mealtimes.

"Not that that improved his dinner conversation in the slightest," Kelly complained to Nrraa and Mrrva the next afternoon. She made grunts and woofs to demonstrate. "Now that he's got vocabulary and syntax, he complains because he only has present tense verbs!" She rolled her eyes in histrionic resignation.

"But zey are working togezzer," Nrrna murmured, and the two women sighed once again with relief.

When the matter of planning for the upcoming Snake Hunt would have interfered with language lessons, Todd reluctantly acceded to Robin's pleas that he could handle the pre-Hunt arrangements. Kelly offered to give her young brother-in-law a hand. That work gave her a respite from Todd's current preoccupation. Robin proved not only completely conversant with the complexities of the big event but efficient in checking minor details to forestall accidents. Todd and Hrriss, as Hunt Masters, would spare a few moments to answer his questions and go over his work schedules and estimates, but that was one less worry for them.

Todd, Ken, Hrriss, and Hrrestan, separately or as teams, escorted Gringg visitors around Doonarrala or accompanied volunteer linguists up to the huge Gringg vessel to build vocabulary and language links for the translation voders. The Alreldep scout ship which had been assigned years before to Todd and Hrriss was back in service, shuttling people up without having to go through Barnstable, Greene, or Castleton. Only two of the smaller Gringg, like Eonneh and Koala, were small enough to fit in the scout. Hrrestan tried hard to get permission to put a temporary grid in the Gringg cargo bay, but Hrrto was totally opposed to the notion. Todd and Hrrestan did, over a great outcry from Barnstable and Prrid, give permission for the Gringg to use their own ship-to-surface transport, the smallest of the ones they'd seen on their initial visit. It was a cumbersome vehicle, like a great box, and looked totally out of place on the common of First Village where it had space to land.

Hearing about this, some of the more vocal dissidents made strenuous objections on grounds of noise, pollution, and possible damage to the expanse of grass which doubled as a playing field. But the vehicle was quiet, emitted no noxious fumes, and used an air cushion for landing and resting, leaving no marks despite its mass. The Gringg pilot, an oddly misshapen individual, smaller than any other adult Gringg, courteously asked for landing and departure permissions every time and remained in the vehicle, though Buddy, alias Buddeeroagh, was quite willing to show anyone through it.

Alec told his father that one day he had counted nineteen men and women, all of whom had the odd gait of spacefarers, requesting permission to board.

"None of 'em are from any of the villages, Dad. Me, I think that old Admiral's busting his britches to find out something against the bear people. Isn't he?" Alec asked his father, cocking his head with a shrewd look in his eyes.

"You might think that," Todd answered cautiously, busy assembling the latest Gringg sounds on flash cards. Once again he reflected that children often saw more than their parents. "Why were you counting in the first place?"

"Aw, Allie, me, Hrr, and Hrruni were chatting with Buddy. He kept getting interrupted by these jokers when he was showing us this neat game. You know, if we could charge 'em for a visit, we'd make a pile!"

"You've been listening too much to your uncle Jilamey, I think," Todd replied, amused by his son's acumen but privately embarrassed at such gall, "but we can't charge for . . . ah . . . curiosity!" When his son's face contorted in dismay, he added, "And the navy is here to protect us."

Alec gave a snort. "Ha! Then they should spend their time doing that instead of nosing about our planet's guests!"

"Well said, Alec!" and he ruffled his son's tangled curls and then had to wipe his hand. "What have you been into?"

Alec finger-combed his hair, inspecting the results. "Some sort of oil er somethin'. Musta got it when Buddy showed me how their drive works!" Alec beamed suddenly, but his eyes were twinkling with slight malice. "He didn't show anyone but us kids!"

Todd decided he didn't need to worry about Spacedep's interest in the Gringg vessel when the pilot displayed such discretion. He also decided that letting the village children tag along with Gringg visitors would be a subtle way of disrupting the surveillance Barnstable and Greene had set up. What was the old tag? *Qui custodiat?* Who watches the watchers? The kids of Doonarrala!

So the almost daily unofficial visits by Eonneh and one or more of his fellow scribes to gather information and understanding of their new friends took on a new perspective. Of course, there were some diehards who wouldn't subject their children to "such influences," but these were fewer than Todd expected. When Alec casually mentioned the presence in the group of some youngsters Todd knew had been prohibited, he did have a qualm or two of conscience but decided their independence of mind should not be discouraged.

The positive reaction of the youngsters was also a grand buffer between the Gringg and the doomsayers who had managed to arrive from both Hrruba and Terra.

Somewhere underneath the busy exterior, Todd knew he was exhausted, but he'd hardly ever been so enthusiastic about a project in his life. Well, not since he'd been six.

The Gringg and the majority of Doonarralans were as delighted as he, co-operating like a dream. Frictions that had been caused by disagreement about the spaceport were mainly discarded by the generally held desire to establish relations with the aliens. The barriers of speech and unfamiliar custom were dropping farther and farther every day.

Sumitral, far from showing impatience with the laborious progress, made it a practice to interact every day with one of the male scribes, or with Grizz aboard the Gringg vessel. The Gringg captain herself had not yet set foot on Doonarrala, nor had any of her female department heads, preferring to save that portentous event, Todd was made to understand, for the day when she could make an official entrance, able to speak for herself.

Todd was grateful for her forbearance. His office received enough complaints from the very vocal Human and Hrruban minority who reacted negatively to the tercel males who had requested permission to wander about. The gigantic females would only cause a bigger stir and more friction. But he did identify most of the possible troublemakers and set up contingency plans to prevent outbursts from those quarters.

Todd also had reason to be very grateful to Jilamey Landreau, who set up entertainments and unofficial meetings at his hilltop home, well out of the way of Todd and those working on the language project. Superficially Jilamey seemed to be working both ends against the middle, soothing the disappointed members of the interrupted conference while making no bones about his Gringgophilia. He evidently made much of his being included in the first contact group.

The austere Barrington 'copted down daily to bring private and encouraging reports to Todd. Todd took these with a grain of salt, knowing Jilamey's enthusiasms, but Barrington's manner of reportage allowed him to hope that much of what Jilamey said was true. Especially when Barrington relayed Jilamey's firm opinion, one Barrington seemed to support, that the Gringg's only objective was to establish trade relations.

It was on this point that Jilamey urged patience until the translation problem could be solved, and how he managed to keep the frustrated delegates from leaving Doonarrala. Ironically, Tanarey Smith became one of Jilamey's converts, especially after Landreau persuaded Eonneh to escort the shipbuilder around the *Wander Den*, a rough translation of the Gringg vessel's name.

Todd could not ignore the undercurrents of dissatisfaction, even among Gringg supporters, that the talks about the space facility had been put hold. When he had time, he gave some thought to that. As a child, he had absorbed his father's views about planetary cohabitation; as an adult, he shared his father's opinion about any intrusive invasions of Hrruban lands on the planet. All right, it was Human greed that his father feared and it was the Hrrubans who had initiated the spaceport project. But did it matter which species encroached? If the rule applied on Doonarrala, it applied for both!

Had the arrival of the Gringg now altered the equation? No. Although he was optimistic about the outcome, the Gringg hadn't been officially allowed to open trade on Doonarrala. Todd, well-conditioned by Captain Ali Kiachif over the years, considered trading a different matter entirely from occupation or habitation. The crunch came in discussions of *where* the spaceport could be sited.

Todd knew how cramped and inadequate the old Hall at the Spaceport was for the volume of commerce that flowed in and out of it. Something had to be done to expand the facilities. No one wanted a larger complex at the original landing site, oozing toward the First Villages, ruining the peaceful valley. So a new location was imperative. Each time Todd mulled over the problem, he still found himself opposed to siting a larger port anywhere on the lovely subcontinent that was now called Hrrunatan. *That* should be left as the natural memorial park to the old First Speaker, which he, and all Doonarralans, had intended for it to be. He finally decided to leave the sore subject for another time, when he was thinking clearly and logically, not so emotionally nor—he admitted to himself—close-minded. His brain was already working overtime trying to cope with a difficult new language.

Gradually the daily sight of the large, shaggy strangers moving about with their Human or Hrruban escorts took the edge off the "fearsome hairy monsters" appellation. The Gringg became the "big bears," or Bruins, to most Doonarralans. But xenophobic pessimists somehow began arriving from Terra and Hrruba, and familiarity was not going to appease them. They visited every village, Hayuman and Hrruban, whispering against the "fiendish Gringg." They muttered about "murders most vile" and "devastated worlds," but would slip away before they could be closely questioned.

Todd worked all the harder to get the one tool that would throttle doubters and doomsayers both, and allow the Gringg to speak for themselves. Couldn't people wait for that, instead of stirring up unnecessary fears and forecasts?

The voder that Cardiff had designed with Koala was a brilliant piece of audio-engineering. It made use of the tiny Gringg resonator, memory chips, and other components from both Terra and Hrruba in common use on Doonarrala, all fitted into a compact case seven centimeters by two by five. Worn about the neck on a cord, it "heard" what the wearer said and repeated it in Gringg or human. Its creators nicknamed it growl box, or simply, the growler.

Cardiff, with the help of two of the university engineers, worked long hours to turn out six of the growlers so that Ken, Todd, and Hrriss could discuss Gringg objectives with Grizz, Honey, and Panda. The session was filmed, and although Barnstable had a fit at being excluded and decried the secrecy in which the interview was conducted, Sumitral pointed out that not even he, as Alreldep head, had been included, in an attempt to provide as relaxed an atmosphere as possible. Once again, Sumitral reinforced the perogative of Reeve and Hrrestan to conduct their own planetary affairs. There had been some heated reminders that the Gringg vessel was the concern of Spacedep.

"I could agree with you if it carried armament," Sumitral had replied suavely. "It carries only peaceful visitors!"

For Todd and Ken particularly, the session was a golden moment, for they established relations and exchanged meaningful data.

First: that for many spans of time (which Todd and Ken thought meant generations, since the Gringg travelled in family groups), the Gringg had been actively searching space for other sentient species as well as suitable resource planets. (It was a particular joy for the Doonarralans to learn that the Gringg had eschewed planets which probes reported showing habitations suggesting the basic intelligence of indigenous species.) The Gringg also required the availability of certain minerals and soils on a colonial world, for, despite being omnivorous and able to digest more substances than Hayuman or Hrrubans could, they had to have a certain range of dietary supplements.

Two: they were quite open about the direction of their homeworld; galactically speaking, north by northeast, though the speed at which their ships moved was still not translating accurately. They provided "strips" which, fed through a device, enlarged the data into star maps. The difference in eye structure made these difficult for Hayumans or Hrrubans to decipher, and Koala was working on an apparatus that would compensate for the different optics.

Three: they would be happy to establish trade with both Hayumans and Hrrubans. Which put Todd right back on the horns of that unresolved dilemma of an adequate spaceport now that there would be three species using it.

Four: it was confirmed that they had found their way to this sector of space by following ion trails, detected by their own equipment. When they had come upon the Doonarralan warning devices, they realized they had finally discovered a sophisticated culture, which they approached cautiously, but openly. They were overwhelmingly relieved to discover they were not the only sentient species in the galaxy. And there was great jubilation when they realized that they had encountered two such species!

"We are joyous to not be alone," Grizz had said during the conference, bowing her head almost to her knees to signify deep emotion.

Hayuman and Hrruban were hard put not to burst out in cheers. Instead, they gripped hands with the Gringg, allowing their broad grins to demonstrate how happy they were.

"All a little too pat," Admiral Barnstable told Greene and Castleton when they viewed the tape. "Buddy-buddy, lovey-dovey, but all too pat!"

"Especially as we can't read their star maps," Greene added, as if that fact vindicated his distrust of the bearfolk.

"Considering they've come into this sector of space from a different quadrant, you couldn't read them even if they had the same optics as we do," Grace Castleton felt obliged to remark. She knew these two wouldn't have believed anything the Gringg said, even if they'd agreed to drop buoys all the way back to their homeworld, like crumbs that marked the way out of a cave in some old children's tale. Even loosely translating their distances, the Gringg homeworld was one helluva way back in on this arm of the Milky Way.

When the tape was shown in every village on Doonarrala, there was considerable rejoicing, and some doubts were allayed. Copies were dispatched by courier to both Amalgamated Worlds and Hrruban High Councils: Inevitably that brought back the issue of a larger spaceport.

"Zodd, we must resolve this between us," Hrriss said in Low Hrruban when he managed to find Todd alone in his office.

"Yeah," Todd agreed unenthusiastically, exhaling a long sigh as he tossed his pen across a desk covered by little piles of flash cards. He managed a half-smile for Hrriss, his dearest friend. "Can't bury my head in a snake nest any longer. Not if we want to keep the Gringg."

"First of all, Zodd, you have to agree," Hrriss said patiently, settling on the edge of Todd's desk as he had so many times in the past, "it is not Hrruban encroaching on unused space. It is Gringg needing space"—he dropped his jaw at this play on words—"for the very size of them. But more importantly, they provide a neutral factor, cancelling the sort of single-race intrusion you dreaded. In a triangle, all sides are equal."

"Only if it's an isosceles," Todd said, weary to his bones with disputations and arguments, and mostly fearful of a resumption of the estrangement from Hrriss which had cost him much mental anguish.

"Equal sides," Hrriss repeated, his eyes liquid and pleading. "Equilateral."

"Two of us don't quite equal a Gringg."

"What can equal a Gringg?" demanded Hrriss, throwing up his hands in comic dismay.

"They *are* to be friends, are they not?" Todd said, suddenly propelling himself out of his chair. He gripped Hrriss by the arms, needing to have all half-doubts dismissed. He *had* to proceed positively, thinking optimistically; by sheer will power bringing about what he so intensely desired. That method had worked before.

Hrriss' hands returned his grasp and then pulled him forward into an embrace, thumping Todd on the back as was the Hayuman custom.

"Yesss, friend of my heart, yesss! Even as thou and I," Hrriss added in High Hrruban. Then, in the less formal speech, he added, "As I have told you hundreds of times now, not all of the Hrrunatan is beautiful."

Todd frowned as he released his friend. "Where?"

Hrriss gave a sigh. "Where we have always wanted to put it, only you would never let me explain . . ."

"I knew, I knew." Todd flapped his hand dismissively, then suddenly stopped himself and smiled with chagrin at Hrriss' careful expression. "I'm doing it again, aren't I? But you do mean that rocky area on the east coast where that massive subsidence was?" When Hrriss nodded, relieved that his dear friend for once was willing to discuss the problem, Todd said, "But that wouldn't be large enough . . ."

"If one filled in the lagoon that was formed by the little subsidence islands and extended a firm base to those islands . . ." Hrriss explained with the weary patience of someone repeating a well-rehearsed argument, and waited for his friend's reaction.

Todd turned away, shaking his head sharply from side to side, but then slowing the motion as his sense of fair play forced him to examine that compromise. "It would take years . . ."

"To expand, yes, but not to set up the initial facility . . ." Again Hrriss watched his friend's face, seeing indecision increasing. "The beautiful part of the Hrmnatan would be intact, untouched . . . untouchable!"

"If that could only be enforced . . ." Todd began reluctantly.

"Why not?" Hrriss said, shrugging his tawny shoulders and dropping his jaw. "The terrain is perfect. The first precipice, where the subsidence began, is a natural barrier to the interior, and we will see that the traders abide by our laws."

"Traders are born to bend laws," Todd said, but he knew that was a weak argument. He shook his head one more time. "All right. Put the port there, but seal off the rest of the continent!" He shook a stern ringer at Hrriss' grinning countenance. "I find so much as an ounce of ship's flotsam or the trace of fuel discharge on the mainland . . . I suppose you've got rough sketches all ready?"

Hrriss growled a laugh. "Jilamey used them as a device to keep the discontented occupied while we struggled with our growls."

Todd made a disgusted noise in his throat and rolled his eyes at such complicity. "Only, I'll have nothing to do with it. I hereby empower *you* to attend any meetings on my behalf! My heart simply isn't in it and I've *got* to increase the working vocabulary. I'm much more useful doing that. And, one more thing, I don't even want spaceships overflying the Hrrunatan. They come in from the east. That sort of racket would be disrespectful to Hrruna."

"Ah, but"—Hrriss raised a digit, claw half-extended—"Hrruna was a far-sighted progressive."

"So you say—" Todd caught himself as he was about to embark on the arguments he'd initially used to try to stop the project. With a laugh, he put his fingertip on the claw and gently pushed it back in its sheath. "A triangle *is* the most stable geometrical figure." Another thought caught him. "Great snakes! We'll have to enlarge Treaty Island facilities, too, to accommodate the Gringg."

"So we will. So we will," Hrriss replied equably.

Besides conscripting one of the local manufactories to turn out the voder parts, Todd managed to get the local high school and university, as a work-experience for their students, to assemble the translation devices in their electronics shop classes under the direction of Lieutenant Cardiff. Cardiff was a find. If Todd could have replaced his Spacedep pension, he would have been happy to give him a place on Doonarrala. But Cardiff liked travel and he was used to the military life.

"Maybe I'll retire here, friend," he told Todd. "Meantime, you've got a thousand of these growl boxes ready to go."

The crew complement of the orbiting Gringg leviathan numbered one hundred fifty-four, so the remaining devices were split evenly among Humans and Hrrubans. Over protests from the contentious of both homeworlds, Todd insisted that a number be set aside for children. Much debate had shrunk his proposed allotment from one hundred to thirty, but he was satisfied. The point had been made to Alreldep that, once again, the children of Doonarrala were going to play an important part in the missions of peace. In spite of a cry of nepotism, four growlers were assigned to the elder two of Hrriss' children and to Todd's twins.

Twenty-seven days after the project began, Todd asked Barrington to bring Jilamey down to the manufactory.

"But don't tell him why," Todd instructed, trying to maintain an expression of innocence. The tall, thin manservant regarded him with a calm demeanor, but Todd could perceive a twinkle.

"Of course not, sir," Barrington assured him, and departed in the small air-craft.

Jilamey was a child when it came to mysteries, in no time, the personal heli was back, scattering dust as it descended next to the factory door. Landreau barely allowed it time to touch down before he sprang out, calling for Todd and Hrriss. With broad grins, they met, one on each side as they guided him into the building. Barrington followed at a more sedate pace.

"What's the secret?" Jilamey demanded. "Old Silence-is-golden back there wouldn't give me a clue!"

Without speaking, Todd escorted him into the quality-control room. At his nod, Lieutenant Cardiff came forward, bearing a small device attached to the center of a soft, flexible strap.

"In rrrcognition of srrvice above and beyond ze call of duty," Hrriss said formally, "zo wit, keeping ze nuisances out of our furrr, we want you to have ze first working speech zranslator."

"Truly?" Jilamey gasped, looking from one friend to the other. Todd wore a face-splitting grin as he nodded. Enchanted, Jilamey held still while the voder was fastened on, then cleared his throat. "My dear friends, this is ever so super!" The sound echoed, expanded, and dropped several octaves through the speaker. Jilamey jumped. "This will need some time to get used to," he said, covering the voder input with his hand, but his eyes were glowing. "I sound like a bassoon."

Lieutenant Cardiff took a sonic probe to the side of the voice box. "Your voice is not as deep as some, sir. I tried to leave a little personality in each one."

"How's it work? I warn you"—Jilamey peered out of the corner of his eye at the technician—"I'm dreadful with machinery."

"Well, it transposes the pitch of your voice, compresses your range a little," Cardiff said. "Gringg don't hear as many of the upper tones as we do. It has a full language memory, with plenty of bytes left for expansion. You'll notice a bit of a pause—that'll take time to get used to—between the words out of your mouth and the Gringg equivalent from the growl box. It'll translate Terran into Gringg or Hrruban, whichever you set it for. At least the words that it currently recognizes. Otherwise it defaults to Middle Hrruban, since Hrriss said you're fluent in that."

"We'd like them to learn one language at a time," Todd said.

"One language I speak better than any other"—Jilamey laughed—"and that's trade. I've been contacted by a consortium on Terra. I say, Todd, there's a bit of unfair play going on. The Hrruban trading contingent grows with every grid operation and, if it weren't for the presence of Kiachif, Horstmann, and that crowd that got here originally, you and Hrrestan would be in for real trouble from Terra. However," he added, swiftly shifting mood again from the semi-critical to the self-satisfied, "I managed to salve injured feelings and, if I say so myself, managed quite a coup." He preened a bit, which set his shirt to shimmering with a cascade of subtle color shifts. "I've been appointed agent for the biggest and most diverse consortium of AW."

"Congratulations," Todd said, grinning. "The Gringg'll never know what hit them."

Jilamey pretended modesty, but was quick to make a demand. "When *can* we get down to the nitty-gritty? I've been arguing day and night on your behalf, but, since you've solved the voder problem, when are we going to get to *trade?* That financier Hrrouf is like a Momma Snake, and I hear old Hrrto just gridded back in."

Although Jilamey could be discreet, neither Todd nor Hrriss mentioned that Second Speaker was here because he had insisted on a private conference with Grizz. That was the only way they could pacify the Hrruban after he'd received his copy of the initial voder-assisted conference. The same concession would not be granted to Barnstable, on the grounds that he was only an admiral and not the temporary head of the Hrruban world.

"You will be happy to learn that the original spaceport conference can be reconvened," Todd told Jilamey.

"Wow!" Jilamey rounded his eyes and dropped his jaw in astonishment. "I thought you'd never relent."

"The Gringg constitute a new factor," Todd said obliquely. "Hrriss has been deputized to stand in for me."

"Ahha!" Jilamey waggled a ringer in Todd's face. "I knew you'd figure out how to renege."

"I haven't reneged, Jilamey," Todd said with an edge of rancor. "But"—he waggled his finger in Jilamey's face—"if we want to trade with the Gringg—and we do—the old Hall and spaceport are totally inadequate. And letting the Gringg come in and out of Doonarrala obviates the necessity for their knowing the coordinates of our respective homeworlds. I still don't like to see the Hrrunatan—"

"Corrupted." Jilamey finished off one of Todd's well-known objections. "But old Hrruna would have approved of consorting with the Gringg. You know that! And by utilizing that rocky eastern coast, your preserve will be sacrosanct."

Todd sighed. "Hrriss made that point, too."

"Humph! At least the Gringg have made you two friends again, haven't they?" And Jilamey peered anxiously into Todd's face.

"We have never been *not* friends, Jilamey."

"Still and all, you can't get me to believe that things weren't pretty strained there, just before the *Wander Den* put in its serendipitous appearance."

"Leave off, Jil," Todd said, and pushed the carton of voders at him. "These are for your guests. We're giving everyone a day to get accustomed to the growlers. Show them how they work, and put them to use tomorrow. When I told Grizz that the voders were ready, she assured me that her delegates would be here directly after lunch. I'm taking hers up to the *Wander Den* this evening."

He did not say that he'd also be taking the Second Speaker in the scout for his meeting with Captain Grizz.

Waiting until the old port facility was relatively vacant, Hrriss and Hrrto gridded there from First Village and got on board the scout just before Todd made a more public appearance. He whistled as he loaded the cartons of growl boxes, and waved affably to those who noticed him. The tower gave him clearance, and he made no mention of passengers.

As usual, Grizz had been cooperative about meeting Second Speaker, styled to her as the "Oldest Elder" of the Hrrubans. Hrriss also managed to convey that the Elder was . . . nervous about spaceships, which was the nearest he could manage with a limited vocabulary, to offset any lack of Stripe that Hrrto might display when finally faced with the reality of the huge Gringg captain.

"Weddeerogh," Grizz had told him and, using two fingers, pantomimed her son meeting and escorting the visitor to a private place to talk. "Two," she signed, holding up two digits and sliding her hands sideways, one above the other, making it plain that she and Hrrto would be the only ones.

Todd could tell by the tense look on Hrriss' face that his friend was not entirely happy about that. This meeting would be quite a test of old Hrrto's Stripe! Hrriss had hoped to be an observer. Still, Hrrto *had* insisted! Todd hid a grin and indicated that Hrrto would have the growlers to help the conversation.

Grizz did the Gringg equivalent of relieved smiling and much snapping of her claws in and out of their sheaths. Todd just hoped she would refrain from doing that in Hrrto's presence.

However, when they arrived at the Gringg bay, Weddeerogh stood there by himself, looking comparatively small and harmless. He was also wearing a growler, and someone had tied a reef knot in the cord that had been designed to encircle adult Gringg necks. The knot stuck out behind one ear and made him quite appealing. Hrrto reacted appropriately, by dropping his jaw in a half-smile, though he was clearly stunned by the size of the bay and the immense boxy shuttle-craft parked there.

On the short trip from the planet's surface, Hrrto had practiced with the voder, getting accustomed to the growling guttural reaction to his spoken words.

"Good evening," he now said, inclining his head to the cub. "You are my escort?"

Weddeerogh began to growl, and then his voder started off with "I am"—there was no equivalent for his name—"male child of captain. Come with me!"

With that, the cub did an about-face that Greene couldn't have faulted and strode toward the interior.

"You will wait for me," Hrrto said to the two friends with great dignity and turned to follow his guide.

They were about the same height, though the Hrruban was longer in the leg. As they disappeared through the iris of the lock, Todd wondered if he ought to have warned Hrrto once more about the size of adult female Gringg. He felt Hrriss touch his arm, and the laughter in the cat man's eyes suggested that he entertained similar thoughts.

"I wonder if he will howl," Hrriss said mischieviously.

"Well, he demanded a private audience," Todd said and then began to unload the cartons. As soon as Hrrto and his guide had reached their destination, Eonneh and Koala—and probably half the crew—would arrive to receive their growlers and practice before tomorrow's talks.

Hrrto had been much encouraged by the size and dignity of his escort. The creatures at least understood the basics of courtesy. The stumpy legs of the Gringg made its hind end waggle as they moved down the corridor—rather like a young cub, not quite leg-long. Still, the creature wore a harness that even Hrrto could see was beautifully crafted. So he had been accorded a senior official as his guide. That was as it should be.

With these thoughts, he tried not to notice the dimensions of the hall they traversed. Door panels slid aside at their approach and they went down another, larger hall. Then his guide paused, used partially extended claws to scratch at a door. This slid aside, and bowing from his waist, he made a sweeping gesture for Hrrto to enter.

He began to growl, which translated to "Captain . . ." and then some incomprehensible syllables of which all Hrrto understood was "grizz." Well, Captain would do well enough, so Hrrto swept his robes up deftly and stepped over the threshold. There he stopped and didn't even hear the panel slide shut behind him.

The room was twice the size of the Hrruban High Council Chamber and looked even larger because it was painted a light shade of yellow and was virtually empty except for a pile of cushions; a magnificently ornamented chair and footstool, which his stunned mind told him must be for him; and two small side tables, each crowded with exquisite dishes piled high with tidbits.

But the room was otherwise filled with the most immense living shape Hrrto had ever seen. Its coloring was a sinister dark brown, nearly black, against which the icy shards of its teeth gleamed dangerously. Its head seemed almost to brush the high ceiling, and the frightening roar that came from its mouth—before the voder took over—resounded in the chamber.

Blinking, and rocking back on his heels, Hrrto nevertheless heard Middle Hrruban words that made sense to him.

"Welcome, Honored Second Speaker Hrrto," it said, managing to speak his name with a proper roll of the *r*, a feat few Hayumans accomplished properly. "I am captain of the *Wander Den*. You may call me Grizz as your friends do."

No friends of mine, Hrrto thought, trying to find some mental balance. *Why hadn't Hrriss had the courtesy to warn me of its* size?

"Be seated. Be comfortable. We talk." The words rolled out of the voder, reverberating. As if puzzled by a lack of response, the creature held up the device, and with the tip of a very sharp claw, made a minute adjustment—which Hrrto doubted even as he saw such a delicate movement performed—to one of the dials. "Too loud. Roars are not good for friendly talk."

Hrrto appreciated the adjustment just as he realized that he could not hesitate any further or be a disgrace to his Stripe. He bowed as deeply as he felt he should and dropped his jaw, remembering that Hrriss said the Gringg understood that as a positive action. He thanked the ancient gods that he had not permitted any witness to accompany him—especially Mllaba, who had been quite incensed at being left behind.

Steeling himself for the next action in this ordeal, Hrrto managed a creditable and stately progress to the chair which a massive furred paw indicated. It was only then that he realized the creature had been standing. It now squatted down, with its own peculiar grace, to the pile of cushions, and gestured again for him to be seated.

Still in a state of shock, Hrrto realized he would have to step up on the footstool in order to seat himself. He was wondering about the dignity of this as he did so, but once he was seated and turned toward this Captain Grizz, he found himself at eye level with her. Yes, Hrriss and Zodd had said that the captain was a female. He'd forgotten that detail. Out of nowhere he was reminded of an absurd joke that Zodd Rrev had told in his presence, about citrus fruits that grew so large that eight of them would equal a Human dozen. One of these Gringg was certainly a full dozen.

With an effort of will, Hrrto slowed his heartbeat and his quickened breath and looked her straight in her odd red eyes, pupilless but glistening with intelligence. He couldn't deny that!

"You are . . . (*gracious? kind?*) very good to receive me, Captain," he said, wishing that the voder would not hesitate in its translation. Would that be considered a sign of weakness? No, her device did the same thing.

Now she gestured to the bowls on the side table.

Growling; then the voder explained, "All Hrruban foods. Enjoy!"

She reached for her own table and took a gobbet of something, conveying it neatly to her mouth. Grateful for the diversion and the courtesy thus shown, Hrrto selected a tiny crisp-fleshed fruit and became more relaxed, for clearly these Gringg had taken the time to discover his preferences. They both chewed companionably.

"You were long on your way here?" Hrrto asked, abruptly deciding to be social in manner. His previously rehearsed speech was totally inappropriate.

The Gringg nodded her great head, dropping her jaw as a Hrruban would, but he wished her black lips did not retreat over her very white fangs. He reached down for a handful of refried meat cubes, another favorite tidbit. "Grrrr . . . two cubs born to me and a long time between them. I am captain."

"I see," Hrrto said, nodding at such information. "Will you return to your homeworld or a colony?" He hoped the voder translated "colony."

"Grrruuph . . . We are on peaceful mission for long as possible," she replied. "We wish to trade. With Hrruban, With Hayuman."

Subtle, too, Hrrto thought, putting his species before the Hayuman. But that was as it should be.

"Grrrummmm . . . glad to find two for one trip," and she dropped her jaw again.

Hrrto paused a moment, decided she intended to be humorous and dropped his jaw. Then, deliberately over his next words, he scooped up more of the meat cubes, nibbling delicately. He had long ago learned how to eat without exposing his own dental equipment.

"You have seen many other worlds, planets, systems . . ." All three nouns came out in assorted groans and growls. "Have you?" he added, making that a question rather than a statement.

The captain nodded, running her tongue over her teeth, fortunately with her mouth closed. Evidently they had several courtesies in common.

"Many. Not enough water for Gringg. Too much land is not needed. But land has certain minerals, earths, no smart peoples. We are a water people. Hrrubans like water worlds?"

Clever as well, Hrrto thought, considering this a deft ploy to gain knowledge of his homeworld.

"We are land creatures," Hrrto said, finally settling back in the chair and finding it comfortable. His back muscles had started jumping from inner tensions. "We are hunters. Are you?"

Another nod. "Eating is necessary."

One answer led to another question, and Hrrto found himself able to ask, and receive answers, to many queries. What he so desperately wanted to ask—about the Gringg ship drifting derelict off a shattered world—did not come to his lips. Such a query would have been inappropriate, he told himself; certainly not consonant with the social nature of this meeting, and probably would be deftly parried by the captain. Far better for him to think of trade, and most particularly of the need for purralinium, though he had to be most adroit in his questions concerning that desperately needed commodity. The captain readily admitted how many planets they had surveyed, but not what the surveys had discovered. She discoursed on many matters, some of her conversation marred by the insertion of growls, snarls, and woofs where the voder could not accommodate a translation.

"On your way, did you discover dwarf systems? Or do you have enough ores and minerals on your own planet?" Hrrto finally inserted as casually as possible. Only systems shattered by novas contained the purralinium with the impurities that could be used for matter transmission.

"Reh! Yes," the captain said, nodding her great head. "Three," and she held up three huge digits. "We always look for new . . . ah grrrmmm—metals, earths, useful raw materials."

"I see!" Hrrto could hardly contain his excitement over such news. Surely in one of those systems, there would be the purralinium the Hrrubans had long sought.

"Do you?" asked the captain politely.

"One always *looks*," Hrrto said, waving one hand in an airy gesture, dismissing that topic. "We search space, too. You must come from very far away."

"Our scribes try to find time parallels so can be accurate. No wish to keep back any information. Only special words not available yet."

Throughout their hour-long meeting, she appeared at ease and did not evade discussion of any topic Hrrto touched upon.

Finally, after noticing she had finished the contents of the bowls on her table, he realized that it would be diplomatic of him to bring the meeting to a close. She was graciousness itself, and the young Weddeerogh, her male cub, waited outside the door to guide Hrrto back to the bay, and his transport back to Rraladoona.

All in all, as Hrrto took his seat in the scout ship, he felt the meeting had gone well. The possibility of locating one of those nova-blasted systems was the brightest part of the hour. More important, he had survived it!

The next morning, when Second Speaker arrived at the Treaty Center with his entourage and swept into the Chamber, he had second thoughts. He had spent a night tossing and turning on his pallet, and he was one who usually found sleep easily. He had rehearsed query and answer many times. He also tried to figure out how to acquire the coordinates of one of the nova systems. Yet that would require very adroit maneuvering on his part. But, as he tossed and turned, a solution came to him. The scientist Hurrhee, who was one of his own Stripe, would surely be invited to attend any technological sessions. Hurrhee was completely trustworthy, in that he held science as the premier dedication of his life. He could certainly introduce the topic of nova-blasted systems. Perhaps the Gringg might even have samples of ores, earths, and minerals they hoped to trade. A simple survey would reveal whether or not the purralinium fit Hrruban requirements. Yes, that was how to handle that problem. Accepting judicious amounts in return for trade items would not arouse any suspicions.

Satisfied with that solution, Hrrto once again composed himself to sleep, only to find himself distressed by a second anxiety. Despite the evidence on the tape shown him by the Hayuman admiral, he could not equate such brutality with the courtesies shown him by the captain. Of course, her manner and charm—yes, she had been charming in her own fashion—might be serving her own ends by allaying his doubts, but Hrrto could not quite believe such duplicity. Certainly not from someone who had assigned her own flesh and blood as his guide. Had she come to Hrruba, he would have assigned his second-generation offspring as her guide.

Mllaba, of course, had wanted a word-by-word account of the meeting. He had touched on the details, privately wondering what her reactions would be when she was face to face with the stupendous reality of Captain Grzzeearoghh. That would teach her humility. Casually, he asked her to arrange a discreet meeting with Hurrhee as early as possible the next morning, before the Trade Conference began, and for once, she did not ask why.

The next day, the wide hall of the Treaty Center—almost as wide as a corridor on the Gringg vessel—was well populated with little knots of Hayumans and Hrrubans chatting amiably. Hrrto, walking with great dignity, sensed the air of pleased anticipation. In front of the chamber assigned to the spaceport talks, he recognized the fair-haired female captain of the *Hamilton* and the Hayuman commander. If there was purralinium to be had by congress with the Gringg, he would have to rethink that uneasy alliance.

Greene turned a precise half-bow in his direction, to which Second responded. The Hayuman had kept Hrrto's aide fully informed as to the progress of the Spacedep fleet toward Rraladoona. Neither that squadron nor the three Hrruban defense ships were close enough yet. Now Hrrto wondered if that action had been as necessary as the Spacedep person had insisted. Would it ruin the good start he had made with the captain and, at the worst, deny the Hrrubans a possible source of purralinium? If he had only been able to ask her about Fingal and the dead, orbiting Gringg ship! Maybe having both navies there was *not* a bad idea. If the Gringg *were* as peaceful as they seemed, he could always say that policy had required him to inform the Hrruban navy and they had acted without his orders. Yes, that was it. On the other hand, the naval presence might forestall any devious Gringg scheme. Either way, he would be considered wise. Overnight reflections had not entirely dispersed his anxieties, but his little chat with Hurrhee had been most productive.

After briefing the scientist, he had reviewed the morning dispatches, which included almost insolent demands from Hrruban manufacturers and traders of all commodities to open dialogue. They clamored that they *must* have first choices, with such an obscene single-mindedness that for once Hrrto found himself disgusted with Stripes, wide and narrow.

He was here now, officially and publicly, to initiate trade talks with Captain Grizz. Hurrhee was primed to include ores as part of any trade payment. Once matters were underway in that session, Hrrto could then gracefully retire to the spaceport conference. He couldn't quite leave such negotiations to Prrid, Mrrunda, Hrrouf, and the others who had gridded in for that purpose. Only after he was sure that both meetings were proceeding with dispatch, might he then be able to get back to Hrruba and promote his personal ambitions toward First Speakership.

Mllaba was almost treading on his heels as she escorted him to the Trade Conference room. To his relief, the immense and shaggy Gringg had not yet arrived, though huge square cushions on the floor gave notice where they were to sit.

"Your place should be at the head of the table," Mllaba whispered, guiding him toward one end of the great oval board.

To their surprise, Hrrin was already seated at the end of the oval. He regarded them with glittering eyes when they approached, showing no signs of vacating his seat.

"Greetings, Honorrred Speaker," he said in proper High Hrruban, rising and bowing gracefully. "I have been deputized as Rrraladoonan spokesperson, but I will, of course, defer . . ."

"I had expected Hrrestan—" Second began.

"Ah, but he is conducting the spaceport affairs," Hrrin said smoothly. "It was our understanding that you would not stay here long, but go on to the more important conference."

Mllaba hissed slightly in Hrrto's ear. Sometimes she could be annoying about what was due his rank.

"We have arranged ourselves according to our origins," Hrrin went on, gesturing to the Rraladoonans seated to his right and the Hrrubans, onward to the Terran delegation of captains and Jilamey Landreau further along the table.

The room was full enough of bodies right now, and Hrrto jerked his shoulders and switched his tail, trying hard not to remember how the Gringg captain had dominated a room not much larger than this.

"Most commendable," Second said with an absent frown. In ordinary circumstances, protocol would have required a Hrruban to allow him the dominant place for however long he chose to stay in the meeting. Hrrestan would have automatically deferred, but this Hrrin was more Rraladoonan. Hrrto decided to ignore Mllaba's hissing. To demand protocol in a mere trade meeting would appear petty. It was more important for him to be prominent in the spaceport considerations than to bicker about what to buy from whom and at what price.

Noting that Hurrhee was present, Hrrto spared a glance for Nrrena, seated to the scientist's right. She was an intimate of Fifth Speaker and bore watching. She must not think that these seating arrangements constituted a discourtesy. Determined to put the best face on the situation, he nodded with great dignity to Hrrin. "How wise to show, even here, that Hrruba is distinct from Terra."

"I am so glad that you approve, sir," Hrrin said, once again making a courteous gesture to the chair placed well along the outer curve of the great table.

Smiling graciously to Nrrena and two Hrrubans he did not know, Hrrto moved to that seat. It was, he was relieved to note, more ornate than any of the others at this segment of the table. He settled himself in the deep chair, flicking his tail out under the armrest. Mllaba was growling under her breath as she sat behind him on a small seat she pulled from those ranged along the wall.

Hrrto looked around with practiced casualness. Zodd Rrev occupied the other end of the table. Hrrto noticed that neither he nor Hrrin sat at the exact head, but angled off slightly from the table's axis. He wondered what precisely that indicated in the negotiations to come. The Rraladoonans had their own agenda, he had no doubt, and were clever enough to push it through in spite of the best efforts of homeworld diplomats. See how they had begun by forestalling him.

Then he realized that he was directly opposite an as yet unoccupied place which had no chair. He would be facing a Gringg. He steeled himself for that, wary after last evening's encounter. That inadvertently brought to mind the Spacedep tape as well as last night's insomnia. Again, he saw the devastated landscape, and the floating frozen corpses, and could not control a shudder down his spine. Firmly, he put that vision out of his mind. To cover his spasm, he fiddled with the voder straps. Everyone here was wearing the contraptions, of course, and he devoutly hoped that Hrrin—or would it be Zodd Rrev who moderated this meeting?—made certain that only one person spoke at a time. Otherwise the resultant cacophony would be nerve-racking.

The Hayuman admiral noisily entered the chamber now, and took his place obliquely across from Hrrto, with curt nods to everyone in the room. The bearded Codep trader and the stout independent trader followed with the Alreldep admiral and the small Hayuman male from Terra and a gaggle of others he'd never seen.

Jilamey Landreau interested Hrrto. His spies had informed him that Landreau was well connected in government, industry, and the arts, and had tremendous credit. His financial acumen was much respected despite his youth, for none of his ventures ever seemed to lose money. Landreau dressed much more colorfully than any negotiator or diplomat should, in Hrrto's opinion; almost Hrruban in style. At least the Hayuman understood the order of precedence, as he greeted Hrrto first on entering the room.

"Second Speaker, you honor us by your presence!" Landreau said, bowing with hand on heart. His warm brown eyes held a twinkle. "Why, good morning, Commander Greene! You're looking well."

The Hayuman commander offered a meaningless pleasantry and swung immediately back to the Spacedep admiral. Landreau slouched into the seat between the scarlet-haired banker and Todd Reeve, and began a cheerful conversation.

More, totally unknown Hrrubans arrived, bowing sharply to Hrrto from the doorway. Then Prrid emerged from the group and proceeded to his side of the table.

"I must be here to welcome the Gringg captain," Prrid murmured in High Hrruban in Hrrto's ear. "Then I will join you in the spaceport discussions. Mrrunda attends it now."

Hrrto approved with a nod, and Prrid seated himself. The Space Arm commandant, too, would be facing Gringg. Hrrto mulled over Prrid's probable reactions to Captain Grizz. Quite likely it would only reinforce Prrid's doubts about the Gringg's real purpose in approaching Rraladoona.

There was a stir and a hubbub of voices in the corridor outside. Todd Reeve observed it, too. Hrrto tilted his ears toward the door and rolled them back again as he felt an uncomfortable sensation at the back of his neck.

"I think our third party has arrived," said Reeve, rising.

Hastily, Hrrin, as co-host, sprang to his feet. Into the chamber swung Grizz, looking even larger than before. Hrrto had to restrain an impulse to lean back, away from her. She was truly overwhelming as she strode into the room. The floor seemed to bounce with the weight of her and her four companions.

Someone, thought Hrrto, ought to tell her to keep her lips over her fangs, despite the fact that an open mouth was for her species, like his, a sign of friendliness. Then Hrrto noticed that the stripe fur of every single Hrruban bristled with an instinctive reaction. Except for his, he was excessively pleased to note. He could also hear the fault whistle of lashing tails as Grizz's head brushed the top of the doorway. The resounding roar she used for a voice filled the room, overpowering the efforts of the small translator at her throat to compensate. Hrrto's heart pounded. So bizarre for the female of a species to be larger than the male. She quite dwarfed the males in her entourage.

"Hold it, hold it there, Grizz," a narrow, dark-skinned Hayuman said, running up to the giant beast with a small tool. "We're getting harmonics here, lady bear."

Lady bear? Hrrto was taken aback by such familiarity, such lack of basic decorum. Beside him, he could sense Mllaba's tension. He gave her a warning glance to settle the fur on her nape, but when he turned to Prrid, the naval commandant had already smoothed himself. Good Stripe, that Prrid.

With five Gringg, the room became suddenly as crowded as a package of fish, and he could see more in the corridor. They were so imposing that just a few of them looked like an invading army. Perhaps calling the Space Arm had not been such a bad idea. The Hayuman made adjustments to the captain's speech device and stepped away.

"That . . . good, gggrrr, better, best," said the Gringg, swinging a huge paw to touch the male gently on the shoulder. Her voder had modified her speech to a much more pleasing pitch.

Without the subsonics exacerbating his nerves, Hrrto relaxed. Strange that just sound could produce such effects. But others looked very much on their guard. Merely the presence of the immense Gringg held an aura of threat. Did they count on that?

"Wrrrfgruh . . . I grrreet you all," Grizz said, turning her head to include all the occupants of the table. "Hayumans and Hrrubans both."

"On behalf of Doonarrala," Todd Reeve said, "I greet you, Captain Grzzeearoghh, and welcome you to the first in a series of talks which, we deeply hope, will benefit us all."

The device at his throat translated his words from good Middle Hrruban into inarticulate growls and coughs. Hrrto laid back his ears. Some of the growling fell below his range of hearing, and sound shocks flew up and down his spine.

The great captain inclined her head. Todd swept his hand around the room to include the cushions on the unoccupied side of the table. "I hope these will be adequate."

The captain nodded absently in approval as she asked, "Two peoples are you Hayumans and Hrrubans?"

"That is corrrect, Madam Captain," Hrrin replied, courteously. "Here on Rraladoona we proudly sharrre a world, but we are of separate origins and species. If you and your prrrty will be seated, we shall begin."

"No. Two rooms are needed," the Gringg said, and folded her paws over her chest with a gesture of finality. "I have brought two pairs of Gringg, to speak to you separately."

"But why?" Todd asked, surprised.

"Here are two peoples. We honor your individuality. It is possible you each need different things from us, that you supply us with different items or units. It is only courteous to give individual attention to each of you. Therefore, two separate negotiations shall be held." The translator punctuated the Hrruban phrases with growls and hums, but Grizz's meaning was clear.

Hrrto felt his ears lean backward. This was not proceeding according to plan. And yet, without the Hayumans in the room, the subject of purralinium could be brought up without fear that the Hayumans would understand its importance to the Hrruban economy.

Be that as it may, Hrrto did not entirely trust this new development. These aliens were dangerous. Did they intend to divide and conquer, to promise vital goods and services to the Hayumans in private, cheating the Hrrubans of equal opportunities? Purralinium was not the only raw material Hrruba lacked. Depressed, Hrrto could see complications looming.

Admiral Barnstable seemed no happier with the Gringg captain's proposal, for he leaned across the table toward Reeve.

"Conference, Rrev," he ordered in High Hrruban. Quickly, Reeve turned to the towering Gringg and made a deep bow.

"A moment's pause, Captain," Reeve said through the translator and beckoned urgently to Hrrin. "We had not expected a division."

The Gringg lifted a paw in acceptance and sat down on the cushions, waiting with cheerful patience.

Second Speaker, Hrrin, and Mllaba joined the Admiral, Greene, Captain Hrrrv, Castleton, the two Reeves, and Hrrin and Kiachif in the furthest corner from the Gringg. Mllaba's nape hair stuck straight out in agitation. Greene looked grim; Castleton, curious.

"This will not do, Reeve," the Admiral muttered as they assembled. "I insist that we establish a single round table for any trade agreements. Each of our two races must have absolutely identical treatment and consideration. No covert clauses."

"Nonsense, nails, and nuts," Captain Kiachif said, scoffing at the red-faced Spacedep official. "That'd be the end of free enterprise—see if it isn't. Why not let it be their way? What's the harm of it? If we don't like what they have to offer, we insist on a joint parley tomorrow, if you follow me. Nothing's to stop us from convening, comparing, and combining."

"Nor am I comfortable with zis," Hrrto said, covering his voder with one hand. "I prefer open confrrrnce."

"But isn't zis preferable, Second Speaker?" Hrrin asked. "Hrruba's individuality maintained, and ze same for Amalgamated Wrrlds."

Hrrto glared, but he could detect no note of sarcasm in the Rraladoonan's voice. Those born on this colony planet really did lack many of the basic courtesies and tact which he felt his due.

"It is a dangrrrous ploy," agreed Captain Hrrrv, eyes gleaming.

Reeve dismissed that remark. "If we want the Gringg to feel comfortable among us, we should do our best to accommodate a reasonable request. I concur with Captain Kiachif. Let's go along with the Gringg's wishes today. We can use, uh—" he glanced around for a view of the hall—"the conference room in the research library as the other chamber. It's just down the hall and around the corner from the spaceport business."

"This is not as planned," Second said, reverting again to High Hrruban in his dismay. "Hrruba and Terra must take the lead here, not these strangers."

"It would seem, Honored sir," Ken Reeve said, replying in the same language, "that we must oblige our guests—today, at least."

Only because the privacy suited Hrrto's needs did he give consent. Graciously leaving the Hrrubans in possession of the Treaty Chamber, Todd led the Hayumans, the Gringg captain, and one of the pairs of males out of the door and away to the right.

Hrrto watched them leave. Could he trust any one of the Hayumans to give him an accurate account of what transpired in their session? Possibly his erstwhile allies in Spacedep would not dissemble too much. Still, if he could get the purralinium, he might just win the election on that score. He caught Nrrena staring at him. His direct and haughty glance made her look away again, her chin lowered in momentary embarrassment. How dare Fifth's representative look askance in his direction! He nodded just once at Hurrhee, who gave the barest of nods in understanding.

As soon as the Hayumans and the three Gringg had gone, Hrrin gestured for the others to be seated. With only two Gringg in the room, everyone seemed to breathe more freely.

"As long as we are now together," he said in Middle Hrruban, dropping his jaw in a pleasant smile, "perhaps we should begin by introducing ourselves."

To Todd's surprise, the engineer Koala was waiting a little way down from the Treaty Chamber with Commander Frill, Lieutenant Cardiff, and a few other Gringg males whom Todd hadn't met before.

"Afternoon, Mr. Reeve," the burly xenotech said, grinning. "Didn't think you'd be free."

"Frill and I are going to show Koala the sights," Cardiff explained. "These are a few of her assistants. We've got a powwow later with a consortium of scientists from your colony and both cruisers. Nothing sensitive, of course, just general stuff, like that resonator of theirs. Good luck!" He escorted the troop of Gringg down the corridor toward the landing field. "You can raise me by belt radio if you need to!" he called over his shoulder.

"Thanks, Lieutenant," Todd replied. Weddeerogh waddled shyly up to Todd and touched his hand with a wet, black nose, then turned to bestow the same greeting on Ken.

"Hello, little guy," Todd said, pausing to ruffle the cub's pate hairs. "Welcome to Doonarrala." Then he turned to Grizz, and turned his voder on again. "The other room is just down here, Captain."

"Morra," Grizz said, looking down on them fondly from her great height. "I do not discuss trading matters. I seek to visit your home village. Much has been told me that I wish to see with my own eyes," she said in slow Hrruban. The translator produced remarkably accurate pronunciation. "These two"—she pointed a claw at Eonneh and another Gringg, a male with silky gray fur—"I trust to make best trade speech for us types."

"Of course," Todd said, surprised on the one hand but pleased on the other. He'd wanted Grizz to see for herself what her emissaries had. "I'll see you're gridded up to First Village. My wife, Kelly, and Nrrna, Hrriss' mate, will be delighted to host you in our homes. Allow me to send a message for them to meet you."

"You are most very kind," Grizz said, pausing between words to remember what was appropriate to say.

"Are you sure that is wise, Reeve?" Greene demanded, hand over his voder input. "Sending a . . . a being of her stature to a civilian habitation unescorted?"

Todd understood exactly what the commander really meant, and refused to acknowledge it.

"I admit it might be considered rude to ship the highest-ranking official of a delegation somewhere without the correct entourage, but perhaps," he said, with a bow and a smile to Grizz, "under the circumstances she will forgive me. She will be met on arrival, of course, by my wife, who is, by the way, an Alreldep representative, and quite capable of handling our new friends."

Barnstable shot both of them a look of annoyance, and Todd understood that the criticism must actually have come from him. Spacedep's paranoia was beginning to wear upon Todd. Grizz, who had followed only part of the swift, low-pitched conversation, showed her fangs amiably. The gesture made most of the Human delegates shiver, and Todd grinned back at her.

"I forgive without reserve, Todd Reeve," Grizz said. "I and my son look forward to seeing the beauties of your home which these others have described to me. And this one"—she patted her son's shoulder—"is eager to swim in Doonarralan waters."

"Well, Admiral, Commander," Todd said, "don't let me keep you from your duties. The spaceport conference is just down the hall, you know." Then he turned to Sumitral, Ali, and Jilamey. "You all know the place we're to use. Why don't you show our Gringg negotiators the way? I'll join you soon as I can."

After he had called Kelly to tell her to meet her guests, he conducted Grizz and her cub out of the Treaty Building and to the grid facility. As there seemed to be no limit to the weight a grid could shift, he did not worry about the mass of a female Gringg.

But the mass of the personage to be gridded quite shattered the composure of the bored grid operator. The slim female Hrruban on duty froze, her neck hair bristling, and gaped in shock at the pair to be transported to First Village.

"Zis grid is only for small shipments," she protested, anxiously glancing over Todd's shoulder at Grizz.

"Oh, come now, the captain masses no more than some of those 'visitors' you've been bringing in all week," Todd said, cocking an eyebrow at her. Then he pointed to the schedule hung above her control board. "You've got an opening of almost ten minutes before you receive the next pallets. Captain Grzzeearoghh is a person of importance. She shouldn't have to hang about here with you, now should she?"

"No, sirrrr, no!" the Hrruban gasped. "Step up onto ze platfrrm, most honrrrred guests, please!" She gestured the Gringg between the slim transmission pillars and fumbled to key in the coordinates.

"I know you'll enjoy your visit, Captain," Todd said, waving. "Kelly will be waiting for you!"

"G'bye!" Weddeerogh said, waving both his paws energetically. As the mist rose and began to swallow him up, he squealed on such a note that the grid operator laid back her ears.

The conference room which Todd entered on his return was providentially carpeted, floor and walls, in a warm, burnt orange that complemented the golden woods of the furniture frames. The padding on the walls would baffle some of the more annoying overtones of Gringg speech. The chairs, upholstered in the same handsome orange, were set around a well-polished table of golden hardwood. Several computer monitors on swivel boards occupied positions on the tabletop and could be turned to face any direction.

Someone had brought in the cushions which the Gringg preferred and placed them on one side of the large square table. Ken Reeve, the merchant captains, Sumitral and Jilamey, and some Humans Todd didn't know were occupying the chairs on the opposing side. Todd was annoyed to find Commander Greene also present. Barnstable was eating his cake in the spaceport discussions and having it, too, with Greene here to listen to trade talks. Todd did recognize several Doonarralan representatives of the craft- and farm-collectives. These men and women were trying not to appear awed by the company in which they found themselves.

"Are you comfortable now?" Sumitral was asking. "I would be happy to sit on the floor. We could move the table."

"Eye to eye, please, is Gringg way," Eonneh said politely. "Sofas are fine for Gringg, chairs for you, thank you." The translator had picked up the unfamiliar word "cushions," and given the Gringg the closest equivalent it had. "New friends, I am Eonneh, named Honey by a child of this world. I approve the name, as I consider it the first step to close links with your people. This is Krrpuh. You call him Coypu—easier to say."

Todd had to restrain a broad smile. He recalled, and cherished, the memory of the Gringg being assigned "bear" names by his twins and Hrriss's two eldest. The youngsters took the naming responsibility very seriously, having made a list of every synonym or cognate for "bear" that could be found in Terran philology. He remembered Hrrunival being peeved that his planet had no corollary creature. They matched names as closely as they could to the Gringg sounds, delighting the recipients.

"We welcome you, Honey and Coypu," Todd said formally and started introducing those present. He could hear rapid footsteps on the marble floors as latecomers hurried to the new venue.

As Todd recited the Humans' names, the Gringg sniffed subtly in the appropriate direction, obviously pairing scent with face. Sumitral raised the corner of his mouth in a wry smile as he realized what they were doing. Horstmann was the only one who seemed slightly uneasy. Jilamey, seated at the far comer beside Honey, winked as Todd named him. The tool-and-die maker from Rompiel was frowning abstractedly, trying not to stare at the two Gringg. Commander Greene spoke in low, urgent tones to Horstmann, who turned a shoulder on him; then the navy man stared piercingly at Todd. Todd tried to ignore Greene. The man's blatant Human chauvinism grated on him.

Todd had had a furious discussion about Greene with Barnstable after returning to the *Hamilton*, concerning Greene's near-disastrous antics on the Gringg ship. That the aide had been responsible for initiating the intruder probe was bad enough, but carrying an explosive device onto a vessel assumed to be peaceful defied all reason. Todd had made it clear to Barnstable that either act could have compromised matters beyond recall, and he insisted that Greene be left behind on the flagship whenever Barnstable came groundside. The Admiral refused, demanding his right to such escort as he required. He resented Todd's criticism of a member of his staff, and pointed out again that Doonarrala's priorities and Spacedep's were not identical. Todd hoped he wouldn't have to go all the way to the Amalgamated Worlds Council to keep Spacedep from causing more trouble.

During the weeks of research on the voder, Greene had been around and about on Doonarrala, always maintaining his distance from Todd, but always there, like an annoying itch Todd couldn't get rid of. Since none of the ursine guests had mentioned Greene, Todd decided that they hadn't noticed the burly commander, or were choosing to ignore his surveillance. The Spacedep officers hadn't been subtle when following the Gringg, as if they'd hoped for some kind of incident which would allow them to step in and take command.

Nothing had happened, and Todd hoped Greene and his spies had gotten bored stiff.

Honey seemed to be in good spirits. He had visited Doonarrala nearly every other day, touring schools, factories, and farms, and spending much time in the villages. He was easily the most recognizable of the Gringg. His companion, who moved with a ponderousness dilatory even for a Gringg, seemed to be older than Honey, with a majestic, slow bass voice that was so low it rumbled through Todd's very bones. Both of them had small computer devices with sculpted depressions, which were probably operated by the rhythmic manipulation of claws, something like the device used by an old-time court reporter. As usual Honey held his ubiquitous tile-like tablet. Jilamey, at Honey's elbow, was keeping a close eye on the Gringg, waiting for him to draw or write something with the double-looped pen that lay atop it on the table.

By then, the tardy delegates had arrived, slightly breathless, and more time was taken up by introductions.

Of the seven newcomers, five were clearly alarmed by the size of the Gringg, and although they were wearing voders, only one had practiced with his device. And Todd instantly marked Emil Markudian, a swarthy-faced man with a prominent, hooked nose and black eyes, as trouble. His companion, for the man seemed unwilling to move away from Markudian's side, was Brad Ashland, and he was not only plainly terrified by the aliens, but his eyes had the glitter of the xenophobe.

When he noticed them darting quick glances at Greene, he decided they bore close scrutiny. Well, he should have expected something like this after Barnstable's little confrontation of assorted blow-ins at Kate Moody's office. The others who had arrived in the wake of Markudian seemed to be legitimate, since they all carried portfolios with the logos of major, diversified Terran or colonial companies. Two found Jilamey's presence distinctly unsettling. Remembering how chuffed Jilamey had been about his coup, Todd grinned to himself and then turned the meeting over to Admiral Sumitral, seated directly opposite the Gringg envoys.

Once introductions of the new arrivals had been made, there was a perceptible pause. Todd sensed an electrical tension rising among them, veiled excitement. *I feel as if we're about to start a high-stakes poker game*, he thought. *Who's going to bluff whom?*

"We begin from ignorance," Admiral Sumitral said, rising to address the Gringg. "You have been among us for many days now and seen us going about our work and play. We know nothing about your world, and desire similar information."

"Ah," said Coypu, resting his paws on his large belly, "very kind of you to ask. Our world is much like this, gravity heavier and more water in many big pools. We are four ships to explore. Long, long, long"—and he nodded his head to emphasize the span—"looking. It is good, great news to find two at once!" He dropped his jaw and looked about him, his eyes twinkling.

"You say your objective is to trade, yet you admit that you are very far from your homeworld. How can you possibly trade profitably over long distances?" Commander Greene wanted to know.

"Big ship," replied Coypu succinctly. "We come prepared with offerings. Trading is good with peaceful people. You have much here which will be tradable."

"Such as?" Greene demanded sarcastically.

"You are out of order, Commander," Sumitral said, turning slightly so that his body shielded him from the Gringg. He had covered his translator and spoke in a low but carrying tone, somehow managing not to move his lips very much. "As Spacedep personnel, you are present only to observe!"

"We have seen much here on Doonarrala that will be very appreciated on our world," Honey added. "We are peaceful traders."

"It's very easy to say that you come in peace," Markudian spoke up, his deep voice smooth but holding an edge.

That statement elicited quiet gasps around the table. Todd had seen no signal from Greene, but that didn't keep him from suspecting the two might be acting in concert.

Sumitral regarded Markudian with an expression of mild surprise and astonishment, but it was Coypu who answered.

"It is easy to say what is true," Coypu said, either not offended or deliberately not understanding Markudian's implication. Now he lifted his paws. "We come far from our homeworld, seeking new worlds, hopefully new peoples."

"You are peaceful types, also," Honey said, looking around the table and nodding his appreciation of that fact. "It is very good for Gringg to see that two different species can live in peace without acchggt-spppput . . ." He turned to Coypu as his voder could not give a suitable translation of the Gringg word.

". . . without tearing the collar?" Coypu suggested.

"Tearing the collar?" Sumitral asked, pointedly asking for an explanation.

Coypu touched his ornate neckpiece with one delicate claw. "Yes, to tear off the collar of a Gringg is to start fight, but only if there is no other honor choice."

"Oh, similar to throwing down a gauntlet . . . a glove . . . a hand protector," Sumitral said, ignoring the mutters from some of those nervous about this discussion. "Of course, duels with lethal weapons have long been considered against the law as well as against common sense."

Coypu seemed oddly pleased to hear that. "With us, too, the custom has declined. There are nearly always other choices. We enjoy peace. Gringg do not like to exert themselves. Peace takes much less energy than combat, do you not agree?"

Todd laughed at the beautiful simplicity of the statement. "War is too much trouble?"

"War?" Coypu asked, for the word had been carefully omitted from the voder's lexicon.

"War," Greene said, jumping at the opportunity, "is when many tear the collar and join a fight; the winners take all. A great exertion," he added sarcastically.

"War is a thing of the past for both species. It was always a useless exertion," Sumitral said in such an icy voice and with such an icy stare directed at Greene that the commander subsided, mostly in surprise at the Alreldep admiral's intensity.

"Good! Good!" Coypu said seriously. "I tire if I think about it. Cooperation takes so much less work."

"Then Gringg have had wars?" Markudian asked, leaning forward.

"Long ago," Honey said negligently, "to protect the family pool and the landing place, and our young when there was not enough to eat."

That mildly delivered statement brought quite a reaction around the table. Todd and his father exchanged concerned glances,

"Then, during the Great Heat, we were forced to seek refuge in the deepest caves. It was then that we were forced to eat many things other than the beasts which had been our natural food," Honey went on, blithely unaware of the effect his first statement was having. "When we emerged from the caves, we turned to the sea and began to hunt the big fish. Little ones, too, which are often very tasty."

"But you *were* cannibals?" Markudian demanded, with such an air of superiority that Todd knew the man was there to cause whatever trouble he could. Unfortunately Honey had just handed him a perfect opening.

As Sumitral was trying to explain the word "cannibals" to Honey, Todd leaned toward Markudian.

"The emphasis was on a trade vocabulary, Mr. Markudian. We cannot, and will not, at this time, accept the discussion of side issues."

When Honey and Coypu finally understood, they both looked mournful.

"When we were very young beings, long, long, long ago, before we learned to think what we were doing, before we learned how much easier it was to work together instead of separately," Honey said, leaning forward, paws crossed over his chest in humility—"we Gringg did many stupid things we do not like to remember doing. Perhaps this happened to Hayumans, too, when your species was learning wisdom?"

"Not cannibalism," Markudian said firmly.

Sumitral gave a droll chuckle. "Mr. Markudian, you are obviously not much of a student of Terran history or you would realize how wrong you are on that point." Then Sumitral bent a stern look upon the man. "But you cannot be so young as to be ignorant of the Siwannah Tragedy, in which humans caused an entire race to suicide. I also feel that you speak out too hastily, Mr. Markudian, and I advise you to think very carefully the next time you feel obliged to criticize." Then he turned to Honey and Coypu. "We also had to learn to cope with famines. I trust there is no famine on your homeworld now that has sent you out on your long journey."

"No, not famine," Coypu said. "We wish to find new worlds. We wish to trade with same peaceful people."

"Let's get back to trade talk, shall we?" asked Jilamey a bit impatiently, giving Markudian a very jaundiced look for his interruptions. "Let's talk about what sort of payment we'll use for trade items."

"Excellent idea, my dear Landreau," Sumitral said. He turned to the Gringg. "In trading with our Hrruban friends, we use certain minerals and metals on which we have agreed to a value."

"Do you not use symbolic currencies?" Coypu asked. There was a murmur of surprise among the merchants.

"Yes, of course we do," Jilamey said, "but our credits would be worthless to you in your own system, so let us find other values for barter."

Ken Reeve said, "Eonneh and I have discussed molecular structures of certain metals and minerals that we would like to acquire in moderate quantities. What mediums have value for you?"

"We discuss a common trade currency?" Honey asked mildly, rattling his claws in the holes of his computerlike device. "Held perhaps on this planet in a central place for all three to use? With . . . ahccccgg . . . writings that can be strictly kept accurate?"

Ashland looked stunned. Jumping from cannibalism in a distant past to modern finance was too big a leap for him. Markudian's expression became darker than ever.

"A banking system is, of course, an excellent idea," Sumitral said, raising his eyebrows in silent query at the two, who blinked agreement.

"If you become permanent trading partners with us . . ." Jilamey began slowly, allowing the possibility to sink in, "a central place would simplify all transactions."

"Trading partners for a long time we want," Honey replied, and gave them a huge white grin.

Kiachif whistled. "For critters who've never seen other aliens before, you sure take the long view."

Honey bowed to Kiachif, inclining his long torso. "We are hopeful creatures, and in that hope much discussion occupied our long travels and what to do if we find others." He hiked one shoulder in a very human gesture. "It passed the time, and now we discover that it was wise to plan for such acchtgg . . . possibles.

For now"—he spread his big paws—"we put theory into practice. It is not much different to the trading we do between our homeworld and its young."

"Young? You have colony worlds?" Sumitral said.

"Or subjugated worlds?" Greene asked, his eyes glittering.

Honey looked down at his voder, and Coypu looked puzzled.

"Acchgg?" Honey asked in query.

"That's quite enough from you, Greene," Sumitral said with the first flash of temper Todd had ever seen him display.

"You have set up colonies of Gringg on your young worlds? Yes, both Hayumans and Hrrubans have done the same. Have you found worlds with the different species?" Ken asked quickly, smiling.

"You are the two first we have ever met. The other worlds were empty of *intelligent* lifes," Coypu said, and even the translator echoed the regret in his manner. "Creatures with no thought of more than full stomachs, or things that were inedible, even for Gringg. Each has its place on that world. We do not interfere unless threatened."

"And if threatened, what do you use to protect yourself?" Greene asked, ignoring Sumitral's exclamation of aggravation.

"We are able to defend ourselves," Honey said blandly, and unsheathed his claws. Coypu retracted his lips, uncovering his white fangs. "We are larger than any edible creature we have met."

"And not as dumb," Jilamey said, giving Greene a look of pure disgust.

"How many colony worlds have you now?" Sumitral asked before Greene could continue.

Honey held up four fingers. "Four! One with very good water." His jaw dropped and he gave himself a wiggle that suggested total approval of it.

"Far from here," Coypu added. "A very long journey, but not impossible to make for Hayumans."

"We are translating our maps to yours," Honey said. "Slow because of vision differences and because we are far from the star patterns we know and guide our ships by."

"Let's stick with trade values," Todd said, and leaned across the table to Honey with the chart he had been making on his keypad. "What's of value to you might not be as valuable to us, so we'll need to establish the variables and work out percentages of increased value for temporary rarity of stock and other factors. This one time, I hope you will accept the values we use to pay for traded things between Hayumans and Hrrubans. We think the values are fair."

"It is just what I expect of the peoples who live together in peace," Honey replied. His simple frankness drew mutters from the other delegates.

Todd was relieved that the two Gringg had evidently not caught the blatant animosity in Greene's words and manner. "We can discuss the subject of values in more detail at the end of the meeting so you can key it in your own language."

Suddenly Horstmann, who had been growing more impatient, slapped both hands down on the table to divert attention to himself. "Let's also cut this confounded cackle. Let's find out what commodities you Gringg are interested in. And what you have to offer us. Those resonators Cardiff used in these voders would make a good start. Small, powerful, and I haven't ever seen anything like 'em from Terra nor Hrruba. Can we do a deal on them?"

"Any technological items will first have to be cleared by the Scientific Council of Amalgamated Worlds," Greene said.

Jilamey brushed that contingency aside. "Not according to the Doonarrala Treaty, they don't, Greene. Look, Honey, you've had time over the last weeks to see just what's available on Doonarrala, which I think is a fair sampling of goods drawn from both Hayuman and Hrruban. Technology? Medical or scientific processes? Tools?"

"We have many desirable commodities to trade, as well as the product of our skills," Eonneh began ponderously.

"Good," Kiachif said. "My ships don't like to make the trip back to ol' Terra empty. Give us a f'rinstance or two, friend."

"Also, our four young—colony—worlds have many valuable minerals in quantity. To trade here are listed molecular patterns with Gringg names. Some I do not see in use here or do not recognize. Maybe we bring you new stuff?" Honey dropped his jaw, suddenly a little like Kiachif, anticipating a major trade deal. Todd put his hand to his mouth to hide a smile. "Our friend Chilmeh has spoken to us also about gaining credit from the sale of drawings and works of art. We are pleased to see that you consider these things to be of value. Culture has value on your planets even as it has on ours. We feel that we may also learn technology stuff from you, sharing information. Already we have share technology"—he tapped the voder with the tip of one claw—"with Lootcardiff." Sumitral, Ken, and Todd openly grinned at the combination of rank and name. "We are happy to share information freely in exchange for also you share freely with us."

Greene and Markudian both began to protest, but Ashland was eager to know "information about what?"

"You can't want just cultural things and to share," Jilamey said. "That could be very one-sided and we insist on giving equal value to trading partners."

Honey inclined his head. "You give equal value sharing with us the delights of this planet of Doonarrala."

Todd could see Greene interpreting that to mean acquisition, and hastily intervened.

"Peaceful people deserve proper hospitality when their intent is good," Todd said, and Sumitral stared Greene back down into his seat.

"The matter has been discussed thoroughly among the captain's staff and by space-transmission with the motherworld," the golden Gringg said. "What we search most earnestly—besides peaceful people—is a source of protein, for"— he turned his deep red eyes on Markudian—"we are civilized peoples who do not I eat meat of each other. Especially when here you have many delicious proteins."

Greene's mouth was open in amazement at Eonneh's dry humor.

Eonneh showed all his teeth. "Hayumans seem to have the most superior idea of what is a good thing to eat."

"Well, as it happens, Honey," Jilamey said, beaming from ear to ear, "we process a lot of protein in nutritious and delicious forms, and I happen to represent a large consortium which can provide you with a wide range of truly delicious and healthful comestibles . . ." His voder faltered on that word. "Stuff to eat—eatables, edibles," he hastily explained.

Coypu gave a startlingly deep grunt, signifying pleasure, for he had dropped his jaw. "Good. We wish to import to our world bulk or packaged largenesses of snake meat, fishes, beef, poultry, and of course, the stuff you name popcorn. It is not high in protein, but it is most entertaining to watch it cook and it can be seasoned in many flavors."

"Food?" Sumitral asked weakly. "You want food? Not technology?"

"Morra," Eonneh assured him. "If at all, some forms of Gringg electrics—"

"Electronics," Todd corrected.

"—electronics are more efficient than yours."

"You think that?" Markudian said indignantly.

"Our scientists know that after talking with yours," Honey replied. "Scientific fact is fact for all of us."

"A science conference just is not possible at this point in time," Greene said flatly. "Discuss food all you want. That's safe enough."

"Nonaggressive science is also safe," Sumitral said with equal firmness. He put his hand over his translator. "If they have no ordnance, Greene, then why not discuss science? Now that we know what their need is, I think you can step down from that Red Alert you're on."

"Just so long as *we're* not the food resource they have in mind," Greene said, but he also covered the voder as he added in a savage tone, "These peaceful people of yours are not as peaceful as they've all conned you into believing."

With that, he rose from his chair and stalked from the room.

After Greene's ominous remark, Todd was relieved to see the back of him. He was undoubtedly going off to report to Admiral Barnstable. Greene's crack about the Gringg eating Humans was asinine—especially when the snakes were larger, more numerous, and far tastier.

"You don't require metals?" Markudian asked, surprised.

"Yes, some metals are in short supply with us, and please to give us samples of all you use," Honey said. "But mostly we need foods," and he leaned forward, an earnest expression on his face. "Already, many on the homeworld are most eager to try Doonarralan snake meat. Having heard the praise it has from those who have taste it here, it will be a much sought-after delicacy. Perhaps you can show us how to breed the snakes on one of our worlds. One snake can feed several Gringg. As we learn to know each other better, I am sure there will be other goods we want, but for the present, we are eager to obtain largenesses of Hayuman-manufactured eating stuffs. That is all."

"Unbelievable," Markudian said, staring perplexed at the Gringg.

Jilamey threw back his head and let out a delighted laugh. "After all of our posturing and careful management, timid questions, and demand for sureties, food is what they need!" The Reeves and Kiachif chuckled with him.

As the Hayumans and the Gringg left the room, Hrrto was for a long moment too annoyed to gather his thoughts. The only advantage to the new arrangement would be the privacy to mention purralinium—if the Gringg had it. There wasn't a Hrruban here who didn't realize how vital it was to replenish the supply of that transuranic ore. Even Hrrin would appreciate that. But Hrrto saw that he would have to remain here longer than he had anticipated, to be sure the negotiations secured them at least the hope of the grid metal. Mllaba was also irritated. It wouldn't be her preference to be stuck discussing trade when she considered the spaceport conference a better place for Hrrto to show his merits. But her irritation also stemmed from the presence of the two Gringg across the table from her who were settling their big haunches into their cushions. Beside him, Hrrin sat with folded arms, watching as if he expected the Gringg to spring forward in an assault.

The subsonics in their voices were not entirely masked by the voders, from the keener Hrruban hearing, so the buzz and annoying vibration were still present, heavy in the air. At Hrriss' tactful reminder, the Gringg had been careful to modulate the volume of their speech, but they could do nothing to cushion the impact of their mere presence. Hrrto was rapidly developing a painful headache, one of the first in a long and healthy life. He tried to concentrate on what Hrrestan, who chaired the meeting, was saying.

Hrrestan was assisting the Gringg in their translations when the limits of the programmed vocabulary failed. Hrrto felt some respect for the colony leader's ability to retain what sounded to him like the roar and sputtering of malfunctioning motors. He was feeling yet another painful twinge, when Mllaba leaned toward him, her hand over the translator input grille.

"I dislike the uncouth way they sniff at us, Speaker," Mllaba hissed under her breath. She spoke in a very high-pitched whisper which the Gringg were unlikely to hear. "So primitive."

All the homeworld Hrrubans attending the trade meeting were initially disturbed by the Gringg behavior, but as the aliens proved to be affable and intelligent, they began to relax. Hrrto did not—torn between the need to introduce purralinium and memories of that tape. He wanted to be able to at least warn these Rraladoonans—since they were, in the final analysis, also Hrruban—that the Gringg were dangerous; warn them not to rush into discussions that would display their vulnerability to the Gringg; warn them to learn as much about Gringg customs and culture as the Gringg were learning about theirs. But he could not yet speak of that tape, not until the combined navies were in position. They were still some days away. Until then, Hrrto was forced to dissemble. He also had until then to discover the coordinates of systems that might produce purralinium. With difficulty, he turned his attention to the proceedings.

While Hrrestan was basically a sensible Hrruban, he appeared to be badly infected with young Rrev's enthusiasm. Perhaps, Hrrto thought, it might be wise to tell Hrrestan about that damning tape. Hrrestan was of an old Stripe and did not deserve the fate that might await other Rraladoonans when their seemingly cultured and civilized visitors showed the violent side of their natures. But Hrrestan was so honorable a Stripe that he might feel obliged to impart that information to Rrev. No, no warning to anyone until the fleet was in place.

Then the aliens produced a computer program showing molecular diagrams of the minerals they were ready to use as trade mediums. Hrrto shot a warning glance at Hurrhee, who was already trying to see what was on offer.

"These ores are available in quantity now from our mining worlds," said the one called Kodiak. "We have printed diagrams for you to compare with your molecular data. If you require any of these ores, we are pleased to offer them to you as goods for barter against our own requirements."

"I am sure we can come to agreeable terms for all parties," Hrrestan said.

"Indeed we should," Hurrhee murmured, flicking a confirming glance at

Hrrto. "We have often found a use for this"—he extended a nail to delicately single out one item—"impure as it is."

Hrrto inwardly sighed with relief. They did have purralinium to offer.

"What is Hurrhee doing here?" Mllaba demanded in an annoyed undertone to Hrrto. "He's a scientist, not a trader."

"He is here at my command," Hrrto murmured back, protruding the claw of his fifth digit to indicate the need for discretion.

Suddenly Mllaba became extra alert and leaned as far across the table as possible to get a view of the slate. Under the table, Hrrto pulled her roughly back. She nearly hissed at him, so great was her indignation, but one look at her superior's eyes and she obeyed, though stiff with the insult just given her. Hrrto ignored her manner. Nothing must indicate to the Gringg how important the purralinium was to the Hrrubans.

Although Kodiak and his partner, a black-and-white Gringg whom the children called Big Paws after Zodd's sister's cat, were speaking very clear Middle Hrruban, modulated into audibility by the voders, the edge imparted by the subsonics of Gringg speech wore on Hrruban nerves.

Hrrto wondered how long he would have to remain in such an ambience.

"Yes, you do have goods that might form a trade currency," banker Hrrouf said with extreme affability, his tail tip switching. Ah, Hrrouf had noticed the purralinium, too. And, in his high position in the financial world, he would know about the lack of new supplies of the metal. "What is it you would require in exchange?"

Big Paws regarded the Hrruban amiably and folded his enormous hands on the table.

"You appear to be comfortable without the clothes used by Hayumans to cover their skin. We Gringg also do not need coverings. We admire the way that the Hrrubans adorn their natural fur with the most striking ornamentation. Most especially I like these harnesses of hide." The black and white Gringg put out a claw and plucked at the strap of the handsome harness Hrrouf was wearing. "The variety of these and of other pretty stuffs are most desirable to us. Such will be need to be made much larger to fit Gringg, but we wish to trade for quantities of harness. Plain and with many sparkle stones."

"What?" Hrrouf demanded, unable to believe his ears.

Other Hrruban representatives were equally astounded, and if Hrrestan and Hrrin managed to hide their amusement, few of the others—expecting to trade advanced technologies of all kinds with the Gringg—saw the humor of the announcement.

Second Speaker sputtered, his headache forgotten. "Garments? Jewelry? Ornaments? You must be joking!"

"What is joking?" Kodiak asked, looking up from his electronic keypad. He turned to Hrrestan for clarification.

"He asks if you tell him something that is not true to make him laugh," Hrrestan explained solemnly.

Kodiak returned his dark-red gaze to Second Speaker. "Morra, very, I do not joke."

"This is what you wish to receive in trade from us? Not technology?" asked Nrrena. "Hrruban technology is famous. You must have observed the transport grids—"

"Sst!" Hrrouf hissed at her in a high whistle. The merchant stopped, embarrassed.

"Ah, yes," Kodiak said casually, observing the byplay. "The transport system. But it does not interest us. We travel fast enough and are comfortable doing it. Items of wear and personal adornment are more important. And we insist to be told new styles and modes."

Hrrto wondered at Kodiak's dismissal of the "transport system." Could it be that they *knew* the special use for purralinium and had matter transporters on their own worlds? And if they did, would they trade any of that precious commodity to the Hrrubans? Many of the Gringg had used the grids, getting about Rraladoona, but no reports had been made by any of the operators that the Gringg had shown any interest at all in the workings of the grid, or had even looked closely at either the purralinium columns or the floor grid, though these were, in any case, thickly coated by the conducting material.

"This is outrageous," Nrrena said in a growl, rising from the table. Her tail swished angrily, lashing her sides, and her eyes all but shot sparks. "I was made to understand that this was a high-level trading conference, not a fashion show. I have the honor to wish you a good day." The Hrruban made a bow to Second Speaker and strode stiffly from the room. Second was glad to see her go. She would report back to Fifth that the conference had been a charade. When Hrrto arranged for substantial quantities of purralinium, she would look a fool, Fifth would lose face and Hrrto gain it in the contest for the Speakership.

"Perhaps all should go," Hrrin suggested sourly, "and put an end to this pretense."

"Have I offended?" Kodiak asked Hrrestan.

"No, friend," Hrrestan assured him. "That Hrruban represents manufacturers on our homeworld and elsewhere. There is nothing in these current talks which interests her." Hrrestan also suspected that Nrrena would be grateful to get out of the range of Gringg speech. Kodiak accepted his explanation.

"Ah," the Gringg said, returning a bland gaze to those left at the table. "May we then negotiate terms? It is now to work out equivalencies of value, against that which we offer for that which we want." He ended up facing Hrrestan, who gestured courteously toward Hrrto.

"I may not speak for Hrruba," Hrrestan said. "I have lived on Rraladodna for over thirty years. It is the Second Speaker for External Affairs whom you must address." He bowed deferentially. Hrrto was pleased and mollified.

"Very," Kodiak said, and turned to face Second. Mllaba sat up straight beside him. "So you are empowered to act on behalf of all Hrruba in these matters?"

"I do not understand what he said," Mllaba snapped, turning to Hrrin. "Please translate once more."

With a little less patience for her, Hrrin repeated the Gringg's question.

Kodiak's brow ridges lowered halfway over his eyes, concealing all but a crescent of angry red irises. "I believe that the delegate understood me," he said, his voice shifting very slowly to a menacing growl. "We have come in good faith to this meeting. It is not the Gringg way to give offense or take insult. Lootcardiff caused this device to translate perfectly. As a Gringg scribe, my honor required me to practice diction until perfection came. Does this female have hearing problems? That is the only acceptable reason."

The word "reason" came out in as close to a snarl as a Gringg had so far mouthed. Mllaba jumped in her seat. She glared at Kodiak, her yellow eyes ablaze.

"You wrong me," she said in a low, dangerous voice. "My hearing is extremely acute and the roars you make injure delicate tissue. You know that certain sounds you cause unpleasant reactions in us Hrrubans. Perhaps you deliberately use them to upset us."

"Enough!" Hrrestan said, raising his voice. Hand over his voder, he turned to Mllaba, but his attitude was clearly cautioning. "There is not a thing wrong with my hearing, Mllaba, and I think you are the one deliberately upsetting the smooth progress of this meeting."

"Why should I?" Mllaba demanded.

"That I do not know," Hrrestan replied sternly, "but as I am moderator of this meeting, I will have no further obstruction from you."

"I am assistant to—"

"In this meeting," Hrrestan said calmly but forcefully, "rank has been suspended to the greater benefit of all Hrruba. Or have you had trouble, Honored Assistant to Second Speaker, which you are embarrassed to admit?"

Mllaba drew a deep breath in through her nostrils at what was perilously close to a direct insult to the Second Speaker. Hrrestan waited, his eyes intent on Hrrto, as though Mllaba did not exist.

"I have had no trouble understanding the Gringg," Second said, his eyes slit- ted. "I do find their voices and their presence oppressive."

"Oppressive?" Hrrestan asked, with mischief in his eyes. "How can you find oppressive a species which is so very interested in fashion?"

Mllaba's tail tip lashed.

"If the price is right," Hrrin said, deliberately trying to lighten the tension in the room, "we Rraladoonans are delighted to supply as many harnesses as the Gringg wish. Since"—he turned to the disappointed representatives—"we sup- ply our homeworld with many such items, we may need to import skilled work- ers to supply the demand."

"Then we have wasted our time?" asked the senior Stripe of the merchants.

Hrrestan bowed graciously. "Consider it but the first offering in a trade that may develop in unexpected directions, and have the imagination to come for- ward with other examples of our *culture*"—he gave the last word considerable emphasis—"which might appear attractive or interesting to our large friends."

Then Mllaba, using a coaxing and wheedling tone, spoke up, her manner so abruptly altered that Hrrto decided his clever assistant must finally have grasped the significance of Hurrhee's presence and remarks.

"Hrruban textiles are much admired by Hayumans, since you are interested in adornment. A swift message and we can have many beautiful things to show you," she said at her silkiest.

"We Gringg are content to see all you will offer," Kodiak said, showing all his teeth in an affable smile.

"So," Hrrouf broke in, "you will not object if we ask for metals, ores, and suchlike as payment for our cloth, leather, and jewels?"

Kodiak lifted one shoulder. "Metals we have much of and can cheerfully trade them for what we wish of yours. Shall we talk of relative values now for such bartering?" He turned his slate and held it up so that all could see it. Gringg symbols were on the left-hand side of the slate, Hrruban equivalents on the right. Purralinium was mid-list. "These are in order of value to us."

Titanium was at the top, and Hrrto recognized the symbols for tin, zinc, germanium, platinum, and some transuranics before purralinium. How many leather belts and neckpieces would be traded for enough purralinium to manu- facture another grid? The very concept was bizarre!

He found himself holding his breath as weights and measures were being discussed. To his dismay—for surely Hrrestan knew their plight—the colony co- leader was settling for too low a quantity of metal. Or was he merely being cau- tious? Then Kodiak mentioned bulk figures for finished leathers that nearly made Hrrto drop his jaw. There would be more than enough purralinium. Now he worried that Hrrestan might ask only for that metal and signal its value to Hrrubans. But Hrrto had underestimated the leader's acumen.

Suddenly he began to fret that Hrrestan would get the credit for such dealing, and that he, Second Speaker, who had laid the groundwork in his initial conference with the Gringg captain, would not gain the face he deserved. Restlessly he drilled claw tips on the table until he saw what he was doing and forced his fingers to be still. That precious metal in return for acres of cloth, no matter how beautifully woven, seemed almost indecent. Could the Gringg really be so naive? Or their holdings so rich that they could make such ludicrous exchanges? That was a possibility that hadn't occurred to him before. Those rich in goods thought nothing of exchanging what they didn't need for what they coveted.

"We do not deplete your stores with such large orders?" Big Paws asked courteously. "We can space shipments so that each is full of what is required. With Hrrubans we trade for what the Hayumans do not show or seem to need. Therefore no bad feelings may happen. We are peaceful folk. We wish for peace everywhere around us."

Hearing those oft-repeated words, Hrrto felt the pressing need for some air.

"If you will permit me to withdraw?" Hrrto asked, and received a courteous nod from Hrrestan and a vague wave from Kodiak. He shot Mllaba a glance to signify she was to be careful, and left the room.

In the hallway, where fresh air flowed lightly in from the doors and open windows, his head seemed to clear. *Peaceful folk, peaceful folk, wishing for peace around them.* The repetition made him nauseous. Perhaps calling the fleets was not a wise idea. The prospect of almost unlimited quantities of purralinium was worth a certain risk, was it not? Ah, but with the navies in place, perhaps such information would be easier to obtain. Yes, that was the way to move now. They could show the tape to the Gringg and force them to admit to these atrocities—they had already admitted to being cannibals, hadn't they? Show them that their hypocrisy was discovered, and make them reveal what weapons had caused such destruction. With the fleet pinpointing one unarmed ship, surely they would accede to all demands. Before another Gringg ship could reach the heliopause of Rraladoona, they would have built defenses against such ordnance . . . Why should Hrruba defend Rraladoona at all? The thought suddenly occurred to Hrrto. Why not evacuate all Hrrubans? If the Hayumans were foolish enough to wait for Gringg vengeance, so be it.

But what if the Gringg should discover the Hrruban homeworld? Hadn't that fat captain been a whisper away from admitting that he knew where the Hrruban home system was? Hrrto had never fully subscribed to either the Decision or the Treaty, though he had been forced to give verbal agreement. Under his Stripe, he had known eventually they would live to regret it.

And what were the Hayumans wresting from the Gringg while Hrrubans were selling *harnesses and collars?*

Unable to resist, he found himself walking toward the other negotiating room. He heard voices ahead, and slipped forward, close to the wall.

He peered out from around a column and saw the small Hayuman, Landreau, in animated conversation with the fat and fair-haired trader, Horstmann. Horstmann was patting his protruding midsection with satisfaction which, at this time of day, could have little to do with the pleasures of the table.

The trader's voice rang loudly in the empty hall. "Even calculating in the cost of fuel and modifications to the cargo space, we could clear a pretty bundle. If I can get impactors, freeze-dry whatever, that'd increase space available. If we pack in drones, they'd take ores, refined or half, even raw for some of the unusual stuff, and your principals will be damned pleased with the results, Landreau."

"We can always use a steady new supply," Jilamey said, his eyes narrowed as he calculated. "Spaceships don't build themselves, you know, besides requiring hills of metal. So, if they'll trade us . . ." and, in a low voice, he began to enumerate items which Hrrto had to strain to hear. In shock, he thought he heard Jilamey name purralinium. "That newest colony of theirs hasn't begun to deliver the quantities that assays suggest are available. And they haven't even thought of the concept of in situ space refineries. We got a lot we can teach them."

Half-reeling with the shock of such infamy, Hrrto moved off toward the open door. The Hayumans were obviously being given the more important trade items while the Hrrubans were being palmed off with trifles. He could not return to the Hrruban conference until he had recovered his poise.

He was halfway there when he heard angry voices coming from the chamber where the spaceport talks were being held.

"It would be foolish *not* to consider Gringg facilities, Admiral," Lorena Kaldon was saying in an aggravated tone. "Much easier to start off with buildings suited to their needs . . ."

"I am not discussing the Gringg," Barnstable said angrily, and Hrrto could hear him striding away, his booted steps echoing in the marble hall.

Hrrto heard Kaldon give a totally exasperated sound, the quick noise of steps, and a door that was closed as firmly as a slam. He hurried back to the Hrruban trade conference, pausing to arrange his robes and wondering just how many lengths of such expensive cloth it would take to garb a Gringg. How many *trmbla* of weight made a new grid?

His return coincided with the end of the formal talk, Kodiak and Big Paws rising from their cushions with a grace that Hrrto envied. They were physically large but all too clearly athletic. Polite farewells were made, with Hrrestan and Hrrin doing most of the talking, arranging additional meetings so that tomorrow the Gringg could see, and perhaps order, varieties of ceremonial harnesses.

Hrrto managed to drop his jaw as the occasion demanded, and by wrapping his tail about one ankle under his robes, managed to keep that appendage from giving any hint of his agitation.

As the others started leaving the room, he gave a little sign to Mllaba to wait, and she made a show of gathering up her books, checking on items until they were alone.

"I think that the Gringg have given the Hayumans purralinium," he told her, speaking in the merest whisper.

"Just as if they knew what Hrruba needed the most," Mllaba replied in angry exasperation. "While they deal in harnesses with us," and she stamped a foot while her tail switched violently.

"Is it possible the Gringg have developed matter transmission?" Hrruba asked, having to voice his worst fear.

"Really, sir," and she spoke impatiently, "even our matter technology was a chance application. The circumstances are unlikely to be repeated by Gringg paws."

He gave her an odd look. "And the Hayumans keep trying! Let us hope the scientists of both do not get together on such a project."

"Highly unlikely, not with Spacedep controlling all technology."

"I must have a few words with Hurrhee," Hrrto said as he finished gathering up his own notes. "Catch him before he leaves." Hurrhee would tell him what the Hayumans did with purralinium and whether they used the metal in its pure or impure state. "We must remain the only species in the galaxy with transport grids."

"As you say, Speaker," Mllaba agreed.

Recalled from a more pleasant occupation to be an observer, Commander Frill found himself growing sleepy through the talk of electronics, and the endless displays on the small computer screens of circuit diagrams which to him looked all alike. It wasn't really his subject. He excused himself for a breath of air and wandered out of the computer lab.

The corridor was lined with windows along this side of the building. Opposite the doors of the computer lab was a view of a stand of picturesque forested hills overlooking the landing pad. Frill could see the great hulk of the

Gringg shuttle on the tarmac, an ostrich among chickens. There was someone lurking around it with a furtive air. Frill went out to investigate.

From the door, Frill could see that the man snooping around the shuttle wore the uniform of a Spacedep officer.

"Lieutenant!" the commander bellowed in his best parade-ground voice. The man turned slowly. Frill didn't recognize him. He must have been one of Barnstable's suspiciously increasing entourage.

"Sir?" the lieutenant said, tapping his brow diffidently.

"I don't think you're supposed to be touching that, son," Frill said. "Come on inside."

"Yes, sir!" the marine said. He snapped off a more creditable salute and strolled, not too quickly, into the building. "Good day, sir!" he said, marching purposefully up the long corridor.

"Carry on," the commander said vaguely, and turned away. He glanced back over his shoulder at the retreating lieutenant, but the man was gone. Puzzled, Frill went back to the conference.

chapter eight

By midafternoon, exchange rates had been decided and some groundwork laid for an exchange board. Honey was also deftly inquiring what sort of warehousing would be available until a sufficient amount of goods had been accumulated to make a voyage to the homeworld profitable. Ali was trying very hard to negotiate a contract, but Honey was sidestepping him neatly, suggesting that they would prefer to build their own facilities on Doonarrala if some unoccupied space could be found. By dinnertime, Todd had a deep respect for Honey's skills as a negotiator. The Gringg fought hard for concessions from the Amalgamated World-based traders, and won a few, even from Ali Kiachlf, who Todd thought would never yield.

"Such a facility not being currently available, we meet you halfway and do ship-to-ship transfers at designated points in space," Honey said in conclusion. "It will save transit time. From here it is far to the Gringg worlds."

"The same goes on our side," Kiachif said. "No trip, no tax or tariff. That's fair. But there's still a need for full transits, or else how are we to meet your folk and find out all about you for ourselves?"

Honey grinned, showing his fangs. "Reh," he said, noting the terms on his tablet. "We seek only equity."

"None of this is final until we check with Earth," Markudian warned, not for the first time. "It's subject to approval by the trade authorities and the Amalgamated Worlds Council."

"As you say, as you say," Honey agreed, nodding his great head. He had been incredibly patient with the man's continual complaints and criticisms.

Todd wondered why Barnstable and Greene had picked so obvious an agitator. Even Honey had displayed brief annoyance at Markudian's constant interruptions and trivial complaints. But, Todd supposed, that's why the man was there, to try and disrupt the meeting as much as possible. That Markudian had failed was due as much to the Gringg's unshakable affability as Todd's own determination not to let such ploys develop.

A loud, insistent clicking sound arose from the vicinity of the Gringg's collar.

"Communication device?" Ken whispered to Todd.

"Sounds more like a timer," Todd said. "I'll bet Kodiak and Big Paws just heard one of those, too."

Todd's surmise was correct. Honey carefully finished the last of his hieroglyphs and glanced up to nod at the assembled Hayumans.

"That is all I may do today, friends," he said. "I thank you most very. I will be able to give you final numbers when I have presented these terms to Captain Grzzeearoghh. She is who decides what is best for Gringg."

Todd rose and bowed to the Gringg. "On behalf of the people of Terra and Doonarrala, I thank you for coming, Honey and Coypu."

"Doonarrala," Honey said. "Have I not heard the Hrrubans say Rraladoona? Which name for your world is right?"

"Both, really," Todd admitted. "Each of our species had their own name for the planet Hayumans called it Doona, the Hrrubans, Rrala. Now we each use both names combined, but putting the one from the original language first."

Honey pursed his rubbery black lips. "You defer in all ways regarding a common language to the Hrrubans, it makes sense to settle on one name, everyone use it."

"You know, Honey, you're right," Todd said, nodding. "Possibly we've just hung on to both names to please our respective over-governments. We really should be concentrating on unity. It's an acknowledgment that we're all one world, after all. Calling people Doonarralans or Rraladoonans is just another way of identifying them as Hayumans or Hrrubans, and that shouldn't be a consideration anymore. It was a point that hasn't arisen before. From this moment, I'll only use Rraladoon. It puts my native tongue second, but that should demonstrate how much I value peace and unity."

"Like Gringg," Honey said approvingly.

Ashland looked astonished and Markudian glowered. "Really, Reeve, I think you take too much on yourself."

"No, he's right," Sumitral put in. "The name ought to have been standardized a long time ago. I agree we should be calling this colony by the Hrruban-derived name. I don't think Reeve's co-leader, Hrrestan, will object," he added with a grin.

"Then so will the Gringg," Honey agreed. He and Coypu arose with more grace than their lumbering bodies suggested they were capable of. "We will speak to you again soon." Without further ceremony, they withdrew.

The Hayumans remained in place. Markudian was still out of sorts, drumming his fingers on the tabletop. Looking worn out, Ashland stared out the door after the Gringg. Even Ali Kiachif was subdued. Jilamey glanced up at Ken and Todd with bemusement.

"Did I just negotiate a concession for half an ocean of canned fish?" he asked, "For a small fortune in rare minerals."

Ken pushed back his chair and stretched his long arms toward the ceiling, listening to his ribs crack. "One man's trash is another's treasure. I don't know about you, but I'm desperate for a cup of coffee."

"Seconded," Jilamey said at once. "We've been here hours. Let's see if there's anything left to eat in the dining hall."

"Dammit," Horstmann said fervently, "I hope there's something to *drink*."

"I could swim a sea of mlada and never sink, if you get me, friends," Kiachif agreed.

The urge for refreshment had brought the Hrrubans to the dining hall as well. A few of the delegates from the spaceport conference stood in a corner, eating from plates heaped with cold meat and salad. They gravely acknowledged the Hayumans as they entered. The rest, locked in a deep discussion with Second Speaker, paid no attention to the new arrivals. Someone tapped Hrrto on the shoulder. Surprised, the Speaker turned to face Admiral Sumitral.

There was an awkward pause of a few moments. Sumitral recovered first. "A most fruitful afternoon, wouldn't you say, Speaker?" he asked amiably.

"Most interrrsting," Hrrto said. "Ze Gringg are most skilled at ze arrrt of negotiation, zough zis is not zeir native language." His voice displayed signs of strain.

"I trust you won some concessions from them?" Sumitral asked delicately. "Your own skills are not to be decried."

"You are most kind," Hrrto replied, bowing.

"Somebody find me a drink," Barnstable said plaintively, sinking down at a table. "Jonny?"

Greene stood up, looking about him for a refreshment cabinet. Todd rose to get drinks for the party, listening closely.

"Did you find their terms favorable?" Sumitral asked Hrrto.

"I am surre as much as you yrrrself did," Second replied, equal to Sumitral's courtesy. Now that he had the chance to ask what the Gringg had offered the Hayumans, his nerve failed him. He could not stand the humiliation of admitting what the Gringg had asked of them. He kept his eyes fixed on Sumitral's mild gray eyes, hoping he would speak first.

Todd found the wet-bar cabinet and poured out a good shot of Doonan-distilled whiskey for the Admiral. The sight of open bottles attracted a number of the negotiators, and Todd found himself at the center of an eager and grateful group, dispensing liquid comfort. Hrriss gave him a drop-jaw grin from the edge of the throng, and held up a jug of plain juice. Todd nodded enthusiastically.

"A spot of mlada," Kiachif requested, with a pretended whine like an old man. "Not too small, and don't you dare dilute it, laddie."

In the center of the room, the careful maneuvers went on, the tension growing. Greene hovered at Sumitral's elbow as if to snatch back any incautious statements the head of Alreldep might make.

"Might one ask what commodities were discussed?" Sumitral suggested.

"I do not zink I am at liberty to reveal zat at zis time," Second said blandly. Mllaba stared open-eyed at the Hayumans.

"Perhaps I should not, then, either," Sumitral said, but Todd could tell his curiosity was aroused. Hrrto was being more than usually cagey.

Ken and Hrriss stood next to the drinks cabinet as Todd poured another draft for Ali Kiachif. The captain inhaled that libation and held out his glass for a refill. Jilamey broke away from the group in the center of the room.

"I can't stand it any longer," Jilamey said to Hrriss under his breath, watching the two senior administrators waltz around one another. "What did they ask for? You must have got some humdingers."

"In a way," Hrriss replied, but his big green eyes were brimming with mischief. "But change yrrr expectations down razzer zan up!"

"You, too?" Todd asked. "The Gringg asked us for food!"

"Not what anyone was expecting," Ken said, "but I was charmed by it and trust Landreau here to have food processors and big freezer units in that consortium of his. The Gringg don't want our technologies; they seem content with their own. But they do want rather basic, simple items we have in quantity, and cultural things. Is that why Hrrto can't get the words out of his mouth?"

"Yes," Hrrestan replied, with a fit of low, grunting laughter. "Hrruba has been requested to send this yearrr's fashions in hrrnss and jewelled szraps, and the heavy cloth of which Hrrto's robes are made. Custom-made size giganzic, please, in quantity."

Kiachif grinned, his narrow, bearded jaws opening in amusement. "They were ready to say no to bombs and bullets, but they didn't have a position prepared on beef or baubles!"

"I am sure zey would have classified it as potenzially dangrrrous and not fit frr exprrt if zey had considered it," Hrrestan said, his voice hoarse with merriment.

Jilamey exploded in a fit of the giggles. "And when you look at the two of them out there, neither one able to spit it out—" He waved a hand, unable to continue speaking. He watched them for a moment; then his voice changed. "On second thought, I don't think this *is* so funny."

"Neither do I," Todd said, breaking away. Hrrestan, with a nod of agreement, followed him.

"I'll have to put the matter to the Amalgamated Worlds Administration on Earth before we can discuss this further," Sumitral was saying. "In the meantime, I am glad to see we continue with the spirit of cooperation that has characterized this world of Rraladoon for over thirty years."

"Pardon me," Todd said, edging adroitly between the two diplomats, "I see little evidence of cooperation in your faces but a lot of wariness. Speaker Hrrto, would you like to know what the Gringg asked for in our talks?"

"Reeve, no!" Markudian cried, outraged.

"Markudian, yes!" Todd said, rounding on him. "I see this as a real test of Rraladoonan integrity, not Hayuman/Hrruban competition. Consider this," he went on urgently, looking around the circle. "One of the reasons the Gringg thought we were a single species was the way we worked together. I was delighted by that because it showed we'd learned to trust each other. But the first stir of the pot from outside, and we separate into distrustful—and greedy—strangers." Todd stared at each one in turn, his glance gliding over Greene's smug expression. "So let's reinstate the honesty we have always used in dealings on Rraladoon."

"Prrrhaps if we begin again," Hrrestan suggested, "knowing zat we arrre among friends, who will not judge against you no mazzer what occurred?"

Sumitral was silent for a long time, then bowed deeply to Second Speaker. "Hrrto, old friend, I don't know whether I've been gulled or not. The Gringg asked us to ship them tons of comestibles from Earth and its colonies. They want fish, and beef, and chicken. Oh," he added, with a wry grin at Todd, "and popcorn."

Hrrto cleared his throat and ground his back teeth a moment before he could bring himself to reply. "From us"—and the words seemed reluctant to leave his mouth—"zey wish fine cloth, leather, and jewels for zose collars zey prize so much."

"You worked the more equitable bargain," Jilamey said. "Jewels cost more than popcorn and fish."

"Only on Earth," Ken Reeve said, grinning. "Here we pick 'em up like popcorn."

The tension in the room melted away like fog. Todd relaxed and grinned at Hrrestan.

"You should not have admitted such," Mllaba said, glancing at Hrrto but careful not to let Todd or any of the others catch her eye.

"I agree with the little lady," Barnstable said to Sumitral.

Todd grinned. "The truth is, we all feel a little absurd. Right?"

"Ze Gringg do not wish Hrruban, technology," Hrrto said, his tail giving an emphatic switch.

Sumitral grinned. "They didn't want any of ours either. Not even for purposes of comparison. I admit that I'm a little puzzled."

"Maybe they are satisfied with the technology they have," Grace Castleton suggested from the fringe of the group. Neither of her superiors seemed to agree. Todd thought it was a fair assessment.

"Don't be so naive, Grace," Greene put in acidly. "Any objective observer could see that by asking for such trivia they are determined to allay suspicion."

Todd glared at him. "Greene, you're not what I'd call an objective observer," he said. "On the other hand, you've been extremely suspicious from the get-go. Have you any reason that you're not sharing with us?"

"Grrrene is not ze only one who does not believe zeir asserzhons of peace," Hrrrv said, breaking in. "To me"—he put his fist against his chest—"zey are so very *not* curious about our technology, zat alone makes me suspicious. Or have zey been given prrivate brrriefings?" He stared a challenge at Todd, who felt his hands balling involuntarily into fists. Hrrrv stared coldly, awaiting action.

Hrrestan immediately stepped between them, putting a hand, claws sheathed, on each.

"Captain, I find such an accusation as insulting as Zodd does," Hrrestan said in High Hrruban. "For this one Hayuman, the safety of this planet has always come first, nor would he ever, ever, jeopardize it. You will withdraw the remark. Now!"

Unobtrusively, Hrriss had moved to one side of his friend; Hrrin, the other. For one tense moment, Hrrrv looked as if he would disobey, but then, with minimum courtesy, he indicated his withdrawal by nodding briefly.

"We beg your pardon for the intrusion," a booming voice said from the door. Hrrestan's hand fell away, and Todd spun around. The Gringg had returned. Honey stepped forward, gesturing to two of the other males to enter the dining room. Between them dangled a Spacedep lieutenant, struggling and angry. His uniform was mussed and he had a bruise on his cheek. "We return this Hayuman male to you. He had unaccountably found his way onto our ship."

"He what?" Todd exploded.

"He was concealed behind a storage hatch," Kodiak said. "But we smelled him. I knew immediately which Hayuman he was. I had smelled him before. He walks behind that one." Kodiak pointed at Greene.

Putting up his hands to quiet the room, Hrrestan came toward the Gringg. He touched the arms of the two holding Greene, and they released him. With a tight grip on the Spacedep lieutenant's arm, he bowed to Honey and Kodiak.

"We thank you for rrrsstoring him to us. He surely became lost and disoriented. We will see zat he does not wandrrr again."

Fortunately, the Gringg chose to accept Hrrestan's explanation.

"Then we wish you good day," Honey said with a toothy smile at the assembly. The Gringg left, and the room seemed suddenly larger.

As soon as the door closed, Lieutenant Bouros shook off Hrrestan's grip and stood at attention. Greene eyed him with annoyance.

"Detected by smell," Hrrrv said in disgust. "A fine job of concealment, Terran-male. No Hrruban would have been so stupid."

"What in hell did you think you were doing, concealing yourself on the Gringg shuttle in the first place?" Todd demanded, looming over him.

"I don't answer to you, sir," the officer said, staring straight at the wall ahead of him.

"Reeve, this is a Spacedep matter," Barnstable said, pulling Todd aside and lowering his voice. Greene and Ken closed in on them.

"If he answers to you," Todd turned to confront Barnstable, "did you order him to penetrate the Gringg ship? Spying on them is no way to establish trust between our two peoples."

"The more we know about them, the more secure we feel in forming closer relationships," Barnstable said, his brows drawing down over his eyes.

"Ev, that's Alreldep's job, not yours," Sumitral said, mastering his irritation. "And to allow him to go without neutralization of body odor?" Sumitral rolled his eyes. "Have you learned nothing about the Gringg? Even the kids here know the Gringg have a keen sense of smell. Or don't they issue deodorants in your navy?"

"Reconnaissance seems an obvious course with unknowns like the Gringg,"

Bouros said, still staring straight ahead. "The ship wasn't secured, sir. It was easy to do a recon."

"A recon might have been acceptable," Sumitral said, though his expression was dubious.

"But you had hidden, hadn't you," Todd said, "intending to remain on board. For what purpose? To fumigate them into submission by overpowering them with your body odor?"

"Now that was uncalled for," Barnstable said, indignant, though clearly he wasn't happy that one of his men had been apprehended.

"So was this marine's illegal entry," Todd said, then addressed the lieutenant. "You may be under the Admiral's orders, but by all that's holy, while you're on this planet you are also under mine as planetary leader." Todd went on, his fury unabated. "The next time you overstep yourself, mister, you'll be subject to my authority."

"And mine," Hrrestan said with equal threat.

The marine kept his face carefully expressionless.

"Have we made ourselves clear, Admiral?" Todd added, turning to Barnstable but looking at Greene, too. "We're trying to forge an alliance with these beings, and there are to be no more juvenile war games during the proceedings."

"Has it never occurrrred to you," Hrrestan added, "zat ze Gringg will likely *tell* you morrre zan you could ever discoverr by spying?"

"With all respect, Leader," Greene said, "I doubt that very much."

"I wish zo know morrre about ze Gringg zen zey have told us," Hnrv muttered sulkily. "As yrrr prrrecious Hayumans say, 'Know yrr enemy.' "

"Better, *recognize* who is your enemy," Todd said to the Hrruban captain, and swung a fierce gaze toward the Spacedep officers, which gave him the satisfaction of momentarily startling Hrrrv. He did catch the odd glint in Hrrrv's eyes, but he couldn't interpret it. "If you'd realize there are no enemies here at all, we could progress on all fronts!" He eyed the Spacedep officers with the same fierce gaze, but clearly, he'd taken much of the wind out of their sails. He allowed his temper to cool. He'd said enough, and to the point, for one day. He'd best withdraw.

"Now, if you'll excuse me, I have other matters to attend to." With a bow to the assembly, Todd left the dining hall.

"A little strong, was that not?" Hrriss asked mildly, following Todd toward the grid. His naturally quicker pace kept him abreast of the Hayuman, who was still dissipating his anger.

"Aargh!" Todd said, stopping and twining his hands into his hair. "I wish they'd all pack up and go home, and let us handle the diplomatic relations. We'd achieve fair terms and a treaty, and they'd never have to leave Terra!"

"Or Hrruba," Hrriss said thoughtfully. "I don't know how zings went with ze trade discussions, but ze spaceport talks were constantly interrupted by Barnstable's objections. I zought he was an advocate."

Todd grinned. "Only if Spacedep's allowed its little bureaucracies. And with the Gringg a new factor, he's likely to insist on a heavy Spacedep presence."

Hrriss shook his head. "No, it's somezing else. We know zey do not trrrust the Grringg, but zeir paranoia is worse zan just mistrrust."

"And probably all a part of why Greene had an agent infiltrating the Gringg shuttle." Todd flattened his lips into a grim line. "I shouldn't have been so glad to see Greene leave our trade talks—where, I might add—he and that Markudian lackey of his were doing their damnedest to mess things up."

"He objected to selling zem food?"

"As much as Hrrto objects to selling them ornaments from Hrruba."

The two old friends grinned at each other.

"Greene had a notion that perhaps they wanted *us* for food," Todd said, with a shadow of distaste at being reminded of that incident.

"Ho! So long as you promised zem Rraladoonan snake, you skinny creatures are safe," Hrriss said with a laugh.

"All fooling aside, Hrriss, I think the Spacedep personnel bear closer watching. But come on," he said, with a sudden lightening of mood. "We've got to get the lists of Teams drawn up for the Hunt, or you'll see a hell of a hullabaloo when the snakes swarm!" He grinned at his best friend. "I wonder if the Gringg would like to participate. Not that we've a horse up to such weight."

"Ze way zey move, zey don't need a hrrss," Hrriss replied.

Todd's eyes twinkled. "Speaking of moving, c'mon! Race you to the grid!"

Forgetting for the moment that they were adults, with children and responsibilities, the two abandoned themselves to the familiar contest of their childhood. Todd was laughing by the time he caught up with Hrriss at the pillars.

After Todd had stalked out, most of the other delegates found excuses to leave. Jilamey Landreau collared Admiral Sumitral and led him away, talking excitedly about the tons of fish and snake which the Gringg would need. Hrrestan was deep in discussions with the craftsfolk about the availability of large quantities of well-tanned leathers, and they all left together. Only Castleton, Barnstable, Greene, Second Speaker, Hrrrv, Mllaba, and Bouros remained.

Greene spoke to Bouros. "You're dismissed, man. Report back to Earth." He turned to Barnstable. "We can't use him again now that Reeve and the others have seen him."

"Stupid way to be caught," Castleton said with a half-smile. "Especially after we saw them use their olfactory senses to differentiate between us."

"Bouros is not a clumsy operative," Greene replied, annoyed at her comment. She shrugged.

"Well, Castleton, see what your specialists can do to overcome that problem," Barnstable said, giving her a sour glance. That startled her, but she nodded her head in acceptance of the commission. "Somehow or other, we have got to gain more evidence against the Gringg that will hold up in the World Court. Grace, have we gotten anything new from the exploration ship?"

"Nothing yet, Admiral," Castleton said. "I renewed the request with an urgent tag on it through secured transmission again this morning."

"Confound it, we need that data." Barnstable pulled a chair away from the dining table and sank into it.

"Trivia!" Second Speaker burst out suddenly. Grace stared at him, wondering if he was accusing them. The Hrruban began to pace, showing all the agitation he had concealed while Sumitral and the others were present. His tail lashed back and forth. "The Gringg ask us for trivia. What does it mean?"

"It means," Barnstable said, "that they intend to keep up this charade until the last minute. The pretense is wearing my nerves to a nubbin."

He sat back in his chair and wiped his face with a handkerchief. Castleton knew precisely how he felt. After weeks of maintaining the *Hamilton* in a continual state of Yellow Alert, she was tired. Shore leave to the surface of Doonarrala was limited, and the crew were taking it hard. Frail Frill, one of her most loyal officers, had asked to be released from his duties planetside because it was causing jealousy among the personnel who had been denied permission to downside. Grace had been grateful for the presence of Jon Greene, who had lent her his deep well of strength during the alert. His consideration was only part of his attractiveness. He was the most zealous patriot she had ever met. All his actions and decisions were considered in the light of what was best for Humanity. Grace admired him, but found herself unable to agree completely with him about the treachery of the Gringg. Her own observations belied what the archive tape had shown; her own instinct disagreed with that proof. Still, she watched the computer scopes every day, tracking the approach of the Spacedep squadron. It was still too far away to be picked up on sensors. Nor was anything else closing in, which took care of the notion that the Gringg were waiting for reinforcements. Perhaps they needed none, whether for peace or war.

"What are the Gringg waiting for?" Mllaba asked, her yellow-green eyes wide.

"A display of physical aggression?" Castleton suggested. "They don't act, they react. If we don't press them, they might never attack us."

Barnstable waved away the notion. "How far off is the fleet now?"

"Six to seven more days, sir."

"Right. From now on, tighter security. But I still want a look at what they're hiding on that ship!"

"I have an idea how to accomplish that, sir," Greene said. "If you'll allow me a free hand."

"What? All right, Greene. Carry on."

Castleton paused, wondering how to phrase her feelings. "Sir, after having listened to them today, I hesitate to admit it, but I . . . I like the Gringg. Hearing them talk, it's hard to believe that they caused the destruction of an entire planet. Their behavior differs so greatly from what appeared on that tape. If I hadn't seen it, I'd never be convinced that they are dangerous."

"Besides that tape they are so big!" Hrrto exclaimed. "And so loud!"

Barnstable planted a firm finger on the tabletop. "Cunning, too. All that openness and charm . . . right up to the moment they're ready to take over this planet!"

Such an emphatic pronouncement silenced the others.

"Only a week, maybe less," Hrrrv said in a tone of some desperation, "and we'll have a superior force in Rraladoonan skies. Zen we will ze authority"—he paused and drew his lip back from his teeth—"zat will wring ze zruth from these 'bears'!"

"Reeve and Hrrestan can be removed as planetary leaders," Barnstable said, rubbing his hands together in anticipation, "as unfit to govern . . . since they've extended hospitality to so clearly a menacing species, endangering the citizens of both species."

"Speaker Hrrto and Captain Hrrrv, you would of course support this move for any doubting Hrrubans," Greene put in. "With an intelligent and dedicated administration, we'll soon put things to rights. We might even consider removing the Reeve family from Doonarrala as subversives, detrimental to the well-being of the colony, since they seem to be forever leading it into dangerous situations."

Just giving voice to that possibility gave Greene a certain measure of satisfaction. Grace Castleton regarded him with shock. She had no idea his dislike of the young planetary administrator went that deep.

"And Hrrestan with him," Mllaba said, "since he also espouses zese same courses."

"I do most respectfully suggest that you act only on provocation," Grace Castleton said carefully. "This is an independent and autonomous planet. We still don't have proof that *these* Gringg pose a threat to the planet or either of our worlds."

"I don't like hearing such sentiments from you, Castleton," Barnstable said, eyeing her fiercely.

The captain inclined her head a moment. "I am of course required to comply with any orders you may give me, Admiral," she said in a colorless voice, "but I would not be acting in *your* best interests if I did not play devil's advocate."

"Oh? Well, there's that," Barnstable said, mollified. "The Gringg protestations of their pacific nature are hypocritical," he went on, "and the basis for trade with them ludicrous. Only consolidates my distrust of 'em. I'll have conclusive proof all too soon that they're dangerous! Why, the size of them alone makes them physically superior . . . I mean . . . well, you *know* what I mean! We've got to make these fool Doonarralans see that these bear types are the most dangerous species Mankind has ever encountered. Why, they could dominate the known galaxy. That cannot be allowed!"

"It will not, sir," Greene assured him.

By the time Todd reached home that evening, he was tired and wanted nothing more than a quick dinner and enough time to review the day's tumultuous and astonishing incidents. He could smell the dinner, but as soon as he swung in the door, he felt the atmosphere crackling.

"Oh, Lord, what've I done wrong now?" he murmured. The house only felt like this when Kelly was ready to scalp him.

"Ah!" She leaped from the kitchen and stopped abruptly in the middle of the living room, fists dug into her hips. " 'Would you mind entertaining Captain Grizz and her son, dear?' " She did a good imitation of Todd, further warning of his being in deep trouble with her. " 'Oh, all I have to do is entertain them this afternoon, show them how we live?' " she said, mimicking her own wifely reply. "But"—and now she advanced on him, her head down, her glower intense— "does my beloved husband drop me one little word of the essential difference between the bears I've met and our noble Captain Grizz? No, nary a word does he say!" With a practiced flick of her hand, she caught his outstretched hand with the hard edge of a whipped tea-towel. It stung, and even as he began retreating, she flicked the towel again, catching him even harder on the leg.

"Now, sweetheart . . ."

"Don't 'now, sweetheart,' me!" She snapped the towel again, and this time he ducked because she was aiming at his neck and she'd had too much practice at that art. "Only one phrase . . . just one phrase was necessary. 'Sweetheart, the females are bigger than the males.' "

"But you *knew* that," Todd said, reaching for the door to put it between him and her attack. "You knew that! We told you she was immense . . . that the males are tercels. I know we said it."

"But you didn't say it *then!*"

With unexpected force she jerked the door free of his grasp and he stood there, feeling vulnerable.

"Sweetheart, you're good at remembering details . . ." he began. Then panic swept through him. "Nothing happened, did it? With Grizz and Weddeerogh?" Surely someone would have got word to him about that.

Kelly turned on her heel. "No, nothing happened except Nrrna, Mrrva, and I were paralyzed with shock for five minutes. Even the grid operator was affected . . ." And then Kelly couldn't maintain her angry pose any longer. She burst out laughing, doubling over and clutching her sides.

"I don't think Grrirl, who was on the grid controls then, will ever forgive us," she said, wiping her eyes on her former weapon, "because he really did lose it . . . even if Nrraa and Mrrva pretended he hadn't. Even if you'd said something in your message, we still wouldn't have been prepared for the size of Grizz and Teddy." Her giggles were slowly subsiding. "He's adorable! All I could think of was 'a Bear of Very Little Brain . . .' "

"Huh?"

"You know, Winnie the Pooh." She stared at her husband. "My mother read me those stories when I was a kid and I read them to our children . . . don't you remember? Eeyore . . ."

"And the tail that's all he's got," and Todd now remembered the charming stories. "*What* name did the kids give Weddeerogh?"

"Teddy," Kelly said firmly. "Not my idea. Winnie ought to have been obvious, but those kids of yours latched onto Teddy Bear and there was no arguing them out of it. My word, but he can eat. 'Sing ho for a Bear, sing ho for a Pooh,' " she sang. " 'I'll have a little something in an hour or two.' He can move in here any time his mother's away . . . Swims like a dolphin. So does she . . ." Another burst of laughter, and tears were now streaming down Kelly's face. "Thank goodness you dredged the lake last year or it wouldn't have been up to her knees and she does so love to float, flat out. We'll got to go to the seashore next time she's free or perhaps demonstrate how we shoot the river rapids."

Kelly collapsed onto a couch, then patted it for Todd to sit beside her.

"Sorry, love, but I had to get it out of my system. I mean"—she shook her head in remembered amazement—"I didn't think the grid could take anything that big!"

"*That* particular grid, as you well know, can handle a whole village. So, what was the captain's reaction? She wasn't offended?"

"I believe she thought we weren't sure how to greet her appropriately and instructed us," Kelly said, snuggling up to him. "And Teddy was no problem at all—especially after he saw Hrrunna. After that, when he wasn't in the water, he was rocking her. Thank goodness they eat anything, and almost everything. I'll have to do a major resupply tomorrow. Another thing, Grizz wouldn't come in here . . . she figured our floors weren't up to her weight . . . but she looked in through every window. On tiptoe she could even see into the dormer rooms." Kelly stifled another bubble of laughter. "She seemed to approve—but mainly of the lake. Thank goodness you and Hrriss dredged that lake!" she giggled. "How did your day go?"

"Well, now that you mention it, I am glad we dredged the lake," he replied at his most casual. "Gringg love water sports. There's the ocean, too. I'm not sure they have tidal seas . . ."

"Yes, but what do they want to trade?"

Todd affected a very serious expression. "Not what we expected at all." He wondered how long he could play this one out before he told her the "awful truth."

Once the details of trade items became public knowledge, there was great competition to show the Gringg what Rraladoon craftsfolk and farmers had to offer. Since the old Hall would be more inadequate than ever with even a few Gringg inside, every village offered its green as marketplace. Nearly half the Gringg on board the *Wander Den* wished to participate actively in trading, so no village had a chance to feel deprived or neglected.

The remaining Gringg were interested in other facets of life on the planet. Their wishes were accommodated despite continued vehement protests and ominous warnings from Spacedep. Gringg were "adopted" for a day by people in every line of work. With scrupulous impartiality, Kelly and Nrrna acted as secretaries for such engagements. So it was not surprising that when Shhrrgahnnn asked to have a closer look at some of the four-footed beasts which were in such continuous use by Hayuman and Hrruban, Kelly asked her brother to oblige him.

"Only if the smell of a Gringg doesn't freak my patients out," Mike Solinari, a veterinarian, replied.

"The Gringg smell pleasant," Kelly remarked, a trifle sharply, "and my house pets and our horses have exhibited no reaction to their presence." She didn't add that dogs pretended the mountain of flesh wasn't there and the cats remained well beyond the range of even Teddy, but they hadn't exhibited a "physical" reaction.

"Well, sick stock doesn't respond normally. That voder contraption unnerves *me*," Mike said, "and I understand its purpose."

However, Kelly did agree to wait and help if the Gringg freaked out Mike's patients. So, early on the scheduled morning, Kelly Reeve delivered the guest to the hospital for a trial meeting.

"Now, bro," Kelly said, introducing the Gringg, "your niece and nephew have renamed him Cinnamon."

"I can see why," Mike replied affably. "He's got hair the same color as we do." Mike's poll was fiery red, much brighter than Cinnamon's, though both could be termed red. Where Kelly was dainty and slenderly built, Mike's features were heavier and his frame carried extra bulk. He had a friendly, open face that wore a grin of anticipation as the Gringg climbed awkwardly out of the Reeve family hovercraft.

"Cinnamon, this is my brother Mike," Kelly said, holding onto the Gringg's arm. Then she gestured toward a tall, hollow-chested Hayuman with black hair and a broad, blunt nose, and a narrow-striped Hrruban. "Bert Gross, who's also a veterinarian, uh, animal doctor, and Errrne. He's an intern. Studying to be an animal doctor."

"Fardles, he's a monster!" Bert muttered, nevertheless extending a hand to the Gringg. "Greetings, or whatever." The Gringg touched his claws gently to the middle of the man's palm. Bert drew back, pretending to make sure all his fingers were intact.

"I am most pleased," Cinnamon said after the usual preliminary growlings came through the voder. He showed his long, white teeth, and all three doctors swallowed.

"Bet he brrrush zem a lot," Errrne quipped weakly.

"I've never seen anything with red eyes before that wasn't stark raving mad," Gross added.

"All right!" Kelly said, keeping an affable grin on her own face, just as glad that neither Bert nor Errrne had translators. "Let's see what effect Cinnamon has on the stock. Today I've got to touch a lot of bases!"

"I dunno," Bert Gross said, muttering under his breath. "I've been hearing rumors that these guys are pretty dangerous."

"Oh, horseapples," Mike said. He liked the Gringg on sight. Cinnamon seemed friendly and curious, not threatening as some of those in-flow visitors from Earth had suggested. The Gringg stood looking around him, sniffing the air, nostrils wrinkling ever so slightly.

"I guess the barn does smell kind of pungent," Mike said with a grin, and wondered if the voder translated the tone in which words were said, or meant. "It's a warm day, and we haven't mucked out our patients' stalls yet," he explained to the Gringg. "Come along. You don't have to do any of it, but we can talk to you while we work."

The isolation stables were in a big airy barn that had ventilators along the roof line, to circulate air through the building without chilling the patients below. Sensing the visitors, some of the sick horses and mules started whickering nervously, and one animal kicked the partition in its stall. Mike promptly marched Cinnamon out again, while Kelly exclaimed in some dismay until Mike and Cinnamon re-entered the barn through the downwind door.

"Can't be too careful," he explained to his slightly puzzled guests, keeping his tone low, hoping the voder translation would be equally quiet. It was. "Horses are delicate. There are a couple of high-risk mares in foal. I don't want them to abort. Say, here's a fellow who's only in for a sore leg. Have a look." Leaning over the stall door, he beckoned the Gringg close.

A low hiss of admiration escaped Cinnamon's lips as he gazed at the young bay horse standing on the straw. The animal looked up from the hay it was lipping, wisps hanging from its muzzle as it gave the unusual shape a long stare before it started to chew again, but it didn't panic. It twitched its dark satin coat here and there as if flies troubled it, and raised its white-bandaged leg, curling the hoof under the protection of its body.

"See? No reaction at all," Kelly said, "I'm off!" And she departed before anyone could delay her.

"The creature is very beautiful," Cinnamon said, speaking more softly through the translator than Mike would have thought possible. "What is such an animal used for?"

"We ride them," Mike explained, gritting his teeth as the voder squawked back. The gelding switched its ears and rolled its eyes apprehensively, but didn't do more, since it also heard Mike's familiar voice, "We use them as non-polluting—well, non*toxic*-polluting—transportation around here. They run on hay instead of batteries, and besides, they can be good friends to you. Some of this type"—he pulled Cinnamon across the aisle to a sick cow—"are reared as food animals and their hides are used for other things."

Cinnamon gave the cow only a cursory glance and went back to admire the horse. "They are like gentleness and night and wood," Cinnamon said, struggling for Hrruban words to express his admiration. "Hrrrsses must surely be the most lovely creatures on Rraladoon." He spoke the new word with a trill that enhanced the Hrruban pronunciation.

"Well, we kind of like them, too," Mike said, a little overwhelmed to be on the receiving end of poetry so early in the morning. "Stay and see how we care for them. I've got to spend some time in the surgery this morning. Bert, you have the comm." He passed his voder over so that any queries Cinnamon had could be understood. Then, with a nod at the others to begin their work, he left for his office.

Cinnamon watched intently as Errrne and Bert hauled out soiled straw and spread fresh, doled out medication, checked bandages, and generally cared for the ailing hoofed animals. When the round device on the wall had its two indicators pointing directly skyward, work ceased, and Mike returned to collect the Gringg.

"Do you have any questions about what you've been seeing today?" Mike asked.

Considering, Cinnamon rolled his fleshy lower lip. "I want to know what is the purpose of this place. I have watched you. Why have a vet-er-i-nar-y hospital when you eat animals? Why not just eat the ones who can no longer serve you?"

Errrne and Gross thought this was the funniest thing they'd ever heard. Mike shut them up with an eloquent glance.

"You don't farm animals, do you?" Mike asked rhetorically.

"Morra," Cinnamon replied. "Only plants such as grain, vegetables, and fruits. All of our meat is caught wild. There is plenty of game around us, and we are good at preserving that which is uneaten."

"Well, there are more reasons to have animals than for food," Mike said. "Not all animals make good eating."

"Can you show me some?"

"No, I can't. Every beast we raise has a double purpose. These, for instance," Mike said, drawing Cinnamon to the sheepfold, "we raise for the fleece on their backs which makes our clothes." Capturing one of the merinos, he showed Cinnamon the depth and fineness of the wool and then demonstrated the difference with a hardier mountain sheep. The Gringg gingerly felt each fleece, nodding as he appreciated the different textures.

"The captain will want to know about these," he said.

The Gringg was careful to input all new vocabulary into the memory of the voder at his throat. By the end of the morning, he could discuss what he had learned with intelligence and a measurable degree of clarity.

"These bruins are smart," Bert commented, impressed.

"Tape-learning," Errrne said, shrugging his plush-covered shoulders. "He is amassing a bluffrrr's guide, zat is all."

Errrne looked puzzled when Cinnamon shoved away the chair beside their table in the lunch room. Then he realized that the Gringg was quite capable of reaching the table even parked on the floor beside it. Not knowing how much a Gringg ate, Mike had made arrangements with the cafeteria cook for double quantities of everything. As he watched the Gringg eat, though daintily enough for all his size, Mike was a little sorry that he hadn't made that triple. Cinnamon exclaimed with pleasure over everything he tried, and ended up consuming as much as all three Rraladoonans put together. When his plate was empty, he was clearly though politely looking around for more.

"You eat more than my brother Sean," Mike said, with respect, leaning over to speak through the voder around Bert's neck. "I didn't think anything short of a Great Big Momma Snake could pack it in tighter."

"Everything had a most delicious flavor," Cinnamon said, rolling back on his tail and running the tip of a claw between his teeth for stray morsels. "I admire also the variety of textures and aromas."

Mike grinned. "The grub is good here. What's Gringg food like?"

"We eat protein, carbohydrates, starch coming from different sources. I will show you some of our eatables at another time. Now I must be curious about all aspects of our new friends, who are so very different from Gringg."

"You can say that again," Bert said, surveying the alien with a narrowed eye, forgetting that he was wearing the voder.

"Why must I repeat it?" Cinnamon asked, drawing his brows together over his snout.

"Uh," Bert said, and looked to his friends for help. Mike guffawed.

"It's a colloquialism," Mike explained, taking hold of the voder by the cord around Bert's neck and bringing it to his mouth. "He means he agrees with what you said."

"Would it not be simpler to say 'I agree'?" Cinnamon asked, and the men laughed again.

It was impossible for anyone passing through the lunch room to miss the shaggy hulk of the Gringg. A few eyed Cinnamon warily and hurried on. Mike recognized those as interns from Earth. Most of the usual Rraladoon staff, however, stopped to be introduced. Cinnamon's head kept turning back and forth, trying to follow multiple conversations, Mike decided he was happy to be in the midst of everything. One by one, the medics and visitors recalled appointments, and disappeared, leaving the four of them alone at their table.

"Okay," Bert asked. "So, Cinnamon, what do you want to do this afternoon?"

"I wish to learn more about the pretty hrrrsses," he said eagerly.

"You and everybody else," Mike said, pushing away from the table with a

mock sigh of exasperation. "Come on. We've got Mrs. Lawrence's hunter gelding in for an abscess on his rump. He's pretty calm. I don't think he'll spook at
the sight of our pal here."

In the treatment barn, Mike greeted Nita Taylor, one of their veterinary assistants, who was washing out a bucket under the pump at one end of the horse
barn. "Got a visitor here to see Amber."

Nita glanced over her shoulder, then stood up to take a full-faced stare at the
Gringg. She was a willowy girl of middle height with light-golden skin and dark
brown eyes and hair. The things most people noticed about her were her perfect
cupid's-bow lips, and the fact that she was as shy as an urfa. She nodded, tilting
her head toward the stall.

"No problem," she said, collecting her wits. "Like you ordered, I changed the
dressing before feeding this morning so it might need replacement."

The chestnut horse stood half asleep in the sun. Mike hopped over the fence
and approached with soothing sounds, running one hand down its back and to
the rump. Its eyelids fluttered as it shifted a leg, denoting it was aware of Mike.

"Hey, watch he don't cowkick you, Mike," Bert said, nervously, "if he catches
sight of Cinnamon!"

"He's all right," Mike assured him, turning to catch the tie-rope and halter
in one hand.

The horse came fully awake and nosed at Mike's chest. He pushed away the
gelding's muzzle.

"You're almost better, fella," he said affectionately. "Another couple of days
and you can go home."

Cinnamon walked halfway around the fence to get a better look at the animal's face. Mike noticed the visitor was being very careful to stay downwind.

"We call horses the wealth of Doona," Mike explained, patting the gelding's
cheek. "No one in the galaxy raises better stock than we do: jumpers, hunters, or
just riding hacks."

"How is it ridden?" Cinnamon asked.

"I will show you," Errrne volunteered, taking a headcollar and lead rope
from those on the peg of the turn-out field. As the Gringg watched, the Hrruban
quietly approached an animal grazing just beyond the sick gelding. Deftly he
slipped on the halter, then tied the rope onto the far side to make an impromptu
rein. Then, with the ease of long practice, Errrne leaped to the horse's back and
coaxed it into a walk.

"You hold on with your knees," Mike explained. "You don't need a saddle
unless you're riding a long distance. Then it's vital for your comfort and the
mount's. They've got sharp spines."

"Ah," the Gringg said, his eyes glued to the graceful form of horse and rider. Errrne coaxed the beast to a fast trot, then into a canter, which increased to a gallop.

"That Hrruban rides like he was part of the critter," Bert said admiringly. "He breaks horses freelance."

"He does what to hrrrsses?" Cinnamon asked anxiously, tapping the voder. Bert laughed as he tried to explain.

" 'Break' is not the literal translation," Mike said, his eyes dancing.

"Hello?" someone called.

"Back here!" Mike shouted back.

Footsteps ticked and scratched on the concrete floor of the barn. Nita blushed suddenly. Mike noticed her reaction with a grin. If she knew those boots just by sound, the wearer had to be Robin Reeve. The younger Reeve was a smaller, slighter copy of Todd. He had the same intense blue eyes, dynamite with the engaging grin that got him out of trouble as often as it got him into it.

"Afternoon," he drawled, then noticed the visitor. "Well, hi!" he greeted the Gringg. "I'm Robin. Which one are you?"

"I am this one," Cinnamon replied. "I am called Cinnamon."

"Welcome, well-met, and well-named," Robin said cheerfully. "As our old friend, Kiachif, would say. Are you enjoying Rraladoona so far?"

"Reh! Very especially the hrrrsses," Cinnamon said enthusiastically.

"Glad to hear it," Robin replied. "We're all horse-crazy here."

"Robin is my brother-in-law," Mike said. "His brother is married to my sister."

"A most complicated explanation of a simple relationship," Cinnamon observed.

"Sometimes it's very complicated," Robin agreed. "Say, Mike, I've got a sow in the flitter out front. She's due to farrow any time now, but she's running a temperature. I'm afraid she'll lose the litter."

"How in hell did you get a sick, pregnant pig into a hover?" Mike demanded.

"It's only because she knows she's my favorite that she trusted me enough. I have this way with women. Oh, hi, Nita," he said, mischievously peering at her sidelong from under his sweeping black lashes. Nita bent the bow of her delicious-looking lips into a shy smile, then retreated to the isolation stall.

"I'd better take a look at your pig, then," Mike said, grinning. "I hope she hasn't decided to give birth right in your car."

Robin looked alarmed. "I hope not! It's my sister Nessie's car."

Cinnamon barely noticed the two Hayumans depart, so entranced was he with the ruddy-coated gelding. He was mentally composing a poem to the species, and to this specimen in particular, when the Hayuman Bert Gross pulled at his forelimb fur.

"If you want to see some more horses, we've got a whole bunch of them in a corral over to the other side of the building," Gross said, studiously casual.

"Reh!" Cinnamon exclaimed, picturing a sea of the beautiful animals. "I would be most grateful."

The Hrruban pulled Gross to one side. "What are you up to?" Errrne said in a low voice.

"I'm gonna show our guest," Gross said with careful emphasis, "a whole *lot* of horses."

Errrne, understanding the joke at last, dropped his jaw in a big grin. "Let us go!"

The paddock contained some thirty animals, huddled together near the feed troughs. One tiger-spotted appaloosa stood near the gate, scratching the side of his nose on the post. It glanced at the Hayuman and Hrruban without interest, but started violently and snorted at the sight of the Gringg. As Cinnamon came closer, the horse retreated until it was well within the crowd on the other side. It wheezed a warning sound. All the others in the pen looked up and stared with wary brown eyes at the stranger.

"These are all two-year-old geldings," Gross said.

"They are not hrrrsses?" Cinnamon asked, puzzled. "When is a hrrrss not a hrrrss?"

"Is that a joke?" Bert asked, elbowing his Hrruban companion. "Uh, when a horse—ah, forget it. Yeah, they're horses. Nice, aren't they?"

"Reh," Cinnamon breathed. He felt a deep affection rising in him for the big liquid eyes, slender limbs, and smooth pelts of these animals. Oh, what very attractive creatures they were. "I understand why Rraladoon prizes them so."

"Why don't you just go in and get acquainted with them?" Bert asked, opening the gate and standing back to courteously gesture him through. "They're all well handled."

"Oh, I would like that," Cinnamon said, and stepped into the paddock. Bert shut the gate behind him.

"What if he hurrrrts zem?" Errrne whispered.

"Don't worry," Gross muttered back. "They won't let him get anywhere near 'em."

The veterinarian's prediction almost came true. Wearing a beatific expression, Cinnamon walked toward the herd. Instantly, it split into two groups and cantered past him toward the opposite side of the corral.

The Gringg was disappointed that the animals were so shy around him. His new friend had assured him that they were friendly. Perhaps he was just too unfamiliar. If he allowed them to smell him, they would become used to him and come close enough to touch.

Extending one paw forward very slowly, Cinnamon walked toward the horses again. For the first ten paces, they stayed where they were, watching him approach. He had not observed before that their huge brown eyes were edged with white under the lids. He took another step, and one of the bigger animals tossed its head. That seemed to set off the others, who cantered away in a bunch, skittering and neighing, leaving the Gringg facing nothing at all. Patiently, he turned about and tried his approach again.

Try as he might, Cinnamon could not get close enough so that any of the lovely animals could sniff at his paw. Intent on his task, he could hear the gasps and bursts of sound made by the Doonarralans behind him, but he did not see them slapping one another on the back. He tried another approach: when the herd was downwind of him, he stood still, allowing the slight breeze to carry his scent to them.

The musk of his fur made a few of the horses rear and toss their heads, but they didn't bolt or show other signs of alarm. In a few moments, they calmed down completely except for a twitch here and there. Slowly, very slowly, Cinnamon moved closer with his paw out. As before, as soon as he was within a Gringg-length or two, the herd melted to either side of him and fled. Patiently, Cinnamon tried again.

"We could let this go on all day!" Gross said, red-faced with laughter. Errrne grunted breathlessly beside him.

Over and over, the same actions were repeated: the bearlike Gringg walked toward the herd, which split up and ran away from him. The Rraladoonans were enjoying themselves immensely. It was funnier each time it happened, and the Gringg's disappointment increased their pleasure. Then one of the horses in the paddock began to rear and whinny. Its eyes showed wide arcs of white, and its nostrils were flared.

"What's with that one? It's spooking badly now," Gross said, pointing. "I don't want it jumping the fence."

At first there seemed to be no reason for the horse's growing anxiety. As the herd split one more time, the two men outside the pen saw why.

"A mare's in zat bunch!" Errrne cried.

"Oh, fardles, and her colt is there, too," Bert said, hurrying to jump the fence. The mare cut out of the herd and made straight for the Gringg, swinging her head back and forth, showing her teeth.

"Cinnamon, get out of there!" he yelled. "Back off!"

The Gringg stood waiting for it, his eyes wide with joy.

*   *   *

Even trained as he was for accurate recall, Cinnamon was not ever able to describe exactly how the collision came about. One of the hrrrsses came out of the herd, directly toward him. Welcoming, he put out a paw for it to sniff, but greeting him was not what it intended. He saw a flash of eye, then teeth, then hard, round hooves flailing at his face. It cut his muzzle, making him bleed. The hooves struck him on the shoulder, the chest. Cinnamon's paw came up to protect his face, and hit the mare's head instead. Her neck broke with an audible snap. As Cinnamon watched, stunned, she sank to her knees and, rolling to one side, lay still. A half-grown horse trotted out of the herd, and stopping uncertainly halfway there, it emitted a tentative whinny, which grew sharper when there was no reply. Cinnamon realized with horror that this was her young. He had killed a mother horse and left an orphan.

He threw back his head and wailed his grief. Then the horses began to stampede!

The instant the wild howling started, Mike and Robin exchanged a look and raced toward that side of the building. They'd never heard such a sound before—a cross between a siren and a foghorn, a very insistent and unhappy foghorn—but they knew it meant trouble.

In the stableyard, there was a penful of hysterical horses hammering themselves against the far fence, and Mike's two junior associates staring with horror at the Gringg.

"What happened?" Mike demanded, looking from one to the other. "Why's he yelling like that?"

"That beast killed a horse," Bert Gross said, pointing wildly at Cinnamon, who was sitting on his haunches in the corral beside the body of the dead mare. "They're dangerous! He broke her neck with one swipe!" He hoped that Mike would take his story at face value. Neither he nor Errrne wanted to confess their part in the tragedy.

"Better get Todd," Robin said grimly.

The Hayuman and Hrruban traders, chafing from their enforced idleness while awaiting the outcome of the postponed conference, had spent a lot of time in the pub of the Space Center. The Center wasn't a large building, though additions had been made as trade to Doonarrala increased. In fact, there was more pub than spaceport facility. Ali Kiachif made it a point to stop in at least once a day and swap lies with whoever was hanging about. Any of his captains who needed to drop a private word in his ear could find him there, and many potential problems were quietly defused in that milieu.

Fred Horstmann and a couple of the others involved in the conference were having an afternoon drink with Kiachif. The subject, as it had been for weeks, was the Gringg.

"I can't guess whether they're funning us or not," Morwood said. He was a middle-ranker, a Codep shipper who had been out a fair number of years. He wanted most of all to get a cargo and leave the planet. He'd been here far too long.

"Fun? For fish, flesh, or fowl?" Kiachif asked, ripping the seal off a fresh bottle of mlada and pouring himself a glassful. "I'd say they're telling the truth."

"But it sounds like a joke," Horstmann offered, taking a pull on his beer. "Hard to believe they'd settle on such simple stuff, if you understand me."

The other traders grinned. "You've been around Kiachif too long," Captain Darwin said, looking open and innocent when the Codep chief turned a surprised glare on him.

"Not so simple, but it's a foot in the door, to be sure, a foot in the door," Ali said. "Nothing will do but fresh and new, which will keep our ships in the spacelanes. I like that well enough, if you follow my reasoning, and you do."

The debate went on, with about two thirds of the spacers firmly in the Gringg's corner, and the others uncomfortable and unsure of the new aliens' motivations. It was shaping up to a fine brawl, when Kiachif spotted Jon Greene walking through the security gate toward the landing bays.

Thank the Stars I outrank him, Kiachif thought. *I dislike him more than I hate stale bread and water. And I hear he's sweeties with Grace Castleton, though you'd think a lass of her rank would have better taste.* Greene was sure set on roiling up ill-feeling, and Kiachif knew, from his sources, that the commander'd come an alm's ace to making an intergalactic incident *happen.* Which would have been bad for new trade possibilities and *that* was not on in Kiachif's lexicon.

It's time he had a piece of my mind handed him, Kiachif decided. He gulped what was left in his glass and excused himself.

"I'll be back," he called to the publican. "Another bottle of the same, to be waiting." The man snapped the towel he was plying on the inside of a glass pitcher, and nodded.

The mlada was burning a pleasant warmth in Kiachif's stomach as he made his way through the chilly concrete corridors. He told himself he preferred a quiet life, but a good mill always helped the blood run warmer. If Greene didn't tell Kiachif why he was trying so hard to queer things, it wouldn't be for want of persuasion—of one form or another. He might even persuade the commander to show good manners.

Around the corner, the corridor was empty. His prey had a good stride on him; Greene must be pretty far ahead. Kiachif passed the control room. He waved a hand in at the door, and kept walking. One of the female technicians, a young woman with chocolate-dark skin, nodded to him. She was having a quiet talk with someone who wasn't visible from the doorway. A lover's chat, perhaps? Kiachif slowed down as he recognized the man's voice: the importunate Commander Greene.

He doubled back and put his ear next to the doorpost.

Whatever was going on in there, it wasn't love talk. He heard Greene say something about sensors, followed by a low and indistinguishable question. Chancing a quick look inside, Kiachif saw the woman shake her head.

"No, sir. It's all been by the book, I swear," she said. She sounded panicky, and her skin had a moist look of stress Kiachif did not like to see.

"And the records of the scans have all been filed under coded seals?" Greene's voice was smooth and low, but there was an unmistakable threat in it.

"Yes, sir." The woman's throat constricted on the second word, sending it up an octave. Kiachif's eyes went wide.

"Blank that screen!" Greene commanded. Hastily, she reached for the control, and the sensor pattern she'd been monitoring vanished. Kiachif hadn't had time for a good look at it, but he fancied he could reconstruct it, given time. There'd been three ships on the screen—three ships with the yellow data-prints of heavy weaponry. Fleet ships? But where bound, and why?

"It's a crime to reveal secure data to anyone without the correct classification," the commander said, continuing his harangue.

"I know that, sir," the technician said. "I'd never do that, sir."

"Good," Greene said, standing up and moving into Kiachif's line of sight. He leaned over her in an ominous fashion. That he scared her was obvious from her distraught expression. "See that you don't. You are to keep me or Admiral Barnstable posted on any change, but no one else, do you understand? An infraction of the regulations could put you into a one-by-two cell in a military prison on Earth for ten years."

The woman's eyes widened until Kiachif thought they'd pop right out of her head.

"Well, if that gall don't grease a goose's gizzard," Kiachif muttered. Abandoning his listening post, he strode boldly into the office.

"Afternoon, pretty lady," Kiachif began cheerily, as if he hadn't a care in the world. "I've got a ship coming in from Tau Ceti way. Wondered if you could give me a vector and an ETA. If it's no trouble, that is. Oh, hello, Greene. Leaving, are you?"

The Spacedep commander fixed Kiachif with a hostile stare. He was clearly unhappy to have been interrupted before he had totally cowed the poor girl.

"I was just going," he said. "Remember what I said," he told the technician. "Security!"

"Yes, Commander," the technician replied unhappily. She watched Greene leave, then turned to Kiachif, beads of sweat visible on her forehead. "How may I help you, Captain?" she asked, readying her hands on the keyboard at her station. Her voice petered out, and she swallowed.

"Is that rattlesnake giving you trouble, my dear?" Kiachif asked kindly, sitting down on the edge of the chair Greene had just vacated.

"Oh no, sir," she said quickly.

"Now, now, you know, I don't believe you at all, if you follow me," Kiachif said, his voice soothing. "That one has no manners. I'm sure that asking nicely would have gotten him the selfsame smiling service from a nice lass like you." He glanced up at the digital clock. "Ah, you're nearly off shift, aren't you?"

With a grateful look of near-fainting relief, she glanced the same way. "Fifteen minutes," she said with a sigh and a sagging of her shoulders.

"Well now, you wouldn't think of joining an ol' space captain for a tot or so of mlada, would you? A sort of thank-you for checking up on my ship? You look like you could do with a jolt, if you know what I mean."

She shot him a tentative smile. "I don't know as I should . . ."

"Why not? Your shift will be over, duty done, and a little relaxation's in order. You've been under quite a strain, with all the shipping in and out, and many's the glass I've had that's taken the weariness out of me in such a situation. So I recommend it highly to you, if you know what I mean."

After Greene's manner, the kindly old captain whom she'd known for years soothed her rattled nerves. A drink or two in pleasant company *was* just what she needed right now. She swiped back her hair with a shaking hand. "Oh, Captain," she said in a low voice suffused with desperation. "I'd like that very, very much."

chapter nine

Since everyone on board the *Wander Den* was so busy that there wasn't even company for swimming, Weddeerogh asked his mother if he could visit the young people at the Double Bar Gemini Ranch. Grzzeearoghh thought that an excellent idea and immediately inquired of the Hayuman Zodd if this could be arranged. Todd asked Kelly, adroitly in the presence of Alison and Alec, but fortunately his wife was amenable to the notion even without the pressure of their pleas.

"I told you Teddy could come any time," she said. "Pop over and tell Nrrna, will you, kids? Is Grizz coming, too?" she added, immediately cataloguing what she had on hand in the freezer.

"No, just Teddy," Todd said. "With all the adults out and about trading or kibitzing, the little feller's likely to be lonely."

"Little feller?" Kelly mocked with a sly smile, and raised her hand to ear level.

"Comparatively," Todd said, grinning. "Buddy'll drop Teddy off right here. Save you a trip into town."

"Fine by me, as I thought the air cushions on the flitter would burst the day we collected the little feller and his sweet mommy from the grid." Kelly favored her husband with a sardonic look for the surprise she'd had when *all* of Grizz and her not-so-small cub had emerged from the mist.

"I'll clear up as much as I can in my office today," Todd said, "so I can join in the fun."

"Ha! Where were you when I needed you!" Kelly exclaimed, rolling her eyes but smiling. "Teddy's no problem, but *what* should I fix for him to eat this time?"

"Ask the gang," Todd suggested as he left.

News of Teddy's imminent visit sifted through other items of interest so that when Buddy skillfully landed the big Gringg shuttle, there were unofficial observers, too, as the five eager youngsters bounded to greet Weddeerogh. He had put on his best fish-scale collar and, at his dam's urging, brushed his fur until it gleamed. He had also shortened the cord of his voder so that it no longer prodded his ear or the back of his head.

Not that the voder could handle the shrieks and shouts of delight from the two Hayumans and three Hrrubans. He didn't even try to say the phrases of gratitude his dam had had him prepare.

"C'mon," said the Alec one, grabbing his hand and starting to pull him away from the house. "The (garble) just hatched and you've never seen baby (garble) before, Teddy."

Alison, Hrruna, and Hrrunival, either pushing or pulling him, started him on the way to the barn while the smallest Hrruban followed, wide-eyed.

"I must give your parent . . ." Teddy began, the translator stuttering at first until the Hrruban came out.

"Mom said you'd want to see the (garble)!" Alec said, tugging harder.

Teddy could see Kelly on the porch, waving for him to go with the children, so he felt completely excused from the courtesies his dam had insisted he perform in acceptance of family hospitality.

He found the newly hatched "chickens" (and he dutifully added that noun and "bantie" as "mother of chicks" to the vocabulary), delightful creatures, although he couldn't hear them peeping, as the others could, no matter how he fiddled with the voder.

Then he was taken on a tour of the hrrrses in the barn, and he pleased everyone by remembering the names he had been given on his previous visit. He wondered how long it would be before he could mention swimming in the lake again, but no, there were other newborn creatures for him to meet . . . katzz and kitthhhens. He did know the word "katz". . . small furry being. Well, he must uphold the honor of his father, who was one of the most renowned linguists on their homeworld, so Teddy girded himself to remember the personal names of these new species. It wasn't easy to pick up new words: the Hayuman children talked so fast and the Hrruban brothers and sister interrupted them constantly, making it difficult for the voder to keep up.

"Here they are, Teddy," Hrruna said, beating the others to the place where the katz had kitthhhens.

Four tiny four-legged animals swarmed over Teddy, their mouths opening and closing, though the voder didn't pick up the sounds. Hrruna lifted one up to him and instructed him on how to handle the soft, squirmy things. It sniffed at him, as was proper, so he sniffed, very carefully, at it.

"(Garble) behind the ears," Hrruna said, and demonstrated. He asked her to repeat the first word and then added it to the rapidly increasing line of new vocabulary.

He gently extruded one claw only, because his digits were much larger than Hrruna's, and applied the appropriate pleasure. He could feel a rumbling through the palm of his paw.

"She's prrrring," Hrruna told him proudly, and he took this to mean the small creature accepted him.

"What is this kitthhhen? How big does it grow?" Teddy asked just as a larger, black and white creature of the same species came bounding over the hay-strewn place to investigate him. It sniffed at his feet, and courteously he squatted, bringing his head down to its level to get its scent.

"That's how big it grows," Hrrunival said. "Cats are from Earzz and are not intelligent."

"They are so," Alec replied with some heat "Kasha's very intelligent."

"For a cat," Hrruna agreed, shooting a quelling glance at her brother.

"At least as intelligent as you, Hrrunival," Alec went on tauntingly.

As he evidently expected, Hrrunival charged at Alec, who lithely twisted out of the way and streaked for the wide-open barn door, Hrrunival in close pursuit. Clucking (rather like the chicken had), Alison removed the kitten from Teddy's paw.

"We'd better make sure the fight's fair," she said, and with Hrruna and Ourrh, who hadn't yet addressed the Gringg cub, she followed the boys. The little Gringg had no choice but to follow as fast as he could waddle. At the door, Alison looked back.

"Wait, Hrruna! We're leaving Teddy behind!"

"Ooops! He can't run verry fast, can he?" Hrruna observed, slowing down.

"He's doing the best he can," Alison replied.

Alec suddenly remembered his manners and grabbed hold of Hrrunival, evading the punch that came his way. "C'mon, let's do something that's fun for all of us. Hey, Teddy, what do you want to do?" he called out.

"I would like to swim," the cub said. "Swimming here last time was much pleasure."

"Should we try the creek this time?" Alec asked his twin.

"No, he wouldn't get very wet in the creek," she replied, scanning the girth of their guest.

The ducks on the farm pond scattered with noisy protests when the children, stripped naked, waded into the water and started to splash one another. Teddy unfastened his collar and laid it and his voder on those of his hosts.

"Confirmed," Lieutenant Gallup whispered, crawling on his knees and elbows into the ditch where Lieutenant Walters crouched. His long, sallow face was filmed with sweat under the camouflage makeup, and his brush-cut black hair was dusty. "The Gringg cub *is* there, with the Reeve and Hrruban kids. They're swimming in the pond, mother-naked."

"And the pond is right out in the open," Walters said, squinting through the tall grass into the sunny yard. His light blue eyes were two pale spots in an irregular stripe of black greasepaint. Raising his scope, he scanned the grounds of the Reeve and Hrriss farms. "D'ja see anyplace we can grab him alone?"

Gallup shook his head. "Not so close to the houses. The kids'll set up a ruckus. We'll have to wait until they're farther away. Too bad the pond's visible, 'cause they've all stripped off comms and voders. Damn!"

"Let's ooze down there anyhow. That fancy collar of the cub might be interesting to examine. Can't know what sort of technology's hidden in it. All the bruins wear something of the sort all the time they're downside."

Under a sky bluer than any he had ever seen, Teddy dived and swam and played with his new friends in water that smelled of fragrant grasses and weeds. It tasted unusual but very nice.

The Hayumans and Hrrubans taught him games by demonstrating between themselves how they were played. One required each swimmer to keep away from one chosen to be "tagger." Alison lost that draw, and the game required lots of splashing and swimming and shrieking for those eluding the tagger. Another game made use of a colored ball which the players were required to catch with their hands. Teddy had to be careful of his claws, which inadvertently unsheathed to make the catch, indenting the surface of the ball. It made him realize how fragile Rraladoonan toys were, as were the persons of Rraladoona. It was also very difficult to throw the squishy ball any great distance, depriving him of the advantages that strength and speed gave him in the other contests, to the evident joy of the younger Hrruban. Hrrunival was so determinedly competitive that Teddy started losing on purpose to keep the young felinoid from feeling bad. The object of the game was to get the ball over cross poles at each end of the relatively oval pond. After a certain number of these objectives had been attained, Hrrunival gestured for Teddy and the others to join him at his end of the pond, pantomiming that they should now swim as fast as possible to the other end. Bored, Ourrh went back to the house. Teddy wished that the voder was waterproof. He was losing valuable words which he was certain no other Gringg would collect.

The children quickly discovered that though Teddy couldn't move as quickly as they could on land, none of them could touch him for speed in the water. His big paws scooped waves out of his way, and his powerful tail gave him extra thrust. No matter what kind of a head start he allowed the others, he was always at the other side of the pond before any of them were halfway across.

"No fairrrr!" Hrrunival cried, spitting out a mouthful of duckweed at the end of another unsuccessful race. "He's got a ruddrrrr behind!"

"You've got a tail, too," Alec told him. "Use it!"

"Mine does not wrrrk zat way. Also, all my furrr is so wet, it holds me back. Your bare skin is an advantage."

"Teddy's got fur, too," Alison said, shaking her black mop out of her eyes. "Lots more than you do, that holds liters more water."

"I'm tired of losing," Hrrunival said, pouting and splashing with his arms. "What if we have a test whrrr Teddy swims, and we run on ze bank? We'll see who's fastrrr all over."

This motion was carried as a good idea and the alteration explained to Teddy. He never objected to staying in water. The Rraladoonans climbed out of the pond and shook the water from their skins and fur. Taking his voder from the pile, Alec named himself as official starter.

"Okay, once around the pond to this point here," he said, drawing a line in the soft earth down to the waterline with his toe. "If anyone falls down or gets hurt, the race stops right there."

"Agreed," Teddy said. This Hayuman was most careful of the safety of others.

"Okay," Hrrunival said. The girls nodded.

Teddy braced his toes in the thick mud. The others bent down with one foot behind, their hands touching the ground on either side of their forward feet.

"On your mark, get set, GO!" Alec shoved off, running. His long legs gave him an immediate lead over the two Hrrubans and his sister. Teddy thrust off powerfully from the bank and plowed across the pond.

Alec was a swift runner. Hampered by having to avoid reeds and water plants, Teddy needed to concentrate closely on his stroke to keep up with him.

He could hear the Hrruban boy yards behind them, grunting with frustration as he drove his short legs to their fastest pace.

A small fish, disturbed from its hiding place among the reeds, leaped into the air like a rocket, directly underneath Teddy's face. Thinking of the predatory fish on his motherworld, he jumped up to avoid it. It fled him. Sputtering, he rolled over in the water to clear his nose and mouth. Alec gained a few paces and Hrrunival was closing faster now. Teddy kicked to right himself onto his round belly, and paddled furiously to regain the lead. He was nicely buoyant, but the water plants all around him were dragging at his fur, slowing him down.

Only a few lengths to go. He spat weeds out of his face and sucked in a deep breath of air to sustain himself for one final burst. In three strokes, he crossed the shallow line etched in the bank. Alec was still right beside him. Alison and Hrrunival were nearly together, coming in second. Hrruna was dead last. Teddy heaved himself out of the water and stood dripping to congratulate Alec.

"It's a tie!" Alec said, slapping him on the back and splashing all of them. "You're fast."

Teddy reached for his voder and put it on. Alec repeated his last words.

"You are . . . fast, too," Teddy said. "I worked hard, but we both won." He turned to Hrruna. "I am sorry." He meant to console her for losing, but Hrruban words failed him.

The girl seemed to understand his intentions perfectly well. She shook her head with cheerful resignation. "It is all rrright. I nevrrr win," she said, "so it does not bozzer me."

Hrrunival was not such a good loser, but he tried to cover his disappointment. "Well, that . . . was a good . . . contest!" he panted, still short of breath. "Wanna . . . zry rrriding hrrses?"

"Yes! But I do not know how," Teddy said, looking around for his collar. Surely he had put it right with the voder. No, there it was on the bush. He shrugged, not too concerned that it was other than where he thought he had left it. The children finished dressing and strapped on their voders and belt-radios.

"I'll teach you," the young Hrruban said, condescendingly patting Teddy on the arm.

"Hrrrrrrunival," Hrruna said, fuming with embarrassment at her brother's tone. "You haven't ze patience to teach anyone to *hop*."

Not looking back, he twitched his tail at her and led Teddy away, water still dripping off their fur. (Alec and Alison followed, grinning.)

"Close, but no luck," Gallup muttered under his breath as they watched the children leave the pond. "Didn't have long enough to check anything on that collar.

Good thing I got it to hang on the branch." He and Walters had been within meters of the pond when the children climbed out.

"Commander Greene wants that little bear stat," Walters said. "Figures questioning the kid's our best chance to find out what the Gringg are really doing here. He might even be our ticket aboard their ship, if his folks want him back safely."

"The Hrruban kid said they're going riding."

"Couldn't be better," Walters said, grinning. His teeth glinted. "We'll let 'em get clear of the yard, jam the kids' comms and be ready to snatch the bear. He's sure to fall off a time or two and we ought to be able to isolate him from the others. The flitter's waiting for us just this side of the woods."

Teddy had already been introduced to Tornado and Fairy, the twins' mounts. Looking over the other mares and geldings, Alec and Alison tried to choose one for their guest while the Hrrubans went back to the stables for their own ponies.

They came back, leading their mounts, before Alec and Alison had decided which horse suited Teddy best.

"We need something so bomb-proof you could drop a Big Momma Snake on its back and it wouldn't spook," Alec decided.

"That's Teabag, then," Alison said.

"What saddle, though?" Alec asked, critically examining their guest's body.

"We'll look for something," Alison said. "Hrruna, will you saddle my gray for me, please?"

"Ssure," the obliging Hrruban said and expertly threw a pad and then a saddle over Alison's gray pony mare. Hrrunival went so far as to help bridle her. Teddy stood to one side watching, feeling considerable respect for his new friends.

Teddy was unused to the idea of having pets larger than he was. Yet the hrrrsses, who stamped an occasional heavy and dangerous-looking foot down on the concrete floor of the building, seemed content to serve. There were no longer large animals on Teddy's homeworld, though his dam had told him there had once been many different kinds. How lucky were Rraladoonans to have such a variety. Then Alec came out of the barn with his bay animal.

"Now, Teddy, watch me! This's how you mount," Alec cried, and sprang into the saddle, wiggling from side to side to show how secure his saddle was. "There! See how easy that is?"

"Alec, you nit," his sister admonished him. "Teddy couldn't vault that. He'll need to mount from something."

"Yeah, I guess he would," Alec said, dismounting and looking around for a suitable surface. "Sorry, Teddy, we were just about born in the saddle."

The mental picture this evoked for Teddy made him gasp. He could not picture his dam awkwardly poised over the back of an animal. Surely it could not be true! Alec caught his expression of open-mouthed horror and started to laugh. Teddy realized his statement had been a joke, and added sheepish staccato grunting to the merriment.

Alison looked him over with a measuring eye.

"And Teddy's a different shape from us, not much leg. There's no way he could rise at the trot," she said, turning to her twin. "But old Teabag's a pacer, isn't he?"

"Say, wouldn't a pack saddle give Teddy a lot of support?" Alec suggested. "I mean, remember when we used them for jousting-saddles when we played knights and ladies?"

"Ze very zing," Hrruna said. "We can pad it wiz extra blankets and a sheepskin."

"Worth a try," the redheaded boy said. He jumped off his horse, ran up to the end of the barn, and came back laden with a strange contraption and an assortment of blankets and numnahs.

Together, the twins prepared his mount, the golden-brown hrrrss named Teabag. The children explained that Teabag was a "single-foot," which confused Teddy, who could see that the animal had four legs, just like all the other hrrrsses. He was a bigger animal than the children's ponies. And his back, where Teddy was to sit, was higher off the ground.

"Daddy always gives Teabag to people who've never been on a horse before," Alison explained with gay reassurance. "He knows more about riding than we do," and she giggled.

Her preparations complete, she signalled Teddy to approach. Teabag turned his head to eye this unusual form, and he breathed noisily between his lips. Each time the small Gringg attempted to get close to the horse, the animal edged his backside away. Then Alec pulled sharply on the reins.

"Get up there," he ordered, and the horse sidled close to the bales of hay that had been piled in the form of a mounting block for Teddy's benefit. "Jump up on these, Teddy, and we'll get you in the pad. We've even got a neck strap for you to hang onto. No one's ever fallen off Teabag."

"Safe as houses," Hrrunival said, snickering a little as Teddy dutifully climbed up on the bales.

"Throw your right leg over," Alec said, pushing against Teabag's right side so the old horse couldn't dodge his would-be rider.

Teddy managed that, though he could feel himself stretching the skin between his legs. Maybe Gringg were not meant to ride horses, even if Hrrubans could. Still, it was not uncomfortable and there was support for his lower back and a slot for his tail to fit through, too.

"Yeah, the pack saddle even has a tail hole," Alec told the others. He grinned up at Teddy. "Now, these are called reins. Reins. They guide the horse. Pull left and he'll go left, pull right and he'll go right Pull both reins back hard and he'll stop."

"Ol' Teabag'll stop more zan he starts," Hrrunival said with another snigger.

Teddy nodded, trying to assimilate the knowledge while the horse moved from side to side under him. Inadvertently he clutched both reins, leaned back, and convulsively tightened his legs against the sides of the animal.

"Whoa there, Teabag," Alec said, grabbing at the bridle by the bit. "Hey, you did just right then, Teddy, leaning back and tightening your legs. You'll be a rider in next to no time. Just sit deep in the, ahemm . . . pack saddle. Grab on to the crosspiece, here—" Alec showed him the leather-covered bar. "All you have to do on ol' Teabag is sit and let your body move with the horse!"

"I will try," Teddy promised.

"Oh, Alec, I'm not sure if he'll be able to stay on," Alison said, frowning at the shortness of the Gringg's leg despite stirrups shortened to the very last hole in the leather.

"He'll do fine," Alec said, nodding his head with assurance. To justify such confidence in his abilities, Teddy determined that he would.

"Here we go!" said Alec as he once again vaulted to Tornado's back. As soon as he saw the others were mounted, he dug his heels into the horse's flanks and Tornado moved forward. Teddy, right behind him, followed his example. To Teddy's absolute delight, Teabag immediately obeyed, forcing his rider forward. Startled, Teddy grabbed at the crosspiece and that gave him a feeling of more security. Then they were all out of the barn and walking briskly away from the yard. To his surprise, Teddy enjoyed the movement. It was exciting. The hrrss smelled good, too, always a propitious sign. He felt that it might not be a bad thing after all to be born in the saddle.

"Where do we go?" he asked.

Alec swivelled around to face him. "How about just down to the river and back?" he suggested. "We'll go near the marsh. Maybe see some drrr-frogs?"

"Toward the marsh," Gallup said, scrambling out of the hollow on hands and knees. "Ready to deploy the jammer."

Walters was right behind him. Keeping their distance, they trailed the string of horses. The five young riders kept their horses to a slow steady pace, moving farther and farther from the security of the ranch houses. When they were far enough ahead, the two Spacedep men dropped away to one side, pacing silently through the standing crops until they paralleled the little group.

"Be ready to grab him," Walters said.

The path was a worn ribbon of earth drawn through flower-strewn meadows, skirting golden crop-fields and going over green hills. Where the path was level with the surrounding terrain, the horses walked abreast. Alec and Alison sat so naturally in the leather cradles that they appeared to be part of the animals. Hrranival would occasionally hurry his hrrrss forward ahead of the others, then turn back to rejoin the formation. Nobody minded the pudgy Hrruban's plunges and darts, least of all Teabag. It was a peaceful day. Avians winging in the sky sang sweet chirrups, and the breeze smelled delicious and intriguingly different. Teddy felt happier than he could ever remember. He wanted to stay on Rraladoon forever and ride hrrrsses every day until he rode as easily as Hrrunival did. The children chatted and laughed, asking Teddy about life on his world and matching his experiences with some of theirs.

"I am sad," said Teddy. "I am sad to know that in the future I will be too big to ride these beautiful creatures. This is more fun than anything I have ever done!"

The four other children regarded him with sympathy.

"Would plow horses be big enough?" Alison asked her brother, eyeing the young bruin.

"Uh . . ." Alec said, measuring Teddy with an eye. "Not for a really fully grown-up Gringg. Not Captain Grizz's size, for sure. But Teddy is a male and will never be that big."

"What was it like to come all this way in a starship?" Alison asked then.

Teddy's Hrruban vocabulary did not include many superlatives, so it was difficult to find the words to explain.

"I was not yet born when the voyage started," he said, no longer aware of the hesitation in the voder turning his Gringg into their Hrruban, "but I have been travelling all my life. Always stars around us, some very bright and big. Some dim. We came to one place where there was nothing but big rocks in orbit. My sire said that the sun had burst open in one great whoosh. We have orbited several planets, but I was told they were not right for Gringg. Then I had to learn what was right for Gringg, which is right for Hayuman and Hrrubans, too. Much more fun to see than to learn." And he made a broad gesture, dropping his jaw to show them how happy he was. "Were you born here on this planet?"

"Yup, all of us," Alec said. "Mom was, too, but Dad was born on Earth. And hated it."

"Earzz?" asked Teddy.

"Yeah, Hayumans originate on Earth and—"

"Hrrubans come from Hrruba," finished Hrrunival.

"But you are Rraladoons?"

"We all are," Alison said from where she rode slightly behind Teddy. "Let's see if Teddy can manage to trot a bit, okay?"

When they pushed their horses to faster movement, Teddy made a tentative grab for the crosspiece, but Teabag seemed to flow forward and soon Teddy released his hold, leaning back so his tail would keep him steady.

"Hey, Teddy, you're doing just great," Alison called, but somehow Teddy did not trust his balance enough to turn around and thank her.

Soon they pulled the horses back to a walk, for they had reached a forested area and could no longer ride spread out. Teddy's fur was beginning to dry in long rats and tangles. He combed at a few of the worst knots with his claws, fearing the thorough brushing at the hands of his sire if he arrived back at the ship so untidy. Eonneh was never unkind, but he was merciless with tangles in his cub's thick fur, and smoothing them out sometimes hurt Teddy. Eonneh threatened, not seriously, to plait all of Teddy's fur and leave it that way if he could not keep it neat. Working carefully with one hand, he undid a mass of stringy fur and extracted a strand of lakeweed. It smelled interesting, so he tasted it. Not bad.

Hrrunival was behind him now. He was careless and inclined to show off. Without a strong hand to control it, his hrrrss had its snout almost up Teabag's tail, probably continuing some private argument on-going between the two animals. Teabag kicked backwards with one hoof to discourage the untoward familiarity. Hrrunival's mount reared and whinnied a protest, moving in again. Teabag stopped short, making Teddy rock violently forward in the saddle, and turned to snort, as if to demand the other hrrrss leave him alone. Instead, he caught a sniff of hot, wet bear, and his eyes rolled white. The hnrss's neck arched, its nostrils flared, and Teabag swung his head forward.

"What is he doing?" Teddy shouted, alarmed, clutching for the saddlehorn.

Alec turned to look, and his eyes went wide. "Hold him! Hrrunival, grab his lead. Teddy, pull back on the reins!"

"It does no good!" Teddy bellowed.

The sound of the Gringg roar was the last straw. The spooked gelding shot off along the trail with Teddy bouncing on his back. The little Gringg struggled to hold on, gripping as hard as he could with his knees to keep from tumbling off. He pulled at the reins, but the horse refused to respond to the pressure. It was running away as fast as it could from the funny smell.

"Come on!" Alec shouted, spurring Tornado after the wailing Teddy. "We have to stop them before they hit the marsh. There could be early snakes rising."

The other three wheeled to follow. They were responsible for Teddy. How could they ever go home again if their guest got hurt? The ground in the swamps was notoriously unsafe. The horse could slip on the unsteady path, both mount and Gringg ending up in deep, viscous mud. And what would they say to Grizz if Teddy got eaten by a snake?

"The horse bolted with him," Gallup radioed to Walters, now a dozen meters behind him. "We've got him alone. Deploying jammer."

"Following," Walters said. "Stay out of sight. Radio silence, now!"

Keeping their eyes open for the other children, the two men pelted down the hill, following the runaway horse and rider into a stand of young trees at the edge of the meadow.

Teabag charged off the path down into a deep gully, twisted down the sloped sides, then bounded across a narrow but fast-flowing stream. One of his hooves slipped on a stone in the middle of the brook, throwing Teddy forward. Anchored by only his frantic grasp of the crosspiece, the reins had somehow got wrapped about his arms, effectively tying him in the saddle with just enough slack to let him bounce with every jolt of the runaway horse.

"Help!" he cried and shifted one paw, his claws instinctively extending so that he dug into Teabag's neck. The horse, already frightened, now reached the stage of terror where all he wanted to do was rid himself of what was on his back. Teabag charged up a bank and headed directly into a thicket, hoping to brush the predator off. Teddy had to cover his face with both hands to protect it against the thin branches that whipped past. The reins wound tightly around his palm jerked again and again as Teabag tossed his head wildly from side to side. He brushed against tree trunks and shot through bushes, snorting and neighing furiously. The Gringg, afraid of being thrown off, shifted his grasp to the crosspiece again, digging his claws into the wood beneath the leather and shut his eyes tight.

"Hurry!" Alec shouted. Tornado crested the bluff overlooking the summer-creek and came to a halt. The other horses cantered up beside him.

"Where's he gone?" Alison demanded.

Hrruna scanned the woods on the other side of the stream and pointed to where the bracken was disturbed. "Zere!" she cried.

"We can't get zrough zere," Hrrunival said, gawking. "It is solid forrrrst. Ze hrrses won't obey if we zry to frrce zem in."

"You're right," Alec agreed. "Teabag must have been scared so much he just went through like a rocket. We'll have to go around on the path and hope we catch up with them."

He guided Tornado down the gully and up the other side so that they skirted the woods. They found the path, which was marked by yellow streamers tied around two small trees flanking its entrance to show it had been widened and cleared of dangerous plants. As hers was the steadiest horse of the four, Alison urged Fairy in first, leaving Alec to bring up the rear.

Once under the roof of leaves, the group scanned the area to their right, looking for clues of Teddy's passage. There was nothing moving in the woods except for an urfa that looked up, chewing, with tender leaves sticking out on either side of its narrow jaws. It fled when Hrrunival sat up high in his saddle and yelled.

"Teddy! Teddy! Can you heeaaaarrrr meeeee?"

There was a slight echo as the trees caught his cry, but no answer.

Alison led them as fast as she dared. The path was narrow, and wound to avoid big trees and fallen trunks. Several small brooks cut through the floor on this side of the Bore River. The riders forded the streams, only centimeters deep.

The four took turns calling out. "Teddy!" "Are you all right?" "Answer us!" "Teddy!" "Teddy!"

"If we don't find him soon, we'll have to call for help," Alec said, peering ahead as he felt along his belt for his handset.

"Oh, no," Hrrunival protested, as his friend pushed the signal button. "Do not. I will get in zrouble. It is all my fault. My hrrss made his nrrvous, and it rrran away. Please let us find him first."

"We'd better," Alison said, looking at Alec, stricken. She punched furiously at her handset. "My communicator's not working."

"Neither is mine," said Alec with an eloquent groan. "Mom will feed us to the snakes!" He shouted out again, "Teddy! TEDDDDIEEEE!"

"Can't . . . keep . . . up," Walters called to Gallup. The horse with the young Gringg was well ahead of them, vanishing in the thick cover of shrubs and trees. "You go on. Going . . . for . . . car!" Walters slowed to a stop, and bent over to catch his breath.

"Aye!" Without looking back, the other Spacedep man shouldered his light pack and kept running.

The forest thinned eventually, fading away to whippy saplings and high grasses flattened where the deer and urfa slept at night. Alison led them around to the right, toward, as Alec put it, "Teabag's probable trajectory." Beyond the woods, the ground was soft and soggy. The riders skirted the edge of the bright green patches of bog, hoping that by staying close to trees, which their fathers had told them liked "to keep their toes dry," they would be able to stay out of the clutch of quickmud.

About a hundred meters from where the path left the woods, Hrrunival's sharp eyes spotted the first signs of Teddy's passage. A long streamer of dark fur hung on the point of a broken twig about two meters into the forest on their right. To the left, the mud was churned up. Green-tinged water already filled hoofprints that pointed arrow-straight into the heart of the marsh.

"There could be snakes! We've gotta find him," Alec moaned, voicing what all of them were already thinking. It was early, but even a Big Momma Snake might be wriggling out there. "If anyone's afraid, you'd better go home now. Get Mom, or Aunt Nrrna, or go call Uncle Robin or Uncle Dan."

"I'm not afraid," Hrrunival said at once, though his green eyes were saucer-sized and his tail lashed.

"Nor I," Hrruna cried. Alison just shook her head.

"Okay," Alec said, taking a deep breath. "Here we go."

The land changed around Teddy. First, branches stopped hitting him in the face and feet. Then, stinking, sticky mud got thrown up at him by the hrrrss's hooves. Suddenly, the mud changed to wet sand, then very dry sand. Teabag's feet foundered and slid. Teddy cried out as the hrrrss fell down and rolled on top of him. He wasn't hurt, because the sand was so soft, but he was scared by all that weight on him. Suddenly it lifted, yanking the reins one more time, and they ripped free of Teddy's hands.

Teabag scrambled to his feet and shook himself vigorously, splattering sand everywhere. Realizing that at last he was free of his rider who was floundering in the sand beyond him, the horse made straight for the safety of his home barn.

"Stop!" Teddy called to him. "Don't go! I am lost!"

The Gringg roar only served to speed the gelding on his way.

Teddy pulled himself up out of the sand and brushed at his coat. Now it was not only matted, but dust and grit were ground in all the way to the skin. He scratched at his belly, which emitted a deep, rumbling sound.

"They did not feed me yet," Teddy said wonderingly, "and I am hungry." Such a thing had never happened to him before. But what was there to eat in this hilly desert overlooking the smelly marsh, or in the big river he could see down the hill to his left? If his new friends were here, he could have asked them. This was their world. They would know what to eat here.

Wait, there was a smell! It was faint because the air was so dry, but he was sure he had caught it.

The breeze that carried the scent was coming from behind him. He turned and clambered on all four paws up the dune. At the top, he saw a dark-furred being with its head busy over its front paws. It was eating! Teddy was so excited that he scrambled toward it.

The crest of the dune gave, and tumbled him bawling with surprise into the bottom of a sandy cup. In the midst of a sandy nest of eggs, a mda looked up, startled. When Teddy appeared at the top of the next dune, it met his eyes.

"Are you Gringgish?" Teddy asked hopefully. It was unlikely that more true Gringg had come here, but he might be one of the sort of Gringg that lived here. It was not impossible, Teddy thought, remembering katz and Hrrubans. "I am Weddeerogh, of the *Wander Den,* cub of Grrzzeeraoghh and Eonneh. Can you help me? I am hungry and lost. What are you eating? It smells good. Can I have some?"

The mda, accustomed to living by itself and avoiding creatures that talked, was taken aback to hear unfamiliar sound emitted by another mda. It eyed Teddy with suspicion. The animal was fully his size, Teddy noted, and obviously meant to attack to defend its find. But surely courtesy would require this Gringgish creature to offer him some?

"Please. I am only a little Gringg. Will you not share?" Teddy waited politely. The strange Gringg did not reply, other than to start a low growling which reverberated in gibberish through the voder. Confused, but unwilling to leave a source of food, Teddy rolled back on his tail and settled in to wait.

That calculated act suddenly unnerved the mda. Attack it could understand, and knew how to defend itself. But the smell of this creature was different, subtly menacing. Suddenly the mda decided that it had had enough egg. Growling with annoyance, it picked its way gingerly across the hot sand and disappeared among the marsh plants.

That was a decision of sorts, Teddy realized, galumphing down and up the hill of sand toward the good smell. If the strange Gringg had none of his words, this was his way to tell him it was all right to share, and that he wouldn't measure how much food Teddy ate.

The stranger had already eaten many eggs, to judge by the number of shells strewn around, but the nest contained many more, half-uncovered in the sand. Teddy picked one up carefully and it sagged around his handpaw. He sniffed and the smell was good, not tainted by unpleasantness. His father had told him that most of the food the planet offered was good for Gringg to eat. Reassured by both smell and paternal remarks, he tore it open with his claws. He plunged his muzzle into the heart of the egg and drank the delicious yolk. Extending his long tongue, Teddy licked his lips and square muzzle with pleasure. There were enough eggs here to make several good meals for a small Gringg. He would not be greedy. He'd eat only enough to take the edge off his hunger. He picked up another egg, pierced one end of the shell, and sucked the contents out. That way he would keep his face fur clean.

He had emptied quite a few eggs in this fashion when he heard hoofbeats. Teddy stood up and, peering over the dunes, saw Alec approaching on Tornado. He pulled so hard on the reins that Tornado stood up on two hind legs, which delighted Teddy.

"He's here!" Alec cried, and the others quickly joined him. "But you're in the dunes, Teddy! We've got to get you out of here! It's dangerous."

"You've found him?" Alison cried in relief. "And Teabag, too? Is he all right? What's he doing?"

Alec squinted at the little round figure, who was waving something white at him. "Teabag's not here, but Teddy's eating snake eggs."

They climbed up to meet him, panting in the dry air. Teddy was ecstatic that his friends had found him.

"Have some!" he said. "These eggs are good to eat, and I am so hungry. The strange Gringg let me have some. Are you hungry?"

"Well, yes," Alison admitted, but looked queasily at the raw egg. "But we usually eat these cooked."

"Ooh, cooked!" Teddy opened wide red eyes. "That would be good, also!"

"I like zis little guy," Hrrunival said. "He's got class!"

"Wait," Alec said, squatting down beside Teddy. He, too, refused the egg, so Teddy felt obliged to eat what he had opened. Then Alec looked at him queerly. "What other Gringg?"

Teddy swallowed a mouthful of yolk and pointed the way the stranger had gone. "He never spoke to me, but that is not unheard of," he said.

Hrrunival scrambled to look at the tracks that led away from the snake nest. "It was a mda!" he gasped. "And it left you alone?" His voice cracked on the last word.

"Reh. It did not speak to me, but we have not been introduced."

Alison was laughing. "Mda can't talk. They're not intelligent."

"Like the katz?" Teddy asked,

"Not like cats at all," Alison said, her face screwed up in earnest. "Mda're dangerous carnivores, Teddy."

"What is carnivore?"

"It eats meat!"

"So do I eat meat!" the young Gringg protested.

Hrruna, ever cautious, was checking the perimeter for snake signs. "I see no tiddlers, but zere are ozzer nests already made. We should go away as quickly as possible."

"It's zoo earrrly for anyzing but tiddlers," Hrrunival said, holding his head up to sniff the breeze.

"Snake Hunt is only dayz away," his sister reminded him.

"But not yet."

Since no one moved away, Teddy went back to eating eggs. They were so delicious, he could not understand why his friends did not want to share them. Nor why they kept looking around them nervously at the dunes.

Gallup spotted the white-eyed horse with the torn pack saddle plunging toward him on the swamp trail. The young Gringg had been thrown off, then. He had only to find the cub now. The horse saw him and shied away, continuing its panicked gallop down the track. Gallup palmed sweat out of his face and kept moving. He surveyed the path for footprints, but there were none except those the horse had just left. It must be heading for home. All he had to do now was follow its tracks back to the cub. The stink of the marsh was dying away as the terrain sloped up and into less fertile soil. Ahead of him were the snake dunes. Wonderful Spacedep maps warned him against going into the desert unarmed. The big Rraladoon snakes were capable of eating an entire horse, let alone a winded lieutenant.

As he topped the next rise, he looked down onto the dunes. And there, on the top of one of the sandy hillocks was the little bruin. Alone, too! A perfect opportunity! Gallup reached for his side arm. If the kid agreed to come quietly, Gallup wouldn't have to use force, but after a chase like that one, his patience was gone. The kid was looking down, busy with something messy. Gallup crept around the edge of the dune, staying just out of sight.

Behind him, he heard rhythmic pounding on the sand. He jumped into cover just in time to avoid being seen by the four youngsters riding out of the woods. The little Gringg glanced up and waved. Gallup snorted in annoyance at the lost opportunity. By mere seconds. He hoped Walters would get to him quickly with the flitter. He checked his tracer stud to see that it was still working. This was their last chance to grab the Gringg. He and Walters would have to carry him off in full view of the other children. If they protested, he'd have to take care of them, too.

Kelly was busily preparing a big lunch for the kids, who would surely be hungry after swimming. It was only as she walked into the living room that she realized there were no sounds coming from the direction of the pond. She had also just realized that there was a horse tied up to the door-post and a hovercar on the drive, when the doorbell rang.

"Who—?"

"Kelly, my dear!" She opened the door to see Jilamey Landreau, finger poised over the bell for a second stab.

If she'd thought that Jilamey had toned down his wardrobe in the years since she had first met him, she was profoundly mistaken. He was dressed in bright, bull-angering red that stood out from the surrounding landscape like an out-of-season poppy. Still, when Kelly considered it, the color was perfectly becoming to him. She didn't know why she thought men shouldn't wear bright colors.

"Hello, dear Jilamey," she said, leaning over to collect a kiss. "Barrington, this is an occasion." The gentleman's gentleman was waiting down beside the hover. He was clad in sober brown, a color that blended into the scenery as thoroughly as his master's garb did not.

"Mrs. Reeve." Kelly thought for a horrible moment Barrington would bow to her, but he only nodded.

"Old Caution there insisted on following me here in the car," Jilamey said plaintively. "You see why I don't bring him to Rraladoon very often? He mothers me, Kelly. Make him stop."

Kelly shook her head. "You need it sometimes, sweetheart. Come in, both of you. Where are Todd and Hrriss?"

Jilamey laughed. "Oh, likely in their office in the government building," he said. "I thought I heard something about 'too much to do before Snake Hunt' as they left."

"Sometimes, I wish they were both twins," Kelly said, her hands on her hips. "I love having these visitors, but I wish that things would calm down a little so I could see my husband once in a while." She sighed. "I can't damn the man for having priorities, but it does get a little lonely."

Jilamey laughed and seized her hand. "Now I know you're telling a fib, beautiful lady. Where are the children?"

"I'd just realized that it was too quiet out there," Kelly said. "Teddy, Grizz's cub, came today. With all the mighty discussions at full spate, no one has time for the youngster. Well, they won't want to miss their favorite uncle."

"Good!" Jilamey said. "I have a special present. It finally arrived from Terra on the latest shuttle."

"Good heavens," Kelly exclaimed, going over to the comunit and punching in the twins' codes. "What is it?"

"A model airplane, made from blueprints from centuries ago. It really flies! I tried it from the roof of Alreldep block."

"Only you could get away with that!" Kelly said, all too aware of the repressive character of Terran society. "That's funny. There's no answer." She punched in the code again, thinking she had gotten the signal wrong. "Nothing."

Nrrna arrived with her sleeping cub, greeting Jilamey graciously before she saw the anxious expression on Kelly's face. "Somezing is wrong?"

"I told those children to take their radios!—No, they did take them," Kelly said, glancing at the rack which held only one, hers. "I remember the Cats picking them up as they went out the door."

"So why do zey not answerrr?" Nrrna asked anxiously.

"I don't know," Kelly said, biting her fingers. "Oh, wait, maybe they're out in the barn. No need to turn the units on there. Only, surely we'd hear them . . ." She looked anxiously at Jilamey.

"Barrington? Search the barn for the youngsters, would you?" Jilamey said, and his servant moved with great alacrity, covering the distance to the main barn in seconds. "He keeps fit," Jilamey remarked as he gently extracted the comunit from Kelly's hand and punched in a sequence. "Just a little trick I learned . . . to see if the units are broadcasting. Ah, that's odd. There's interference from somewhere."

"A jammer?" Kelly cried, really alarmed now.

"Could be natural . . ."

"Maybe David's seen them." Kelly ran to her computer and called the ranch manager on the land lines. "He hasn't seen them at all," she said, severing the connection. "I wonder . . ." She punched in another number. "Todd? Hi. Are the children with you?"

"No," Todd told her. "Are they on their way here? I'll keep a lookout for them."

Kelly winced, for suddenly she was sure that the kids were in trouble. But Todd had broken the connection before she could tell him that. Then Barrington mounted the steps to the porch.

"I'm sorry to report that there is no sign of the children in the barn or the pond. Further, five stalls are empty. Would that be significant?"

"It would! Oh God," Kelly said, "they should have *told* me they were going riding. And with a total novice in tow, too."

"The hovercar could be used to search," Barrington offered.

"And I can summon my personal heli from the house," Jilamey added. "We'll find the children in next to no time, Kelly. Don't you bother your head." He took the comunit back and called for his pilot to bring the heli immediately to the

Double Bar Gemini. Then he strode to the wall where the big map was tacked. "Hmmm, let's see. Where do the children usually ride, Kelly?"

She shrugged. "They ride everywhere."

"But not everywhere with a complete novice like Teddy."

Kelly frowned, glancing at Nrrna for help. "No, they would probably go across the meadows and into the forest . . ."

"Well, that would require the heli. Barrington, you take the road toward the village in case they went that way. Your children are very resourceful, Kelly, Nrrna. I wouldn't worry—yet! No sooner do we leave than they'll come back, having done a tour of the meadow for Teddy's sake."

Not quite convinced, Kelly and Nrrna nodded uncertainly, each thinking of all the dangers that could befall five small children on Rraladoon so close to Snake Hunt time.

Just then, four things happened: a riderless horse clattered into the barn-yard, Ourrh was found in the barn, asleep in the hay, Jilamey's heli arrived, and so did the big Gringg shuttle.

chapter ten

Although Kelly and Nrrna waved frantically at the shuttle, it took off once it had deposited Grizz.

"Oh, Lord! And that's Teabag coming in all a-lather, too." Kelly groaned, hiding her face in her hands.

"With a pack saddle on?" Jilamey inquired, mystified.

"When I get hold of those twins, I'll larrup them to within an inch of their lives," she said so fiercely even Barrington regarded her in some surprise. "Jilamey—" She pushed the entrepreneur toward the porch. "You meet the captain, be gracious, offer her food and drink, while I see what I can find out from Teabag."

"He talks?" Jilamey said to Kelly's back as she strode off to intercept the gelding, wearily plodding toward the safety of his stable.

"No," Nrrna said, her eyes flashing, "but ze mud on him and ze grasses caught in ze girt will tell us where he has been. The young Gringg cub would be more comfortable riding a pack saddle zan a normal one. At least, zat Hrrunival cub of mine had some sense!" She was not one bit less annoyed than Kelly, though her aggravation was expressed by the lashing of her tail.

As he obediently went to greet Grizz, Jilamey mused on the maternal trait that caused each of the women to blame her own offspring for whatever had happened to Teddy. He devoutly hoped nothing had, for it might have a devastating effect on the delicate negotiations now in progress.

"How nice to see you, Captain," he said cheerfully. "Didn't realize you were expected. Kelly's had to go tend to that loose horse," he added, waving in that direction. "Are you hungry or thirsty? Kelly offers you hospitality. You've been here to the ranch before, I understand? Great place, isn't it."

Teabag, only too grateful to be home, allowed Kelly to approach him, especially as he had just stepped on the longer of the broken reins and answered the tug on his bit. But that was the least of the details she observed. The blanket under the pack saddle looked to have been sliced by a sharp object; Teabag's neck bore shallow scratches. His hide was sticky with half-dried sweat, so he hadn't come from all that far; the still slightly wild white eye he gave her as she caught up the shorter dangling rein proved that his fright hadn't been that long ago. She soothed him as she examined the claw marks on the crosspiece and noted the scratches on the thick leather of the reins, but apart from his scratches, there were no other bloody spots. Kelly tried to reassure herself that falling off a horse was part of learning how to ride. Probably even ol' bomb-proof Teabag had found a Gringg too much to bear. A real all-out howl from a fallen Teddy might well have made Teabag bolt. Nonetheless, spooking was most uncharacteristic of the docile Teabag. She felt his legs—warm but not hot, so no tendon damage. Her hand came away with swamp mud, the stink apparent even at arm's length.

"Well, clues of sorts," she said, still trying to reassure herself that Teddy had merely fallen off. In the swamp—which Teabag would have avoided on his own—Teddy would at least have had a soft landing. But *why* didn't the kids call in? Ask for reinforcements? Why were the comunits dead? That was disturbing. Quickly then, she stripped off the saddle, dropped some feed in his manger, and left Teabag in his stable to recover.

Jilamey and Grizz were booming at each other on the porch as she returned to the house. Kelly gritted her teeth. The truth was always preferable, even if it showed her up as a less than careful guardian.

"I am so sorry, Captain. The children have all gone off, on horseback, I believe, though the last time I looked they were all in the pond," she said, and managed a smile. "I didn't realize you'd be able to join us or I'd have kept them about the place."

"Grrgggl . . . the meeting ended sooner than expected," Grizz said amiably, glancing toward the pond.

"And you thought of a swim, no doubt," Kelly said, managing to act casually. "Well, while you're indulging yourself in some well-earned relaxation, we'll just go back along the trail and hurry the kids in. Here's Nrrna, too, Captain—" Turning her back briefly on the Gringg, Kelly beckoned furiously at the Hrruban to join them. "How fortunate you came by heli, Jilamey," and she firmly tucked her arm in his, elbowing him to fall in with her scenario.

"Easiest way to travel speedily," Jilamey said on cue. "This won't take long," he added as he guided Kelly toward the vehicle where Barrington waited.

"Any instructions?" Barrington, who had just rejoined, asked as they began to board.

"Oh, would you please man the communications channels, Barrington?" Kelly said, scrambling into a window seat. "And keep trying the kids' frequency." She gave him the code and he bowed politely.

The small craft lifted off and Kelly's heart did a flip as she saw Grizz, dwarfing Nrrna's slight figure, standing in the yard.

"Where do you think they went?" Jilamey called over his shoulder from the co-pilot's seat as they cleared the trees. The heli's engine was reasonably quiet, but no way to silence the *whup-whup-whup* of rotors tearing the air had ever been discovered.

"They must have taken a trail ride," Kelly shouted back and remembered then to turn off her voder before she damaged her eardrums.

"Then they might just have turned their handsets off?" he asked.

"No, a call alert would get through. Nothing did," Kelly said, disturbed by that. "Those units'll even continue broadcasting near high-power sources."

"Think they went mda-watching?" Jilamey asked.

"They wouldn't dare!" Kelly exclaimed, horrified. "Or maybe they would, the rascals. They were dying to show off the whole planet to Teddy."

"Would they have known to keep the pace slow for Teddy's sake?"

"Alison and Hrrana have more common sense than the three boys so they'd have kept to a reasonable pace. Turn toward the swamps, Jilamey. It was swamp-mud Teabag had on his legs."

"Swamp? This close to Snake Hunt?"

"Yes, I know." Kelly grimaced. "But Teabag wouldn't spook at any old tiddler."

"What about a Big Momma?"

Kelly shook her head impatiently. "I'll skin them, I will, when I find them. Let's backtrack Tea's probable route home. He came in on the swamp road."

"No sooner said than done, milady," said Jilamey.

"Look, where the terrain opens, can we skim to see if I can spot hoofprints?" Kelly asked, reaching for the case that held binoculars.

Jilamey, had taken the controls and was a deft pilot. In the soft ground of the track, Kelly could make out the darker color of disturbed ground in the even pattern made by a single-foot. Skimming along as far as they could until the bushes grew too close, she could also see where the tracks were those of a gallop stretch.

"Well, he was still running scared here," she said as Jilamey lifted the heli above the thick shore growth.

Now she scanned more widely as they passed over the marsh toward the dunes.

"This is getting all too close to snake-hatching grounds, isn't it?" he asked.

"It certainly is," Kelly said, leaning forward with the field glasses.

Jilamey had just angled the heli up and over another line of drifts, and a wide prospect spread before them. She caught her breath at the oh-so-welcome sight of a handful of small figures crouched on a blanket on a dune ridge. Slightly below them were five horses, apparently tied to a driftwood log. "And there they are, the scamps! Teddy's with them." Only then did Kelly admit to herself how terrified she had been that he'd be missing. "Set down!"

With one eye on the tracer screen and the other looking out for riders, Walters drove the small flitter around the edge of the dune where Gallup was waiting. He killed the quiet hum of the motor, and the small vehicle coasted silently to a halt. Gallup gestured for him to climb out, and pointed up the hill at the five youngsters. Walters nodded and swung the pack off his back.

"This place is full of snakes," he whispered. "Damn near stepped on one that was sleeping! They give me the creeps."

"Shh!" Gallup said, flattening himself on his belly on the hot sand. Together, they inched up toward the crest of the dune where the children were waiting.

The *whupping* of heli blades startled them. Hastily, Gallup and Walters burrowed into the sand and covered their heads with their arms. The copter set down on the sand hill between them and the children.

"Aw, hell!" Walters exclaimed, slamming his fist into the hot dry dust. "Commander Greene is going to be furious!"

Gallup plucked at Walters's collar. "Come on, we have to get out of here before they spot us." He reached into his pack and switched off the jammer.

Together, the two men crept backwards down the hill to the flitter.

"Snakes!" Kelly cried, pointing.

There were only a few, and relative tiddlers at that, but they were gathering just out of sight of the cluster of children. Kelly knew that the smaller reptiles wouldn't attack something big by themselves, but when they were hungry after laying their eggs, and there were a bunch of them, they'd been known to trap urfa or even small mda and rend the animals apart. Jilamey whirled the craft around so that the fine sand blew directly into the faces of the waiting snakes. Most of them fled over the dunes and into the marshweeds before he landed.

Kelly sprang out, ducking under the still-whirring blades. "There you are! Teddy, you're all right?" She fumbled to turn on her voder. "You've had us worried half to death," she scolded, running a hand down Teddy's sticky matted fur before she turned on her twins. "Why didn't you let us know you were in trouble?"

"We *tried*, Mama," Alison said, ducking her head in shame. "We tried."

"We did, Mom," Alec said stoutly, reinforcing his sister. "And we made sure the red 'charged' light was on before we took them off the rack. They just wouldn't work when we tried to call you."

"Well, you nearly caused an interplanetary incident, young lady," Kelly said sternly, but she hugged her daughter and ruffled Alec's hair before she plucked Alison's radio out of the belt clip. She thumbed the switch and then stared at the unit. "It's working now," she added expressionlessly.

"It wasn't before, Mama, honest!" both twins clamored, tugging at her arm.

"Alley tells ze exact truzz," Hrrunival said, twitching his tail for emphasis.

While it was just like these rascals to stick together, Kelly knew that they were always truthful. She compressed her lips tightly.

"Furthermore, you all know how dangerous the dunes can be at this time of year, so why under the sun did you bring Teddy here of all places?"

"We didn't *bring* him, Mom," Alec began in an exasperated voice, as if she had added insult to the injury of underestimating his common sense. "Teabag did, and Teddy didn't have much choice." Alec pressed his lips against a grin. "We followed."

"Well, then, young man, what spooked Teabag to run off?"

Alec shrugged his shoulders. "I was leading, Alison behind me, then Hrrunival with Hrrana now beside Teddy."

"Teabag just took off," Hrrana murmured, obviously upset and feeling responsible.

"Well, no one has been hurt and Teabag got home. Teddy, did Teabag actually run away with you?" Kelly turned back to the victim and only then saw the yolk streaking the fur around his muzzle. It gave him a ludicrous Pooh Bear look. "He'd had a little something this hour or two." The verse rattled unbidden through her mind.

Teddy shrugged, so reminiscent of Alec that Kelly had trouble keeping a straight face. "Grrbble . . . the hrrss did not like me on its back. It took time for it to fall me off as I clung tightly."

Well, Kelly thought, *since he's all right, there's no need to make an intergalactic incident out of this.* "So you've found snake eggs, have you, Teddy? Do you like them?" She grinned because his eyes sparkled and he dropped his jaw.

"Gracckle . . . Very tasty indeed. May I take some back? My dam would find them as tasty as I do."

Alec gave an exasperated snort. "We've been trying to get Teddy to move, but he's stuffing himself."

"Can we get started home now?" asked Hrrunival. "It's not much fun sitting around watching someone else eat when you're hungry, too."

"You'll be hungrier by the time you've ridden home," Kelly began, thinking that would be adequate discipline for this escapade.

Just then the horses neighed in alarm and began pulling at their reins which were tied to a driftwood log.

"Kelly, look out!" Jilamey cried, pointing violently even as he reached for whatever hand weapons the heli carried.

As swiftly and inexorably as a tsunami, a medium-sized tiddler boiled over the ridge of the south-facing dune, flowing its leaf-patterned sinuous body toward them with incredible speed.

Because they were beside her, Kelly gave her two children a shove toward the heli before she reached for Teddy, who hadn't even risen at Jilamey's warning cry. Hrrunival and Hrruna ran to safety. Teddy first had to rock himself to his feet, even with Kelly yanking at him. The snake, feeling the vibrations, moved in on them.

"Oh, fardles, Teddy, GET UP! That thing wants you for lunch!" Reflexively, she pulled out her belt knife, jumped in front of Teddy, and faced the oncoming snake. She just hoped Jilamey had a snake rifle in his heli. The worst she could do to the snake with her knife was deflect it briefly. But Teddy had to be protected.

Then the snake was close enough to stare directly into her eyes, pinioning her almost hypnotically. She didn't recall ever being this close to one when on foot before or armed with such an inadequate weapon. She stared with helpless fascination as its maw opened, the jaw unhinged as it widened, showing its extraordinary gullet. Gunfire, deafening in the usual silence of the dunes, startled both her and the snake. Sand kicked up almost in her face, and there was the smell of explosive propellant in the air. The snake was distracted.

"Move away, Kelly, so I can get a clear shot!" Jilamey shouted. He was sighting down a heavy-caliber hunting rifle. "You know I'm a lousy shot."

"I'll forgive you," she shouted back, "if you kill it!"

Kelly and Teddy dodged, getting out of the direct line of fire. The entrepreneur fired again, this time catching the snake in the tail, causing it to thrash back and forth in pain. Then it raised its head and stretched its jaws wide again, moving toward Jilamey. Teddy needed little urging from Kelly now, as she hauled him to the top of the nearby ridge and slid down the far side. They both lost their balance in the loose footing and ended up rolling down into the next valley.

"*Aaaaaaggghhh!*" Teddy cried, his vodered voice echoing in her ears. Above, below, beyond, and behind her, she heard the repeated boom of the rifle discharging.

She was still trying to spit sand out of her mouth and clear her eyes when Jilamey slithered down beside her, a wisp of smoke curling up from the bore of the rifle.

"It's okay. It's as dead as I could get it."

Kelly got her eyes clear of sand, but that didn't seem to help. She was at the bottom of a gully covered with sand, looking at what seemed to be a dozen people, their features foreshortened by height and darkened by the sun behind them. In a moment, they coalesced into four, then two, then one Jilamey. She released the fierce clutch she had on the Gringg cub and rose to her knees.

Teddy unrolled easily and waddled to his feet. "That was fun," he said. "I want to come back here and roll down hills again."

"Teddy, not here!" Kelly said firmly. "This is the breeding ground for those snakes. You could have been killed."

"Why didn't you tell me to defend myself from it? I was not afraid, and I am strong enough to have rendered it harmless," the cub said calmly.

Kelly started to protest that he was only a child, and then realized that the Gringg cub was probably a lot stronger than she, and might well have been a match for the tiddler. But snake-killing was not likely to be considered a desirable occupation for a species that said it did not like violence.

"Well, I knew Jilamey had a rifle and I certainly don't want to risk your hide on any snake-wrestling!"

"Oh, that is what one does with these snakes? Wrestles? I like wrestling. I'm good at it," Teddy said, looking disappointed that he had not been allowed to show his prowess.

"Fardles!" Kelly muttered under her breath and continued to de-sand herself. "Actually, Teddy, I think your dam expected you to play with our young, not wrestle the wildlife." She got to her feet and extended her hand to the cub. "But let's leave here *now*, because I really don't care to run into anything bigger than that one."

"How big do they come?" asked Teddy, intrigued.

"That one was small . . . a tiddler. Some of them are immense. The ones we call Great Big Momma Snakes are much, much bigger." She indicated girth with her hands.

"Oooh," Teddy said, impressed.

When they got to the top of the dune, he exclaimed in dismay, "It smashed all the eggs." There was yolk all over the place, and crumpled shells, for in its death throes the snake's body had convulsed, completely destroying the nest.

"We'll find more another time, Teddy. Come on. Your mother's waiting for you at the ranch. Let's go." Kelly gave him a gentle shove toward the heli.

"You didn't mention the mda," Alison muttered at Alec as they watched the dying snake.

"Do you want to be grounded for the rest of your life?" Alec replied.

"Well, no . . ."

"Then, shh!"

"Well?" Jilamey asked, steadying Kelly through the sand to the heli.

"Well, what?" she asked. There was sand down the back of her blouse, inside her trousers, and inside her boots. She was itchy and thirsty, and she didn't know whether to skin her children alive or just never let them out of her sight again.

"My second snake," Jilamey said plaintively, pointing to the twitching corpse. The children were admiring it and arguing amongst themselves over its length and probable weight. "After nine Hunts and not for want of trying, I have slain another snake. Might it count toward the Coming of Age Ritual?"

Kelly laughed, her voice echoing over the empty land. "Oh, I'm afraid not, Jilamey. I wish it did, you were so heroic. But it's got to be an official kill or capture during the Hunt itself, or we'd have poaching during the early season by obnoxious youths who want to make sure they qualify. Cheer up," she added, seeing his crestfallen expression. "It'll be good enough for a feast. We'll have a barbecue. Grizz'll enjoy fresh snake steak, and so will I. I only have to defrost the sauce."

Jilamey brightened. "I like barbecued snake!"

When the snake's corpse finally settled to an occasional twitch, they heaved it into the heli. It exuded a slightly musty odor, but the trip back to the ranch wouldn't take that long.

After settling Teddy inside the craft, Kelly turned to the other youngsters.

"You five go straight home, now," she said, shaking her finger at them. "No diversions, no detours. Got that?"

Two "Yes, Moms" from the twins and a meek "Yes, Aunt Gelli," from the three Hrrubans.

She let a grin break the scowl of disapproval on her face. "I'm just glad you're safe," she said, kissing each one in turn.

"I just wish they hadn't fibbed about those comms. This could have been very serious," Kelly said softly to Jilamey as he lifted the heli. Teddy had his nose pressed tight against the plasglas, watching the kids ride off.

"They don't lie as a rule, Kelly," Jilamey said. "Could someone actually have been using a jammer for some reason?"

"I'd prefer that explanation, but it isn't likely." She sighed. "Well, nothing really bad happened."

At the house, Grizz was on her feet, a living tower, waiting for the heli to land. Making a most peculiar-sounding ululation, Teddy climbed out of the aircraft almost before it had set down, and hurtled toward his dam. She embraced him fiercely, throwing him up in the air without effort and neatly catching him as he squealed with delight. Jilamey whistled at the careless exhibition of strength.

"And we've got a special treat for you," Kelly shouted over the slowing rotors as she walked toward the Gringg. "Fresh Doonarralan snake, courtesy of Jilamey's hunting skills. We'll have a real feast tonight."

The captain shook her head. "Morra. Please to take me immediately to the government offices. I have had an urgent communication from Eonneh. There is trouble. I must be there."

"Quiet!" Todd shouted, waving the crowd down. "One person, tell me what happened."

His office was full of angry people. The bad news had travelled all over the colony in the time it had taken Mike Solinari to inform him of the incident. Admiral Sumitral had come on the run from his office when he heard the commotion. Second Speaker arrived shortly afterward, with Captain Hrrrv and several of the visitors from Hrruba behind him. The rest were Rraladoonans of both species, all arguing at the top of their lungs. In the middle of it all was the Gringg male, Cinnamon, who said nothing and sat despondently waiting for whatever would happen to him.

"Mike!" Todd said. "The rest of you, quiet!"

"My two assistants and I were showing Cinnamon around the veterinary hospital," Mike began, shouting at first but lowering his voice as the others stopped talking to listen. Dr. Adjei, head of Veterinary Services, stood at Mike's shoulder behind Robin. "He was our special visitor today. I had morning surgery, so I left Cinnamon with my assistants, Dr. Gross and Intern Errrne. They took him around the place and ended up at the corral where we were holding about thirty animals, mostly geldings. I heard a howl and came running. The Gringg, Cinnamon, was in the corral"—Mike shot a furious glance at his erring employees—"with the dead mare at his feet."

"He killed it," Bert Gross burst out. "With one punch!"

"You're out of order, Gross," Todd told him sternly.

The plump woman from Humanity First! pounded on Todd's desk and thrust an accusing finger at Cinnamon. "This monster should never have been allowed to go unsupervised among decent beings! It could have been one of us!"

"It was an accident," Robin Reeve said firmly. "Cinnamon has repeatedly said so."

"I will recompense for its loss," Cinnamon said miserably. "I will adopt its youngster and nurture it."

"It'll need a foster mother of its own kind," Mike Solinari explained, but the spontaneity of Cinnamon's offer softened his harsh expression. "There's a couple of mares who have lost their foals. We can put the colt in with one of them. That part'll be all right."

"But he killed . . ."

"Ma'am, it's upsetting, but can we put the incident in perspective?" Todd asked politely.

"What perspective is that, Reeve?" Greene asked sardonically. He stood with fingertips poised on Todd's desk, not as loud or insistent as the angry woman, but somehow much more menacing. "That one of these gigantic aliens of yours killed a horse, or that he did it with one blow? They can break necks with as little effort as it takes for you or me to brush away dust. You've sown them among the population of a civilian planet like poisonous weeds. Where in this perspective do we find responsibility?"

"Oh, very picturesque, Commander," Robin Reeve said, applauding with sarcastic exaggeration.

Greene showed no signs of impatience or temper. "As Admiral Barnstable has repeatedly requested, these creatures should be sequestered."

"Locked up like wild beasts?" Hrrestan said, shaking his mane. "Unrrrea-sonable. You would not lock up a Hayuman for killing a hrrss. You would fine him and set him frrree. So would a Hrruban trrrbunal."

"Only in cases where malicious inzenz does not exist," Second Speaker Hrrto said. He was as far away from the Gringg as the dimensions of the room, and the crowd, would allow. Todd was relieved to observe that Barnstable was not present. "Ze question now remains if ze Gringg intended to kill."

"Why would he? And let me remind you that in our laws," Todd said, "as in yours, a suspect is presumed innocent until proven guilty. Prove that Cinnamon acted in malice."

"Our laws forbid violence," Eonneh protested, making his way forward to stand beside his colleague. The room seemed to shrink around them. The animal rights woman from Terra let out a squeak of surprise and retreated behind Mike and Robin, who exchanged a glance of disgust.

"I am sorry," Cinnamon repeated, staring at his big paws reproachfully. "I strove only to push away the hrrrss's attack. It hit me with its feet, here." He showed a torn patch on his coat where the mare's hooves had struck his chest, and the gash on his broad muzzle. "I did not realize I had struck it so hard until I heard—" And somehow he imitated the precise sound of a bone breaking. Everyone in the room shuddered. "I grieve to have killed a harmless animal, especially one prized so highly by our new friends. My hosts assured me that the hrrrsses were eager to have friendship. I sought only to make friends with the beautiful animals."

"Dr. Gross," Todd said, keeping his voice level and consequently forcing the crowd to hush to hear him. Inwardly, he was ready to roar with fury that a petty, though tragic, incident had given such fuel for trouble.

Bert Gross came forward and cleared his throat. His face was red, and he nervously rearranged his hands from pockets to belt to hip; his right hand twitched toward Cinnamon, and ended up scratching the nape of own his neck.

"Well, he, I mean the Gringg, went right into the corral, and he started chasing the herd around and around. Anyone with sense wouldn't have done that. Then the mare charged him, defending her foal. He struck her down like swatting a fly."

"It is so," Errrne said with a terse nod.

"Why didn't you stop him," Dr. Adjei asked, his eyes narrowing, "when you saw the herd reacting? You had the voder."

"Why would you leave ze Gringg alone in ze corrrrl in ze first place?" Hrriss asked. He had stood beside Todd, silent until now.

"Huh?" Gross looked at his Hrruban comrade. Errrne lifted both hands palm up, shrugging.

"I heard them." A very soft voice came from within the muttering crowd.

"You were a witness?" Hrrestan asked, glancing around the crowd. "Come forward."

A slender girl in a soiled coverall raised her hand. "I saw. Juanita Taylor. I work at the animal hospital."

Robin elbowed his way through the crowd to escort her toward the desk.

"Will you tell us what you heard?" Hrrestan asked her in a kind voice.

Nita blushed deeply, but Hrrestan kept his big green eyes fixed on her deep brown ones. "Dr. Gross invited the bear, I mean, the Gringg, to see a herd of horses on the other side of the barn. I . . . I didn't mean to be eavesdropping, but the barn's open all the way through, and there's an echo."

"No one's accusing you of anything, Nita," Todd said in a gentle voice. "You're helping us."

The girl nodded, and swallowed nervously. "They told him to get into the corral and get close to the horses. It was their idea. They were laughing about it. I didn't realize that anything was wrong until I heard the stampede, and then the mare screamed."

"So you say that the two Rralandoonans led him to believe the situation was controllable, and then failed to act responsibly and in time to prevent a tragic occurrence?" Admiral Sumitral asked.

"That's a leading question!" Bert Gross protested.

"You watch too many courtroom videos, Bert," Ken Reeve told him. "Will you answer, Nita? Just tell the truth."

"Well, my dear?" Sumitral prompted.

Nita nodded, not looking at the men. "I think they were trying to play some kind of joke on . . . Cinnamon, but it backfired. That mare was very protective of her foal. We had trouble getting close to her, and she knows us."

"So the mare reacted out of fear of a stranger," Todd said flatly. "I think that sums things up pretty well, don't you, Hrrestan?"

"I agrrree," Hrrestan said. "If it was not frrr zis witness who has come brrravely frrrwrd, zeir dishonor would nevrrr be discovrrrd, since ze Gringg would continue to believe he was guilty of a crrrime."

"We," said Todd, including Hrriss at his side, "apologize, Cinnamon, that you were subjected to such infantile behavior."

"Hey!" Bert Gross protested. Errrne hissed. Todd met their glares with a cool stare. Both of them suddenly found something else to look at.

"I'll talk to the two of you later on," Todd said, his voice cold. "But I think Dr. Solinari might have something to say to you first."

"You're damned well right," Mike said grimly.

"I have a restoration to make," Cinnamon insisted, inclining his big head. "I did not mean to cause a loss of life. I wished to make friends."

"I am positive of that!" Todd replied earnestly.

"You are most courteous," Eonneh said, bowing.

"Is that all?" Greene asked. "You stand here and compliment one another ad nauseam, when this alien has shown the dismaying ability to destroy without effort?"

"Not at all," Todd said, as if he had noticed the Spacedep commander for the first time. "As Cinnamon has already offered to make restitution, what else could be demanded of him? A day in the stocks? A month of bread and water? Mike'll determine the value of the mare and how much fostering the colt will cost, and Cinnamon will pay what he owes. End of matter!"

"In whatever way becomes possible, I will make the value good," Cinnamon promised.

"You forget the loss of use of a valuable brood mare and any subsequent earnings," Greene said.

Cinnamon nodded his head obligingly. "That, too, is fair and can be decided. I await the decision."

"But we have formulated no schedule of payment or value," Second Speaker said, looking distressed.

"You can't just let these . . . *aliens*"—Greene larded the word with repugnance—"buy their way out of any incidents. This one involved only the death of an animal. You let the Gringg wander where they like. What happens—"

"We Gringg will cooperate in any way we can," Eonneh interjected, looking intently from Greene to Second Speaker to Todd. "The just reparations for accidents must be decided, clearly stated, and set down. This regrettable incident is unlikely to be repeated, but we Gringg are big and accidents can happen no matter how careful we try to be in our excursions."

Greene rolled his eyes, and was gathering himself to speak, when Hrrestan held up his hand.

"Agreement must be formulated with all dispatch," Hrrestan said, "so zat justice—unlike zis . . . inforrmal and crrowded hearring—can be calmly and sensibly rendered on any matters zat could be required. A tribunal of one each of our zree species should do very well, should it not, Zodd? Sumitral?"

"Now wait a minute—" Greene said.

"You are not, Commander Greene, a resident, norrr even a frequent visitor to Rraladoon," Hrrestan said, gently but firmly dismissing the man's protest.

"We Gringg agree," Eonneh said, looking from one to the other, "justice must be clearly stated and set down. It is the only fair way in which we can interact, now or in the future."

"A second Decision at Doona," Todd said, with a grin at his mentor. Today's accident—so nearly a tragedy—had provided a major forward step in the tripartite relationships. The Rralandoonans in the crowd cheered, but not all the visitors looked pleased by the outcome.

"Impossible situation," Greene protested, realizing he had lost control of the situation. "There are ramifications you cannot understand—" He broke off suddenly.

At Second Speaker's side, Mllaba stared at the commander, her huge eyes glinting, and a hot flush rose from Greene's collar to flood his face unbecomingly. In his presence, almost with his cooperation, the ridiculously naive Doonans had struck a bargain with their would-be destroyers. They proposed galactic policy with a dangerous species, and were grinning like idiots. Sumitral, beside them, who should have been wary, was behaving just as foolishly.

"This whole thing is an inappropriate response to the situation," he said through clenched teeth.

"Not at all." Todd raised his voice to be heard over the hubbub. "The malice was not on Cinnamon's side. If he had deliberately destroyed property, it would have been necessary for him, as it is for anyone on Rraladoon, to be disciplined in some fashion. However, we have established—haven't we?—that he was the victim of an ill-conceived trick."

"Hear! Hear!" Mike cried.

Robin, breaking off his quiet but intense conversation with a blushing Nita, echoed the vet's sentiment, glaring at the dissenting expressions of faces in the crowd.

"Since it seems that Rraladoon is fast becoming a popular spot for aliens to meet"—Todd went on, injecting some levity into the discussion, for which he was rewarded with a few grins—"it behooves us to consider contingency plans and guidelines until formal proceedings can be initiated. This is my world, and I am the Hayuman leader of it. Hrrestan, as my Hrruban colleague, do you concur?" Hrrestan nodded, his gleaming eyes never leaving Greene's face. "I could almost suspect"—Todd paused significantly, though he pointedly did not look in the commander's direction—"that the whole incident was manufactured by those intent on causing trouble between our people and our new friends. Our *guest*"—Todd emphasized the word—"has been most gracious, considering he was the butt of a bad joke. End of incident. Now, you all, clear out of here, and tend to your own business. Not mine!"

Greene stood staring at the desktop, then looked up to meet Todd's eyes.

"I . . . I agree with you, Reeve," the commander said, nodding his head slowly. "You should not have become involved with a tempest in a teapot. Delicate relationships between our three races should not be fractured. As Human colony leader, you are in a superior position to facilitate such guidelines. Spacedep wishes to offer any assistance you require."

Todd gawked at the Spacedep officer's sudden change of direction. He was unable to detect any sarcasm in Greene's earnest face.

"That's very wise of you, Commander Greene," Sumitral said. "And the sooner we can devise final terms the better. In the meantime, let us extend immunity to these stray visitors of ours until we have achieved a proper treaty with the Gringg." He sighed. "If only they came in a slightly smaller package, there'd be less objection!"

The officers were talking in a tight group as Robin and Mike were urging people to disperse, joking that the show was over for the day.

"Or were they less dangerous," Mllaba said, staring at the dejected Cinnamon. "It is not merely ze sheer size of the Gringg zat is off-putting."

"Not to menzion ze zurprize of zeir trade items," Hrrestan said.

Hrrto was shaking his head, and his tail tip twitched convulsively. He spoke Middle Hrruban in a low voice. "Perhaps if all business was conducted by comlink, there would be less need for protection."

"Why, Honored sir, when they offer no violence?" Hrrestan asked. "I think some responsibility devolves on us—to be sure they are not victimized, as they were today."

That aspect had clearly not occurred to Hrrto. "Yes, yes, I take the point, Hrrestan. But . . ." And he sighed heavily. His priorities were in constant turmoil. Only the prospect of the essential purralinium remained of constant importance. "It always depends *who* the victim is, doesn't it?" he added enigmatically.

"Hall's cleared now, so goodbye. I've got a hospital to run," Mike Solinari said over his shoulder as he firmly pushed the last of the curious out the door.

"Especially when the victim does not realize he has been made one," Hrrestan said, looking at the retreating figures of the veterinary contingent. "The laws of Hrruba are far more stringent than are needed here on Rraladoon, Second Speaker. Diplomatic immunity should be tendered. The terms of such immunity are already known to both Hayuman and Hrruban. Let us examine them first. Then we must learn the law forms of our visitors, so that there is no ambiguity or misinterpretation." As he spoke to Hrrto, Hrrestan leaned away from Greene, as if he hoped the commander would take the hint and depart. "We of Rraladoon will be honored to mediate such discussions if that would solve the current dilemma of jurisdiction."

Mllaba nudged Hrrto. "Such a project would greatly enhance your prospects for election, Speaker!"

"I . . . yes, of course it would, Mllaba," he told her testily. Then he turned to Hrrestan. "Justice for all is the primary purpose of the Council," he said. "And also of our allies on ze Amalgamated Worlds Council."

Greene, who had not taken the hint to leave, entered the discussion, also using Middle Hrruban. "Diplomatic immunity is certainly a good point at which to start, since we are all familiar with its workings. I was for a while attached to Spacedep Legal, so I would like to assist."

His offer surprised every one in the room, so that he was able to glance meaningfully at Mllaba without comment. She nodded, understanding that the two of them must have a private conference.

"Then it's settled," Sumitral said cheerfully. "Ah, Captain Grzzeearoghh, we've been expecting you. There's a matter of great importance I wish to broach to you."

Todd glanced up. The enormous Gringg filled the doorway, her red eyes nearly sparking. Behind her were her cub, Kelly, Jilamey Landreau, and Landreau's servant, Barrington.

"What matter is that?" Grizz asked carefully, her sweeping glance having taken in the forlorn Cinnamon. Eonneh went to her side and began to speak in a low voice. Grizz bent over him, and waved her claw now and again in assent.

"If I may," Admiral Sumitral began, nodding to Todd and Hrrestan for permission. Then he approached the Gringg captain. "As Honey undoubtedly informed you, there has been a slight mishap involving Cinnamon, which has been resolved under our laws. As guests of this planet, Rraladoon, you are now granted diplomatic immunity, the ramifications of which I will gladly explain to you. I can safely assure you that this will be immediately ratified by the governing body of Amalgamated Worlds."

Somewhat stunned by Sumitral's announcement, Hrrto forced his way over and said, "And by the High Council of Hrruba."

As he heard himself saying such words, he wondered that he had so spontaneously promised what he would have to argue at his most eloquent, in the Council, to obtain. And yet, all he had to do now was mention purralinium to them and they'd agree to any measures needed to procure the metal. Nevertheless, he had been forced to take an action which he ought to have discussed, at least with Mllaba, before committing himself. Could the Hayumans and Zodd Rrev have cunningly maneuvered him into agreeing? Or was it that Sumitral had once again made the Second Speaker of the High Council dance to his tune as if Hrrto were a mere apprentice in the halls of diplomacy? Perhaps both. Sumitral had always been a formidable mediator, and young Zodd had indeed grown up.

Then Hrrto wondered at the sudden shift in Greene. It had been the commander all along, declaring that the Gringg could not be trusted. What could be the reason behind such a switch? Then it occurred to him that under the guise of diplomatic immunity, "escorts" could be assigned to any Gringg on the planet—to ensure that the immunity was observed. *Ahh,* thought Hrrto, *that Greene is quick, clever, and shrewd. He had got the better of Sumitral, Hrrestan, and Rrev, and used the concession to forward his own aims.*

"Of course," he continued, hoping his pause had not been overlong, "all three interested parties, plus their homeworld representatives must be present to discuss a Trade Agreement—in the same chamber."

Grizz gave him a brilliant smile, her long fangs gleaming. "Of course, Second Speaker Hrrto," said the pleasant voice of the voder. "It would not be correct or courteous any other way."

Second Speaker bowed to the Gringg leader, suddenly feeling that twice in a short space of time he had been manipulated by a clever strategist. Zodd and the two Hrrubans were not laughing, but he thought they might be close to it.

"I would be most interested in a treaty between us all, especially if it will facilitate trade practices here on Rraladoon," Grizz said, addressing both diplomats. She put a maternal claw on her cub's head. He grinned up at her lovingly. "My son has been telling me how delicious are the eggs of the native species of snake of Rraladoon. How glad I would be to trade with Rraladoon for such a commodity."

"Now that you mention our friend the snake," Jilamey said, addressing everyone who remained in Todd's office, "I happen to have a delicious specimen which we can barbecue tonight. You are all invited to partake of the unique taste of Rraladoonan snake, a real delicacy. I feel a lot of policy can be discussed over a friendly sparerib or two, eh?" He winked at Kelly.

"You two are never, never, *never* to leave your handset off again," Todd said, towering over his offspring with uncharacteristic anger. Alec and Alison studied the ground and each other's shoes for a moment, then peeked up at Todd. "If there had been an accident, no one would have known where to find you until it was too late!"

"But everything came out all right in the end," Alison offered, fluttering the thick lashes of adoring golden eyes at her father. "We stayed with Teddy to make sure he'd be all right until Mama found us." She could sense him softening, and nudged Alec with her elbow. Her twin added the earnest plea in his blue eyes.

"Honest, Dad, the radios were working when we left! It's not our fault they failed," Alec said.

Kelly spotted the silent communication between her children and interjected her own comment. "It doesn't matter how it came out; it's how it began. Promise, or you'll never get to ride Hunt until you're old and gray. Promise!"

"She means it," Jilamey said, lounging in the porch seat while Barrington, elegant as ever, sliced snake up into manageable portions for the barbecue grills. "She nearly made me stay behind from my first Hunt because I didn't want to carry a handset."

The twins sighed and matched glances. They knew they hadn't been remiss but couldn't prove it. Being accused of a lie was almost worse than getting chased by snakes.

"I promise," Alec said at last. Alison nodded.

"We'll check and double-check from now on. We're very sorry to have caused trouble. And we washed Teabag and the other horses down and groomed them real good."

"And so you should have, kids. But it isn't what happened, it's what might have," Todd said, hunkering down to the children's eye level. "Teddy's a stranger here, and we trusted you to look after him. Your responsibilities make it imperative that you remember things like making sure that your equipment is functioning properly. You were unable to call for help, or notify anyone as to your location. Think of your mother and me. We'd have been devastated if anything happened to you."

The thought had passed through the twins' minds. They threw their arms around Todd, who hugged them tightly.

"We'll never let it happen again, Daddy," Alec said in a low, tight voice. Over their shoulders, Todd glanced up at Kelly.

When Teddy had emerged from the Gringg shuttle at the Double Bar Gemini, he was also visibly chastened. He stood, scuffing one foot in the dust, waiting for his friends to come out again to play. Hrrana and Hrrunival had been assigned extra chores by Nrrna as their punishment. Kelly watched Teddy mooch around the grass kicking a stone, bored and lonely. She relented.

"All right," she said, and the Alley Cats perked up. "Go and play, but when I call, you come right in, understand? I'm counting on you to help me with all the guests we're having tonight. You're my best assistants."

"Yes, Mama!" Like twin bolts of lightning, Alec and Alison raced down the steps calling to the small Gringg.

"And we wanted children, didn't we?" she said, taking Todd's hand and squeezing it as they watched the children play together on the grass.

"We did, and I wouldn't have it otherwise, even with double trouble," Todd said, gathering her under one arm and enfolding her tightly. "It's not an easy job, but I love it."

The smell of roasting meat made a tantalizing atmosphere for the negotiators who gathered over the course of the next hour or two. Robin and Jilamey acted as chief cooks, turning hunks of meat on the broad grills, and explaining to the Gringg what "barbecue" meant. Big Paws, the black and white Gringg, couldn't seem to stay away from the fragrant, spitting roasts. He stayed close, chatting with the chefs.

"I have had only preserved snake," Big Paws said, with a sidelong glance at a smallish steak, only centimeters from the edge of the grill, as if he'd swipe it if backs were turned. "I am looking forward to tasting fresh meat."

"This'll be the best," Robin said expansively. "Reeve family recipe. There's a secret to cooking snake to bring out the true flavor. First, you sear the sides of the meat, then season—"

"No. Season, then sear," Jilamey said, interrupting.

"Right," Robin said. "Then cook for four to eight minutes on a side."

"How is it a secret if he knows?" Big Paws asked, pointing to Jilamey.

"I'm practically family," the entrepreneur said, grinning. He sliced off a piece of rare steak and held it out on a roasting fork to the Gringg. "Taste."

The bite disappeared in a twinkling. "Delicious!" Big Paws exclaimed, licking his chops with his long brown tongue. "I would like to have much more of this. Is this barbecue the only way of preparing it?" He looked dubiously at the glowing coals.

"Whatever way rocks your jollies. Tell you what, come along on Snake Hunt," Robin suggested. "If you catch your own snake, you can cook it any way you want."

"Oh, I would love that," the Gringg said, his eyes lighting up. "I will make the suggestion." He raised his voice, already quite loud enough to be heard all across the yard. "Captain Grzzearoghh, may I suggest a concept to you?" The black and white Gringg lumbered off toward his leader. Robin grinned at Jilamey and went back to turning steaks.

Hrriss passed among the guests with pitchers of lemonade and beer, filling glasses. He stopped to offer refreshment to Ali Kiachif, who looked at the contents of the two carafes, and shuddered.

"Unfermented fruit squeezings! Don't you have a decent tipple for a *man*?" the old spacer asked, reaching for the beer.

"I'm sure I will find something," Hrriss said, dropping his jaw, amused.

"So you're the chief meeter, greeter, and feeder for tonight?" Kiachif asked. "Where's your tail-twin? Scrubbing dishes?"

"Zalking," Hrriss replied, with a dropped-jaw grin for his long-suffering friend. "I am sure he would razzer be washing dishes. Zodd is engaged in deep talks with my father, Second Speaker, the Gringg, Spacedep, and Alreldep, so I offer hospitalizy on behalf of us both."

"Ah, one of you is as good as the other," Kiachif said airily. "And I saw your assorted offspring going about handing out baked taties, salad, and fruit like very pros. You're raising 'em right, young Hrriss, so you are."

"Thank you," Hrriss said, extremely gratified. "I will see if there's any mlada in the house."

"Ah, this picnic is doing wonders for calming overstretched nerves, so it is." Kiachif sat down on the porch seat to wait.

Mllaba and Greene left their seniors engaged in the informal Treaty talks, and made their way surreptitiously to a spot as far removed from the party as possible. Grace Castleton and Captain Hrrrv were at the end of the fence waiting for them. There was a small tray table before each of them. Hrrrv's platter was empty, and looked as if it might have been licked clean. Castleton's food was virtually untouched. She toyed with a beaker, picking it up and putting it down again without drinking from it. She felt she couldn't force anything past the tightness in her throat.

"I could not zink what you were doing, Greene, in agreeing to enter formal discussions with these creatures," Mllaba said, as soon as they were out of earshot of the party. "But it was cleverly done. We can szretch out zuch dialogues for many weeks."

"Glad you caught my drift," Greene said smugly, settling onto a chair beside Castleton. She glanced up at him with an abstracted smile. "And it had the effect of disarming Reeve's objections. The Admiral was very pleased when I reported back to him. The bruins have sworn to abide by a peace accord. Now they'll have one, and Admiral Barnstable is personally involved in drawing it up. It gives the fleets time. This diplomatic immunity also allows us to keep track of where the Gringg go. They'll have escorts everywhere. If once they show what they are capable of, we'll have witnesses!"

"How does the meeting go?" Hrrrv asked in a low voice.

"Second Speaker has become caught up in the dream laid out by Hrrestan and Rrev," Mllaba said, her eyes gleaming with faint disgust. "He will lose the election if he does not take care. All of them are so enamored of the concept of unity that no one listens to reason."

"They'd sign tonight if the Admiral wasn't there," Greene said, grinning with malice. "He insists on discussing each clause in the Diplomatic Immunity Handbook over and over again, then letting himself be talked into the original wording already set down."

"But very slowly," Mllaba said, laughing in short, breathy grunts. "A very cleverrr man, for a Hayuman. The Immunity Agreement will not be finished tonight. And yet they continue to look upon his involvement as helpful!"

The other two joined in the laughter, but it had a forced ring to it. Castleton took a sip from her drink, but did not taste it. The thought of deliberately sabotaging a safeguard for both Gringg and themselves worried her, almost more than the up-coming confrontation when the naval support ships arrived. Despite the tape, she found much to admire in the Gringg.

"Now Reeve has committed himself," Greene said, "the confrontation with the Gringg will make him look the idealistic fool he is. All we have to do now is stall. When the fleets arrive . . ."

"They're close," Grace said quietly. "The Terran fleet is within twenty-four hours of making orbit."

Greene looked at her, almost for the first time, and his expression changed from triumph to concern as he saw how worried she was.

"What's wrong?" he asked.

"Nothing," Grace replied carefully, glancing at the two Hrrubans. "All ship-shape, and observing radio silence."

"Ze Hrruban fleet will arrive just outside ze heliopause a few hours later," Hrrrv added.

"Very good," Greene said. "The Gringg are most likely to strike when we expect it least. Possibly while we conclude agreements and treaties they never had any intention of signing. We'll hold up the final agreement as long as possible until both fleets are in position."

"It cannot be held up long," Mllaba said. "Ze movement toward accord is inexorable. Ze Gringg, Sumizral, and Rraladoon are in agreement. Zere are reasons why Second Speaker will sign zat I cannot discuss, but no one will oppose him in ze Council."

"Then that trade agreement could be the last thing any Human or Hrruban does on Doona," Greene warned. "Admiral Barnstable has sent sealed orders to open fire on that *Wander Den* of theirs the moment their reinforcements arrive, or at the first hostile sign."

"Zousannds of lives are at risk," Mllaba added. "We have to stall until ze ships are in place to defend zem. Ze Gringg shipz must be blown apart before zey can attack."

"We shall be ready," Greene said, leaning over and speaking in a low voice so the others had to listen very closely. "Then we'll support Hrrto by telling the Council that he was on the right side—the side of caution—all along. The Admiral has the tape to justify our actions. That's our ace in the hole. Barnstable also wants to sabotage that scientific get-together planned for tomorrow."

"It is already being zaken care of," Mllaba said, her yellow-green eyes watchful in the twilight. "I attend ze conference again in ze mrrning."

"Good! This charade has gone on long enough," Greene said. "In the meantime, we pretend to cooperate and thus allay suspicion until our fleets are in position."

"Then we demand the truth of the massacre in the Fingal system," Hrrrv said, flourishing his claws. He stood up, bowed to Mllaba, and left.

"I, too, must go," Mllaba said. "Ze Council expects me to report on ze Treaty's progress." Her black robes whispering over the long grass, Mllaba glided away. Like a shadow, she passed between the hulking figures of Gringg and Hayuman, and disappeared between the gateposts.

"Jon, what if we've been wrong?" Castleton asked Greene suddenly, in the thoughtful silence that followed the Hrrubans' departure. Her voice was too loud, and she forced herself to lower it. "What if they truly are peaceful creatures? What will the Gringg think when our forces surround them? They'll feel betrayed. They'll never trust us again."

Greene put a gentle hand on her wrist, and she shuddered slightly. "You've seen the tape, Grace. We can't ignore that proof. We have every right to demand an explanation, and to take reasonable precautions."

"I still don't agree with your conclusions," Grace said. "I'll fight, and even die, if I have to, to protect Humanity, but I still can't bring myself to believe in the Gringg threat. I'll just be doing my job." She lowered her gaze, and sat staring at the ground between her feet.

"Yes," Greene said, moving closer to her. They were now knee to knee. She was aware of the warmth in his eyes and the scent of his skin mixing with the cooler aromas of the night air. "After tomorrow we might be very busy . . ."

"Or dead," Grace said, her eyes fixed on his.

"But not without having fought good battle," Greene said. He held out his hand to her. "Let's go back to the ship . . . and form our own plan of action."

With a sad smile, she nevertheless took his hand.

chapter eleven

Commander Frill courteously pushed back his chair and rose when Mllaba entered the conference room. He wasn't sure if protocol for a Speaker of the High Council applied to his personal assistant, but it was better to err on the side of courtesy. Mllaba spared him an annoyed expression, then made straight for his side of the table. He remained standing until she had taken a chair, and he assisted her in drawing it to the table. Cardiff, on his other side, glanced up at the Hrruban, but his conversation with a pair of Gringg engineers and the technician from the Hrruban warship did not falter. The Gringg were arguing a complex point about drive engines that the Hrruban couldn't believe, but wanted to. Vocabulary was not yet adequate for high technology, so most of the dispute was carried out in mime, with each side making subtle alterations in the technical diagrams showing on the computer screens set between them. Cardiff's talk was peppered with untranslatable military and Earth City Corridor slang that a couple of the Gringg were beginning to repeat back to him.

Hurrhee, the chief scientist from Hrruba, interrupted his talk to pay heed to Second's assistant. He was, as Frill understood it, a medium-wide Stripe, which put him among the upper class on Hrruba, but Mllaba was his superior. She muttered a long, low stream of grunts and growls at him, flipping off the control on his voder. Hurrhee submitted to that action, but Frill frowned and pricked his ears, though he only recognized a few of the glottal changes as belonging to High Hrruban rather than Middle. He wished he knew that dialect, because whatever it was she was saying, it sounded important.

"What is it, madam?" Hurrhee asked with just a touch of asperity. "I am in a most interesting conversation. I do not wish to get left behind in the details."

The assistant's gold-green eyes glinted with impatience. "What have you learned?"

"About their grasp of matter transport technology?" The military tech glanced up at the words. Mllaba stared around her in alarm, but no one else had comprehended.

"Yes," she said. "Speak in concepts, not terms."

Hurrhee lowered his voice. "Most interesting, madam. I spoke in a general way about crystalline focusing systems from deliberately impure mineral complexes. Those"—he nodded toward the hugest Gringg, a female, who sat beside the Hayuman scientist and a large, brown-patched male Gringg—"began to study the false diagrams I gave them. To my great delight, they have an idea how to prolong the life of the tuning crystals, madam. But I am now absolutely positive that the purralinium they are willing to trade us has the impurities we so urgently need. Though that metal did not come up in conversation, the darkskinned Hayuman has made a suggestion that could very well result in still further protection for our supplies."

"What?" Mllaba replied, deeply troubled. "How could he? Hrruba has sought such advances for centuries."

"But a fresh eye," Hurrhee said in a grunting whisper, "may see things a jaded one cannot. I am most enthusiastic about pursuing this discussion. And Sixth Speaker for Production was eager that I should continue."

"If the Hayumans suspect what aim you serve, they will be in possession of valuable information regarding gr—that technology," Mllaba said sternly. "Discredit anything which comes too close."

Hurrhee shook his graying mane, disbelievingly. "But should these things be secrets, madam? Science is the only universal language which cannot lie. Sooner or later they might deduce it on their own. The Hayumans seek it now, and I believe the Gringg have a fair idea that purralinium is what powers the grid systems. The large female has asked several leading questions. I hate to keep putting her off, since who knows what advances she may lead us to?"

"But it could be advances the Hayumans might be able to share to the disadvantage of Hrruba, and that must not be. Our secrets must remain our own. Can you not equivocate?"

"No," Hurrhee said bluntly, but still in a whisper. "The facts would swiftly bear against me. There is more. A few of the naval Hayumans are quite upset about it, and in fact tried to speak out against open discussion."

"Could you tell what the subject was?"

Hurrhee shook his head slightly. "I think it had to do with spaceship technology, maximizing poor resources for greatest effect. It may well be, madam, that both our technologies are short of essential metals to increase our respective transportation mediums. In my deepest heart, I feel cooperation, total cooperation, would benefit us more than the current secrecies."

Mllaba eyed him coldly. "Then it is as well that you are not in any position to make policy," she said in a voice devoid of expression. "Follow the instructions given you and do not deviate."

"Madam," Hurrhee replied with great dignity, "how can I, in my capacity as a leading scientist, ignore the chance to gain advantages which will result in massive leaps forward in many fields? I must know what these Gringg have to say, and to do so, I must be honest."

"Honesty!" Mllaba was astonished. "What is that when our security is at stake?"

"False security, I would say," Hurrhee replied haughtily.

Mllaba didn't trust herself to speak further. An outburst here would only serve to disgrace her office and that of the Speaker she served. Angrily, she pushed back her chair and stalked out. Hurrhee watched her depart, then returned to his discussion.

"Ah, Koala," he said, pleasantly. "Now, where were we?"

"Hrrestan, may I speak to you?"

At Second Speaker's voice, the Hrruban co-administrator glanced up from a stack of angry messages scattered across his desk, then rose hastily to his feet. The older male seemed agitated. "But of course, Honored Speaker. Please be seated. How may I serve you?"

The Hrruban settled himself into the padded chair opposite and attempted to compose his thoughts. "May I take you into my confidence, Hrrestan? You have always held the Hrruban cause dear."

"This sounds ominous, Speaker Hrrto," Hrrestan said, infusing a light tone into his voice. "It is true, I act for the best of all Hrrubans, but also to secure prosperity for my Hayuman neighbor."

"My request does not run counter to either of those purposes," Hrrto said. "You are aware of the scientific conference going on in the Treaty Center?"

Hrrestan inclined his head. "But of course. Your interest honors us. What is your request?"

"It is not a simple one to explain. I must tell you I disapprove of the openness which pervades there. Instead of discussing generalities, as I thought the conference was meant to do, the participants seem to have gone straight on to sensitive topics, discussing engineering and space sciences as if they were exchanging recipes."

"Scientists do tend to become enthusiastic about their pet topics," Hrrestan said. "If you wanted them to learn only names and formulae, that could have been done with simple teaching tapes, instead of allowing free-thinking beings to participate. The Gringg have their own sciences, some in advance of ours, from what I have been told. Evidently our own inventors and technicians have discovered they can proceed quickly to the satisfyingly and interestingly complex."

"No! That is not the way it should be operating," Second insisted, raising his voice almost to a shout. He stopped, surprised at his own lack of prudence. "There are reasons why we should be more discreet. I . . . I cannot be more candid at this time, but I am greatly worried that indiscretion reigns with creatures unknown to us a mere four weeks ago." Second Speaker allowed his alarm to color his tone, then controlled himself and went on firmly. "We take quantum leaps before we understand walking with them as partners. So much is at stake here."

"Indeed, but what exactly alarms you so?" Hrrestan asked earnestly.

"I beg your pardon?"

"From what I have heard, there has been accord and much exchange of information among our scientists, while others are busily discussing trade agreements. What specific problem agitates you so, Second Speaker?"

"Mllaba has been attending on my behalf while I dealt with the diplomatic immunity affair," Hrrto said in a testy tone; he had the right to use his assistant as an information gatherer. Hrrestan did not react adversely. Perhaps he, too, had spies. "Her sources suggest that the Gringg may have already deduced the workings of our grid transport system!" He paused to let Hrrestan absorb the significance of that before he continued. "We know they have impure purralinium on offer as barter. We must obtain all, *all* of the material. We cannot allow the Hayumans to have any. Surely I do not need to remind you why."

"Pure purralinium is also on offer, and the Hayumans seem much more interested in that," Hrrestan said soothingly. "They like quality and insist on the purest assays."

"But the danger exists, and you should know by now how Hayumans can grasp a single word and end up with a statement! If they *ever* connected the impure purralinium with our grid technology—!" Second Speaker threw his hands up at the thought of such a catastrophe. "Mllaba has tried to slow the talks or divert them from discussions that would inevitably lead to its disclosure, but she has been unsuccessful. These scientists are so single-minded! Therefore, you must disband the science conference!"

"I must not do that. For shame, Speaker Hrrto," Hrrestan said, his large eyes flashing. "For shame that you will not allow the Gringg to prove themselves as strong and supportive allies. If they can deduce our poor technology by casual examination—as our Hayuman friends have never yet managed to do—and yet have offered their friendship and their assistance instead of taking advantage of us, you should be pleased and grateful instead of treating them with distaste and fear. I shall be proud to have them as friends, which is much more preferable than making them rivals or potential enemies. As you have said, I support Hrruba, and I say that Hrruba would benefit greatly by frank and honest inter-action with such a race."

Hrrto regrouped his arguments. "But you do not fear them yourself? You do not find their size frightening?"

"Not at all," Hrrestan said, his jaw dropping in a slight smile. "Their voices are annoying, but they cannot help that. We become accustomed, and nape hair no longer rises when they speak too loudly. If they are large of stature, what of it? They are intelligent, caring beings. Yesterday, at the incitement of my grand-child, one of the Gringg picked me up and held me in the air like an infant. You were at the barbecue; you might have seen it yourself. It was a game the two of them were playing together, and yet the Gringg is the size of a large hrrss. My rambunctious grandson considered him a playmate. If my children and their offspring trust them, can I do less? Children are most intuitive. The Gringg value the same things we do, hold life as dearly. I find a great basis of mutual un-derstanding already."

"I see," Hrrto said slowly, realizing that he could form no alliance with this person. "Thank you, Hrrestan. It has been most instructive speaking with you."

Hrrestan rose and bowed deeply. "I am always glad to be of service."

Hrrto left the Government House and made his way to the grid in the heart of the First Village. The mist obscured his vision for a moment, matching the muzziness of his thoughts. Hrrestan had always appeared such a sensible Stripe, even if he seemed to have wasted his opportunities, choosing to be a mere co-leader on an agricultural planet. Furthermore, nothing Hrrto had seen or heard of the Gringg, even the unfortunate hrrss accident, contradicted their con-tention of pacific nature. The horrific tape shown to him by Spacedep seemed more and more of a fantasy. And they had purralinium.

Throughout the weeks since the Gringg had arrived, Mllaba harped at him that revealing the Gringg's inherent evil would serve to propel him into his world's highest honor. Yet he continually temporized and did not reveal the existence of that damning tape. At this moment, he too had difficulty seeing them as evil. And yet, if he was wrong, he was risking the destruction of a Hrruban colony. He had almost told Hrrestan about the tape. Would that omission cost lives?

Few people of any species were in the corridor of the Federation Center. Hrrto walked soft-footed into the Council Chamber and took the same seat he had occupied the day of the trade negotiations. The chamber was empty, for which he was grateful. He wanted solitude to mull over the conversation with Hrrestan.

In the final analysis, Hrruba had to have whatever purralinium the Gringg had! He could even use that as his excuse for withholding vital evidence.

"But why, Tom?" Todd asked, puzzled and unhappy. The emigration request Tom Prafuli had just handed him was possibly the worst document to cross his desk. A totally unexpected and unwelcome surprise.

Tom Prafuli pushed the sheets toward Todd. His solemn, dark brown eyes were mournful. "Just sign the emigration order, will you, Todd? Don't take it personal. Get it over with."

The colony co-administrator took the pages in both hands and met the other man's gaze. "Tom, we've been friends for more than twenty years. We grew up together; we suffered through university exams together. I don't want to see you take off on an impulse like this."

"It's no impulse," Prafuli said, straightening his thin shoulders. "Sigrid and I talked it out all night, but a month of nights arguing won't change our minds. We want to get off Rraladoon. We don't like the change the neighborhood is taking." The colonist made a meaningful gesture with one hand, holding it high above the ground beside his head.

"The Gringg?" Todd asked, astonished. "Tom, you're one of the greatest proponents of diversity I know. The Gringg will make great friends and allies. They're harmless."

"Oh, yeah!" the rancher said, bitterly, and Todd could almost see tears starting across the man's shiny dark eyes. "Ask Crystal Dingo how harmless they are."

"Crystal Dingo?"

"My mare. My prize brood mare that was. She's the one who's going to be cheval steaks and a tanned hide today. But my mare is just the beginning, isn't she? I hear you're giving a big prime chunk of Rraladoon to those Gringg."

Todd stared. "What? Who told you that?"

"There's a Hrruban going around saying that you're going to plant those bruin-monsters right in the middle of town, taking our land away for them, and fardle anyone who protests. I'm not one for racial or species solidarity, Todd—you know that—but I think these Gringg are plain dangerous. Just like that Hrruban said. A lot of people are listening close to him, and what he says makes sense. I've been hearing worse, too. They're killers."

"That's bull," Todd replied staunchly, suppressing the rise of anger at such ridiculous gossip, "and you know it, Tom. Even if one of them wanted to settle right here, they'd have to take unclaimed land. That's in both the Decision and the Treaty. You know how I feel about them, don't you?" Todd put a little heat in his words because Tom had been pro-spaceport.

"Well, there's those that say you're thinking of them before your own folk, Hayuman or Hrruban."

Todd eyed him. "If you weren't hurting, I'd take exception to a crack like that, Tom."

"You can take what you like, so far as I'm concerned. You can give them my ranch when I'm gone. I don't want to be anywhere near them. Let me go, Todd," Prafuli begged. "I heard through the bulletin board that they're taking applications for homesteaders on Parnassus. We're already booked on a ship heading in that direction next week."

"I wish you'd reconsider," Todd said, sensing even as he spoke that his attempt was going to fall flat. "Snake Hunt is only a week away. We'd miss you if you left before it started."

Prafuli shook his head. "Thank God, because that's how we can get out of here *now*, when we want to. I'm not the only one who feels this way, Todd. I'm just the only one who's going right now. You ought to get out there and listen to your friends."

Without further protest, Todd signed and affixed his seal to the form and handed it back to the rancher, who left the room without saying another word.

When the sound of Prafuli's retreating footsteps died away, Todd got up from his desk and stared out the window for a moment. Usually the view relaxed him enough so he could think. The vast garden, changing with the season and overlooked by the grand presence of Saddle Ridge, was a most soothing view. This morning, though, the garden was flooded by a gathering crowd. Among them he could pick out the probable dissidents by their pallid complexions, somewhat scorched across noses and cheeks by the sun. All this past month there had been a steady stream of agitators swelling the original numbers, troublemakers Todd was sure Barnstable had gridded in.

He really hadn't thought they'd have much effect on dedicated Rraladoonans, but Tom Prafuli had proved him wrong. Unfortunately Rraladoon had never seen the need for any exclusion policy for "undesirable" visitors, much less professional agitators. Whoever had the money—or the interest—to come to Rraladoon was made welcome. Right now, with so many arriving for New Home Week and the Snake Hunt, and every Rraladoonan involved in those affairs, there wasn't a spare someone to screen the spurious from the serious. Wryly Todd thought that those who took in paying guests for the New Home Week festival would be making good money.

He vowed that once New Home Week and the Snake Hunt Festival, which was its finale, were over, he'd start weeding out the agitators on the grounds they were disturbing the peace. Which they were.

As he watched, in full view of the crowd, some of these new "activists" unfurled banners and stapled them to poles of green rla wood. Todd squinted to read the badly printed messages snapping in the light breeze: *Gringg Go Home, Two's Company—Three's a Crowd! . . . Doona for Doonans.*

That last slogan was obviously contrived by Earth-dwellers, since they didn't even use the current name for the planet. Todd recognized many neighbors and people he knew from all six villages. No one seemed to protest the waving banners, and that saddened him.

Once the banners were erected, the group hoisted the poles and began to march in a large oval, obstructing the pedestrian walkways to the building. Todd forced himself to watch several circuits, listened to them chanting their slogans, then turned back to his desk.

His mail was full of messages of complaint: the Gringg were an unwelcome and threatening presence. He erased most of them as soon as he saw their content, stunned by the depth of ill-feeling. A half-dozen suggested that he step down from office immediately and allow a "responsible, right-thinking Terran" to take over before disaster struck. Where had his wits been all these weeks? He'd been so convinced that the best possible outcome for all Human- and Hrrubankind was to form a partnership with the new species that he'd ardently pursued that goal. Had he been so wrong to inflict his world-view on the rest of his people? Was his idea of galactic unity so unwelcome to the majority?

Hrriss slipped into the office. "Arre you ready to go yet, Zodd? My father would like to take a few moments to talk wiz you befrrr ze conference begins. What is ze mazzer?"

Todd looked up at him, his blue eyes wide with confusion and hurt like those of a lost child.

"The first real test of my government, and I don't know if I've failed my responsibilities or not." He told Hrriss about Prafuli's visit. "I've forced my judgment on others, without caring what happened to anyone, or what anyone else thought." He threw up his hands, paced fitfully to the end of the room, and spun self-accusingly on his heel.

"You have not failed," Hrriss assured him. "Hrrestan has had such messages, too, and he is paying no heed zo zem. Zere is bound zo be malcontents who will not wait frr all to come out right. How many of zose messages were signed by villagers?"

"More than I like to count." Todd felt suddenly unworthy of the office Hu Shih had ceded to him.

"You always assume zat you are ze one who is wrong," Hrriss said with a gentle grin as he opened the door. "Let me suggest a little experiment. Ask zese folk what zey zink."

Todd's personal staff consisted of two Hrrubans and a Human, whose workstations were in the outer office. They looked up as Todd and Hrriss came out. The office manager, Kathy Hills, fluttered her long blond lashes at him in a demi-flirt, then stopped when she noticed his expression. Her large blue eyes filled with concern.

"Todd, what's wrong?"

He wasn't very sure how to frame the question. Anyway, these people were loyal to him personally. It was those who had no connection to him that he had to reassure.

"Er, Kath, are you comfortable with the idea of allying with the Gringg?"

"That's a funny question," she said, a little puzzled. "Sure. Why?"

"Well, I . . . would it trouble you to have them as permanent trading partners? Neighbors? Friends?"

Kathy laughed. "Well, I can't imagine being closer to anyone than I am to my two best Hrruban friends. It'll be a shade difficult," she added with a giggle, "to be on the same level as a Gringg, but every one of them I've met so far has been polite and curious and really rather interesting. Need you ask?"

"Well, yes," Todd said. "It seems I do need to ask. I should have done it before."

Mrrowan, at the desk across the room, exchanged pitying glances with Kathy and Hrriss, and shook her head.

"Zodd, you can be so blind sometimes. We zrust yrrr judgment. We sure wouldn't work so hard for you if we didn't!"

Barrough, beside her, his jaw halfway to the floor in amusement, nodded agreement.

"We can't be considered a good cross section in a random poll," he said. "But we get out and about when you haven't got us slaving over hot consoles here. So we do know that the majority will follow you and Hrrestan. We elected you to succeed Hu Shih, didn't we? And most of the people I know"—he turned to get emphatic nods from the two females—"think you're handling a difficult situation very well. Any fainthearts don't know how good they've got it here."

"Thank you," Todd said, his shoulders relaxing somewhat, though the tight knot in his gut remained. "I needed to hear that. I was half-convinced that I've been ignoring what's been going on right around me. I'm not going to bull it through without the approval of the people who live here."

"And you are not," Mrrowan insisted. "Rraladoon exists as it does because we've always helped each other. You have had help from many people zese long weeks of zeaching ze Gringg to speak our language. Zose are not disapproving. It has been a prrject we have all shared. And enjoyed."

"Tom Prafuli's emigrating," Todd said, still ashamed of that disappointment.

"So?" Barrough demanded with a shrug. "He was never really a Rraladoonan. He only came here to hunt Snake. We can do without his kind."

"And you're letting that upset you?" Kathy demanded, screwing her face up in disgust. "You amaze me, Todd! Let it run off your back, the way you did the other stupidities that have been perpetrated. You're on the right track. Don't you doubt it!" Her expression turned fierce.

"I second that!" Barrough and Mrrowan chorused. "But it is nice of you zo ask," Mrrowan added, dropping her jaw in a big grin.

"I zold him he was mad," Hrriss said, his eyes alight.

"No, they're not exactly disinterested parties," Admiral Sumitral said when Todd consulted him on the matter, "but loyal enough to you to warn you if the matter was getting out of hand. So why are you letting one emigration give you second thoughts?"

"It just made me realize that not everyone agrees with the policy Hrrestan and I have been following. I mean, bringing the Gringg along as quickly as we can, opening our homes, our businesses, our lives, to them is good for interspecies relations, but are we doing the right thing for the greatest good of the people on the planet we administer?" Todd asked, and paused.

Hrriss grunted low in his throat, but it was Sumitral who answered.

"Would I"—the diplomat touched his chest—"have backed you so solidly if I felt you were *not* acting in the best interests of a planet which is very dear to my heart?"

That rhetorical query wrung a wry smile from Todd. "You'd be the first to set me straight, I guess."

"If I hadn't firrrst," Hrriss said, twitching his nose and whiskers.

"I admit that it can be unnerving to see people carrying such unflattering banners round and round your office," Sumitral agreed, "but surely you saw how many of them are not even residents?"

"It's the ones who were that upset me. There were letters demanding that I step down. Kelly's reported rumors all over the complaint board."

"Pay no azzention to zem," Hrriss said. "Zey do not speak for ze majrrity."

"Do you, in your mind and heart, doubt the merits of what you're doing?" Sumitral asked, leaning forward over his folded arms.

"No! Not for a moment," Todd said. "Not for myself! But I'm not acting for myself anymore—or alone."

Sumitral smiled. "You are acting for the good of Rraladoon and that has always been an instinct with you, and with Hrriss. Remember that. Ignore the dross. Myself, I have trusted very few in my life . . . a survival technique. But I trust you, and Hrriss, and certainly Hrrestan. And oddly enough, I also trust the Gringg. Call it professional instinct. That's why I'm backing you. And, to give you a little encouragement"—Sumitral pulled up a file on his desk computer and swung the screen around for the two friends to see—"I'll give you the straight facts from homeworld newsprints. Here's the result of an opinion poll circulated by the Amalgamated Worlds Council on Earth. You see, in the beginning when the first data about the Gringg's arrival began to circulate, a general poll showed seventy-five percent were against getting involved with them. But look at the demographics: most of them are oldtimers, who grew up when there weren't even Hrrubans on the horizon, when settling space meant hardship and terror. The young people, between sixteen and twenty-five, were ninety-two point seven in favor of getting to know the Gringg better.

"Now, after the initial reports"—Sumitral allowed a tiny smile to touch his lips—"and I might add, after a little judicious salting of news programs with tapes of you two and other Rraladoonans interacting in friendly, nonthreatening activities with the Gringg, teaching them Middle Hrruban and playing with them, there's a forty percent swing in the oldest demographics, and anyone under sixty is ninety percent or better in favor of forming a Treaty with the Gringg. This is what I based my platform on when approaching the Council, and that's how I won approval to offer them both diplomatic immunity and a trade agreement." Sumitral tapped the screen with a stylus. "Don't doubt yourself, Todd Reeve. You've the backing you need. And an interstellar reputation as a fine example of Hayumankind and a role model for aspiring youngsters."

"Zere, you see?" Hrriss asked, whacking Todd solidly on the upper arm with the back of his hand.

With such reassurances, Todd was finding it hard to hold on to his gloomy mood. Hrriss was grinning widely, his jaw dropped almost all the way to his breastbone.

"I'm not sure I like having an interstellar reputation," Todd said in a low grumble.

"You should have thought of that when you were six," Sumitral said, with the ghost of memory liming a smile on his face. "Now, come, take your optimism into the negotiating room with you. You can deal with the rumormongers when the job is done."

In their dress uniforms, Sumitral, Todd, and Hrriss shouldered their way out of the building past the protesters and walked quickly to the transport grid. Ignoring the cries at their backs, Hrriss set the controls. The mist rose around the three of them, obscuring the ring of dissident Hayumans and Hrrubans. Todd was never more grateful to see the plain white walls of the Federation Center. He nodded a greeting to the grid operator, a young Hrruban male with a very pointed face and narrow-striped tail.

"We'll meet the Gringg on the landing pad," Sumitral said.

As they emerged from the grid facility, they were surprised to see the crowds on the Treaty Center grounds. A handful of Alreldep regulars in their maroon uniforms stood guard on the concrete apron attached to the building, around a grand table with three pens and inkwells but only two seats, for the public signing of the Treaty between Terra, Hrruba, and Gringg.

Most of the Hayumans and Hrrubans waiting near the landing pad were Rraladoonans, waiting eagerly to view the signing. Many had brought seating, while others had spread blankets on the ground. There was a buzz of pleasant talk which stilled as the official escort arrived. To one side, however, Todd was dismayed to see yet another cluster of protesters. This bunch suddenly pushed their way through the scattered onlookers, right up to the boxy Gringg shuttle, waving their posters. These featured caricatures of Gringg, ill-drawn as well as defamatory. One showed a Gringg tearing apart a small body, obviously a Hrruban cub. Another featured a mass of Gringg, wearing extravagant collars and harnesses, trampling down both Hayumans and Hrnibans, exaggerated paws reaching toward a table heaped with food stuffs.

Ken Reeve, Jilamey Landreau, and Ali Kiachif immediately stepped up to the shuttle hatch, daring the mob to start something. A phalanx of the commercial space crews emerged from behind the shuttle, their hand weapons still bolstered but ready, and formed a sort of barrier.

Jilamey waved to Todd and Hrriss and gave one of his outrageously cocky grins.

"Damn!" Todd muttered under his breath.

"Well, I didn't expect this!" Sumitral muttered under his breath.

"I did, after the crowd around my office. Kiachif and Horstmann dragooned their crews into guard duty," Todd replied out of the side of his mouth. "I'd hoped it was just talk. Damn 'em for using pictorial insults."

"Since it's all too well known that the Gringg have concentrated on spoken, not written language, that's one way for them to make their points."

"And Eonneh's in the shuttle and has probably faithfully drawn what's on the posters for posterity," Todd said, his tone savage with frustration. Even as he'd been speaking, he'd been surveying the faces of the orderly Rraladoonans, estimating the numbers. "Wait a sec!"

He held up his hand to delay the others in the formal escort. Then he took a step toward the dissidents.

"You're not citizens of this planet," he said, rapidly scanning the protest group to find the leader. "You have no right of protest here." Then he turned to the friendlier faces, and raising his voice, added, "I recognize a lot of you from previous Snake Hunts. How about removing the vipers in our midst? I think they need to go back to whatever hole they emerged from. Quietly! Out of respect for the rules of hospitality!"

Before the protesters could rally effectively to defend themselves, their posters were confiscated and their persons bodily removed by willing hands. Some loud and outraged cries drifted back. Todd waited a bit, grinning at Sumitral.

"All right, that's out of the way. Let's proceed with the scheduled formalities."

As soon as Todd, Sumitral, and Hrrestan approached the Gringg shuttle, the door slid open. A buzz started, this time a welcoming one.

Waving cheerfully and with a pleasant smile showing all her fangs, Grizz alighted, her powerful legs making the long step easily. Todd sighed, hoping that the Gringg had not been there very long.

Honey and Kodiak followed Grizz, turning to help Teddy down the tall steps.

A hearty cheer rose from the crowd and some laughter. Grizz twitched her ears and seemed to scan the gathering, but her fanged smile remained in place—the same fanged smile that had been caricatured on one of the posters. Todd hoped that the Gringg might just dismiss those as bad Rraladoonan art. The Gringg and officials had taken no more than a few steps, when suddenly a fist-sized rock winged past Todd's head, ricocheting off the side of the shuttle. A clatter of pebbles hit the ground around them.

Todd swung immediately in the direction of the assault. A man, tawny-skinned but with the sallow complexion that spoke of limited exposure to the sun, threw another rock straight at Grizz.

Anticipating its trajectory, Todd jumped up with one hand high and caught the rock. He swore as it stung his fingers. Teddy squealed with fear. The Gringg immediately closed about the cub, hiding him from any further attack.

There were cries of "Shame! Shame on you!" from most of the onlookers, and agitated movements in the crowd as a number of them chased after the assailant.

By all that's holy, Todd resolved, *I'll find some punishment to fit this crime, all quite within my authority as co-leader.* A glance at Hrrestan told Todd that the Hrruban had the same uncompromising opinion. The sharp chunk of granite he'd had caught would have done some damage had it reached its target, no matter how tough Gringg hide was.

"I'll want to see that man when you catch him," Todd said aloud and gestured to two of the crewmen to follow through.

Todd dropped the stone to the ground and, with his boot, ground it into the dirt.

"My sincere apologies, Captain," he said in a ringing voice. "Let us proceed with the order of business."

Then, flexing his stinging fingers, he raised his arms and gestured for the crowd to give way. A respectful aisle immediately opened up, wide enough for the Gringg and escort to proceed. That such an incident had occurred at all rankled deeply in Todd, marring what should have been a great occasion.

With Kiachif, Jilamey, Ken, and Hrriss flanking the aliens, they marched toward the Center, the space crews forming a guard behind them.

The Treaty Chamber door swung wide to admit Hrrto's erstwhile allies, the Hayumans from Spacedep. Of those expected at the noon hour, they were the first to arrive. Barnstable, in his dress blues, nodded sharply to Hrrto as he slid into the chair opposite, and surveyed the room. The only other occupant was Mllaba, who sat discreetly against the wall, allowing her senior to mull over his thoughts by himself. Greene waited patiently as Barnstable seated himself, then escorted Castleton to her chair on the other side of their senior commander.

"Well, Speaker Hrrto?" Barnstable asked. "Anything to report?"

"I have spoken to Hrrestan. Ze conference goes on unhindered, and a Treaty seems imminent whether we will or will not apprrove," Hrrto said, but his voice was distant. "If we are right, zis means zere are only hours left. I can do nothing more. Despite all advice to the contrary, the High Council wants to trade with zese Gringg."

That was true enough, for once Hrrto had mentioned the existence of purralinium, the High Council would hear of nothing but an agreement—any agreement—that would augment the dwindling supplies.

Mllaba, in her chair by the wall, glared at the floor with glowing yellow eyes, but said nothing. Hrrto had not requested her presence at that High Council meeting and he knew she was certain that he had mishandled that meeting. No matter. His conversation with Hrrestan had caused him to alter more than one long-held opinion. He had even altered his desire to win the upcoming election: such crashing responsibility for all sorts of unexpected incidents had lost any appeal.

"Withhold your approval," Greene said. "The Treaty will require signatures from all three governments."

"I am not sure zat will be possible," Hrrto replied. "Nor zat it will mazzer."

"But it can," Barnstable said urgently, his eyes glittering. "Think of it: the Gringg have given us a map of their systems. They have claimed hundreds of planets. If you don't sign, all the provisions *and* the safeguards become null and void. Hrruba could take over valuable mining planets—even habitable worlds. Considering what they did on Fingal, the Gringg don't deserve to colonize more worlds."

"No," Second said wearily. "I am too old for war. Nor am I one to take anozzer's worlds. We Hrrubans, too, have put such greed behind us. But ze others will sign ze Treaty anyhow. It will not matter if I sign or not."

"It will matter, Speaker," Greene assured him. He held out a small datacube. "I have the tape from our exploration ship. It proves that the Gringg ship did fire on Fingal Three, destroying at least one of the cities on the surface and several of the satellites. The weapons we have suspected all along must be hidden somewhere aboard that leviathan. Our combined fleets are hours away. They must not hesitate to attack."

"Is zis wise?" asked Hrrto. "It is not us who will die." *And*, he thought, *we are so close to gaining new supplies of purralinium.* He closed his eyes in despair.

"Too many will die if we don't act. You saw that tape," said Greene through gritted teeth. "These Gringg are deceivers and vicious killers. I can sense it every time I'm close to one of them."

Grace Castleton, sitting by Greene, angled her body away from him. As close as they had been the night before, she felt uneasy about contact with him just now. She was weary of trying to argue with Jon. He kept on the same theme and would see no other logic. For the first time since she'd received her own commission, she found her command onerous, as her private opinions could not interfere with her obedience to orders from the Admiral. Barnstable was as rabid against the Gringg as Jon, wholeheartedly willing to believe evidence she found spurious.

"We need more time," Mllaba said. "Just a few hours and ze fleets will be here to support our views. We need a diversion. Now is ze time to show Rrev and Hrrestan zat tape!"

"And Admiral Sumitral," Castleton added.

"Those confounded, optimistic hand-in-friendship fanatics won't believe it," said Barnstable, dismissing the leaders of Rraladoon with a gesture. "Alreldep is full of fools who can't see a real threat when it weighs half a ton and has claws."

"Yes," Greene said promptly, "but showing them the tape buys us time. They'll demand proof of its authenticity and we can drag that out as long as we want to. Let 'em rant and rave a while. That'd be to our benefit. And I've arranged one more delaying tactic. Those should eat up the hours we need for the fleet to get into position."

Everyone nodded in agreement, and nervously settled back to wait.

As soon as they were safely past the crowd, Teddy started to whimper, having managed to control his terror until the safety of the Treaty Center was in sight.

"Here, Teddy," Jilamey said, stroking his shoulder, handing the cub a handful of peppermint humbugs he happened to have in his pocket. "Can't imagine how those layabouts got here! Must be some fringe nuts."

Far more reassured by something to put in his mouth, Teddy stuffed in as many candies as he could and so forgot his earlier fright.

Having emerged unscathed from that incident, Todd was dismayed to find an even more substantial number of onlookers surrounding the meeting hall. But this time there were neither placards nor stones. Disconcertingly there were people, carrying tri-d cameras and flashing seemingly legitimate reporter idents, who wanted to ask the Gringg questions—a tiresome but necessary interview. Todd tried to appeal to them to wait until after the formal signing, but the protests were so loud that he relented. Voders were passed over to the reporters, which Todd hoped would prove so irksome to use that the newsgatherers would depart. Instead there was a barrage of inane questions, the kind of tripe that made Todd's innards roil.

"Captain Gringg, how did you feel discovering not one but two sentient races inhabiting this planet?" "Do we differ from other species you've encountered?" "How long was your journey here?" "From what part of space do you originate?" "What's your homeworld like?" "How many cubs would you have in a life span and doesn't it interfere with your professional duties?" "Why was Middle Hrruban used as the bridge language?"

"I wasn't informed that news-gatherers had landed here," Todd murmured to Hrrestan.

"Nor was I, but it is never wise to annoy zose who broadcast news," Hrrestan said.

"If such broadcast is ever aired on Earth and Hrruba," Todd said, feeling uneasy about the unexpected delay. He glanced down at his wrist chrono. They were already late for the scheduled arrival time, but he agreed with Hrrestan that it wasn't politic to irritate news-gatherers. How many of those quickly flashed credentials might prove bogus? And *how* did so many arrive so propitiously? As if he needed to go far to find an answer to that question. What did Barnstable and his crowd think they'd achieve by these delaying tactics?

However, when he and Hrrestan suggested that the interview had gone on long enough, there was immediate protest.

"This isn't half enough of an interview, Reeve," protested one of the more aggressive Human interrogators.

"Our people, too, need to know ze facts," a Hrruban of very narrow Stripe chimed in.

"What news channel do you represent?" Todd asked, holding out his hand for their credentials. "My office was *not* informed of your arrival, and any interview should have been cleared first with me or Hrrestan. We could then have allotted sufficient time for a proper interview. Now, we've given you as much as we can. After the ceremony's over, I'll arrange a longer session for you with Captain Grizz and her crew."

Todd cast a significant look at the commander of the Alredep honor guard, and immediately his troops moved in to form a barrier between the Gringg and the news-gatherers. Then Todd and the others politely herded their guests into the building.

"I know who planned that little diversion," Todd muttered to his father. "I just don't know why!"

"The 'why' worries me, too," Ken said.

"I must check the records of ze grrrid operrators," Hrrestan said. "Zere have been too many unauzorized uses of zat facility!" He twitched muzzle and whiskers, and his tail lashed angrily.

When they reached their destination, Todd sighed with relief, thinking as he did so that maybe such relief was premature.

"Who was so kind as to arrange a press interview?" he said, glancing around those already seated at the table.

"There were no news-gatherers when we entered," Barnstable said, glancing up casually from his personal clipboard. "Just the usual bunch of onlookers one would expect."

"Surely"—Greene grinned smugly—"you want as much publicity as you can get on such a momentous occasion? Surely you don't wish to keep any of these negotiations secret?"

"Surely, you don't expect me to believe you didn't arrange it, Greene," Todd countered with an insincere smile.

"Please, let us put aside rancor," Hrrestan said in Middle Hrruban, hand raised for silence. "Will you not all sit down? This is the final phase of our negotiations. I have here three copies of the Treaty worked out between Admiral Sumitral, Captain Grzzeearoghh, Second Speaker Hrrto, Admiral Barnstable, myself, and Zodd Rrev. The suggestions and input come from many quarters and have taken days to compile. I ask you all to glance over this document to ensure that all the salient points discussed have been included to your individual satisfaction."

It was only when Hrrestan sat down that he realized half the room was more interested in the ornate timepiece at one end of the room—admittedly a fine piece of engineering, since it registered the precise time in the administrative centers on Hrruba, Earth, and Rraladoon. He had the distinct sense that only the Gringg and Rraladoonans had paid any attention to his brief words. While he was not of a Stripe that took offense at minor snubs and slurs, he was decidedly uneasy about the atmosphere in the chamber. He glanced at Speaker Hrrto, who had his eyes carefully averted.

To Hrrestan's surprise, the Spacedep commander asked to be recognized. He nodded to Greene, and the Hayuman rose.

"The agenda of this meeting does not allow sufficient time to read every clause of this weighty document," Greene said, making a show of the effort it took for him to raise the weight of the thick document. "There were many points that had to be discussed in great detail. We will need more time for a thorough reading than you have allowed."

"I must point out, Commander, that you are not an official member of the Trade Treaty Committee," Hrrestan said in Middle Hrruban for the voder to translate. "You were present only as an observer for the Admiral, who was involved in another discussion."

"However, as the Admiral's appointed representative, surely I may speak to that point?"

There was the slightest edge of smug superiority about Greene's manner that irritated Todd. The commander was obviously initiating yet another delaying stratagem. *Why?* The question was beginning to obsess Todd.

"You attended all the meetings, that is true," Hrrestan said, replying with dignity. "You had ample opportunity to bring up any points then for clarification. Read!"

As Greene quickly riffed a few pages, and then held the document open, it was clear to Todd that the man was totally familiar with the contents.

"On page fourteen, clause five, subsection twelve, there is an ambiguity in wording that I feel ought to be clarified," and he read it out.

"I hear no such ambiguity," Hrrestan said. "And furthermore"—he tapped the keys on the terminal nearest him—"here is a transcript of that particular discussion. You will note that the wording is exactly as it was decided upon at that meeting."

"Ah, I see that you are correct," Greene said, all affability even as he turned pages again to a new section. "Would you also check paragraph nine, clause three, Honored co-leader? Now is *that* as it was decided? I really do feel there's been an error in the quantity of lithium with respect to trade weights."

Todd began to fidget, but a glance from Hrrestan suggested to him that his colleague would allow only so much of Greene's disputation.

"No," Jilamey said bluntly. "That's written as decided upon, Commander. And you know it!" He pointed an accusing finger at Greene.

"I do, Mr. Landreau?" Greene asked, all innocence.

"You forget, Greene, that I have an eidetic memory," Jilamey said.

Captain Grizz raised her brow at the new word, and Jilamey leaned across the table to clarify the term.

"Ev," Sumitral said, turning to Barnstable, "what is all this in aid of?"

"Well, you can't expect me to sign a faulty or error-strewn Trade Agreement, now can you?" Barnstable said, raising his eyebrows at Sumitral. "And I never approve of a document I haven't read thoroughly."

"Your approval of this document is not required," Todd said bluntly. "This is Alreldep business. You are here as an observer Admiral, and on our sufferance."

Barnstable raised his eyebrows in placid amusement at the warning.

"But I," Hrrto said firmly, "wish to read the text before it is signed." Second Speaker glanced round the table. "I would be failing in my duty to my Stripe and my position were I to dispense with such a formality"—he bowed courteously to Hrrestan—"for such a momentous document."

Todd had to stifle his impatience. The conspiracy of delay which he had suspected was now proven. Spacedep and Second Speaker were clearly working together to slow the proceedings down to a crawl. Fortunately the Gringg seemed unconcerned by the delay. So Todd offered the oval mass of the Gringg-language copy to Eonneh, who brought it to Grizz. She flipped to the first page of the document and began to read.

Most of the Hayumans crowded around Admiral Barnstable, who had pulled the Basic-language copy over in front of him. Kiachif put a pair of spectacles on his nose and peered down them at the pages, scanning as Barnstable read to himself.

Just then, the first quiet, decorous intrusion of Spacedep aides began, the first with just a whispered message for Greene, the second and the third bringing him message cubes, which he read before passing them to Barnstable for his perusal.

Mllaba stood behind Second Speaker as he read slowly. She hissed, startled as Jilamey Landreau sidled up to look over Hrrto's other shoulder.

"Too much of a crowd over there," he said, smiling at her winsomely. "Just as well I can read formal High Hrruban as easily as Basic."

"Provisions for trade, galactic court, common currency based on table of values . . ." Barnstable muttered to himself after spending several minutes thumbing through the pristine pages. "Wait just a nanosecond, here—what is this?" he demanded, planting an indignant finger in the middle of one page. "What is this about a panel for scientific interchange to be chaired by the Gringg?"

"At my humble suggestion," Honey replied. "The Gringg see that Hrruba and Terra require an arbiter of scientific matters to ensure most efficient development of important technology. We will do this for you, in exchange for a place among you."

"Never!" cried Barnstable. "Ridiculous! Afroza, you can't sign this," he boomed at Sumitral.

"I can, Ev, and I shall," Sumitral said. "I have the permission of the Amalgamated Worlds Council to do so."

"But a seat on the Joint Supervisory Council overseeing trade!" Barnstable's face turned bright red with aggravation.

"If the Gringg trade with you," Grizz asked, "is it not fair to allow us a small say in the laws and privileges? We will agree to abide by them. If we governed, would you not expect such a courtesy?"

For that Barnstable had no objection. "I . . . suppose so."

"We keep faith," Grizz replied. "Even as you have asked us, we have kept our ship in the same orbit you recommended many weeks ago."

Greene was surprised to have that fact raised. Could the Gringg suspect? Had they instrumentation powerful enough to see through the large Rraladoon moon which was obscuring the approach of the fleets?

For another half hour everyone read quietly while Todd and Hrriss became more uneasy. Todd drummed his fingers on the tabletop. Every legitimate signatory for this Trade Agreement had been intimately involved and had approved each day's finished negotiations. *Why* delay the inevitable? Or did those messengers mean the Spacedep contingent were waiting for something more?

Greene had edged forward and was perched on the edge of his seat, turning an occasional worried glance at Captain Castleton, who responded with small shakes of her head.

"And what is this?" Mllaba asked a few minutes later, pointing over her senior's arm at a statement near the end of the document. "A section of Treaty Island to be designated as an Embassy of the Gringg?"

"Of course," Todd said. "As we discussed at length last Tuesday afternoon, they will have ambassadorial status to Rraladoon. It's an acceptable compromise, since they are not actually members of our Hayuman-Hrruban alliance. No, change that to 'federation.' An alliance suggests there is an enemy to ally against."

To Todd's surprise and concern, Castleton visibly winced at his wording. She looked almost guilty, but he continued with his explanation. "They are entitled to have a base for their trading houses and a diplomatic compound. I'm still not at all happy to see the Hrrunatan inhabited, but that part of the continent's useless for anything else, so it might as well be a spaceport, and the Gringg are to have their own quarters there as well as here in the Treaty Center." He looked around the table at the troubled expressions. "Look, you'll have to accept that the universe isn't composed of only two sentient races anymore"—he stared significantly at Greene—"or just one. We've been sought out by a third. One day there may even be more." He kept his grin at their dismay to himself. "That portion of the text was agreed on yesterday morning."

"And you agreed to this?" Barnstable demanded of Hrrto. "When? After I left? How could you?"

Suddenly stung by the Hayuman's presumption, Hrrto struck back.

"Hrruba does not answer to Earth for its actions," he replied. "It sounded quite reasonable to me when I discovered how much that would benefit Hrruba you Hayumans would deny us."

"Now, wait!" Barnstable roared. "*We* deny *you*? What about you and your precious grids?"

"Just a moment, Admiral," Kiachif said soothingly. "To be just, judicious, and nonjudgmental, there are processes we deny the Hrrubans and could very well offer without any loss to ourselves, if you understand me. Our new cryogenic techniques for one thing."

"That's top secret, military only!" Greene said, narrowing his eyes at the Codep captain.

"As if we have a constant call for frozen soldiers," replied Kiachif with a snort.

"If we may be allowed to mediate this point—" Grizz began pleasantly, with her paws folded over her belly. "The function of trading is to sell to others what they do not themselves have. Both parties should gain in the exchange."

"So let's exchange," Jilamey said eagerly. "Let's exchange spaceships for grid systems. Amalgamated Worlds would gain what they need and Hrruba would be able to explore more efficiently. That'd be the greatest trade—and the greatest gain—possible." He beamed around the table, apparently unaware of the frozen, outraged silence.

"And, under special auspices, that might very well be possible," Hrrto said. Mllaba nearly choked and jumped from her seat to whisper urgently in Second Speaker's ear. After only a few words, he pushed her from him.

"D'you mean that, Second Speaker?" Jilamey asked, incredulous.

Just then two ensigns hurried quietly into the meeting room and placed a communications unit on the floor next to Barnstable. Todd noticed that the unit was operational.

"Now just a moment, Barnstable," Todd said, rising from his chair. "This is a closed session and that thing is on broadcast. You two"—he pointed to the ensigns—"get that out of here, on the double."

Hrriss indicated his distaste with a swish of his tail. Hrrto, usually a stickler for protocol, glanced up and seemed to draw in on himself.

Todd's order was ignored as, hard on the heels of the Spacedep technicians, uniformed Hrrubans brought a similar unit for Hrrrv.

"Just what is going on here?" Todd demanded, glaring at Barnstable and Hrrrv. Neither answered him. "I want an answer, or, by all that's holy, you'll leave this meeting!"

"Not until you've seen what we can now show you, Reeve," Greene said, pitching his voice louder, his eyes fixed on Todd. "You've lost this one, Reeve. You and your all-for-one, one-for-all!" He sneered. "You've lousy judgment, Reeve."

"In what respect, Greene? or by the powers of the office Hrrestan and I hold, you'll be off this planet and you'll never get back on it!"

Out of the corner of his eye, Todd saw the smug grin on Barnstable's face. He nodded at Greene, an obvious signal to continue.

"Yes, you've erred catastrophically in the matter of the Gringg. These great, peace-loving creatures you're so eager to invite everywhere! That you're stupid enough to trust."

Sumitral and Hrrestan both leaped to their feet.

"If you fault Reeve's judgment, then you fault ours, too," Sumitral said in a cold, hard voice.

"You're obviously getting a little too old to practice basic common sense, Sumitral," Barnstable said. "If you resign now, we can probably see that your long service is suitably rewarded."

"My what?" Sumitral's face was expressionless, but his tone was unforgiving.

"You've all made the mistake of taking the Gringg at face value," Barnstable said. "And it is a mistake! Which Spacedep and the Hrruban Arm can at least control."

"You had better explain yourself, Admiral," Todd said, anger rising to a barely controllable pitch.

"Indeed you better, and immediately," added Sumitral.

"Now!" Hrrestan's single word held overtones of threat, causing the Gringg to respond by standing taller.

"Before those naval snips coming in behind the moon get into a position to cause both us and our Gringg friends considerable discomfort," Ali Kiachif said, his black eyes flashing with warning. He removed from under the table a small but powerful receiver which he had obviously been monitoring.

"What?" Todd said, thunderstruck. "Space fleets? Ali, why didn't you tell us?"

"Just got the confirmation I've been waiting for. I thought this laddie buck"—he jerked a thumb in Greene's direction—"was up to no good, so I've kept an eye and ear pricked until he overstepped himself. You, too, Admiral."

Todd turned on Barnstable. "I demand to know on what grounds you have brought armed ships into Rraladoonan space!"

Sumitral drew himself up in regal dignity. "If you have data you've been concealing from us during these negotiations, you must now reveal why you are obstructing the progress of these peace talks."

"The data was *classified*"—Greene stressed the verb—"until it could be confirmed. It is now. I contend that in your naive and ingenuous fashion, you have put all of Humanity and Hrrubanity at risk."

"And that you, in your usual warlike and suspicious nature, have arbitrarily decided we need to be defended by two space fleets. Humpf." Kiachif's black eyes sparkled with outrage and indignation.

"Ev, what have you done?" Sumitral asked, distress and disbelief spread across his face. "How could you supersede my authority in this matter?"

"I have rectified—and not arbitrarily—a serious error of the current civilian government—" Barnstable turned toward Todd, levelling a finger at him.

"You have negligently placed the civilians of this planet in grave mortal danger. Therefore I declare martial law on this planet. I am taking over here. Two cruisers are approaching the Gringg ship and have orders to fire if it moves or they detect any unusual emissions. Furthermore, the entire fleet will take action in one hour if I do not cancel the mission with a code word known only to myself." The Spacedep Admiral glared at Grizz as he finished speaking and Todd realized just how frightened the man really was.

At this point a squad of heavily armed Human marines and another of even more heavily armed Hrruban soldiers entered the Chamber. Mllaba smiled with intense relief.

"Guards will be here in minutes to take these Gringg into protective custody until we can search their ship." Greene pointed at Grizz and Honey as he spoke, signalling the marines. One immediately tried to remove Grizz's collar. Honey attempted to prevent it, but withdrew when a laser rifle was thrust in his face.

"How dare you?" Todd said furiously, rushing over to place himself between the marines and the Gringg. "We're on the verge of making lasting peace with these people. We've already begun commercial transactions!"

"You are so naive, Hayuman," Mllaba said, her voice coldly insulting, "opening the way to the Gringg domination of Hayumankind and Hrrubankind. Because that's the climate you were preparing—or did they make it worth your while?"

The marines had removed the collars of all the Gringg now, even Teddy's, though he had tried to resist. His dam had given one shake of her head. Sniffling, he had allowed it to be removed, though he kept his eye on the side table where it lay. Then marines took up positions behind the now-shocked Gringg, their rifles pointed at the large aliens' backs. At that, Teddy slipped from his chair and nestled under his dam's arm. Eyes straight ahead, she cuddled him.

Todd ignored Mllaba's snide insult "Domination?" he asked, wanting to guffaw out loud as he glanced at the passive Gringg. If she had chosen to, Grizz by herself could have overcome both squads, without requiring the help of Honey or Kodiak, but she remained quiescent—almost amused, Todd thought (Or were the loud and conflicting exchanges jamming her voder with meaningless sounds?)

Barnstable continued. "Spacedep is in possession of data that proves a Gringg ship destroyed a planetary civilization in the Fingal system."

Sumitral sat bolt upright. "I have received no information on such an incident!"

"The matter was classified but we have the tape of the exploration group, tape showing the devastated planet, *with a dead Gringg ship orbiting it.*" Barnstable enunciated that phrase with intense satisfaction at its effect on the Rral-adoonans. Almost patronizingly, he continued. "Further examination proves that the weapons that killed the population and destroyed the cities came from that ship."

"What proof is there the Gringg actually were the aggressors?" Todd demanded.

"Quite enough, Reeve. More than enough," Greene observed drily. "We missed the shot but can see the smoking gun."

"Then the evidence is circumstantial?" Hrrestan asked, stiffening his shoulders under his formal attire.

"They *were* there!" Barnstable said defensively. "The remains of their ship are still in orbit. The race they wiped out did inflict mortal damage on the ship, which is why we have proof of their infamy."

"And when did this happen?" asked Kiachif. "How many eons ago?"

"That hasn't been ascertained yet," Grace Castleton said, speaking for the first time. Greene gave her an odd look, then hurriedly took over the explanation.

"What we have is from a scout ship . . ."

"Which only has limited scientific capacity," Sumitral said in a crisp tone.

Greene glared at the Alreldep official. "The fully equipped naval team sent to conduct a thorough investigation of the system hasn't had time to reach Fingal yet."

"And for this you want to put Rraladoon under martial law?" Todd protested.

"It is for your own protection," Greene answered, looking pleased at Todd's dismay, "since you aren't showing the sense to protect yourselves. Spacedep is doing its job, risking lives to rescue you from your folly."

Todd spun to confront Barnstable. "As the representative of Rraladoon, I order you to end this nonsense. There is no clear threat and you have no basis for the illegal actions you've taken, including letting an unauthorized war party into Rraladoonan space."

The Gringg were now looking around nervously, their subsonic rumbles adding to everyone's agitation.

"He's right," Kiachif agreed. "These are bears, not bombs or brigades."

"They aren't bears," Barnstable said. "They're an alien race—strangers."

"I have always made myself personally responsible for Grizz and the others," Todd added. "Send those guards out. I know these people, and they are a threat to no one."

"Gone native again," Greene said to Todd with such repugnance the room was completely silent for several seconds.

"I have evidence of a clear threat as I've told you all along," Barnstable said. "Sit down, Reeve."

"If you're accusing me of being a closet Gringg, then this won't surprise you, either."

With lightning fingers, Todd reached out and wrenched the corner of Greene's collar away from the body of his tunic. There was an audible gasp from Grizz and the rest of the Gringg. Greene recoiled, wondering if Todd was about to strike him, then sat very still. He had been present for Honey's explanation of the Gringg custom, and knew precisely what the gesture meant. Second Speaker and his aide looked puzzled, and glanced at Todd for enlightenment.

Todd spoke intensely, to Greene alone. "I challenge you to personal combat. I resent your interference. I deplore your attempt to embroil me and my world in your petty, secret bureaucratic games. You have tried and condemned an entire race on the basis of an isolated incident and no evidence. Do you realize that if they weren't so peaceful, you might have just given them cause for retaliation? You've insulted the captain, scared her cub, and have they moved a muscle?"

"How could they?" Greene demanded with a sneer, "with lasers aimed at them?"

Todd laughed again. "Haven't you seen how fast the Gringg can move when they want to? Have you any genuine notion of their physical strength? Grizz alone could account for every marine in this room and bend those laser barrels into pretzels. But I've a quarrel with you, Greene. And I mean to get it settled right now!" He poked a hard finger into Greene's sternum. "Knives or bare hands?"

Greene hesitated, shocked at Todd's wrath. "Knives or bare hands? That's barbaric . . . that's—"

"Barbarians have a keen sense of honor, you stupid button jabber." Todd cut him off with a ferocious smile on his face that made him look not unlike a hairless Gringg. "I do, too, and there are many on Earth who have considered me an arrogant barbarian. But I'm willing to fight for what I believe in. Whereas you are preparing to initiate a bloody and unnecessary war, and turn a very profitable colony on its ears with martial law! Well, I'm willing to fight for self-determination. Are you as willing to fight for your beliefs, Greene? Is individual combat too immediate, too undignified for you? In your hearing, the Gringg said that 'tearing the collar' has long been considered unacceptable. Or didn't you understand that?"

Greene was stunned by the onslaught of Reeve's tirade. He glanced down at his torn collar and up again at the relentless glare of Reeve's hard eyes. He'd never been challenged before; not since he'd been a very young boy. He hadn't won that fight either. Physical training as an officer had always been isometric. For the first time, he was aware of Todd as a man who was physically fit and was known to have wrestled with and killed a large Doonan snake.

The two men stood facing each other for long moments. Castleton moved her hand to her side arm, only to be answered by a threatening growl from Hrriss.

"Zis is between the two of zem," he said.

"Enough!" the Admiral said in a thundering voice. "Jon, Reeve, sit down! The very idea of a physical contest between the two of you is repellent."

The two men remained eye to eye for a moment; then Greene spoke.

"I . . . decline your challenge, Reeve."

"There speaks a really brave man," Ken Reeve said. Greene eyed him, looking for sarcasm, but the colonist's face was as sincere as his voice. "Maybe we can all have the courage to refuse to fight when there are alternatives."

"Admiral Barnstable, you will show us that incriminating tape, *now!*" Sumitral demanded, so forcefully that he had the instant attention of everyone in the room. Then he turned to Hrrto. "I count on your support, Second Speaker," he said to him. "An individual, as well as a species, is innocent until proven guilty. The Gringg are here to speak for themselves. The tape, please—" He held his hand out to Greene. "Somehow I feel certain that you have it to hand." As if in a trance, Greene fumbled at a tunic pocket and drew out a tape, laden with security seals. "Thank you. But—" Sumitral raised his hand—"no matter what transpires here, this Gringg and her crew are to be allowed to proceed out of this system without hindrance. Do I make myself clear?" His cold gaze fell on the Spacedep officers. "Or by all the powers and the favors I can call in in the Amalgamated Worlds, you'll be sorry!"

The silence was profound.

"Grurghgle . . ." Eonneh's voder began, "I have not completely understood all that was said, but I did hear you mention a destroyed Gringg ship, did I not? I would very much like to see this tape you speak of."

Barnstable and Greene exchanged cynical glances, but Second Speaker looked decidedly uneasy. When Mllaba wanted to whisper in his ear, he pushed her away.

"Well?" Todd asked pointedly.

With quick deft fingers, Sumitral slipped the tape into the appropriate slot and keyed it to play on the table projection. Todd was not the only one in the chamber who watched in horror as the camera skimmed over the dead surface of the planet, then followed a searchlight through the heart of a cold, dark ship. The faces of the dead Gringg swam out of the blackness and disappeared again.

Eonneh and Grizz were still, watching, their mobile faces for once devoid of expression.

"Hold that image," Grizz said suddenly, pointing an unsheathed claw as the recorder skimmed along the hulk's battered exterior She peered closely at the picture, then leaned back in her chair, her face saddened. She gave Eonneh a brief nod.

"We can identify this sad ship," Eonneh said in a slow, solemn tone. "It is the *Searcher* and was commanded by Captain Vrrayagh, an ancestor of our captain. It left the motherworld many long Revolutions ago. We had only two brief reports from Vrrayagh. The first when the *Searcher* arrived at that system and discovered the planet was torn by a massive war, its peoples fighting against one another. When the Gringg attempted to make contact and sent a shuttle to land in the largest remaining city, it was immediately attacked and destroyed." Eonneh bowed his head briefly. "Then, even as the two armies still fought each other, they turned their weapons also against the *Searcher*. Whatever armament was used was immensely powerful, and the *Searcher's* engines were destroyed. The second and last message told us this, and that the crew would defend themselves as well as they could, but, if no further message came from the *Searcher*, this planet was not to be approached again." Honey bowed his great head, and Grizz put a sympathetic hand on his back. "It was a long time ago, and for some considerable Revolutions, we worried that these hostile people might trace the *Searcher* to our motherworld. But no one came. A brave captain, Zeeorogh, volunteered to make a solo mission to that system in case our people had survived but were without communication. She found the world—and the *Searcher*—lifeless. Perhaps if the *Searcher* had not returned the attack, it might have been allowed to depart in peace. Perhaps, our people might even have mediated the quarrel that started such total conflict. But in those early days of our exploration program, our ships were armed. No longer. Better the loss of one ship than encourage retaliation or indulge in lethal exchanges which require so much expenditure of energy."

"How wise of you!" Sumitral said softly. "So we are the first life forms—and with the events of the day I am not sure I can say either of our species are as intelligent as they should be." He shot an almost malevolent glance at Greene and another at Mllaba. "We are the first life forms you have encountered face-to-face. I deeply regret this misunderstanding. Though to be perfectly fair, the evidence would give a military mind cause to make exhaustive inquiries." He glanced briefly again at the Spacedep contingent.

"Reh," Grizz said, nodding solemnly. "It would cause concern when similar strangers appear in your skies. Vrrayagh's ship was left where it had died, and it is our custom to take those cubs who would arm our ships to see what this can cost. Gringg cubs learn that lesson at once."

"How tragic to encounter a race bent on self-extermination," Kiachif said in a sympathetic voice.

"Reh. It became a great sadness to all Gringg," Honey said. He bowed his large head in deference, but then lifted it again and smiled at Kiachif. "It is why we were so happy to meet the Rraladoonans and that they came to welcome us, without loss of life."

Sumitral looked at Todd with a wry expression. "Their experience is not so far from ours in the Siwannah Tragedy."

"Gringg, Hayuman, and Hrruban have a great deal in common," Todd said. He breathed a deep sigh of relief that his faith in the Gringg had not been misplaced, that he had not been mistaken to trust his gut feelings about them. He felt a tremendous surge of elation.

"So, zey are trrruly friendly," Second Speaker said to Hrrestan, respect in his eyes. "You were right to trust."

"Trust is worth more than any other treasure of spirit, mind and heart," Hrrestan said, nodding sagely.

"But what about those parts of the ship you would not let me enter?" Greene asked. "What's hidden in that mass of water at the center of your ship? Why did you pull me away when I went to investigate?"

"You did not ask to go," Honey replied, surprised. "It is our custom to ask permission before viewing another's domicile. What do you wish to see? The bottom of our swimming pool?" He broke into a loud, grunting laugh, joined by his mate and cub. "Most certainly, if you can swim, you are welcome to come see that or any part of our ship, any time. Come now!"

Greene flushed, but said nothing.

"But why do you want such trivia as food and clothes from us?" Barnstable asked the Gringg, breaking the uncomfortable silence. He was still looking for reasons to doubt.

"With all due respect, Admiral," Kiachif said with a huge grin, "you stick to running spaceships and leave this to us trade captains. Whatever the customer wants, if he's willing to pay for it, I'll convey it to him. Trade is important for more than just the items we transport. Trade opens minds as well as credit sources. It brings new customers together and circulates goods, which means more goods get made, and more gets traded to satisfied customers, anywhere in this galaxy that we can navigate to."

"Reh," Eonneh said, showing his teeth in a brilliant white grin. "No misleading was meant. It is not the items themselves which are important to the

Gringg, but the act of exchange, leading up to the exchange of all things: goods, then techniques, then ideas. We understand the confusion, and we forgive without grudge."

"I was misled by another's enthusiasm," Barnstable said, glaring at Greene. "There are some who always see the downside of situations."

"Sir—" There was a humble tone to Greene's voice. "I thought that, based on the information I had, I was acting in the best interests of us all."

Castleton turned to look at him with a surprised but pleased expression, her eyes glowing.

"Look, Greene," Todd said, facing the chastened officer, "it's your job to err on the side of caution. Just stick to that, avoid explosives, and leave us planetary types to do ours."

Greene's face flushed, and his lips were pressed tight. He turned to Barnstable. "Sir, I wish to tender my resignation and accept full responsibility for my actions, authorized and unauthorized."

"You acted under my authority, so I bear the responsibility, too, which is to safeguard this colony as I would our homeworld. I did as I thought advisable under the very . . . unusual circumstances. And that's that!" He turned toward Hrrto and Hrrestan, then muttered brief, crisp orders into the communicator. "Red Alert's cancelled and my units are returning to previous duties."

"I have done ze zame," Captain Hrrrv said with an impassive expression and dulled eyes.

Barnstable exchanged a glance with the Hrruban captain and cleared his throat. "With your permission, Captain Grizz—" he said, and she nodded, lowering her eyelids briefly. He cleared his throat again. "I would welcome a full tour of your ship and its facilities. I believe Captain Hrrrv would, too." He even attempted a smile at the Gringg.

At a gesture from Castleton, the marines returned the Gringg's collars, shouldered their weapons, and filed out of the room. Hrrrv's squad followed.

Barnstable swivelled his chair to face Greene.

"In view of the unauthorized actions you personally initiated which put civilians in danger, I accept your resignation, Jon. What may serve a combat officer well is simply no good in an aide. Perhaps you're more suited for other duties."

"If I may suggest an alternative for Commander Greene, Admiral," Captain Castleton said, her manner devoid of emotion, the *Hamilton* has an opening for an executive officer. Commander Fletcher's tour of duty is over in two weeks' time. I would certainly accept Commander Greene as a replacement."

Barnstable's snowy eyebrows rose high on his forehead, and he favored her with a paternal smile. "Whatever you say, Grace. It looks like someone has to keep a leash on him."

"I won't let him out of my sight for long, sir," Castleton said. Her eyes met Greene's, his expression changing from stern endurance of disgrace to surprise. He pushed back his chair and stood up.

"Request permission to be excused for a moment, sir?" he said, saluting both Barnstable and Castleton. Grace looked queryingly at the Admiral, and he flicked his fingers for her to answer.

"Granted, mister," Castleton said. Without another word Greene stalked from the room.

Todd leaned sideways to Hrriss. "Whaddya want to bet there won't be any protesters awaiting our departure?"

"I never bet on a sure thing!" Hrriss wrinkled his nose. "Hope no one will need ze grid for ze next few hours."

"Admirrrral," Hrrestan said severely to Barnstable. "In all this confrontation, I have seen that Spacedep has been closely involved. Why should it be necessary to start trouble where there isn't any?"

Barnstable glared at the tabletop. "You have to admit that that tape was pretty damning. What else was I to do to protect the colony?"

"You could have informed ze colony leaders of your suspicions," Hrrestan said fiercely. Then he turned to Second Speaker.

"And for you, a Speaker of the High Council, to go along with such machinations!" Hrrestan said. Todd heard the hurt and suppressed anger in his colleague's voice and trembled as he had when he and Hrriss were small, caught by his friend's father, doing something they knew they shouldn't. "We must learn to see all beings as potential friends, for we are terribly alone in the void of space. No offer of friendship should be rejected out of hand. See what you nearly did, destroying the peace both our species have enjoyed. For the sake of Hayumankind, for the sake of all Hrruba, for our hopes for the future, we must never come this close again to disaster!"

Hrrto gazed at him thoughtfully. No one spoke, for Hrrestan's words struck home in every heart.

Sumitral broke the silence. "Well, gentlefolks, we do have some business to conclude here. Are there *now* any changes to be made to the Trade Agreement?"

Silently, Barnstable shook his head. Second Speaker glanced up and blinked. "No."

Grizz spoke for the first time, smiling. She had been watching and listening to the whole interchange with the greatest of interest, and now beamed upon Todd. "I find all to be very well."

"Then let nothing delay the signing," Sumitral said urgently. "Shall we make this official?"

"All in favor?" Todd said. The vote was unanimous. A moment later, he sent a clerk running to the Duplication Office with the approved copies of the Tripartite Trade Agreement.

The party went outside to the prepared table. The Alreldep guard withdrew to each corner and stood proudly flanking the officials, obviously relieved to be back on ceremonial duty. It was such a momentous occasion that Todd felt quite six years old again. He could almost feel Hrruna's reassuring presence as that six-year-old helped to formulate the Decision at Doona.

As they neared the table, Todd could see that the news-gatherers were gone and those that remained were smiling with friendliness, eager to be present at an auspicious occasion. Grizz, accompanied by her two scribes and her son, took her place at the end of the table and rolled her haunches gracefully onto the pad provided. Sumitral took his place opposite her and waited until Second had seated himself at the center of the table.

Todd, Hrriss, and Hrrestan opened the copies of the Trade Treaty Agreement and placed one before each of the signatories. Ken Reeve dipped the archaic pens into the inkwells and handed them ceremoniously to each delegate.

"Hayumans, Hrrubans, and Gringg," Sumitral said, turning to the crowd. "I welcome all of you to witness the signing of this historic trade agreement between our three peoples. This is only the beginning of what I hope will be a long and fruitful alliance."

There was a wild cheer. The deep voices of the Gringg boomed louder and lower than the rest of the crowd. Flowers, brought along specially for the occasion by Rraladoonans, were thrown into the air like confetti. A handful of fragrant stephanotis landed on the treaty table in front of Second Speaker Hrrto.

"An omen, Speaker?" Mllaba whispered the question in his ear.

"I believe so, Mllaba," Hrrto said, nodding.

When the Trade Agreement was placed before him with the page open to the complex and beautiful seal of Hrruba, ready for his signature, Hrrto took up the pen and signed. He felt relieved, strangely at ease, as if more had been settled that day than the peaceful accord of three diverse and independent races.

". . . For our hopes for the future, this must not be!"

The tape ended, and the lights came on in the High Council Room. Hrrto glanced around at his fellow High Council members. Sixth Speaker was looking irritated, Fifth thoughtful. The sergeant-at-arms was smiling slightly. At a glance from Hrrto, he snapped his jaw closed and assumed a properly blank expression.

Second Speaker rose and placed his hands on the desk. "This concludes the file I have been assembling on Hrrestan, son of Hrrindan. You have had copies for your personal review, and heard personal witnesses testify to his wisdom and devotion to Hrruba. I nominate him for the seat of First Speaker of the High Council, and withdraw my own candidacy in his favor."

Gasps and muttering from the rest of the council, Mllaba looked absolutely livid, but suppressed her anger as best she could even if she couldn't control the twitching of her tail.

Hrrto did not entirely regret that he was unable to help her advance further, but he no longer envied anyone who must sit in the First Speaker's chair. The power—which old Hrruna had rarely invoked—was simply not worth the attendant responsibility. Younger, stronger shoulders would bear the burdens better. He would be remembered, however, perhaps as often as Hrruna, as the Stripe who had secured unlimited quantities of purralinium from the Gringg. It would be enough.

"He is a younger, stronger person, impartial and possessed of great patience and wisdom. With all humility, I would serve the Council and Hrruba best by remaining as Second Speaker. In that capacity, I can cement the relationships with the Gringg which I have already begun. Therefore, as temporary Council leader, I direct the sergeant to commence the voting for the First Speakership."

Each member placed his hands on the hidden panel below the level of the table. The blind monitor at the head of the table would tally the votes without revealing who had cast them. The sergeant stood up.

"The nominees for the position of First Speaker are Fifth Speaker for Health and Medicine, Sixth Speaker for Production, Carrdmarr, an industrialist and philantropist of Hrruba, and Hrrestan, Village and Colony Leader of Rraladoona and Chief Liaison Officer to Hrruba," the sergeant intoned. "For Fifth Speaker?"

One light went on at the tally board.

As tradition dictated on Doona-Rraladoon, the construction of new quarters—in this case the Gringg Embassy—became a community affair.

The site chosen for the Gringg compound was a woody area near the northern sea on the banks of the Treaty River, the major artery on the small continent.

From all over Rraladoon, trunks of the fast-growing rla trees were brought in and cut to size according to the blueprints drawn up by a team of indigenous architects and the Gringg. Vats of strong smelling rlba bubbled in several places on the site. Hayumans and Hrrubans in respirators with brushes full of the sticky sap treated the timbers, which became strong as iron and rigid in their newly cut shapes, yet still light enough to be hauled about by two sturdy workers or one Gringg. Other teams carried the finished beams and wall sections to the builders. It was all going by the numbers.

While those workers prepared the building materials, heavy loading equipment that had been used to build the Center and the Councillors' Residences had been rolled down, and were now in use excavating a deep swimming hole, with dams at each end to keep the level suitably high.

In the spirit of cooperation, artists from every village worked alongside the Gringg scribes to stencil and paint handsome, colorful designs as soon as the walls were ready.

When Todd arrived that morning on the site, he estimated that there must have been five hundred people pitching in to help. He was inordinately pleased by that—another subtle vote of confidence in himself and Hrrestan. When he and Hrriss had put out the word that volunteers were needed, the response had been so overwhelmingly enthusiastic that they'd had to set up two shifts. Feeding the large crew presented no problem; over a hundred households had offered to supply meals.

"At this rate, it could be finished in two days," Todd told Hrrestan, who was sitting at a safe distance from the sawyers, going over the blueprints. Amid loud cries to keep clear of danger, workers raised the pylons for the foundation. Gringg, using mighty hammers, almost casually pounded them into the ground. From where they sat, Todd could see how enormous the finished complex would be. But then, the Gringg liked a lot of space. The curved archways were a lot like the halls on their ship.

"As quickly as the rlba sets," Hrrestan agreed cheerfully in Low Hrruban. "It is hot enough to dry the sap, but not too hot. Donations of furnishings have also been coming in. Have you noticed them? I asked Kelly and Nrrna to take careful notes so the donors can be thanked."

The generosity of the Rraladoonans was indeed impressive. Piles of tapestries, cushions, carefully boxed works of art, even some electronic entertainment equipment, lay upon outspread tarps under a vast expanse of waterproof canvas. The period of settled weather had been chosen intentionally, but with such fine gifts, no chance was being taken. Kelly and Nrrna climbed around the heap of goods, compiling a rough inventory.

"Hey, the pickings are great! The Gringg'll be able to furnish several embassies with what's come in," Kelly called to Todd, waving her clipboard.

Todd grinned, and held up a hand, still slightly yellowed from last week's bruising rock. Hrrestan glanced at it.

"Kiachif tracked the culprit down."

"He did?" Todd was surprised. "Is he still breathing?" he asked, knowing Kiachif's penchant for making the punishment fit the crime.

Hrrestan grinned. "Kiachif *is* careful to keep his customers. The man is from a trading company which does a lot of business with Spacedep. With all the false rumors being circulated, he evidently believed that the Gringg were going to be allowed sanctions that would ruin his business."

"So, what punishment fit his crime?" Todd asked, seeing Hrrestan was amused.

"Tell, tell, tell!" Kelly cried, coming over to join them.

"Kiachif demanded a cut-rate for all merchandise he is now empowered to supply at the spaceport." Hrrestan's dropped jaw indicated how well he approved of the solution, and Todd's smile was just as big.

Kelly turned wide eyes on her husband. "You've given up fighting the spaceport?"

"Well," Todd said, dragging out the word and the suspense, "a triangle is a much more stable construction than a two-sided affair." He heaved a sigh. "And with the Gringg mediating, I don't foresee the problems that obsessed me when the project was first suggested."

"The Gringg have done us many favors," Hrrestan said, and answered a hail from a group of workers, leaving the two Reeves together.

"That's a tremendous relief, darling," Kelly said, giving him a firm hug and a long kiss. "You don't know how Nrrna and I have worried . . ."

"Oh, yes, I do," Todd said, and held her tightly for a long moment more when she would have disengaged. "Yes, I know," he added more softly, "and I've blessed you for letting me make up my own mind."

"Humph," she said, struggling out of his embrace. "As if *any* agency but you will make up *your* mind!" Todd followed her as she went back to inventory-taking. "So when will that start?"

"Right after Snake Hunt," Todd replied, with a broad sweep of his arm. "Which will be soon. Ben Adjei predicts it'll start in two days at the most"

Kelly gave a groan of dismay. "Oh, lordy, will we have time to finish the Gringg house?"

Todd laughed, waving his hand at the hustling workers. "I don't see why not. At least they'll have a roof over their heads. They're as eager to join the Hunt as anyone else on Rraladoona right now." He grinned broadly. "That'll be some sight! Gringg tackling Big Momma Snakes."

Nrrna looked up from note-taking. "Hrriss says to tell you zat ze Sighters say ze snakes are gazzering on ze sea marshes. Some are even heading for ze dunes."

"Good, good!" Todd said, nodding.

Nrrna grinned. "Ze children have talked of nozzing else all day. Zey arre eager to show Zeddy what a G.B.M.S. looks like."

"From a safe distance, I hope." Todd looked around. There were numerous children on the site, but he couldn't spot his twins. "That reminds me: where are they?"

Kelly glanced up. "Hmm? They were around here just a minute ago, with Teddy in tow. Together with Nrrna's two, they're so inseparable I'm starting to think of them as the Fearless Five." She stood up and called out the twins' names.

"Over here, Dad," Alec's unhappy voice came from around the back of the tarpaulins.

Todd found the five youngsters sitting together in a heap. Hrruna had her tail wound firmly around Teddy's leg, and Hrrunival was sandwiched between the Alley Cats with his head on Alison's lap. All of them wore glum expressions.

"So what's wrong here, Cats?" Todd asked.

"Daddy, couldn't Teddy stay here with us?" the twins asked in hopeful unison. "We're afraid if he goes away, we'll never see him ever."

"Well, since his mother's a starship captain as well as a fully accredited consul to Rraladoona, she might be spending a lot of time either in the embassy or running cargoes between our world and his," Todd explained. "So you might get to see him as often as you do Ali Kiachif."

"That'd be okay," Alec said. He had screwed his face up under his mop of red hair, hardly daring to let hope show.

"You may be absolutely certain that we will be staying in touch with our Gringg friends," Kelly promised, sitting down on the tarp's edge beside them.

"How?" Alison asked.

"How?" Todd echoed, beating Alec's identical query.

Kelly smiled. "Oh, Grizz has signed on my computer bulletin board. Her engineer and that marvellous Cardiff worked out a conversion program. Her entries will be holographic or audio/video for a time, but the Gringg have all the parameters to create a congruent written-language program. I gave them a lot of read-and-listen books to help them connect the spoken to the written word."

"What kind of books?" Todd asked, eyebrows raised, seeing the mischievous gleam in his wife's eyes.

Kelly affected innocence. "Very simple ones to start with. Children's books, like *The Three Bears*, and *Winnie the Pooh*."

Todd laughed and hugged her close. "Thank you, love."

"But of course! I don't want to lose touch with them either," Kelly said, and reassured the children with her smile. "So you can message to Teddy as often as you want."

"I'm glad," Alison said, seizing Teddy's paw. "I like him."

Teddy blinked at her shyly. "I like you too, Alison."

"And me?" Hrrunival demanded, determined not to be left out.

"And you. All of you." The young Gringg bestowed rib-cracking hugs on each of his dear friends, which left them gasping for the breath to giggle.

"Teddy is going to be able to ride out on Hunt with us tomorrow, isn't he, Dad?" Alec asked, his tone demanding an affirmative. "Hrriss said he could have that old plodder of his."

Todd scowled. "It may not be tomorrow. And it might not be safe. Have you considered what Captain Grizz thinks of all this?"

"Oh, she wants to go, too," Hrruna said. "She is very interested in snake eggs. Teddy told her about his lunch that day."

"Please, Dad?" "Please?" "Please, Uncle Zodd?"

"We will stay back where it is safe," Hrruna promised, opening large green eyes at him. Todd sighed.

"Let's talk it over with your parents later."

"Oh, there you are!" Ken Reeve said, peering in under the makeshift tent flap. He held up his camcorder. "Part of the frame is up, and they're setting the braces for one wall. I thought I'd immortalize this historic moment of galactic cooperation. I'm looking for models to show the scale of the building," he said, glancing meaningfully at the children. "Any volunteers?"

"Oh, yes!" exclaimed both Alley Cats at once, springing to their feet.

They dragged the rest of the Fearless Five behind them, although no one required much urging. Kelly and Todd, holding hands, followed more slowly.

With the same Hrruban and Hayuman skills that had raised the Friendship Bridge, a mighty, cavelike building—translated from an architectural design by Honey—was already starting to take shape. Part of the first level, which would support a solidly buttressed terrace, was cantilevered over the river, so that the water-loving Gringg could dive into the warm, tropical water from their dwelling. Todd admired its handsome lines as much as he did its symbolism.

"Gosh, your own swimming hole, right inside your house!" Alec said, catching the gist of the design immediately. "Hey, Dad, this is a great idea! Can we run a walkway right to the swimming hole? It would be terrific!"

"You wouldn't say that in no-see-um season," Todd said with a mock grumble.

"Aw, Dad!" the twins chorused.

Hrriss and Eonneh pulled themselves away from their conference with the senior builder, a heavy-set Gringg with a graying mane and muzzle.

"Are you pleased with what you have wrought, friend Zodd?" Hrriss asked.

"More and more," Todd said, waving a hand at the building framework. "That's a grand design, Honey, functional and impressive."

The architect sighed. "It is not often such an opportunity is given. I am sorry I shall never live in it." But he eyed his design with evident satisfaction. "Others shall stay as the permanent residents. I and my mate and offspring will only be occasional visitors."

"Well, you'll be welcome whenever you part space to come here," Todd said. "We've certainly enjoyed your visit."

"I contemplate with great sorrow the ending, and I thank you for the invitation to join in the Hunt festivities."

"Couldn't, and wouldn't, leave you out of them," Todd said instantly. "It's just too bad we don't have horses strong enough for you to take part in the Hunt itself."

"Zat is so," Hrriss added, dropping his jaw in a broad grin. "You make even a Big Momma Snake zink twice about attacking."

"I will enjoy what is possible," Eonneh said, with the usual equanimity of the Gringg, "from the shuttle."

"Well, then, Fate protect any snake that gets in your way. In any case, you'll be more than welcome, if only to keep our assorted offspring from haring away to find big snakes by themselves," Todd said with a laugh. "This is the time to see Rraladdon at its best, during New Home Week. Every Rraladoonan who can scrape up the fare from Earth or one of the colonies comes home. We'll introduce you to as many as you can tolerate meeting. They'll spread the word about our new trade allies with no need for tall tales and embroideries. That I can promise!"

chapter twelve

Two mornings later, sighters landed their light helicraft outside Todd's bedroom window just after dawn to inform him that the hundreds of female snakes were nearly finished with their egg-laying in sandy dunes. Between one breath and another, Todd roused out of a sound sleep to full organizational mode. As he dressed, he reviewed one or two points that he wanted Robin to check out, but despite the overlapping problems with Spacedep and the Gringg, long familiarity with Snake Hunts assured him that they were ready for the snakes. Robin was a good organizer and meticulous with details, so Todd anticipated few problems. But then, the snakes might not cooperate. They could create glitches almost as if they were testing the Hayumans and Hrrubans who had invaded their traditional routes. Years of coping had provided ample experience to handle anything that could possibly happen. He hoped!

Fortified by a good breakfast, he and Hrriss reined their Hunt horses in the middle of the village square in front of the Assembly Hall. The peripheral support personnel—Sighters, Beaters, Lures, Wranglers, and First-Aid crews—as important as the Teams who herded the snakes along the way, were all accounted for. The complements of the individual Teams were still assembling, their Team leaders checking each person to ensure that gear was in proper order and appearance. The Aids were well supplied with traditional medical gear, plus big tubes of the healing salve vrrela, good for any general wound, but a sovereign remedy for rroamal poisoning. The mere touch of the toxic vines was enough to raise large welts even on furred skin. Team members carried tubes of the salve as well, but it wasn't just Team riders who blundered into the poisonous weed.

Experienced Hayuman and Hrruban hunters wore "chaps and straps" to protect them against rroamal and the thin whips of young branches that scored flesh on a hell ride through the forest. Hardhats were buckled across chins and inspected for soundness. Where a Team had green riders, one member was assigned as "wrangler" to assist those who might have trouble controlling their horses in the excitement of the Hunt.

The square was crowded with double the indigenous population of Rraladoon, included many who got vicarious thrills from observing those who were qualified to participate in the Hunt, as well as visiting dignitaries from planetary governments all over Hrruban and Hayuman space.

Not only did the Hunt provide a real boost to the treasury of the colony, it attracted enough competent people to help the resident conservationists drive the snakes safely back to their natural preserve with a minimum of loss. Even when there had been few riders to control the thousands of reptiles moving, wholesale killing had been prohibited; the most ardent ProLife fanatic admitted to the necessity for discreet culling of a species whose females each laid hundreds of eggs, a large proportion of which survived natural disasters.

The decision of a safety kill or capture of a certain number of snakes was the prerogative of the Hunt Masters, requiring split-second decisions during the high excitement of the Hunt. Fresh snake meat was a delicacy, generally only available during Hunt season or when marauding young males attacked outlying farms.

Todd and Hrriss checked with each Team leader that all riders had snake sacks and operational handsets. Someone always forgot these essentials. As usual, there was one young rider who protested having to wear a poxy belt unit which he was certain would hamper him. Hrriss gave him the cold-eyed stare of a person who did not wish to argue.

"No handset, no Hunt, young man," Hrriss said firmly. Grumbling gracelessly, the Hayuman took the unit and retreated out of sight of the Masters of the Hunt.

The onlookers framed the main square, keeping a judicious distance from the heels of excited horses cavorting and showing off. Old hands at this Hunt, like Todd's Gypsy, Hrriss's Rrhee, and the old mares that Errala and Hrrin used, calmly circulated, miraculously avoiding a kick or a bite.

"Sappers?" Todd asked, checking his pad.

"I have hrrrd from Hrrol," Hrriss confirmed, pointing a sharp claw at his pad to underscore that entry. "She says zey have finished laying mine charges under bridges, and blockading with fences, zorns, and razor wire over all other accesses leading to vulnerable targets. Zey are spread out along ze route for stragglers, particularly the old Space Center." Hrriss, was not above grinning at Todd over that. "Lures are ranged along the route, and zere are relief and backup riders ready to accompany the Teams."

The Lures, mounted on dirt bikes, were trained in their function—to attract renegade snakes of any size and "lure" them back to the main drive. Their bikes and persons were liberally smeared with bacon fat, redolent and irresistible to snakes.

"Great," Todd said. "We've got about half an hour before we have to ride out. I'd better let the guests get into position." He informed the heli pilots.

The excited clamor, mostly from fast-time Hunters—duffers in Rraladoonan parlance—vied with the hacking sound of copter blades beating the air, the impatient whinny of the occasional horse, and the general babble among old friends reuniting after long separation as Rraladoon prepared for its annual event. While duffers were permitted to accompany hunting teams, they could not participate in the more difficult and dangerous occupations of Beater or Lure, though over the years, some off-world Hunters who showed the proper amount of care and skill could be "promoted" to Hunter status. Few had the patience to be accorded that honor. Many of the duffers who joined in only wanted to have a crack at "one of the big ones," a Great Big Momma Snake, reptiles that reached up to sixteen meters in length. For the ardent predator, the Rraladoon snake provided a sufficiently dangerous prey, and there were many who wanted the accolades that came with bringing in either two live snakes or twelve intact eggs. For a Rraladoonan, it was a Coming of Age Ritual but Hunter-mentalities of all ages vied to meet that challenge.

Pet ocelots, who hunted alongside their masters and mistresses, now huddled underneath horses' bellies or sat on pillions behind their owners' saddles. Hrriss was running a new ocelot this year, Gerrh; a cub of his two beloved pets, Prem and Mehh, who were getting too fat and lazy to run beside horses. The spotted cat sat bolt upright on back of the shifting mare, his tail curled around his haunches much as his master's was. Most Hrrubans tucked their long tails down inside chaps or bandaged them to one leg to prevent accidents.

As one of the Masters of the Hunt, Todd stood up in his stirrups, one hand on Gypsy's neck to steady him. In a stentorian voice, he ran through his usual caveat.

"We are not here to decimate the snake population. If that's your intention, you can stay right here, in this square when we move out," he announced, eyeing the crowd. "The Hunt is for the purpose of controlling the flow of the snakes, driving them back into the salt marshes after they've spawned. When those females come off the dunes, they're hungry! There is plenty of food for them in their regular habitat. Our task is to prevent them from stopping off for a snack on the way." There was appreciative laughter from the crowd.

A timid hand went up among the riders. "But what if a snake attacks me?" a young Human visitor asked. Her riding coat was so new Todd fancied he could see the mark on the cuff where the bar code had been.

"If you should be so unlucky as to have a snake attack you, call in your position and then get out of the way as fast as your horse can carry you; and a snake-chased horse really moves! If flight's not an option, shoot as straight as you know how," Todd said. "That one's for the stewpot. If a snake attacks and gets a taste of blood, it'll go for any hunter near it next year. We call them 'renegades' and they're killed to prevent real trouble later. The snakes that proceed peaceably back into the marshes are to be left alone. Don't provoke them! You don't know what they're capable of. Do not mingle in the main swarm; just flank it. You don't want a snake running up your horse's leg to get a chunk of you!" He grinned then. "I assure you Rraladoonan horses will do their best to keep you clear all by themselves. If you hot-dog, endangering yourself, your mount, or anyone else, the leader of your Team has full right and responsibility to sideline you for the duration. If you don't want to spend the rest of the day in a snake blind, listen to your leader and obey any orders. He or she knows how to save your life. Any questions?'

There were a lot of brash mutters as the inexperienced Hunters mulled over Todd's remarks. It got louder and more intense as the Gringg, led by Kodiak, appeared on foot over the span of the Friendship Bridge.

Fifteen or twenty of the huge aliens had elected to join the Teams, to the amazement and enthusiasm of some of the returning Rraladoonans, and the nervousness of others. Todd was unhappy to see that there was still some distrust among his folk for their newest allies, but he hoped the Gringg performance in the Hunt might alter die-hard notions.

Since there were no horses up to the weight of an adult Gringg, they had agreed to work as assistants to the Beater Teams, whose task was to make enough noise to scare an escaping snake back into the mass. The job was by no means a sinecure. Since the Beaters drove tractors and other light farm machinery fitted with heavy snake-bars, the crews were equipped with noisemakers, flails, and, for use as a last resort, heavy-caliber handguns, anything that could persuade a snake to return to the stream heading south toward their natural habitat.

Todd had Kodiak brief the other Gringg on the safety procedures and then pointed out which driver each Gringg would accompany. Beater Teams One and Two, stationed nearest the spawning sands, got two Gringg apiece.

"Heavy artillery," said a grinning Mark Dautrish, the wheelman for Beater One. He reached down to give Big Paws and Koala a hand up into the cab of the wide-bucket heavy-duty tractor, one of the largest on the planet. It was effective in blocking snakes' escape routes among the marsh grasses, and Mark was wizard in the things he could make his rig do, should push come to shove.

"Move 'em out!" Todd cried as he saw all the Gringg on board their designated vehicles. He pumped a fist in the air. With a roar of engines, the Beaters departed to take up their positions, followed by the Lures, mounted on nippy dirt bikes that looked all too flimsy for the work they had to do.

With Grizz and Eonneh riding in the farm hover truck, Kelly drove slowly enough for the five children to follow on their horses. She also didn't want to bottom the truck with all the weight it currently carried. With her huge arms folded neatly across her belly, Grizz sat with the utmost dignity in the front seat, her bulk crushing Kelly up against the door—rolling the window down gave Kelly the opportunity to lean her upper torso outside. Honey, filling the rear seat, was armed with his ubiquitous pad and stylus. The youngsters were leading Kelly's mare, Calypso, and Alison had a lead rein on Teddy, who was mounted on Rock, the calmest horse in Hrriss' stable. This time the young Gringg sat on a much more professionally modified pack saddle, cushioned by deep fleeces and surrounded by rolls of canvas that acted like a safety belt, preventing him from falling out of the saddle. As the truck reached the square, Kelly hooted the horn to clear a space for her to maneuver the truck inside the crowd, and waved furiously to get Todd's attention. Hrriss noticed her and trotted over.

"Nrrna and the farm managers are lined up at the ranch fences with heavy guns and dynamite in case of tiddlers! Where do you want us?" she called over the din.

"You and ze children go wiz Llewellyn Carn's Beaters toward Boncyks' farm," Hrriss said, checking them on his list, "wherrre the woods end."

"Right you are!" Kelly saluted cheerfully and set the hover truck moving in the right direction. In her rearview mirror, she could see the youngsters urging their horses after her, east toward the river, disappearing among the houses and trees at the edge of town.

"Four Zeams filled and dispatched, twenzy-seven to go," Hrriss informed Todd.

"There you are!" Jilamey exclaimed, forcing his horse through the crowd. The entrepreneur was clad in new and flamboyant riding gear that had nevertheless been chosen with the perils of the Hunt in mind. His hand-unit radio and voder were clipped to crossed bandoliers in the center of his chest where they wouldn't interfere with free movement. After Todd's initial reproof, Jilamey always wore every bit of the compulsory Hunt safety gear, even adding a few pieces of equipment that he considered necessary. His saddlebow was hung with quivers, one full of short spears, another of crossbow quarrels to fit his custom-made, fast-reload weapon, including some marked with the red seal for high explosive. The sedately clad Barrington followed closely behind his master in the small, but very speedy flittercar. Responding to an over-the-shoulder nod from Jilamey, he parked the vehicle beside the Assembly Hall, and disappeared inside.

"Old Overprotective's going to help cook this time!" Jilamey said with an impish grin that made him look like a balding faun. "Out of my way at last. I'm ready, able, and oh-so-willing! Bring on the snakes!"

"Good to see you," Todd said, chuckling. "Now that you've arrived, our Team is present and accounted for. Take a position next to Hrrin and Errala." Jilamey nudged his horse until it edged in between the two Hrrubans.

"We musst all move to our assigned places," Hrriss said.

"Then, my old friend, let us go!" Todd's grin was as much for the memories of past Hunts as it was for the present one. The stresses and problems of the recent past were all behind them. This Hunt was *now!*

A Sighter flew in overhead. The copter swooped low, facing the Hunt Masters. Through the open hatch, Dar Kendrath waved wildly to get Todd's attention. He pointed to his wrist and held up one finger, then five more. The main swarm would reach the dunes in about fifteen minutes.

"That's cutting it close," Todd said to Hrriss, giving Dar the thumbs-up sign that he understood the message. He stood in his stirrups, twisting around at his waist. "At the trrrrrot, forward!" he yelled, swinging his arm over his head in an age-old gesture.

Dar veered his craft out of the way of the oncoming horses. The second Sighter chopper, a good distance from the throng, followed a moment later.

Hrrula, at the head of Team Two, with Robin Reeve as his second riding behind him, wheeled his horse around. His Team was full of visiting duffers, some of whom were reasonably good riders, but Hrrula was competent at keeping Team members from coming to grief.

"Moving out," the Hrruban said, his sharp teeth flashing brightly in a wide smile. "See you at ze salt mrrrshes!"

Jilamey paired off with Hrrin as Team One moved out. As Todd and Hrriss led them along the well-worn river trail, they could hear the two of them shouting excitedly to each other about grids and ships. That left the one recently promoted Hunter, a man named Harris, riding beside Hrrin's mate, Errala, with Jan and Don, Team One's Wrangler and sharpshooter, bringing up the rear. Team One was lighter in personnel than most of the other groups of Hunters, but as the team that took responsibility for steering the lead snakes, they needed to be able to peel away and move faster than any other.

Todd held them to a fast trot until they reached the head of the desert, where the snakes laid their eggs. The weather was slightly overcast, which was a minor blessing. Bright sunshine meant hours of hot riding. Gerrh twitched nervously on his pillion, reacting to the strong odor of snake which a slight breeze wafted down the river path. Errala covered her sensitive nose with a citrus-scented cloth, and coughed. Team One cut along the trail past the other teams in place. As Todd and Hrriss passed, each leader acknowledged their readiness.

The radio crackled on Todd's hip.

"They're swarming!" Leah Kalman's shout came through clearly. "Teams Six and Seven spreading out."

Todd squeezed his legs into Gypsy's sides and lifted him into a gallop, heard his team follow his lead. They arrived at the edge of the marsh in time to see Mark Dautrish rolling up his big tractor with its wide bucket inches above the ground. No snake could squirm through that space.

Several young tiddlers, none more than four meters long, broke in that direction. At the sight of the sharp metal, they thought better of it and cut away toward Todd. Hrrula's team was circling around to the north.

"Yow!" Todd exclaimed, his gaze sweeping the heaving multitude of snakes.

"Numbers have increased beyond estimate," Hrriss called in Low Hrruban. "More must have survived than usual. Good for us that we can trade the excess to the Gringg now they've gotten a taste for the flavor."

"This swarm's going to take real handling, partner," Todd called back and then began shouting orders to the other riders. "Spread out! Contain them. We've got to keep them rolling or they'll stack up here and we'll have the devil's own time!"

Big Paws had his powerful body crouched so low to the ground that he was almost on all fours. But his fangs and claws were bared, and the small snakes that had tried to scoot out past him quickly reversed, and he herded them back to the marked route. When a three-meter tiddler made a hasty break to dive between his legs, he seized it at the back of the neck, and flung it bodily into the main stream of snakes leaving the dunes. He glanced up and waved at Todd.

"Fun!" he cried.

The subsonics in his voice, which tended only to disconcert or annoy the

Hayumans and Hrrubans, seemed to cause a violent reaction among the reptiles. At the sound of his rumbling roar, several that were headed in that direction stopped where they were and doubled back on their own lengths.

"Look at zat!" Hrriss said gleefully. "A new deterrent! Zey must dislike Gringg vibrrations!"

Todd, vigorously applying his quarterstaff to curtail breakouts, grinned back. "Keep up the good work, Big Paws!"

"Reh!" the Gringg chortled, flinging another four-meter snake overhand. It struck the ground on its nose and hastily sought refuge among its fellows, slithering away as quickly as it could from the gigantic black-and-white terror.

Todd wheeled to follow the vanguard of the reptiles through the woods. The snakes were relatively placid up near the dunes, in strong contrast to the way they would act later on, when they were tired and the clutching hunger had fully kicked in. Then they became dangerously cunning. The slightest breath of air which carried rumors of a quick meal caused them to take any reasonable chance to avoid the Hunters and find food.

"Ware!" Todd cried, pointing at a pair of very small snakes, probably at the dunes for their first clutches, who zipped around the front of the tractor.

"I'll get the one on the right!" Jilamey shouted, waving his crossbow over his head and spurring his horse through the marsh waters after the snake. He aimed and loosed the bolt, but the quarrel struck mud, missing the tiddler completely. His horse slipped, nearly precipitating him into the fetid waters. Jilamey was improving, but he would never be a match for Kelly, and Todd missed her support on the Team. She certainly wouldn't have missed an easy shot like that, but she had offered to cart the captain around.

A roar sounded from behind the farm machine, and one of the young snakes came sailing over the top of the tractor to land in a heap on the path. Todd jumped. Don swore.

"Fardle it, I didn't think they could fly!"

"Compliments of Koala," Dautrish called to the Team. "She missed the other one, though!"

"I'll call ahead!" Todd said, and thumbed the switch on his handset. "One escapee, heading west from the dunes."

"Got it, Todd," replied Leah Kalman and broke the contact.

The river road became a living, writhing sea of reptilian bodies. Todd kneed Gypsy to the edge of the marsh grasses, loping alongside the leading snakes and keeping the foot of his quarterstaff poised for use. His Team fanned out in single file behind him, riding herd.

A flashgun popped to one side of the path. Todd caught the glare out of the comer of one eye. A margin Hunter, turning back a tiddler that had strayed between the cordon of horses as they entered the woods. The terrain here favored the snakes, who could disappear without trace into the undergrowth by virtue of their natural protective patterning. It took quick eyes to make sure none of the leaders strayed, encouraging others to follow it. Not for the first time, Todd was grateful to the river for bordering one side of the snake run, keeping the Hunters from having to double up Teams along this section.

A low ridge of rock rose up in the middle of his path. Avoiding the obstacle, Todd hugged the opposite side and came out ten feet behind the lead snakes. He urged Gypsy forward. Once they came level again, the experienced horse dropped back to a trot.

From behind him came the raucous snarl that told him that Gerrh had joined the hunt. He risked a quick glance over his shoulder. The young ocelot had leaped from his perch and was after a three-meter-long tiddler that was attempting to go the wrong way around the rocky upthrust. Hrriss cantered by his pet and administered a thwock! to the snake's head with the butt end of his spear. It coiled up and headed into the stream without further hesitation. Gerrh galloped after his master and leaped neatly back onto Rrhee's back.

The ridge had provided one of the few breathers the Hunters got on the trail, where geography did their work for them in keeping the snakes from straying. After that, the long hot ride was made even more dangerous by low branches which knocked against Todd's helmet and shoulders while he tracked the swift-moving snakes along their way.

He passed the first of the snake blinds: one of the small, well-sealed rlawood cottages smeared with the citrus perfume that kept snakes from smelling the contents. The broad window at trailside was filled with spectators staring out at him through field glasses.

"Todd, I've got a lively one here," Don called through the handset. "Could use your help."

With one hand, he laid the reins along Gypsy's neck and turned him around, while he lifted the small communications unit to his mouth.

"Hrriss, take point. I'm circling back to help Don."

"Rrright!" The friends passed in mid-gallop, Hrriss spurring Rrhee to catch up with the lead snakes.

Far back along the line, Jan was overstretched, herding much more of the cordon of young reptiles than she could really handle as Don went in pursuit. The sharpshooter waved to Todd as he approached, and pointed at the five-and-a-half-meter snake he was pacing. As steady as if he were sitting on still ground, Don's rifle aimed at the back of the reptile's head.

"The damned thing won't go back in line!" he called. He ducked a branch. "I've got a bead on it, but I don't want to kill it if it's just ornery."

"Crank a ground shot next to its head on the right," Todd said, unlimbering his quarterstaff to help prod.

He called for a Lure to come and assist. Nodding, Don squeezed the trigger, and a puff of dust kicked up on the right of the snake's nose. With a violent check, the snake turned a sharp corner and veered toward the stream, but over five meters of body was a lot to maneuver. The tail whipped around and struck Don's galloping horse, knocking it off its feet.

"Wheeee-ee-ee!" the gelding screamed, falling onto its side. Don jumped off and, cursing, rolled into a stand of bushes. He emerged, brushing himself off. Todd raised his flashgun and reined Gypsy to a stop between the fallen horse and rider, standing guard.

The incident attracted the attention of more tiddlers. Todd shot off flash after flash of brain-searing light to divert the predatory snakes while Don helped the gelding to its feet and regained his saddle. Suddenly, a leather-clad Lure on a cycle burst out from among the trees and began riding a serpentine trail between Todd and the mass of snakes. Across her shoulders was a fresh sheep hide, inside out. The heavy scent of blood got the slow-witted attention of the stray snakes, and they followed the Lure, who led them to the main stream. The bike tilted to an angle and roared down the riverbank, out of the snakes' reach.

"Whew!" Don said. "Thank heavens for loaves and little fishes."

"Ow, this thing gets hot," Todd said, letting the flashgun fall on its strap against his chap-covered leg, and airing his gloved hand. Don swung up and leaned over to slap Todd on the shoulder.

"Thanks, friend," he said, reining the horse toward the perimeter of the snake cordon. "I'm not even bruised." Team Two was coming up fast behind them, and Don paced in a couple of beats before Hrrula arrived.

Todd turned Gypsy inland and galloped onward to come level with Hrriss. He passed another group of Beaters with Cinnamon. They were sweeping the snakes back onto the path with brooms, flails, and in the Gringg's case, his own big feet. A jab here, a prod there, and the tiddlers stayed in the boundaries of the swarm. Cinnamon waved and called out happily as he and Hrriss passed.

The day was going well. No injuries or losses had been reported yet from up the line. The most serious problems would probably arise on the Boncyk farm, still some klicks ahead.

Kelly felt as if they'd been waiting for hours in the meadow near the Boncyk farm, but she knew it hadn't been more than one. It just seemed longer, because the children, antsy with anticipation, were on the verge of driving her crazy. She'd known all along the folly of bringing youngsters into the heart of a Snake Hunt. Carn had brought up her horse, so at least she had a chance of chasing them down if necessary. Staying back with a Beater Team was simply the best way for them, and their guests, to see the action without getting hurt. She'd explained the roles of each of the hunting Teams and the auxiliaries. The Gringg listened with careful attention, but the children, who'd heard it repeated for years, were bored.

"Now, if anything goes wrong," Kelly repeated again and again, hoping her instructions stuck in the minds of the excited children, "you pull back! Get out of the way of the Hunters! Immediately! Is that clear?"

"Yes, Mom."

"Yes, Aunt Gelli."

"Yes, Kelly," Teddy promised, wiggling deep into the sheepskins.

Somehow she wasn't totally reassured. In the hour since they'd taken up positions, the five youngsters had made friends with the Beaters, galloped up to take a look at the Boncyk farm, and found the nearest citron-covered snake blind. Alec came galloping back with a report of who was inside it, watching for the snakes to come by.

"That Admiral is in there," her son announced. "The cranky one with white hair."

"Alec!"

"In a blue uniform," Alison said. "Well, he grumbled at us."

"Admiral Barnstable?" Kelly asked. "Huh. Whaddya bet he's here more to keep an eye on the Gringg than the snakes!"

She hadn't her voder on just then, but nevertheless looked over to where Grizz sat at her ease in the soft meadow grass. The captain daintily plucked a tiny yellow flower between two claws and examined it closely. Delicately, she extended it to her mate, sitting with his shaggy golden side pressed against hers.

"See here, Eonneh, the five-petal structure. Most attractive, is it not?" she asked, her red eyes gentle.

"Most attractive," Eonneh replied, accepting the flower. Their claws intertwined.

There's more going on there than a botany lesson, Kelly thought, with a silly smile of approval on her face.

"They're coming," called Llewellyn Carn. Kelly stood up in her stirrups and let out a sharp whistle for the children.

"Come on!" yelled Alec, and headed Tornado uphill.

Seeing his friends respond, Teddy wheeled the lethargic Rock in a wide loop, and at a dignified plod, followed Alec back toward the threshing machine.

Admiral Barnstable, pacing around outside the snake blind, felt unwilling to enter the reeking enclosure until it was absolutely necessary. He noticed that there was some commotion up on the high meadow where Mrs. Reeve and her horde of children were waiting. Hastily hiking up the dusty path, he called out to her.

"What's going on?"

"Please get back to the blind, Admiral," Kelly shouted. "The snakes are coming."

"If you're safe, I'll be safe," Barnstable said, panting a little as he reached the crest of the low hill. The Reeve woman had a small arsenal's worth of primitive weapons arrayed on her sheepskin-padded saddle. There was a strong smell of animal sweat and excrement coming from across the lea to the right. Looking down the hill toward the farm buildings, Barnstable saw a thin, dour-faced farmer and his family waiting on horseback, behind an odd assortment of heavy farm machinery that had been rolled up to the low fence. What a ridiculous barricade, he thought. He turned back to eye the two adult Gringg, seated on the grass nearby, who met his gaze pleasantly.

"Aren't you carrying any defensive weapons?" Barnstable demanded. "These snakes are highly dangerous and excitable."

"Why will you not believe that we have no such tools?" Honey asked, then held up his paws. He flexed his digits, and the sharp claws gleamed in the gray sunlight. "These natural fittings are all we need."

The sounds of galloping, and a curious, terrifying hiss, came from the edge of the woods. Mrs. Reeve tensed, and raised a loaded crossbow. Barnstable turned.

Out of the thin forest came a dappled, tossing, undulating reptilian river. Barnstable's heart started to pound in his chest and his mouth went dry. He sucked his cheeks for saliva. This was like the prelude to a battle. Beside him, the enormous farm machine revved its engine and bucked down the slope toward the snakes.

Two horses, looking amazingly small next to the swarm, cantered along, prodding an occasional snake that tried to break free. What Reeve and Hrriss were doing looked almost easy. For all their admonitions about the dangers involved in the Hunt, it looked like there was nothing more to herding snakes than quick reflexes and concentration. Barnstable was unimpressed.

Then the wind changed to the southwest. Instead of blowing into their faces from the salt marshes, the shift brought a miasma of heavy, stinking air direct from the byres behind them. Barnstable gagged.

"What is that appalling stench?" Barnstable asked, pinching his nostrils shut.

"Pigs," said Kelly amiably. "Boncyks raise China and Poland pigs. No help for it now"—an urgent note crept into her voice—"the snakes have the scent."

The tumbling tide of snake shifted until it was heading directly towards them. Everett Cabot Barnstable had a sudden change of heart regarding the difficulty of managing thousands of snakes as the whole boiling wave of them seemed to come straight at him. For the first time in his life, he experienced gut-twisting terror.

"Llewellyn!" Kelly shouted, angling her steed between Barnstable and the stream. The horses, having caught the snake stink, were dancing frantically about, their riders controlling their antics with unconcerned skill. Teddy bounced up and down like a ball in his high saddle.

"Behind me, Kelly," Carn shouted, raising his hand unit. "Lures! Edge of the Boncyk farm! Now!"

The thresher rolled around the crest of the hill and headed for the outbuildings. The huge machine moved down like an avalanche, pushing the snakes away. A cluster of the reptiles avoided the Beaters by going every which way at once, and looped uphill at speed.

"They're headed to Mr. Boncyk's farmyard!" Alec cried. "Can we go help?"

"No!" Kelly exclaimed. "You stay right here or—!" She left the threat of dire punishment hanging.

Then a three-meter tiddler attempted a fast break around the wheels of the thresher. Carn promptly lowered the boom on it and Kelly shot the crossbow bolt directly into its brainpan. The snake lashed about in muscular spasms, but it was no longer a threat. One of Carn's assistants dismounted and stuffed the writhing corpse into a snake bag.

Todd and Hrriss galloped by, their attention on the fan of stragglers who were enticed by the strong swine smell. Hrriss growled orders into his handset for Don and Jan to keep the rest of the snakes moving down the path to the marshes.

Having learned by bitter experience in the early years of their homesteading just how tempting their stock was to snake, Wayne and Anne Boncyk prepared for the worst. In fact, as individual defenders went, they had more personnel massed on their property than any other farm on the route. As luck would have it, their prize sows tended to farrow every year about the same time as Snake Hunt. But the shrewd and aggressive sows had learned to defend their piglets against these wriggling predators. The females were ruthless and attacked any snake that crossed into their tract, chopping them into squirming pieces with sharp little hooves.

The males were even more aggressive, charging at any snake, no matter what its size, that dared impinge on their territory. Todd had nicknamed the swine herd Wayne's War Boars, euphonious even if there were more sows than boars.

Just to the right of the line of outbuildings, the pigpens were surrounded by high, lightweight but sharp-edged, metal barriers that could rip open the belly of any snake trying to crawl through. Wayne left the spoor of snake blood on them year after year to try and scare off new marauders, though Todd and others warned him that it worked just the opposite way. Snakes happily consumed their own dead. But to get to the barriers, let alone the sties containing the piglets, the snakes had to pass the cordon of angry boars.

Todd counted the boars ranged along the white metal fence, and gave up at thirty, each averaging about 275 kilos. Two black and white Border collies ran up and down the line, using The Look to keep the pigs from wandering away before the battle began.

"C'mon, Reeve! Get these snakes out of here," Wayne cried, hoisting his bow to his shoulder. That was the signal to his crew. They pressed forward to help the Hunters form a strong cordon against the advancing mass of snakes. With hand gestures, Todd directed them to the best points to reinforce the defenses around the byres.

"Where're the rest of the barricades?" Todd demanded, looking at the bare rear edge of the pens.

"Got a stand of new olive trees," Wayne said, pointing beyond the pen to a grove of young saplings with gray-green foliage. "I don't want them snakes mowing them down."

"For life and love, Wayne," Todd said in a groan, slapping himself in the head. "Snakes don't eat olives, they eat meat!"

"The boars'll get 'em," the stockman assured him.

The inrush of stragglers made for a lively few minutes, to the joy of Jilamey Landreau, who'd been somewhat disappointed with the tame atmosphere of this year's Hunt. Once on the Boncyk property, the Hunters and snakes were within a few kilometers of the marshes, the end of the journey, which meant that Jilamey had only a short time in which to secure his second snake to complete his Rite of Passage, or go without for another year. Snake sack in hand, the Human was casting frantically about him for a likely catch.

"Jilamey!" Todd shouted. "Help Anne!"

With a guilty start, the younger man wound the sack around his saddle horn and kicked his horse over to where Mrs. Boncyk and two farmhands were fighting off tiddlers who were slithering around the pen looking for any weakness. The open edge drew the wily squirmers like a magnet. Boars rushed to protect their families, getting underfoot of the horses and squealing fiercely whenever a quarterstaff blow meant for a snake struck one of them in the back. Jilamey prodded escaping snakes until they retreated far enough upwind to lose the pig-redolent air. Most departed hastily for the marshes. One struck back at his quarterstaff. Anne Boncyk raised the crossbow at her knee, and fired.

The quarrel hit the ground under the snake's jaw, missing it by feet. Anne reined her horse away, not quite believing she'd missed.

Hurriedly, Jilamey kicked his horse over and bashed the surprised snake over the head with his quarterstaff, which made it recoil and double away.

"Aim a little higher," he called. "I make that mistake myself."

"My darned sights must be off," Anne swore, fiddling with the cross hairs.

There was a tremendous explosion on the opposite side of the barn. Todd grabbed for his radio.

"Anybody! What was that?"

"Sapper mine," Kelly's voice replied. "A horde of tiddlers was moving in between the house and the granary. The survivors are stopping to eat the carrion. You won't have to worry about this avenue for a while. Team Two's moving up! I just saw Hrrula."

"Thanks, hon," Todd said, replacing the unit on its clip. He gestured to Don to move out to the opposite end of the grounds to check that no small snakes were trying to sneak around the far end of the building.

Hrriss had had his eye on a good-sized Momma Snake that moved up among the ranks of younger reptiles. The smell of delicious fresh meat just beyond the barrier tempted it away from the road home. At present, the huge snake was staying out of range of Hrriss' sharp spear, but still trying to make a break for the pigpens. Gerrh leaped down to join the boars hunting small snakes. The pigs grunted at him, but didn't attack, accepting him tentatively as a fellow predator.

Inside the smelly enclosure, the sows were running round and round their mud patches, screaming challenges to the snakes outside; detailing in Pig—Todd grinned to himself—just exactly what they'd do to any reptiles they got.

The screams of the attacking boars as they stomped tiddlers to death added to the din as the Hunters tried to restore order. Todd's horse slipped slightly on the bloody pieces of one snake. The boar who had killed it was eating some of the flesh with savage grunts of pleasure. Todd held tight with his knees as Gypsy recovered and got to more secure footing. Then he chased four live snakes away from a damaged portion of the fence that lay tilted, leaving a tempting rent through which a small snake would squeeze.

"We are here," Hrrula's voice called through the radio link.

"Good," Todd replied. "I want to split this stream of snakes into two parts, send 'em around the farm and down into the swamps. Can you set up a blockade just below the fence with the Beaters to deflect them?"

"Will do," Hrrula affirmed.

Hrriss' Momma Snake made one more effort to escape before he harried it beyond the farm. Once it was upwind of the pigs, the smell of salt air touched its sensitive tongue and nostrils, reminding it that there were easier meals elsewhere.

"He's down, he's down!" the handsets screeched. With a final swipe at a pair of tiddlers who'd just decided to leave, Todd grabbed for his radio.

"Report! Who is it?"

"Hrrula," wailed the voice, evidently one of Team Two's duffers.

"It's me, Todd," Robin's voice exclaimed, interrupting the hysterical outcry. "Hrrula got spun off when a snake twined a foreleg. He's okay, but there are a couple of Momma Snakes coming around your side of the barn with a flood of tiddlers. I'll join you as soon as I've got him up again. Llewellyn's blocking the path. Five Lures just came out of the woods to help. Hey, it's the Biker Babes!"

"Thanks, Robin," Todd said, smiling grimly. His eyes met Hrriss's over the pigpens. They were in for a tough fight. Momma Snakes were tough and canny, having survived many years of Snake Hunts, and they were *big*.

Another charge exploded noisily, alerting them that more snakes had tried to enter the vulnerable farmyard. Not for the first time, Todd cursed Boncyk, who refused to move his pigs to a more secure location during the farrowing season. The sharp whine and buzz of motorbikes cut through other noises, marking the arrival of the all-female team of Lures Robin had nicknamed the Biker Babes.

Robin had been right to call the mass of snakes a flood. The very ground undulated with a hissing carpet that inexorably flowed toward the sties. The dry grass beneath the snakes sounded as if it were on fire. All the Hunters who were free moved to intercept them.

"Blockade in position, Todd," Llewellyn Carn reported by radio. "Hope you can handle what's up there!"

The smaller reptiles braided in and out between the hooves of the horses, causing even some of the Hunt-hardened mounts to dance nervously. Not even seasoned horses liked a snake twining up their legs, so most were lashing out, fore and hind. The eleven-meter length of the first Momma Snake slithered into view, making directly for the War Boars. She wouldn't be intimidated by their hooves or their cries of defiance, as she could swallow one whole while on the move. Todd fretted that the few Hunters he had on hand might not be equal to her determined challenge.

Then the second of the Momma Snakes appeared around the edge of the barn, pursued by Anne Boncyk and Kelly. They loosed crossbow bolts, hitting it along the back just below the head, which distracted it, but didn't really slow it down. Hrriss and Jan joined the chase.

"In!" Kelly called to Todd. "This one's a real trier."

"Where are the children?" Todd asked, looking about him in panic. The ponies would be vulnerable to this Big Momma.

"Back there!" Kelly gestured. "With the Gringg!"

Now the cluster of five young riders and their horses, with their gigantic escort, galloped up the rise. Not allowed to carry more dangerous weapons, the Alley Cats and Hrriss's children did have dart guns and slingshots with which they were uncannily expert. Keeping their horses moving at a good distance and parallel to the snakes, they used darts and sling-propelled rocks to distract them from their intended prey and drive them along.

Teddy threw rocks, too. His pad-fingers were too big to fit inside the trigger-guard of a needler, but the stones he threw had the force of a bullet. He hit one snake broadside with a hand-sized stone that opened a bleeding wound on its back. At the smell of blood, several larger snakes swarmed over their unlucky mate, and it was torn to pieces.

"Good shot, Teddy!" Jilamey called. He was reloading his crossbow. "Look out, someone! Get that one!"

Attracted by the new rich musk from Gringg fur, a four-meter tiddler made for Teddy's horse. No one was nearer than Jilamey. Not stopping to think, he spurred his horse forward until he was nearly on top of the reptile before he struck at it with his quarterstaff. The snake evaded his blow and wound up the shaft onto the saddle before he could drop it. Jilamey went for his knife, but the snake trapped his arm. He let out a roar of pain just as the snake opened its huge maw to engulf his head.

"Morra! Chilmeh!" Teddy cried. The little Gringg leaned over toward Jilamey's saddle and grabbed the hissing snake around the throat with one paw. Hauling its head away from Jilamey's body, he began to batter the snake with his other handpaw, his claws rending the thick scales as if they were no more than cotton. Blood spurted, and the snake hung limply in his grasp. Jilamey, rubbing snake spit from his face, stared down at it. Teddy raised his eyes to the Hayuman, almost surprised as Jilamey at what he had done.

"Thank you," Jilamey said sincerely. As he scrubbed at his face, he could feel his heart hammering in his chest. The muscles of his squeezed arm tingled, and he wiggled the fingers to ease them. "Thank you very much."

"Rehmeh," Teddy replied. "I am sorry I got blood on your coat."

"Think nothing of it," Jilamey said, shaking his head in wonder. "You saved my life. You're a real hero, little bear!" He gave a shaking laugh. "People have always warned me about losing my head over Snake Hunting."

A roar from Grizz attracted their attention. The two adult Gringg had caught the Momma Snake that Hrriss was chasing. Grizz had caught it by the tail and was now working her claws up its back to the head. Meanwhile Eonneh tackled its wide-open jaws, attempting to shut them. The Momma had been all set to swallow the War Boar it had stunned. The immense snake writhed in a furious attempt to dislodge one or the other of its attackers.

"DON'T LET IT GO, GRIZZ!" Robin roared. "It'll be twice as dangerous now it's tasted pork blood."

All the farm Hunters converged upon the scene, peppering the snake with quarrels, while at the same time Eonneh was closing its mouth by the simple expedient of locking his claws right through its tough skull and jaw. Gradually its frenzied thrashing subsided to an occasional twitch. Only then did the two Gringg let go, without noticing the very respectful expressions of the other Hunters.

"Great kill, Gringgs. Thanks. But that's one down and still one to go," Wayne said grimly.

The remaining Momma Snake had turned at bay. It was coiled in a huge knot at the corner of the sty, ready to spring on whatever puny creature dared to attack. Todd estimated the snake at a good twelve meters or he'd lost his eye. In that posture and cornered, it would be a bitch to kill. It could strike out in any direction, and even if all of the Hunters charged, it was capable of inflicting considerable damage.

He and Hrriss signalled to the Team to form a circle around the snake. If there was any way to get it moving, they might be able to drive it downhill into the marshes without killing it.

Just then, Jilamey's horse buckled to its knees and sent him over its head, right into a mass of squirming tiddlers trying to brave the bloodstained barriers around the olive grove. The horse got up and, squealing, fled its immediate danger. Flailing his arms and legs, Jilamey desperately sought to get to his feet. Like living ropes, the snakes impeded his efforts, tripping him until he was up against the light metal blockades. With a cry, he slipped again into the midst of them. Todd spurred Gypsy into the tiddlers, brandishing his quarterstaff from side to side.

That distraction gave the Momma Snake its opportunity. It launched out of its coil at the smallest creatures it could see: the children. Trained in evasive actions, the Alley Cats and Hrriss's cubs scattered their horses in their mad dash, leaving Teddy behind on the old, slow-moving Rock. While Teddy tried to urge Rock to *move*, the powerful snake skimmed the ground toward him, as relentless as lava, as fearsome as lightning. Todd and the others wheeled and hurtled toward the vulnerable pair. Teddy let out a deafening squeal that startled old Rock more than the approaching snake. He reared, adding his own scream of terror, and walked backward on his hind legs right up against the wall of the grain barn. The Gringg cub had learned his lesson about holding on. His legs were locked firmly on the pack saddle, but he didn't know what to do except hang on.

"Mama!" he cried. The voder at his throat made it a weak, high-pitched whimper.

Horses were fast, but Gringg could move with astounding speed when necessary.

"Weddeerogh!" Grizz cried, streaking forward to fall on the snake's back.

It dragged her for yards, then strained to a halt as the Gringg clawed her way, up to its head, repeating the tactic that had been so successful with the other Momma Snake. She threw one massive arm around its neck, wrapped the other one across her wrist, and squeezed. And squeezed. And squeezed.

The snake's long body whipped dangerously from side to side, making it too perilous for anyone to approach to help her. The Gringg hung on, rolled over and over in the dust by the muscled strength of her prey. As Todd and the others watched in astonishment, the serpent's frenzied movements grew weaker and finally ceased. The great coils gave one more convulsion and then lay still. Shakily, Grizz rolled off the dead snake and lay on her back. Eonneh rushed forward to help his mate to her feet. Teddy dismounted and hurried to his parents, dragging the unwilling horse behind him by the reins.

"That," said Robin Reeve, the first to regain his voice, "was the most amazing thing I've ever seen in my life. Ever."

"I warned you how dangerous—" Barnstable began, then stopped, aware of the sudden, almost hostile repudiation of his audience. He cleared his throat and began again. "You are correct. It was an astounding feat of strength. The Gringg make formidable Hunters."

Todd leaned over and slapped the Spacedep man on the back. "Now, that admission has made my day, Admiral!"

"You may be *sure*, Reeve, that I never intended that," Barnstable said, eyeing Todd warily.

"Oh, I'm sure." Todd laughed. "Well done, Grizz," he called. The Gringg, clutching her cub and mate close to her massive chest, beamed at him, showing all her fangs.

"Isn't anyone going to congratulate me?" Jilamey called, rising to his feet from the dust. "I'm going to pass my Coming of Age Ritual at last!" He held up not one, but three snake bags, tightly tied and wriggling.

"You young fool," Boncyk said with a groan, bowing over his saddlehorn in despair. "You've flattened half my new olive trees!"

A beaming Hu Shih took his place of honor on the dais at the Snake Hunt feast that evening in the Assembly Hall. His wife Phyllis, tiny and exquisite, sat beside him in a Hrruban robe of red tissue silk spangled with gems. The presentations for successful Hunters had taken place, with a special round of applause for Jilamey Landreau and his bag of three. But the roar of approval when Grizz was given her medal was deafening.

Then the servers began distributing the dishes which had been tantalizing everyone with their aromas. Jilamey sat at the Reeve family table in the front row below the dais, proudly showing off his Coming of Age medal with its four wiggly ribbons.

Hu tapped his water glass with the side of his fork, and waited for silence.

"Thank you, friends," he said, beaming. "I've been asked to say a few words. This is a triple celebration. Today we celebrate yet another successful Snake Hunt, a festival I have always enjoyed, as it marks the climax of New Home Week, the very first of the traditional Rraladoonan festivals. Rraladoon—the name has passed through many changes over the years: Doona, Rrala, Doonarrala, Rraladoona, It is really time we settled on one designation to be used by everyone. Rraladoon demonstrates our unity as one people, despite our different biologies. 'Wee be of one people, thou and I,' as an ancient poet once said— now and forever.

"The second reason for celebration is the historic Trade Agreement signed with our newest allies, the Gringg. I welcome their captain, Grzzeearoghh—" The name set him coughing. "Dear me," he said when he recovered, "I hope I said that right, and all her crew, and hope they make many more trips here to visit us and enjoy their beautiful new residence on Treaty Island."

"Here, here!" Ken Reeve shouted from his table near the dais. Pat Reeve raised her glass to clink against her husband's. Jilamey, and Commander Frill, seated at Ken's particular request at the Reeve family table, joined them.

Teddy, urged on by his parents, came forward with a heap of tissue-wrapped bundles. He stopped next to Hrriss, waiting with pleading, scared red eyes until the Hrruban took the top bundle.

"Zank you, young Zeddy," Hrrestan said gravely.

The young Gringg sketched a clumsy half bow, made all the more endearing by the roundness of his figure, and moved on to Todd, then one by one to each of the original party visiting the Gringg ship. Commander Frill was delighted to be included, and patted the cub on the shoulder. Teddy's last delivery was to Greene, sitting at one of the front tables with Grace Castleton.

"What is it?" Greene asked, handling the package as if it might explode in his hands.

"It is a collar," Teddy replied shyly, "like mine." He scooted back to his place on the dais beside Grizz and Honey.

"That's sweet," Grace Castleton said, with a warm smile for Teddy, and elbowed the unresponsive commander. "Put it on, Jon!" He reddened, but complied.

"This is in recognition," Grizz announced in Middle Hrruban, the voder raising her voice to a tolerable pitch for the guests, "of our first friends here on Rraladoon, and in hopes for the many yet to be made."

She waved graciously, acknowledging the wild applause and cheers. Todd immediately unwrapped his gift and put it on, preening. Gringg-sized, it hung over his shoulders like a shawl. Hrriss donned his. Each collar was beautifully and individually decorated. Grinning at one another at the tableau they made, they leaned over toward the Gringg leaders.

"Beautiful," Todd said fervently. "Thank you."

"It is our pleasure," Honey replied. "You have given us many gifts, most treasured of all being the gift of friendship."

Hu Shih smiled, and put up a hand for attention. "And thirdly, we celebrate, a little prematurely, the fortieth birthday of Todd Reeve. I know it's two weeks away, Todd, but surely you'll forgive an old man for rushing things a little." The crowd chuckled, and Hu continued. "He is the very calendar of our life here on Rraladoon, and the symbol of our unity, our friendship with our neighbor the Hrrubans. I am proud that he is my successor as Colony Leader. He has secured my safety and my enjoyment in retirement. Let me assure you that I'll continue to vote for him any time he runs for re-election. Happy birthday, Todd, and long life to you." Hu Shih sat down amid applause and cheers.

The Alley Cats left their seats between their two sets of grandparents and mounted the dais, joined by Hrriss's children. Alison pushed Alec, who presented a gift-wrapped box to Todd.

Alec cleared his throat "We have a special present for you, too, Dad."

"It was our own idea," Alison added.

"Why, thank you," Todd said, really touched by the gravity on their faces. He opened the box.

"It's from us, too," Hrrunival put in. Hrruna, behind him, nodded vigorously.

"What is it?" Hrriss asked, noticing a suspicious hint of moisture in Todd's eyes. Todd held up a rope tail, unmistakably braided together by small, inexpert fingers, but colorful with ribbons interwoven with the sisal.

"It's beautiful, kids," he said, his voice husky with emotion. He tied it around his waist and tugged the knots taut. "What do you know? It fits!"

The children gave him kisses and hugs, made shy by the onlookers, and hurried off to return to their places by their grandparents.

"Speech, speech!" Hrriss cried, clapping his hands together. The cry was taken up by the rest of the room. "Speech!"

"My friends," Todd began as he rose. He pointed at the collar and the rope tail. "If my age is the calendar, then this is the composite picture of the makeup of Rraladoon: part Hrruban, part Hayuman, and now part Gringg, but all very, very happy and grateful. Thank you so much."

"Lions and Hayumans and Bears, oh my!" Kelly chortled. Everyone laughed.

Overwhelmed by a deep feeling of joy, Todd sat down. Kelly, Hrriss, and Nrrna raised their glasses to him. "Happy birthday, my love," Kelly whispered. She was dressed in a glowing, green silk dress that fit her slender form to a degree that was almost illicit. "My present's waiting for you at home." She raised her eyebrows wickedly, and Todd grinned.

Second Speaker Hrrto, seated at the end of the dais, rose. "May I speak, Mr. Hu?" he asked politely.

"But of course, Speaker," Hu Shih said, startled, but in perfect High Formal Hrruban. "We'd be honored by your words."

"It is I who am honored," Hrrto said, bowing. Then he changed to the Middle Hrruban that most of those in the room would understand. "I have a most important announcement to make. I do not wish to diminish the last presentation, but there is a fourth reason for celebration tonight. You are aware that our beloved First Speaker, Hrruna, became one with the Stripes some months ago. We have all mourned his loss, I more than I knew at first. An election was held last night for his successor. The results affect you more"—he dropped his jaw slightly in the equivalent of a Hayuman grin—"than you might think."

"Old Hrrto looks almost happy," Todd whispered to Hrriss. "He must have won the election after all."

"Finally," Hrriss replied, with a grin of relief. "He'd be a better First Speaker than most—not that there was a lot of choice."

Silvery mane gleaming in the lantern-light, Second looked noble and somewhat fragile, except for the totally uncharacteristic gleam in his eye.

"This is a most happy day for me as well," he went on in Middle Hrruban. "I am proud to announce that the Hrruban who will pass into the First Speakership is revered for his wisdom. He is known to have trod a difficult but just path in the best interests of both Hrruba and Rraladoon. He is well known to you all. It is perhaps as well"—again there was that brief, amused drop of the jaw—"that he is not a member of the High Council at present, which I believe is one reason why many of my fellow Councillors felt able to vote unanimously in his favor." His smile broadened as he deliberately tantalized his breathless audience. "By that admission, you know that it is not I who won such an honor. I find myself content to remain Second Speaker and serve First. But I did sincerely believe for some time that I was the only suitable candidate.

"Over the course of the last two months, I have watched and been impressed by another whose achievements I brought to the attention of the High Council. They have seen the merit of my arguments. Consequently, I can announce to you that the duly elected First Speaker of the High Council of Hrruba is"—he paused to turn to the recipient—"Hrrestan, son of Hrrindan."

The surprise was so complete that gasps rippled through the room before yells and cheers broke out and the entire assembly rose to its feet, clapping their hands raw and making the Gringg cringe from the wild whistlings.

A dazed Hrrestan got to his feet, shaking his head at Hrrto as if he could not believe such an honor would fall to him. Then with a snap of his head and a straightening of his lean shoulders, he held up his hands. As silence finally fell in the hall, Hrrestan seemed unable to find words. Into the stillness, tiny Hrrunna, who could have no understanding of the honor just bestowed on her grandsire, purred a childish question. "Rra?"

Hrrto chuckled at the baby's reaction. "It is auspicious that Hrruna's namesake also approves."

Then, with a formal bow of unusual humility, Hrrto presented Hrrestan with a small box. Hrrestan opened it, his eyes widening in surprise. The audience gasped as he held up the great blue sapphire which had been Rraladoon's present to Hrruna.

"Where's Mrrva? She should be here," Todd murmured to Kelly, and started to beckon Alec to him.

"She is here," Hrriss said, drawing his attention to the rear of the dais. The graceful Hrruban woman, her mane whitening slightly around her sweet face, was clad in the most exquisite diaphanous red robe. She joined her mate, looking up at him with great pride as she adorned him with his new badge of office. Another round of cheers and applause followed that little ceremony. Todd was so affected by the tableau that he could feel involuntary tears starting in his eyes.

Hrriss wound his tail around Todd's knee and gave him a companionable squeeze. Todd threw his arm over his best friend's shoulders. Kelly and Nrrna joined the hug, insinuating themselves into the embrace and clasping their hands across to one another. The baby sat in the middle, gurgling happily.

"What a splendid tribute! So long deserved," Kelly whispered.

Todd nodded and sniffed surreptitiously. All his life, he'd respected the Hrruban who was, in many ways, a second father to him. Without Hrrestan's guidance, Todd might not have grown up to take over the responsibilities that had been predicted as the fate of the exuberant, disobedient six-year-old colonist. Hrrto was right. There was no one else of all the high-ranking wide Stripes that Todd had met during his nearly forty years who was better suited, or trained, to accept the First Speakership. He overcame his thickened throat and added his cheers to the prolonged accolade.

"I am honored beyond speech," Hrrestan said when the applause abated enough for him to be heard. "I do not presume to take the place of First Speaker Hrruna, for he was unique in the history of both our worlds, and certainly of this one. But I *will* do my utmost to live up to the honorable principles he endorsed.

"The one regret I have is that my appointment to the position of First Speaker will limit the amount of time I may spend here, among my friends and family on Rraladoon. I will never give up my home here, so it is a good thing that our new friends, the Gringg, have come to us with the materials to make more, and more efficient, grids. So efficient, in fact, that we will be extending this technology to our longtime allies and partners, the Hayumans. And it is the Gringg who have brought us the means to share that technology with Hayumans."

The applause which followed this announcement was thunderous. Hrrestan, beaming, resumed his seat.

"Couldn't think of a better cat for the job," Ali Kiachif said, toasting him with mlada and draining the glass dry. He beckoned to one of the young Hrrubans helping to serve at the feast. "Give me another shot of liquid headache, son."

Todd had one more announcement to make, and stood, raising his hands for quiet.

"The spaceport planning committee will meet tomorrow—tomorrow afternoon," he said with a grin, "giving the delegates some chance to recover from the party tonight." He held up a hand-sized holographic projector. "I have something else that should be public knowledge now. May I have the lights off, please?"

The lights dimmed as Todd triggered the holograph, and a map appeared on the dais before the head table. Each species' claimed systems showed in a different color: amber for Hrruba, red for Gringg, and green for Amalgamated Worlds. "Now, the moment of truth!" He touched the relevant key, and three spots began glowing in the heart of each nebulous blob. The crowd let out a collective gasp.

"Reeve, that's classified!" Barnstable roared in protest, jumping to his feet at his place on the opposite end of the dais.

"Not really," Todd said. "Not for years. It's long been possible to extrapolate the location of the home systems from radio-telescope transmissions. I tried it myself. There is Earth, there is Hrruba, and there is the Gringg homeworld. We're going to be open and aboveboard now. We've agreed that the homeworlds will be off-limits to the uninvited, but who knows what the future will bring? Oh, and there," Todd said, pointing to a small blue spot glowing gently in the center of the map, "there's Rraladoon."

"Like the nucleus of a molecule," one of the Hayuman scientists observed aloud. "I hope it's a stable one."

"Oh, I doubt it," Todd said, shaking his head, to the shock of the scientist and the assembled guests. "A stable molecule is a closed system. We have to be open." He gestured at his fellow Humans. "It all started with one race of sentient beings. Then there were two, and now there are three. It's only a matter of time before there are four, then ten, then fifty. . . ."

"Stop!" Barnstable protested, his face flushed. Then he took a deep breath and managed a weak grin. "Take it easy, Reeve. Some of us can take only so much . . . incredible news at a time."

"Then let us become a homogenous whole," Hrriss said, his eyes sparking merrily. "Let the party begin!"

The "Doona/Rrala Ad Hoc Band" had a guest instrumentalist among their number: Artos, the Gringg lutanist. He confessed to having learned the Rraladoonan system of musical notation only recently.

"But I can play harmony if required," he added.

"You'll play solos, if I have anything to say about it," said Sally Lawrence, smiling at him winningly. "Ready, everyone? A-one, a-two, a-three!"

They struck up dance music. After listening carefully for a handful of bars, Artos added a delicate but intricate descant to the melody. Everyone listening smiled and started snapping fingers or stamping to the tempo.

"C'mon, Koala," Lieutenant Cardiff said, urging the Gringg engineer out onto the dance floor. "Show us how you do it."

The rangy technician and his giant friend were soon the center of a dozen or so couples merrily stepping along. The children joined hands with grandparents and danced in a circle around them. Teddy spun into the circle holding hands with Ken, and Hrrunival coaxed Kodiak to join with him and Hrruna.

Off to one side away from the musicians, a couple of Hunters who'd started their party not long after dismounting from the ride had adopted Cinnamon, and were telling him tales of being misunderstood in their lives.

"I broke my mother's heirloom teapot when I was a child," one of them said sadly. "Was an accident. Coulda happened to anybody. Have some mlada. You don't have to worry about a hangover, do you? Your eyes are already red."

"My eyes are always red," Cinnamon said, puzzled. "Is this another joke on me?"

The Hunters grinned. "Yeah, Br'er Bear, but a harmless one. Have a drink."

Tentatively Cinnamon accepted their hospitality, sipping, and then, liking the taste, upending his glass.

"Thassa good bruin!"

Ben Adjei collected the pool as the winner for the thirtieth year running, having made the most accurate guess of the onset of snake migration. First-time visitors paid off with groans. Mike Solinari was among the losers, but he anteed up with good grace.

"I don't know," he said, shaking his head at the senior veterinarian. "I think you have some arcane set of motivators to know just when they'll come, because it's never the same hour any two years in a row."

"I've spent a lot of time studying my subject, lad," Ben said, clapping the younger man on the back. "Live, learn, and one day you might guess, too."

On the dance floor, Robin Reeve tapped Grace Castleton on the shoulder. She and Jon Greene executed a gliding turn and stopped.

"Can I help you, young man?" she asked.

"You're a ship's captain," Robin said, his words slightly slurred. He had his arm firmly tucked around Nita Taylor's waist. "Could you marry us?"

"Oh, Robin," Nita said, blushing. "That's an ancient custom."

"But still a valid one, I'm pleased to inform you," Grace said, smiling fondly at the two young people. "I can see that you're both of an age to know your minds. So if you wish, I'd be delighted to officiate. But it'd have to be done aboard my ship. You don't want to leave the party so soon, do you? We certainly don't." Greene whispered in her ear, and she blushed. "Perhaps later, Exec."

A few steps away, Barnstable was recounting the events of the Snake Hunt to a circle of listeners. "Never seen anything like it in my life. Snake comes up and tries to eat a rider, slithers right up the horse's a—" he glanced at his wife beside him and she gave him a long-suffering look—"er, rump. The beggar—I mean, Gringg—just yanked it off by the tail and battered that reptile about the head with her paws until it was dead as a mat! Nothing but her paws! Now I believe they don't need any personal armament."

"Ah, young Reeve," Ali Kiachif said, shouting at Todd and Kelly above the raucous music of the Doona/Rrala Ad Hoc Band. "Congratulations to you and greetings to you, lovely Kelly. My glass must have a hole in it, if you understand the problem. The mlada's all gone."

"I'll find you some," Todd said, laughing. Spotting one of the servers, he directed the girl toward Ali. Arm in arm, he and Kelly wriggled through the crowd to the dance floor. Hrriss and Nrrna were already there, gracefully gliding to the music.

"Todd Rreev," Grizz called. The Gringg captain towered head and shoulders above everyone else in the room. "Todd Rreev, Hrriss? A moment of your attention?"

Todd and Hrriss rose from the table where, over a glass or two, they and Hrrestan, Sumitral, Fred Horsimann, Jilamey, Barnstable, and Kiachif had been having an unofficial roundtable about the spaceport facilities. Kelly glanced at Nrrna.

"Should we go?" she asked Grizz.

"Morra," the Gringg replied. Several of the other Gringg filed in around them, surrounding the table like an impromptu forest. "It is a most interesting thing to tell you. You will like to hear it. Rrawrum, my communications officer, has just called me." She tapped her collar with a foreclaw. "Another species has just attained an orbit around our homeworld. They are so unlike us that they cannot communicate anything except that like us, they arrive in peace." She shot Todd a knowing glance. "And yes, our people have determined that their ship has no weapons, although they do have meteor shields."

"*Another* race?" Kiachif demanded. "Another kind of alien? Not like us, or them, or you?"

"Reh." Grizz smiled, her rubbery black lips peeling back to show all the sharp white fangs in her mouth. "Since you Rraladoonans seem to be able to master new languages with little trouble . . ." She glanced at Todd when he groaned. "That is a proven ability, Zodd, so our leaders, who have been vastly impressed by the voder and all your courtesies to us, have managed to convey the spatial coordinates of Rraladoon to these new creatures."

"Your leaders did what?" Todd asked, half-appalled but also finding himself ready to accept a new challenge. After all, with Hrrestan as First Speaker, there would be harmony with that world.

"They are proceeding with all dispatch here to this Treaty Planet," Grizz said. "It is the sensible solution to a problem we Gringg are not capable of solving."

"Look, Grizz, we can only do so much," Todd began, temporizing only because he didn't want to appear eager.

"But you did so well in greeting us, putting us at our ease, showing us how two species can live in harmony."

"But we treated you badly," Barnstable said, joining them. "We distrusted you."

"You only acted with caution, as a Gringg would," Grizz assured him. She nodded her big head in approval.

"Great stars," Barnstable exclaimed involuntarily, and then looked around him, as if embarrassed to be complimented so publicly by someone he had, until just recently, held in great suspicion.

"I wonder what kind of joy juice they might bring with them," Kiachif mused, sloshing the thick amber liquid which Eonneh suggested he try. "I mean, every civilized species has something or other to ease the pains to which flesh— of any kind—is susceptible."

"What do zey look like?" Nrrna asked.

"We do not know," Grizz said. "A description and other details will follow."

Todd's mind boggled at the hundreds of possible shapes an alien species could have. Kelly nudged him with her elbow.

"I wonder if they have young," she said, assuming a most innocent expression.

"And if zeir young will play with ours," Hrriss added, enjoying the bemused expression on his best friend's face.

Admiral Sumitral of Alreldep grinned broadly at Todd. "Prime your children, Reeve and Hrriss. Alreldep can't seem to get anything done without their assistance."